## 3 NOVELS
# The Moonshine War
# Gold Coast
# City Primeval

# ELMORE LEONARD'S

# DOUBLE DUTCH TREAT

INTRODUCTION BY BOB GREENE

ARBOR HOUSE / NEW YORK

Manufactured in the United States of America

10 9 8 7 6 5 4 3 2 1

Library of Congress Cataloging in Publication Data

Leonard, Elmore, 1925–
Double Dutch treat.

Contents: City primeval—The moonshine war—Gold coast.
I. Leonard, Elmore, 1925–     . City primeval. 1986.
II. Leonard, Elmore, 1925–     . The moonshine war. 1986.
      III. Leonard, Elmore, 1925–     . Gold coast.
1986.   IV. Title.
PS3562.E55A6   1986      813'.54      85-26774
                    ISBN 0-87795-804-1

*For Joan, for Joan, for Joan*

# CONTENTS

# INTRODUCTION
## By Bob Greene

I find myself being wary whenever a writer is the recipient of a sudden burst of publicity. My thought is not that the writer is especially good; rather, my instinct is that the person has probably hired a fancy press agent, and that the press agent has done a creditable job. The hype is just that; a new star has been created, but both the star and the newly famous project will probably be forgotten in a month—usually rightfully so.

I will confess that this is the way I felt when the novel *Glitz*, by Elmore Leonard, was published to lavish acclaim and publicity. With the release of *Glitz* Leonard suddenly became inescapable in the media, and it was almost impossible to pick up a national publication without seeing his name. Newspaper feature sections ran long stories about him, and he even ended up on the cover of *Newsweek*. This Leonard was hot, all right.

I figured that Leonard was destined to be the media darling of the season, and silently congratulated him for his publicity coup. I had no desire to read *Glitz;* after all, in cases like this it's the publicity that matters, not the book. One day, though, I purchased a copy of *Glitz.* I didn't read it right away; it sat there on a table for weeks on end. I was almost angry at myself for having given in by buying it. I had fallen for the great American publicity machine.

Finally, though, I read it. Boy, did I read it. And the first thing I did after finishing it was to hurry to the bookstore to purchase other novels by Leonard. I wolfed them down one after another; I found out that Leonard had been writing for more than thirty years, and had written twenty-three books.

I was a little embarrassed, coming so late to the Leonard fold. Here were all these books—they had been around for years, and I was just learning how good Leonard was.

And how good is he? Incredible, that's all. As a person who makes his living by trying to put words on paper, I am in awe of the guy. Elmore Leonard's books are sheer entertainment—but at the same time they maintain total respect for the reader. There are days when I know I should be doing something else, but I can't make myself put down the Leonard book I am reading at the time.

After I'd read my first few Leonard books, I went around telling people about him. I found out quickly that a lot of folks already were well aware of his skills. The question troubled me: Why was it that Leonard had not become a major literary star before *Glitz?*

I think it's this: he defies categorization—and when you do try to categorize him, you are invariably wrong. For instance, when you look for his books on the paperback racks, you usually are able to find them in the "mystery" section. That immediately brings to mind writers in the tradition of Raymond Chandler and Dashiell Hammett—writers of tough-guy detective fiction.

That's the kind of writer I assumed Leonard was before I tried him. In fact, I had passed his books in stores several times, and not picked them up—I'm not all that much a fan of hard-boiled private eye novels. But Elmore Leonard is way beyond that—his books have such texture and life, they're unlike anything you can pigeonhole. I can see why this worked against him for so long; a good but sad rule of thumb is that if you can't describe a writer's stuff in one sentence, then it will be hard to sell him. That had been Leonard's problem; happily, those days are all over now.

It strikes me that even in this introduction, I have not managed to convey what it is that makes Leonard so special. Let me put it this way: given the chance to see the most popular movie of the season, watch the most popular television show of the season, or read an Elmore Leonard novel that I know absolutely nothing about in advance, I'll go with the Leonard novel every time. He's just that much fun.

And now you are in that lucky position: you have a book in your hands, and between the covers of this one volume are three Elmore Leonard novels. I'll get out of the way; you've heard enough from me. Enjoy yourself. As if you needed encouraging.

# CITY PRIMEVAL: HIGH NOON IN DETROIT

In the matter of Alvin B. Guy, Judge of Recorder's Court, City of Detroit:

The investigation of the Judicial Tenure Commission found the respondent guilty of misconduct in office and conduct clearly prejudicial to the administration of justice. The allegations set forth in the formal complaint were that Judge Guy:

1. Was discourteous and abusive to counsel, litigants, witnesses, court personnel, spectators and news reporters.
2. Used threats of imprisonment or promises of probation to induce pleas of guilty.
3. Abused the power of contempt.
4. Used his office to benefit friends and acquaintances.
5. Bragged of his sexual prowess openly.
6. Was continually guilty of judicial misconduct that was not

only prejudicial to the administration of justice but destroyed respect for the office he holds.

Abridged examples of testimony follow.

On April 26, Judge Guy interceded on behalf of a twice-convicted narcotics dealer, Tyrone Perry, who was being questioned as a witness and possible suspect in a murder that had taken place at Mr. Perry's residence. Judge Guy appeared at Room 527 of police headquarters and told the homicide detectives questioning Perry that he was "holding court here and now" and to release the witness. When Sergeant Gerald Hunter questioned the propriety of this, Judge Guy grabbed him by the arm and pushed him against a desk. Sgt. Hunter voiced objection to this treatment and Judge Guy said, before witnesses, "I'll push you around any time I want. You're in my courtroom, and if you open your mouth, I'll hold you in contempt of court." Judge Guy then left police headquarters with Mr. Perry.

In testimony describing still another incident the respondent gave the appearance of judicial impropriety by his harassment of a police officer.

The respondent had presided over a murder case in which one of the three codefendants was Marcella Bonnie. The charges against Miss Bonnie were dismissed at the preliminary examination.

Judge Guy was talking to Sgt. Wendell Robinson of the Police Homicide Section about the forthcoming trial of the codefendants and revealed how he had met Miss Bonnie in a bar and thereafter spent the night with her. He went on to say that "she was a foxy little thing" and "better than your average piece of ass."

Sgt. Robinson was quite surprised and chagrined to hear a judge boasting of his sexual participation with a former criminal defendant. As a result, Robinson prepared a memorandum about the incident, which he forwarded to his superiors.

The respondent learned of this memorandum and exhibited his vindictiveness by improper and heavy-handed efforts to impair Robinson's credibility, referring to Sgt. Robinson before witnesses as "a suck-ass Uncle Tom trying to pass for Caucasian because he's light-skinned."

Attorney Carolyn Wilder testified to the events in *People v.*

*Cedric Williams.* The charges in this preliminary examination, held June 19, were "second-degree criminal sexual conduct and simple assault," and Ms. Wilder, counsel for the defense, had stated clearly that her client would go to trial before entering a reduced plea. However, the respondent, Judge Guy, requested the defendant and his counsel to approach the bench, where he stated that if the defendant pled guilty to the lesser charge of assault and battery—a misdemeanor—he would be placed on probation and that would be the end of it.

"I'm street, just like you are," the judge said to the defendant, "and your attorney either doesn't have her shit together or your best interests at heart." Whereupon he sent the defendant and Ms. Wilder out into the hall to "talk the matter over."

When they returned to the bench and Ms. Wilder still insisted on a trial, Judge Guy said to the defendant, "Look, you better take this plea or your motherfucking ass is dead." When Ms. Wilder informed the bench that her client would, under no circumstances, plead to the lesser charge, Judge Guy berated the defense counsel, threatened her with contempt and stated: "I see now how you operate. You want your own client to be convicted . . . obviously pissed off because a black man got a little white pussy in this case."

Again in testimony Carolyn Wilder told how she attempted to serve a notice of appeal on Judge Guy as a favor to another attorney, Mr. Allan Hayes. The judge berated Ms. Wilder for one half hour calling her "a non-dues, honkie liberal," who had disrupted the orderly process of his courtroom.

Ms. Wilder: "At the time I asked if he was going to hold me in contempt. He did not respond but continued his berating monologue. When Mr. Hayes entered, having learned what was in progress, the judge addressed him at the bench, saying, 'I want you to explain to this honkie bitch who I am and I want her to understand I won't put up with any bullshit ego trips.'"

Sometime thereafter, the respondent, in a mellower mood, asked Ms. Wilder for a date, which she refused. Judge Guy responded to her refusal with a tasteless and insulting inquiry as to whether she was a lesbian. Thereafter, whenever Ms. Wilder came into court, the respondent would seize upon the opportunity to verbally embarrass and harass her.

\* \* \*

That Judge Guy abused his contempt of court power was witnessed in an incident that involved Sgt. Raymond Cruz of the Detroit Police Homicide Section.

On this occasion Judge Guy ordered a twelve-year-old student to be locked up in the prisoner's bullpen for causing a disturbance in the courtroom during a school field-trip visit. Sgt. Cruz—testifying at the time in a pre-trial hearing—suggested the judge make the boy stand in a corner instead. At this the judge became enraged, held Sgt. Cruz in contempt of court and ordered him to spend an hour in the bullpen with the boy.

Sometime later, with the court in recess, Judge Guy said to Sgt. Cruz before witnesses, "I hope you have learned who's boss in this courtroom." Sgt. Cruz made no reply. The judge said then, "You are an easy person to hold in contempt. You had best learn to keep your mouth shut, or I'll shut it for you every time."

Sgt Cruz said, "Your honor, can I ask a question off the record?" The judge said, "All right, what is it?" Sgt. Cruz said, "Are you ever afraid for your life?" The judge asked, "Are you threatening me?" And Sgt. Cruz said, "No, your honor, I was just wondering if anyone has ever attempted to subject you to great bodily harm."

Judge Guy produced a .32-caliber Smith & Wesson revolver from beneath his robes and said, "I would like to see somebody try."

The record indicates that on several occasions Judge Guy abused members of the media by communicating with them in a manner unbecoming his office. The findings of the Tenure Commission with respect to this allegation state in part:

"Miss Sylvia Marcus is a reporter for *The Detroit News*. In his courtroom and before witnesses, Judge Guy subjected Miss Marcus to discourtesies of a crude nature . . . engaged in an undignified harangue about her newspaper being racist and, further, warned her 'not to fuck around with him.' "

In summary, the Judicial Tenure Commission warned:

"A cloud of witnesses testifies that 'justice must not only be done, it must be seen to be done.' Without the appearance as well as the fact of justice, respect for the law vanishes.

"Judge Guy has demonstrated by his conduct that he is legally, temperamentally, and morally unfit to hold any judicial position.

"By reason of the foregoing, it is our recommendation to the Supreme Court that Judge Guy be removed from the office he holds as Recorder's Court Judge of the City of Detroit and, further, that he be permanently enjoined from holding any judicial office in the future."

At a press conference following the release of the Tenure Commission opinion, Judge Guy called the investigation a "racist witch-hunt organized by the white-controlled press." In the same statement he accused the Detroit Police Department of trying to kill him, though offered no evidence of specific attempts.

Alvin Guy stated emphatically that if the State Supreme Court suspended him from office he intended to "write a very revealing book, naming names of people with dirty hands and indecent fingers.

"Remember what I'm saying to you if they suspend me," Guy added. "The stuff is going to get put on some people, some names that are going to amaze you."

# 1

One of the valet parking attendants at Hazel Park Racecourse would remember the judge leaving sometime after the ninth race, about 1:00 A.M., and fill in the first part of what happened. With the judge's picture in the paper lately and on TV, he was sure it was Alvin Guy in the silver Lincoln Mark VI.

Light skin, about fifty, with a little Xavier Cugat mustache and hair that hung long and stiff over his collar and did not seem to require much straightening.

The other card involved was a Buick, or it might've been an Olds, dark color.

The judge had a young white lady with him, about twenty-seven, around in there. Blond hair, long. Dressed up, wearing something like pink, real loose, lot of gold chains around her neck. Good-looking lady. She had on makeup that made her look pale in the arc lights, dark lipstick. The valet parking attendant said the judge didn't help the lady in. The judge got in on his own side, giving him a dollar tip.

The other car, the dark-colored Buick or Olds—it might've been black—was pretty new. Was a man in it. The man's arm stuck out the window—you know, his elbow did—with the short sleeve rolled up once or twice. The arm looked kind of sunburned and had light kind of reddish-blond-color hair on it.

This other car tried to cut in front of the judge's car, but the judge kept moving and wouldn't let him in. So the other car sped off down toward the head of the exit line, down by the gate, the man in a big hurry. There was a lot of horns blowing. The cars down there wouldn't let the other car in either. People going home after giving their money at the windows, they weren't giving away nothing else.

It looked like the other car tried to edge in again right as the judge's car came to the gate to go out on Dequindre. There was a crash. Bam!

The valet parking attendant, Everett Livingston, said he looked down there, but didn't see anybody get out of the cars. It looked like the judge's car had run into the front fender of the other car as it tried to nose in. Then the judge's car backed up some and went around the other car and out the gate, going south on Dequindre toward Nine Mile. The other car must have stalled. A few more cars went past it. Then the other car made it out and that was the last the valet parking attendant saw or thought of them until he read about the judge in the paper.

Leaving the track, all Clement wanted to do was keep Sandy and the Albanian in sight.

Forget the silver Mark VI.

Follow the black Cadillac, the Albanian stiff-arming the wheel like a student driver taking his road test, hugging the inside lane in the night traffic. It should've been easy.

Except the Mark kept getting in Clement's way.

The ding in the fender didn't bother Clement. It wasn't his car. Realizing the guy in the Mark was a jig with a white girl didn't bother him either, too much. He decided the guy was in numbers or dope and if that's what the girl wanted, some spade with a little fag mustache, fine. Since coming to Detroit, Clement had seen all kinds of jigs with white girls. He didn't stare at them the way he used to.

But this silver Mark was something else, poking along in the center lane with a half block of clear road ahead, holding Clement back while the Cadillac got lost up there among all the red tail-lights. The jig was driving his big car with his white lady; he didn't care who was behind him or if anybody might be in a hurry. That's what got to Clement, the jig's attitude. Also, the jig's hair.

Clement popped on his brights and could see the guy clearly through the rear windshield. The guy's hair, when he turned to the girl, looked like a black plastic wig, the twenty-nine-dollar tango-model ducktail. Fucking spook. Clement began thinking of the guy as a Cuban-looking jig. Oily looking. Then, as the chicken-fat jig.

Sandy and the Albanian turned right on Nine Mile. Clement got over into the right lane. When he was almost to the corner the silver Mark cut in front of him and made the turn.

Clement said, "You believe it?"

He followed the taillights around the corner and gunned it, wanting to run up the guy's silver rear-end. But instinct saved him. Something cautioned Clement to take her easy and, sure enough, there was a dark-blue Hazel Park police car up ahead. The Continental shot past it. The police car kept cruising along and Clement hung back now.

He saw the light at the next intersection, John R, change to green.

The Albanian's Cadillac was already turning left, followed by several cars. Now the Mark was swinging onto John R without blinking, making a wide sweep past the Holiday Inn on the corner. Clement began to accelerate as the police car continued through the intersection. He reached the corner with the light turning red, heard horns blowing and his tires squealing and thought for a second he was going to jump the curb and shoot into the Holiday Inn—a man on the sidewalk was scooping up his little dog to get out of the way—but Clement didn't even hit the curb. As he got straightened out he floored it down John R, beneath an arc of streetlights and past neon signs, came up behind the lumbering Mark and laid on his horn. The chicken-fat jig's head turned to his rear-view mirror. Clement pulled out, glanced over as he passed the Mark and saw the jig's face and his middle finger raised to the side window.

My oh my, Clement thought. I'll play a tune on your head, Mr. Jig, you get smart with me.

Except he had to be alert now. The next light was Eight Mile, the Detroit city limits. Sandy and the Albanian could turn either way or make a little jog and pick up 75 if they were headed downtown. If they made the light Clement would have to make it too. Else he'd lose them and have to start all over setting up the Albanian.

The Eight Mile light showed green. Clement gave the car some gas. He glanced over, surprised, feeling a car passing him in on the right—the Mark, the silver boat gliding by, then drifting in front of him as Clement tried to speed up, seeing the light turn to amber. There was still time for both of them to skin through; but the chicken-fat jig braked at the intersection and Clement had to jam his foot down hard, felt his rear-end break loose and heard his tires scream and saw that big silver deck right in front of him as he nailed his car to a stop.

Sandy and the Albanian were gone. Nowhere in sight.

The chicken-fat jig had his head cocked, staring at his rear-view mirror.

Clement said, "Well, I got time for you now, Mr. Jig, you want to play . . ."

The girl turned half around and had to squint into the bright headlights.

"I think it's the same one."

"Sure it is," Alvin Guy said. "Same wise-ass. You see his license number?"

"He's too close."

"When I start up, take a look. If he follows us pick up the phone, tell the operator it's a nine-eleven."

"I don't think I know how to work it," the girl said. She had lighted a cigarette less than a minute before; now she stubbed it out in the ashtray.

"You don't know how to do much of anything," Alvin Guy said to the rear-view mirror. He saw the light change to green and moved straight ahead at a normal speed, watching the headlights

11

reflected in the mirror as he crossed Eight Mile and entered John R again, in Detroit now, and said to the headlights, "Out of Hazel Park now, stupid. You don't know it, but you're going *down* town—assault with a deadly weapon."

"He hasn't really done anything," the girl said, holding the phone and looking through the windshield at the empty street that was lighted by a row of lampposts but seemed dismal, the storefronts dark. She felt the jolt and the car lurch forward as she heard metal bang against metal and Alvin Guy say, "Son of a *bitch*—" She heard the operator's voice in the telephone receiver. She heard Alvin Guy yelling at the operator or at her, "Nine-eleven, nine-eleven!" And felt the car struck from behind again and lurch forward, picking up speed.

Clement held his front bumper pressed against the Mark, accelerating, feeling it as a physical effort, as though he were using his own strength. The Mark tried to dig out and run but Clement stayed tight and kept pushing. The Mark tried to brake, tentatively, and Clement bounced off its bumper a few times. The Mark edged over into the right lane, the street empty ahead. Clement was ready, knowing the guy was about to try something. There was a cross-street coming up.

But the guy made his move before reaching the intersection: cut a hard, abrupt left to whip the car off his tail, shot into a parking lot—no doubt to scoot through the alley in some tricky jig move—and Clement said, "You dumb shit," as headlights lit up the cyclone fence and the Mark nosed to a hard, gravel-skidding stop. Clement coasted in past the red sign on the yellow building that said *American La France Fire Equipment.* A spot beamed down from the side of the building, lighting the Lincoln Mark VI like a new model on display.

Or an animal caught in headlight beams, standing dumb. Clement thought of that, easing his car up next to and a little ahead of the Mark—so he could see the chicken-fat jig through his windshield, the jig holding a car telephone, yelling at it like he was pretty sore, while the girl held onto gold chains around her neck.

Clement reached down under the front seat, way under, for the brown-paper grocery bag, opened it and drew out a Walther P.38 automatic. He reached above him then to slide open the sunroof and had to twist out from under the steering wheel before he could pull himself upright. Standing on the seat now, the roof opening catching him at the waist, he had a good view of the Mark's windshield in the flood of light from above. Clement extended the Walther. He shot the chicken-fat jig five times, seeing the man's face, then not seeing it, the windshield taking on a frosted look with the hard, clear hammer of the evenly spaced gunshots, until a chunk fell out of the windshield. He could hear the girl screaming then, giving it all she had.

Clement got out and walked around to the driver's side of the Mark. He had to reach way in to pull the guy upright and then out through the door opening, careful, trying not to touch the blood that was all over the guy's light-blue suit. The guy was a mess. He didn't look Cuban now; he didn't look like anything. The girl was still screaming.

Clement said, "Hey, shut up, will you?"

She stopped to catch her breath, then began making a weird wailing sound, hysterical. Clement said, "Hey!" He saw it wasn't going to do any good to yell at her, so he hunched himself into the Mark with one knee on the seat and punched her hard in the mouth—not with any shoulder or force in it but hard enough to give her a drunk-dazed look as he backed out of the car. Clement stooped down to get the guy's billfold, holding the guy's coat open with the tips of two fingers. There were three one-hundred-dollar bills and two twenties inside, credit cards, a couple of checks, ticket stubs from the track and a thin little 2 by 3 spiral notebook. Clement took the money and notebook. He leaned into the Continental again, bracing his forearm against the steering wheel, pulled the keys from the ignition and said to the girl giving him the dazed look, "Come on. Show me where your boyfriend lives."

They drove over Eight Mile to Woodward and turned south, Clement glancing at the girl sitting rigidly against the door as he gave her a little free advice.

"You take up with colored you become one of them. Don't you know that? Whether it's a white girl with a jig or a white guy with a colored girl, you're with *them,* you go to their places. You don't see the white guy taking the little colored chickie home or the white girl neither. He ever come to your place?"

The girl didn't answer, one hand on her purse, the other still holding onto her gold chains. Hell, he didn't want her chains, even if they were real. You start fooling around trying to fence shit like that . . .

"I asked you a question. He ever come to your place?"

"Sometimes."

"Well, that's unusual. What was he in, numbers, dope? He's too old to be a pimp. He looked like a pimp, though. You know it? I can't say much for your taste, Jesus, a guy like that— Where you from? You live in Detroit all your life?"

She said yes, not sounding too sure about it. Then asked him, "What're you gonna do to me?"

"I ain't gonna do nothing you show me where the man lives. He married?"

"No."

"But he lives in Palmer Woods? Those're big houses."

Clement waited. It was like talking to a child.

They passed the State Fairgrounds off to the left, beyond the headlights moving north to the suburbs, going home. The southbound traffic was thin, almost to nothing this time of night, the taillights of a few cars up ahead; but they were gone by the time Clement stopped for the light at Seven Mile. He said, "This ain't my night. You know it? I believe I've caught every light in town." The girl clung to her door in silence. "We turn right, huh? I know it's just west of Wood'ard some."

He heard the girl's door open and made a grab for her, but she was out of the car, the door swinging wide and coming back at him.

"Shit," Clement said.

He waited for the light to change, watching the pale pink figure running across Seven Mile and past the cyclone fence on the corner. All he could see was a dark mass of trees beyond her, darker than the night sky, the girl running awkwardly, past the fence and down the fairway of the public golf course, Palmer Park Municipal—running with her purse, like she had something in it, or running for her life. Dumb broad didn't even know where she was going. A Detroit Police station was just down Seven a ways, toward the other side of the park. He'd been brought in there the time he was picked up for hawking a queer and released when the queer wouldn't identify him. If he remembered correctly, it was the 12th Precinct.

Clement jumped the car off the green light so the door would slam closed, turned right, cut across Seven Mile in a jog to the left, and came to a stop at the edge of the golf course parking lot. The girl was running down the fairway in his headlight beams, straight down, not even angling for the trees. Clement got out and went after her. He ran about a hundred yards, no more, and stopped, even though he was gaining on her.

He said, "What in hell you doing, anyway? Getting your exercise?"

Clement extended the Walther, steadied it in the palm of his left hand, squeezed off a round and saw her stumble—Jesus, it was loud—and shot her twice more, he was pretty sure, before she hit the ground.

Anybody standing there, Clement would have bet him the three rounds had done the job. Except he saw the girl, for just a second, sitting in a Frank Murphy courtroom fingering her chains. Better to take an extra twenty seconds to be sure than do twenty years in Jackson. Clement went to have a look. He saw starlight shining in her eyes and thought, That wasn't a bad-looking girl. You know it?

Walking back to his car Clement realized something else and said to himself, You dumb shit. Now you can't go to the man's house.

# 2

"I think you're afraid of women," the girl from the *News* said. "I think that's the root of the problem"

Raymond Cruz wasn't sure whose problem she was referring to, if it was supposed to be his problem or hers.

She said, "Do you think women are devious?"

"You mean women reporters?"

"Women in general."

Sitting in Carl's Chop House surrounded by an expanse of empty white tablecloths, their waitress of somewhere, Raymond Cruz wondered if it was worth the free drinks and dinner or the effort required to give thoughtful answers.

"No," he said.

"You don't feel intimidated by women?"

"No, I've always liked women."

"At certain times," the girl from the *News* said. "Otherwise,

16

I'd say you're indifferent to women. They don't fit into your male world."

Wherever she was going the girl writer with the degree from Michigan and four years with *The Detroit News* seemed to be getting there. It was ten past one in the morning. Her face glistened, her wine glass was smudged with prints and lipstick. The edge remained in her tone and she no longer listened to answers. Raymond Cruz was tired. He forgot what he was going to say next—and was rescued by their waitress, smiling through sequined glasses.

"I haven't heard your beeper go off. Must be a slow night."

Raymond touched his napkin to his mustache and gave her a smile. "No, it hasn't, huh?" And said to the girl from the *News*, "One time Milly heard my beeper three tables away. I had it on me and didn't even hear it."

"You weren't feeling no pain either," the waitress said. "I come over to the table. I said isn't that your beeper? He didn't even hear it." She picked up his empty glass. "Can I get you something else?"

The girl from the *News* didn't answer or seem interested. She was lighting another cigarette, leaving a good half of her New York strip sirloin untouched. She already had coffee. Raymond said he'd have another shell of beer and asked Milly if she'd wrap up the piece of steak.

The girl from the *News* said, "I don't want it."

He said, "Well somebody'll probably take it."

"You have a dog?"

"I'll eat it for breakfast. Here's the thing," Raymond said, trying to show a little interest. "A man wouldn't say to me, 'I think you're afraid of women.' Or ask me if I think women are devious. Women ask questions like that. I don't know why, but they do."

"Your wife said you never talked about your work."

His *wife*— The girl from the *News* kept winging at him, coming in from blind sides.

Raymond said, "I hope you're a psychiatrist along with being a reporter—you're getting into something now. In the first place she's not my wife anymore, we're divorced. Is that what you're writing about, police divorce rate?"

"She feels you didn't say much about anything, but especially your work."

"You talked to Mary Alice?" Sounding almost astonished. "When'd you talk to her?"

"The other day. How come you don't have children?"

"Because we don't, that's all."

"She said you seldom if ever showed any emotion or told her how you felt. Men in other professions, they have a problem at work, they're not getting along with a customer or their boss, they come home and tell their wives about it. Then the wife gives hubby a few sympathetic strokes—poor baby—it's why he tells her."

The waitress with the gray hair and sequined glasses, Milly, placing his shell of beer on the table, said, "Where's your buddy?"

The girl from the *News* jabbed her cigarette out. She sat back and looked off across the field of tablecloths.

"Who, Jerry?"

"The kinda sandy-haired one with the mustache."

"Yeah, Jerry. He was gonna try and make it. You haven't seen him, huh?"

"No, I don't think he's been in. I wouldn't swear to it though. Who gets the doggie bag?"

The girl from the *News* waited.

"Just put it there," Raymond said. "She doesn't take it, I will."

"I have a name," the girl from the *News* said as the waitress walked away. Then hunched toward him and said, "I think your values are totally out of sync with reality."

Raymond sipped his beer, trying to relate her two statements. He saw her nose in sharp focus, the sheen of her skin heightened by tension. She was annoyed and for a moment he felt good about it. But it was a satisfaction he didn't need and he said, "What're you mad at?"

"I think you're still playing a role," the girl said. "You did the Serpico thing in Narcotics. You thought Vice was fun—"

"I said some funny things happened."

"Now you're into another role, the Lieutenant of Homicide."

"Acting Lieutenant. I'm filling in."

"I want to ask you about that. How old are you?"

"Thirty-six."

"Yeah, that's what it said in your file, but you don't look that old. Tell me . . . how do you get along with the guys in your squad?"

"Fine. Why?"

"Do you . . . handle them without any trouble?"

"What do you mean, 'handle them'?"

"You don't seem very forceful to me."

Tell her you have to go to the Men's, Raymond thought.

"Too mild-mannered—" She stopped and then said, with some enthusiasm, making a great discovery, *"That's* it—you're trying to look older, aren't you? The big mustache, conservative navy-blue suit—but you know how you come off?"

"How?"

"Like someone posing in an old tintype photo, old-timey."

Raymond leaned on the table, interested. "No kidding, that's what you see?"

"Like you're trying to look like young Wyatt Earp," the girl from the *News* said, watching him closely. "You relate to that, don't you? The no-bullshit Old West lawman."

"Well," Raymond said, "you know where Holy Trinity is? South of here, not far from Tiger Stadium? That's where I grew up. We played cowboys and Indians over on Belle Isle, shot at each other with BB guns. I was born in McAllen, Texas, but I don't remember much about living there."

"I thought I heard an accent every once in a while," the girl from the *News* said. "You're Mexican then, not Puerto Rican?"

Raymond sat back again. "You think I was made acting lieutenant as part of Affirmative Action? Get the minorities in?"

"Don't be so sensitive. I asked a simple question. Are you of Mexican descent?"

"What're you, Jewish or Italian?"

"Forget it," the girl from the *News* said.

Raymond raised a finger at her. "See, a man wouldn't say that either. 'Forget it.' "

"Don't point at me." The girl's anger rising that quickly. "Why wouldn't a man say it, because he'd be afraid of you?"

"Or he'd be more polite. I mean why act tough?"

*"I* don't carry a gun," the girl from the *News* said, "and I'm not playing the role, you are. Like John Wayne or somebody. Clint

Eastwood. Don't you relate to that type? Want to be like them?

"Do I want to be an actor?"

"You know what I mean."

"I'm in homicide," Raymond said. "I don't have to make up anything; it's usually dramatic enough the way it is."

"Wow, is that revealing." She stared with a look that said she knew something he didn't. "You're almost in contact with your center. You catch a glimpse of it and the transference is immediate. I have to be this way because of my job—"

"I don't like to look at my center," Raymond said, straight-faced.

"A smart-ass attitude is another defense," the girl said. "I think it's fairly obvious the basic impediment is all this *machismo* bull-shit cops are so hung up on—carrying the big gun, that trip. But I don't want to get into male ego or penis symbols if we can help it."

"No, let's keep it clean."

The girl studied him sadly. "I could comment on that, too, the immediate reference to sexuality as something dirty. It's not a question, Lieutenant, of keeping it clean, but I guess we should try to keep it simple. Just the facts, ma'm, if you know what I mean."

He wondered if it was safe to speak. Then took a chance. "I'll tell you what influenced me most, once I joined the force. The detective sergeants, the old pros. You had to be in at least twenty years to make detective sergeant. Now, we don't have the rank anymore. You don't wait your turn, you take a test and if you pass you move up."

"Like you did," the girl from the *News* said. "A lieutenant with only fifteen years seniority. Because you went to college?"

"Partly," Raymond said. "If I was black I might even be an inspector by now."

The girl from the *News* perked up. "Do I hear resentment, a little bias, perhaps?"

"No, you don't. I'm telling you how it is. The old pros are still around; but they've been passed up along the way by some who aren't pros yet."

"You sound bitter."

"No, I'm not."

"Then you sound like an old man. In fact you dress like an old man." The girl from the *News* kept punching at him.

Dressing this afternoon, knowing he was going to be interviewed, Raymond had put on the navy-blue summer-weight suit, a white short-sleeved shirt and a dark-blue polka-dot tie. He had bought the suit five months ago, following his appointment to lieutenant. He had grown the mustache, he would have to admit, to look older, letting it grow and liking it more and more as it filled in dark and took a bandit turn down around the corners of his mouth. He felt the mustache made him look serious, maybe a little mean. He was five-ten and a half and weighed one-sixty-four, down fifteen pounds in the past few months. It showed in his face, gave him a gaunt, stringy look and made him appear taller.

The girl from the *News* brought it back to impressions, images, the possible influence of certain screen detective *types*, and Raymond said he thought movie detectives looked like cowboys. A mistake. The girl from the *News* jumped on that, said it was revealing and wrote something in her notebook. Raymond said he didn't mean real working cowboys, he meant, you know, the jeans, the denim outfits some of them wore. He said Detroit Police detectives had to wear coats and ties on duty. The girl from the *News* said she thought that was a drag.

They didn't seem to be getting anywhere. Raymond said, "Well, if that's it . . ."

"You still haven't answered the question," the girl from the *News* said, giving him a weary but patient look.

"Would you mind repeating it?"

"The question is, why can't a cop leave his macho role at headquarters and show a little sensitivity at home? Why can't you separate *self* from your professional role and admit some of your vulnerability, your fears, and not just talk about your triumphs."

It was the first time he had heard anyone use the word. *Triumphs.*

"You know, like"—lowering her voice to sound masculine—"'Well, we closed another case, dear. Let's have a drink.' But what about your resentments, all the annoying, picky things that're part of your job?"

Raymond nodded, picturing the scene. "Okay, I come home,

21

my wife says, 'How'd it go today, dear?' I say, 'Oh, not too bad, honey. I got something I want to share with you.' "

The girl from the *News* was staring at him, a little hurt or maybe resigned. "I was hoping we could keep it serious."

"I'm serious. You're the wife. You say, 'Hi, honey. Have anything you'd like to share with me?' And I say, 'As a matter of fact, honey, I want to tell you something I learned today *about* sharing, as a matter of fact.' "

The girl from the *News* was suspicious, but said, "All right, what?"

"Well, a young woman was murdered," Raymond said solemnly. "Cause of death strangulation, asphyxia due to mechanical compression, traces of seminal fluid in mouth, vagina and rectum—"

The girl from the *News* said, "God."

"So today we talk to a couple of suspects and one of them agrees to cop if we'll trade off with nothing heavier than manslaughter. We dicker around, offer him second degree and finally he says okay. He says actually it was his buddy that killed her. His buddy's fresh out of the joint and very horny. See, what happened, they met the girl in a bar and the guy making the statement says she was all over him. So they take her out in a field and after the first guy's done he lets his buddy have seconds."

"Lieutenant—"

"That's what he said, let his buddy have seconds. Well, the buddy gets in there and won't stop. I mean he just keeps, you know, going. Make a long story short, the girl starts screaming and the buddy panics and strangles her to shut her up. But, he's not sure she's dead. What if she comes to and identifies them in a lineup? So, they find this big chunk of concrete that'd been used to anchor a fence post—weighed about a hundred pounds—and they pick it up and drop it on the girl's face. Pick it up, drop it on her face again."

The girl from the *News* was reaching for her big mailbag purse.

"Pick it up, drop it. When we found her, we thought maybe a semi had run over her. I mean you wouldn't believe this was a girl's face."

"I don't think you're funny."

"No, it isn't funny at all. But then the guy said in his statement—"

The girl from the *News* was walking away from the table.

"He said, 'This is what I get for playing Mr. Nice Guy and *sharing* my broad with my buddy.'"

He walked across Grand River to Dunleavy's. Jerry Hunter was at the bar with a girl who was resting her arm on Jerry's shoulder, close to him but acting bored. She took time to look Raymond Cruz over while he placed his doggie bag on the bar and ordered a bourbon.

Hunter said, "Where's your girlfriend?"

"They have a new thing," Raymond said. "They invite you to dinner. Then just before the check comes they get mad and walk out. Leave you with a forty-two-dollar tab."

The girl with Hunter said, "Is he one, too? He's kinda cute."

Hunter said, "She's trying to figure out what I do for a living."

"If anything," the girl said, moving slightly to the jukebox disco music. "Don't tell me, okay?" She narrowed green-shadowed eyes as she moved with the beat. "If we were over at Lindell's—who's in town?—you might be ballplayers. Except they never wear ties. Nobody wears ties." She stopped and gave Hunter a shrewd look. "Tie with a sport shirt, suit coat doesn't match the pants—you teach shop at some high school, right? And your buddy"—looking at Raymond Cruz again—"what's your sign?"

There was an electronic sound close among them, faint but insistent, a mechanical voice saying *beep beep beep beep*—until Raymond opened his coat and shut it off. Going to the payphone he heard the girl saying to Hunter, "Jesus Christ, you're *cops*. I knew it. That's the next thing I was gonna say."

Everybody knows everything, Raymond Cruz thought. How'd everybody get so smart?

# 3

Because of the lights Raymond Cruz thought of a movie set. The overhead burglar spot and the headlights illuminating the scene. He thought of an actor in a television commercial saying, "The victim's suit is light blue, the blood dark red and the gravel a grayish white." He thought of a movie running backward in a projector, seeing the uniformed officers sucked into the blue and white Plymouths and the squad cars and the EMS van and the morgue wagon yanked out of the picture. Stop there—leaving the silver Continental and the murder victim. He heard Jerry Hunter say, "Well, somebody finally did in the little fucker."

It was difficult to think of Alvin Guy as victim.

"When I talked to Herzog," Raymond said, "the first thing I thought was how come it hasn't happened before this?" He stood at the edge of the scene with Hunter and his executive sergeant, Norbert Bryl. "Who found him?"

"Car from the 11th," Bryl said. "The judge'd called nine-eleven on his car phone, but the operator couldn't get the location. Then a few minutes later a woman on the next street over there, 20413 Coventry, she calls at one-thirty-five to report gun-shots."

"How about witnesses?"

"Nothing yet. Wendell's talking to the woman. Maureen's around someplace. American La France doesn't have a night number, but I don't think Judge Guy was here buying fire equipment."

"The squad-car guys make him?"

"Yeah. They couldn't tell by looking at him, but his wallet was lying there."

Raymond said, quietly but earnestly, "If they knew it's Guy then why didn't they pick him up and dump him in Hazel Park? It's two blocks away."

"Lieutenants aren't supposed to talk like that," Bryl said. "It's a nice idea though. Their body, their case. The squad-car guys didn't know for sure he's dead, so they call EMS. EMS comes, they take one look, call the meat wagon."

Hunter said, "They don't know he's *dead?* He took about three in the mouth, two more in the chest, through and through, big fucking exit wounds—they don't know he's dead."

Uniformed evidence technicians were taking Polaroid shots of the body and the Mark VI, measuring distances, drawing a plan of the scene, picking up betting ticket stubs, credit cards, cigarette butts; they would haul the judge's car to the police garage on Jefferson and go over it for prints, poke around in all its crevices. One of the morgue attendants, in khaki shirt and pants, stood watching with a plastic body bag over his shoulder. Bryl began making notes for his Case Assigned Report.

It was 2:50 A.M. Alvin Guy had been dead little more than an hour and Raymond Cruz, the acting lieutenant in the navy-blue suit he had put on because he was meeting the girl from the *News*, felt time running out. He said, "Well, let's knock on some doors. We're not gonna do this one without a witness. We start dipping in the well something like this we'll have people copping to everything but the killing of Jesus. I don't want suspects out of the file. I want a direction we can move on. I want to bust in the door while the guy's still in bed, opens his eyes he can't fucking believe it. Otherwise—we're all retired down in Florida working for the Coconuts Police Department, the case still open. I don't want that to happen."

Norbert Bryl, the executive sergeant of Squad Seven, Detroit Police Homicide Section, had his graying hair razor-cut and styled at "J" Roberts on East Seven Mile once a month. He liked dark shirts and light-colored ties, beige on maroon, wore wire-frame tinted glasses and carried a flashlight that was nearly two feet long. Bryl plotted a course before he moved.

He said, "You don't want to rule out robbery as the only motive."

"Fires through the windshield and hits Guy in the mouth," Raymond said. "I want to meet this robber before he gets into something heavy."

The acting lieutenant left a few minutes later to find a telephone and report to Inspector Herzog. They did not talk about murder over radios.

Wendell Robinson, in a three-piece light-gray suit, came out of the darkness holding a small brown paper sack. He said, "You doing any good? . . . I talk to the woman on Coventry call the nine-eleven? I say, I believe you heard some gunshots. The woman say yeah, and I saw the man done it. Earlier he was out in the alley and I saw him with his gun. I ask her which man is this and she told me he lives down the street, twenty-two five-eleven. I go down there, get the man out of his bed and ask him about a gun he has. Man frowns and squints like he's trying to get his memory working. Says no, I don't recall no gun. I say well, the lady down the street *saw* you with a gun, out'n the alley. You come on downtown we'll have a witness lineup, see if she can pick you out. The man say oh, *that* gun. Yeah, old thing I was looking to shoot rats with. Yeah, I found that gun yesterday, right in the same alley." Wendell held up the bag. "Little froze-up Saturday night piece, blow the man's hand off he ever fire it."

"They lie to you," Hunter said. "They fucking lie right to your face."

Another man sitting in a car had been shot to death in front of the Soup Kitchen, corner of Franklin and Orleans, and the shooter—they learned later—had waited around to see the police cars and the EMS van arrive before he hopped on a Jefferson Avenue bus and went home.

There were people here, hanging around the unmarked blue Plymouth sedans, who had thrown on clothes or a bathrobe to come out and watch. Most of them seemed to be black people. Women holding their arms like they were cold. Figures silhouetted by the street light on the corner. It was a clear night, temperature in the mid-60s, warm for October.

Hunter, running a finger beneath his sandy mustache, stared openly at the watchers, studying them. When he turned to Bryl he said, "If it's robbery, why'd the judge pull in here?"

"To take a leak," Bryl said. "How do I know why he pulled in. But he was robbed and that's all we got so far."

"It was a hit," Hunter said. "Two guys. They set him up—see him at the track, arrange a meet. Maybe sell him some dope. One of 'em gets in the car with the judge, like he's gonna make the deal, the other guy—he's not gonna shoot through the window, his partner's in the line of fire. So he hits him through the windshield. With a .45."

"Now you have the weapon," Bryl said. "Where'd you get the .45?"

"Same place you got the piss he had to take," Hunter said. "Any way you put the judge here, for whatever reason, it's still a hit."

"This other man in the car," Wendell Robinson said, "he sitting there while the judge's calling the nine-eleven?"

"You guys're hung up on details," Hunter said. "We're talking about motive. Did the shooter have a motive other'n robbery?"

"Okay, I'm gonna give you the job, make up the list of suspects," Bryl said, "if you have enough paper and pencils and you have about a month with nothing to do, because you know how many names you're talking about? Every lawyer ever had a case in front of Judge Guy. Every guy he ever sent away. Everybody in the Wayne County Prosecutor's office. Every police officer— I'll be conservative—half the police officers in the city. Put down about twenty-six hundred names right there. Anybody even knew the prick, it's gone through their mind."

Wendell Robinson said to Hunter, "Idea upsets him."

"Yeah, he don't want to think about it," Hunter said, "but it was a fucking hit and he knows it."

Maureen Downey appeared out of the dark now and stood listening, holding a notebook and purse to her breast the way young girls carry school books. When Hunter noticed her she said, "If it was a hit, why'd he drive in here?"

"To go the bathroom," Hunter said. "Maureen, let's get out of here and find a motel."

She said, "Let's see if we can get a positive I.D. on the other car first."

Hunter said, "You think you're gonna impress me with that detective shit, you're crazy. You're a *girl*, Maureen."

"I know I'm a girl," Maureen said. She smiled easily and was never shocked, by words or bullet wounds. She had the healthy look of a brown-haired, 110-pound marathon runner and had been a homicide detective five of her fourteen years with the Detroit Police Department. Hunter would remind Maureen she was a girl. Or Hunter would tell her she was just one of the dicks. Hunter liked to play with Maureen and see her perfect teeth when she smiled.

Bryl used his flashlight to poke her arm and said, "What other car, Maureen?"

They waited as Raymond Cruz walked over to them from the Plymouth. He said, "Who wants another one?" Keeping his voice low. "Twenty-five-to-thirty-year-old white female, no I.D. Well dressed, shot, possibly raped, burn marks—what look like burn marks—on the inside of her thighs. Found her in Palmer Park half hour ago."

"Insect bites," Hunter said. "They can look like burn marks. Remember the guy—what was his name—the GM exec. Looked like he'd been burned, it turned out to be ant bites."

"Somebody lying in the weeds a couple of days, maybe," Raymond said. "This one's fresh. Car from the 12th spotted a guy out on the golf course, two o'clock in the morning. They put a light on him and he runs. Start chasing him and almost trip over the woman's body."

Bryl said, "They get the guy?"

"Not yet, but they think he's still in the park."

Hunter said, "Tell 'em they want to I.D. the lady, go across Woodward—what's the name of that place?—where all the hookers and the fags hang out."

"I asked Herzog, he said no, she doesn't look like a hooker. Probably she was dumped there. So—we can have her if we want. Herzog says how's it look here? I told him I don't know, we could be around all day and still use some help."

Maureen said, "We've got a second car at the scene. Young guy hanging around—wait'll you hear the story."

Raymond took time to give her a warm look that was almost a smile. "I turn my back a few minutes, Maureen, what do you do? Come up with a witness. Is he any good?"

"I think you're gonna like him," Maureen said, opening her notebook.

In his statement Gary Sovey, twenty-eight, explained how his car had been stolen the previous week and how a friend of his happened to see it this evening in the parking lot of the Intimate Lounge on John R. Gary said he went over there with a baseball bat to wait for whoever stole it to come out of the lounge and get in the car, a '78 VW Scirocco. Gary stated that he waited in the vicinity of Local 771 UAW-CIO headquarters, which is between the Intimate Lounge and the American La France Fire Equipment Company. At approximately 1:30 A.M. he saw the Silver Mark VI traveling at a high rate of speed south on John R with a black Buick like nailed to its tail. He heard tires squeal and thought the two cars had turned the corner onto Remington. He was on the north side of Local 771, in other words away from the American La France parking lot, so he didn't actually see what happened. But he did hear something that sounded like gunshots. Five of them that he could still hear if he concentrated. Pow, pow, pow, pow-pow. About a minute later he thought he heard what sounded like a woman screaming, but he isn't positive about that part. Was he sure the black car was a Buick? Yes. In fact, Gary said, it was an '80 Riviera and he would bet it had red pin-striping on it.

"The part about the woman screaming—" Raymond stopped. "First—did he get the guy who stole his car?"

Maureen said it turned out the car had been there two or three days, abandoned, and the Intimate Lounge owner was about to call the police. So Gary was still mad.

She said, "I like the part about the woman screaming too. We can talk to Gary about it some more."

Raymond said, "If there was a woman with the judge and the guy's gonna shoot her anyway, why didn't he do it here?"

Hunter said, "Took her to the park, fool around a little first."

Bryl said, "I love to listen to you guys. You take the bare possibility a woman was even here and you make her the one found in the park. Two separate shootings with no apparent nexus at all except they were both shot about the same time. The judge here, the woman four, five miles away in Palmer Park."

"Across the street from Palmer Woods," Raymond said, "where the judge lived."

It stopped Bryl for a moment. He said, "Okay, you want to believe it, that's fine. If there's a connection we'll know by this afternoon, but right now I'm not gonna jump up in the air and get all excited. You now why?"

As he spoke they separated, moving aside to let the morgue wagon roll out to the street, and Raymond didn't hear the rest of what Bryl said. He didn't have to. Norb Bryl wasn't going to jump up in the air because he was Norb Bryl—who weighed evidence before giving an opinion and kept hunches to himself. He would say, "We don't even know absolutely for sure from the medical examiner the cause of death and you're talking about a nexus." Bryl had established his image.

Raymond Cruz was still working on his.

Thirty-six years old—what do you want to be when you grow up? He wanted to be a police officer. He *was* a police officer. But what kind? (This is where it became gray, hazy.) Uniformed? Precinct commander? Administrative? Deputy chief someday with a big office, drapes—shit, why not work for General Motors?

He could be dry-serious like Norbert Bryl, he could be dry-cool like Wendell Robinson, he could be crude and a little crazy like Jerry Hunter . . . or he could appear quietly unaffected, stand with hands in the pockets of his dark suit, expression solemn beneath the gunfighter mustache . . . and the girl from the *News* would see it as his Dodge City pose: the daguerreotype peace officer, now packing a snub-nosed .38 Smith with rubber bands around the grip instead of a hogleg .44.

How did he explain himself to her? Pictures could jump in his head, as they did right now, clamor for him to tie in the two killings, because he knew beyond any doubt there *was* a nexus and ballistics and lipstick on cigarette butts would prove it . . . Or, tests would prove nothing and that's why there were bored, cynical policemen who seldom ever hoped and were never disappointed . . . if you wanted to get into poses. Tell her there were all different kinds of policemen just as there were all different kinds of priests and baseball players. Why would she tell him he was posing? Playing a role, she said. You had to know you were doing it before you could be accused of posing. The gunship colonel in that Vietnam movie who wore the old-fashioned cavalry hat— what's his name, Robert Duvall—strutting across the beach, taking his shirt off to go surfing while the VC were shooting at him—*that* was posing, for Christ's sake.

Raymond Cruz said to his sergeants, watching the morgue wagon drive off, "Who wants to go to Palmer Park? . . . Maureen?"

Alone together in the blue Plymouth neither of them said a word until they were almost to the park. Maureen assumed Raymond was going over the case, sorting out evidence, understandably withdrawn. Which was fine. She never felt obliged to talk, make up things, if there was nothing to say.

Maureen Downey wrote a paper in the ninth grade entitled "Why I Want To Be A Policewoman Someday." ("Because it really sounds exciting . . .") She had to leave Nashville, Michigan, to do it, entered the Detroit Police Academy and was assigned, for nine years, to Sex Crimes. Jerry Hunter would ask her why she supposed she was chosen for it and study her through half-closed eyes. He would ask her about deviates and weird fetishes and Maureen would say, "How about a guy who licks honey off of girls' feet?" Hunter would say, "What's wrong with that? . . . Come on, Maureen, give me a really weird one." And Maureen would say, "I'm afraid if I give you a raunchy one you'll try it."

She was comfortable with all the members of the squad, maybe with Raymond a little more than the others; which didn't seem to make sense, because most of the time he was pretty quiet, too. But when he did talk he said unexpected things or asked strange questions that didn't seem to relate to anything.

Like suddenly, after long minutes of silence, asking her if she had seen *Apocalypse Now.*

Yes. She liked it a lot.

"What'd you like about it?"

"Martin Sheen. And the one on the boat, the skinny one that almost died of fright when the tiger jumped out."

"You like Robert Duvall?"

"Yeah, I think he's great."

"You ever see a movie called *The Gunfighter?*"

"I don't think so."

"Gregory Peck. It's pretty old—it was on the other night."

"Not that I remember . . ."

"There's a part in it," Raymond said, "Gregory Peck's sitting at a table in the saloon, his hands are out of sight, like in his lap, and this hotshot two-gun kid comes in and tries to pick a fight, needles Gregory Peck, you know, to go for his gun, so the kid can make a name for himself."

"Did Gregory Peck have a big mustache?"

"Yeah, kinda. Pretty big."

"Yeah, I think I did see it. It was a lot like yours."

"What?"

"His mustache."

"Kind of. Anyway, Gregory Peck doesn't move. He tells the hotshot kid if he wants to draw, go ahead. But, he says, how do you know I don't have a .44 pointing at your belly while you're standing there? The kid almost draws, you can see him trying to make up his mind. Does Gregory Peck have a gun under there or not? Finally the kid backs off. He walks out and Gregory Peck sits back in the saloon chair and you see what he had under there was a pocket knife, paring his fingernails."

"Yeah, I did see it," Maureen said, "but I don't remember much about it.

"That was a good picture," Raymond said, and was silent again.

# 4

When Sandy Stanton first told Clement about the Albanian, Clement said, "What in the hell's a Albanian?"

Sandy said, "An Albanian is a little fella with black hair and a whole shitpile of money he keeps down in his basement. He says in a safe inside a hidden room. You believe it?"

Clement said, "I still don't know what a Albanian is even. What's he do?"

"His name's Skender Lulgjaraj—" pronouncing it to rhyme with Pull-your-eye.

"Jesus Christ," Clement said.

"And if I spelled it you wouldn't believe it," Sandy said. "He's a little black-eyed doll baby that loves to disco. Owns some Coney Island hot dog places and tells me about all this money he's got every time I see him."

"How many times is that?"

"I been seeing him at discos for months. Dresses nice; I think he's doing all right."

"Well, let's go over and have us one with everything," Clement said.

"Wait till I find out if he's for real," Sandy said. "Skender wants to take me to the race track.

That had sounded pretty good. See what kind of a spender the Albanian was. Clement would tag along in Sandy's other boy-friend's car and Sandy would introduce him later that night—like they just happened to run into each other.

Except Clement ran into something else.

Del Weems wasn't exactly Sandy's other boyfriend, but she was staying in his apartment while he was out of town giving management seminars. Clement was staying with her.

Clement had never met Del Weems. He prowled around the man's apartment learning about him: studying weird prints and pottery and metal sculptures the man had acquired as a member of the Fine-Art-of-the-Month Club and trying on the man's Brooks Brothers clothes, size 42 suits, size 36 pants, the length not too bad but the bulk of the garments obscuring Clement's wiry 160-pound frame. Sandy said he looked like he was playing dress-up, trying on his dad's clothes. She said a boy with his build and his tattoos ought to stick to Duck Head bib overalls. They'd laugh and Clement would come out of the bedroom wearing yellow slacks and a flowery Lily Pulitzer sports jacket Clement said looked like a camouflage outfit in the war of the fairies and they'd laugh some more: the thirty-four-year-old boy from Lawton, Oklahoma, and the twenty-three-year-old girl from French Lick, Indiana, making it in the big city.

Sandy had met Del Weems when she was a cocktail waitress at Nemo's in the Renaissance Center (and had quit after six months because she could never find her way out of the complex with all its different walks and levels and elevators you weren't supposed to use—like being in Mammoth Cave—you looked way up about one hundred feet to the ceiling, except the RenCen was all rough cement, escalators, expensive shops and ficus trees.) Del Weems was a good tipper. She started going out with him and staying over at his apartment, at first thinking Clement would love Del's specs: forty-seven, divorced management consultant, lived on the twenty-fifth floor of 1300 Lafayette, drove a black Buick Riviera with red pin-striping, owned twelve suits and eight sport coats; she hadn't counted the pants.

Clement had asked what a management consultant was. Sandy said he like put deals together for big companies and told corporate executives—the way she understood it—how to run their business and not fuck up. Clement was skeptical because he couldn't picture in his mind what Del Weems actually did. So when the man went off on this latest seminar and Clement came to stay, he pulled the man's bills and bank statements out of the teakwood desk in the living room, studied them a few minutes and said shit, the man didn't have money, he had credit cards. Clement said you stick a .38 in the man's mouth—all right, partner, give me all the money you been raking in off these fools, and what does the chicken fat do? Hands you his VISA card. Shit no, it had to be cash and carry. Ethnics were the ones, Clement said. Ethnics, niggers, anybody that didn't trust banks, had a piss-poor regard for the IRS and kept their money underneath the bed or in a lard can. Ethnics and dentists.

That's why the Coney Island Albanian sounded good—if Clement could ever get close enough to check him out. In the meantime, cross off the chicken-fat consultant as a score, but use his place to rest up and get acquainted with the finer things in life. Drink the man's Chivas, watch some TV and look out at the twenty-fifth-floor view of Motor City. Man oh man.

The Detroit River looked like any big-city river with worn-out industrial works and warehouses lining the frontage, ore boats and ocean freighters passing by, a view of Windsor across the way that looked about as much fun as Moline, Illinois, except for the giant illuminated Canadian Club sign over the distillery.

But then all of a sudden—as Clement edged his gaze to the right a little—there were the massive dark-glass tubes of the Renaissance Center, five towers, the tallest one seven hundred feet high, standing like a Buck Rogers monument over downtown. From here on, the riverfront was being purified with plain lines in clean cement, modern structures that reminded Clement a little of Kansas City or Cincinnati—everybody putting their new convention centers and sports arenas out where you could see them. (They had even been building a modernistic new shopping center in Lawton just before the terrible spring twister hit, the same one that picked Clement's mom right out of the yard, running from the house to the storm cellar, and carried her off without leaving a trace.) Clement would swivel his gaze then over downtown and come around north—looking at all the parking lots that were like fallow fields among stands of old 1920s office buildings and patches of new cement—past Greektown tucked in down there—he could almost smell the garlic—past the nine-story Detroit Police headquarters, big and ugly, a glimpse of the top floors of the Wayne County jail beyond the police building, and on to the slender rise of the Frank Murphy Hall of Justice, where they had tried to nail Clement's ass one time and failed. Clement liked views from high places after years in the flatlands of Oklahoma and feeling the sky pressing down on him. It was the same sky when you could see it, when it wasn't thick with dampness, but it seemed a lot higher in Detroit. He would look up there and wonder if his mom was floating around somewhere in space.

Sandy stayed with the Albanian all night and came home to the high-rise apartment about noon with a tale of wonders—a secret door, a room hidden away in the basement—aching to tell Clement about it.

And what was Clement doing? Reading the paper. Something he never did. Sitting on the couch in his Hanes briefs, scratching the reddish hair on his chest, idly tugging at his crotch, hunched over and staring at the newspaper spread open next to him, his mouth moving silently as he read.

"You reading the *paper?*"

Clement didn't even look up. Now he was scratching the bright new blue and red tattoo of a gravestone on his right forearm that said *In Memory of Mother*.

"Hey!"

Hell with him. Sandy went into the bedroom and changed from her silk shirt and slacks to green satin jogging shorts and a T-shirt that said, *Cedar Point, Sandusky, Ohio.* She looked about seventeen, a freckled, reddish-blond 95-pounder with perky little breasts. Sort of a girl version of Clement, though a lot better looking. Not the type, at first glance, some management consultant would keep in his stylish apartment. But look again and see the fun in her eyes. It gave a man the feeling that if he turned her little motor on she'd whirl him back to his youth and take him places he'd never been.

Back in the living room she tried again. "You still reading the paper?"

You bet he was, every word for the second time, wondering how in the world he hadn't recognized the judge last night—the face with the little tango-dancer mustache staring up at him from the front page. He had shot and killed Judge Alvin Guy and didn't have a thing to show for it. Not even peace of mind now. If there wasn't a reward for shooting the little dinge he ought to get a medal, *some*thing.

Sandy Stanton said, "Well, I saw the secret room and I saw this little safe he's so proud of. I think me and you could pick it up without any fear of getting a hernia. But it was weird. I mean the room, with all these cots folded up and a fridge, one tiny room like full of canned goods . . . Hey, you listening or what?"

Clement sat back on the couch, exposing the pair of bluebirds tattooed above his pure-white breasts. When they had first met three and a half years ago at a disco, Clement had said, "You want to see my birds?" and opened his shirt to show her. Then he'd said, "You want to see my chicken?" When Sandy said yes he pulled his shirt out of his pants and showed her his navel in the center of his hard belly. Sandy said, "I don't see any chicken." And Clement said, "It's faded out; all that's left is its asshole."

He nodded toward the picture in the paper. "You know who that is?"

"I saw it," Sandy said. She looked from the bold headline, JUDGE GUY MURDERED, and the grinning photograph to Clement's solemn face. Her mind said, Uh-oh, what does he care? And edged toward the answer, saying, "He couldn'ta been a friend of yours. Why you taking it so hard?"

Silence.

Uh-oh.

Sandy said, "Hey, quit biting your nails. You want to tell me something or's it better I don't know?"

Clement said, "Wouldn't you think they'd be a bounty on the little fucker? A reward you could claim?"

"*Who* could claim?" Sandy waited while Clement bit on the cuticle of his middle finger, left hand, like a little boy watching his dad read his report card.

"You know how many people," Clement said, "would pay money—I mean real money—to have this done? Jesus."

"Maybe somebody did pay."

"Nuh-uh, it was done free of charge. God *damn* it."

"Oh, shit," Sandy said, with a sigh of weariness. "Don't tell me no more, okay?"

She was in the kitchen, Clement was still scratching, biting his nails, staring at the grinning ex-judge, when the security man in the lobby called. He was an older colored man that Sandy liked to kid with, calling him Carlton the doorman. They didn't kid around today, though. Sandy came out to the living room.

"Maybe they come to give you the medal."

Clement hadn't even heard the buzzer. He looked up now. "Who's that?"

"The police," Sandy said.

# 5

Raymond said to Wendell Robinson, "You want to be the good guy?"

"No, you be the good guy," Wendell said, "I'm tired and grouchy enough to be a natural heavy, we need to get into that shit."

Raymond said, "What're you tired from?" But didn't get an answer. The door opened and a girl in a Cedar Point T-shirt and satin shorts was looking at them with innocent eyes. Raymond held up his I.D.

"How are you doing? I'm Lieutenant Raymond Cruz, Detroit Police. This is Sergeant Robinson. We understand—the man downstairs says you name's Sandy Stanton?" Very friendly, almost smiling.

The girl gave them a nod, guarded.

"He said Mr. Weems is out of town." Raymond watched the girl's wide-eyed expression come to life.

"Oh, you're looking for Del."

Raymond said, "Is that right, Sandy, he's out of town?"

"Yeah, on business. I think he went out to California or some-place."

"You mind if we come inside?"

"I know it sounds corny," Sandy said, as though she hated to have to bring it up, "but have you got a warrant?"

Raymond said, "A *warrant*—for what? We're not looking for anything. We just want to ask you about Mr. Weems."

Sandy sighed, stepping out of the way. She watched the two cops, the white one in the dark suit and the black one in the light-gray suit, glance down the short hallway at the closed doors as they went into the living room: the white cop looking around, the black cop going straight to the windows—which is what almost everyone did—to look out at the river and the city. The view was sharply defined this afternoon, the sun backlighting the Renaissance Center, giving the glass towers the look of black marble.

Raymond didn't care too much for the colors in the room: green, gray and black with a lot of chrome. It reminded him of a lawyer's office. He said, "I understand you drove Mr. Weems to the airport."

"The day before yesterday," Sandy said. "What is it you want him for?"

"You drive him out in his car?"

"Yeah . . . why?

"Buick Riviera, license PYX-546?"

"I don't know the license number."

"What do you do for a living, Sandy?"

"You mean when I work? I tend bar, wait tables if I have to."

"You use the car last night?"

"The Buick."

"No, as a matter of fact, I didn't," Sandy said. "I went to the race track with somebody."

"What one, over in Windsor?"

"No, out to Hazel Park."

She saw the black cop turn from the window. He looked like a suit salesman or a professional athlete. A colored guy who spent money on clothes.

The other one was smiling somewhat. "You win?"

Sandy gave him a bored look. "You kidding?"

"I know what you mean," Raymond said. "Who'd you go with?"

"Fella I know. Skender Lulgjaraj."

Amazing. That white cop didn't blink or make a face or say, Lul-what?

"What time'd you get home?"

"It was pretty late."

"Skender drive?"

There, again, like he was familiar with the name. "Yeah, he picked me up."

Raymond frowned, like he was a little confused. "Then who used Mr. Weems' car last night?"

He had a little-boy look about him, even with the droopy mustache. The dark hair down on his forehead . . .

"Nobody did," Sandy said.

She watched them give her the old silent treatment, waiting for her to say too much if she tried to fake it or tried to act innocent or amazed—when all she had to do was hang tough and not act at all. It was hard, though; too hard and finally she said, "What's wrong?"

Raymond said, "Did you loan the car to somebody?"

"Uh-unh."

"Did Mr. Weems, before he left?"

"Not that I know of. Hey, maybe it was stolen."

"It's downstairs," Raymond said. "You have the keys, don't you?"

"Yeah, someplace."

"Why don't you check, just to make sure."

Oh shit, Sandy thought, feeling exposed now in her shorts and T-shirt and bare feet, wanting to walk over to the desk and pick up the keys, but having no idea in the world what Clement did with them—trying to picture him coming in then. No, *she* had come in and he was sitting on the couch reading the paper—the paper still lying there pulled apart. She said, "Gee, I never know what I do with keys," and got away from them, starting to move about the room.

Raymond said, "Maybe we can help you," and began looking around.

"That's okay," Sandy said, "I think I know where they are. You all sit down and take it easy." She made herself *walk* down the short hallway, dark with the doors closed, went into the master bedroom and shut the door behind her.

Clement was stretched out on the king-size bed. He put his hands behind his curly head as Sandy entered and wiggled his toes, showing her how cool he was.

"They gone?"

"No, they're not gone. They want the keys."

"What keys?"

"The fucking car keys, what do you think what keys?" Her whisper came out hoarse, as though from a bigger, huskier woman.

"Shit," Clement said. He thought a moment, watching her feel the top of the dresser. "They got a search warrant?" She didn't answer him. "Hey, you don't have to give 'em no keys."

"You go out and tell 'em that," Sandy said. She had the ring of keys in her hand now, moving toward the door.

"Well, it's up to you," Clement said. "You want to give 'em the keys, go ahead."

Sandy stopped at the door. "What else'm I supposed to do?" Her whisper a hiss now.

"Give 'em the keys," Clement said. "It don't matter."

"What if they find your prints in the car?"

"Ain't no prints to find." Clement's arms were reddish-tan, his body pure white, his bluebirds and ribs resting against the green and gray swirls of Del Weems' designer bedspread. Sandy started to open the door and he said, "Hon? I had sort of an accident parking the car when I come back."

"I love the time you pick to tell me." Sandy took time herself to raise her eyes to the ceiling, giving her words a dramatic effect. "What'd you hit?"

"You know those cement pillars?" Clement said. "I scraped one of 'em parking, took a little paint off the fender—if they was to ask you how it happened." He paused, letting her stare at him. "Why don't we keep it simple, say you did it. How's that sound to you?"

Raymond Cruz looked at the desk, wanting to open the drawers. He looked at the metallic stick figures on the glass coffee table.

He looked at the newspaper lying open on the couch and then over to the dark hallway. What if he walked in there and started opening doors? . . .

Sandy Stanton. He could see the name in a typewritten report, a statement. He tried the name in his mind. Sandy Stanton. He tried it with Norb Bryl saying the name, Sandy Stanton, and then with Jerry Hunter's voice, Sandy Stanton. The name, just the name, was registered in his mind from a time in the past. He walked to the window and looked out. Then turned again, abruptly, and was facing the room as Wendell came out through the dining-L from the kitchen, Wendell shaking his head.

Raymond motioned to the window. "You can see 1300 from here."

"I noticed," Wendell said. "You can see the window of the squad room."

Past the Blue Cross building and beyond the dome of old St. Mary's to the granite nine-story municipal building, police head-quarters—1300 Beaubien—to a window on the fifth floor, above the police garage.

"You notice," Raymond said, "that's 1300 and this is 1300?"

"No shit," Wendell said. "I notice something else, too, while I'm busy noticing. You got hold of something in your head you're playing with."

Raymond frowned at him, amazed. What was going on? Everybody, all of a sudden, reading him.

"You're laying back, savoring it," Wendell said. "You gonna share it with me or keep it a secret?"

Amazing. It was spooky. Raymond thought of the girl from the *News* and said, "You tell your wife what you do?"

Now Wendell was frowning. "What I *do?* You mean tell her everything? Do I look like I want to get shot with my own gun?"

"How do you know what I'm thinking?" Raymond said.

"I don't. That's why I'm asking."

"But you said—like I was on to something."

"Some kind of scheme," Wendell said. "When you lay back and don't move around—you understand?—but look like you want to be *do*ing something? It means you ready to spring. Am I right?"

"Sandy Stanton," Raymond said.

"Cute little lady."

"Where've you heard the name?"

"I don't have the recall you do," Wendell said, "but it's familiar, like a movie star or a name you see in the paper."

"Or in a case file."

"Now we moving," Wendell said.

"Albert RaCosta," Raymond said.

Wendell nodded. "Keep going."

"Louis Nix . . . Victor Reddick. And one more."

"Yeah, the Wrecking Crew." Wendell was still nodding. "I know the names but they were a little before my time."

"Three years ago," Raymond said. "I'd just come over to Seven."

"Yeah, and I came like six months after you," Wendell said. "I read the file, all the newspaper stuff, but I don't recall any Sandy Stanton."

Coming into the living room Sandy said, "What're you doing, talking about me?" She held up the ring of keys. "I found 'em. But if you want to take the car—I don't think I can let you. I mean you haven't even told me why you want it."

Raymond said, "You're sure, Sandy, those're the keys to the Buick?"

"Yeah." She held them up again. "GM keys. He's only got one car."

"When's the last time you drove it?"

"I told you—when I took him to the airport."

"The car was in good shape?"

"Yeah, I guess so."

"No dings in it or anything?"

"Oh," Sandy said and made a face, an expression of pain. "Yeah, I guess I scraped the fender, you know, on the cement down where you park. Del's gonna kill me."

"Getting into a tight place, huh?"

"Yeah, I misjudged a little."

"Which fender was it you scraped, Sandy?"

She held her hands up in front of her and looked at them, trying to remember if shitbird, lying on the bed in his bikinis, had told her. "It was . . . this one, the left one." She looked from the white cop to the black cop and back to the white cop, wanting to say, Am I right?

"You're sure?" Raymond asked her.

Shit, Sandy thought. "Well, I'm pretty sure. But I get mixed up with left and right."

"You live here, Sandy?"

God, it was hard to keep up with him. "No, I'm just staying here while Del's gone, like apartment-sitting."

"Anybody staying with you?"

She hesitated—which she knew she shouldn't do. "No, just me."

"Is anybody else here right now?"

Christ. She hesitated again. "You mean besides us?"

"Uh-huh, besides us," Raymond said.

"No, there isn't anybody here."

"I thought I heard you talking to somebody—you went out to the bedroom."

Sandy said, "I don't think you're being fair at all. If you aren't gonna tell me what you want, then I'm gonna ask you to please leave. Okay?"

"You were at the Hazel Park track last night?"

"I already told you I was."

"You see, Sandy, a car that sounds like Mr. Weems' Buick— maybe the same license number—was involved in an accident out there. About one o'clock."

Sandy said, "You're *traffic* cops? Jesus, I thought this was something more important than *that.*"

"Like what?" Raymond asked.

"I don't know. I just thought . . . two of you come up here, it has to be, you know, something important." Sandy began to feel herself relax. The white cop was saying, well, they have to check out the car first, see if it might be the one, before they get into anything else. Probably—Sandy was thinking at the same time— it was a car that looked like Del's and had almost the same license numbers. That *could* be what happened, a coincidence, and shit-bird in the bedroom had nothing to do with it. There were all kinds of black Buicks, it was a very popular color this year . . . she told the white cop that, too, and the white cop agreed, nodding, and then he was saying, "Oh, by the way . . .

"You seen Clement Mansell lately?"

Like a total stranger coming up to you and saying your name—she couldn't be*lieve* it because she could look right at the white cop and was positive she had never seen him before in her life; he *couldn't* know anything about her. She felt exposed and vulnerable again standing there barefoot with no place to hide, no way to lay it over again and be ready for the question. Still, she said, "Who?"

"Clement Mansell," Raymond said. "Isn't he an old friend of yours?"

Sandy said, "Oh . . . you know him? Yeah, I recall the name, sure."

Raymond took a business card out of his suit-coat pocket. Handing it to her he said, "You see him, have him give me a call, okay?" The white cop and the black cop both thanked her as they left.

In the elevator Wendell said, "Clement Mansell. You name the Wrecking Crew and save the best one. I don't know how I forgot him."

Raymond was watching the floor numbers light up in descending order. "I probably shouldn't have done that."

"What, ask her about him? We all stunt a little bit."

"If it's Mansell I want him to know. I don't want him to run, but I want him to think about it. You understand what I mean?"

"Man could be back in Oklahoma, nowhere around here."

"Yeah, he could be in Oklahoma," Raymond said. His gaze came down from the numbers to the elevator door as it opened. They walked out of the alcove, across the lobby to the desk where the doorman sat with a wall of television monitors behind him. Raymond waited for him to look up at them.

"You didn't tell us somebody was with her, Miss Stanton, twenty-five oh-four."

"I don't believe you ask me," the doorman said.

Wendell said, "How long he been staying with her, uncle?"

The middle-aged black man in the porter's coat looked at the younger, well-built black man in the three-piece light-gray suit. "How long is *who* been staying with her?"

"Shit," Wendell said. "Here we go."

6

One time Clement was run over by a train and lived. It was a thirty-three-car Chesapeake & Ohio freight train with two engines and a caboose.

Clement was with a girl. They were waiting at a street crossing in Redford Township about eleven at night, the red lights flashing and the striped barrier across the road, when Clement got out of the car and went out to stand on the tracks, his back to the engine's spotlight coming toward him at forty miles an hour. Yes, he was a little high, though not too high. He was going to jump out of the way at the last second, turned with his *back* to the approaching train, looking over at the girl's face in the car windshield, the girl's eyes about to come out of her head. Instead of jumping out of the way Clement changed his mind and laid down between the tracks. The train engineer saw Clement and slammed on the emergency brake, but not in time. Twenty-one cars passed over Clement before the train was brought to a stop and he crawled out from beneath the twenty-second one. The train engineer, Harold Howell of Grand Rapids, said, "There was just no excuse for it." Clement was taken to Garden City Hospital where he was treated for a bruised back and released. When questioned by the Redford Township Police Clement said, "Did I break a law? Show me where it says I can't lay down in front of a train if I want?"

Clement said it was like conditioning, preparing for the ball-clutching moments of life while building your sphincter muscle. After lying in front of a freight train you can lie in bed in your underwear while two cops are visiting, asking about a certain black Buick—and while a mean-looking Walther P.38 automatic is hidden nearby at that very moment—and not worry about making doo-doo in the bed.

See, just as he knew he could easily have jumped out of the train's way—as he explained it to Sandy—he knew he had time to skin through this present situation and get rid of the gun—though he hated to do it—before the cops came back with a warrant to search or impound the car. He admired the cops' restraint these days in not opening bedroom doors or looking inside cars without a warrant. Cops had to go by the rules or have their evidence thrown out of court. It gave Clement, he felt, an edge: he could grin at the ball yankers, antagonize them some, knowing they had to respect his rights as a citizen.

But who in the hell was Lieutenant Raymond Cruz? Clement studied the business card, then looked out the bedroom window and squinted toward the police headquarters building.

"I don't know any Lieutenant Raymond Cruz."

"Well, he knows you."

"What's he look like? Regular old beer-gut dick?"

"No, he's skinny almost."

"Raymond Cruz," Clement said thoughtfully. "He's a greaser, huh?"

"Well, he's sort of dark, but not real. He seems quiet . . . Except, it's funny, I get the feeling there's some meanness in him," Sandy said. "Otherwise he's kinda cute."

Clement turned from the windows to look at her, idly scratching himself. "He's cute, huh? I got to see a De-troit homicide dick that's cute; that'll be one of my goals in life." He said then, "I guess you better get dressed."

"Where we going?"

"Want you to drive over to Belle Isle for me."

"Now wait a sec—"

"I'll tell you where the gun's hid down the garage. Up over one of them beams? Put it in your purse—it's in a paper sack so it won't get your purse oily or nothing—go on over to Belle Isle and park and come walking back across the bridge partway. When there's no cars around—'specially any blue Plymouths—take the sack out of your purse and drop it in the river."

"Do I have to?" Sandy turned on her pained expression. Clement just looked at her, patiently, and she said, "I ought to least have a joint first. Half a one?"

"I want you clear-headed, hon bun."

There wasn't any grass in the apartment anyway. Down to seeds and stems. She'd have to stop at the store on the way and pick up a baggie.

Clement tucked Raymond Cruz's business card into the elastic of his briefs and took hold of Sandy's arms, sliding his hands up under the satiny sleeves and tugging her gently against him. He said, "What're you nervous about, huh? You never been nervous before. You need one of Dr. Mansell's treatments? That it, hon bun, get you relaxed? Well, we can fix you up."

"Mmmmm, that feels good," Sandy said, closing her eyes. She could feel him breathing close to her ear. After a moment she said, "I have to do it, huh?"

"You want us to be friends, don't you?" Clement said. "Don't friends help each other?"

"I think I feel another little friend—"

"See, Homer don't pout or wimp out on you. He's always there when you need him. 'Specially when I'm hung over some, huh? You can hit him with a stick and he won't go 'way."

"Does it have to be in the river?"

"Can you think of a better place? You get back, sugar, we'll go see your Albanian. How's that sound?"

Tell 'em anything long as you tell 'em something.

Women were fun, but you had to treat them like little kids, play with them, promise them things; especially Sandy, who was a good girl and never let him down. Clement kissed her goodbye and looked at his situation as he got dressed.

He'd have to leave here in the next day or so. He'd miss the view, but there was no sense in being easy to reach. Man, they were swift this time. Or lucky. He couldn't recall a Lieutenant Raymond Cruz. Maybe if he saw the man's face. Get rid of anything incriminating, like the gun. Which was a shame; he loved that P.38.

Clement picked up his pants from the floor and dug out what he'd scored off the judge. The money, three hundred forty bucks, was clean, no problem with it. He'd left the checks in the wallet; he couldn't see himself peddling a dead man's checks. The little 2 by 3 spiral notebook—it was thin, like pages had been torn out—had names and phone numbers in it, also columns of figures and dates, impressive amounts up in the thousands with a lot of dollar signs, but meaningless to him . . . until he came to a right-hand page—the second to last one in the notebook—and a phone number jumped out at him.

W.S.F. 644-5905.

The initials and numbers gone over several times with a ballpoint and then underlined and enclosed within a heavily drawn square.

To make it special, Clement thought. He didn't recognize the initials, but the number was sure familiar, one he had seen not too long ago. But where?

Two officers from the Major Crime Mobile Unit—in street clothes, in a black unmarked Ford sedan—were assigned the surveillance of the Buick Riviera, license number PYX-546, located in the lower-level parking area at 1300 Lafayette East. They were given mug-shot photos of Clement Mansell, 373-8411, full face and profile, the photos bearing a '78 date. If he got in the car, Mansell was to be approached with caution and taken into custody for questioning. If he refused, resisted or tried to drive off, the officers were to arrest him, but under no circumstances search the car. If a woman got in the car they were to follow, keep her under close surveillance and call in.

Which is what the MCMU officers did when Sandy drove off in the Buick, took Jefferson to East Grand Boulevard, turned left—going away from the Belle Isle bridge—and proceeded to a bar named Sweety's Lounge, located at 2921 Kercheval. The subject went inside, came out again in approximately ten minutes with a middle-aged black male and accompanied him next door, to 2925 Kercheval, where they entered the lower household of a two-family flat.

MCMU called Homicide, Squad Seven, and requested instructions.

# 7

Technically, Squad Seven of the Detroit Police Homicide Section specialized in the investigation of "homicides committed during the commission of a felony," most often an armed robbery, a rape, sometimes a breaking and entering, as opposed to barroom shootings and Saturday night mom and pop murders that were emotionally stimulated and not considered who-done-its.

The squad's home was in Room 527 of Police Headquarters, a colorless, high-ceilinged office roughly twenty-four-by-twenty that contained an assortment of ageless metal desks and wooden tables butted together, file cabinets, seven telephones, a Norelco coffeemaker, a GE battery-charge box for PREP radios, a locked cabinet where squad members sometimes stored their handguns, two banks of flickering fluorescent lights, a wall display of 263 mug shots of accused murders, a coatrack next to the door and a sign that read:

*Do something—*
*either lead, follow*
*or get the hell*
*out of the way!*

A very old poster, peeling from the column that stood in the middle of the squadroom and left over from another time, stated, *I will give up my gun when they pry my cold fingers from around it.*

It was 2:30 in the afternoon when Raymond Cruz returned to the squadroom. The investigations into the deaths of Alvin Guy and the young woman found in Palmer Park were less than thirteen hours old.

Raymond hung up the suit coat he'd been wearing for the past twenty-four hours, crossed to the unofficial lieutenant's desk in the corner—the desk facing out to the squadroom, beneath the room's only window and the air-conditioning unit that didn't work—and listened.

Norb Bryl's desk faced the lieutenant's. Bryl was on the phone—taking notes and saying, ". . . keyhole defectment, bullet found in anterior cranial fossa . . ."—talking to someone at the Wayne County morgue.

Hunter, also on the phone, had a young black guy sitting at his desk who was the suspect/witness in the Palmer Park murder. They sat almost knee to knee, the young black guy slouched low, wearing a white T-shirt and a plaid golf hat with a narrow brim that he fooled with as he waited for Hunter, who was waiting for someone to come back on the line. No one else was in the squadroom.

Still waiting, Hunter said to the young black guy, "Twenty-five years old and all you got are some *traffic* tickets? You must've been in the army a while."

Raymond watched the young black guy give a slow shrug without saying anything.

Hunter said, "Let's see your hair."

The young black guy raised his hat above his head and held it there.

"We'll call it nappy," Hunter said and made a notation on the DPD Interrogation Record lying on his desk.

"It's Afro," the young black guy said.

Hunter said, "An *Afro?* It's a shitty-looking Afro. We'll call it a nappy 'fro." He straightened then and said into the phone, "Yeah? . . . *Darrold* Woods? . . . Okay, give me what you got." Hunter nodded and said yeah, uh-huh, as he made notes on a yellow legal pad. When he finished, Hunter picked up a Constitutional Rights Certificate of Notification form and said to the young black guy, "How come you signed this Donald Woods? You lied to me, Darrold"—sounding a little hurt—"try to tell me you're cherry and they got a sheet on you, man. First thing, I'm gonna erase this zero 'cause it's a bunch of shit."

Darrold Woods was saying, "Two larceny from a person reduced from larceny not armed and a little bitty assault thing . . ."

And Hunter was saying, "Little *bit*ty . . . little bitty fucking tire iron you used on the guy . . ."

Bryl put his hand over the phone and said to Raymond, " 'Cause of death multiple gunshots . . . two slugs, one with copper jacket recovered intact within the spinal canal, the other one in his head . . ."

Raymond said, "Judge Guy?"

Bryl nodded and said into the phone, "Okay, how many holes in the girl, Adele Simpson? . . . You sure? . . . Can't find any more, uh?" He put his hand over the phone and said to Raymond, "It's looking good. Maureen's already taken the slugs over to the lab."

Hunter was saying to the young black guy, "How well did you know Adele Simpson?"

"I never seen her before right then."

"You took her purse—what else?"

"What purse you talking about?"

"Darrold, you had Adele Simpson's credit cards on you."

"I found 'em."

Hunter said, "You gonna start shucking me again, Darrold? We're talking about murder, man, not a little half-assed assault. You understand me, mandatory life . . ."

Raymond got up from his desk. He walked over to the young black guy in the plaid golf hat and touched him on the shoulder.

"Let me ask you something, okay?"

The young black guy didn't answer, but looked up at the lieutenant.

"The woman's lying there dead—is that right?"

"What I been tryng to tell him."

"What did you burn her with?"

The young black guy didn't answer.

"Shit," Hunter said, "let's put him upstairs."

"I just touch her a little," the young black guy said then, "see if she's alive."

Hunter said, "What'd you touch her with, your dick?"

"No, man, nothing like that."

"They're doing an autopsy on her," Hunter said. "Now they find any semen in her and it matches your blood type—then we got to ask you, Darrold, you rape her before or after you shot her?"

"I *didn't* shoot her. You find a gun on me? Shit no."

"Where'd you touch her?" Raymond asked.

After a moment the young black guy said, "Like around her legs."

"Just touched her a little?"

"Yeah, just, you know, a little bit."

"You touch her with a cigarette?" Raymond asked.

"Yeah, I believe it was a cigarette."

"Lit cigarette?"

"Yeah, was smoked down though, you know, like a butt."

"Why'd you touch her with a cigarette?"

"I told you," the young black guy said, "see if she's alive, tha's all."

Raymond went over to the coffeemaker, picked up the glass pitcher and walked out.

Maureen Downey, coming along the hall, raised a file folder she was carrying. She looked eager, pleased.

Raymond waited for her.

"Pathologist reports," Maureen said.

"How about the lab?"

"They're still comparing, but as far as they're concerned the slugs're identical."

"What kind of gun?"

"They got frags from the woman and two good ones from Guy, the casing intact . . ."

55

"Norb told me."

"Nine-millimeter or a .38. You know what they're leaning toward and looking into now?" Maureen was beaming.

"Walther P.38," Raymond said.

Maureen's grin dissolved. "How'd you know?"

"November, seventy-eight," Raymond said, "the shooting in the drug house on St. Mary's—"

Maureen's eyes came alive again.

"Remember? Two slugs were taken out of the woodwork, from a P.38."

"My God," Maureen said. "You don't suppose—"

"I sure do," Raymond said. "Go on back to the lab, get 'em to do a comparison, the slugs out of the wall with the slugs from Judge Guy and Adele Simpson."

"It sounds too good to be true," Maureen said.

"If they compare," Raymond said and continued down the hall and around the corner to the sink in the janitor's closet where he rinsed out the glass percolator and filled it with fresh water—aware of the good feeling, the rush of excitement he would have to contain, the feeling telling him—without any doubt or pauses or maybes—that all the slugs would compare. He saw Clement Mansell in a green-red-and-yellow Hawaiian sport shirt standing before the judge's bench. He saw Clement Mansell turn and walk out of the courtroom, grinning at everybody.

8

They were quiet men who discussed murder in normal tones.

Robert Herzog, Inspector of the Homicide Section, seated at a glass-topped desk in his glass-walled office: twenty-nine years a policeman, a large man with a sad face, a full head of gray hair. And Raymond Cruz, whose gaze came away from the window when Herzog asked him if the glare bothered him.

"No, it's fine."

"You look like you were squinting."

The window, directly behind Herzog, facing south toward the river, framed late afternoon sunlight and the top half of a highrise in the near distance.

"So what do we know about Adele Simpson?"

"Worked for a real estate company, divorced, no children. Lived alone, apartment over near Westland, dated a couple of guys from the office. One of them married."

"Can you tie in either of the guys to Judge Guy?"

"I don't know yet, but I doubt it."

"You're gonna need help on this one. I'll see what I can do."

"I don't know . . ." Raymond said, easing into it, wanting to hear his own theory out loud and not rush it or leave anything out. Herzog was looking at him expectantly now; but he knew Herzog would ask the right questions and let him take his time.

"Maybe it was luck you gave us both cases," Raymond said. "I mean the two investigations might've never been related, but the first thing we did was look for a nexus and there it was. Same gun was used on Guy and Adele Simpson."

"So," Herzog said, "you assume the same guy did 'em both, but you don't know if it was revenge or jealousy or what."

"Actually," Raymond said, "I'm not too anxious about motive right now. Take the most obvious approach, you'd say it's a hit and the girl, it's too bad, happened to be with the judge."

"How do you know the girl was there?"

"Witness heard five shots, exactly five. Then a woman scream, though he's not positive about it. Three slugs in Guy plus two exit wounds, two slugs found in the car upholstery, in the back-rest of the seat. Two matching slugs were taken from Adele Simpson's body. They caught her in the back, shattered her spine and were deflected into her lung. A third gunshot was through and through."

"But the scream," Herzog said, "didn't necessarily come from Adele Simpson."

"No, I wouldn't want to offer it in court," Raymond said, "but we've got a valet parking attendant at Hazel Park by the name of Everett Livingston who tells us Guy left there in his silver Mark VI with a blond lady wearing like a pink dress, gold chains, and dark lipstick. Which matches Adele Simpson."

Herzog said, "What's Everett doing parking cars?"

"Everett remembers the judge because he knows him by sight. And, because the judge was involved in a little bumper tag with a black car that was either a Buick or an Olds."

"He describe the driver?"

"He described the driver's left arm—sort of sun-burned with reddish hair, sleeve turned up. Which brings us to Gary Sovey— white, twenty-eight years old, he saw a black Buick Riviera push-ing or racing the judge's car down John R."

Herzog said, "Where do you find witnesses like that?"

"It gets better," Raymond said. "A guy was standing on the corner of Nine Mile and John R, one-thirty this morning, when a black late-model GM car, possibly a Buick, nearly jumped the curb and almost ran over his dog taking a leak. License number, the guy says, PVX-5 something. Lansing doesn't have a Buick with a PVX-5 something number, but they sure have a PYX-546 . . . Buick Riviera registered to a Del Weems who lives right over there in that building."

"What building?"

Raymond nodded toward the window. "Thirteen hundred Lafayette East."

Herzog swivelled to look over his shoulder at the high rise and came back to the desk again. "Del Weems have red hair on his arms?"

"I don't know what color hair he's got. He was out of town last night."

"Then why're you telling me about Del Weems?"

"He's got a dinged front left fender," Raymond said.

"That's interesting," Herzog said.

"And he's got a young lady living in his apartment who was out at Hazel Park last night."

"The lady have red hair?"

"Sort of, but more blond than red. No, the young lady wasn't in the Buick, she was in a Cadillac with—you ready?—Skender Lulgjaraj."

Herzog said, "That's kind of a familiar name."

"Skender's Toma's cousin."

"Ah, Toma," Herzog said, "the Albanian. We haven't heard from him in a while, have we?"

"No, at the moment the Albanians are quiet," Raymond said. "We talked to Skender and he said yes, he was at the track with a young lady, but wouldn't give her name."

"Why not?"

"It's the way they are, a very private group. But it doesn't matter," Raymond said, "we know it's the same young lady who's living in Del Weems' apartment, the guy who owns the Buick Riviera, and the young lady's name is Sandy Stanton." Raymond waited.

Herzog waited. He said, "I give up. Who's Sandy Stanton?"

Raymond said, "Let me take you back to November, seventy-eight, to a little house on St. Mary's Street . . ."

"Ah, yes," Herzog said.

". . . where you could get top-grade smack when everybody else was dealing that Mexican brown—an evening in November and three white dudes walk in off the street a little past eleven . . ."

Herzog said, "Albert RaCosta, Victor Reddick . . . let's see if I can remember. Louis Nix . . ."

"He was the driver," Raymond said. "You're saving the best for last, aren't you? Everybody does that."

Herzog seemed to smile. "And Clement Mansell."

"And Clement Mansell, yes, sir," Raymond said, "with the reddish hair on his arms and the bluebirds. Remember the bluebirds? Well, Clement's address at the time was also Sandy Stanton's. Somebody, I think Norb, talked to her. I didn't, but I remember seeing her in court . . . then this afternoon."

Herzog was moving ahead, thinking of something else. "Louis Nix was killed with a P.38, wasn't he?"

"We *think* he was," Raymond said, "but we only got a frag for the test—remember? Not enough to say conclusively it was from a Walther. But—you remember something else? The woodwork in the house on St. Mary's?"

"The woodwork . . ." Herzog said.

"The frame around the opening between the living room and the dining room," Raymond said. "Two slugs from a Walther were dug out of the woodwork, but the gun wasn't found on the scene. We found *vic*tims, three of 'em. Guy by the name of Champ, who ran the house. Guy by the name of Short Dog, eighteen years old, he was the doorman. And Champ's little girl, seven years old, asleep in the bedroom at the time, killed by one shot that went through the door."

"I remember the little girl," Herzog said. "And the same gun did all three of 'em?"

"Yes, sir, but not the Walther, a Beretta .22-caliber Parabellum. The gun was found in the back alley, no prints, if you recall. But when Louis Nix copped he identified the Beretta as belonging to Clement Mansell."

Herzog said, "I vaguely remember that part. Is it important?"

"I don't want to leave anything out that might be," Raymond said. "What happened—somebody in the neighborhood heard the shots, called in, a squad car arrives and Louis is sitting out front in a van with the engine running. By this time, Clement and Ra-Costa and Reddick had gone out the back, leaving Louis sitting there not knowing what's going on. So, we offer Louis a deal and he gives us his three buddies. Reddick and RaCosta were convicted, got mandatory life. Clement Mansell was also convicted, but he appealed on that federal detainer statute—you remember that?"

"Yeah, sort of. Go on."

"Court of Appeals reversed his conviction and Clement walked."

"Something about another charge against him," Herzog said, trying to remember.

"I think the prosecutor blew it," Raymond said. "At the time Clement was arrested the feds wanted him on some shitty little charge, auto theft, transporting across a state line—he was taking a Seville down to Florida—so Clement's lawyer gets him to plead guilty to the federal indictment and they send him to Milan for nine months. While he's there, he's brought back to stand trial on the triple and he's convicted. Louis Nix took the stand, told how they planned the whole thing, how Clement had the Parabellum, everything, and off they go to Jackson, mandatory life. All three of them appealed, naturally. Reddick and RaCosta are turned down; but Clement gets his appeal and wins and you know why?"

Herzog said, "This is the detainer part."

"Right—because when a prisoner is serving time and he's got another indictment pending in another court, he has to be brought to trial within a hundred and eighty days, otherwise"—Raymond paused, getting the thought clearly in his mind—"if he has to wait any longer it could produce uncertainties in the mind of the prisoner and fuck up his rehabilitation."

"That's how the statute reads?"

"Words to that effect," Raymond said. "If you recall, about that time Recorder's Court was in a mess, the docket overloaded. Well, the trial that convicted Clement Mansell and the Wrecking Crew didn't come up until the hundred and eighty-*sixth* day after

they were arraigned. Clement's lawyer filed on the grounds of the
detainer statute and he walked . . . after being convicted without
any doubt . . . even after Reddick and RaCosta testified the murder weapon, the Parabellum, was Clement's and that it was Clement who killed the two guys and the little seven-year-old girl . . .
The guy walks because he was brought to trial six days late while
being held in federal detention . . . which fucked up his peace of
mind and rehabilitation."

"Who was his lawyer?"

"Carolyn Wilder."

Herzog said, "Ahhh—" and nodded and seemed to smile.
"That's a very smart woman. I've watched her and I can say I've
always enjoyed it. Clement's got the mandatory hanging over
him, nothing to lose. She knows the Recorder's Court docket's all
fucked up, so she hands him to the feds hoping six months'll go
by before he's brought back for the triple."

"And makes it by six days."

"Figuring the prosecutor's office isn't counting or might not
even be thinking of a detainer," Herzog said. "Yes, that's a very
smart woman."

"Clement walks," Raymond said, "and a couple weeks later
Louis Nix is found shot in the head. *Up* through the head with a
gun that was stuck in his mouth . . . very, *very* likely the same gun
that put the slugs in the woodwork on St. Marys Street and the
same gun, I like to believe, that killed the judge and Adele Simpson. A Walther P.38."

"I'd like to believe it too," Herzog said.

"Well, the lab's fairly sure, but they want to test the gun before
they'll say absolutely."

"Where'd the gun come from?"

"Champ, the guy that was running the house," Raymond said,
"his wife said Champ carried a Luger. Only it didn't turn up at
the scene."

"A P.38 isn't a Luger," Herzog said, "but I see what you
mean."

"Right, it looks like one and the woman wouldn't know the difference. So we place a P.38 at the scene of the triple three years
ago. Say Clement lifted it off the guy. We find the same gun used
in a double that went down this morning. The victims were at the

race track, so was Clement's girlfriend, Sandy Stanton. The car she's driving around in right now—as a matter of fact— it's possible we can place it at the race track last night and at the scene where the judge was killed."

"So why didn't you impound the car?"

"We will, soon as Sandy gets done riding around. She just went over to a house on Kercheval."

"Grosse Pointe?" Herzog sounded surprised.

"No, no, way this side, twenty-nine twenty-five, off East Grand, next to a place called Sweety's Lounge. Maybe she's a junkie, but I don't think so. We'll check the place out."

"If Mansell did use the car last night," Herzog said, "she could be riding around with the gun."

"It's a judgment call," Raymond said. "Do you pick up the car, go over it, or follow Sandy around and do the car later? If Clement used it I assume he's wiped it down. But anything he might've missed'll still be there for the evidence techs."

Herzog nodded; yes, it was a matter of judgment.

"MCMU's doing the surveillance," Raymond said. "If it's apparent, I mean Sandy drives down to the river or stops by a trash barrel, they'll jump her. But I don't want to panic anybody right at the moment, including myself. I don't want to go bust in the wrong door and have Clement take off on us."

"He could've already," Herzog said.

"That's right," Raymond said, "or he could be in that highrise over there, twenty-five-oh-four. If you remember Clement, he's got very large balls. The papers at the time called him the Oklahoma Wildman, but he's more like a daredevil, a death-defier . . ."

"Evel Knievel with a gun," Herzog said.

"That's right, he likes to live dangerously and he likes to kill people."

Herzog said, "Well, if you don't get him with the gun, the Walther, who do you get him with?"

"That's it," Raymond said, "we got an arm with reddish hair sticking out a car window, but I never heard of a lineup of just arms. No, we got to get him with the gun in his possession, I know that."

"You seem very calm about it," Herzog said. "It can't be lack of desire."

"No, I'm trying to hold back from kicking in doors," Raymond said. "I don't want to blow it and see him walk like he did the last time."

Herzog said, "Why'd he shoot Guy?"

"I'm gonna ask him that," Raymond said, "soon as I get him sitting in the corner. He never appeared before Guy, so I don't think it's something personal. He saw him at the track, maybe Guy was winning, and Clement set something up. Maybe. Or, the way I'm inclined to lean, somebody paid Clement to do him.

"Or," Raymond said then, "he was out at the track because Sandy was there with Skender and they're setting up the Albanian. Same kind of thing Clement used to work with the Wrecking Crew. Find some ethnic storeowner, guy who might be taking his money home . . . the Wrecking Crew pays a visit, beats the shit out of the guy after they turn his place upside-down, and walk out with his savings. I think Clement's still at it."

Herzog said, "How about arrests since the triple?"

"Nothing. Clement's been a suspect—shit, he's always a suspect, but nothing new on the computer. 'Less you want to count a drunk-driving charge. He got it in Lawton, Oklahoma, last spring. Oklahoma sent it to Lansing and Lansing revoked his license."

"Well, if you catch him driving without it . . ." Herzog said. "I'm gonna be off next week, drive up to Leland with Sally."

"Taking her kids?"

"No, that's the whole idea, get away alone. If we can work it."

"What do you need, a sitter?"

"No, her kids're old enough. It's the mothers. Sally's mother asks her who she's going with, she says me. Alone? Yeah, just the two of us. Her mother'd have a fit."

"Why?"

"Why?" The large man behind the desk who had been a policeman twenty-nine years seemed self-conscious, vulnerable.

"Because we're not married. Last winter, trying to get to Florida for a week? The same thing. I tell my mother I'm going with Sally, my mother says, 'Oh, are you married now?' Sally's forty-nine, I'm fifty-four, both of us divorced. Our kids have traveled all over the country with their boyfriend, their girlfriend . . . see, it's the grandchildren and they accept that. But if Sally and I tried to do it—"

"You're kidding," Raymond said.

"Is you mother still living?" Herzog asked him.

"Yeah, in Daytona."

"Okay, try it. Tell her you're coming down with a woman you're very fond of but you're not married to, see what she says. 'You mean the two of you're traveling *alone* together?' Shocked, can't believe it. I know you're not as old as I am," the Inspector of Homicide said, "but I'll tell you something, we're in the wrong fucking generation."

# 9

Mary Alice, Raymond's former wife, called at 6:20. It was dark outside. He had come home to his apartment in bright fall sunlight, stepped into the shower . . . and now the sun had vanished from the living room window. He could see his reflection, the white towel wrapped around his middle. Mary Alice told him the roof was leaking again in the family room. She described what the water was doing to the walls and the carpeting, how it was impossible to dry the carpeting completely and take out the stain.

He wanted to say, "Mary Alice, I don't give a fuck about the carpeting . . ." But he didn't. He said, "What do you want me to do about it?" Knowing what she was going to say.

She told him she wanted him to pay to have the roof repaired and the carpeting replaced, speaking to him without using his name. Also, she needed a new clothes dryer.

His first-floor apartment was on the south edge of Palmer Park, across from a heavily wooded area, about three-quarters of a mile from where Adele Simpson's body was found and a mile from Judge Guy's residence. He said, "Mary Alice, I don't think you understand. We're not married anymore. You have the house, I don't have anything to do with it now." She started to speak again, using her quiet, almost lifeless tone, and he said, "It hasn't even rained lately."

She said he shouldn't have given her the house in the condition it was in—getting an edge to her tone now. She always had the edge ready for when she needed it. A pouty edge. She could tell him what they were having for dinner and sound defensive, conspired against. She said she would get some estimates—not having heard a word he said—and let him know. Raymond said fine and hung up.

He sliced the leftover New York strip sirloin into thin pieces and fried them in a hot skillet, watching the pieces sizzle and curl, thinking of the girl from the *News*, picturing her face the way it had appeared, soft, pleasant, before taking on a sheen and her features became sharply defined. He had looked at her as a possibility, a very attractive girl. But with acid-etched opinions that came out and changed her looks. She could be right, though.

You know it? Raymond thought.

And then thought, No, there was no way in the world he could have talked to his wife and told her how he felt.

In the first place she didn't like the idea of being a policeman's wife. She wanted him to sell life insurance like her dad and join her dad's Masonic lodge and go deer hunting with her dad and remodel the back porch into a family room with an acoustical tile ceiling and use some of her mom and dad's maple furniture. The marriage counselor they visited six times said, "Have you considered having children?" Mary Alice told him she'd had two early miscarriages. She did not tell him she refused to even consider trying again and would begin love-making with reluctance and remain detached while Raymond slowly, gently, tried to involve her to the point of losing herself. (Which had nothing to do with not wanting to have children.) In her detachment, in the automatic, monotonous movement of her hips, she would remain wherever she was, alone.

The marriage counselor asked Raymond if he had always wanted to be a police officer. Raymond said no, he had wanted to be a fireman, but didn't pass the test. The marriage counselor asked him if he had ever had a homosexual experience. Raymond said, "Well—" The marriage counselor said, "Tell me about it." Raymond said, "Well, when I was working Vice I'd go into the Men's room of a gay bar; I'd stand at the urinal and when a guy would come up next to me I'd take out a salt shaker and shake some of it, you know, down like right in front of me. And if the guy rolled his eyes and rubbed his tummy I knew I had a collar." The marriage counselor stared at him and said, "Are you serious?" Raymond said, "Look, I like girls. I just don't like *her*. Don't you see that?"

He ate the fried steak with sliced tomatoes and onions and a can of Strohs. He wasn't tired. He hadn't slept since yesterday morning, but he wasn't tired. He thought about going out. The prospect still gave him a strange feeling after twelve years of married life. He thought about the girl from the *News*. He thought about Sandy Stanton and wondered how he might run into her somewhere. He thought of girls he had met at Piper's Alley on St. Antoine, the Friday after-work place, girls who came with toothbrushes in their purses. He thought of girls and saw glimpses of pleasure in strange apartments, chrome lamps turned down, macrame and fringed pillows made of wool, drinking wine, performing the ritual to the girl playing coy or seductive, giving him dreamy eyes, saying undress me and getting down to the patterned bikini panties, wondering why none of these girls wore plain white ones, most of them big girls, bigger than the girls he remembered in college sixteen years ago, the girls acting coy all the way to bed then accepting the decorator-patterned sheets as a release point and turning on with moans like death-throes and dirty words that took some getting used to, though girls in bars said fuck all the time now and when the girl would say do-it-to-me, do-it-to-me, he would think, What do you think I'm doing? Never ever completely caught up in it, but aware and observing, giving it about seventy percent . . . He remembered the girl from the *News* saying he was old-fashioned—no, old-timey; but it probably meant the same thing. The girl who knew everything . . .

The phone rang.

The woman's voice, quiet, unhurried, said, "Lieutenant, this is

Carolyn Wilder. I understand you're looking for a client of mine, Clement Mansell."

Raymond saw her in a courtroom, slim in something beige, light-brown hair—and had recognized her voice—the good-looking lady with the quiet manner who defended criminals. He said, "How about if you bring him in tomorrow morning, eight o'clock."

"If you don't have a warrant, why bother?"

"I'd like to talk to him," Raymond said.

There was a pause, silence.

"All right, you can talk to him in my office, in my presence," Carolyn Wilder said. "If that doesn't suit you, get a warrant and I'll see you at the arraignment."

He asked her where her office was. She told him the 555 Building in Birmingham and asked him to please come within an hour.

Raymond said, "Wait, where'd you get my number?"

But Carolyn Wilder had hung up.

# 10

"See, a blackjack's the best," Hunter said. "Put it in your pants pocket, you know, right against your thigh. You don't have a blackjack, then you move your gun around, stick it in front by your belt buckle. You start dancing close with the broad, watch the look on her face."

Raymond said, "You horny tonight?"

Hunter said, "What do you mean, tonight? I've always wanted to try one of these broads out here. Husband's a vice-president with General Motors, bores the shit out of her . . . Look-it that one, fucking outfit on her."

They were in Archibald's on the ground floor of the 555 Building—shoulder to shoulder with that after-work cocktail crowd, the young lawyers and salesmen from around the north end and the girls that came from everywhere—Hunter with visions of restless suburban ladies looking for action, waiting to be dazzled by the homicide dick with the nickel-plated 9-mm Colt strapped to his belt.

Raymond said, "You know how old the bored wife of a GM vice-president would be?" He finished his bourbon and placed the glass on the bar. "I'm going up. Clement parked across the street. Tan Chevy Impala, TFB seven-eighty-one."

"Probably stole it," Hunter said.

"The phone's over there by the men's room."

"I saw it when I came in."

"Clement leaves before I do, I'll call you."

Raymond walked out of the bar, edging past the secretaries and young executives, and took an elevator up to seven, to Wilder, Sultan and Fine, celebrity names around Detroit Recorder's Court, criminal lawyers venturing into the corporate world now, out seventeen miles from downtown, into contracts and tax shelters and a brown leather lobby with copies of *Fortune* and *Forbes* on glass tables.

He went in past the row of clean secretary desks and covered typewriters to an office softly lighted where Carolyn Wilder and Clement Mansell were waiting—Clement watching him, beginning to grin, Carolyn Wilder saying, "Why don't you sit down."

He concentrated on observing, noticing Clement's shiny blue and red tattoo on his right forearm. Clement in a sport shirt sitting at one end of the couch with his elbows drawn back, limp hand in his lap, a faded denim jacket on the couch, next to him. Raymond saw a file folder on the coffee table, a pair of glasses with thin dark frames. He noticed the line of Carolyn Wilder's thigh beneath a deep-red material, one leg crossed over the other, the criminal lawyer and her client sitting away from the desk at the other end of the room, the lawyer relaxed but poised in a leather director's chair, open white blouse with the dark maroon suit, tailored, soft brown hair with light streaks almost to her shoulders . . . brown eyes, saying nothing now . . . somewhere in her mid-thirties, better looking, much better looking, than he remembered her.

She said, "You don't seem especially interested, Lieutenant. Are you bored?"

It was in his mind: Pick Clement up and throw him against the wall, hard enough to put him out, then cuff him and say to her, No, I'm not bored.

Get it done.

Raymond didn't say anything. He looked from Carolyn Wilder to Clement, who was staring, squinting his eyes at him.

Clement said, "I don't recall your face."

"I remember yours," Raymond said and stared back at him, looking at a point between Clement's half-closed eyes.

"I should know you, huh?"

Raymond didn't say anything. He heard Carolyn Wilder sigh and murmur a sound and then say, "This is in connection with the Guy murder?"

Raymond nodded, turning his head to her. "That's right."

"What have you got?"

"Witnesses."

"I don't believe you."

"A car."

Clement said, "Shit, he ain't got any witnesses. He's blowing smoke at us."

"The racetrack and the scene," Raymond said.

Carolyn Wilder turned to Clement. "Don't say anything unless I ask you a question, all right?" And to Raymond, "Are you going to read his rights?"

"I hadn't planned on it," Raymond said.

Carolyn Wilder looked at him a moment and then shrugged. "He's not going to say anything anyway."

"Can I ask him a question?"

"What is it?"

"Was he driving around in a Buick Riviera last night, license number PYX-5-4-6?"

"No, he's not going to answer that."

Clement looked from his attorney to Raymond, enjoying himself.

"Can I ask if he's seen Sandy Stanton lately?"

"Is it her car?" Carolyn Wilder asked.

"A friend of hers."

"I don't think you can put together even circumstantial evidence," Carolyn Wilder said. "And he's not going to say anything, so why bother?"

Raymond looked directly at Clement now. "How you doing otherwise?"

"Can't complain," Clement said. "I'm still trying to place you. You have a mus-tache that time—what was it, three years ago?"

"I just grew it," Raymond said and was aware of Carolyn Wilder staring at him.

"You were heavier then." Clement began to nod. "I remember you, the quiet fella, didn't say much."

"It wasn't my case. I don't think I ever spoke to you directly."

"Yeah, I remember you now," Clement said. "What was that reddish-haired fella's name? Not reddish, kinda sandy."

"Hunter," Raymond said. "Sergeant Hunter."

Clement was grinning again. "He tried every which way get me to say I pulled the trigger. Was in that little room with all the old files?"

Raymond nodded, feeling a strange rapport with the man that excluded the woman lawyer, made her an outsider.

"He had me in there, I thought he was gonna punch me through the wall. He never laid a hand on me, but he come close, I know he did. You ask him."

Raymond said, "You been anywhere since Milan?"

"I think we should all go home," Carolyn Wilder said, stirring in the director's chair, about to get up.

"Milan wasn't too bad," Clement said. "You know, there was some famous people there one time. Frank Costello—some others, I can't think of the names right off."

Raymond said, "You been staying out of trouble?"

"Long as I got this lady here," Clement said. He squirmed, getting comfortable. "I'd like to hear how you think you're gonna lay the judge on me."

Carolyn Wilder said, "That's all."

Clement looked at her. "He can't use anything I say. He hasn't read me my rights." Smirky, having a good time.

"You can say anything you want," Raymond said, "I won't hold it against you." And gave Clement a friendly grin.

Carolyn Wilder stood up, brushing a hand down to smooth her skirt.

"He's dying," Clement said. "Got this idea of what happened

to the judge and can't get nobody to—what's the word, corab . . . corobate it?"

"Corroborate," Raymond said. "You hang around courtrooms and county jails you learn some words, don't you?"

"Become a jailhouse lawyer," Clement said. "I met a few of them here'n there."

Carolyn Wilder said, "Lieutenant . . . good night."

Raymond got up. "Can I use your phone?"

She nodded toward her desk, a massive dark-wood dining room table set against Levolor blinds and chrome-framed graphics.

Raymond walked across the room, picked up the phone and dialed a number. He waited and then said, "Jerry? You gonna meet me downtown? . . . I'll see you." And hung up, wondering as he turned from the desk if they heard Hunter's voice, Hunter saying, "Fuck you, I'm not leaving here, man, this is the *place.*"

Clement was saying something to Carolyn Wilder, both standing now, Clement with his hand on her arm, and Carolyn frowning as she stared at him, as though trying to understand what he was telling her—twenty feet from Raymond Cruz—and now she pulled her arm away abruptly, amazed or shocked, and said, "What!" and Clement was shrugging, saying a few parting words as he turned and walked out of the office.

There was a silence. Raymond moved toward her. He said, "What's the matter?"

But she was still in her mind and didn't answer. She was not the woman lawyer he had watched in court, but a woman caught off balance, a girl now, vulnerable, a girl who had just been grossly insulted or told a terrible secret. Raymond wanted to touch her and the words came out easily.

"Can I help you, Carolyn?"

It surprised him, using her first name, and yet it sounded natural and seemed to touch an awareness in her. She looked at him in a different way now, not with suspicion as much as caution, wanting to be sure of his tone, his intention.

"Did you happen to hear what he said?"

Raymond shook his head. "No."

"Any part of it?"

"No, I didn't."

He watched her pick up the file from the coffee table and come past him to her desk, saying, "He's a beauty." Sounding tired.

"He kills people," Raymond said.

She looked at him now. "Tell me about it. You've been a downtown cop long enough—I know I've seen you around—so you know what my job is and I know what yours is."

"But can I help you?" Raymond said.

She hesitated, staring at him again, and seemed about to tell him something. But she hesitated too long. He saw her gaze move and come back and move again and now she was sitting down at her desk, looking up at him with a bland expression.

"I think you mean well . . ."

"But it's none of my business," Raymond said. He picked a Squad Seven card out of his coat pocket and laid it on her desk. "Unless he scares you again, huh? And you admit it."

"Good night, Lieutenant."

He said, "Good night, Carolyn," and left, feeling pretty good that he hadn't said too much, but then wondering if he shouldn't have insisted on helping and maybe said a lot more.

Hunter used the phone next to the men's room, staring at the slim girl in the fur vest and wide leather belt as he called MCMU directly, the Major Crime Mobile Unit. He told them a tan '79 Chevy Impala, Tango Fox Baker 781, was heading south on Woodward and would cross the overpass at Eight Mile in about twelve minutes. He told them to check the sheet on the car, apprehend the driver and take him down to 1300, Room 527. MCMU asked Hunter on what charge and Hunter said, "Driving without an operator's license."

He returned to the bar, worked his way in next to the stylish girl in the fur vest and said to her up-raised profile, "If we can't fall in love in the next twelve minutes, you want to give me your number and we'll try later?"

The girl looked over her shoulder to stare at him with a mildly wistful expression. She said, "I'm not against falling in love, sport; but I'm sure as hell not gonna hustle a cop. I mean even if I thought you'd pay."

# 11

They let Clement sit alone in the interrogation/file room for about forty minutes before Wendell Robinson went in to talk to him.

It was close to 10:00 P.M. Raymond Cruz crossed his feet on the corner of his desk and closed his eyes to the fluorescent lights . . . while Hunter made coffee and told about Pamela and the rough time Pamela was having trying to make it with all the goddamn amateurs out there giving it away, selling themselves for Amaretto on the rocks, Kahlua and cream . . . Raymond half listening, catching glimpses of the Carolyn Wilder he had never seen before this evening, wondering what Clement had said to her, wondering if—at another time, the right time—she'd be easy to talk to.

\* \* \*

76

The windowless file room, about seven-by-eleven, held three folding chairs, an old office table and a wall of built-in shelves where closed case-records were stored. On the wall directly behind Clement was a stain, formless smudge, where several thousand heads had rested, off and on, during interrogations.

Wendell said, "How well you know Edison?"

Clement grinned. "Detroit Edison?"

"Thomas Edison."

"I never did understand nigger humor," Clement said.

"Man whose car you were driving this evening."

"That's his name? I just call him Tom. Only nigger I ever knew owned a Chevy. He loaned it to me."

"He a friend of yours?"

"Friend of a friend."

"I understand he's a doorman. Works over at 1300 Lafayette. That where your friend live?"

"I forget which friend it was's a friend of old Tom's."

"Sandy Stanton lives over there," Wendell said. "She's a pretty good friend, isn't she?"

"You know everything, what're you asking me for?"

"She a friend of yours?"

"I know her."

"She loan you the Buick last night?"

"It tickles me," Clement said, "you people trying to act like you know something. You don't have shit, else I'd be over'n the Wayne County jail waiting on my exam."

"We want to be ugly, we could get you some time over there right now," Wendell said. "Driving after your license was revoked on a D.U.I.L., that's a pretty heavy charge."

"What, the drunk-driving thing? Jesus Christ," Clement said, "you trying to threaten me with a fucking *traffic* violation?"

"No, the violation's nothing to a man of your experience," Wendell said. "I was thinking of how you'd be over there with all them niggers."

"Why is that?" Clement said. "Are niggers the only ones fuck up in this town? Or they picking on you? I was a nigger I wouldn't put up with it."

"Yeah, what would you do?"

"Move. All this town is one big Niggerville with a few whites sprinkled in, some of 'em going with each other. You'd think you'd see more mongrelization, except I guess they're just fucking each other and not making any kids like they did back in the plantation days . . . You want to know something?"

"What's that?"

"One of my best friend's a nigger."

"Yeah, what's his name?"

"You don't know him."

"I might. You know us niggers sticks together."

"Bullshit. Saturday night you kill each other."

"I'm curious. What's the man's name?"

"Alvin Guy." Clement grinned.

"Is that right? You knew him?"

Clement said, "Shit, I could tell you anything, couldn't I?"

"There was a window in there I'd have thought seriously about throwing him out," Wendell said, and Raymond nodded.

"I know what you mean."

"Man doesn't give you anything to hook onto. You understand what I'm saying? He jive you around with all this bullshit, you don't know who's asking who the question. See, he does the judge, then goes home to his bed. We been up two days and a night."

"Go on home," Raymond said.

"I'll stay on it, you want me to."

"We'll let the old pro take a shot," Raymond said, looking over at Hunter. "The old reddish-gray wolf. What do you say? If we can't shake him tonight we'll turn him loose, try some other time."

Hunter got up from his desk. He said, "You want to watch, see how it's done?"

There was no clear reason why Hunter was the squad's star interrogator: why suspects so often confided in him and why the confessions he elicited almost always stood up in court. Maureen said it was because the bad guys got the feeling he was one of them. Hunter said it was because he was patient, understanding, sympathetic, alert, never raised his voice . . . and would cite as an example the time last winter he questioned the suspect, young guy, who admitted "sort of strangling" two women while "overcome with cocaine." The young guy said he thought this belt one of them had was a snake and wanted to see what it would like around their necks; that's how the whole thing had come about, while they were sitting on the floor tooting and having a few drinks. But he refused to tell what he did with their bodies. Hunter said, well, the bodies would show up by spring, when the snow melted, and added, "Unless you're some king of animal and you stored them away for the winter." Hunter noticed the suspect appeared visibly agitated by this off-hand remark and quickly followed up on it, asking the suspect if he liked animals or if he was afraid of them or if he related to animals in some way. The suspect insisted he hated animals, rats especially, and that when he went out to the abandoned farmhouse a few days after and saw that rats had been "nibbling" on the two women he immediately took measures to prevent them from being "all eaten up." He cut the bodies up with a hacksaw and burned them in the coal furnace. He was no animal . . .

"What you do," Hunter said, "you see your opening and you step in. You don't let the guy out until he's told you something."

"Remember this room?" Hunter asked Clement.

"Yeah, I remember it. I remember you, too."

"Still put grease on your hair?"

"No, I like the dry look now," Clement said.

"Good," Hunter said. "You messed up the wall the last time—all that guck you slicked your hair down with."

Clement looked over his shoulder at the wall. "Don't you ever clean this place up?"

"We hose it out once a week," Hunter said, "like at the zoo. Get rid of the stink."

"What're you," Clement said, "the heavy? First the nigger and then you. When's the good guy come in?"

"I'm the good guy," Hunter said. "I'm as good as it's gonna get."

"You haven't read me my rights."

"I figured you know it by heart. You want me to read 'em to you? Sure, I'll read 'em."

Hunter went out into the squad room. Raymond Cruz sat at his desk with his eyes closed. Hunter poured himself a mug of coffee, picked up a Constitutional Rights form and went back into the file room, sat down and read the first paragraph of the document to Clement.

"You know your rights now? Okay, sign here." Hunter pushed the document over to Clement with a ballpoint pen.

"What if I don't want to sign?"

"I don't give a shit if you sign or you don't sign. I'll put down you refused, give us a hard time."

"But why do I need to sign it?"

"I just told you, asshole, you don't."

"I'm in here for questioning as . . . what?"

"You were arrested."

"For not having a driver's license? What's this got to do with it?"

"While in custody the defendant's record was examined with reason to believe he might be involved in a homicide under investigation and was detained for questioning."

"Detained—I can hear you," Clement said. "And then my lawyer stands up and says, 'Your Honor, this poor boy was held against his will, without any complaint being filed and was not read his rights as a citizen.' Buddy, I don't even know why I'm here. I mean, nobody's told me nothing yet."

"You're in here, Clement, because you're in some deep shit, that's why."

"Yeah? Friend of mine was in this room one time, he refused to sign and nothing happened to him."

Hunter said, "Look at it from the court's point of view, Clement, all right? . . . Which looks better, we get a warrant and arrest you for first-degree murder, which carries mandatory life? Or, we report you came to us voluntarily to make a statement. Under no duress or apprehension you describe the circumstances—"

Clement began to smile.

"—under which a man lost his life, telling it in your own words, putting in whatever mitigating factors there may be, such as your mental or emotional state at the time, whether there was some form of incitement or threat to your well-being . . . What're you grinning at?"

"You must think I went to about the fifth grade," Clement said, "buy that load of shit. I don't have to say a word to you. On the other hand I can say anything I want and you can't use it because I ain't signed your piece of paper. So what're we sitting here for?"

"It's a formality," Hunter said. "I got to give you the opportunity to make a statement. You don't, then I take you down the garage, stand up against the wall and beat the shit out of you with the front end of a squad car."

Hunter said to Raymond Cruz, "Fuck—we don't get him with the piece, we don't get him."

"He sign the sheet?"

"No, but what difference does it make? He's not gonna say anything. He knows the routine better'n we do."

"I'll give it a try," Raymond said. "Go on home."

"No, I'll stick around."

"Go on. What're we doing, we're just chatting with the guy."

"Clement . . . how you doing?"

"You're in trouble," Clement said. "Carolyn told you, you guys don't talk to me without her."

Raymond said, "You spend the night here, she might be a little mad when she finds out, stamp her feet maybe. But she knows it's part of the business. We see a shot, we have to take it. Listen . . . let's go in the other room. You want some coffee?"

Clement said, "I wondered who the good guy was gonna be."

He sat at Hunter's desk swivelling around in the chair, unimpressed, until he spotted the mug-shot display, the 263 color shots mounted on the wall and extending from Norb Bryl's desk—where Raymond sat—to the coatrack by the door. Raymond sat sideways to the desk facing Mansell, ten feet away, who was turned sideways to Hunter's desk.

"Poor fuckers," Clement said. "You put all those people away?"

"About ninety-eight percent of 'em," Raymond said. "That's this year's graduates, so far."

"About ninety-eight percent niggers," Clement said. "The fuck am I doing sitting here?"

"You want me to tell you?" Raymond said.

"I wish somebody would," Clement said. "I can guess what your heart's desire is, but I *know* you don't have nothing good else I'd be across the street."

"I might've jumped the gun a little."

81

"I believe you jumped the hell out of her."

"You know how you get anxious."

"Got to stay cool," Clement said. "Evidently you got somebody made a car somewhere—"

"At the scene, for one."

"Yeah?" Noncommittal.

"And at the Hazel Park track," Raymond said. "The car belongs to Del Weems, a friend of Sandy Stanton."

"Yeah?"

"She's staying at Del Weems' apartment, using his car sometimes."

"Yeah?"

"So are you. I know I can place you over at 1300 Lafayette if I talk to enough people. And there's a good chance I can put you in the car at Hazel Park, the same time the judge was there, same night he was killed." Raymond looked at the wall clock. "About twenty-two hours ago . . . What did you think when we got on you this fast?"

"You got a tape recorder going someplace?"

Raymond raised his hands, helpless. "For what?"

"Won't do you any good if you have." Clement looked up at the ceiling and raised his voice as he said, "You can't use anything I'm saying, so fuck you!"

"I can hear you fine," Raymond said pleasantly. "I'm not trying to pull anything, legal or otherwise. I just thought you and I might save some time if we know where we stand."

"That sounds like it makes sense," Clement said, "except I think it's pure bullshit. There's no way I can be doing myself any good sitting here. This is a miserable fucking place, you know it?"

"You never went before Guy, did you?"

"No, I was never in his court."

"So it couldn't be anything personal."

"Jesus, you got your mind made up, haven't you?"

"The only other reason I can think of, somebody must've paid you." Raymond waited. Clement didn't say anything. Raymond smiled slightly. "That person finds out you're in custody I think it would clutch him up some . . . the kind of situation you get into when two or more people are involved in a murder. Like the guy that was shot in front of the Soup Kitchen, the promoter. You remember him? This past summer. Who was convicted? The shooter. Not the guy that arranged it. He copped and we gave him immunity."

"Jesus Christ," Clement said, "you're starting to sound like that other chicken-fat dick, giving me this scary story like I got grits or something for brains."

"I guess I ought to come right out with it," Raymond said.

Clement nodded. "I think you'd feel better."

"Okay," Raymond said, "what's gonna happen as soon as we put you in the Buick—we already have the Buick at the scene—you'll want to start talking deal. You'll give us something if we'll ease up a little. Except by then it will probably be too late. We settle for Clement Mansell, he gets the mandatory, that's it. Did somebody pay him? Who knows? Or more to the point, who cares? See, there isn't that much wrath, you might say, or righteous indignation involved. Some people think the guy who did the judge ought to get a medal instead of a prison term. But it's a capital crime, so we have to go through the motions. I want you to understand now we *will* nail you down, there isn't any doubt about that . . . *unless,* before we put in all these hours and get pissed off and cranky and unreasonable . . . you say okay, here's what happened, here's the name of the guy that put up the fee . . . *then* we could probably do something for you. Talk to the prosecutor about second degree, maybe even get it down to manslaughter and put the mandatory on the guy that hired you. You see what I mean?"

Clement leaned his right forearm on the desk and stared across the ten feet at Raymond Cruz.

"You got a nice, polite way about you. But underneath all that shit, you really want my ass, don't you?"

"I don't have a choice," Raymond said.

"You feel this as something personal? I mean this particular case?"

Raymond thought a moment; he shrugged.

"Shit no," Clement said. "What's bothering you, three years ago you guys blew it. You had me convicted on a triple, air-tight with witnesses, and I walked. That's been bothering the shit out of you. So now you're gonna try and get me on this one to make up for it. See, now it *does* get personal. Right? You don't care who hit the judge, you just want *me.* Am I right or wrong?"

Raymond took his time. He said, "See, we're finding out where we stand."

"Am I right or wrong?"

"Well, I have to admit there's some truth in what you say."

"I knew it," Clement said. "You got no higher motive'n I do, you talk about laying things on the table, see where we stand. You don't set out to uphold the law any more'n I set out to break it. What happens, we get in a situation like this and then me and you start playing a game. You try and catch me and I try and keep from getting caught and still make a living. You follow me? We're over here in this life playing and we don't even give a shit if anybody's watching us or not or if anybody gets hurt. We got our own rules and words we use and everything else. You got numbers, all these chicken-fat dicks that'd rather play the game than work; but I got the law to protect me and all I got to do is keep my mouth shut, don't associate with stupid people and there's no way in hell you're gonna lay this one on me . . . or any of the others."

Raymond nodded, thoughtful but at ease, alert but not showing it. He said, "You know what, Clement? I think you're right." There was a silence. "What others?"

And again, a silence.

Clement leaned on his arm that rested along the edge of the desk, as if to draw a little closer to Raymond Cruz.

"You know how many people I've killed?"

"Five," Raymond said.

"Nine," Clement said.

"In Detroit?"

"Not all in De-troit. One in Oklahoma, one in Kansas."

"Seven in Detroit?"

"That's right. But five—no, six of 'em was niggers."

"Counting Judge Guy."

"Count who you want. I ain't giving you a scorecard lineup."

"When you were with the Wrecking Crew, huh?"

"Most by myself. Well, kind of by myself. Other fella didn't do shit."

"Going into dope houses, huh?"

Clement didn't answer.

"Like the one on St. Mary's, the triple?"

Clement didn't say anything.

"I don't mean to pry," Raymond said. "You arouse my curiosity." He sat back in Norb Bryl's stiff swivel chair and placed his legs on the corner of the desk. "It's interesting what you said, like it's a game. Cops and robbers. A different life that's got nothing to do with anybody else."

"Less we need 'em," Clement said. "Then you get into victims and witnesses. Use who you can."

"But what it comes down to," Raymond said, "what it's all about, I mean, is just you and me, huh?"

"That's it, partner."

"Some other time—I mean a long time ago, we might have settled this between us. I mean if we each took the situation personally."

"Or if we thought it'd be fun," Clement said. "You married?"

It took Raymond by surprise. "I was."

"You got a family? Kids?"

"No."

"So you get bored, don't have nothing to do and you put more time in on the job."

Raymond didn't say anything. He waited, looking at the wall clock. It was 11:15.

Clement said, "You ever shoot anybody?"

"Well . . . not lately."

"Come on, how many?"

"Two," Raymond said.

"Niggers?"

He felt self-conscious. "When I was in Robbery."

"Use that little dick gun? . . . I been meaning to ask why you put the rubber bands around the grip."

"Keep it from slipping down."

"Cheap fuck, get a holster. Shit, get a regular size weapon first, 'stead of that little parlor gun."

"It does the job," Raymond said. It sounded familiar: a table of cops at the Athens Bar drinking beer.

Clement said, "Yeah?" and let his gaze move around the squad room before returning to Raymond Cruz, sitting with his feet on the desk. "Say you're pretty good with it, huh?"

Raymond shrugged. "I qualify every year."

"Yeah?" Clement paused, staring at Raymond now. "Be something we had us a shooting match, wouldn't it?"

"I know a range out in Royal Oak," Raymond said. "It's in the basement of a hardware store."

"I'm not talking about any range," Clement said, staring at Raymond. "I was thinking out on the street." He paused for effect. "Like when you least expect."

"I'll ask my inspector," Raymond said, "see if it's okay."

"You won't do nothing of the kind," Clement said, "cause you know I'm not kidding."

They stared at each other in silence and Raymond wondered if this was part of the game: who would look away first. A little kids' game except it was real, it was happening.

He said, "Can I ask you a question?"

"Like what?"

"Why'd you shoot Guy?"

"Jesus Christ," Clement said, "we been talking all this time, I think we're getting someplace—what difference does it make why? Me and you, we're sitting here looking at each other, sizing each other up—aren't we? What's it got to do with Guy, or anything else?"

# 12

Some months before, a story in *The Detroit News Magazine*, part of the Sunday edition, had featured eight "Women At Work" in which they described, beneath on-the-job photos in color, exactly what they did for a living. The women were a crane operator, automotive engineer, realty executive, homemaker, attorney, waitress, interior decorator and city assessor.

The attorney was Carolyn Wilder, photographed in an ultra-suede jacket leaning against her dining-table desk. Framed on the wall behind her and almost out of focus was an enlarged printed quotation that read:

> *"Whatever women do, they*
> *must do twice as well as men*
> *to be thought half as good.*
> *Luckily, this is not difficult."*

CHARLOTTE WILTON
MAYOR OF OTTAWA, 1963

Set in two columns beneath the photo, the text read:

CAROLYN WILDER, Attorney, Senior Partner of Wilder, Sultan and Fine, Birmingham.

"At one time I thought I was an artist. In fact I attended The Center for Creative Studies three years, believed I could draw, paint adequately, set out with my portfolio and found work in the art department of a well-known automotive ad agency where the word 'creative' was heard constantly but appeared exiguously, if at all, in their advertising; married a 'creative' director and was both fired and divorced within fifteen months on two counts of insubordination. (No children, a few samples.) The switch to law is an involved tale: though I did have clear visions, goals, that saw me through the University of Detroit Law School and two years with the Legal Aid and Defender Association. The latter prepared me for criminal law as it is served in the Frank Murphy Hall of Justice on a daily basis. My clients, for the most part, are charged with serious felonies: varying degrees of murder, rape, armed robbery and assault. Seventy-nine percent of them are acquitted, placed on probation, or, their charges are dismissed. Implicit in the question I'm most frequently asked—why am I in criminal law?—is the notion that women by nature abhor violence and would never, under any circumstances, help violent criminals remain at large. The truth is: criminals are a police problem; individuals accused of crime are mine."

Another notion, that life can be simple, if you base it on a fairly black and white attitude about behavior, appealed to Carolyn in providing answers to dumb questions. It made her sound at least curt when not profound and helped develop her courtroom image as an incisive defense counsel. Wayne County prosecuting attorneys referred to her, not altogether disparagingly, as the Iron Cunt. She might say hello on an elevator; she might not. She would never, under any condition, give her view of the weather. When facing her in court the prosecutor had better have his case documented far beyond implications or dramatic effects or Carolyn would counterpunch him to a decision with pure knowledge of law. Recorder's Court judges were known to sit up straighter, listen more attentively, when Carolyn was working their courtrooms.

\* \* \*

Raymond Cruz ran into her on the fifth floor, where two of the Frank Murphy courtrooms were holding pretrial examinations and witnesses and families of defendants were waiting in the corridor.

It was 11:00 A.M. Raymond was coming out of an exam, having identified the photograph of a woman, bound and gagged with a pantyhose and shot twice in the back of the head, as Liselle Taylor, and testified that upon showing the photo to Alfonso Goddard, Mr. Goddard denied knowing the deceased until, after several hours of questioning, he stated: "Oh, yeah, I *know* her. See, you asked me if she was my girlfriend and I said no to *that,* because she wasn't my girlfriend, we was only living together, you understand?" . . . There were two more exams scheduled this week . . . five cases in the squad's "open" file . . . when Carolyn Wilder stopped him, taking him by the arm in the crowded corridor.

She said, "Don't ever do that to me again. I don't care if you just wanted to buy him a drink, when I say you can only talk to a client in my presence it means exactly that."

Raymond touched her hand on his arm, covering it with his own in the moment before she drew it away.

"What did he tell you?"

"He was arrested—how you used that drunk-driving charge—"

"We let him go didn't we? Listen, I don't even know how he got home. But if he keeps driving without a license he's gonna get in serious trouble."

Carolyn didn't smile. She seemed genuinely disturbed, her esteem damaged. Raymond stepped quickly, quietly, inside her guard. He said, "What did Clement tell you last night? In your office."

And there was the vulnerable look again, a glimpse of the girl who could be uncertain, afraid.

"If he scared *you,* and I mean that as a compliment, then he said something pretty bad."

"You're out of line. Whatever my client says to me, if you don't know, is privileged information—"

"Yeah, but it wasn't like that. He didn't confide something, he scared you. The look on your face—you could have filed a complaint for assault. Or improper advances, lewd suggestions . . . Let me tell you something if you don't already know it." Raymond looked around. He took Carolyn by the arm then and guided her through the waiting people, held doors open and followed her into an empty courtroom.

"You want to sit down?"

She went into one of the spectator rows that were like widely spaced church pews, sat down, crossed her legs beneath a gray skirt, smoothing it, and turned on the contoured bench to face him or to keep some distance between them.

"What?"

"Clement Mansell killed the judge and Adele Simpson. We know he did."

"All you have to do is prove it," Carolyn said.

Raymond took time to gaze all around the courtroom before looking at Carolyn again. He said, "Just quit being the lawyer for a minute, all right? Clement Mansell has *killed* nine people. Four more than we know of and seven more than he'll ever be convicted for. He isn't a misguided boy, somebody you can defend, feel sorry for. He's a fucking killer. He likes it. He actually *likes* killing people. Do you understand that?"

Carolyn Wilder said quietly, "Even a fucking killer has rights under the law. You said last night, 'He kills people.' And I believe I said, 'Tell me about it.' We both know the purpose of this room. If you feel you have a case against Mansell, let's bring him in and find out. Until then, leave him alone . . . All right?"

The lady lawyer rose from the bench.

Raymond was dismissed.

He had felt this way standing before judges who had the final word and would pound a gavel and that was it. He had felt the urge to punch several judges. He had once felt the urge to punch Alvin Guy just as he felt the urge now to punch Carolyn Wilder. It seemed a natural reaction. The strange part was—he realized now, in the same moment—he did not have the urge to punch Clement Mansell.

He could see himself killing Mansell, but not hitting him with a fist, for there was no emotion involved.

It stopped him, brought him back to where he could say something and not be afraid of his tone, of an edge getting in the way. She had moved past him and was almost to the door.

"Carolyn? Let me ask you something."

She waited, half-turned, giving him a deadpan look. No person inside. Let him try to get through if he could.

"How come in the hall before, you said, 'Don't ever do that to me again'? About picking Clement up and bringing him in. How come you didn't say don't ever do that to *him* again?"

Carolyn Wilder turned without a word and walked out.

Raymond felt better, but not a whole lot.

# 13

Norbert Bryl said, "You didn't question him in the room?"

"Nobody was here by then. I sat right where you're sitting, he was over at Jerry's desk."

Hunter said, "Jesus, I better check the drawers."

Bryl said, "What've you got that he'd want?" And swivelled back to Raymond Cruz. "So how'd you get to the nine people?"

The phone rang. Hunter said, "Take that, will you, Maureen? Act like you're the secretary."

Maureen, at her desk next to the file-room door, said, "Sure," and picked up the phone. "Squad Seven, Sergeant Downey—"

Wendell Robinson entered with a young black male wearing a T-shirt and a wool watchcap, motioned him into the file room to wait and closed the door. "Another boyfriend of Liselle Taylor. Says he believes Alfonso killed her, and if we can get his traffic tickets tore up—like three hundred dollars' worth and a suspended license—he'll tell us things so we'll believe it too."

"Tell him what the food's like across the street," Hunter said.

"He's been there. Probably likes the food."

Raymond said, "Before you go in—what'd Clement say to you, something about having a black friend?"

"He said one of my *best* friends," Wendell answered. "I said what's his name? He wouldn't tell me."

"Yeah—" Raymond, thoughtful, looked from his desk to Hunter. "He mention a friend to you?"

Hunter said, "How could that asshole have a friend?" But then squinted, closing one eye. "Wait a minute. He *did* say something. He wouldn't sign the rights sheet and he said, yeah, he said he had a friend who wouldn't sign it either and nothing happened to him."

"The Wrecking Crew," Raymond said, "they ever use a black driver?"

No one answered him.

"Then before the Wrecking Crew. You see what I'm getting at? He knows a black guy who was brought in here. The black guy wouldn't say anything about whatever it was. Which could be the reason Mansell thinks of him as a friend. Why, because the black guy wouldn't talk? A matter of principle? No, because the black guy wouldn't talk about Mansell. How's that sound?"

"That's not bad," Bryl said. "Let me go consult the great computer, see what it says."

Raymond said, "Check with Art Blaney in Robbery. He's got a memory better than a computer. Ask him if he recalls a black guy that ever ran with Mansell."

Bryl went out. A uniformed officer stood holding the door open. He said, "Judge Guy was shot four times with a .38, right?"

Hunter looked up. "Five times."

"Shit," the uniformed officer said, "I went and played four-three-eight."

The door swung closed.

Hunter said, "Probably boxed it, too, the dumb shit."

Raymond said, "He tells me he's killed nine people. I say, oh, in Detroit?"

The door swung open. A black officer in shirtsleeves, wearing a

.44 magnum revolver in a white shoulder rig, came in with a stack of papers, licked his thumb, took off the top sheet and said, "Who wants it? Schedule for the play-offs, nine-thirty, Softball City. Homicide versus Sex Crimes."

The door swung closed.

Maureen hung up the phone. "MCMU. Mansell and Sandy Stanton just left 1300 Lafayette in a cab."

Inspector Herzog listened with his hands clasped as though in prayer, fingers pressed together, pointing straight up.

"He's telling me he's killed nine people," Raymond said, "without going into detail, two there, seven here, and I'm trying to get him to be a little more specific. With the Wrecking Crew? He says no. Well, we know he performed the triple on St. Mary's and that was with the Crew. So what he meant was none of the others. But he was with *some*body. He said the guy was along but didn't do anything."

"This is the black guy?" Herzog asked.

"He didn't say he was black," Raymond said. "He only told me another guy was along. But he told Wendell he had a black friend. See, first he keeps throwing 'nigger' in Wendell's face, then he tells him, 'One of my best friends is a nigger.' He tells Jerry he's got a friend who was questioned here and refused to say a word or even sign the rights sheet. He tells me a guy was with him when he killed some people and now we put the pieces together and Norb consults the computer, checking out Mansell in depth, all his arrests for whatever, all the times he was picked up on suspicion, brought in for questioning, to see if he's got a black guy in his past anywhere."

Raymond's gaze moved to the window framing Herzog's mane of gray hair. He could see the top floors of the highrise in the near distance.

"Incidentally, Clement and Sandy, about an hour ago they took a cab out to the Tel-Twelve Mall. They went inside, MCMU lost them."

"They're not using the Buick," Herzog said. "How come?"

"I think he cleaned it up," Raymond said, "doesn't want to touch it again."

"Maybe you should've picked it up yesterday."

"Well, as I mentioned to you," Raymond said, "it was a judgment call. MCMU followed Sandy around, they're pretty sure she didn't dump anything. And if they *hadn't* followed her, then Mr. Sweety wouldn't be the important man he is today."

"Who's Mr. Sweety?"

"You remember yesterday Sandy went to a place on Kercheval, Sweety's Lounge?"

Herzog nodded. "Came out with a guy and went in the house next door."

"Came out with Mr. Sweety and went to *his* house," Raymond said. "It's where he lives."

"I think you said yesterday the guy's black."

"Yes, and according to the sheets on Mansell, so is a guy by the name of Marcus Sweeton who did some work with Clement back when he first came here and before he joined the Wrecking Crew. Sweeton's had two convictions—one probation, two years on a gun charge—and I guess he's not looking forward to that third fall, because he's been pure ever since, now operates Sweety's Lounge."

"How'd he get a liquor license?"

"It's in his brother's name. Sweeton says he's only a bartender; but he runs the place and lives next door with his girlfriend, Anita. The brother works out at Chrysler Mound Road. So we know Marcus is the original Mr. Sweety of Sweety's Lounge. Art Blaney remembers him—"

"What do we need a computer for with Blaney?" Herzog said.

"That's what I said to Norb. Art looks up at the ceiling, it's like he wrote some notes up there. What do you want to know? Marcus Sweeton, a.k.a. the Dark Mark, Sweetwater, a couple more and Mr. Sweety. He makes about fifteen grand a year from the bar and another twenty-five or thirty from drugs, nothing worth busting, little neighborhood store."

"This is how he stays pure," Herzog said.

"Well, it's relative," Raymond said. "Pure compared to going in someplace with a gun. Art says Mansell used him as a bird dog. Mr. Sweety would go in a dope house—very friendly type of guy—sit around and chat a while, pass out some angel dust, tell a few jokes—that's the way they worked. Get 'em laid back on the dust, then Clement comes in and takes 'em off easy—all these clowns sitting around grinning at him."

"How many times can you do that?" Herzog said.

95

"In *this* town?" Raymond said. "You put all the dope stores on a computer the printout would reach down the hall, down the stairs, out onto Beaubien—"

"I get the picture," Herzog said. "So now you've got a possible witness to one or more of these nine killings Mansell claims he did. Are you trying to tie in Mr. Sweety to Judge Guy and Adele Simpson?"

"Not necessarily," Raymond said. "See, the original idea, find out who this old buddy is, tie him in to Mansell as an accessory and get him to cop on one of the earlier murders. Just in case we don't get Mansell on the current one, the judge and Adele. I thought, ah, use a lead Mansell himself gave us and doesn't even know it. Bring him in and watch his mouth fall open."

"I'm not gonna hold up my vacation on that happening," Herzog said.

"No, I said that was the original idea," Raymond said. "But now—what *is* this? Mansell shoots the judge and Adele and the next *day* Sandy Stanton goes to see the old buddy, Mr. Sweety. What's going on here?"

"So you *are* trying to tie him in."

"Yeah, but not necessarily in the way I think you mean."

"I'm not sure I know what I mean," Herzog said.

"Look at it this way," Raymond said. "If Mansell was hired to do the judge and then he hired Mr. Sweety to drive for him—"

"Then why didn't Sweety get a car?"

"That's the first question. The next one—since Mansell knows we've made the Buick, would he tell Sandy to drive over to Mr. Sweety's house in it the next day?"

"I don't know," Herzog said, "would he?"

"Or—did Sandy go over there on her own?"

"For what?"

"I don't know."

"Why don't you ask her."

"I'm going to," Raymond said, "soon as she gets home."

"But then she tells Mansell and he'll know you're on to Mr. Sweety. How do you get around that?"

"It's a game, isn't it?" Raymond said. "Nothing but a game . . . Why don't I go find Clement and shoot him?"

Herzog said, "That's the best idea I've heard yet."

# 14

Clement bought a ten-shot .22 Ruger automatic rifle, a regular $87.50 value for $69.95, and a box of .22 longs at K-mart in the Tel-Twelve Mall. He went over to the typewriter counter and asked the girl if he could try one. She said sure and gave him a sheet of notepaper. Clement pecked away for a minute, using his index fingers, pulled the notepaper out of the Smith-Corona and took it with him. He saw a black cowboy hat he liked, put it on and walked out with it . . . down a block to Red Bowers Chevrolet where Sandy Stanton was wandering around the used car lot in her high-heel boots and tight jeans.

She saw him coming with the black hat on, carrying the long cardboard box sticking out of the K-mart sack and said, "Oh, my Lord, what have you got now?"

He told her it was a surprise and Sandy brightened. "For me?" Clement said no, for somebody else. He looked around at the rows of "Fall Clean-up Specials" and asked her if she'd picked one out.

Sandy led him to a Pontiac Firebird with a big air scoop and the hood flamed in red and gold, sunlight flashing on the windshield.

"Isn't is a honey? Looks like it eats other cars right up."

Clement said, "Sugar, I told you I want a regular car. I ain't gonna street race, I ain't gonna hang out at the Big Boy; I just need me some wheels in your name till things get a little better. Now here's seven one-hundred-dollar bills, all the grocery money till we get some more. You buy a nice car and pick me up over there—if I can make it across Telegraph without getting killed—where you see that sign? Ramada Inn? I'll be in there having a cocktail."

Sandy got him a '76 Mercury Montego, sky blue over rust, with only forty thousand miles on it for six-fifty plus tax and Clement said, "Now you're talking."

A boy who was born on an oil lease and traveled in the beds of pickup trucks till he was twelve years old would be likely to have dreams of Mark VIs and Eldorados. Not Clement. He had driven, had in his possession for varying periods of time in his life, an estimated 268 automobiles, all makes and models, counting the used '56 Chevy four-barrel he'd bought when he was seventeen and the used TR-3 he'd bought one time when he was feeling sporty; all the rest he stole. Clement said cars were to get you from here to there or a way of picking up spending money. If you wanted to impress somebody, open their eyes, shit, stick a nickel-plated .45 in their mouth and ear back the hammer.

Clement drove back downtown and over to Lafayette East, but didn't go to the apartment. Sandy said she wanted to get some Vernor's. So while she was in the supermarket down the street from the apartment building, Clement found a telephone booth with a directory and look up Cruz . . .

Cruz, Cruz, Cruz . . . no Raymond Cruz, which he didn't expect to find anyway, but there was an M. Cruz—the kind of initial-only listing women thought would prevent dirty phone calls—and Clement bet twenty cents, dialing the number, that M. Cruz was Raymond Cruz's former wife.

\* \* \*

MCMU called Raymond Cruz. Sandy Stanton was back, crossing the street toward 1300 Lafayette with a bag of groceries. Alone. A 1st Precinct squad car got him over there, up the circular drive to the entrance, in less than four minutes. Sandy was in the lobby, pulling Del Weems' credit-card bills out of the mailbox, when Raymond walked in.

"Well, hi there." Sandy gave him a nice smile.

Raymond smiled too, appreciating her, close to believing she was glad to see him.

"What brings you around, may I ask? Del isn't back yet, if you're looking for him."

Raymond said, "No, I'm looking for you, Sandy." And she said, oh, losing some of her sparkle. They went up to 2504. Raymond walked over to the skyline view while Sandy ran to the bathroom. She was in there a long time. It was quiet. Raymond listened, wondering if she was flushing something down the toilet. She came out wearing her satin running shorts, a white T-shirt with a portrait on it, barefoot, saying she had to get out of those tight designer jeans. Saying she wished uncomfortable outfits weren't so fashionable, but what were you supposed to do? You had to keep up. Like with cowboy boots now. Back home she'd worked at a riding stable at Spring Mills State Park and wore cowboy boots all the time, never dreaming they'd be the fashion one day and you'd even wear 'em to shopping centers . . . Sandy talking fast to keep Raymond from talking and maybe he'd forget why he came. It did give him time to identify the portrait on her T-shirt and read the words SAVE BERT PARKS.

She hesitated too long and he said, "Where's Clement?"

"Well, so much for the world of fashion," Sandy said. "I don't know where he is."

"You drop him off someplace?"

"You think I'm dumb or something? I'm not gonna tell you a thing. If I didn't have a kind heart, I wouldn't even be talking to you . . . You want a drink?"

Raymond was ready to say no, but paused and said sure and went with her into the kitchen that was like a narrow passageway between the front hall and the dining-L. She asked him if Scotch was all right. He said fine and watched her get out the ice and pour the Chivas. Sandy opened a can of Vernor's 1-Cal ginger ale for herself. She said, "Ouuuuuu, it sure tickles your nose, but I like it. You can't buy it most other places but here."

Raymond said, "You have any grass?"

"Boy—" Sandy said. "You never know anymore who's into what."

"You have trouble getting it?"

"What do you want, my source?"

"No, a guy in the prosecutor's office I know has a pretty good source. I was thinking maybe I could help you out, I mean if Mr. Sweety isn't coming through."

"Man oh man," Sandy said. "I think I better go sit down. You're scary, you know it?"

"Looks like Mr. Sweety's in some trouble."

"Jesus, who isn't?"

"Have to be careful who you associate with."

"*That* is the truth," Sandy said. "I think I might be running around with the wrong crowd. Let's go in the other room; I feel cornered in here."

"I just wanted to ask you something," Raymond said. "See, we're gonna be talking to Mr. Sweety. He was supposed to be working the night the judge was killed. Maybe he was. But we do know you have something going with him—"

Sandy said, "Have something *going*?"

"You went to his house yesterday—"

"To get some dope. You already said—you *know* he's a source I use. You just said so."

"Yeah, but why would Clement send you over there?"

"He *didn't*. He didn't even know I went." Sandy paused. "Wait a sec, you're confusing me. I did go over there yesterday to score some grass. Period. It's got nothing to do with anything else."

"Clement let you use the car?"

"It isn't *his* car, it's Del Weems'."

"I know, but I wondered why he'd let you go there."

"He'd didn't *know* I went. I already told you that."

Twice, Raymond thought. He believed her because he wanted to, because it was reasonable. He didn't like to come onto facts that appeared unreasonable and have to change his course.

He liked it that she was upset and he kept going now. "I mean considering everything," Raymond said. "Here we've got a car that was identified at a murder scene, Del's Buick . . ."

Sandy rolled her eyes—little girl standing there in her satin running shorts, nipples poking out at Bert Parks on her T-shirt. Skinny little thing—he felt sorry for her too.

"What's the matter?" Raymond asked.

"Oh, nothing . . . Jesus."

"We don't have Clement in the car yet, but we know Clement did both the judge and the girl, Adele Simpson."

"Now it's starting to snow," Sandy said, "and we're hardly into October."

"Ask him," Raymond said. "But here's the thing. Would Clement like to know you were over there in the car, the Buick, seeing a man who used to work with him and could be a suspect in Guy's murder? You understand what I'm saying?"

"Do I under*stand?* Are you kidding?"

"So it isn't so much Clement doesn't know you went over there," Raymond said. "You don't *want* him to know."

"If you say so."

"Why don't you want him to know, Sandy?"

"He don't like it when I smoke too much grass."

"Like when you get nervous or upset?"

"Yeah, usually."

"Well, the way things're going, Sandy," Raymond said, "I think you better hit on a couple pounds of good Colombian."

# 15

Clement had never ice-skated, but he could see the Palmer Park lagoon would be a good place. It wasn't a big open rink, like most. It was a pond, several acres in size, with wooded islands in it to skate around. A good place to dump the Ruger when he was finished with it. He parked by the refreshment pavilion and cut through the woods along Merrill Plaisance Drive to where he had hidden the rifle in some bushes a few minutes before.

It was almost six o'clock; getting dark in a hurry. He picked up the rifle and moved up to the edge of the trees where he could look directly across Merrill Plaisance, across the narrow island separating the drive from the residential street and the front of the four-story, L-shaped apartment building that was 913 Covington, the home of Lt. Raymond chicken-fat Cruz—with the sad mustache and the quiet way about him, which could be politeness or just empty-headed dumbness.

Clement had said to the woman's voice on the phone, the cop's former wife, "What's Ray's address again? I lost it ... And the apartment number? ... Oh, that's right on the first floor, huh?" Then had got the name of the building manager off her mailbox and called her saying this was Sgt. Hunter: they were planning a surprise party for Lt. Cruz; the guys were gonna drop in and then, when he wasn't looking, reach out the window and haul in this present as a surprise, a stereo outfit, and he wanted to know which window to put it outside of. The landlady said in this neighborhood they better put a policeman with it or they would be the ones surprised when they reached out to get it.

There were three windows: one with an air-conditioning unit, one with a plant, one with raised venetian blinds, close to the sidewalk on Covington.

Ten past six.

The landlady had said he was usually home by six-thirty the latest, unless he didn't come home. Her apartment was next to his and if she was in the kitchen she'd hear his door slam and then sometimes she'd hear him playing music ... Didn't he already have a Victrola? ... A little cheap one, Clement told her, which was probably the truth.

Look for a medium-blue four-door Plymouth. Clement heard cops didn't use their own cars on the job because no one would insure them.

Twenty after. There was a last trace of red in the sky. The front of the building was without definition now, a few lights showing in apartments. Clement practice-sighted on Raymond Cruz's dark windows. Range, about fifty yards. But a tough shot with the cars going by in front of him, on the park drive.

Maybe this Raymond Cruz did use his own car. Or lieutenants got a different color than that shitty medium blue. Clement didn't worry about odds or luck. Something happened or it didn't. The man would come home or he wouldn't. If not tonight, tomorrow. Clement didn't plan on waiting around forever; but a little patience was good and more often than not got rewarded.

That's why Clement wasn't too surprised or especially elated when he saw the light go on in Raymond Cruz's apartment. Sooner or later it was supposed to. Clement put the Ruger against a tree and lined up his sights on the figure moving inside the apartment, Clement waiting for a lull in the traffic ...

Raymond had come into the apartment building from the alley, walked through to the foyer and got his mail: *Newsweek*, a VISA bill, a bank statement, a thick window-envelope from Oral Roberts, Tulsa, Oklahoma, addressed to Mr. M. Cruz, and a folded piece of notepaper.

In his apartment Raymond dropped the mail on the coffee-table, went into the kitchen with *Newsweek* and got a can of Strohs out of the refrigerator. He drank from the can as he glanced through the magazine on the counter, learning that beer was now discovered to cause cancer along with everything else. In the living room again he sat down at the end of the couch by the floor lamp he'd bought at Goodwill Industries. He picked up the mail from the coffee table, threw back the bill from VISA and the bank statement, laid the Oral Roberts envelope on his lap and opened the piece of notepaper that was folded three times. The typewritten message said:

SURPRISE
CHICKEN FAT!!!

Raymond would replay the scene, what happened next, and at first believe the guy was right outside because the timing was that good . . . sitting there looking at the typed words, wondering . . .

And the front window and the lamp exploded, the glass shattering, and he was in darkness, instinctively rolling off the couch, catching a knee on the coffee table, trying to yank the snub-nosed .38 out of his waistband that was tight on his hip, crawling toward the window now, the flat sounds of reports reaching him, erupting through fragments of glass, thudding into the wall, six, seven shots—he got his legs under him, turned and ran for the door . . . down the hall, out the front entrance. Cars were going by on the park drive, headlights on, making faint humming sounds. He crossed Covington to the island, kept going, heard a car horn and brakes squeal and he was into the trees, in darkness, with no sense of purpose or direction now, no sounds except for the cars going past on the park drive.

In the apartment again he picked up the phone, began to punch buttons. He stopped, replaced the receiver. If Sandy was home with the Buick, what was Clement driving? Could it have been someone else? No. He sat in semidarkness, a light showing in the open doorway to the hall.

Raymond picked up the phone again and punched a number.

"Mary Alice, I just want to ask you a question, okay? . . . No, I don't have time to get into that. Somebody called and you gave him my address. Did the guy have kind of a southern accent? . . . I know you didn't know who it was. Mary Alice, that's why you're not supposed to give out . . . No, you just tell them you don't know. Last night, did a lady call? . . ."

Jesus Christ, Raymond said. He put the phone, in both of his hands, in his lap and could hear her talking. He saw streetlight reflections in the jagged pieces of windowpane. Raising the phone again he heard her pause and said, quickly, "Mary Alice? Nice talking to you."

He called Squad Seven. Maureen answered and he asked her to look in his book and give him Carolyn Wilder's phone number. Maureen came back and said, "Six-four-five . . ."

And Raymond said, "No, that's her office. Give me her home number. And the address." He got out his pen and wrote on the back of the Oral Roberts envelope as Maureen dictated. Maureen said, "Why would she have an office in Birmingham if she lives on the east side?"

Raymond said, "You want me to I'll ask her. But I got a few other questions first."

He dialed Carolyn Wilder's home number. Following the first ring her voice came on. "Yes?"

"You were waiting for me to call," Raymond said.

"Who is this?"

He told her and said, "I'd like to talk to the Oklahoma Wildman, but I don't know where he is."

"He isn't here."

It stopped Raymond. "I didn't expect him to be."

There was a pause. "He *was* here," Carolyn Wilder said. "He left a few minutes ago."

Raymond said, "Carolyn, don't move. You just stepped in a deep pile of something."

# 16

Carolyn Wilder's home on Van Dyke Place, off Jefferson, had been built in 1912 along the formal lines of a Paris townhouse. During the 1920s and '30s it had changed from residence to speakeasy to restaurant and was serving a limited but selective menu—for the most part to Grosse Pointe residents who knew about the place and were willing to reserve one of ten tables a week in advance—when Carolyn Wilder bought it as an investment, hired a decorator and, in the midst of restoring a past splendor, decided to move in and make it her home.

Standing in the front hall, facing the rose-carpeted stairway that turned twice on its way to the second-floor hall, Raymond said, "It looks familiar."

The young black woman didn't say anything. She stood with arms folded in an off-white housedress, letting him look around, the lamplight from side fixtures reflecting on mirrored walls and giving a yellow cast to the massive chandelier that hung above them.

"You look familiar too," Raymond said. "You're not Angela Davis."

"No, I'm not."

"You're . . . Marcie Coleman. About two years ago?"

"Two years in January."

"And Mrs. Wilder defended you."

"That's right."

"We offered you, I believe, manslaughter and you turned it down. Stood trial for first degree."

"That's right."

"I'll tell you something. I'm glad you got off."

"Thank you."

"How long ago was Clement Mansell here?"

There was a pause, silence. "Ms. Wilder's waiting for you upstairs."

"I was just telling Marcie," Raymond said, "your house seems familiar, the downstairs part." Though not this room with its look of a century later, Plexiglas tables, strange shapes and colors on the wall, small areas softly illuminated by track lighting. "You do these?"

"Some of them."

The room was like a dim gallery. He was sure that most of the paintings, not just some, were hers. "What's this one?"

"Whatever you want it to be."

"Were you mad when you painted it?"

Carolyn Wilder stared at him with a look that was curious but guarded.

"Why?"

"I don't know. I get the feeling you were upset."

"I think I was when I started."

She sat in a bamboo chair with deep cushions of some dark silky material, a wall of books next to her, Carolyn half in, half out of a dimmed beam of light. She had not asked him to sit down; she had not offered him a drink, though a cordial glass of clear liquid sat on the glass table close to her chair and a tea-table bar of whiskeys and liqueurs stood only a few feet from Raymond.

"Marcie married again?"

"She's thinking about it."

"I bet the guy's giving it some serious thought too. She live here?"

"Downstairs. She has rooms. Most of it's closed off though."

He turned from the abstract painting over the fireplace to look at her: legs crossed in a brown caftan—some kind of loose cover—her feet hidden by a hassock that matched the chair.

"Are you somebody else when you're home?"

"I'm not sure I know what you mean."

"You go out much?"

"When I want to."

"I have a hard question coming up."

"Why don't you ask it?"

"Are you working at being a mystery woman?"

"Is that the question?"

"No." He paused.

He was aware that he had no trouble talking to her, saying whatever came to mind without wondering what her reaction would be or even caring. He felt a small hook of irritation, standing before the woman in shadow, but the irritation was all right because he could control it. He didn't want to rush the reason he was here. He would hit her with it in time; but first he wanted to jab a little. She intrigued him. Or she challenged him. One or the other, or both.

He said, "Do you still paint?"

"Not really. Once in a while."

"You switch from fine art to law . . . On impulse?"

"I suppose," Carolyn said. "But it wasn't that difficult."

"You were divorced first—is that where the impulse comes in? The way the divorce was handled?"

She continued to stare at him, but with something more in her eyes, creeping in now, something more than ordinary interest. She said, "You don't seem old enough to be a lieutenant; unless you have an M.B.A. and you're somewhere in administration. But you're homicide."

"I'm older than you are," Raymond said. He walked toward the chair, moved the hassock with his foot and sat down on it, somewhat half-turned from her but with their legs almost touching. She seemed to draw back against the cushion as he made the move, but he wasn't sure. He could see her face clearly now, her eyes staring, expectant.

"I'm almost a year older. You want to know what my sign is?" She didn't answer. He picked up the cordial glass and raised it to his face. "What is it?"

"Aquavit. Help yourself . . . but it's not very cold."

He took a sip, put the glass down. "You watched this lawyer handle your divorce, thinking, I can do better than that . . . Huh?"

"He agreed to their settlement offer," Carolyn said, "practically everything, let my husband have the house, a place in Harbor Springs, charged ten thousand and billed me for half."

Raymond said, "And treated you like a little kid who wouldn't understand anything even if he explained it."

Her eyes held. "You know the feeling?"

"I know lawyers," Raymond said. "I'm in court about twice a week."

"He was so condescending—he was oily. I couldn't get through to him."

"You could've fired him."

"I was different then. But at least it turned me around. I actually made up my mind to get a law degree—listen to this—and specialize in divorce and represent poor, defenseless, cast-off wives."

"I can't see you doing that."

"I didn't, for very long. I decided if I wanted to work with children I should work with real children. I even felt a tinge of sympathy for that jerk who represented me; he'd probably become conditioned to vacuous outbursts and treated all his women clients exactly the same. Eventually I found my way into the Defender's office and Recorder's Court."

She was more relaxed now, not making a pretense of it.

"I've always liked to watch you," Raymond said. "You never seem to get upset. You're always prepared . . . full of surprises for the prosecutor." He placed a hand on the brown cotton material covering her knee.

Her eyes, still calm, raised from his hand to his face.

"But you're fucking up, Carolyn, and it isn't like you, is it?"

"If I tell you Mansell was here this evening," Carolyn said, "it means I'm not going to discuss his involvement in *any*thing until you produce a warrant and he's placed under arrest."

"No, it means you're telling me a story," Raymond said. "Clement wasn't here." He watched her expression; it didn't begin to change until he said, "He was outside my window at 6:30 P.M. trying to blow my head off with an automatic rifle. Otherwise—if he was here at the same time, then Clement's into bilocation. And I'm getting off the case."

Carolyn took her time, as if studying him before she said, "You saw him?"

"No."

"How many people, do you think, you're directly responsible for sending to prison? In round numbers."

"I don't know—five hundred?"

"Then count their friends, relatives—"

"Lot of people."

"You have the gun whoever it was used?"

Raymond shook his head.

"Do you have the gun that killed Guy and the woman?"

Raymond almost smiled. He said, "Why?"

"You know you're not going to get Mansell unless you can produce the murder weapon and prove it's his and even then you're going to have a tough time. On this new allegation, a suspicion of an attempt—what have you got? Did anyone see him? At 6:30 it's already dark. Where are you going to even look for a witness?"

"Carolyn," Raymond said, getting used to saying the name. "Clement wasn't here."

"What I said to you on the phone," Carolyn said, with a hint of irritation now, in eye movement more than tone, "is not something you can enter as evidence, even if you recorded the conversation. You know that, don't you?"

"You lied," Raymond said.

"God *damn* it—" She seemed to come up from the cushion, but in the next moment she was composed again. "If I don't care to admit I made a statement, whether to protect my client or because of the particular interpretation I believe you might give the statement, then I'll rephrase it to the best of my ability and memory."

"Why did you lie?" Raymond said.

"Jesus Christ, are you dense or something?" Finally with a bite to her tone. "If you intend to use whatever I said then I'll flatly deny it."

Raymond got up, giving her a chance to breathe, maybe bring her guard down a little. He went over to the tea-table bar, found a cordial glass and concentrated on pouring aquavit into it, up past a crisscross design in the crystal.

"I'm not threatening to use what you said in court. I'm not threatening, period." He sipped the clear liqueur from the rim of the glass and came back to the hassock, watching the glass carefully as he sat down again. "All I'm trying to do"—looking at her now—"see, I have a feeling that Clement, that time in your office, scared you to death . . . holding something over your head. He called you this evening and did it again. Scared you to the point of covering for him. Then you have a couple of these and calm down and you're the lawyer again and you start using words on me, try and dazzle me with your footwork. But it doesn't change Clement, does it?"

She said quietly, "I can handle Clement."

He wanted to grab her by the arms and shake her and tell her to wake up. Fucking lawyers and judges who used words and a certain irritating tone and there wasn't a thing you could do about it . . .

Holding the cordial glass helped. He took a sip and placed it on the table next to hers. It was hard, but he was going to play this with her. He said, "A man by the name of Champ who packed a Walther P.38 thought he could handle Clement and Clement took him out. Remember? Three years ago. I'll bet Judge Guy, calling the nine-eleven in his car, the judge thought he could handle him too. Clement's holding something over your head, he's threatening you or extorting you and you're letting him do it."

Carolyn picked up her glass and he knew she was going to dodge him.

"He did tell me something interesting," Carolyn said. "That you want to meet him somewhere and have it out. Just the two of you."

"He said that?"

"How else would I know?"

"There are stories," Raymond said, "the cop takes off his badge and they settle it man to man in the alley. If you think it's like

111

that—no, this is Clement's idea. You look at my living room window you'll see he's already started."

"You're saying what, he challenged you to—what amounts to a duel?"

"He didn't give me his card or slap my face or anything, or give me a choice of weapons; but it looks like he leans toward automatic rifles. This is your client I'm talking about. The one you can handle."

Carolyn said, "What're you going to do about it?" Quietly but with new interest.

"I'm gonna keep looking over my shoulder, for one thing," Raymond said. "I'm not gonna turn a light on with the shades up."

"What does the department say about it?"

"The police department?"

"Your inspector, commander, whoever you report to."

"I haven't told anybody yet. It just happened."

"Are you going to?"

"I'm gonna report the shooting, yes."

"You know what I mean. Are you going to tell them Clement challenged you?"

Raymond paused. "I haven't thought about it."

"What's the difference in the way you look at Clement Mansell and the way I do?" Carolyn said. "I tell you I can handle him. You imply to me, in effect, the same thing, that it's a personal matter."

"There's one big difference," Raymond said. "I've got a gun."

"I know. That's why I think the idea appeals to you," Carolyn said. "Mano a mano. No—more like High Noon. Gunfight at the O.K. Corral. You have to go back a hundred years and out west to find an analogy. But there it is."

He thought of the girl from the *News*.

He said, "I don't know—" and paused. In his mind the allusion to a western scene, the street, men with guns approaching, dissolved and now he saw kids playing guns in a vacant lot near Holy Trinity, before the places where they played disappeared beneath a freeway, seeing the same kids in school then, a little blond-haired girl named Carmel something, on a dismal fall afternoon in the fifth grade, dropping a note on his desk that said *I Love You* on ruled paper, like an exercise in Palmer Method—

kids sharing secrets—a long time ago but still clear in his mind, part of him now as he sat in dimmed light with someone else who had a secret. He wondered if she had close friends or someone she spoke to intimately.

She said, "What don't you know?"

"I thought of that, it's strange, what you said. When I was talking to Clement he kept making the point that I wasn't any more interested in upholding the law than he was in breaking it—"

"*He* said that?"

"Yes, that it was a personal thing between us that didn't have anything to do with other people."

"Did you agree?"

"I said, 'A long time ago we might've settled this between us.' And he said . . . 'Or if we thought it might be fun.'"

Staring intently she said, "You haven't told this to the people you work with. But you've told me."

She came up from the silky cushion, close to him now but closed in on herself, arms against her body, hands clasped on her knees.

"You said the other night in my office, 'Can I help you?' You said it twice. Both times, the way you said it, I came so close to telling you, I *wanted* to—"

Her eyes were brown, the pupils dilated in the dim light, making her eyes appear dark and cleanly defined, like eyes in a drawing that were accentuated, inked in except for a small pale square to indicate reflected light, a soft sparkle.

"Everybody," Raymond said, "has to have somebody to tell secrets to." He liked the delicate line of her nose, the shape of her mouth and saw where he would go in and take part of her lower lip, biting it very gently.

She said, "I make assumptions—I think I know you, but I don't. You say, 'fine art.' You say, 'if he's into bilocation . . .'"

Raymond said, "But he isn't, is he?"

She didn't answer.

"Let me help you."

She continued to look into his eyes, into the deep end of a pool, gathering courage—

"Carolyn, I give you my word . . ."

She said, "Hold me . . . please."

# 17

They made love in a bed with white sheets and a dark oak head-board that towered to the ceiling. They made love almost at once, as though they missed each other so much they couldn't wait, hands moving, learning quickly, and when he entered her she breathed a sound of relief he had never heard before—even in the beds with decorator pillows and designer sheets, with the girls who would groan dramatic obscenities—none of them came out of themselves the way Carolyn did. Raymond moved with her, involved, but aware of himself too, because he couldn't believe it was happening, he couldn't believe it was Carolyn Wilder moving and making the sounds, thrusting, arching up with her head back, straining in faint light that let him see her face in a way she would never see it or recognize herself, Raymond seeing a secret Carolyn and then, for a moment, seeing her eyes open, seeing her awareness. He wanted to say something to her. He said, "I know you." The moment became a brief silence that was gone as her eyes closed again and then became something that had happened a long time ago.

They remained in darkness, in silence for several minutes, Raymond holding her, seeing the faint outside light against window shades across the bedroom. He heard her say, very quietly, close to him, "God, that was good." He thought of ways to reply but said nothing. She would feel him holding her, his hands moving gently, stroking; she would know what he felt.

Finally she said, in a voice that was a murmur but clear in the silence, "In my office the other night, when you were on the phone—" She paused. "He said, as he started to leave he said, 'When do I get the money?' I looked at him, I didn't know what he was talking about. He said, 'The hundred thousand you promised me for killing the judge.' I said 'What?' I couldn't believe it. He said, 'Don't try and act dumb to get out of paying me. I have proof the judge was putting the stuff on you.' I said, 'What do you mean?' But that was all. He said something else like 'I'll be in touch,' and left."

"Then tonight," Raymond said, "he called you—"

"He called this morning, too. Tonight he called just a few minutes before you did. He said, 'I've been at your place the past hour if anybody wants to know.' I didn't say a word to him; I hung up the phone. He called back within a minute and said, 'Look, if I take a fall on the Guy thing, you're going with me.' This time I told him if he was worried about it he'd better get a lawyer, because I was no longer representing him. He said . . . 'Oh, yes you are.' He said if it even looked like he might be convicted he'd sign a statement that I had paid him to kill Guy and he'd—words to the effect that he'd produce enough evidence to substantiate it or at least give credence to a motive."

"How can he do that?"

"That's what's interesting about it, he thinks he can implicate me." Carolyn turned enough to see his face in the darkness. "This is in confidence, right?" Raymond didn't say anything. "I'm not telling you something you can use anyway."

He was aware of a strange feeling—even with her breast against his arm and their naked thighs touching—that the lawyer was returning, that the woman who had let go was pulling in

115

again, regrouping, perhaps not even aware of it herself as she lay in his arms.

Carolyn said, "I mean if I filed a complaint against him, say on the grounds of extortion, it would be my word against his. Which would be considerable, but not nearly enough to convict him. He'll put on his dumb-hillbilly act and say I misunderstood him. Clement is very good at playing dumb."

Raymond said, "Let's go back a little bit. First, he wants a hundred thousand or he'll cop, swear you paid him to kill Guy."

"I think," Carolyn said, "considering he's an opportunist, Clement's first thought is to capitalize on Guy's death." She paused. "Whether he killed him or not."

Raymond told himself to wait, be patient. Ignore, for the time being, the warning trying to tighten up his insides.

"But now he's a suspect and he's telling me to use every effort to keep him out of jail—I presume free of charge—or else he'll take me with him."

"When did he tell you this?"

"This morning, he called me at my office."

"What'd he say exactly?"

"He said he knows and can prove I had some kind of bribe scheme going with Guy, that I paid him off for acquittals or reduced sentences. *But,* because I testified against Guy before the Tenure Commission, helped to get him thrown off the bench in fact, I'm supposedly one of the ones Guy threatened to expose. He was going to write a book, 'name names of people,' Guy said in the paper, 'with dirty hands and indecent fingers.' Clement will say I had Guy killed to keep him from writing the book."

"Clement thought up all this?"

"Everybody misjudges him," Carolyn said. "That's how he gets away with what he does, why he's . . . fascinating, really." She stirred, bringing her arm out from beneath Raymond. "Would you like a drink?"

Carolyn left the bed naked and came back wearing the brown caftan. She handed Raymond a glass of aquavit and turned on the night table lamp before getting into bed again to rest against the headboard. When Raymond placed his hand on her thigh she raised her glass and sipped the clear liqueur. He had never thought of women using men other than to get carpeting and appliances. He had said to her, "I know you," and she had said nothing in return. He wondered what he felt about her beyond the fact he liked her eyes and her nose and her body. He wondered if he had been genuinely moved or if he had only wanted to mount and subdue the dignified, distinguished lady lawyer, or if it had been the other way around and it was Raymond Cruz who had been seduced.

"Is he *saying* he has proof you were involved with Guy," Raymond said, "or does he have something?"

She turned, leaning against the headboard, to look at him, holding her glass in two hands. "Are you asking *was* I actually involved, and could there be some valid bit of evidence?"

"I'm asking what he's holding over you."

Carolyn paused. "Well . . . if, for example, you found my name in Guy's address book . . . name, phone number and figures that could be interpreted to represent amounts of money, perhaps, by some stretch of the imagination, a list of payments made to him, Guy—and you were looking for a suspect, someone who might have contracted for Guy's murder—would you consider that evidence?"

Raymond shook his head. "Not by itself . . . Did you see the address book?"

"What address book?"

"The one Clement, I assume, lifted off the judge."

Carolyn was still looking at him, at ease against the headboard. "I said what if you found my name in his book. I didn't say Clement took it, did I?"

"We've come a long way," Raymond said, "but I get the feeling we're back where we started. You were scared to death of him a little while ago—"

"I'm still reasonably afraid," Carolyn said, "enough to know that I have to be very careful with Clement. But that doesn't mean I can't handle him."

"You don't have to *handle* him. All you have to do is make a statement, Clement admitted to you he shot the judge."

"Because he's trying to capitalize on it," Carolyn said. "I told you before, that doesn't mean he actually did it."

"But he *did!*" Raymond spilled some of the aquavit, pushing himself up on the pillow to get to Carolyn's level. She watched him brush at the wet spot on the sheet.

"Don't worry about it," she said quietly, "the bed's going to be changed." She lounged against the dark wood of the headboard while Raymond sat erect, stiffly, bare above the sheet around his waist. She said, "Look, we've confided in each other because sometimes we feel the need. You said before, everybody has to have somebody to tell secrets to. I've told you things I wouldn't tell my partners and you've told me things, you've indicated, you aren't going to tell your people. You have your game with Clement and I have mine. We both will admit he's an unusual study, a pretty fascinating character, or neither of us would be quite so uniquely involved. Isn't that true?"

"You told him to find another lawyer," Raymond said.

"Yes, but he won't. He not only needs me, he likes me . . ."

Raymond listened to the lawyer and the women talking at the same time.

". . . But he *is* going to have to realize, once he gets this extortion-blackmail bullshit out of his head, that I charge a fee, and if he's not willing to pay it he *will*, indeed, have to go somewhere else." She seemed to smile, though it was a bland expression. "We can play our games, but it still has to be within the context of the jobs we're paid to do. You can't expect me to give you information about my client, just as I don't expect you to shoot him down without provocation . . . Agreed?"

"I guess we are back where we started," Raymond said.

"Why? Where did you expect to be?"

He paused and said, "I don't know," as he got out of bed and then stood naked looking down at her. "But aside from all that, how was the fuck?"

"Let me put it this way," Carolyn said, her eyes moving up his body to his face, "it was about what I expected it to be."

# 18

Mary Alice had said to him, "You don't care about anybody else; you only think of yourself."

Bob Herzog had said to him, "You know what I admire about you? Your detachment. You don't let things bother you. You observe, you make judgments and you accept what you find."

Norb Bryl had said to him, "You spend two hundred and ten dollars on a *blue* suit?"

Wendell Robinson had said to him, "I don't mean to sound like I'm ass-kissing, but most of the time I don't think of you as being white."

Jerry Hunter had said to him, more than once, "What's the matter you're not talking?"

The girl from the *News* had said to him, "I think you're afraid of women. I think that's the root of the problem."

The woman, Carolyn Wilder, had said to him, "It was about what I expected it to be."

He had put on his blue suit and left her house because he couldn't think of anything to say. All the way home he had tried to think of something that would have nailed her to the antique headboard, her mouth open; but he couldn't think of anything. He went to bed and woke up during the night thinking of lines, but none of them had it. Until finally he said to himself, What're you doing? What difference does it make what she thinks?

He was working it out slowly, gradually eliminating personal feelings.

But it was not until morning, when he walked into his living room and again saw broken glass, that he finally realized what he should have said to her and it amazed him that it had nothing to do with him, personally.

He should have told her flatly—not trying to be clever, not trying to upstage her with the last word—that if she continued to play games with Clement the time would come when Clement would kill her.

It was that clear now in his mind. He did not believe for a moment she had had any kind of a kickback scheme going with Guy. She had not denied it directly, because she would feel no need to, would not dignify it. Carolyn Wilder, of all the Recorder's Court defense lawyers he knew, would be the last one to ever get involved in back-court deals. Especially with Guy.

He pried flattened chunks of lead from his living room wall and knew by looking at them they weren't from a P.38. When his landlady came in, approaching the window as though something might again come flying through the broken glass, he told her it was probably kids with a BB gun, over in the park. The landlady seemed to have doubts, questions, but asked only if he'd reported it to the police. Raymond reminded her he *was* the police. She told him he would have to pay to have the window replaced.

That morning, Raymond sat at his desk in a gray tweed sport coat he had not worn since spring—since dieting and exercising—and the coat felt loose, a size too large. He reviewed the Judicial Tenure Commission's Report on the investigation of Judge Guy, seeing familiar names, Carolyn Wilder's appearing several times.

He did not tell his squad about the shooting—whether it was an attempt on his life or a challenge—not because he considered it a personal matter, but because he didn't want to spend the morning discussing it. He was quiet this morning, into himself, and they left him alone. They made phone calls. They worked on other cases. They looked at hard-core sex photos they had picked up during the evidence-search of a victim's house: exclaiming, whistling, Wendell pretending to be sick; Hunter studying one of the photos and Norb Bryl saying to him, "You go for that kinky stuff, huh?" Hunter saying, "Jesus Christ, what kind of pervert you think I am?" And Bryl saying, "Oh, one about six foot, sandy mustache, green-striped shirt . . ." At noon, Raymond told them he was going to skip lunch.

After they had left he took off his sport coat, unlocked the plywood cabinet next to the GE battery charger and hung his .38 snub-nose with the rubber bands around the grip on a hook inside the cabinet. He brought out, then, a shoulder holster that held a 9-mm blue-steel Colt automatic with a hickory grip, slipped the rig on, adjusted it snugly beneath his left arm and put on his sport coat again, now a perfect fit.

# 19

Sandy woke up lying on her side, feeling Clement cuddled close to her and something hard pressing against her bare behind.

She said, "Is that for me, or you have to go to the bathroom?"

Clement didn't answer. She hadn't heard him come in last night. When she shifted to her back, turning her head to look at the Oklahoma Wildman, he made a face with his eyes still closed and said, "Get off me."

"Pardon me, did I touch you or something? . . . You have a big time last night?" No answer. "Well, I was somewhere, too, if you think I was sitting home."

Clement's little-boy face looked red and swollen; his breath smelled of sour-mash whiskey.

"The Wildman all tuckered out? You big shit, where'd you go?"

Clement opened his eyes, blinked a few times to focus, seeing noon sunlight in the window and Sandy's frizzy hair sticking out golden from the pillow. He said, "I went to that place out Wood'ard . . . took me back home it was so good." Clement's mouth was partly open against the pillow and he talked as though he had a toothache or had just eaten Mexican peppers.

Sandy said, "What? . . . What place?"

He worked his mouth to loosen the stickiness. "Line up your Albanian, I'm ready for him now," Clement said. "You all be sitting there when I walk in. You introduce us . . . we'll look into this business."

"*What* place?"

"Uncle Deano's."

"Jesus Christ," Sandy said, "he's Al*ban*ian, he doesn't like country. He likes disco."

Clement stared at his little partner, waiting for what she said to make sense.

Finally he said, "Honey? . . . I want to talk to this man, I don't want to dance with him."

"Well, what if he doesn't want to go there?"

"Hey, aren't you with the good hands people?" Clement inched his own hand over as he said it and caught Sandy between her slender legs. "Aren't you?"

"Cut it out."

"Why, what's this?" Clement closed his eyes as he felt around. "Whiskers? You growing whiskers on me?"

"That hurts."

"Yeah, but hurts good, don't it? Huh? How 'bout right there? Feel pretty good?"

Sandy rolled toward him, pushing out her hips, then stopped. "I ain't gonna do it less you brush your teeth,"

"Come on," Clement said, "we don't have to kiss. Let's just do it."

Clement laid around the rest of the day while he thought and stared out at Motor City. Sandy sat at the desk to write a letter to her mother in French Lick, Indiana, that began "Dear Mom, The weather has been very warm for October, but I don't mind it a bit as I hate cold weather. Brrrr." And stopped there. She rattled the ballpoint pen between her front teeth until Clement told her to, goddamn it, cut it out.

She went over and turned on the TV and said, "Hey, *Nashville on the Road* . . . my God, anybody ever tell you you look like Marty Robbins? You and him could be twin brothers." Clement didn't answer. Sandy turned to him again after a few minutes and said, "That doesn't make any sense, does it? Marty goes, 'Would you like to sing another song for us?' And Donna Fargo—you hear her?—she goes, 'I can't hardly pass up an offer like that.' What offer? Marty didn't offer her nothing." Clement was staring at her, hard. Sandy got dressed and left the apartment without saying another word.

What Clement thought about was a hundred thousand dollars and the possibility of prying it out of Carolyn Wilder. He heard himself saying to her, "Here's how it is. You give me the hunnert or else I send the cops this notebook, has your phone number written in the judge's hand, the initials of your company . . . Wilder, Sultan and Fine . . . I tear a few pages out of the book so on the lefthand page facing your number and all're these amounts of money, payments, dates and arrows pointing over to you. What do you think?" She had hung up the phone. That's what she thought. She was a tough lady. She didn't get wimpy or act scared for no good reason. She listened and then hung up the phone.

Sandy came back after a couple of hours and glanced at him as she turned on the television. He didn't even look at her, just continued to stare out the window.

Clement thought and thought and finally—with the sun going down and the tall glass stacks of the Renaissance Center turning silver—he said to himself, Jesus Christ, you think too much. *That's* the problem, you dumb shit. Thinking.

What was the quickest, surest way to get money off a person? Stick a gun in their mouth and ear back the hammer. Your money or your life, partner. Hell, that's the way it's always been done throughout history and around the world. Take it and git.

If Carolyn won't go for the con, shit, it was a dumb idea anyway, knock her on her ass, straddle her and let her look into the barrel of a Walther—except, shit, he'd gotten rid of it.

Well, some other gun then.

Which reminded him, he'd have to go shopping before meeting Sandy's Albanian. Go in some nigger bar and make a purchase. He thought of Marcus Sweeton and said to himself, no, stay away from Mr. Sweety for the time being. Sweety had hard bark on him, but he had been messing with dope lately and he wasn't sure where Sweety stood on matters of trust and not fucking an old buddy. Who *could* you trust these days? He looked over at Sandy curled up on the sofa watching Mike Douglas. Bless her heart. Clement told her to go ahead and watch her program, he'd fix supper.

They dug into fried steaks breaded country-style and served with Stove Top Dressing and Miller High Life in the dining-L while the city outside turned dark and began to take on its evening glitter. It was Clement's favorite time of the day. He said, "All right, I'm paying full attention now. Tell me about Albanians."

Sandy said, "Okay, you know where like Italy is, how it sticks down? Al*ban*ia is over on the other side of it."

Clement thought, Jesus Christ— But he had asked for this and he said, "Yeah?" shoveling Stove Top into his mouth and sounding all ears.

"The Albanians that live *here*," Sandy said, "are mostly— you'll get a kick out of this—the really hardass ones that wouldn't live under the Turks or the Communists or somebody. See, so they came here."

"What's hardass about 'em?"

"Well, like Skender says, it's like if you do something to his brother you're doing it to him. I mean they really stick up for kin if anything happens to them. Like a husband beats up his wife? She goes home, tells her dad. The dad goes looking for his son-in-law and shoots him."

"Is that right?"

"But then the brother of the son-in-law shoots the dad and the dad's son, the brother of the guy's wife, shoots the brother of the husband. And sometimes they have to get somebody from Yugoslavia, where most of the hardass ones are, to come over and settle it, it gets so mixed up and confusing with everybody shooting each other."

"Where'n the hell are we," Clement said, "De-troit or East Tennessee?"

"A bunch of 'em live in Hamtramck mixed in with all the Polacks," Sandy said. "Some others live out in the suburbs, Farmington Hills, all over. There're more Albanians here than any place in the United States, but they still have these old ways. Skender says it's called *besa*, like the Code of the West."

"The what?"

"*Besa*. It means like a promise. Like, I give you my word. Or sometimes he refers to it as 'the Custom.' "

"Shit," Clement said, "how come I never heard of 'em?"

"Skender says, 'If someone kills my brother and I do nothing, then I am nothing. I can never'—how'd he say it?—'put my face out among my people.' "

"That's the way he talks?"

"Listen, they're very serious. They get into one of these blood feuds, they have to hide out to stay alive. That's why Skender has the secret room. He built it himself four years ago."

"I think he's giving you a bunch of shit," Clement said, digging into his dressing.

"Really." Sandy was wide-eyed. "I saw the room again. It's hidden down in the basement behind a cinder-block wall that doesn't even have a door."

"Yeah? How you get into it?"

"He turns this switch that's like part of the furnace, up above it, and the wall—you hear this motor hum—and part of the wall comes open, real slow. That's where the safe is . . . with forty thousand dollars inside."

"He show it to you?"

"He told me it's in there."

"Uh-huh," Clement said. "Well, if it's a secret room, what'd he ever let you in there for?"

Sandy got up and went into the kitchen. She came back with her purse. "I've been trying to tell you I went out with him last night, but you were into your thinking time. Who am *I?* I'm not important. Well, take a look at this, buddy." Sandy brought a small blue-felt box out of her purse, opened it and placed it next to Clement's beer glass—where the overhead light would reflect off the diamond in tiny glints of color.

"Skender wants to marry me."

Clement chewed, swallowed, took a sip of beer and sat back with the ring pinched between his fingers.

"What's it worth?"

"Almost four thousand."

"Bullshit."

"You a diamond expert now? I had it appraised over at the RenCen. That's where I went while you were thinking. It's worth three thousand seven hundred and fifty dollars. Plus tax."

"He *proposed* to you? . . . What'd you tell him?"

"I said I'd have to ask my brother."

Before he left the apartment Clement went into Del Weems' closet and picked out one of his sports jackets, the pink and yellow and green Lily Pulitzer model. He took it down to the lobby with him, handed it cross the desk to Thomas Edison, the doorman, and said, "Hey, Tom, this is for you. Case I don't see you again."

The doorman, who had seen the coat on Del Weems throughout the past summer, said, "You leaving us?"

"Yeah, time to move on. Feel like I'm living in a fish bowl—people watching every move I make."

"Yeah, well, I don't know as I can take this coat."

"Don't be bashful," Clement said. "It's for letting me use your car . . . shit, for being a good guy. I'll tell you something. I know white people that've been personal friends of mine for years I couldn't count on like I have you. You wear it and watch all the colored girls' eyes light up."

It was nearly eight o'clock and Thomas Edison was going off duty. The night man was standing with him at the desk. They watched Clement walk over to the bank of elevators and get in, going down to the garage. As the door closed, Thomas Edison said to the night man, "What did he say to me?"

"What you think he said," the night man answered. "It was mighty white of you, boy."

Thomas Edison took the card out of his pocket that the black detective—Wendell Robinson was the name—had given him, picked up the phone and dialed the number on the card for Homicide, Squad Seven.

He said, "That redneck motherfucker you looking for's driving a '76 Mercury Montego, light blue, old beat-up piece of shit . . . What? . . . Wait now, I'll tell you what. You ask me one question at a time, my man, and I'll see if I can give you the answers. How that be?"

# 20

Raymond came out of Sweety's Lounge and walked up to the house next door, 2925, the lower flat. Dull light showed in the windows; the porch was dark. He rang the bell. The black man in the velour bathrobe who opened the door said, "How you doing?" stepping aside. "Come on in."

Raymond wondered if the guy thought he was someone else. He walked in, smelled incense and turning saw clear plastic covers on the furniture, heard Motown music he couldn't identify coming from somewhere in back, saw a photograph in an illuminated frame of a young man with long light-brown hair parted in the middle and a full beard. Raymond came all the way around to face the black man, Mr. Sweety, standing now with the door closed behind him, Mr. Sweety raising a hand to rub his face thoughtfully and giving Raymond a flash of gold rings.

"You're not working tonight," Raymond said.

"Yeah, I'm working. I just ain't working *yet.*" He was studying Raymond, eye to eye with him, though Mr. Sweety was much heavier and when Raymond looked at the dark velour robe trimmed in beige and red he thought of draperies. Mr. Sweety said, "We ain't gonna bullshit each other, are we? You look like you might chew some plug, officer, but I doubt if you smoke what I got."

Raymond was showing his I.D. now. As he said his name his beeper went off.

Mr. Sweety said, "I like that. Got sound effects. You want to use the phone it's in the back hall there."

When Raymond came back in the room Mr. Sweety was sitting at one end of the couch with his legs crossed, smoking a cigarette. He said, "I didn't think you was the dope squad. They come in, you should see the outfits, shirt open down to here, earrings, some of 'em . . ."

Raymond sat down across from him. He looked at the photo in the illuminated frame again.

"What kind of car you drive?"

"Eldorado. You want the license? S-W-E-E-T-Y."

"You own a '76 Montego?"

"No, never did."

"You know anybody who does?"

"Not offhand."

"How's your buddy Clement Mansell doing?"

"Oh, shit," Mr. Sweety said, tired, shaking his head. "I knew it."

"What's that?"

"I mean I was afraid we gonna get to him. I haven't seen the wildman in, I believe, a year or so. Man runs too fast. I settle down, give up the craziness."

"You saw his girlfriend the other day."

"Oh, yeah, Sandy come in, Sandy like her weed. She come in time to time."

"Sandy tell you why he did the judge?"

"Sandy don't tell me nothing. Little jive chick run in run out."

"We can close you down," Raymond said.

"Man, I know that."

"Send you out to DeHoCo for a year. I thought you might want to trade."

129

"What am I gonna trade you? I don't have nothing to give's what I'm saying."

"The little jive chick ran in," Raymond said, "but she didn't run right out again, she stayed a while. Didn't she?"

"Sampling the goods. You know women, they like to shop."

Raymond hesitated, then took a chance. "How come she doesn't want Clement to know she was here?"

The question caught Sweety unprepared. Raymond saw it, the startled look in the man's eyes, there and then gone.

"You seemed confused. What's the problem?"

"Ain't any problem."

"Why would Clement care if she came here?"

"I wouldn't know if he does or he don't, where his head's at these days."

Get off of it, Raymond thought. His gaze moved to the Scandinavian-looking guy in the photo and back to Mr. Sweety. "Why do you think he killed the judge?"

"I don't know as he did."

"Yeah, he did," Raymond said. "But he didn't have anybody driving for him. That make sense to you?"

"Man, come on, I don't know nothing, I don't *want* to know nothing."

"What reason would he have?"

Mr. Sweety sighed. "You have to ask him that."

"I did," Raymond said.

"Yeah? . . . What'd he say?"

"He said what difference does it make. Those were his words," Raymond said. "What difference does it make?"

"You talking to him like that, what you talking to me for?"

"Because you'd like to help me," Raymond said. "You'd like to get the wildman off your back, for good. But you're afraid if you give me something, Clement's liable to find out." Mr. Sweety didn't say anything. After a moment, Raymond got up. "Can I use your phone again?"

In the dark hallway the moving beat of Motown sound was closer now, coming from a bedroom. Raymond held one of his cards toward the light to read a phone number written on the back, then dialed the number.

A male voice answered. "Lafayette East."

"Let me speak to Sergeant Robinson, please." Raymond

waited. When he heard Wendell's voice he said, "Where are we?"

"Got a call out on the Montego," Wendell said. "Told 'em to get the number, see if it's on the sheet and tell MCMU where the car's at. But you see the problem?"

"Which one?" Raymond said. "That's all I see are problems."

"They spot him out in Oakland or Macomb County some-where," Wendell said, "then the local people got the case. They pick him up for driving without a license, but they can't take a weapon out of the car less it's in plain sight. Say they do. Then he's out of our jurisdiction on some halfass gun charge. You un-derstand what I'm saying?"

"Tell 'em—" Raymond paused. "I'm not worried about juris-diction right now. But we have to be sure it's admissible evidence. We find a gun on him, first it's got to be the right gun, then it's got to stand up in court the search was legal and the only sure way is if you take him in on the traffic charge and set a bond and he doesn't make it. Then you can go through the car when you list his possessions. Otherwise, you say you had reason to believe he was carrying a murder weapon—based on what? Shit," Ray-mond said. "I can see us losing him again on a technicality."

"He won't have the gun on him anyways," Wendell said.

"He probably won't, but what's he doing, driving around? Where did he get the car? . . . How about Sandy Stanton?"

"Went out, hasn't come back."

"What's your friend say about letting us in the apartment?"

"Yeah, Mr. Edison says fine. Wants to know if we have a search warrant, I told him you're handling that."

"Everybody's into legal rights," Raymond said. "We see some-thing we want we'll get a warrant and go back. How about the Buick?"

"Hasn't moved. Nobody's gone near it."

"Okay, call a truck, have it picked up. I'll be leaving here shortly."

"I hear the Commodores now," Wendell said. "You and Mr. Sweety spinning records?"

Raymond was thinking. He said, "Listen, let's not worry about Clement, I mean picking him up. Tell 'em just try and locate him and stay close. I'll see you in a few minutes."

He walked back into the living room, looking again at the illu-minated photo of the man with the brown beard and long hair.

"Who's that, a friend of yours?"

Mr. Sweety glanced over. He said, "This picture here?" and sounded surprised. "It's Jesus. Who you think it was?"

"It's a photograph," Raymond said.

Mr. Sweety said, "Yeah, it's a good likeness, ain't it?"

Raymond sat down again, nodding, his gaze returning to the heavyset black man in the bathrobe.

"Are you saved?'

"Man, I hope so. I could use some saving."

"I know what you mean," Raymond said. "There's nothing like peace of mind. But I'm afraid I might've upset you. You're confused now. You don't know whether you should call Clement or not . . ."

"Wait now," Mr. Sweety said, with an expression of pain. "Why would I want to do that?"

"Well, to tell him I was here . . . tell him Sandy was here . . . But then you'd be getting involved, wouldn't you? If I wanted to remain saved," Raymond said, "especially if I was concerned about saving my ass, I think I'd keep quiet, figuring it's better to be a little confused than involved, right?"

"Lift my voice only to heaven," Mr. Sweety said.

"I'd even think twice about that," Raymond said. "You never know, somebody could have you bugged."

# 21

"Yeah, it's dark in here," Clement said, looking around Uncle Deano's, at the steer horns on the walls and the mirrors framed with horse collars. "Darker'n most places that play country, but it's intimate. You know it? I thought if we was gonna have a intimate talk why not have it at a intimate place?" Clement straightened, looking up. "Except for that goddamn pinball machine; sounds like a monkey playing a 'lectric organ." He settled down again. "I'll tell you something else. If our mom hadn't been carried away by a tornado last spring, we'd be holding this meeting in Lawton."

Sandy said to Skender Lulgjaraj, "He means Lawton, Oklahoma."

"Well, hell, he's heard of Lawton, hasn't he? If he hasn't, he's sure heard of Fort Sill . . . Here," Clement said, "make you feel at home."

He took off his K-mart cowboy hat, reached across the table, and placed it on Skender Lulgjaraj's thick head of black hair. The hat sat high and Skender tried to pull it down tighter as he turned to Sandy.

"Hey," Sandy said, "you look like a regular cowpoke."

"I don't think it fit me," Skender said, holding onto the brim with both hands.

"It looks cute," Sandy told him. "Goes with your outfit nice." She reached over to brush a kernel of popcorn from the lapel of Skender's black suit, then picked another one from the hair that showed in the open V of his silky beige sport shirt.

Clement was reaching out, stopping their waitress with his extended arm. He said, "Hey, I like your T-shirt. Honey, bring us another round, will you, please? And some more popcorn and go on over and ask Larry if he'll do 'You Pick a Fine Time to Leave Me, Lucille' the next set? Okay? Thank you, hon." He turned to Skender and said, "Our mom loved that song. She'd listen to it and get real mad and say, 'That woman's just trash, leave four children, *hungry* children, like that.' I believe she loved that song, I'd say just a smidge behind 'Luckenback, Texas.' I *know* you heard that one."

Skender said, "Luke . . . what?"

"He's putting me on," Clement said to Sandy. "You putting me on, Skenny? You mean to tell me you never heard Waylon do 'Luckenback, Texas'? Time we got back to the basics of life?"

Sandy said, "It's 'Time we got back to the basics of love' . . . not life."

Clement squinted at her. "You sure?"

Sandy glanced over at the bandstand in the corner where Larry Lee Adkins and the Hanging Tree—three guitars and a set of drums—were getting ready for the next set. "He just played it," Sandy said. "Ask him."

Clement was thoughful. "He says let's sell your diamond ring, get some boots and faded jeans . . ."

"And he says we got a four-car garage and we're still building on," Sandy said. "So maybe it's time we got back to the basics of love."

"That doesn't rhyme."

"I never said it did. But it's *love*, not life."

Skender, with his cowboy hat sitting on top of his head, would look from one to the other.

Clement grinned at him. "Well, it don't matter. We're here to talk about the basics of love anyway, aren't we, partner?" He paused, cocking his head. "Listen. Hear what they're playing? 'Everybody Loves a Winner.'" Clement half singing, half saying it. "That's a old Dalaney and Bonnie number."

"You're sure full of platter chatter this evening," Sandy said. "You ought to get a job at CXI and get paid for it."

"Well, I got nothing against work. I come a piece from the oil fields to the world of speculation," Clement said, seeing Sandy rolling her eyes as he tightroped along the edge of truth. "But I'd rather see my investments do the work than me, if you know what I mean and I think you do." He looked over at Skender and gave him a wink. "I understand you're in the restaurant business."

"Coney Island red-hot places," Skender said. "I start out, I save eighty-three dollars and thirty-four cents a month. The end of a year I have one thousand dollars. I buy a HUD house, fix it up and rent it to people. I keep saving eighty-three dollars and thirty-four cents a month. I buy another house, fix it up. Then I sell the first house and buy a Coney Island. I buy another house, more houses, fix them up, sell some of them, buy an apartment, buy another Coney Island. In twelve years I have two apartments now I keep for rent and four Coney Island red-hot places."

Sandy reached over to touch Skender's arm, looking at Clement. "Hasn't he got a cute accent?"

Clement said, "Yeah, I 'magine you're paying Uncle Sam a chunk, too."

Skender shrugged. "Yes, I pay. But I have money."

"You ever been married?"

"No, thirty-four years old, I never marry. My cousin Toma and my grandfather, the houseman, the head of the family, they try to get me to marry someone from Tuzi, in Yugoslavia, bring her over here to marry. But I say no and make them very angry, because I want to marry an American girl."

Clement was listening intently, leaning over the table on his arms. He said, "I know what you mean, partner. Nice American girl . . . knows how to fix herself up, shaves under her arms . . .

uses a nice perfume, various deodorants and flavors"—winking at Skender—"if you know what I mean. See," Clement said, "I don't mean to get personal with you, but I got to look out for sis here or I swear our mom'll come storming back from wherever she's at and give me the dickens. I said to her, Sandy—didn't I?—it's entirely up to you. But if this fella is sincere he won't mind satisfying some of my natural curiosity and concern. I said, after all, if you're gonna be Mrs. Lulgurri . . ."

Sandy rolled her eyes.

Skender said, "Lulgjaraj. It's a very common name. When I look in the telephone book I see there are more Lulgjaraj than Mansell. I look hard, I don't see your name. Another question I have, you don't mind, if you sister and brother, why do you have different names?"

"One thing," Clement said, "you can look at us and tell we both got shook out of the same tree, can't you? Well, it's a pretty interesting story how Sandy came to change her name . . . while she was out in Hollywood, was right after the Miss Universe contest . . ."

Skender was nodding, smiling. "Yes?" Sandy was sitting back in her chair, rolling her eyes.

Clement stopped. "I'll tell you, I sure like a man with a natural smile like you got. It shows good character traits." Clement stared hard at Skender, nodding slowly, thoughtfully, as Skender smiled, the smile becoming fixed in an awkward, almost pained expression.

"I'll tell you something else," Clement said. "I've been all over this country, coast to coast to wherever my work as a speculator takes me, but believe it or not, you're my first Albanian . . . Where you living now, Skenny?"

Skender went to the Men's as they got ready to leave. Clement said to Sandy, "I wasn't able to get a gun."

She seemed nervous now, which surprised Clement, and said, "Be nice. You don't have to do it tonight."

Clement said, "Hell I don't. I got seven dollars to my name and no place to sleep."

Clement stayed close behind Skender's black Cadillac, not letting any traffic get between them: straight down Woodward from

Royal Oak into Detroit, east on the Davison Freeway to Joseph Campau and a ride down Hamtramck's main drag, then a right at Caniff to head west, back toward Woodward. Clement thinking, This bird doesn't ever know how to get home. He turned a corner and parked behind the Cadillac in front of a U-shaped, three-story apartment building, 2781 Cardoni.

Skender told them he had been in this place four years. He had moved in right after his brother was shot and killed. Clement paid attention, looking away from the street signs in the light on the corner, and followed Skender and Sandy into the building.

Say he was shot? Clement asked and found out, yes, by a member of another family. It was a long boring story that Clement didn't understand, something about an argument in a bar leading to the shooting of the brother, then a cousin and two from the other family were killed before some guy came over from Yugoslavia and settled the matter.

On the stairway Clement asked Skender if he had shot the two from the other family. But Skender didn't hear him or else ignored the question, telling Sandy, yes, he still lived on the first floor. Sandy wanted to know why they were going up to the second floor then. Skender said wait and see.

Clement couldn't picture this skinny camel-jockey-looking guy shooting anybody anyway.

He seemed to make a ceremony of unlocking the front apartment on the right and stepping back for them to enter. It was a big apartment. Clement was struck by the newness of everything. He thought it looked like a store display and found out he wasn't far wrong.

"For my new bride," Skender said, smiling, showing white teeth and gold caps in the light—Clement getting a good look at him for the first time—Skender sweeping the cowboy hat from his head to present the room. "Decorated with the Mediterranean suit by Lasky Furniture on Joe Campau"—Skender, Clement judged, going about five-nine, a hundred and thirty, maybe shorter, his hair giving him height—Skender showing them the master bedroom then, the other bedroom would be a sewing room—Clement giving Sandy a nudge—the pink and green bathroom, the fully equipped kitchen, ice-maker in the refrigerator, two bottles of slivovitz chilled for the surprise celebration . . .

Sandy looked surprised all right. She said, "Gee, it's really nice."

Clement wasn't in any hurry. He let her walk around the apartment touching wild-animal figurines and the petals of the plastic tulip lamps, looking at the twin stardust-upholstered recliner chairs, looking at the painting of the big-eyed little girl and what looked like a real tear coming down her cheek, while Skender opened a bottle of slivovitz and brought it out to them with his fingers stuck in three stem glasses and the cowboy hat on the back of his head.

Clement kept calling Sandy sis. Saying, "Hey, you're gonna love this place, aren't you, sis?" Or, "How 'bout that sewing room, sis? God darn but he's a thoughful fella, isn't he?" He said, "Man, this is choice stuff" and got Skender to open the second bottle, Clement deciding it tasted something like bitter mule piss, but he wanted the Albanian good and relaxed. Near the bottom of the second bottle he said, "Now what's this about a secret room somewhere? I hope it ain't for locking sis in when she's pouty or mean . . ." Sandy appeared to sigh with relief.

It was about the cleanest basement Clement had ever seen, with separate locked stalls for each of the building's twelve tenants, a big furnace that was like a ship's boiler with aluminum ducts coming out of it and running along the ceiling, cinder-block walls painted light green . . .

Skender said, "Now watch, please."

As though Clement was going to look anywhere else—as Skender reached up to what looked like a metal fuse box mounted high on the wall by the furnace, opened it and snapped a switch to the "up" position. Clement heard a motor begin to hum; he located it in the overhead and followed an insulated wire over to a section of cinder-block wall. About three feet of the wall, from the cement floor to unfinished ceiling, was groaning on unseen metal hinges, coming open right before his eyes, the motor high-pitched now, straining to actuate the massive load. Son of a gun . . .

The room inside was about ten-by-twelve. Clement stepped inside, saying out loud, "I'll be a son of a gun." He saw the floor safe right away. About two feet high, with a telephone and a phone book sitting on top. There was an office-model refrigerator that contained a two-burner range, a record player on a stand, a half-dozen folded-up canvas chairs, a pile of sleeping bags, a table with a sugar bowl on it, prints on the wall of a white seaside village, one of Jesus showing his Sacred Heart and one with a lot of funny-looking words Clement couldn't read. Behind a folding door was a small room with a sink and toilet and shelves stocked with canned goods.

As Clement looked around, Skender turned on the record player. In a moment Donna Summer was coming on loud, filling the cinder-block room with disco music from one of her Greatest Hits.

Clement tried to ignore the sound. He said, "My oh my oh my. You play house down here or you hide for real?"

Skender, smiling, said, "I'm sorry. What?"

"I heard of Eye-talians going to the mattresses—how come I never heard of you people?"

" 'Specially since you read so much," Sandy said.

Clement grinned at her. Little bugger, she was loosening up. That was good; they'd have some fun. He had said to her many times, as he did now, "If it ain't fun, it ain't worth doing, is it?"

She said, "You want me to leave?"

"Hell no, I don't want you to leave. Do we?" Looking over at Skender and seeing him kneeling down at the safe now, opening it—the safe wasn't even locked—and shoving a window envelope inside he had taken out of his inside coat pocket.

Right before your very eyes, Clement thought. You believe it? He would love to be able to tell this later on. Maybe to Sweety. Watch his old nigger face . . .

He said, "Hey, brother-in-law"—feeling a nice glow from the plum brandy and the bourbon he'd had before—"what you got in that box there?" The music wasn't too bad . . .

"I keep some money, some things," Skender drew an automatic out of the safe, held it up for Clement to see. Clement stepped over hesitantly, reached out and let Skender hand the gun to him. He felt Sandy watching, gave her a quick glance.

"This here's a Browning."

"Yes, and this one is a Czech seven-six-five. This little one is a Mauser. This one, I think, yes, is a Smith and Wesson. This one . . . I don't know what it is." Skender was laying the pistols on the floor next to the safe.

Clement released the clip from the Browning, looked at it and punched it back into the grip. "You keep 'em all loaded?"

"Yes, of course," Skender said.

"What else you got in there?"

"No more guns. I keep some money . . ."

"How much?"

Skender looked up at him now, for a moment hesitant, then reached up quickly to keep the cowboy hat from falling down his back. "I put some in last week. I think now . . . four hundred, a little more."

"Four hundred," Clement said. He waited. "Four hundred, huh?"

"A little more."

"How much more?"

"Maybe fifty dollars."

Clement frowned. "You keep money in the bank?"

Skender hesitated again.

Sandy said, "It's okay, he won't tell nobody."

"In a saving certificate," Skender said, taking the envelope out again and opening it to look at a pink deposit receipt, "forty thousand three hundred and forty-three dollars."

Clement said, "That's where your forty grand is, in *savings?*"

"Yes, of course."

"I thought you didn't trust banks."

Skender looked at him. "Yes, I trust the bank. They loan me money when I need it."

Clement glared at Sandy. "Turn that goddamn goat-tit music off!" As she hesitated, startled, he stepped over to the record player and swept the arm scratching across Donna Summer's Greatest Hits. "That disco shit just ricochets off my mind!"

There was a silence.

Sandy said quietly, very slowly, "I think somebody ought to calm down and quit acting like a spoiled brat. You'll live longer."

Skender seemed glad to look at Sandy as she spoke. He said, "I don't understand why he did that."

"Little misunderstanding," Sandy said. "Everything's okay now."

Clement said, calm again, "How much you got in your checking account?"

Sandy grinned and shook her head as Skender looked up at Clement.

"I don't keep much there. This time of the month maybe a few hundred." Skender seemed to prepare himself then and said, "Why do you want to know this?" Hesitant, as though the question might be out of line, an affront to Clement.

"You have a little sister," Clement said, "you want to be sure she's taken care of." He was looking around the room now, hands on his hips.

"You don't have to worry about that," Skender said. "Can I have the gun back now? I put them away."

Sandy was watching Skender. She saw his serious, almost-sad expression now. Disappointed. Or finally getting suspicious.

Clement, still looking around, wasn't paying any attention to him, not even looking at him as he said, "When you're hiding in here and the door's closed, can you open it if you want?"

"Yes, there's a switch." Skender nodded. "There."

Clement walked over to the metal switch housing mounted on the side wall, turned the Browning automatic in his hand to hold it by the barrel and whacked at the housing with the gun butt until it hung loose and he heard some excited words in Albanian. Clement turned and put the Browning on Skender, who was pushing himself up from the floor. "Stay right there, Skenny. Be a good boy." He tore the switch from the wall, threw it out into the basement, then paused and reconsidered what he was about to do. Locking the guy in wasn't going to teach him anything. Introduce him to reality. Clement stepped toward the Albanian.

"You got the EMS number handy?"

Skender was staring hard at him, black eyes glowing. Yes, Albanians could get sore at you, Clement decided. He heard Skender say, "I want you to leave here, now."

"We're going, partner, but first I want to call the Emergency Medical Service."

Skender frowned, taking his time. "Why do you need them?"

Yes, they could get pissed at you, but my Lord, they were innocent about things. Place a level on this boy, up one side and down the other, and get a true square.

"I don't need the EMS," Clement said. "You do."

He heard Sandy say something like, Oh God, as he lifted the

141

K-mart cowboy hat off the Albanian's head and placed the nose of the Browning against the man's hairline, the man's forehead creasing in furrows as he tried to raise his eyes. "Now edge over to the door," Clement said.

The Albanian tried to look at Sandy and Clement wrist-flicked the gun, giving him a backhand whack across the head. Skender came to attention. He began moving on his knees toward the opening in the wall, Clement prodding him along.

"Go on out, then turn around and sit down."

Sandy said, "What're you gonna do to him?"

"Just bring the phone out, hon. There's enough cord. Tell the operator you want the Emergency Medical Service. When they answer, tell 'em to send a van over here to twenty-seven eighty-one Cardoni, corner of Caniff." He looked at Skender, sitting outside the opening in the wall, and said, "Hold on, partner, I'll be right with you."

Sandy hurried out of there with the phone, edging past Skender. Clement followed, roughing Skender's hair with his hand as he came out.

Skender was swallowing. He said something in a language Clement didn't understand, then said, "You are crazy . . ."

"Lay back and stick your leg in the opening," Clement said. "Either one, I don't care." He walked over to the furnace, reached up, and looked over his shoulder as he flicked the switch. With the hum of the motor the wall began to swing slowly closed. He saw Skender, twisted around watching him, draw his leg away from the wall and Clement switched the motor off. He said, "It's up to you, partner"—walking over to him and placing the muzzle of the Browning against Skender's head—"put your leg down or get your fur-cap head all over the basement."

Sandy was saying into the phone, "Hi, we're gonna need an ambulance. I mean we *do* need one, right now . . ."

Clement walked back to the furnace, reached up, flicked the switch on again and watched the wall moving in again, touching Skender's leg now and pushing it up against the stationary section of wall—Skender staring, not believing it was happening to him—and Clement pulled the switch down. As the hum of the motor stopped, Skender looked around, eyes wide with fright and perhaps a little hope.

Clement said, "I want to impress something on you, partner.

I'm disappointed, but I ain't really mad at you, else I'd be pulling the trigger by now. See, but when you're laying in the hospital with your leg in a cast, I don't want you to have any bad thoughts like wanting to tell the police or the FBI or anybody. You do, I'll come visit you again and stick your head in there 'stead of your leg. You hear me? Nod your head."

Sandy was saying, "No, the person didn't have a heart attack . . ."

Clement flicked up the switch and let his hand come down.

Sandy was saying, "Course it's serious . . ."

With the hum of the motor Skender began to cry out. He sucked in his breath, holding it, his face straining, then let the sound come out, his eyes closed tightly now and his face upturned, the sound rising, building to a prolonged scream.

Sandy said into the phone, "Hey, does that sound serious enough for you? You dumb shit . . ."

# 22

Raymond had a vision. Or what he imagined a vision might be like. Herzog told him the Albanian was in the hospital and Raymond saw clearly, in the next few moments, what was happening and very possibly what was going to happen.

He saw the Albanians going after Clement.

He saw Clement running to get his gun, to defend himself.

He saw Mr. Sweety, *yes*, with the gun, the Walther P.38.

He saw Clement holding the gun, the Guy-Simpson murder weapon, and saw himself extending the Colt 9-mm in two hands and saw . . . the clarity of the vision began to fade. He wasn't sure if visions were always accurate. He told himself to back up, look at it again, carefully, beginning at his desk in the squadroom. He remembered . . .

\*　　\*　　\*

Wendell on the phone saying to someone, "What you know for a fact and what you believe, that could be two different things. I want to know what you *know.*"

Norb Bryl saying to a middle-aged woman sitting at his desk, "We can help her, I give you my word as a man." And the woman saying something and Bryl saying, "Well, I hope somebody doesn't kill her."

Hunter saying to Maureen, imitating a voice out of *Amos and Andy*, " 'Yeah, she come up to me and says she wants to pet my puppy.' I'm thinking, ah-*ha*, he got it on with her, before he killed her, right? Isn't that what it sounds like?" Maureen grinning expectantly. "No, the guy's got a *dog* in his car and she wants to pet the dog."

Inspector Herzog coming in, approaching Raymond's desk: "You mentioned, wasn't Mansell's girlfriend—what's her name, Sandy Stanton—going with one of the Albanians?"

This was where the prevision began, Raymond feeling the jab in his stomach, realizing he had forgotten to talk to Skender, to warn him, be careful . . .

Saying "Skender Lulgjaraj," And feeling his stomach knotting.

Herzog saying, "Yeah, Skender. Art Blaney was over at Hutzel visiting his wife. He's going past a room, sees a familiar face. It's Toma. Art looks in, Skender's in traction with a fractured leg. Art wants to know what happened and Toma says, 'He fell down the stairs.' "

Raymond remembered feeling worn out, even with the thing in his stomach, and saying, "Oh, shit . . ."

And Herzog saying, "Let's go in my office."

It was while walking from the squadroom to the office with the view of the river and the highrise that Raymond had his vision.

"I was gonna call him," Raymond said. "I don't know what I was thinking. I know the guy's being set up and I didn't call him."

"Toma says it was an accident," Herzog said. "Maybe it was."

Raymond shook his head. "No—I'm gonna find out what happened, but it wasn't an accident."

"Well, you have hunches," Herzog said, "and most of them turn out to be nothing, so you don't follow up on some." Herzog looked over at a wallboard of newspaper clippings covering the Guy-Simpson murders. "Half those news stories are hunches, speculation. Who killed the judge? . . . Who gives a shit? You notice, there's hardly any mention of Adele Simpson, she's a minor figure. It's all about the judge, what a prick he was. We give them a few facts and, for the most part, they're satisfied, leave us alone and write interviews with people who say, 'Oh, yes, I knew the judge intimately, it doesn't surprise me at all.' They don't care if we ever solve it, they've got so much to write about."

Raymond, reviewing his vision, seemed patient, attentive.

Herzog said, "That girl from the *News,* Sylvia Marcus, she's the only one asks about Mansell. If he's a suspect, where is he? Why isn't he upstairs?"

"I haven't seen her around," Raymond said.

"She's here every day. She picked up on him somehow, maybe getting a little here and there, sees a case folder open on somebody's desk—Sylvia's a very bright girl."

"You think so?" Raymond said.

"Well, she asks good questions," Herzog said. "I have a few myself I've been wondering about. Like the car, the Buick. We seem to be taking this one kinda leisurely."

"I know what you mean," Raymond said. "But you know how long we've been on it? Seventy-two hours. That's all. Since Sandy got back from visiting Mr. Sweety the car hasn't moved—till last night, we took it in, had it vacuumed, dusted. It's like the car's been driven twelve thousand miles with gloves on. Clement's driving a '76 Montego now. He went out last night, but nobody could find him. Didn't come back this morning. Sandy went out, came back early this morning in a cab. We went in the apartment over there last night while they're both out. No gun under the underwear or in the toilet tank. Nothing of the judge's."

"So he got rid of the gun," Herzog said.

Raymond didn't say anything.

"You've been holding back, not wanting to break down the doors too soon," Herzog said. "Meanwhile the guy's riding around in a Montego, you tell me, and might've broken somebody's leg. If you can't get Mansell with the gun, how're you gonna get him?"

"Maybe the gun's still around," Raymond said. "But you're right, I think I've been holding back, being a little too polite, expecting people—you might say—to be reasonable and forgetting a very important principle of police work."

Herzog nodded. "When you got 'em by the balls . . ."

"Right," Raymond said, ". . . the head and the heart soon follow."

Someone in the family had died recently and that's why the Albanians were in black. Coming down the hospital corridor and seeing the figures, Raymond thought at first they were priests. A nurse was trying to remove them from the room, with their packages and paper sacks, telling them only two at a time, please, and to wait in the visitor's lounge. He saw Toma Sinistaj.

Then Toma said something as he saw Raymond Cruz and the delegation in black moved down the hall.

Raymond thought of Toma as a face on a foreign coin. Or he thought of him as a Balkan diplomat or a distance runner. He wore a blue shirt with his narrow black suit and tie. He was about thirty-eight but seemed older; his full mustache was black; his eyes were almost black and never wandered when they looked at you. Raymond remembered this; he knew Toma from several times in the past when Albanians had tried to kill each other and sometimes succeeded. He remembered that Toma owned restaurants, that he carried a Beretta, with license, and a beeper.

Attached to the hospital bed was a frame with an elaborate system of wires that hoisted Skender's plaster-covered leg in the air: like a white sculpture that would be entitled *Leg*. Skender's eyes remained closed. When Raymond asked how he was, Toma said, "He'll be like that a long time and then he'll be a cripple. You know why? Because he wanted to marry a girl he met at a disco place. She tells him okay, but first he has to meet her brother."

"He's not her brother," Raymond said.

"No, I don't think so either. They planned this a long time."

"How much did they get?"

"What difference does it make?" Toma said. "We don't look at it, was it a misdemeanor or felony? You know that. He did it to Skender, he did it to me, it's the same thing. I'm going to look at this Mansell in the eyes . . ."

"It's not that simple," Raymond said.

147

"Why not?" Toma said. "The only thing makes if difficult, you worried you have to arrest me." He shrugged. "All right, if you prove I kill him. You do what you have to do, I do what I have to do."

"No, it isn't that simple, because I want him too," Raymond said. "You're gonna have to get in line. After we're done you can have him charged with felonies, assault, but it isn't gonna mean much if he's doing life. You understand what I'm saying?"

"I understand you want him for killing the judge," Toma said. "I spend some time up on that fifth floor, I talk to people, different ones I know. I understand why you want this man. But if you don't care personally that he killed the judge, then why do you care who kills him? You see the way I look at it? You tell me to get in line. I tell you, you want him you better get him quick, or he'll be dead."

Raymond said, "You always look in their eyes?"

Toma seemed to smile. "If there's time."

"He's killed nine people."

Toma said, "Yes? If you know he kills people, why do you let him? Before I come to this country when I was sixteen I have already kill nine people, maybe a few more—most of them Soviet, but some Albanian, *Ghegs*, my own people. Before the Soviets—before my time, were the Turks; but before the Turks, *always*, we have the Custom. If you don't know about it you don't know anything about me."

"I think of us as friends," Raymond said, wanting the man to know that he understood.

"Yes, you give your word and keep it," Toma said. "I think you know about honor because it doesn't seem to bother you to talk about it. It isn't an old thing in books to you. But maybe honor goes so far with you and stops. Say a policeman is killed. Then I think you want to kill the person who killed him."

"Yes," Raymond said. Basically it was true.

"But you don't understand the honor that even if a man who's smoking my tobacco—he doesn't have to be my brother, but a man I bring into my house—if he's offended in some way then I'm offended. And if he's killed then I kill the person who killed him, because this goes back to before policemen and courts of law. Now—wait, don't say anything, please. A man breaks the leg of your cousin who is like a brother—a very trusting, very nice person—and steals his money. What does you honor tell you to do?"

"My honor tells me," Raymond said, the word sounding strange to him, saying it out loud, "to take the guy's head off."

"You see?" Toma said. "Your honor stops. It tells you something, yes. But you can't say, simply, 'Kill him,' and mean to do it. You say what you *feel* like doing, something more than killing him. But what you would actually do is . . . what?"

"Arrest him," Raymond said.

"There," Toma said. "Well, we're able to talk about it even if we don't see it the same. You don't call me a crazy Albanian."

Raymond said, "How're you gonna find him?"

"We have people looking, some others helping, friends. Some of your own people, some with the Hamtramck police, they tell us a few things they hear. We know what kind of car he has, where the girl lives. We find him, all right."

"What if leaves town?"

Toma shrugged. "We wait. Why does he live here? He likes it? People are easy to rob? If he leaves we wait for him to come back, or, we go after him. Either way."

Raymond looked at the man lying in traction. "How'd he break Skender's leg?"

Toma hesitated, then said, "He broke it very deliberately. You see the Medical Service report?"

"It said he fell down the basement stairs and they found him on the floor. One of the tenants did and called EMS."

"Yes, that was the girlfriend who called," Toma said. "As soon as you came in here—see, I know you're after this Mansell and you figure out he did this; so I'm not going to lie to you, say Skender fell down the stairs. You want that person for murder, but you don't have him. So I know you don't have evidence, and if you don't find some he remains free, even though he's killed two people—no, nine, you say."

"It takes time," Raymond said.

Toma shook his head. "No, it doesn't. Tell me where to find him. It takes only a few minutes."

Raymond didn't say anything.

"For the sake of honor," Toma said.

"Well, it would take care of yours," Raymond said, "but it wouldn't do much for mine, would it?"

Toma studied him with his direct gaze, curious now. "There's more to it than I know about." He paused and then said, "Maybe you *would* take his head off."

"Maybe," Raymond said.

Toma continued to stare, thoughful. "If he resists, yes. I can see that. Or if they tell you, all right, you can shoot him on sight. But if he gives himself up, then what do you do?"

"Turn it around," Raymond said. "You open the door and he's just sitting there. What would *you* do?"

"I'd kill him," Toma said. "What have we been talking about?"

"I know, but I mean if he was unarmed."

"Yes, and I say I'd kill him. What does his being armed or not have to do with it? Are you saying there are certain conditions, rules, like a game?" Toma emphasized with his eyes, showing surprise, bewilderment, overacting a little but with style, letting his expression fade to a smile, that remained in his eyes. "This is a strange kind of honor, you only feel it if he has a gun. What if he shoots you first? Then you die with your honor?" Toma paused. "They call us the crazy Albanians . . ."

It was time to leave. Raymond got ready, looking at Skender again. "Tell me how the leg was broken."

"He tried with a heavy object at first," Toma said. "It was very painful, but it didn't seem to injure him enough. So he raised Skender's foot up on a case, a box, with Skender lying on the floor, and struck the leg at the knee with a metal pipe until the leg was bent the other way. He says he remembered the sound of the girl crying out, saying something, then the sound of the ambulance as he was riding in it, going to Detroit General, and that's all he remembers. This morning," Toma said, "I had him brought here to a doctor I know."

"You say he heard Sandy?"

"The girl? Yes, she cried out something."

"He remember what she said?"

Toma looked at Skender, asleep, then back to Raymond and shrugged. "Does it make any difference?"

"I don't know," Raymond said. "It might."

Hunter was in the blue Plymouth standing at the hospital entrance. He turned the key as Raymond got in . . . held the key, his foot pressing the accelerator, but the car wouldn't start. It gave them an eager, relentless, annoying sound, as thought it was trying, but the engine refused to fire.

"Toma was there. He wants to do Clement himself."

"Who doesn't?" Hunter said. "Fucking car . . ."

"He was talking about his code of honor. Says he's gonna look Clement in the eye and blow him away."

"Tell him, go ahead."

"I said, what if he's unarmed? He says, what's that got to do with it?"

"Drive this piece of shit, you know why they're fucking going out of business." The engine caught and Hunter said, "I don't believe it."

"See, what he couldn't understand, we'd only shoot him if he was resisting."

"Yeah? . . . Where we going?"

"Sweety's Lounge, over on Kercheval. But his point was . . ." Raymond paused. "Well he didn't understand."

"He didn't understand what?"

"I told him the guy's killed nine people and very calmly he says, 'Yes? If you know he kills people, why do you let him?' "

"What'd you tell him?"

"I don't know—we started talking about honor then."

"The Custom," Hunter said. "Fucking Albanians are crazy."

Raymond looked over at him. He said, "You sure?"

A young woman with a full Afro and worried eyes, a scowl, holding a floral housecoat tightly about her, opened the door and told them Mr. Sweety was working. Raymond said, "You mind if we just look in? I want to show him something. That picture over the couch."

The woman said, "What picture?" half turning, and Raymond moved Hunter into the doorway. He waited as Hunter peered in and then came around to look at him as if expecting a punch line. They went down the steps to the sidewalk.

"You see it?"

"Yeah. Picture of some guy."

"You know who it is?"

"I don't know—some rock star? Leon Russell."

"It's Jesus."

Hunter said, "Yeah?" Not very surprised.

"It's a *photo*graph."

"Yeah, I don't think it looks much like him."

Walking next door to Sweety's Lounge Raymond didn't say anything else. He was wondering why things amazed him that didn't amaze other people.

There were white voices in the black bar. Two women in serious, dramatic conversation.

It was dark in here in the afternoon. Mr. Sweety looked like a pirate in his black sport shirt hanging open and a nylon stocking knotted tightly over his hair, coming along the duckboards to the front bend in the bar. The place smelled of beer, an old place with a high ceiling made of tin. Two women and a man sat at the far end of the bar. They looked this way, as Raymond and Hunter came in and took stools, then turned back to the voices coming from the television set mounted above the bar. A soap opera.

Raymond said, "I thought you worked nights."

"I work all the time," Mr. Sweety said. "What can I get you?"

"You want to talk here or at your house?" Raymond asked him. "I don't want to get into anything might embarrass you in front of your customers."

"Don't do it then," Mr. Sweety said.

"No, it's up to you," Raymond said.

"How 'bout if I serve you something?"

"There's only one thing you can give us we want," Raymond said and held up his two index finger about seven inches apart. "It's this big. It's blue steel. And it's got P.38 stamped on the side."

"Hey, shit, come on . . ."

"Sandy told me she gave it to you."

Mr. Sweety leaned on his hands spaced wide apart on the bar so that he was eye-level with Raymond and Hunter seated on stools. Mr. Sweety looked down toward the end of the bar, seemed to wipe his mouth on his shoulder and looked back at Raymond again.

"Sandy told you what?"

"She said she gave you a Walther P.38 that Clement wanted you to hold for him."

"Wait," Hunter said, "let me read him his rights."

"Read me for what? I ain't signing no rights."

"You don't have to," Hunter said. "Those people down

there're witnesses. Then we'll serve you with the search warrant."

As he said this Raymond took a thick number ten envelope out of his coat pocket and placed it facedown on the bar. His hand remained on it, at rest.

Mr. Sweety turned his head back and forth as though he had a stiff neck. "Hey, come on now, man. I don't know shit about nothing. I told him that last night."

"I'll tell you something," Raymond said. "I believe you. I think you got caught in the middle of something and you're naturally a little confused. I would be too."

"I'm not talking to you," Mr. Sweety said.

"I can understand your position," Raymond said, "sitting on a hot gun and here we are coming down on you." Raymond raised his hand from the envelope, palm up. "Wait now. I also see you're still more confused than involved. Sandy laid this on you and you don't know what's going on. She comes in the other day, she tells you Clement wants you to hold the gun for him. But wait a minute. We come to find out Clement doesn't know anything about it. That's straight—listen to me. Hear the whole thing. I told you last night Sandy doesn't want Clement to know she came here. And what do you do? You act very surprised. So I think about it—why would you be surprised? Well, because she *said* it was from Clement. But if Clement doesn't know she was here then he doesn't know she delivered anything. Right? . . . You with me?"

"You losing me on the turns," Mr. Sweety said.

"I know you've got some questions," Raymond said, "but how much do you really want to know? See, all we want is the gun. Now. Listen very carefully. If we have to *look* for the gun, then what we're gonna find is a murder weapon in your possession. Then, you not only get your rights read, you get to see a warrant for your arrest on the charge of murder in the first degree, which carries mandatory life. On the other hand . . . You listening?"

"I'm listening," Mr. Sweety said. "What's the other hand?"

"If you tell us of your own free will some person gave you the gun but you don't know anything about it, whose it is, how it was used, *any*thing, then what we have here is still another example of citizen cooperation and alert police work combining their efforts to solve a brutal crime . . . You like it?"

Mr. Sweety was silent, thinking.

He said, "He don't know she gave this piece to anybody. I mean Clement. That what you saying?"

"That's correct."

"Where does he think it is?"

"Well, I don't think she lifted it off him," Raymond said. "Do you?"

"No way."

"So I think he gave it to her to get rid of and she laid it off on you. It isn't as easy as it sounds, throwing a gun in the river. Maybe she was coming here anyway, you know? Or maybe she told *you* to get rid of it. I'm not gonna ask you that. But if she did, that puts a burden on you. You got to take it out in your car somewhere . . . somebody finds the gun, remembers seeing you . . . the way it always happens. You been around, you know these things. Who wants to be associated with a hot gun. No, I don't blame you." Raymond waited a moment. "You coming to a decision?"

Mr. Sweety didn't answer.

"Where's the gun, at your house?"

"Down the basement."

"Let's go get it."

"I got to call Anita, have her come over here."

Raymond and Hunter looked at each other but didn't say anything. They waited for Mr. Sweety to come back from the phone that was halfway down the bar, by the cash register.

Raymond said, "You feel better now?"

Mr. Sweety said, "Shit . . ."


They got back into the blue Plymouth, Raymond carrying a brown paper bag. He said, "It's work, you know it? It wears you out."

Hunter said, "That's why they pay all that money. Now where?"

"Let's go see Sandy. No, drop me off and get this to the lab. But don't tag it yet, I mean with any names on it."

Hunter held the key turned, his foot mashing the accelerator. "Fucking car . . ."

Raymond waited patiently. He thought back, reviewing the conversation with Mr. Sweety, pleased. Then said, "I think I left the envelope on the bar," and patted his breast pocket. "Yeah, I did."

"You need it?"

"From Oral Roberts," Raymond said. "No, I'll probably be hearing from him again."

# 23

A Hamtramck Police detective by the name of Frank Kochanski picked up his phone and said to Toma, "Where you been?"

"I'm still at the hospital."

"This character you're looking for's at the Eagle. We saw his car by there and I give Harry a call. Harry says yeah, he's in there having a few pops, making phone calls."

"The Eagle?" Toma said, surprised that the man was still in the vicinity of Skender's apartment, little more than a mile from it.

"The Eagle, on Campau," Kochanski said. "How many Eagles you know?"

Toma called the bar. Harry said, "Yeah . . . no, wait a minute, he's picking up his change . . ."

Toma walked down the hall to the third-floor visitor's lounge where the male members of the Lulgjaraj family were waiting.

They watched him unfold a city map, study it for a few moments, then place it on the coffee table and draw a circle with his finger to take in, roughly, Hamtramck and the near east side of Detroit. He said, "He's somewhere in here. But he stays most of the time downtown; I think he'll go there. If he knows how, he'll take the Chrysler. If he doesn't he may take McDougall." Toma paused. His finger began tracing the line that indicated East Grand Boulevard. "But he could go this way, too, from Joseph Campau. We don't know him, so we have to look for him all these places."

About forty minutes later Skender opened his eyes to the beeping sound. It stopped and Toma was standing close to him, touching his face.

"Go back to sleep."

At the public phone Toma called his service, was given a number and dialed it.

"Where is he?"

"In a house on Van Dyke Place. We're at the corner of Van Dyke and Jefferson," the voice said in Albanian.

"Wait for me," Toma said.

"But if he comes out . . ." the voice began.

"Kill him," Toma said.

"I think what happens to niggers is they come up here and find out they can talk back to you," Clement said, "so all they do then's argue. I tole your nigger woman I *know* she's upstairs. I called her office enough times they finally told me she's home. So what're you arguing with me for?"

"I'm never home to clients," Carolyn said. "I'll see you in my office or, more likely, the Wayne County Jail, but not here. So, Clement, you're going to have to leave."

"All you're doing's reading. You sick? I see a person in their bathrobe the middle of the day I figure they work nights or they're sick."

Carolyn took off her glasses, brought her bare feet down from the hassock and placed the glasses inside the book as she closed it on her lap. "I'm going to argue with you, too, if you don't leave," Carolyn said, "and I promise you'll lose."

Clement didn't seem to hear her. He was looking around the room, at the abstract paintings, at the bar, his gaze moving past

Carolyn sitting in the bamboo chair in a beige and white striped caftan, to the beige couch that was covered with pillows in shades of blue. He walked over and let himself fall back into it, his boots levering up and then down, hitting hard on the Sarouk carpet. He pulled a pillow out from behind him, getting comfortable.

"Shit, I'm tired. You know it?"

Carolyn watched him, curiosity soothing impatience, calming her as she studied the man half-reclined on her couch, his head bent against the backrest cushion, fingers shoved into tight pockets now. The Oklahoma Wildman. Born somewhere between fifty and one hundred years too late.

Or a little boy she could hear saying, "I don't have nothing to do." Kicking at the Sarouk, at the ripple, with the heel of his boot, trying to flatten it.

"That carpet you seem determined to destroy," Carolyn said, "cost fifteen thousand dollars."

"No shit?" He looked down at the blue Oriental pattern.

"No shit," Carolyn said. "It's worth much more than that now."

"Why don't you sell it, get the money?"

"I enjoy it. I didn't buy it as an investment."

"How much you make a year?"

"Enough to live the way I want."

"Come on, how much you make?"

"Why do you want to know?"

"You don't keep any money in the house, do you?" Clement grinned at her. "*I* know, it's all in VISA cards. That shit's ruining me, you know it?"

"Am I supposed to feel sorry for you?"

"No, but you could write me a check."

"Why would I do that?"

"You know why."

"Clement, you're a terrible extortionist."

"I know. But there was that chicken-fat judge dead and nothing to come of it. Seemed a shame. Then I see your phone number in his book and I commenced to scheme." Clement squinted. "How come he had your number?"

"He called a few times, wanted me to go out with him."

"Jesus, you didn't, did you?"

"No, Clement, I didn't."

"You ain't a young girl, but I *know* you can do better'n that."

Carolyn said, "This chat's costing you money, Clement. If we're getting into your situation there's a twenty-five-hundred-dollar retainer to think about. If we go to trial, I'll need another seventy-five, in advance."

Clement blinked and squinted. Carolyn watched his act indifferently—Clement shaking his head now.

"First thing you must learn in school, I mean lawyers, is how to turn things around. I come up here to get a check and you tell me you want ten thousand dollars."

"If I'm going to represent you."

"For what? Shit, they're dickin' around, they're never gonna have a case. I'm pulling out, going down to Tampa, Florida, for the winter. But I don't have the stake I thought I was gonna. That's why I need you to write me a check."

Carolyn sat low in the chair studying Clement, her elbow on the arm, her cheek resting against her hand.

"You never cease to amaze me."

"I don't?"

"Always seem so calm. Never upset. How do you manage that?"

"Thinking good thoughts," Clement said. "Go get your checkbook."

"What do you need, a couple hundred?"

Clement squinted at her again. "Couple *hun*nert?" He had come seeking no particular amount. She had mentioned a ten-thousand-dollar fee and that didn't sound too bad. Nice round number. But now—shit, looking at him like he was the janitor, waiting for him to leave so she could open her book again—he doubled the amount and said, "Twenty thousand oughta do it."

Carolyn didn't say anything. She didn't move until he said, "You're pretty calm yourself." Then watched as she came out of the chair, laying the book on the hassock, and went to the desk in the bay of front windows.

With her profile to him, leaning over the desk, she said, "I'm doing this against my better judgment," opening a business-size checkbook and writing now.

Clement was surprised. He'd expected her to give him an argument. He could see the curve of her fanny against the robe. She tore a check from the book and walked across the room, right past him, not looking at him until she was standing in the doorway that opened on the upstairs hall. Clement could see the railing behind her and now she was offering him the check.

"Here. Take it."

Something wasn't right. Clement stared and watched her move out into the hallway now and hold the check over the railing.

"All right, then pick it up on your way out," Carolyn said. "But if you take it, please don't expect me to ever help you again, in or out of court. Understood?"

Clement got up and crossed toward Carolyn. Her extended arm looked pale and naked sticking out of the robe. As he reached her she handed him the check. Clement looked at it.

"This says two hunnert."

Carolyn called over the railing, downstairs, "Marcie?"

"I said twenty thousand. You left out some aughts."

Carolyn turned to look at him. "Even if I could write a check in that amount, do you really think I would?"

"Yes, I do," Clement said. " 'Stead of me rolling up your rug or taking your jewelry—sure, I do."

"But a check—you know I could stop payment as soon as you leave."

"Then I'd come back, wouldn't I?"

"I don't believe this," Carolyn said. "All I have to do is call the police."

"Man, it's hard to get through to some people," Clement said. "Where's your bathroom?"

Carolyn hesitated, then gestured with her hand, a vague motion. "Right there. The first door." She turned with her back to the railing for Clement to go past, then tried to pull away as he took her by the arm.

"Let's me and you go toidy."

"Now wait a minute—" Clement's fingers dug into her upper arm and she called out, "Marcie!"

"She's locked in the pantry." Clement was moving Carolyn along now. "I told you she was arguing with me. People argue— you're a lawyer—you got to make your point or shut 'em up, huh?" He pushed Carolyn into the bathroom and swung the door closed behind them, looking around. "Man, this is some biffy; you could have a party in here . . . big stall shower . . . I like a tub-bath myself, but this'll do fine. Take your robe off."

"Clement?" Carolyn began.

"What?"

"Whatever you're doing ..." She tried a sincere expression with a slight smile. "Can I offer you a little advice?"

"How much's the retainer?"

"No, this is free. Whatever you have in mind"—slowly, with a soft lilt to her voice—"I think you should consider very carefully the position you're in." Clement hooked a finger in the ring of the caftan's zipper. "Clement, be nice, okay?"

"You'd stop payment, huh?" The caftan opened as he pulled down. She tried to hold it closed. He took her two hands and brought them away, standing close, looking into her face.

"I don't have anywhere *near* that much." Carolyn said, still sincere, "so what difference does it make?"

"How much you got?"

"Let's go look in the checkbook."

"Take off the robe first." He let go of her hands.

"Clement, really, if you'll stop and think for a minute ..." His hands slipped inside the rough-cotton garment, moved up her body and felt her elbows come in tightly, her eyes staring into his.

"What you think I'm gonna do to you? ... Huh? Tell me." He moved his thumbs across her breasts. "Hey, your nobs're sticking out ... That feel pretty good? Juuuust brush 'em a little, huh? ... They get hard as little rocks." His right hand moved lightly down her side to her hip, their eyes still holding. "Now what am I gonna do? ... That your belly button right there? ... My, we don't have no panties on, do we?" His voice drowsy. "Tell what you think I'm gonna do to you ... Huh? Come on ..."

Clement drew his right hand out of the caftan, bringing it down past his own hip, curled the hand into a fist, and grunted, going up on his toes, as he drove the fist into Carolyn's stomach.

Once he got her into the shower, the caftan off her shoulders, pinning her arms, Clement gave Carolyn a working over with a few kidney punches and body hooks, a couple of stinging jabs to the face before a right cross drew blood from her nose and mouth and he turned the shower on her. The job was trying to keep her on her feet, glassy-eyed and moaning, Clement doubting she had much air left in her. He gave Carolyn a towel and guided her back to the desk in the window bay, bright with afternoon sunlight.

161

Opening the checkbook, Clement said, "Let's see now how much you want to give me."

He looked at himself in the mirrored walls of the first floor, grinned a little at the hotshot grinning back at him and walked out of there with a check for six thousand five hundred dollars in the pocket of his denim jacket, thinking: I believe you stumbled onto something, boy.

It was sure nice out.

There was a guy standing across the street. A young guy in a dark suit.

It was sure easier than going in with a gun. Pick out the right party, impress on the party why they should not call the police, then go to a downtown bank at once and cash the check. See, then if the bank calls the party to verify the check, the party is still seeing life through pain and fear and would say, you bet it's good—fast.

There were three guys over there now, standing, talking.

Carolyn was probably upstairs looking out the window. Man, but it was a big place. Weird. High picket fence, like spears, all around and a blacktop parking area in the side yard—no grass— like the place had once been a residence, then a commercial establishment of some kind, with its big kitchen and bathroom, then a residence again. His car sat over there all by itself, up against the iron fence.

The three guys across the street, he realized now—looking through the fence at them as he approached his car—were wearing black suits. Dark-haired guys with mustaches and black suits . . .

Jesus Christ, he had never even *seen* an Albanian before yesterday. He said to himself, Oh, shit—wanting to run for the Montego, but making himself walk, not wanting to get anybody excited just yet, least not until he was behind the car on the driver's side and could open the door and reach under the seat.

The three guys were coming across the street. They looked like undertakers. They were opening their black suit coats and reaching inside . . .

Clement was still five long strides from the car when they drew pistols and began firing at him. He couldn't believe it. Right out on the street, three guys he'd never seen before in his life shooting at him through the fence, not asking him to wait-up there, find out if he was the party they wanted—Christ, just blazing away at him! Clement got his door open and saw the windows drilled and patterns form at the same time, the windows shattered but held together. He got the Browning from under the seat, edged to the rear curve of the Montego, extended the Browning over the edge of the trunk and, as he saw them through the widely spaced pickets, the three of them coming toward the drive, he began squeezing the trigger, feeling the gun jump, hearing that hard report in his ears, and saw them scatter, running along the fence on the other side of the drive. Clement got in the Montego, backed up, headed toward the rear of the house and almost braked when he saw the chain across the exit drive—thought, What, you don't want to scratch up your new car?—kept going and tore through those links without even feeling a tug—sailed out hanging a right into the alley and faced another split moment of decision as he saw the end of the alley coming up fast. Turn left, away from the boys in black? Or hang another right and have to drive past the front of the house, where they were presently swarming? To hell with them. He cranked a right . . . saw the blacks suits back in the street again, looking this way, then all three of them aiming with both arms extended, like they knew what they were doing. The sound of the shots came as *pops*, far away, but the windshield blossomed at once in fragmenting circles. Clement floored it right at them. Saw them run for the sidewalk and veered over to jump the curb and sweep along close to the fence. Two of them ducked into the drive, out of the way, while the third set a fence-climbing record, just pulling his legs up as Clement scraped the Montego against the metal pickets, swerved back onto the street and took a couple of more shots in the rear end before he got to Jefferson and turned without stopping into the westbound traffic.

He couldn't believe he had never heard of Albanians.

# 24

Sandy was wearing her Bert Parks T-shirt with tight faded jeans. She let go of the door, resigned, walked ahead of Raymond into the living room.

"We alone?"

"You mean is Clement here? No. But Del called. He's coming back this weekend."

"What's that do to your arrangement?"

"It doesn't do nothing. I move out."

"Clement find another place?"

Sandy seemed worn out. She didn't answer, she moved in a circle, indecisive, before dragging herself over to the couch and curling a leg beneath her as she sank down.

"Tired?"

"Yeah, a little."

"Out late last night, huh?"

"Pretty late."

Raymond came over and sat at the other end of the couch, playing with a folded piece of notepaper now, rolling it in one hand the way you might roll a cigarette.

"I'm tired too," Raymond said. "You want to know where I've been?"

"Not partic'larly."

"First I went to Hutzel . . ."

"What's Hutzel?"

"It's a hospital. Up at the Medical Center."

Sandy held her hands close to her face, idly concentrating on a fingernail, putting it between her front teeth then, holding the nail with her teeth as she twisted the finger.

"I saw Skender."

"Then where'd you go?"

"Skender's in traction. He's gonna be crippled the rest of his life. You can say, oh, what happened? And we can throw that back and forth a while, or you can tell me how you feel about it."

"I don't have to talk to you," Sandy said, "so I don't think I will."

"You know the kind of person Skender is—quiet, very nice guy—"

"Hey, come on." Sandy got up abruptly. She went over to the windows and stood with her back to Raymond, who rolled and unrolled the piece of notepaper between his thumb and fingers.

"What'd Clement call him, the chicken-fat Albanian?" Sandy didn't answer. "You don't have a typewriter, do you? I mean Del Weems."

Sandy shrugged. "I don't know."

He handed her the piece of notepaper.

"What's this?"

"Read it."

Sandy unrolled it, saw:

### SURPRISE
### CHICKEN FAT!!!

and let the paper curl up again. Raymond took it. He left her standing at the window and returned to the couch.

"He leaves the note and shoots up my apartment with a .22.

The question is, was he trying to kill me, or was he just having some fun?"

Sandy turned to the television set that was in the corner between the banks of windows, dialed the knob through the channels, back and forth, stood looking at the screen a moment, then came back to her end of the couch and sat down on her leg, her gaze holding on Bob Eubanks talking to a panel of newlywed wives, asking them what film star will their husbands say *"you* would most like to make whoopee with."

"Who would you?" Raymond said.

"Robert Redford," Sandy answered, watching the television screen. An Oriental-looking newlywed wife also said Robert Redford. The other three said John Travolta.

"One time," Sandy said, with a little more life in her now, "Bob Eubanks asked them what was the most *unusual* place they ever made whoopee? And this girl goes—it's bleeped out, but you can read her lips. She goes, 'In the ass.' And Bob Eubanks goes, *'No!* I mean a place like a location.' I though he was gonna die."

"You ever married?" Raymond asked.

"Yeah, once. This shithead from Bedford. His big ambition was to move to Indianapolis."

"I guess you've seen some sights."

"Not a whole lot worth remembering."

"How old are you?"

"I'm twenty-*three.*" Giving the number an edge of panic in her tone.

"I don't mean to sound square," Raymond said, "but you might consider a different way of life."

Sandy was still gazing at the television screen. "Look at that"—amazed—"all four of the husbands said John Travolta. Jesus. You know how many John Travoltas there are around? If I had my choice, who I'd pick, you know who it'd be?"

"You said Robert Redford."

"No, he's the one I'd like to make whoopee with. No, I mean the one, like somebody I wouldn't mind being married to."

"Who's that?"

"Don't laugh, but Gregory Peck."

"Is that right?"

"I mean a young Gregory Peck."

"Yeah, I've always liked him."

"He's so . . . calm. You want to know something? When you first came here, the first time, you reminded me of him. A younger Gregory Peck—that's what I thought of."

Raymond smiled. "Were you smoking?"

"*No*. I didn't have nothing but seeds and stems. I told you that, didn't I? Didn't we discuss that one time?"

"You've been smoking today though."

"Some, but I don't feel it. God, I wish I did."

"I know what you mean," Raymond said. "Mr. Sweety told us about the gun."

Sandy sighed and seemed tired again. "Here we go."

"A Walther P.38 HP model, made in Germany about 1940," Raymond said. "It's probably been to war, killed some people. But the only ones we know for sure it's killed are Alvin Guy and Adele Simpson. Mr. Sweety says you're the one gave it to him."

"He said that?"

"It's true, isn't it?"

"I don't know—I thought Gregory Peck was cool," Sandy said, "but I think you could give him some lessons. I've been seeing it coming and, I'll tell you the truth, I don't know what to do. If you think I'm gonna testify against Clement—I mean even if he was paralyzed from the neck down and had to be fed with a spoon— even if you *swear* you're gonna put him away forever, like the last time, make me all these promises if I'll say he had the gun, whatever it was that time, and I wouldn't do it and thank *God*, Christ, I didn't, cause he walked out of the courtroom, didn't he?"

"He isn't gonna walk this time," Raymond said, not even convincing himself.

Sandy said, "Bull *shit*, *you* don't know. Practically everybody he knows made him in that house—where was it, on St. Mary's—with that fucking gun and he *walked*. The only way in the world—I'll tell you right now—I'd ever testify against Clement is if he's dead and buried with a stake through his heart and even then I'd be nervous." Sandy got up. "You can send me to jail you want, but I swear I'm not saying one fucking word." She went over to the front windows again and stood motionless, looking out.

Bob Eubanks was saying, "Now, gentlemen, listen carefully. Who will your wife say, of all your friends, is the most oversexed? First names only, please."

Raymond got up. He walked over to the set thinking, Jerry. Turned it off and stood next to Sandy looking down at the city . . . cars coming off the Chrysler Freeway and turning onto Jefferson, the Renaissance Center, people in there coming out of work, conventions, meeting for drinks . . .

"Have you seen him today?"

"No."

"You talk to him?"

"No."

"Why do you stay with him?"

He didn't think she was going to answer; but she said, after a moment, "I don't know." Listless again. "He's fun . . ."

"He kills people."

"*I* don't know that." She started to turn from the windows and Raymond put his hand on her shoulder, lightly, feeling small bones.

"You wish he'd disappear, leave you alone," Raymond said. "You won't make the move because you're afraid to. He scares you to death. So you pretend he's a normal person, maybe just a little wild, and say he's fun. Was he fun when he put Skender's leg up and took the pipe? . . ."

"I'm not saying one fucking word to you!" She tried to turn and pull free, but Raymond put both hands on her shoulders now and held her facing the pane of glass, the view.

"All I want you to do is listen," Raymond said. "Okay?" Relaxing his grip, his hands moving gently over her shoulders before coming to rest. "I wondered, why didn't he kill Skender? He killed the judge, he killed the woman with the judge. You see, I don't think Clement planned it or anybody paid him to do it. He kills in the line of business, or when he feels like it. I think he came out of the racetrack looking for you and Skender—I know you were setting the poor guy up—and I think the judge got in Clement's way, that's all, and one thing led to another and . . . what does Clement do when he gets mad at somebody? Well, he might shoot you. Or, if he halfway likes you or feels sorry for you, he might only break your leg, let you off with a warning. You see what I mean?"

"You answer your own question," Sandy said.

"What question's that?"

"Will I testify against him. You admit he kills people he

gets mad at. Or breaks their leg. What do you think he'd do to *me?*"

"I'm not asking you to testify. Have I said anything about testifying?" Raymond paused. "Are you thinking about something else?"

"Are you kidding—something *else?*"

"I think you're missing the point here," Raymond said. "What happens, say in the next day or so, before we pick him up, Clement finds out Sweety has the gun?"

"Oh, Jesus—"

"He'd want to know how he got it, wouldn't he?"

Sandy came around and was looking up at him with terrible fear in her eyes that seemed almost a yearning. *"Why?* I mean he doesn't have to know that, does he?"

Raymond's hands moved gently on her shoulders. "What were you suppose to do with the gun, get rid of it?"

"Throw it in the river."

There it was. Not something he could use; still, it was nice to hear, verifying what he had put together in small pieces.

"So why'd you take it to Sweety?"

"Because I was going there." She was a little girl again, pouting, resentment in her tone. "I'm not gonna walk out on the Belle Isle Bridge. What am I suppose to be doing if somebody sees me? Standing there on the bridge . . ."

"I know, it sounds easy," Raymond said, "but it isn't. What'd you tell Sweety to do with it?"

"Anything he wanted. Just get rid of it."

"And he looked at it the same way you did. So he hid it down the basement. But weren't you afraid he might call Clement?

"Why would he?" Her tone changed as she said, "Listen, I'm not making a statement—if you think you're being clever."

"I told you, I'm not asking you to snitch," Raymond said. "But how come you didn't tell Clement you took the gun over there?"

"God, I don't know." Weary again. "He gets so picky and irritated sometimes . . ." She turned to the window and Raymond kept quiet, letting her stare at her reflection against the fading light. Almost at once the T-shirt image on the window changed to white and she was looking up at him again. "Wait a minute—if you know where the gun is then you already picked it up, huh? You're not gonna *leave* it there."

"Sandy," Raymond said, "what difference does it make where the gun is? What's that got to do with *you?*"

"He'll find out—"

"Wait. Let me suggest something," Raymond said, "before he finds out *any*thing, tell him you took the gun over there. That's all. You're off the hook."

"But I didn't do anything to get him in trouble—I *didn't*. Will you just, God, explain it to him?" In desperate need of help, but not listening.

"Sandy, look, all you have to do is tell him the truth. You gave the gun to Mr. Sweety. Tell him, because you were afraid. Isn't that right? I don't think Clement was very smart to give it to you in the first place, but that's not your fault. At the time, I can understand him being a little nervous. What is this? He's hardly out of bed, reading about the judge in the paper and we're banging on the door. The gun's down in the Buick or somewhere—he just wants to get rid of it, quick." Raymond paused. "Sandy? Look at me. You listening?"

"Yes . . ."

"Do you see any reason to tell him anything else? Maybe get him excited, as you say, picky and irritated? No, just say, 'Honey, I think I ought to tell you something. I was afraid to throw the gun in the river, so I gave it to your friend Mr. Sweety.' You can say, you know, looking at him very innocently, 'Was that all right, honey?' And he'll say sure, fine. See, keep it simple. But you're gonna have to do it pretty quick. Next time you see him, or if he calls."

"God, I don't know," Sandy said. "I got a feeling I'm in awful deep trouble."

"Well, you go with a guy like Clement you're gonna have some close ones," Raymond said. "What I'd do, if you want my advice, I'd tell him and then split. Go find you a young Gregory Peck somewhere. Twenty-three, Sandy, you're not getting any younger."

"Thanks a lot," Sandy said.

"On the other hand you stick with Clement, you have a good chance of not getting any older," Raymond said. "So there you are."

# 25

Raymond said, "What're we having, a telethon or something?"

Hunter was on the phone. He raised his eyes and one hand, motioning to Raymond, but didn't catch him in time. Raymond was moving from the squadroom door to the coffeemaker.

Norb Bryl was on the phone. He was saying it wasn't the tires, it was the wheel alignment; he said you pay thirty-four hundred dollars for an automobile you expect it to go in a straight line, was that right or wrong?

Wendell Robinson was on the phone, sounding pleasant but in mild pain, saying he had been taking cold showers to keep himself civil; but if someone's old man didn't go back on nights pretty soon, then maybe it wasn't meant to be.

Maureen Downey was on the phone, saying okay, fine, swivelling around from her desk as she hung up to watch Raymond pour a cup of coffee.

"There was a shooting, three o'clock this afternoon. On Van Dyke Place."

Raymond stopped pouring.

"MCMU told us about it, so I called the precinct, just now," Maureen said, "and the sergeant read me the PCR. Three unidentified males, all in dark clothes, dark hair, shooting at an unidentified male driving a light blue older-model car that might be a big Ford or a Lincoln."

"Or a Mercury Montego," Raymond said. "Did he shoot back?"

"They think so, but no reported injuries or fatalities. MCMU's checking the hospitals."

"How was it reported?"

"The call came from the woman next door to two-oh-one, where the shooting took place—in the driveway and out on the street—and we know who lives at two-oh-one, don't we?"

"They talk to Carolyn Wilder?"

"They said they talked to the maid. She said Ms. Wilder wasn't home. But then—"

Hunter, off the phone, said, "We got him by the ass!" and Raymond looked over. "It's the gun, man. Absolutely no question. I'm gonna go pick it up."

Maureen waited for Raymond to turn back to her. He said, "I'm sorry. What?"

"Carolyn Wilder phoned almost a hour ago. She wants you to call."

"Okay." He picked up his coffee mug and started to move away.

"At home," Maureen said.

Raymond stopped and looked at Maureen again, appreciating her timing. "You ask her if she heard the shots?"

"No, but I'll bet you she did."

Raymond went to the unofficial lieutenant's desk beneath the window and dialed Carolyn's number.

"I hear you had some excitement."

"I'd like to see you," Carolyn said.

"Fine. I'll be leaving here pretty soon. You sound different."

"I'll bet I do."

Now he was puzzled. Her voice was low, yet colder than he had ever heard it. "Marcie see what happened?"

"No, but I did."

Raymond didn't say anything.

"Who are they?" Carolyn said.

And now he wasn't sure how much to tell her. "Clement picked on the wrong one this time and it snapped back at him. Why, you want to file his complaint?"

"I would like to laugh," Carolyn said, "but my mouth hurts. Before this sounds even more like farce, why don't we save it until you get here."

Raymond hung up, still puzzled. He said to Norb Bryl, who was standing now, clipping several pens into his shirt pocket, "What exactly is farce?"

"It's a used car that's supposed to drive in a straight line," Bryl said, "but pulls to the left. If you don't need me I've got something to do."

The door closed behind Bryl, then opened again as Hunter came in with a brown paper bag that was grease-stained and could be a bag of doughnuts. He placed it on the lieutenant's desk, pleased. "No prints, but this is the little mother that did it. Absolutely no question."

Raymond looked across the squadroom. He said, "Maureen, if you want to go, you can, it's pretty late; but if you want to stay, lock the door. Okay?"

Wendell said, "How 'bout me?"

"Same thing. You want to leave, go ahead."

Hunter said, "Shit, you got his interest now. Afraid he might miss something."

Maureen came over, hesitantly, and sat at Bryl's desk.

Hunter said, "How come you don't ask me if I want to leave?"

"You're already in it," Raymond said. He looked at Maureen and then Wendell. "We took the gun off this guy Sweety without a search warrant. I'm not worrying it's gonna kick back at us, that's not what I'm getting to. I wanted to find out, you know, without typing up all the papers and pleading with some judge, if this is really the gun or not. All right, we find out it is. No question about it—our friend up in the lab checks it out without entering any names and numbers in the book—we have a murder weapon. Now . . . if we take it to the prosecutor at this point he says, fine, but how do we prove it's Mansell's gun? We say, well, if we're very persuasive we can get this guy by the name of

Sweety to cop. The prosecutor says, who's Sweety? We tell him he's a guy that used to run with Mansell, he's done time and now he's dealing drugs. The prosecutor says, Jesus Christ, *that's* my witness? We say, well, we can't help the kind of people we have to associate with in this business; he's all we got."

"Sandy," Maureen said.

"Right, we've also got Sandy," Raymond said, "but you can pull all her fingernails out, which she hasn't got much of anyway, and she'll still never say a word. Not out of loyalty, but because Clement scares the shit out of her."

"How about if I talked to her?" Maureen said.

"Sure, why not? I'm open to suggestions, But let me review what we've got. An arm that could be Clement's sticking out of a car at Hazel Park. Possibly the same car at the scene, which Sandy has the keys to and we say she gave to Clement. Clement's lawyer, Miss Wilder, looks at us and says, 'Yeah? Prove it.' We can put Clement at another scene, three years ago, where slugs were dug out of a wall from a Walther P.38"—Raymond picked up the paper bag—"right here, our murder weapon. But how do we show it belongs to Clement?"

There was a silence.

Maureen said, "Wow. I think I know what you're gonna do."

Again a silence. Raymond was aware of the four of them sitting in an old-fashioned police office under fluorescent lights, plotting.

Hunter said, "I don't see no other way."

Wendell said, "You want me to talk to the brother, Mr. Sweety?"

"No, it's my responsibility if anybody gets blamed. I'm gonna do it." Raymond said. "At least try to arrange it. Wendell, you know Toma pretty well, the Albanians. Have a talk with him, like we're thinking about busting him for the attempt, we're watching him, you know, so he better not do anything dumb for the next couple days . . . Maureen, you want to take a shot at Sandy, go ahead. I think she wants somebody to talk to and, who knows . . ."

The phone rang.

"Jerry, let's see about putting MCMU on Sweety around the clock now."

The phone rang. Raymond laid his hand on it.

"Put a couple guys in the bar—if they can hang around without getting smashed."

The phone rang.

Raymond picked it up. He said, "Squad Seven, Lieutenant Cruz."

Clement's voice said, "Hey, partner. I got a complaint I want to make. Some crazy fuckers're trying to kill me."

He parked behind Piper's Alley on St. Antoine, a few blocks south of 1300, came through the kitchen with the paper bag and Charlie Meyer, the owner, said, "Raymond," almost sadly, "you don't bring your lunch here. This is a restaurant."

Raymond smiled, gave him a wave and continued out into the main room, looking past plastic fern and Tiffany lamps at the booths of after-work drinkers, a swarm of them at the bar, guys and girls unwinding or winding up for the evening, either way unaware of the policeman with the paper bag who was wondering what it would be like to drop the bag on Clement's table—sitting there, next to one of the front windows in his denim jacket— say to Clement, Here, I got something for you, and as Clement's hand goes inside the bag say, loud enough to stop the room, DROP IT! and pull the Colt out of his sport coat and blow him away.

Clement said, "There he is." Grinning. "You look like a man with pussy on his mind. See something here you like?"

Raymond sat down and placed the paper bag on the table, to one side. Clement had a drink in front of him—in his denims, someone off a freighter or a trail drive—sizing up the house.

"All these boogers come in here looking for quiff, you know it? Their badges and convention tags on, they end up looking at each other, I swear. What's in the bag, your lunch?"

"Yes, it's my lunch," Raymond said. "You owe me seventy-eight dollars for a new window."

Clement grinned. "Somebody shooting at you? Listen, partner, I got people shooting at me too. I see these fellas coming across the street, I'm thinking, what're they, undertakers? Wearing these black suits. What I don't understand is how come I never heard of Albanians."

"Well, they never heard of you either," Raymond said. "But now, it's a question of who gets you first. You want to turn yourself in, I think you'd live longer at Jackson than out on the street."

Clement was squinting at him. "You let those fellas loose like that, shoot at people?"

"You want to file a complaint, stop in the precinct. See, we don't get attempted or assault. Like what you did to Skender."

"Man, you keep on top."

"He'd have to file a charge, but they'd rather handle it themselves."

"And you let 'em?"

"If the man doesn't report you broke his leg, then we don't know about it, do we?"

"Jesus—" Clement shook his head. "You want a drink?"

"No, there's something I have to do yet."

He watched Clement drain his glass and look around for the waitress—not quite the leisurely, laid-back Clement this evening—half-turning and putting his arm on the table, his hand, Raymond judged, about eight inches away from the paper bag. Clement raised his other hand, motioned with it and looked at Raymond again.

"Reason I called you, I want you to understand something. I'm leaving town. I'm not leaving on account of the Albanians and I'm not leaving on account of you either. But I got no reason to sit around here with my thumb up my ass, so I'm moving on."

"When," Raymond asked, "tonight?"

"I *was*—send you a postcard from Cincinnati—till I got jacked around this afternoon and by the time I got to the bank it was closed. All three banks I went to. I just want you to know, partner, I'm not *running*, as you know the meaning of the word. But I'm not gonna wait while you dick around and I'm not gonna exchange unpleasantries with some people I don't even know who they are 'cept they wear blacks suits . . . Can you tell me why they dress like that?"

"One of them died," Raymond said.

"Well, some more of 'em are gonna if I hang around, so tell 'em it's just as well I'm leaving. I just don't want them thinking they run me off, cause they haven't. But shit, I get mixed up with those people—I got no incentive. You understand?" He looked up as the waitress took his glass. "Same way, hon." As she turned to Raymond Clement said, "No, he don't want nothing. That's Jack Armstrong, the all-American Boy." Clement smiled at her and looked at Raymond again. "She don't know shit who I'm talking about, does she?"

"Sandy going with you?"

"I don't know, I suppose. She's cute, isn't she? 'Cept when she gets stoned. I tell her quit smoking that queer shit and drink liquor like a normal person."

"Some people," Raymond said, "you can't tell 'em anything."

"That's the truth."

"But long as they don't tell on *you* . . ." Raymond shrugged and let the words hang.

Clement stared at him.

Raymond was aware of the noise level in Piper's Alley. It surprised him that when he purposely listened to the sound of the place it was so loud. Everybody working at having fun. He said, "Well, I got to get going."

Clement stared at him. "You want me to think you know something I don't."

"You're nervous this evening," Raymond said. "But long as you trust your friends, what're you worried about?"

Clement stared at him. His head turned a little and he stared at the paper sack. He said, "That ain't your lunch, is it?"

"No, it isn't my lunch. Isn't a bag of fry cakes, either," Raymond said. "You want it?"

"Oh, my," Clement said, beginning to grin just a little. "We getting tricky, are we? Want to hand me somebody else's murder gun?" His eyes raised, his expression changing abruptly as Raymond got up from the table. "Where you going? I ain't done yet."

Raymond said, "Yes, you are," and walked out with the sack. He used the telephone in the kitchen, noise all around him, to call Hunter, told him not to move, he'd be right there.

A few minutes later Raymond walked into the squadroom. "Maureen leave yet?"

"Right after you did. I put MCMU on Sweety's place, told 'em to get somebody in the bar and the rest out of sight."

"Good." Raymond opened his address book to "S" and began dialing a number. "Clement made an announcement. He's leaving town tomorrow."

Hunter said, "We better have the party tonight then."

Raymond nodded. "I think we should try." He said into the phone then, "Sandy? This is Lieutenant Cruz. How you doing? ... Yeah, I know, some are better than others. You having a nice talk with Maureen? ... Yeah, well, let me speak to her a minute." He put his hand over the phone as he looked at Hunter. "She says it isn't her day." Taking his hand away, Raymond said, "Maureen? ... Listen, tell her Clement'll probably call or be over in a little while. In fact, any time now, so you better get out of there. Explain to her—she can say we questioned her about the gun, even leaned on her a little, tried to scare her, if she wants. But tell her to keep it simple. She took the gun over to Sweety's, period. That's all she knows. Was she crying? ... Uh-huh, well, tell her if she feels like she's going to to save it for Clement, just in case ... Hey, Maureen? Tell her you wish you were twenty-three again."

"You're all heart," Hunter said.

"I can sympathize with Sandy a little," Raymond said. "I can. But I'm not too worried about her. I mean, if she can hang around with Clement three, four years and she's still in one piece ..."

"She knows how to cover her ass," Hunter said.

"If anything's bothering me at the moment, that I feel a certain responsibility ..." Raymond paused, thoughtful, and looked over at Hunter. "You got Sweety's number?"

Hunter dialed it and stayed on the phone. Raymond picked up his phone and sat back, crossing his loafers on the corner of the gray metal desk. He said, "Mr. Sweety, how you doing? This is Lieutenant Cruz ... What I was wondering, has Clement called you yet?"

"Has *Clement* called me!"

Both Raymond and Hunter moved the receivers away from their ears, looking at each other with expressions of pain.

"Where are you?" Raymond asked. "You at home or at work?"

"I'm home. What you mean has Clement called me?"

"Anita working?"

"Yeah, she's over there."

"Why don't you go help her," Raymond said.

"Why?"

"I think you're gonna be busy tonight."

There was a silence before Mr. Sweety said, "Why is Clement gonna call me?"

178

"When he does," Raymond said, "tell him you're glad he called, you've been wanting to get in touch with him. In fact, you want to see him."

"I want to *see* him? For what?"

"To give him back his gun."

"You *took* the gun! . . . I *gave* it to you!"

Hunter had his eyes and mouth open wide, miming Mr. Sweety's emotional state.

"No, you told us it's in the basement," Raymond said, solemn, straight-faced. "We assume it's still here."

There was a silence again. Mr. Sweety said, "I don't want no parts of that man. I'm getting dumped on—whole big load of shit coming down on me."

"No, you're all right. You have my word," Raymond said. "He comes for the gun, tell him where it is. In fact, how about this? Tell him he'll have to go get it himself, you're busy."

Silence. "I'd have to let him in the house."

"Not if you put the key under the mat," Raymond said and had to smile now, looking at Hunter. A couple of kids getting away with something.

There were tales of heroics and tales of tricky nonprocedural moves, old-pro stunts, told in the Athens Bar on Monroe in Greektown, two short blocks from 1300 Beaubien. Raymond wondered if, not so much the heroes, the tricky movers ever looked ahead and saw replays, recountings: a twenty-year pro, an insider, telling appreciative someday pros that it wasn't to go beyond this table: "So he cons the guy into handing over the gun, has ballistics fire it to make sure it's the murder weapon, then— here's the part—he puts it *back* in the guy's basement, inside the furnace where it was, and has the guy tell the shooter to come get his gun, he doesn't want any part of it. You follow? He's got to make the shooter with the gun or he doesn't make him. He's got to set him up . . ." And the someday pros at the table wait with expectant grins, gleams in their eyes. Yeah? . . .

Then what? Raymond was thinking, riding in the blue Plymouth police car with Hunter.

Go on . . .

Well, the way it should happen: With Mr. Sweety's place under surveillance Mansell walks in, comes out with the gun in his pocket and they shine lights on him and that's it. If he stays inside they ask him to come out and eventually he does, after trying to hide the gun again or pound it apart with a hammer; but they would still have him with the gun, be able to make a case.

But maybe another way it could happen and be told about later in the Athens Bar: For some reason the surveillance is called off ... There could be a reason.

Clement comes out with the gun, the gun loaded, the way it was found. He comes out on the porch and stops dead as he hears, "That's far enough—" He sees Cruz on the sidewalk beneath the streetlight. Cruz with his sport coat open, hands at his sides ...

You're weird, Raymond said to himself.

But he continued to picture the scene as they drove off East Jefferson, hearing, "That's far enough—" and trying to think of what Clement might say then. Yeah, Clement would say something and then he would say something else, something short and to the point and then ...

Hunter said, "We both going in?"

Raymond, holding the paper bag on his lap, said, "No, I'm gonna do it." He was silent for about a block and then said, "He's got another gun. If he was shooting at the Albanians he got another gun somewhere."

# 26

Maureen let Sandy pace the living room in her Bert Parks T-shirt and satin shorts, Sandy shredding a Kleenex tissue, dropping tiny pieces of it but leaving no pattern of a trail. Maybe she had to wear herself out before she'd sit down.

"You jog?" Maureen asked her.

Sandy paused to look at the lady homicide sergeant on the couch in her little schoolteacher navy blazer and gray skirt—like a nun in street clothes except for the gun, Sandy suspected, in the worn brown handbag.

"You kidding? *Jog* . . . no, I don't go sailing either, or play golf. Jesus Christ, do I jog . . ."

"You have a nice trim figure," Maureen said, "I thought maybe you exercised."

"I've been running to the bathroom every ten minutes since your buddy Lieutenant Cruz was here. I don't *need* any more ex-

ercise, I'll tell you." She paced over to the dining-L and back to
the desk in the living room before stopping again to look at
Maureen. "How would you tell him?"

"Just the way Lieutenant Cruz suggested," Maureen said."You
gave the gun to Mr. Sweety because you were afraid to throw it
away yourself."

"It's true."

"So you have nothing to worry about."

"He's gonna ask me if the cops were here, I know he is."

"Well, I'm here," Maureen said. "I asked you if you saw a gun
in Clement Mansell's possession, here or anywhere else, and you
told me no. That's all you have to say. Don't complicate it."

"You don't know him."

"I'll bet I've known a few like him though." Maureen watched
Sandy move to the windows and look out toward the river.
"There's one guy we sent to Jackson keeps writing to me. He says
we're pen pals. I think when he gets out in about seven years he
wants to get together."

"Clement's only been to prison once," Sandy said. "He's been
to *jail* plenty of times, but he's only spent like a year in a regular
prison. He says he won't ever go back again and I believe him.
God, he makes up his mind to something . . . but he's so unpre-
*dic*table. One time we're out at Pine Knob, the Allman Brothers
were there. Everybody, you know, they're drinking beer and acting crazy, rolling joints on their coolers. This boy turns around
and offers Clement a toke? Clement slaps it out of his hand like he
was the boy's dad or something, gives him this real mean look. All
while the Allman Brothers're playing Clement's waving his arms
around to make the smoke go away. Sometimes, I swear, he's like
a little old man."

"You must like him a lot," Maureen said.

Sandy turned from the window. "Shit, I'm scared not to." She
stared off, mouth partly open, then gradually began to grin,
though not giving it much. "He's cute, though, you know it?
God, in bed . . . I think that's where he got his nickname, the
Wildman? I swear, he gets it up, like he says, you got to hit
it with a stick to make it go down." Sandy's grin broadened as
her gaze moved to Maureen and she said, "What're you smiling at?"

"I've had some experience there, too," Maureen said. "I was assigned to Sex Crimes for nine years. I think I saw everything there is to see. I mean, you know, funny things."

"God," Sandy said, "that must've been interesting. Like rapists and degenerates and all? Perverts?"

"Uh-huh, lot of perverts. People you'd least expect."

"Isn't that the way? Like schoolteachers . . . preachers?"

"Uh-huh. A lot of flashers."

"Yeah? Guys with raincoats and nothing underneath?"

"The pros cut the whole front out of their pants," Maureen said."One of the weirdest ones—we got a rape report. Right over in the City-County Building, one of the secretaries was dragged into the stairway and raped, had her clothes torn off. We asked her to describe the guy, if he had any unusual marks or characteristics. The girl said yes, come to think of it, he had an infantile penis."

"God," Sandy said, "a rapist." She sounded a little sad. "Did you get him?"

"We rounded up suspects, repeated offenders," Maureen said, "but first we had to qualify them, if you understand what I mean."

Sandy's face brightened. "Yeah, to see who had an infantile one." She frowned. "How little is infantile?"

"Wait," Maureen said. "A suspect would be brought in, then one of the guys in the squad would tell him to drop his pants."

"Didn't you see any of 'em?"

"Well, a few. But during the investigation I think something like a hundred and fifty-seven penises were inspected."

"Wow," Sandy said, with something like awe. "A hundred and fifty-seven. God . . ." She paused then with a puzzled expression. "Wait a minute. This girl said the guy's joint was infantile, but compared to *what?* I mean her old man could've had a shlong that hung down to his knees. You know it?"

"We thought of that," Maureen said. "Compared to what? We never did get the guy."

"That's really something," Sandy said. "At least you get to meet a lot of interesting people."

"Well, I'm never bored," Maureen said.

When Sandy was alone again she let the silence and dismal evening sky work on her. It was the best time of the day to be depressed. She was able to cry for a few minutes, shredding another Kleenex, made moaning sounds as she went into the bedroom, stood in front of the full-length mirror and studied her image hiding there puffy-eyed behind Bert Parks' big grin.

She said out loud, "You poor thing." She curled her lower lip down and got her chin to quiver and studied the expression. Then parted her lips slightly and opened her eyes wide in a look of surprised innocence. "Well, *I* didn't know. God, I thought you'd be *glad*"—pouty again—" 'stead of being an old meany." Sandy stared at her slumped shoulders, her pitiful expression. She stared for a long silent moment and then said, "Fuck it." She took off the T-shirt and jeans and tried it again, looking at a bra-less image now, hooked her thumbs into the narrow band of her white panties and cocked a hip . . . turned sideways and stared past her shoulder, letting her eyelids become heavy . . . turned full front again and stared with her bare feet apart, hands moving to her narrow hips.

She said, "Hey, are you Sandy Stanton?" and cocked her head slightly. "Yeah, I thought you were. You've got a dynamite body, you know it? I mean anybody can see you've got it together. *Look* at you. You are a fucking groovy chick, you know it? Yeah, I know it. Then what's the problem? What problem? I don't have a problem, you have a problem? . . ."

When Clement came in he said, "Where you think you're at, a nudist camp?" Without a bit of fun in his voice. "Jesus, turn that boresome music off—"

"We a little irritable this evening?"

With a foot-dragging funky step and two whole joints working in her, Sandy got over to the hi-fi just ahead of Clement and saved the Bee Gees from being scratched to death. She said, "What on *earth* is the *matter* with you?"

He walked over to the windows and stood looking out at the downtown lights.

Sandy tried again. "This your thinking time?"

He didn't answer.

"I've been worried about you—sitting here all day. There's such a thing as telephones, you know." Yeah, get a little pissed at him.

Early this morning Sandy had let the EMS attendants into

Skender's apartment building, told them "Down the basement" and got out of there fast. They drove over to Woodward Avenue, pulled up alongside Blessed Sacrament Cathedral and Clement told her to get out, take a cab home. She's said, "What am I suppose to do, stand out on the street like a hooker?" He gave her a shove. She asked him where he was going to stay and he said, "Don't worry about it." In one of his moods.

Evidently still in it. Good. She could think about standing on that Woodward Avenue street corner with all the colored guys slowing up to look her over and get really pissed at him.

She said, "Don't worry about *me*, just think about yourself."

Still looking out the window Clement said, "I *was* thinking about you. Come on over here. You ever been up the top of the RenCen?"

"Course I have. I used to work there."

He put his arm around her bare waist, pulling her in close. "Seven hundred feet up in the air. You sit there with your cocktail and it turns. It turns reeeeeal slow. You look at Canada a while. You look downriver at the Ambassador Bridge. You look over De-troit then as you turn real real slow, giving yourself time to wonder and think about things."

"I didn't throw the gun in the river," Sandy said. "I gave it to Mr. Sweety."

"I know you did."

"You want to know why?"

"I know why."

"How do you know?"

"I talked to him."

"Are you mad?"

"No . . ." He didn't sound too sure about it. "See, when I was up there thinking about you . . ."

"Yeah?"

"I called you up and the line was busy."

Sandy held on, not making a sound.

"I thought, who could she be talking to? Not the Albanian."

"Uh-unh . . ." Sandy said, thinking, Please, God—

"And then it come to me. You were talking to Sweety."

"God, are you smart," She felt herself shaking a little and slipped her arm around Clement. "I know you don't like me to smoke weed, but it's sure good when I'm nervous."

"Tell me what you're nervous about."

"Well, I thought you'd be mad that I didn't, you know, throw the gun away. But I really thought Mr. Sweety would know how better."

"I understand that," Clement said. "But see, then another person knows my business."

"Yeah, but he doesn't really *know* anything. I mean, it's just a gun."

"Well, how come he's nervous and wants me to come get it then? I told him, chuck it in the river you don't want it. He goes, 'I ain't fooling with no hot guns. It's yours, you take care of it.' See, why would he think that gun's hot?"

"Well, maybe the police talked to him." Right away, Sandy knew she had made a mistake, said too much.

"That's a thought," Clement said, giving her a squeeze. "Like they talked to you, huh?"

Even with miles of nighttime lights outside reaching way way off, Sandy felt walls around her, no more room than inside a box, a coffin. It was a terrible feeling. She said, "I was so worried about you today, I didn't know where you were or if anything happened to you or *any*thing."

"They come see you today?"

"Well, this lady cop stopped by. Asked if I knew anything about a gun. But she was real nice about it."

"Tricking you," Clement said.

"Yeah, but I didn't tell her nothing. I *didn't.*"

Clement patted her. He said, "I know you didn't, hon. It's just their chicken-fat ways . . . You been smoking a little?"

"Few tokes is all, now and then." She was surprised, he was making it sound so simple.

"When'd you get it?"

"The other day."

"When you give Sweety the gun?"

"Uh-huh. I just got a little bit."

"Oh my," Clement said with a sigh. "Life can sure play a tune on you you let it."

"I didn't *do* anything wrong."

"I know you didn't, hon. But see what's happened? They got to Sweety and I 'magine made a deal with him. He sets me up or they shut him down, put him on the trailer. I come get the gun, walk out of there and twenty squad cars converge on my ass out of nowhere. 'Throw up your hands, motherfucker!' They'd have to empty their weapons," Clement said, "cause I sure ain't doing hard time. Never have and never will."

"Let's go to Tampa, Florida," Sandy said, "right now."

"I'd like to, hon, but we got some problems. Those goddamn Albanian undertakers shot your Montego all to hell—no, that's something I'll tell you about after," Clement said, Sandy frowning up at him. "First thing, we got to get shuck of the gun."

"Why? Why not just walk away from it?" Sandy was still frowning. This was not turning out simple at all.

"Cause I don't leave behind anything might catch up with me later," Clement said. "If I don't get rid of the gun then I got to be rid of anybody could take the stand against me. I don't think you'd care for that."

"Yeah, but you *know* I wouldn't testify."

"Hon, I know it but I *don't* know it. People change their mind. The only thing perfectly clear in *my* mind, I ain't gonna do time. So the gun goes or you and Marcus Sweeton go. Which'd you rather?"

"I thought everything was gonna be good now." Sandy's voice was faint, sounding as far away as her gaze, the little girl wishing she was out there somewhere, even out beyond the lights of Canada.

"We'll make her," Clement said. "I'm gonna call Sweety back, tell him the arrangements."

"But you said if you picked the gun up—"

"Trust the good hands people," Clement said. "You feel that good hand on you there? Here comes another good hand—close your eyes. Here comes another good hand . . . closer . . . closer . . . Where is it going to land? . . ."

Doing was more fun than thinking. But sometimes thinking made the doing more worthwhile. Like if he had known he was going to do the judge he would have thought something up to make it pay more and the doing would have been more satisfying. When he tried to explain this to Sandy, she said she would just as soon not know what he was thinking, if it was all the same. She turned on the television set and he turned it off.

"What am I saying?"

"I don't *know* what you're saying, or want to."

"I'm saying like in this deal here," Clement said, "there are ways to skin by. Shit, lay in the weeds and let it pass over. Like that Grand Trunk railroad train passed over me. But there also ways of doing it with some style, so you let the other party know what you think of their chicken-fat scheme. You follow me?"

"No," Sandy said.

"Then keep your eyes open," Clement said, "and see if your old dad ain't a thinker as well as a doer."

# 27

Raymond thought of Madeline de Beaubien, the girl who over-
heard the plot and warned the garrison Pontiac and his braves
were coming to the parley with sawed-off muskets under their
blankets and saved Detroit from the Ottawas.

The house could have belonged to one of her early descen-
dants, an exhibit at Greenfield Village that people walked
through looking into 19th-century rooms with velvet ropes across
the doorways, a cold house despite amber reflections in the hall
chandelier and a rose cast to the mirrored walls. The house was
too serious.

That was it, Raymond decided. The house didn't see anything
funny going on or hear people laugh. Marcie told him solemnly, a
funeral-home greeter, Ms. Wilder was waiting for him in her sitting room.

An audience with the queen. No more, Raymond thought,

mounting the stairway, not surprised to find her in semidarkness, track lighting turned low, directed toward squares of abstract colors, Carolyn lying on the couch away from the lights. She told him he was late and he asked, "For what?"

He let himself relax and said, "Let's start over."

"You were going to leave in a few minutes," Carolyn said. "That's what you told me."

"I know, and then we got into something. What's the matter with your voice?"

He did not see her face clearly until he turned on the lamp at the end of the couch away from her and saw the bruise marks and swelling, her mouth puffed and slightly open. Carolyn's eyes held his with a quiet expression, her eyes blinking once, staring at him, blinking again, waiting for him to speak.

"I told you," Raymond said.

Her expression began to turn cold.

"Didn't I tell you? No, you can handle him, no problem."

"I knew you'd have to say it," Carolyn said, "but I didn't think you'd overdo it."

"You didn't? Listen, I'm not through yet," Raymond said. "If I can think of some more ways to say it I'm going to, every way I know how."

She said, "You're serious . . ."

"You bet I am. I told you, don't fool with Clement, but you did anyway."

"I misjudged him a little."

"A *little* . . ."

She began to smile and said, "Do you feel better now?"

He said, "Do you?" Then surprised both of them.

He went to one knee to get close to her and very gently touched her face, her mouth, with the tips of his fingers. He said, "You don't want to be a tough broad." She said, "No . . ." and slipped her arms around him and brought him against her. The faint sound that came from her might have been pain, but he didn't think so.

He said, "I want to tell you something. Then we'll see if we're still friends, or whatever we are. I didn't plan this. As a matter of fact, I came here I was a little on the muscle. I was gonna listen, try to be civil and get out."

"What happened?" Carolyn said.

He liked the subdued sound of her voice.

"I don't know. I think you've changed. Or I've changed. Maybe I have. But what I want to tell you, I think you're too serious."

She didn't expect that, or didn't understand what he meant. "He beat *hell* out of me . . ."

"I know he did," touching her face again, soothing her with his voice and his fingers. "I'm not gonna say it anymore, you know who he is . . . Tell me why he's going to the bank tomorrow."

"He made me give him a check. All the money I had in the account."

"How much is that?"

"Over six thousand."

"What did you say one time, he's fascinating? I'm sorry, I've got to quit that . . . Did you stop payment?"

"No, I'm going to file on three counts and get him for assault, extortion and probably larceny from a person. He took more than a hundred in cash."

"Hold off on it," Raymond said. "Let me bring him up on the homicides, then you can file all the charges you want."

"You'll never convict him," Carolyn said, "unless you have more than I know about."

"Did he have a gun?"

"Not when he was here; at least he didn't show it. But when I heard shots and looked out the bathroom window—I thought it was the police and I remember thinking, Wait, as I went to the window, I want to see him killed."

"Really?"

"It was in my mind."

"Did he have a gun then?"

"Yes, shooting back at them. It was an automatic, a fairly good size. But who are they?"

He told her about Skender, Toma. She knew something about Albanian blood feuds and now wasn't surprised. "On the phone you thought I wanted to file against them on behalf of Clement, while I'm thinking of all the ways I want to see him convicted."

"Let me do it," Raymond said. "I'm close. In fact, it could happen tonight, as soon as I hear something." Looking at her, thinking of Clement, he said, "Did he . . . molest you?"

Carolyn began to smile again, her eyes appreciating him. "Did he *molest* me?"

"Come on—did he?"

Her mood became quiet. "Not really."

"What does that mean, not really?"

"He touched me . . ."

"Make you take your clothes off?"

"He opened my robe—" Carolyn stopped, she seemed mildly surprised. "You know what I'm doing? I'm being coy. I've never been coy in my life."

"No, you've been too busy impressing yourself," Raymond said. "Tell me what he did."

"What're you trying to do, analyze me? He felt me up, but we didn't go all the way." Now Raymond smiled and she said, "You think you have insights, is that it?"

"Maybe, if that's the word. I don't expect to see something and then look and say, uh-huh, there it is. I try to look without expecting and see what's actually there. Is that insight?"

"You're sly," Carolyn said. "I think I have you down and you slip away."

He said, "You have me down . . . where? It's like filling out an Interrogation Record of an Information for Arraignment, you know what I mean? Sometimes the form isn't big enough, or it doesn't ask the right questions."

"You think I presume too much," Carolyn said, "see only what I expect to see. Is that it?"

"I don't know, we can talk about it sometime." He was tired and wasn't sure if he should close his eyes.

"If I make presumptions," Carolyn said, "what about you?"

"What about me?"

"We were making love and you said, 'I know you . . .'"

"I didn't think you heard me."

"What did you mean?"

"Well, it was like I saw *you*. Not what you do or who you believe you are, just you. Does that make sense?"

"I don't know . . ."

"But you didn't say anything, did you? I think you changed back after that and I didn't know you anymore. You became the woman lawyer again who thinks she has to be a tough broad. But look what happens to tough broads." Raymond was silent a moment. "Let me take care of him, Carolyn."

*   *   *

When Hunter called Raymond was sitting on the couch with Carolyn's legs across his lap, both tired of words, on safer ground now but still intimately aware of one another. Carolyn asked if he had always lived here, trying to picture him in another life, when he wasn't a policeman. And Raymond said, "In Detroit? No, I was born in McAllen, Texas. We lived in San Antonio, Dallas. We came here when I was ten." She asked, almost hesitantly, if his father was a farmer and Raymond looked at her and smiled. "You mean, was he a migrant? No, he was a barber. He was a dude, the way he dressed, wore pointed patent-leather shoes." The phone rang then, Raymond waiting for it. He lifted Carolyn's legs and got up. "My dad was fifty-seven when he died."

Hunter said, "Mansell called back, just now. He wants Sweety to bring him the gun."

"Where?"

"It got complicated. Sweety told him he was going to a family thing at his mother's—trying to hurry Clement up, get it over with. Clement tells him to take the gun along with him. Sweety says he isn't gonna touch it. If Clement wants the gun tonight he has to come in the next half hour."

Raymond said, "What difference does it make? The key's under the mat."

"Yeah, he told Clement that," Hunter said. "But what he did was confuse the issue with this going to see his mother and Clement says, okay, he'd just as soon get it tomorrow anyway, sometime in the afternoon." Hunter waited. "You still there?"

"You're gonna have to get Sweety out of there for a while," Raymond said, "keep the story straight. Clement could check, he could still come tonight."

"I don't think he will. It's something he has to do, but it's the kind of thing you put off," Hunter said. "Wendell get hold of you?"

"Not yet."

"He talked to Toma. Toma says he'll kill the guy if he sees him. In other words, fuck you. But he slipped and gave us one. Skender's Cadillac's missing and Toma thinks Mansell's got it."

"Where're you?"

"In the bar."

"He could go in there tonight. I don't mean with the key. He could come in the alley, through the yard, go in a back window."

"Is that right?" Hunter said, very patiently for Hunter. "It turns out the flat next to Sweety's is vacant, so MCMU's spending the night there. Is that close enough? What's the matter, you got a guilty conscience—I'm out here working my ass off, you're with a broad?"

When Raymond returned to the couch he stood looking down at her, uncertain, removed from where he had been only a few minutes before. He said, "My mother's name was Mary Frances Connolly."

He saw Carolyn's face against a blue pillow, composed, looking up at him. She said, "Really?" a little surprised.

"You want to know what she did?"

"She was a school teacher," Carolyn said.

"No, she was called Franny and operated a beauty shop in the Statler Hotel, when it was still there."

Carolyn said, "Do you know what my mother did? Nothing. Why don't you sit down?"

He lifted her legs and got under them, sitting low in the couch, his head against the cushion.

"You want to go to bed, I'll get out of your way."

"No, stay here. You've watched me, but I haven't watched you," Carolyn said. "You like your work, don't you?"

"Yeah, I do," Raymond said.

"You don't get tired of the same thing every day?"

"Well, nobody likes surveillance; but outside of that it's usually, well, each one's different."

"There's surveillance and there's lying in wait," Carolyn said quietly. "I think you're setting Clement up."

He was touching her bare toes, feeling them relaxed, pliable. "You're not ticklish, huh?"

"A little."

"That's the way you are in court, very cool. All the pros make it look easy."

"I said, I have a feeling you're setting Clement up."

"And I have a feeling he knows it," Raymond said, "so it's up to him, isn't it?"

"But you seem fairly certain he's going to come."

"He's gonna do *some*thing, I know that."

"How do you know?"

"We looked each other in the eye," Raymond said.

He smiled and Carolyn said, "My God, you haven't grown up either."

Raymond worked his head against the cushion, getting comfortable. "I was kidding."

She saw him against lamplight, his eyes closed, simply himself now. She said, "No, you weren't."

# 28

At eight o'clock the next morning Raymond phoned Inspector Herzog to report on the surveillance. Herzog, he was told, had left a day early on his vacation. Raymond felt relief. Then tensed up again as he had the call transferred to Commander Lionel Hearn, who was a good police officer, quiet, reasonable, but did not smile easily and this bothered Raymond. Commander Hearn was black. Raymond told him about the surveillance of Sweety's Lounge and residence and the purpose, without offering details. Commander Hearn said fine, and then asked Raymond where he had stationed himself.

Raymond said, "As a matter of fact I'm at Mansell's lawyer's place. It's only about three or four minutes away." Silence. "I want Ms. Wilder to be there if an arrest is made. I don't want us thrown out of court on any surprise technicalities. We're gonna do it absolutely straight." Silence—while Raymond imagined

Commander Hearn putting bits and pieces together in his mind and getting a picture of Raymond in his shirtsleeves, tie off but freshly shaved, a breakfast tray on the desk next to his holstered Colt automatic. The commander said he had never heard of this type of precaution before; was it necessary? Raymond said, "Well, actually Ms. Wilder's not representing Mansell and won't be if we bring him to trial. He hasn't retained her and she's willing to go along; so I think she could serve as a very valuable witness." Silence again.

The commander said, "Well, if you think you know what you're doing, good luck."

Raymond turned to Carolyn and said, "I'm not this casual, not at all."

"You convinced me," she said.

Hunter had gone home at seven and returned just before noon. He kept in contact with Raymond using a phone that MCMU had taken out of Sweety's residence and connected to a jack in the recently vacated flat next door. Along with Hunter there were six MCMU officers in the flat, three armed with shotguns, watching front and rear. There were no automobiles on the street that could be identified as police cars. Hunter called every hour.

At noon he said, "Everything's cool. Sweety's in the bar, the key's under the mat."

At 12:50 Hunter said, "Where'd you sleep, on the couch? . . . Yeah, how come you're changing the subject?"

At 1:55 Hunter said, "I'm gonna have Herzog put you in for a citation. 'Without regard for his own personal safety' . . . You getting much?"

At 2:25 Hunter said, "Black Cadillac went past, turned around up the street, coming back. Here we go. Parking right in front."

"I'm on my way," Raymond said.

"Shit," Hunter said.

"What's wrong?"

"It's not Mansell. It's his dizzy girlfriend."

She was supposed to walk through it, no problem, nothing to get excited about. Fine. Except it took forever to get the front door open while she danced around, dying to go to the bathroom. She couldn't find the basement light switch. She tried to open the hot water heater before she realized it wasn't the furnace. She found the gun, the Walther, and dropped it in the brown leather shoulder bag she'd brought along. Upstairs again when she went to use the phone, it wasn't there. Hey, come on. She found a phone in the kitchen, dialed and said, "The way it's going, I almost forgot why I fucking came in here. It just isn't my day ... Yeah, I got it ... No, I haven't seen a soul." She listened to his voice that was almost a whisper and said, "Hang around for what? You want me to bring it or not?" She looked outside, studying the cars on the street as she was supposed to, and came out looking up and down, dragging the shoulder bag along by the straps, got in the Cadillac and drove off.

Raymond crossed over from Carolyn's gray Mercedes as Hunter and the MCMU officers came out of the flat next to Sweety's.

Hunter said, "You see her? She's so stoned I bet she don't even know she was here."

When Toma looked out and saw the car, he thought of a time when he was sixteen and had sighted down the barrel of a Mauser on a Russian soldier who had got out of his truck to relieve himself—the same distance from the apartment window to the car across the street—and had killed the man with one shot. He had waited three days for a Russian truck. He had been in Skender's apartment perhaps three minutes, getting some books to take to the hospital, and had not looked out the window with the hope or intention of seeing something of interest. But there it was, Skender's black Cadillac.

Sometimes you had to work hard and sometimes it was handed to you. Toma put the books on the windowsill and took out his .32-caliber Beretta. Then saw that he wasn't being handed everything. The person in the car was a young girl with funny-looking golden hair. Smoking a cigarette. Taking her time.

Toma watched for several minutes. Finally the girl got out of the car and slammed the door. Then opened it again and bent over to reach inside, held this pose for nearly a minute, then came out again with a brown leather bag that appeared worn and soft. The girl held it at her side by the shoulder strap as she crossed the street, the bottom of the bag brushing the pavement, and entered the building's courtyard. Toma stepped back from the window. She passed along the walk to the front entrance. Now she stood there. She didn't go into the vestibule, she stood outside, waiting, not more than thirty feet from Toma, who was looking at her back now. She seemed relaxed but didn't move. Toma turned, looking toward the street again.

A gray Mercedes passed slowly. A black Ford passed . . . another one.

He's here, Toma thought.

But how could he be?

Then knew—as he turned to look at the girl again and saw the glass door open and Mansell step outside—*in the basement.* In the room made for hiding.

Or in the apartment upstairs Skender was preparing, furnishing.

Jesus, the man had nerve. Toma went to his knees to raise the window, slowly. The screen was still in place; he'd fire through it. Men with nerve died like anyone else if shot in the right place. But the girl was in the way. He could see only a small part of Mansell. The girl was holding up the big leather purse. Mansell, yes, had a gun in his hand. Toma aimed carefully. But Mansell would move, lean to look past the girl toward the street. Now he was reaching into the purse—Toma thinking, What is this? Is it a show? For a moment he thought he saw a different gun in Mansell's hand.

Why doesn't he hurry?

Now he was going inside, the glass door closing, the girl turning away but taking her time.

It was in Toma's mind to run, *now*, meet him in the hall . . .

But something strange was going on. The girl was walking out of the courtyard with the same uncertain but uncaring stride . . . then stepping out of the way, onto the grass, and Toma saw familiar faces, Raymond Cruz, Hunter, homicide people, and some not familiar, a woman with them—coming quickly along the entrance walk, past his front-row seat.

Yes, like a show, Toma thought.

Raymond Cruz was looking at the girl. He seemed to hesitate. The girl nodded, once. Not nodding hello, but saying something with the nod. Cruz kept going with the others. All of them eager. Of course—because they know Mansell's inside.

It *is* a show, Toma thought.

They were in the vestibule now. He could hear someone buzzing the door open for them.

The girl with the strange blond hair was still in the courtyard, forgotten—looking inside her big purse now, feeling in there like she was looking for her keys as she walked out to the street—past a uniformed policeman getting out of a squad car—and across the street to Skender's Cadillac.

If she had given Mansell a gun and was leaving him here, of all places— *No*, not of all places, the *only* place!

Toma ran from Skender's apartment down the hall to the back stairs, hearing others on the stairs above him. He turned off the light and started down, as quietly as he could, still not certain what the show was about, even though he had thought of a way to end it.

# 29

Standing in the first-floor hallway, the MCMU people hurrying past them, Carolyn said, "Does this happen often?"

They had searched every apartment, every room, every closet in the building and were still going up and down halls past each other. Around in circles, Raymond thought. There was no way Mansell could have gotten out, nowhere between the roof and the basement he could be hiding.

He said to her, "We'll find him."

"But he's not here."

"Yes, he is," Raymond said, with nothing to lose.

Hunter came up to them. He said, "Well?"

Raymond pictured again what he had seen from the car, going past slowly in Carolyn's Mercedes: Sandy at the door, Clement coming out. Going past again . . . going in then as Sandy came out, seeing her nod, accepting it because he was anxious, evidently too anxious . . .

He said, "Where's Sandy?" Hunter looked at him. He looked at Hunter.

Carolyn said, "I don't believe this." She watched Hunter walk off toward the front of the building. "What do you do now?"

"Wait," Raymond said.

"For what?"

Hunter turned and started back. "Hey, you see Toma yet? He's here."

As Carolyn watched, Raymond began to smile.

Toma left the apartment door open; he sat reading one of the books he would bring Skender, a book about the cultivation and care of house plants. When Raymond Cruz and a woman and Hunter appeared in the doorway Toma said, "Well, how are you?"

Raymond said, "Toma Sinistaj, Carolyn Wilder. Ms. Wilder does criminal work, she's one of the best defense attorneys in town. I mention it in case you want to retain her right now and get that out of the way."

Toma said, "You don't want to talk to me alone?"

"I want you to tell me where he is. Right here's fine."

"I'm giving you something, Raymond; but you don't want all your people watching. I could have killed him. You understand that? I came very close. Then I said no."

"Why?"

"You'll see. Or you won't; it's up to you. But I think you better get rid of your people."

A door closed down the hall.

It was quiet in the building now. Toma took them to the basement where he turned on fluorescent lights and let them stand looking around for a moment, preparing his audience.

"He had a gun," Toma said. "This one," opening his suit coat and drawing an automatic from his waistband. "You see it? It's a Browning. It belongs to this family and has killed no one."

"Where is he?" Raymond said.

Toma nodded. "Watch the wall there." He walked over to the furnace, where Raymond was standing, Raymond stepping out of his way, reached up, stretching to his tiptoes, and pulled the switch down.

With the humming sound the wall began to come apart, the three-foot section of cement blocks opening toward them, gradually revealing the room, the record player, the safe . . . Clement Mansell seated in a canvas chair with his legs crossed.

He said, "Hey, shit, what is going *on?* I come down here to put back something Sandy give me she says her friend Skender loaned her for protection and this undertaker sticks a pistol in my back, locks me in here."

"He had the wall already open," Toma said, "waiting in there for you to find him."

"With the Browning?" Raymond said.

Toma nodded. "He wants you to believe he got it from the blond girl with the hair."

"You searched him good?"

"Of course."

"What about in the room?"

"I made sure." Toma hefted the Browning. "This is the only gun he had. There were some in there, but I took them out yesterday."

Clement said, "Are you looking for a gun, it's got P.38 stamped on the side and some other numbers and kinda looks like a German Luger? . . . I haven't seen it."

Pull him out, Raymond thought. No, go in there with him. Tell Toma to close the wall.

"We got Sandy," Hunter was saying to Clement. "Saw her hand you the gun and you hand it back, thinking you're foxing somebody."

"Hey, bullshit," Clement said. "You had Sandy you wouldn't be standing there with that egg smeared all over your face."

Raymond wanted to pull him up out of the chair—where he sat low with one knee sticking out at an angle, his boot resting on the other knee, elbows on the chair arms, hands clasped in front of him—and hit Clement as hard as he could.

The man's eyes danced from Hunter to Raymond, then to Carolyn. He said, "How you doing, lady?" Frowning then. "Jesus, what'd you do to your face, run into something?" His gaze moved back to Raymond. "What the undertaker says, that's my story. I come down here to return a weapon Sandy was given or swiped off her boyfriend. If you think you saw something different or you don't like what you see now, tough titty, I'm sticking to it. There ain't any way in the world you're gonna lay the judge on me, partner, or anybody else. And I'll tell you something, you never will." His gaze moved to Carolyn and he winked. "Have I got 'em by the gonads, counselor, or haven't I? I want to thank you very much for that loan." He patted his jacket pocket. "I got the check right here. Gonna cash her as I leave here for Tampa, Florida, never to return. Which I bet chokes you all up some." With his half-grin he looked at Raymond again. "What do you say, partner, you give up?"

Raymond said nothing. He reached up with his right hand, felt the switch mounted on the wall and flicked it on.

As the wall began to close Clement said, "Hey—" He didn't move right away, he said, "My lawyer's standing right there, shithead." They saw him rise out of the chair now, saying, "Hey, come on, goddamn-it—" They could see his fingers in the opening before he pulled them in. They could see a line of light inside and hear him scream, "Goddamn-it, open this goddamn—" And that was all.

Raymond reached up again. The humming motor sound stopped. There was a silence. Carolyn turned, started for the stairs, and Raymond looked over.

"Carolyn?"

She didn't pause or look back. "I'll be in the car."

He watched her go up the stairs—no objections from her, no emotion—and again there was silence. Hunter approached the cinder-block wall almost cautiously and ran his hand over it. He looked at Raymond and said, straight-faced, "Where'd he go?"

Toma said to Raymond, "You see why I didn't kill him. This way satisfies both of us. For me. it's like Skender doing it to him, which is much better. For you, it seems the only way you're going to get this man who kills people."

Hunter said, "You sure he can't open it?"

"He broke the switch himself when he was here before," Toma said.

Raymond listened as they spoke in low tones, almost reverently, Toma saying, "He prepared his own tomb. There's water, a little food for his last meals, a toilet. He could last—I don't know—fifty, sixty days maybe. But eventually he dies."

Hunter saying now, "We had the place covered, but somehow he slipped out. I don't see any problem, do you? Man disappeared." Toma saying, "It's also soundproof." Then Hunter wondering if after a while there might be an odor and Toma saying, "One of the tenants complains we open the wall and say, 'Oh, so that's where he was hiding. Oh, that's too bad.' "

It's done, Raymond thought. Walk away.

# 30

They had several drinks at the Athens Bar, quiet drinks, Raymond and Hunter alone at a table, with little to talk about until Hunter leaned in to tell what worried him. Like Carolyn Wilder. Would she blow it or not? Raymond said he didn't think so. She had walked out (her car was gone when they left the apartment building) and it was like saying to them, do what you want. Without saying it. He believed she could handle it. Carolyn had learned to be realistic about Clement: she could send him away for assault and robbery, but knew he would come back if she did.

Hunter said, "You want to know exactly what it's like? It's like the first time I ever went to a whorehouse. I was sixteen years old, these guys took me to a place corner of Seward and Second. After, you're all clutched up, you don't know whether to feel proud of yourself or guilty. You know what I mean? And after a

while you don't think of it either way; it's something you did."
Hunter went home to bed.

Raymond walked back to 1300 Beaubien. The snack counter in
the lobby was closed and he looked at his watch: 5:40. The squadroom was locked, empty. He went in and sat at his desk beneath
the window. It was dismal outside, a gray cast to the sky; somber,
semidark inside, but he didn't bother to turn on lights.

He had felt relief as the wall closed and Mansell disappeared;
but the relief was an absence of pressure, not something in itself.
He tried to analyze what he was feeling now. He didn't feel good,
he didn't feel bad. He called Carolyn. She said, "Are you worried
I'm going to tell on you?" He said, "No." She said, "Then why
talk about it. I'm awfully tired. Why don't you call me tomorrow,
maybe go out to dinner, get a little high? How does that sound?"

A little after six Raymond looked up at the sound of the door
opening. He saw the figure in the doorway backlighted from the
hall.

Sandy said, "Anybody home? . . . What're you doing sitting in
the dark?" She came in, letting the door swing closed. "God, am I
whacked out." She dropped her shoulder bag on Hunter's desk,
sank into his swivel chair and put her boots up on the corner of
the desk.

Raymond could see her in faint light from the window. He
didn't move because he felt no reason to. He had not been thinking of Sandy Stanton. He had obvious questions but did not feel
like asking them. He did not feel like getting himself into the role,
being the policeman right now.

"I pulled in the garage downstairs, a guy goes, hey, you can't
park here. I told him it's okay, it's a stolen car, I'm returning it.
The guy at the desk downstairs—what is that place?"

"First Precinct," Raymond said.

"He goes, hey, where you going? I tell him I'm going up to
five. He goes, you can't go up there. I'm thinking, try and get out
of here, shit, you can't even get *in* . . . I thought you'd be looking
for me. I sat in the apartment not knowing what's going on, finally the phone rang. It was Del. He isn't coming home, he's
going to Acapulco. You ready for this? And he wants me to fly
out to L.A. and go with him . . . and bring his pink and green
flowered sport coat that asshole gave to the doorman. How am I
gonna get it back?"

Raymond said, "Is that what you came to ask me?"

"No, I wanted to know if it's okay to go or if you're gonna arrest me or what. I'm so fucking whacked I want to go *some*where, I'm telling you, and sleep for about a week." She made fists, holding them out, and said, "My nerves are like *that.*"

"You left Skender's car?"

"Yeah, I told the guy it really wasn't stolen, it was *sort* of stolen and that you know all about it."

"What about the gun?"

Sandy dug into her bag. She brought out the Walther and laid it on Hunter's desk.

She said, "Do we have to get into it again? I haven't seen shit-bird at all, he hasn't called, thank God, I don't know where he is, if he's in jail or what, and I don't want to know. I'm twenty-three and I got to get my ass in gear and I think going to Acapulco could be very good for me. What do you think?"

"I think you ought to go," Raymond said.

"Really?"

Raymond didn't say any more. Sandy got up with her bag. "I'll just leave the gun here." Raymond nodded. She said, "Listen, I'm not mad at you, I think you've been a pretty neat guy, considering. I know you have a job to do and, you know—so maybe I'll see you again sometime . . ."

Raymond raised his hand to her. As the door swung in, closing off the light from the hall, he brought his hand down and got up. He went over to Hunter's desk and picked up the Walther, hefting it, feeling its weight. He shifted the gun to his left hand and brought out his Colt 9-mm from the shoulder holster, feeling both of the guns now, judging the Colt to be a good half-pound heavier. Two-gun Cruz. In a dark room all by himself. Two-gun Cruz, shit. Sneaky Cruz . . . Dead-ass Cruz . . . Or how do you like Chicken-fat Cruz, chicken fat?

After a couple of hours Clement put Donna Summer's "Love To Love You, Baby" on the record player to hear the sound of a human voice. He inventoried the canned goods, found all kinds of mashed chick peas and pressed meat and not one goddamn thing he liked to eat. There was nothing to drink except water and two cans of Tab and he expected they'd be turning the water off when they thought of it—if the plan was to leave him here. He had thought the wall would open again within a minute or so after it closed. All right, five minutes. Well, give 'em ten. Okay, play the game with 'em, maybe a half hour, which was supposed to give him a good scare. No—what they'd do, he realized after an hour or so, sure, they'd open it up and ask him if he wanted to confess, telling him if he didn't they'd close it up again and take out the motor. The dumb fucks. He'd look scared and say, yes, Jesus, just get me out of here, I'll confess to anything you want. Then come up for the exam and tell 'em to get fucked, the confession was signed under duress and he was not only walking, he was filing suit against the police department. A hundred thousand dollars for fucking up his nervous system. Look how he was shaking . . .

He had been glancing at his gold watch since the wall closed on him at a little after three and he had never seen time go so slow. He'd sit down, he'd get up and pace around a little to the music, then began picturing disco dancers and moved to the beat some more, seeing if he could do it—shit, it was easy—he could *feel* it and wished there was a mirror so he could see himself doing it—shit, dancing all by himself to the nigger girl singing in a secret basement room. Nobody in the world would believe it.

He looked at his gold watch at 6:50, 7:15, 7:35, 8:02, 8:20, 9:05 after some dancing, 9:32 turning off the record player for a rest and at 9:42. It was right after that he heard the sound, the wall moving.

Clement got in the canvas chair facing the opening as it widened, seeing the clean basement a little at a time, the light reflecting off the cement floor it was so clean.

If it was the Albanian, he was dead.

It could be Carolyn, her heart bleeding for him. But she'd be too scared—unless it was somebody she sent. No, it would have to be the cops, come back to make their threatening offer. Clement told himself to get ready to look scared.

He waited. The humming sound of the motor continued. No one appeared. Clement got up out of the chair and approached the opening, inched his head out, looking over at the furnace. Nobody there. Nobody jumped on him when he walked out. He went over to the switch, reached up and flicked it off.

*Who?*

See—it ran through Clement's mind—if it was a friend, the friend would be standing here. And if he wanted to run through his current list of friends, that could only be one person. So it wasn't Sandy. Unless she wanted to help him, but not be associated with him anymore—ran like hell. Or it was somebody like the Albanians who wanted to take him outside, which didn't make sense. Or it was somebody with a guilty conscience, which *could* make sense even though it was hard to imagine.

Clement went up the stairs to the first-floor hall and followed it to the front entrance. He might as well keep going. Anyone meaning to get him would have considered his slipping out the back, so there was no point in getting tricky. Go on out. And he did, walked out to the street, and what did he see sitting there but Skender's black Cadillac.

Now, was it a coincidence, the car was picked up and returned? Or had Sandy left it here this afternoon and took off on foot? Or was somebody tempting him again? Or—wait now—was the gun in there and they'd stop him, arrest him with it?

No. He could be stopped for stealing a car—number two hundred and sixty something—but if there was a gun in it somewhere it would belong to the owner, not him. No prints anyway. Clement opened the driver-side door and felt under the seat. No gun. Just the keys. Did he want to think about this a while or did he want to haul ass?

Clement took the Cadillac south to downtown, got off at the Lafayette exit, just past the giant red Stroh's Beer sign giving warmth to the night sky, and ten minutes later was in the elevator going up to 2504. He hoped Sandy was home and would be able to explain some of these weird things going on.

# 31

Clement still had a key to the apartment that Sandy had given him. He went in and saw lights glittering outside the windows but not one was on in the apartment. He listened a moment and called out, "Hon?"

It was about 10:30; she could be asleep, she had probably smoked enough reefers to send her off early. Clement turned on the light in the hallway as he walked into the bedroom. "Hon bun?"

Nope. The bed wasn't made. That was par—but there weren't any of her clothes lying around. Clement turned the bedroom light on and went over to the closet. It looked like only Del Weems' stuff hanging inside. He went to the dresser, was about to bend down to open one of the drawers she used, but never got there.

He saw the Walther P.38 lying on the dresser about ten inches from his eyes.

She *still* hadn't dumped the goddamn thing. He could hear himself saying, with pain in his voice, "Hon, I don't believe it. Twice now. Are you intentionally trying to fuck me or what?" He had a mind to throw the goddamn thing out the window, man, just to be *rid* of it. Like the goddamn thing had stickum on it. He picked up the gun.

It felt good though. Fired straight and true. He checked the clip, pushed the spring down, saw it was loaded but lacking about two rounds, and punched it back into the grip with the palm of his hand.

He walked into the living room trying to recall something. Fired five at the judge, three at the woman. He had reloaded when he got back to the garage, before he hid it. He seemed to recall he had fully reloaded it. Hadn't he? . . . He turned on the desk lamp. A note written on pale-green paper lay squarely in position before the chair. Clement sat down without touching it, spreading his elbows to get low, close to the note, and laid the Walther to one side.

*Dear Clement:*
*If you read this then you don't know yet I have left. I am not telling you where I'm going for I am leaving you for good as my nerves can't stand any more of your kind of life and I'm getting too old for it. One thing I guess I have to tell you I did not throw the gun away again and I'll tell you why. There was somebody every place I went. I would start to get out of the car and somebody would be there watching. I don't know why but it is not easy to throw away a gun. I have had enough so good-bye.*

*Yours,*
*Sandy*

*P.S. I think you better run!!!*
P.P.S. IT'S TOO LATE.

Clement frowned, staring at the note. Something here was weird. The second postscript was bigger and in a different handwriting. If she scribbled it quick, maybe—but it wasn't like that. It was in big printed letters. Clement felt goosebumps crawl up his arms, over his shoulders and neck, up under his hair. He stared at the notepaper in the soft glow of the lamp, the rest of the living room dark, almost dark, wanting to look up, wanting to look out past the green-shaded glow of light. He had not heard a sound, but he could feel it. Someone else was in the room, watching him.

There was a button switch attached to a light cord that ran along the floor by the front windows. It was behind Clement's chair, so that he had to turn half around and reach over with the toe of his boot. He punched the button and a chrome lamp beamed on, its light rising through the branches of a ficus tree.

Raymond Cruz sat only a few feet away from the tree, in a chair by the side windows.

"Jesus," Clement said, his hand gathering the note, squeezing it into a ball.

"I've read it," Raymond said. "In fact, I wrote part of it."

Clement was still half turned; the desk, with the Walther lying on it, to his left now. "Was it you let me out?" He saw Raymond nod. "Go have some dinner and think better of it, did you?"

"Yeah, I gave it some thought," Raymond said. "That wasn't the way to do it."

"I hope to tell you," Clement said. "I thought what you'd do, open it up and tell me to sign a statement else you'd shut me in there for good."

"I don't want a statement," Raymond said.

Clement cocked his head, looking at him warily. "Yeah? What's this party about then?"

Raymond got up. As he came over to the desk Clement turned in his chair to get both Raymond and the Walther lined up in front of him. "I got something here," Raymond said. His hand went into his coat. "Now don't get excited." The hand came out again holding the Colt 9-mm automatic. Clement sat rigid. Raymond moved the lamp aside and laid the Colt on the desk.

"Pick up yours and I'll pick up mine. How's that sound?"

Clement was squinting but starting to smile a little. "You serious?"

"Stand up."

"What for?"

"You'll feel better. Come on."

Clement wasn't sure. He sensed he should be laying back, not moving too much yet. It was true though, he'd have more choices on his feet. He rose, moving the chair back away from him. They stood now directly across the desk from one another.

"Put your hands on the edge of the desk," Raymond said, "like this . . . Okay, now whenever you're ready, pick up your gun. Or, whenever I'm ready."

Clement said, "You think I'm fucking crazy or something? I don't even know this piece's loaded."

"You checked it in the bedroom," Raymond said, "I heard you. You want to check it again, go ahead. You're short two rounds we fired in ballistics, that's all."

Clement stared, amazed. "You took the gun from Sweety, tested it and put it *back?*"

"With the same live rounds," Raymond said. "You don't trust me we'll trade. You use mine, I'll use yours, I don't care."

Clement's expression seemed bland, open, as though he might be listening or might be off somewhere in his mind.

Raymond said, "This was your idea. Remember?"

"I don't think you're serious," Clement said. "Right *here?* It's too close."

"We can go outside, or up on the roof," Raymond said. "You want to go outside?"

"Fuck no, I don't want to go outside. You got some scheme—I don't know what, but you're pulling something, aren't you? Trying to spook me into signing a statement. Man, you're going way around to do it."

"I don't want a statement," Raymond said. "I told you that. You sign a confession, we come up in court you say it was under duress, coercion, some chickenshit thing. This is fair, isn't it? You said, why don't we have a shooting match. Okay, we're doing it."

"Just grab for the guns, huh?"

"Wait a minute," Raymond said. "No, I think the way we ought to do it—pick up the gun and hold it at your side. Go ahead. I think that'll be better." Raymond brought the Colt toward him and held it pointing down, the barrel extending below the edge of the desk. "Yeah, that's better. See, then when you bring it up you have to clear the desk and there's less chance of getting shot in the balls."

"Come on," Clement said, "cut the shit."

"All right, then you reach for yours and I raise mine," Raymond said, "it's up to you." He waited.

Clement's right hand edged over to the Walther, touched it, hesitated, then covered the grip and brought it toward him, off the table. He said, "I don't believe this."

"Okay, you ready?" Raymond said. "Anytime you want, do it."

"Wait just a minute," Clement said.

They stared, face to face, three feet apart. There was no sound in the room.

"I SAID WAIT!"

There was a silence again before Raymond said, "What's the matter, Wildman?"

Clement put the Walther on the desk and walked away. He said, "You're fucking crazy, you know it?"

Raymond turned, his gaze following Clement as he went around the couch and through the dining-L. He heard Clement say from the kitchen, "You know we could *both* kill each other? You realize that?"

The kitchen was back of the wall that was a few feet behind the couch. Clement could come out again through the dining-L, to Raymond's right, or he could come out from the front hall, to Raymond's left.

Either way, it didn't seem to make much difference.

Raymond moved from the desk over to the front windows, glancing out at the spectacle of lights and reflecting glass, before turning to stand with his back to it. The apartment looked more comfortable at night with the lamps on; Raymond still didn't like the colors though, green and gray.

Clement was saying from the kitchen, "That was interesting, that talk we had in your office. I never done that before with a cop . . . like seeing where each other's coming from. You know it? . . ."

He'll have something in his hand, Raymond thought.

". . . Yeah, that was interesting. Getting down to the basics of life, you might say. I mean our kind of life. You want a drink? . . ."

Here we go, Raymond thought. He didn't answer.

". . . Don't say I didn't ask you. We got some Chivas . . . No, that's it for the Chivas, aaaall gone. How 'bout a beer? Got some cold Miller's . . . That mean no? How come you're not talking?"

It's his turn, Raymond thought, holding the Colt 9-mm at his side, looking at the dining-L, then moving his gaze slowly across the wall that was behind the couch to the entrance hall.

Clement was saying now, "See, what I got out of that talk we had—me and you are on different sides, but we're alike in a lot of ways . . ."

He's trying to put you to sleep, Raymond thought.

". . . You know it? I figured you were a real serious type, but I see you got a sense of humor."

Clement appeared, coming out of the front hall with a bottle of beer in each hand and walked over to the desk. "It might be a little weird, your sense of humor, but then each person's got their own style, way of doing things."

Raymond watched him place the bottle in his right hand on the desk, then, maybe twelve inches from the Walther. The hand remained there.

"I brought you a beer just in case," Clement said.

The hand came slowly, carefully, away from the desk to the front of his denim jacket.

"I got a opener here someplace, stuck it in my jeans. Okay, partner? I'm just going in here to get the opener." He glanced down.

The hand moved inside the denim jacket.

Raymond raised the Colt 9-mm, extended.

As Clement looked up, Raymond shot him three times. He fired, seeing Clement's eyes, and fired again in the roomful of sound, still seeing the man's eyes, and fired again as Clement was slammed against the couch and almost went over it with the momentum but collapsed into cushions and lay there, denim legs stretching to the beer bottle on the floor with foam oozing out of it, his hands holding his chest and stomach now as though he were holding his life in, not wanting it to escape, his eyes open in stunned surprise.

He said, "You shot me . . . Jesus Christ, you *shot* me . . ."

Raymond approached him. He reached down, gently moving Clement's hands aside, felt a handle and drew it from Clement's belt. Raymond looked at it in his hand as he straightened. A curved handle that was fashioned from bone or the horn of an animal, attached to a stainless steel bottle opener.

Raymond went to the desk. He placed the opener next to the Walther, picked up the phone and dialed a number he had known for fifteen years. As he waited he reholstered the Colt. When a voice came on Raymond identified himself, gave the address and hung up.

Clement was staring at him, eyes glazed, clouding over. "You call EMS?"

"I called the Wayne County Morgue."

Clement continued to stare, dazed, eyes unblinking.

Raymond could hear street sounds very faintly, far away.

Clement said, "I don't believe it . . . what did you kill me for?"

Raymond didn't answer. Maybe tomorrow he'd think of something he might have said. After a little while Raymond picked up the opener from the desk and began paring the nail of his right index finger with the sharply pointed hooked edge.

# THE MOONSHINE WAR

# 1

The war began the first Saturday in June 1931, when Mr. Baylor sent a boy up to Son Martin's place to tell him they were coming to raid his still.

The boy was sixteen and had lived in the mountains all his life, but at first he wasn't sure he wanted to go up there alone. He asked Mr. Baylor how he was supposed to get there, and Mr. Baylor said they'd lend him an official Sheriff's Department Ford car. He told Mr. Baylor he had only seen this man Son Martin about twice before, since the man hardly ever showed himself; maybe he'd go up there and tell the wrong person. Mr. Baylor, who was seventy-three years old and sheriff of the county, said to the boy, well, if you go up there and knock on his door and the man answers it is a white man, that's Son Martin. If it's a nigger opens it, that's Aaron, his hired man. Mr. Baylor said, now if you can tell a white man from a nigger you're all set, aren't you?

The boy said, yes, sir, he'd do it; but he asked Mr. Baylor, if they were going to raid the man's still, why was the man being told about it? And Mr. Baylor said, don't worry about that, just tell him.

The boy's name was Lowell Holbrook, Jr. Evenings he wore a white jacket over his big bony shoulders and worked at the Hotel Cumberland as a bellboy, taking the grips and sample cases from the Louisville salesmen and lugging them upstairs. The few times he had seen Son Martin had been in the hotel: the man standing at the desk with his hat on the counter, leaning against it and talking to Mrs. Lyons, the manager. Son Martin was a good friend of Mrs. Lyons; everybody knew that. Some boys said they were more than good friends, that they were going to bed together, but Lowell couldn't picture Mrs. Lyons doing that.

Afternoons Lowell fooled around somewhere, maybe over at the Feed & Seed store, or hung around the courthouse if he wanted to make any extra money. The county people were always sending papers to somebody to have signed and wanting something picked up. They knew Lowell was fast and reliable because he worked at the hotel, and he had run errands for Mr. Baylor a lot of times before. Once he had driven all the way over to Corbin to pick up an important document. He had also been up by Broke-Leg Creek plenty of times and knew the road to Son Martin's place. But he had never been near the house. Some boys had told him, Son catches you on his land he'll blow your head off before asking your name. Lowell didn't think about it backing out of the parking space by the courthouse or driving through town.

The Saturday afternoon traffic kept him busy: the mud-washed cars and old trucks and mule wagons creeping along, the people gawking at the store windows and waving to friends. Nobody had enough money to spend more than a dollar; but, like most Saturdays lately, it was Cow Day and a person could buy a raffle ticket from any of the local merchants and maybe win himself a cow.

Lowell was hoping some of his buddies would see him driving the Sheriff's Department Ford car. Once out of town though, following the blacktop east for seven miles before turning off on a secondary road that climbed up into the scrub hills, Lowell began thinking about arriving at Son Martin's place and getting out of the car. There wasn't anything to be nervous about; Mr. Baylor wouldn't have sent him if there was. But he kept licking his lips anyway and wiping the back of his hand across his mouth. He said in his mind, Mr. Martin, I'm supposed to tell you they're coming up here to raid your whiskey still this evening. Jesus, then what does he say?

All the way up through the hollow the road was narrow and muddy and deep-rutted from the spring rains. It was hard enough staying in the tracks. Then the two foxhounds came bounding and barking out of the thicket, running next to the car and in front of it, so close sometimes Lowell couldn't see them. All he'd have to do was run over one of Son Martin's hounds. Then which did he tell first, about the whiskey raid or the hound? If the hounds would shut up he could hear himself think and study on how to drive this road without going off in the brush.

But the hounds chased Lowell for a mile and a half up through the hollow and didn't break loose until he had reached the clearing and there was the house: a two-story, gray-weathered affair set against the right-hand slope and leveled with stilts so that the porch, on the side of the house as Lowell approached, was as high as a man's head. Beyond the house across the open yard, were the barn and outbuildings and Son Martin's pickup truck over by a shed. Lowell didn't see anything that looked like a whiskey still; there was smoke rising above the house, but that would be from the cookstove. Beyond the cleared land and pasture, the hills were dark with scrub oak and laurel and climbed in hollows and ridges up to the clear afternoon sky. Lowell could just make out the roof of another house way up in the trees. High above were jaggedy-looking sandstone outcrops and several open places that looked like dry creek beds, wide rivers of mud, where the terrible flash floods of '27 had washed away crops and timber. Some of the trees had been hauled out and milled for lumber; but there were still plenty of uprooted trunks lying dead at the edge of the pasture.

Reaching the crest of the road, the hounds streaking ahead of him across the yard, Lowell was going so slow the engine started to lug and he had to shift into second quick. He missed the gear as his foot slipped off the clutch pedal, and the car made an awful metal-grinding noise. Coasting into the yard, punching the shifter looking for second gear, and sounding like a kid just learning to drive, Lowell saw the man on the porch waiting for him, standing with his hands in his back pockets.

The man didn't come down off the porch; he waited for Lowell to get out of the car. Lowell slammed the door behind him. It didn't catch tight, damn-it, but he kept going anyway, around the front of the car to within about ten feet of the porch steps. That was close enough.

"I'm supposed to tell you they're coming to raid your still this evening."

Son Martin didn't take his hands from his back pockets or say anything for a minute. He was wearing a brown shirt that looked like an army shirt. In the daylight he looked younger than the times Lowell had seen him in the hotel; but he knew the man wasn't young at all and must be about thirty-five. It was his hair and his face that made him seem young: full head of hair cut short and clean-looking bony face darkened by the sun. He looked like a soldier, that was it; he still looked like one.

Son Martin turned a little as he said, "You hear?"

Lowell noticed the handle of the Smith & Wesson sticking out of Son's back pocket. Past him, Lowell could make out somebody standing inside the screen door. "I guess it our turn," the man inside answered. The hired man, Aaron.

Son Martin was looking at Lowell again. "Who sent you?"

"Mr. Baylor did." Lowell snapped the answer back.

"In his office, that's where you talked to him?"

"Yes, sir."

Behind the screen Aaron said, "Ask him was anybody else there."

"Wasn't anybody," the boy said. "Just me and Mr. Baylor."

"You work at the hotel," Son Martin said.

The fact that it was a statement and not a question gave Lowell a funny feeling. The man had seen him before and knew who he was. He said, "Yes, sir, I'm on evenings."

"I believe you're Lyall?"

"No, sir. Name Lowell Holbrook, Jr."

"Lila your sister?"

"Yes, sir, she is. She waits table in the dining room." He had never seen Son Martin in the dining room; he had only seen him those few times in the lobby talking to Mrs. Lyons; but the man surely knew things about the hotel.

"Holbrook." Son Martin was placing the name. "Your family used to farm over toward Caldwell."

"Yes, sir, till the floods washed us out." Lowell waited with Son Martin looking at him, then couldn't wait any more. "A year ago me and my sister come over here to live with kin and we was able to get these jobs."

Son Martin kept looking at him until finally he said, "You're here. You might as well stay to supper."

It took him by surprise and gave him the funny feeling again, though now it was funny another way. Here he was talking to Son and being invited to have supper with him. What was so scary or different about Son Martin? Lowell told him he'd had a fair-sized dinner and sure wished he could stay and eat, but he had to get to work.

Driving away he kept glancing at the rearview mirror, at Son Martin on the porch watching him. He didn't wave, just watched. There was no sign of the hounds, which was good. Going down the road through the thicket he remembered he should have asked Son how come Mr. Baylor was warning him about the raid. It didn't make sense, unless Son was paying off the sheriff. But that didn't make sense either. If it was the case Mr. Baylor would tell Son himself, he wouldn't have somebody else do it. People did crazy things where whiskey was concerned. It being against the law to drink wasn't going to stop anybody. They'd fight and shoot each other and go to prison and die for it, so there was no sense in wondering about Mr. Baylor and Son Martin.

It was a relief to see the opening in the scrub growth and the road below him. Lowell kept his foot on the brake, feeling the car sliding in the mud, the rear wheels banging from side to side in the ruts. He said, "Hold her, Bessie," and slapped the steering wheel around making his turn, and right then he had to cut hard to swerve to miss going head-on into a car parked in the road. Not a car, a line of cars, four, *five* of them parked there with the men standing strung out alongside and all of them now staring at him as he went by. Lowell kept going. He looked at the rearview mirror and saw the men and cars getting smaller as he pulled away from them; they were still watching him and some of them were out in the road now. He'd recognized a few of them, people from around here, but couldn't place their names.

He surely wished somebody would tell him what the hell was going on in this world.


Mr. Baylor never could adjust the goddamn field glasses right, so he let his deputy, E. J. Royce, work them. They were on a ridge above the Martin place where they could look down two hundred yards or so through the trees to the cleared land and the outbuildings and the weathered house and the wisp of smoke rising out of the chimney pipe.

"What're they doing now?" Mr. Baylor asked E. J. Royce. The old man squinted into the distance through steel-framed spectacles: a seventy-three-year-old turkey buzzard face beneath a farmer's straw hat; tight mouth barely moving and a hunk of plug stuck in his sunken cheek.

"The nigger just come out carrying something." E. J. Royce spoke with the field glasses pressed to his face. "A pan. There, he just throwed the dishwater out'n the yard. Now he's gone back inside."

"Son come out?"

"No, sir, he's still in the house."

"I want quiet over there," Mr. Baylor said. "If you people can't keep still, bite on your lip or go home."

Somebody must have said something funny, the men laughing and shaking their heads, then hushing up and looking solemn as Mr. Baylor spoke to them: the group waiting a few yards back, in the trees. Mr. Baylor usually deputized these same men, selected from his circle of friends. But on a raid, watching a place or moving in on it, he always called them "you people."

One of them, standing up, said to Mr. Baylor, "He can't hear nothing from where he's at."

Mr. Baylor's steel-rimmed glare turned on the man. "How do you know he can't?"

"Hit's too far," the man said.

"You want to swear on a goddamn Bible he can't hear you? You going to tell me what he can hear and what he can't, him living out here and knowing every sound?" Mr. Baylor was talking louder than the man had talked.

E. J. Royce listened, the field glasses to his eyes, waiting for Mr. Baylor to finish. One time, watching like this, he had said, "Mr. Baylor, the man knows we're coming. What difference is it if we make noise?" And Mr. Baylor's glasses glinted and flashed and his mouth went tight. "Because you don't make any noise on a raid," Mr. Baylor hissed. "That's why." He had been either a sheriff or some kind of county official for over thirty years, since before the year 1900, so he knew what he was talking about.

E. J. Royce said, "Son's come out of the house and gone in the privy."

Mr. Baylor jumped on him. "Well, goddamn-it, whyn't you tell me?"

"It's all right, he's still in there."

"I'll tell you what's all right." Mr. Baylor looked over at the deputy group to make sure they'd heard. The waiting was an important part of it. Mr. Baylor would take out his timepiece and look at it and then look up at the sky. The men would watch him as he did this and he would feel them watching.

"He's come out of the privy," E. J. Royce said.

Mr. Baylor squinted into the dusk. "Doing what?" He couldn't make out a thing down in the yard.

"Buttoning his pants," a man in the deputy group said, and there was a little sniggering sound from the rest of them.

Before Mr. Baylor could jump on the man, E. J. Royce said, "Now he's going toward his pickup truck," and felt Mr. Baylor close to him, the old man breathing, making a wheezing sound. "No, he's past it now, heading up the slope."

"Going to the grave," Mr. Baylor said.

"I reckon so. Yes, sir, that's what it looks like." E. J. Royce waited, holding the glasses on Son as he came up the gentle slope of the pasture. "He's near the grave now. Now he's stepped over the fence and is standing by the post."

Mr. Baylor was nodding. "Every evening. That's something, he does that."

"The light went on," E. J. Royce said. "You see it?"

"God Almighty, I'm not blind."

It was a small, cold light in the dusk, over a way, near the foot of a steep section of the slope, a hundred yards below them and over to the left: a single bulb under a tin shade that was fixed to the top of the nine-foot post. Mr. Baylor and his people could

make out the low fence now and the grave marker and the single
figure standing by the post.

"I didn't see him turn it on," E. J. Royce said.

"The switch is in the house," Mr. Baylor told him. "Aaron
must've turned it on."

One of the men in the group said, "Hardly anybody has 'lec-
tricity in their houses, Son uses it on a grave."

Mr. Baylor shot him a look. It was too dark for the look to do
any good, but he put enough edge in his tone to make up for it.
He said, "You work in a mine and die in a mine you appreciate a
light on your grave, mister. You think about it."

The man said, "It ain't doing the old man any good."

And Mr. Baylor said, "How do you know that? Are you down
there in the dirt looking up? How in hell would you know it ain't
doing any good?" Jesus, people knew a lot.

E. J. Royce let him finish. "The nigger's come out of the
house—going up toward the grave. Son's just standing there."

"Waiting for us," Mr. Baylor said. "It's time."

He led them down through the trees and laurel thickets, not
saying anything now about the noise they were making. As they
approached the pasture Mr. Baylor drew his .44 Colt revolver,
pointed it up in the air, and fired it off.

Aaron looked off in that direction, toward the dark mass of the
hill, and Son Martin said, "He's telling the rest of them down on
the road."

From across the pasture they heard a second revolver report in
the settling darkness.

"They anxious," the Negro said. "They don't want anybody
miss nothing."

Son kept his eyes on a little spot way off and soon was aware of
specks of movement taking shape, the men spread out as they
crossed the pasture, some of them heading for the yard. In the
barn the two foxhounds began barking and yelping to get free. In
a minute then, from the other side of the house, Son picked up the
faint sound of the cars coming up the hollow.

Close to him Aaron said, "Company tonight, everybody welcome."

Son walked along the edge of the grave mound that was covered with stones, to be moving, doing something. He put his

hands in his back pockets. It was getting chilly. Maybe he should have put on a coat. No, he'd be warm enough pretty soon. He said to Aaron, "You might as well get it out."

"How much you think?"

"Lay that part-full barrel on the porch, with some jars."

"Or give them some we cooked yesterday."

"No, out of the barrel tonight."

He could see them clearly now, most of them coming this way, a few straggling toward the yard. Headlight beams moved in the trees as the first car topped the rise out of the hollow. As the next cars followed, pulling into the yard, their headlights caught Aaron walking back to the house. Son waited for the group coming toward him. There weren't many bugs around the post light; it was still too cool. Another month he wouldn't be able to stand here for long they'd be so thick. Another month after that he wouldn't have to. He'd be gone.

Son looked down at the gravestone, at his shadow slanting across the inscription:

John W. Martin
1867-1927
*May he rest ever
in the Lord's
Eternal Light*

He looked up at the repeated sounds of a car horn. Headlight beams crisscrossed the yard with dust hanging in the light shafts; there were voices now and the laughter of grown men out for a good time, the men from the cars yelling toward the ones coming across the pasture. Out of the darkness somebody called, "Hey, Son, you up there?"

He hesitated. "Waiting for you boys!"

Now he set a grin on his face, relaxed it, and set it again, ready to greet them as they came into the light. Then he was shaking E. J. Royce's hand and E.J. was saying, "Son, where you been keeping yourself?"

"I been right here all the time."

"I know you have—I mean how come you haven't been down to see us?"

"You know how it is."

"Sure, up here drinking your own whiskey. Well, a man makes it as fine as you do, I can't say as I blame you."

Mr. Baylor gave E. J. Royce a sharp-pointed elbow pushing between him and the man next to him. He waited as Son nodded, then said, straight-faced and solemn as he could, "Son Martin, we have reason to believe you are presently engaged in the manufacture and commercial sale of intoxicating liquor in violation of the Eighteenth Amendment of the United States Constitution. Is that true?"

"Yes, sir." Son nodded respectfully, going along.

"Then as sheriff of this county I order you to produce it," Mr. Baylor said, "before all these boys here die of thirst."

By the way people came in, Lowell could tell if they'd been to the Hotel Cumberland before. If they walked right over to the main desk, knowing it was back of the stairway and partly hidden, they'd been here. If they came in and looked around the lobby and up at the high ceiling and the second floor balcony and weren't sure where to go, it was their first time.

But the man in the dark suit and hat, carrying the big leather suitcase, stumped Lowell: he didn't walk directly to the desk but he didn't gawk around either. He came in the entrance slowing his stride, holding the bag with a couple of hooked fingers, and seemed to locate the desk without looking for it. He walked over, set his suitcase down, and spread his hands on the counter.

Coming up next to him Lowell said, "Evening," reaching over then to palm the desk bell, hitting it twice. The man looked at him and nodded. He looked tired and needed a shave and was a little stoop-shouldered the way some tall men carry themselves.

Mrs. Lyons came out of the office that was behind the main desk. She said good evening in her quiet tone and opened the register. Mrs. Lyons always looked good, her dark hair was always parted in the middle and combed back in a roll without a wisp of loose hair sticking out. She was the neatest, cleanest-looking person Lowell had ever seen. (And he surely couldn't picture her in bed with Son Martin, or anybody.) He watched her now. Her eyes were something; they were dark brown. Sometimes they sparkled when she smiled and had the warmest look he had ever seen. Though sometimes—watching her closely when she was talking to another person—her face would smile, but her eyes would tell nothing: as if she were looking at the person from behind her smile, or maybe thinking about something else. Whenever he talked to her for any reason, Lowell would have to look over somewhere else, once in a while. She was a lot older than he was, at least thirty, and he didn't know why he'd get the nervous feeling.

The man didn't take his hat off. He bent over and wrote slowly *Frank Long, Post Office Box 481, Frankfort, Ky.* Mrs. Lyons dropped her eyes and brought them back up and asked Mr. Long if he was staying just the night. He shook his head saying he wasn't sure how long he'd be; maybe just a few days. Mrs. Lyons didn't ask him anything else—if he was a salesman or here on some business or visiting kin. The dark eyes went to Lowell as she handed him the key to 205.

Lowell bent over to pick up Mr. Long's suitcase, then put his free hand on the counter as he straightened—God, like there was bricks in the thing. Mr. Long was watching him. He didn't say anything; he followed Lowell up the stairway.

In the room, putting the bag down and going over to the window, Lowell said, "You got a nice front view." He leaned close to the pane, seeing his own reflection over the lights and lit-up signs across the street. Frank Long was looking at himself in the dresser mirror, feeling his beard stubble.

Lowell said, "Can I get you anything else?"

"Like what?" Mr. Long asked him.

"I don't know. Anything you might feel like." He waited as the man took off his coat and tie and started unbuttoning his shirt. "Did you want anything to drink?"

Mr. Long looked at him, pausing a second and holding the button. "Are you talking about soda pop or liquor?"

"Either," Lowell said. "Or both."

"You can get whiskey?"

"Maybe. There's a person I could call."

"Don't you know selling liquor's against the law?" He pulled off his shirt; a line of black hair ran up from his belt buckle and spread over his chest like a tree. His skin was bone white and hard muscled.

"I'm not saying I'd get it. I said maybe there was a person I could call."

"How late's the dining room open?"

ELMORE LEONARD

"Till eight. You want something you'll have to hurry."

Mr. Long pulled a fold of bills from his pocket. He handed one to Lowell. "Tell them to dish up. I'll be down in ten minutes."

"Thank *you,*" Lowell said. "Tonight they got breaded pork chops, chicken-fried steak, or baked ham."

"Ham," Mr. Long said. He let Lowell edge past him and reach the door. Lowell was opening it when he said, "Boy, do you know a Son Martin?"

Lowell kept his hand on the knob. He came around slowly, giving himself time to get a thoughtful frown on his face. The man was unbuckling the straps of his suitcase. Lowell watched him let the two half sections of the suitcase fall open on the bed.

As the man looked at him, Lowell said, "There's a Son Martin lives about ten miles from here. I don't know as it's the same one you mean though."

"How many Son Martin's d'you suppose there are?"

"I guess I never thought to count them."

Frank Long studied him. "This one I know, his daddy was a miner before he passed on. Name John W. Martin. This Son—if it's the one—him and me soldiered together in the United States Army."

"You were in the war with Son?"

"In the Engineers together—if it's the same one."

"Well, it sure sounds like it. John W. was his papa's name."

"You say he lives about ten miles from here?"

"You go out the county road till you see the sign *Broke-Leg Creek*, turn left, second road about a mile or so you turn left again. That takes you right up the hollow where he lives."

The man smiled and it looked strange on his solemn, beard-stubbled face. He said, "Boy, you've been a big help to me." He waited a second and then said, "Hey, you want to see something?"

"What?"

"Something I got here." His big hand unsnapped the canvas cover on one side of the suitcase.

"What is it?"

"Come take a look."

It was strange, Lowell wasn't sure he wanted to. He felt funny being alone in the room with this man.

"I got it strapped in or I'd take it out," Mr. Long said.

"Strapped in?" Lowell stepped toward the edge of the bed. He didn't know what to expect. Least of all he didn't expect to see a big heavy-looking army gun, polished wood and black metal and bullet clips, the gun broken down and each part tied and packed securely. Laying there on the bed with the overhead light shining on it. God. A real army gun they used in the war right there, he could touch it if he wanted to.

"God," Lowell said.

"You ever see anything like that?"

"Just pictures."

"You know what it is?"

"I think it's a BAR rifle."

"That's right," Mr. Long said. "Browning Automatic Rifle. U.S. Army issue." He let the canvas cover fall over the gun. "I expect not many around here have seen one."

"No, sir." Lowell looked up at him now. He hesitated, then said it quickly, before he could change his mind, "What do you use a gun like that for?"

"Hunting," Mr. Long said. "For hunting."

Lowell didn't tell Mrs. Lyons about the gun. When he went downstairs he thought about telling her, but he didn't. Maybe it would make her nervous. If he was going to tell anybody, Lowell decided, it would be Mr. Baylor. Mr. Baylor would know what to do. About a half hour later Lowell saw Frank Long come out of the dining room. He had his hat on and was lighting a cigar as he walked out of the front entrance. He didn't have the suitcase with him.

Lowell said to Mrs. Lyons, behind the desk, "There sure a lot of people interested in Son Martin lately."

She gave him a strange look. It was the closest he'd ever come to seeing something in her eyes.

# 2

There were twenty-three men at Son Martin's place that Saturday night. They were inside the house sitting around the table. They were on the porch where a coal oil lantern hung from a post and where Mr. Baylor's deputies had placed their firearms against the wall. Some were out by the cars. But most of them stayed close to the whiskey barrel that was at the edge of the porch, the spigot sticking out, so that from the ground a man would reach up to fill his fruit jar. They were quiet at first, taking their turns with the jars, sipping the whiskey, tasting it, and thinking about the taste as it burned down to their stomachs. The serious drinkers stood and squatted and spit tobacco on the hardpack at the dim edge of the porch light as though they were waiting for a meeting to start, or waiting out front of a mine company hiring shed: men in broad hats and engineer caps and worn-out suit coats over their Duck Head overalls.

It was a clear night and not too cold and god*damn* that Son Martin could run whiskey. He let his mash set a full six or seven days and didn't put a lot of devilment in it, like buckeye beans or carbide or lye, to hurry up the fermentation. Son took his time; he cooked the beer slowly over a low fire; he used pure copper in the works and limestone spring water to condense the vapor and he kept his still clean. The clear moonshine that came out of the flake stand was run again, doubled through the works, and filtered through charcoal before it was put up to age and mellow in charcoal-blackened white oak barrels. Son aged his run two to four months, which he said was bare minimum to give it color. If you weren't willing to wait, you'd have to go somewhere else and drink clear moonshine. It was worth a wait, E. J. Royce said, because good whiskey was kinder to a person and didn't beat your brains out the next morning. The men E. J. Royce was talking to agreed a hundred percent because they wanted to believe it. Though each man knew if he drank as much as he wanted, he'd feel the pain the next day like a wet leather strap shrinking into his head and his mouth would be stuck together with an awful sour glue taste and he'd drink a gallon of water and six cups of coffee and a couple of bottles of Nehi soda before noon. But tomorrow morning was tomorrow morning. Tonight they'd raided Son Martin's and they were here to drink and confiscate.

Mr. Baylor set aside five half-gallon jars as sheriff of this county and paid Son eight dollars—just about half the going rate—calling it the confiscation price. Mr. Baylor said he wasn't going to sit around all night with these punkin rollers, so he had his stuff put in a car early.

Bud Blackwell was here with his dad and his married brother Raymond. Bud said the whiskey was all right, but he'd tasted better. He said to his brother Raymond and to Virgil Worthman and a couple other boys, where they should be with the whiskey was in town, get themselves some girls, and have a real party instead of listening to the old men talking about closed-down mines and flooded bottom land and tight-assed Herbert Hoover and the goddamn banks. There were sweet girls down there in Marlett waiting, Bud Blackwell said. Jesus, sweet and ready. Or they could ride over to this place in Corbin, near the railroad tracks, where there were girls; he'd been over there with his dad one time—hell no, Raymond hadn't gone, not married a year yet. Bud opened his pocketknife and scratched a little circle in the hard-pack and began flicking the knife at it, sticking the blade every time.

Uncle Jim Bob Worthman, ten years older than Mr. Baylor, sat on the steps for a while drinking whiskey, then went up and took a shotgun from the porch and, swaying in the coal oil light, taking aim, let go both barrels at Son Martin's barn, saying he'd seen a Yankee up in the loft. Bud Blackwell said, Jesus, put that old man to bed before he starts telling about his war; there have been wars since that goddamn war of his. Virgil took Uncle Jim Bob over to their car and talked to him until he went to sleep in the back seat, telling the old man he'd cut the bluebelly dead center and that it was the best shooting ever seen. I hit my share at Lookout Mountain, the old man said. Virgil said, yes, sir, hoping Jim Bob hadn't shot one of Son's mules or one of his foxhounds.

Somebody asked Son if his radio played, they could listen to a program from Nashville. Son said, no, it hadn't worked in some time. The man said, you keep a light burning over a hole in the ground but your radio don't play. E. J. Royce told the man, quietly, to be careful talking about Son Martin's papa. Son takes it wrong, E. J. Royce said, he'll kick out all your teeth.

Then, changing the subject, E. J. Royce wondered that, if Son Martin made the best whiskey, who made the worst? He was just kidding. Moonshiners like the Blackwells and the Stampers and the Worthmans were always making fun of each other's whiskey. One of the moonshiners would say something now and they'd start funning each other. But it was a man on the porch who'd come with Mr. Baylor who said Christ, Arley Stamper; he puts mule piss in a jar and sells it as pure corn. Arley had been in the privy and was coming up the porch steps. He grinned at the man who said it and, as he reached the top step, hit the man full in the mouth with his right fist, took hold of him with his left hand, and hit him again and sent him off the porch. Arley Stamper looked down at the man on the ground and said to E. J. Royce, "E.J., who was that I hit?"

Bud Blackwell took a good drink of whiskey. Holding the fruit jar in front of him, he stared out at the darkness thoughtfully. Finally he nodded and said, "Speaking of mule piss, I wonder which one of Son's animals give us this run."

He didn't look up at Son, who was on the porch, but knew Son had heard him. He took another drink and licked his lips slowly, as if registering the aftertaste in his mind. "Either mule piss or John W. Martin whiskey," Bud Blackwell said. "I bet ten dollars."

Some of the others looked over, knowing what Bud was leading to. They looked up at Son as a stillness settled in the yard, then moved in closer as Son came down the steps toward Bud Blackwell. Bud handed Son the fruit jar and now they watched him raise it and take a long pull, wondering how much he'd already drunk. Nobody was sure what Son could hold; the only thing certain, no matter how much he put away, nobody had ever seen him talkative or loud or open with his thoughts. One time before it was Bud Blackwell who'd said, "The son of a bitch, he could get shitfaced and fall off his porch five times an evening and never say more'n ouch." But maybe this time was different and Son would open up. The word passed into the house Bud was fooling with Son and Mr. Baylor and the others at the table, including Bud's dad, came out to watch. Bud's dad was twisting his mustache and chuckling and shaking his head like it was all in fun, though inside he was nervous and hoping to hell Bud wouldn't get knocked on his ass.

Bud took the fruit jar from Son and held it up to the coal oil glow, facing the audience on the porch. "You claim you run this, is that right?"

Son was patient, knowing what was coming. He said, "I should know, shouldn't I?"

Bud cocked his head, studying the amber inches of whiskey in the jar. "Son, was you taking this to the vet?"

That got some sounds from the people. Mr. Blackwell laughed out loud and then shut his mouth. Son kept quiet.

"Yeah, I see specks of something in there," Bud said. "Like little bugs. Them bugs, Son?"

There was nothing for Son to get angry about, but there was no reason to stand grinning at Bud Blackwell either. He said, "What you're saying, it was either a sick mule run it or else my dad." Son spoke mildly, but it was clear he was laying it out between them and taking Bud head-on. He said, "You either want your skull busted or you want to rile me into claiming my dad made the best whiskey in east Kentucky. Once I do you say, if that's true, prove it. And I say Bud, how can I prove it if he's dead in his grave?"

Bud Blackwell grinned. "That's getting us there. Then I say—go on, you're doing fine—what do I say?"

"You say let's quit talking about the whiskey and drink it."

"Pig's ass I do."

"You say I must be getting drunk cause I'm sure running off at the mouth—I think my daddy better tuck me in bed."

That got some sounds with E. J. Royce saying, "Tell him, Son," and Mr. Blackwell giving E.J. a dirty look. They were watching Bud Blackwell to see what he'd do now, with his mouth tight and no sign of it curling into a grin. But Bud never got his turn.

Aaron appeared out of the darkness, moving through the group in the yard, not saying excuse me or anything until he was next to Son. There he was, barely giving them time to wonder where he came from or what he wanted. Aaron said, "Somebody coming in a car."

Frank Long was aware of the whole scene at once, like walking into a dark room and having the lights go on and everybody yelling surprise. He came up out of the hollow and there were the cars and the house and the man gathered in the dim glow of the porch lamp. The difference was nobody yelled surprise. They stood waiting for him, not making a sound. Long sat in his car a few moments, aware now of the spot of light up on the hill over a mound, over something; he didn't know what it was or much care right now. The men were waiting and if it was a party it surely wasn't in his honor. He couldn't back out now and turn around, so he got out and walked between the cars and when he was in the open, spotting the whiskey barrel now, he said, "I'm looking for John W. Son Martin, Jr. Am I at the right place or have I interrupted a church meeting?"

As a couple of them moved aside there was Son.

Long stopped before he reached the light. He let an easy grin form as he said, "Hey, Son, don't you recognize an old buddy?"

Son couldn't see his face in the dark, but he said, "Frank Long," and saw the man from another time, Frank Long in uniform and leggings and the brim of his campaign hat curling up in front.

Son wanted to act natural and glad to see him; he wanted to raise his voice to match Long's and get that friendly sound in it and hand him a jar and slap him on the shoulder a couple of times and say, "Frank, you old son of a bitch, it's been four years, hasn't it? Summer of 1927, Camp Taylor"—and act like nothing better could have happened than Frank Long appearing out of the dark. Except that the moment he heard Long's voice and felt his stomach knot up, he knew why the man was here.

Son said, "Frank, step over where we can see you."

Frank Long came into the light holding his grin. "You recognized my voice, didn't you? Well, I guess you should, we was in the same tent, how long?"

"Fifteen months."

"That's right, nearly a year and a half. Son, I'd known your voice too. Jesus, I heard it singing and telling stories enough, didn't I?"

"Well, not too much."

"You tell these boys stories, Son?"

Goddamn him, what was he doing? Son forced a little grin and said, "Listen, what I want to know—I thought you were still in."

"Mustered out last fall. I had a bellyful of it."

"I was wondering what—"

But Mr. Baylor, at the top of the steps, called out just loud enough to get their attention, "Son, we never known you was a singer."

Son glanced up. "He means with the other boys in the outfit."

"Oh, I thought maybe you'd sing us a song." Mr. Baylor kept watching him. He could see it or sense it—he wasn't sure which—that Son was holding back and didn't feel comfortable in this man's presence. Son knew something about the man. Or else the man knew something about Son. Mr. Baylor was curious and he was old enough that he could be blunt and not care what anybody thought.

He said, "Mr. Long, my name is Mr. Baylor and I'm sheriff of this county. Whereabouts are you from?"

Frank Long touched the funneled brim of his dark hat. "Well, sir, I'm from all over the state, you might say."

"I might not," Mr. Baylor said, "I'm asking you where you're from?"

"Most recently? I guess that would be Frankfort."

"They say it's a pretty town, though I've never been there," Mr. Baylor said. "Tell me, what do you do in Frankfort?"

"I work for the government."

"Is that the state government?"

"No, sir, the United States federal government."

"I see," Mr. Baylor said. "Well now, I add up all that information and you know what it tells me?"

"No, sir, what?"

"It tells me you're a Prohibition agent."

Frank Long stared up at him. "That's pretty good, Mr. Baylor, you got a keen eye, haven't you?"

"And nose," Mr. Baylor said. "Let's see your credentials."

Long reached into his back pocket for his billfold. Flipping it open he said, "They give me this—card with my picture on it. Not a good likeness though. And they give me Sweetheart." His right hand came from inside his coat gripping a .45 caliber service automatic. He glanced at Son and the men watching him. "You never see one like this? I know Son has in the Army. This beauty will stop a man in his tracks and set him back five paces."

"Boy," Mr. Baylor said to him then, "are you threatening anybody?"

"You asked me for my credentials."

"I see them," Mr. Baylor said. "You see mine up there leaning against the wall. Shotguns and high-powered rifles."

"Yes, sir."

"Any law needs upholding in this county, I take care of it."

"I see that too," Long said, his gaze sliding over to the whiskey barrel. "All these people here your deputies?"

Mr. Baylor was as courteous and nice as anyone had ever seen him. He said, "Yes, they are, and I'll tell you something. They ain't ever seen a Prohibition agent before."

"Is that right?"

"Yes," Mr. Baylor went on, "a revenue man is a rare bird in this county. I mean it's so rare some old boy sees one, you know what he's liable to do?"

"What's that?"

"He's liable to shoot it and have it stuffed and put over his fire-place."

Frank Long shook his head, grinning. "Man, I don't think that would feel so good, getting stuffed."

Bud Blackwell felt it was time he got into this. He said, "You know what we stuff them with?"

But Mr. Baylor wasn't having any Bud Blackwell smart-ass talk right now. He didn't need any Bud Blackwells sticking their nose in his business. He said, "Bud, get Mr. Long a drink of whiskey."

Frank Long looked appreciative. "Well, if you force me to take one."

Mr. Baylor waited until Long was handed a jar and watched him drink some of it. "Kind of good, isn't it?"

"This is all right," Long said, nodding, studying the jar.

"It'd be a shame to pour it on the ground," Mr. Baylor said. "Wouldn't it? Just cause some dried up titless old women don't believe people should drink whiskey."

"Isn't that the truth?" Long finished the whiskey and wiped the back of his hand across his mouth. "Mr. Baylor, as you say, a man is paid to uphold the law. But that don't mean he can't appreciate the finer things in life."

Mr. Baylor said, "Have another drink, Mr. Long."

"I don't mind." He handed the jar to Bud Blackwell for a refill and waited for Bud to take it. "No, sir, you had me wrong. I was passing through, I thought I'd stop and visit is all."

Mr. Baylor adjusted his steel frame spectacles. "I was going to say before, maybe you ought to get your visiting done and start back to Frankfort before it gets too late."

"Well, it's up to Son." Long looked over at him. "I got me a room at the hotel for a day or two."

"It's a good one," Mr. Baylor said. "Hotel Cumberland."

"It seems nice and clean."

"Good food in the dining room. Say, have you had your supper?"

Long hesitated. "Well, I had me a little something."

"Son," Mr. Baylor said, "your friend here's hungry. That's a long car ride from Frankfort.

"Don't be nervous these boys here staring at you. As I said they never seen a federal man close up."

Long grinned, shaking his head. "Listen, underneath this suit there's just a plain old mountain boy. I did most of my growing up down in Harlan County."

"Is that right?"

"Yes, sir, till I went in the U. S. Army."

"Son," Mr. Baylor said, "you going to have Aaron fix him something?"

Son was staring at Frank Long and had been looking at him since the moment he heard the man's voice in the darkness and felt the tight little warning stab deep in his belly. He had listened to Long and Mr. Baylor, every word, as the two of them warmed up and relaxed and if Son wanted to he could pretend everything was just swell and talk and smile and wait for Frank Long—some other time, not this evening—to start hinting and leading up to it, the way Bud Blackwell had started fooling with the idea just a little earlier. Or he could push it in Frank Long's face right now, call him and get it out in the open.

Or, he could think about it some more, not being hasty and maybe regretting it.

Yes, he could think about it and waste time and lose his nerve and in a few minutes he'd be grinning and nodding at everything the son of a bitch said and his face would begin to ache from the grinning. So do it, Son decided. Jesus, do it, will you?

Still looking at the man, he said, "Frank didn't come here to eat supper."

Long's eyes opened, momentarily startled, then his expression settled and he watched Son calmly.

"He didn't come here to visit or talk about old times," Son went on. "He came here to find my dad's whiskey."

Some of the men looked at each other, hardly believing it. Mr. Baylor said, "That old story. Never mind that, Son. Let's get your friend here fed."

"He's not hungry for anything to eat." Son kept his gaze on Long. "He's got on his mind a hundred and fifty barrels of whiskey that's going to come of age this summer—a hundred and fifty barrels of eight-year-old John W. Martin corn whiskey. Isn't that right, Frank?"

Long said nothing; there was no silence for him to fill because Mr. Baylor was already pressing in. He said, "Hell, folks have heard that story and forgot it a hundred times. Who's going to prove John Martin ever put away any whiskey? Son, if he run that much and it's unaccounted for then your daddy drank it is all. Why I remember him drinking two-three gallon a week, drunk it 'stead of water These boys all know that."

Some of them nodded and E. J. Royce said, "Why he'd a sure drunk it afore he ever hid it."

"No," Mr. Baylor said, "that's a story nobody can prove as fact."

Son was patient. He waited and said to Mr. Baylor, "I appreciate it. But Frank already knows about the whiskey."

"I suppose he's heard the story, sure," Mr. Baylor said, "same as everybody else. But that don't make it true."

Son waited again; there was no hurry. He said, "The difference is he heard it from me. One time in Louisville we'd gone in from Camp Taylor, I told him the whole story." Son paused, looking from Frank Long to Mr. Baylor. "You want to know something else? Soon as I told Frank, a second after, I knew I should have bit off my tongue and I started telling myself it was all right because he was probably too drunk to remember any of it. But you know what? Right then, back of some stores in the dark where we'd been doing our drinking, I knew someday Frank was going to come looking for the whiskey."

Nobody said anything. Son's gaze moved slowly from the porch, past the men in the yard to Frank Long. He waited a moment before saying, "But Frank's not going to get it. Not Frank or anybody."

# 3

They said it was toward the end of 1922 and into 1923 that Son Martin's father ran his hundred and fifty barrels of top-grade moonshine and put it away to age a full eight years.

They said he must have been planning it because he bought his white oak barrels three or four years before he ran the whiskey, bought them used at the time the Prohibition law closed the distilleries. They said John W. Martin put up the whiskey as an insurance policy. The old man wasn't going to buy any government Liberty bonds for savings, because it was the government that had taken Son into the Army and lured him into staying after the war was over. He wasn't giving the goddamn government anything. But he would have something to give Son once he got tired of marching around Camp Taylor playing soldier boy. Something worth more than any paper Liberty bonds.

Maybe the old man had put away the whiskey, maybe he

hadn't. All anybody knew was the old man and Aaron and some kin of Aaron's had kept three stills working every day for a year. They'd seen the smoke curling out of the yellow pines above the Martin place and they knew he didn't sell more than a few dozen half-gallon jars during that time.

So, people said, he must have put it away: probably down a mine hole somewhere. While he was stilling, the old man had mined coal more than he'd farmed and they said it must have been part of his plan: dig shafts to hide the barrels in, then cover them up with brush. As a final twist of the story, it was a mine that killed the old man, collapsed and suffocated him to death, not two months after Son had come home from the Army.

Mr. Baylor explained this to Frank Long in the Hotel Cumberland dining room late Sunday morning. Mr. Baylor watching Long eating his fried eggs and ham and hominy and finally calling Lila Holbrook over and ordering a plate for himself, with some hot coffee.

"I want you to understand it," Mr. Baylor said and waited.

Long's eyes raised from his fork. "Understand what?"

"Here's a man had a farm and a nice family, a married son helping him work the farm, two daughters married and living in Tennessee. Everything's just fine till the war come along. Son goes in the Army in 1918. The next year Son's wife, Elizabeth, and his mother both die of the influenza, both of them within a week of each other. Son decides to stay in the Army and the old man is alone."

Frank Long dipped his biscuit in the runny egg yellow. "What's there to understand?"

"I mean the old man working and hoping all these years."

"While Son was taking it easy in the Engineers."

This wasn't something he understood clearly or was sure he could explain, but Mr. Baylor said, "Son had his own reason for staying in, not wanting to come home to an empty house."

"He never talked about his wife any."

"He never talks much about anything," Mr. Baylor said. "That's his way. His daddy was like that. What I'm saying now, what the daddy worked so hard for was *his*, his to sell or leave to Son or drink it all himself if he felt like it. Which is what might've happened."

"I reckon you have all kinds of theories," Long said.

245

"Why they could have sent it to market for all anybody knows."

"A hundred and fifty barrels?"

"There's ways. They could've paid somebody and shipped it out by railroad, hidden down in some coal. Next time you see it it's in a warehouse in Cleveland, Ohio."

"But they didn't," Long said. "They left it to age the eight years."

Mr. Baylor put on a laugh. The steel frames of his spectacles glinted as he shook his head. "I see you don't know anything about whiskey. Four years, eight years, what's the difference in the taste?"

"Maybe nothing, but if the customer believes eight-year-old is better he'll pay for it, won't he?"

"All right," Mr. Baylor said. "Nobody around here has ever seen a trace of that whiskey. Some boys have looked for it. I mean as a game, to see if they could find it, not to steal it. If it's there, it's Son's and nobody else's. Now these smart boys have prowled Son Martin's tract for years and they haven't smelled out a single jar of anything the old man run."

"Then they haven't looked in the right place." Long cleaned his plate with a piece of biscuit and stuck it in his mouth. "Or they come on it and not said anything."

"I'd known," Mr. Baylor said.

"I reckon you're going to keep talking as long as I sit here."

Mr. Baylor hesitated and came in from another direction. "You claim to be his friend?"

"If he don't mind my working for the U. S. government."

"All right, if you're his friend, what'd you tell on him for?"

"They already knew." Long saw Mr. Baylor squinting at him, looking him straight in the eye. He said, "If a hundred people around here know it, a hundred from here to Frankfort can know it too."

"You're telling me the federal authorities know about Son's whiskey and they sent you to find it?"

"That's what I'm saying."

"What're you going to tell your superior?"

"I haven't looked yet, so there's nothing yet to tell."

"Tell them it was a story somebody made up. I seriously advise it."

Long sucked at his teeth. He pulled a cigar out of his breast pocket and bit off the end. "Mister, I believe you told me you're a law officer."

Mr. Baylor was ready. "And I believe you told me that don't stop a man from enjoying the finer things in life. Well, let me put it this way," Mr. Baylor said. "People around here have built their stills and drunk whiskey for more than a hundred years. They believe if a man plows the ground and sows it and raised corn, it's not the place of another man to tell him he can eat it but he can't drink it. That's what we think of your Prohibition law."

"I'm sorry to hear that," Long said easily. "You know I can call on you to help me if I want. I got authority to use you and all the deputies I need."

"You see how many you get."

"Well, I don't know." Long drew on the cigar and exhaled the smoke in a long slow stream. "I was thinking I'd get me some of the stillers to help me."

Mr. Baylor stared at him. "Like the Blackwells and the Stampers maybe?"

"Anybody operating stills."

"I want to be there when you ask them."

"Mister," Long said, "I'm not going to ask. I'm going to tell them. They help me find Son's whiskey or I start busting their stills."

"You got a short memory from last night. Once Son told why you'd come, there was some of them would have shot you full of holes and put you under." Mr. Baylor straightened and was silent as Lila Holbrook placed his breakfast in front of him. He wasn't sure now he wanted it; he'd already eaten breakfast at home. He saw Frank Long looking up and smiling and shaking his head when Lila asked him if he cared for anything else. As she moved away, Mr. Baylor said, "You think about it, you'll recall I got you out of there last night. If I hadn't been there they'd have shot you or run off in the woods nekked and that's a fact."

"They saw my gun," Long said. "If a man had drawn a pistol they'd have seen it again."

"Well, a cocky boy like you, I guess you could bust stills by yourself."

"Or call Frankfort for help," Long said.

"Tell me something." Mr. Baylor was looking him straight in

the eye again. "What do you get out of this? You get a five-dollar-a-month raise? Or they see what a sweet boy you are, they make you state Prohibition director?"

"That'd be something, wouldn't it?"

"Or, you've done your arithmetic and you see a hundred and fifty thirty-gallon barrels, that's—"

"Forty-five hundred gallons," Long said.

"At five bucks a gallon." Mr. Baylor paused, staring across the table at him. "Twenty-two thousand dollars. That right?"

"A little more."

"And the bootlegger he could make, I reckon, a *hundred* and twenty-something thousand. That the figure you get?"

Long shook his head. "Not if I capture it. Poured on the ground, the figure comes to zero."

"Would it please you to see that?" Mr. Baylor asked. "What I mean to say, what is it makes you happy about doing this job?"

"I don't get anything more out of it than my pay."

"Then you must want to see some good boys without a means of making a living and watch their little children go hungry. You want to take food off their table and see them get cholera and rickets. Is that it? Listen, I'll tell you something, boy, they used to farm, every one of them, but on the night of May 30, four years ago, it started to rain—"

"Jesus, I know about the floods."

"Goddamn it, I said it started to rain, I mean rain like it never rained before, all night it never stopped. The creeks overrun and filled the hollers and washed out timber and crops and livestock and roads and houses that had stood a hundred years. Now you can replace those things, but it also peeled away all the topsoil and that you don't replace. You don't grow a market crop on limestone either, or in wore-out pasture fields. So you grow a little corn for stilling and buy whatever other grain you need and pray God some drunken boy don't come along and shoot holes in your cooker. I'm saying, without stills some people around here would starve to death."

Frank Long was looking past Mr. Baylor's left shoulder, through the wide opening of the doorway into the lobby. He said, "That Mrs. Lyons is a good-looking woman, isn't she?"

Mr. Baylor leaned into the table; he moved aside the cold eggs he didn't want anyway. "Did you listen to what I was telling you?"

"Something about it raining," Long said. "Mister, excuse me, will you?" He got up and left the dining room.

Lowell Holbrook was in the lobby emptying ashtrays and picking up the Sunday paper from chairs. He'd traded shifts with the day bellboy so the boy could go somewhere. If Lowell hadn't traded he wouldn't be standing in the lobby with Frank Long coming toward him. He didn't know what to do. He didn't want to talk to the man because he was afraid he'd be nervous and maybe say the wrong thing. But it was too late to pretend he hadn't seen Mr. Long looking this way and raising his head as a sign he wanted him.

Frank Long didn't wait but came over to him. "Didn't I see Mrs. Lyons a minute ago?"

"She left," Lowell said.

"What do you mean she left?"

"I guess she wasn't feeling good. She went home a little early."

"Doesn't she live in the hotel?"

"No, sir. She did for a while. Then she rented herself a little house." Damn—he hadn't wanted to say *sir*. It just slipped out.

"You say rented herself. Don't she live with her husband?"

"No, sir." There it was again. "I guess her husband's dead."

"That's too bad," Mr. Long said. He turned without another word and walked out. Lowell moved over to the door and saw him get in his car.

Now what was he up to?

Talking to him hadn't been so bad. Except the calling him *sir*. Earlier that morning Lowell had called Mr. Baylor from the office when no one was there and told him about the BAR rifle in Frank Long's suitcase and the man saying he used it for hunting.

"I reckon he does," Mr. Baylor had said.

"Wouldn't a gun like that be against the law?"

"Not if you are the law yourself."

Mr. Baylor had told him then that Frank Long was a federal man. "Everybody will know it soon enough," Mr. Baylor had said. "But, Lowell, they don't have to know anything about that gun. All right?"

From the hotel entrance Lowell watched Frank Long drive off down the street, the same way Mrs. Lyons had gone. He thought about the BAR rifle again, upstairs in the room. He pictured himself going up to 205, opening the door with a passkey, and walking out with the whole suitcase.

Then what would he do with it?

There he'd be coming down the stairs as Frank Long walked into the lobby and looked up at him.

No, sir, there were things that were exciting to think about, but nobody with a brain in his head would ever do them in real life.

Frank Long spotted Mrs. Lyons before she was three blocks from the hotel. There, looking at the drugstore window, then moving along to the corner and into the noon sunshine, her dark hair taking on a glint of light: she looked fresh and probably smelled nice, took soapy baths with something in the water like perfume. A good-looking woman with a soft, warm body. Yes, sir, Frank Long decided. He watched her until she was in the next block, then gave the car some gas, got up to her, and swung in close to the curb.

"Mrs. Lyons?" He waited for her to look over. "Hop in, I'll give you a lift."

She didn't recognize him immediately. As she did she said, "Oh, I'm almost there, thank you."

"I don't see any houses along this street."

"The next street where you see the church? I live just up the hill back of there. Say"—now she put a little hint of surprise in the soft, southern-gentlewoman tone of her voice—"how do you know where I'm going?"

"I understand you're not feeling so good."

"I'm just tired I think."

"Then get in, I'll take you."

"Thank you—but I think the fresh air and sunshine will do me more good than anything."

Frank Long grinned at her. "It ain't going to make you look any better than you do."

"Well, thank you very much." Kay Lyons nodded politely and smiled, then let the smile fade as she turned away from him and continued on, hearing the car engine idling at the curb. She wasn't going to look back; not yet. She took her time and didn't glance over her shoulder until she reached the corner. He was still sitting in the car.

Still there as she turned the corner and crossed the street diagonally toward the Baptist Church and walked up the road past the churchyard and the fenced-in cemetery. She knew he was going to follow her, in the car or on foot, to see where she lived. There was nothing she could do about it. If he came to her house and knocked on the door she wouldn't answer. She was tired of smiling and being polite to salesmen and railroad agents and timber buyers in their muddy high-laced shoes: ten hours a day at the hotel, being bright and efficient. If she didn't smile or get a little sparkle in her eyes or make herself laugh—if she just acted natural—they say, "What's the matter with *her?*"

Kay had the feeling her life was slipping by, leaving no more than a few fading pictures in her mind. She saw herself as a little girl, little Kay Worthman, shy and skinny and scared to death of her cousin Virgil. She saw a pretty girl in high school, her hair marcelled into tight curls, honor student, and secretary of her graduating class. She saw the bright, neatly dressed young lady with the good position in the hotel office, assistant to the manager when she met Alvin Lyons, who came through Marlett once a month with his sample case of drugs and pharmaceuticals. She had dated Alvin Lyons whenever he came to town: thirteen dates with him before they became engaged and eleven more before she married Alvin in the Old Regular Baptist Church and left Marlett as Kay Lyons.

The next five years were fading pictures of her life in Louisville:

The red brick duplex on the street of two-family houses; she saw the house in the fall, when it was raining.

The garage that was empty all week with Alvin on the road.

The library books on the coffee table and the bedstand.

The movie theater three blocks from the house; the Ritz it was called.

Alvin coming home with his sample case late Friday evening, the tired smile and the kiss before he took off his hat and coat.

Alvin studying his correspondence course in business every Saturday afternoon at the dining-room table.

Alvin leaving the house every Monday morning before it was light; leaving it the last time.

Finding him in the tightly closed darkness of the garage, lying beneath the car's rumbling exhaust pipe, his body wedged against the double doors.

The last picture of Alvin Lyons was clear and perhaps it would never fade. Kay would see him lying on the oil-stained cement and sometimes she would want to shake him until his eyes opened and say to him, "Why did you do it? Why did you let me think everything was going to be all right? Why did you let me give you six years and then kill yourself?"

She was back where she had started, as bright and efficient as before, now manager of the hotel.

But she was also thirty-one years old and she didn't want to be bright and efficient in the service of others or the manager of a county seat hotel. She wanted to be herself and not have to concern herself with people. She wanted someone to take care of her, someone who was as sensitive and perceptive as she was, someone she could rely on and trust and know would always be there. It seemed so simple. She just wanted everything to be *right*.

The house she had rented for thirty-five dollars a month wasn't at all right. It was dismal inside and smelled old and the floors creaked. The only good points, it was a comfortable walk from the business district and it was private: a tiny one-bedroom place that had once been a tenant farmhouse, sheltered by cedars and overlooking rolling pasture fields out of the back windows.

Crossing the ditch to the front yard, Kay looked back the way she had come, far down the empty gravel road to the cemetery and the red-brick church standing on the corner. There was no sign of him. Soon though, she was sure, a car would drive slowly past the house. The car would turn around and come back and this time would stop.

Kay let herself in the front door. She did not seem outwardly surprised or startled to see Son Martin in the easy chair, but as she closed the door behind her she said, "God, you scared me. I didn't see your truck."

Son had lowered the newspaper and was looking at her from the chair. "It's in the shed. Hey, you're early, aren't you?"

"You were behind the paper," Kay said, "I don't know why, I had a funny feeling you were going to be someone else."

"How many keys to this place did you give out?"

"I mean it. It was an awful feeling."

"Listen, I brought most of a quart jar—if you want something to relax."

"He followed me," Kay said. "Frank Long."

She stared at Son until he got up from the chair and moved to the front window. Looking out, holding open the curtain, he said, "I guess you know who he is and about last night."

"In the lobby this morning," Kay said, "people were talking about it who don't even know you."

"By now I bet it's a good story." Son leaned close to the glass pane to see down the road.

"They say he got Mr. Baylor and his men to help raid your still."

"I don't see a car."

"He's there," Kay said, "somewhere. He wanted to give me a ride."

"What kind of car was it?"

"I don't know. A Ford, I think. He stopped me on the street."

Son looked around as she came over to stand close to him. He smiled a little and said, "Well, sure he would."

"He was in the dining room just before I left. Mr. Baylor came in and they talked for quite a while."

"Have you talked to Frank?"

"No. Only when he registered last night and a few minutes ago."

"Did he tell you he knew me?"

"I heard that this morning. When you were in the Army."

"We weren't good friends, but sometimes we'd go out and have some drinks." Son shook his head, thinking about it. "I've drunk too much with people before, but I never told anybody but him. Kay, why do you suppose I told him?"

"I don't know. I guess because you trusted him."

"I didn't have any reason to. You know, I don't think I even liked him especially. But I told him, the only person I ever told."

"You told me."

"You already knew about it. Like everybody around here."

"But I never thought about it," Kay said. "It didn't mean anything to me until now."

Son half turned from the window. "Listen, why don't we get a little more comfortable."

"What if he comes?"

He touched her hip and slid his arm around her waist. "What if he does?"

"Should I answer the door?"

"We won't worry about it this minute." Son could feel the satin slip beneath her blouse and the edge of her ribs beneath the slippery feeling of the satin. Close to his shoulder her brown eyes were watching him, trusting him, and he could feel her breast and hip pressed against his side, the grown woman with the innocent little girl expression. He said, "If you want to take off your shoes or anything, I'll pour us a couple."

She nodded slowly. "Just a weak one. It might make me feel better."

"That's what I was thinking."

"There's a bottle of ginger ale in the icebox."

Son nuzzled her ear and brushed his mouth across her cheek. "There isn't anything we have to worry about. Not anything." He heard her breath come out softly, then kissed her, holding his hand gently against her face.

In the kitchen Son poured whiskey into two glasses, adding ice-cold ginger ale to Kay's. He drank most of the whiskey in his own glass and half-filled it again. Now Son washed his face and hands at the sink and, with a wet hand, slicked his hair down to the side. Drying off with the dish towel he decided to have another pull. This one he took directly from the quart jar. It tasted better out of the jar; it was a strange thing but it was true. Already he could feel the warmth of the whiskey inside him. He felt good.

All morning he'd felt more alive and sure of himself than he'd felt in a long time. He would probably tell Kay or she would notice it. But if she asked him why, he wasn't sure he could explain it.

Frank Long was the cause. (Tell her *that*.) Because if Frank hadn't walked in out of the dark, Son was sure he would still be smiling with his mouth closed and being nice to people when he didn't want to be. Bud Blackwell might be partly responsible. Bud had started in on John W. Martin whiskey and it had got Son up on the edge. But it was seeing Frank Long that got him to wipe the dumb smile off his face once and for all and say it out loud.

He felt good because now there wasn't anything bottled up inside him, making him afraid to open his mouth. He had admitted to Frank Long in the presence of more than twenty men that his dad had run off the whiskey and put it away. They might have known or suspected it before; that didn't count. Now it was official. Admitting it was telling them straight it was a fact and they might as well quit playing with each other. He had the whiskey and they didn't and that's the way it was. They could fool around if they wanted, but if anybody got serious or got close he'd blow them off with a 12-gauge. Son hadn't said all that last night, but admitting the fact of the whiskey was like saying it and he would tell it again to Frank and to as many revenue agents as Frank cared to bring. They could all go home or to hell or hang around here and try Son Martin out; it didn't matter which.

That was the way he felt now, one o'clock Sunday afternoon, picking up two whiskey drinks in the kitchen of Kay's house and taking them into the bedroom.

She had drawn the shade and was standing in her slip, holding the edge of the shade inches from the window, looking outside. When Son was next to her she said, "I don't see any sign of him." She took the drink and sipped it, holding the glass with both hands, looking up at Son's face.

He said, "Don't think about him. All right?"

"I can't help it."

"He's not going to bother us."

"It's just—feeling him out there."

"He's probably gone away."

"I hope so."

"Listen, why don't we hurry up and finish these?"

He liked her in a slip. He liked her in a slip knowing there was nothing beneath the smooth cloth but her body. He liked pulling the slip up over her hips and seeing her a little bit at a time. He liked it especially this time of day, the house silent and the sunlight flat against the window shade.

He was aware of the quiet afternoon bedroom and was aware of his brown arm and hard sucked-in belly and was aware of the woman nakedness of her pale skin and dark hair, aware that she was with him and around him but also down in alone somewhere behind tightly closed eyes, seeing whatever she was feeling or thinking. He closed his eyes and was aware of a prickle of sweat across his shoulders and after he was down in there with her somewhere holding on and not aware of anything but being

where he was at that moment with his eyes closed tight and trying to make it last, until finally it was quieter in the room than it
had been quiet before.

Close to him, almost whispering, Kay said, "Hold me."

"What am I doing?"

"I mean *hold* me."

"Like that?"

"Yes, that's better."

"My arm wasn't right."

"Hold me tighter."

"How about right there?"

"Just hold me."

"You smell good."

"Tighter."

"I don't want to hurt you."

She worked her body tightly against his and lay still.

"I want to hold you and be held by you every night. Pretty
soon we'll be able to."

There was silence. Son opened his eyes, his face against her
cheek, his gaze on the sunlight framed in the window. "Pretty
soon," he said.

"Maybe in just a few weeks. Let's start thinking about it," she
said. "See if we can set a date."

"Kay"—Son paused—"why all of a sudden?"

She opened her eyes and moved her head so she could look at
him. "Because all of a sudden we don't have to stay in Marlett.
There's nothing keeping us now. We can be married and live anywhere we want."

"We can get married and live up at my place, but you say you
won't do it."

"Because if we set up housekeeping here, we'll stay here, I
know it. I don't want to grow a little vegetable garden and watch
you make illegal whiskey. I want to leave here while we have a
chance, before you think of some reason to stay."

"I've got the same reason I've always had. Maybe I'm dumb or
something, but what's changed?"

She frowned, puzzled. "They've found your dad's whiskey."

"Nobody's found it."

"I mean they know you've got it. Once they take the whiskey,
there isn't any reason for you to sit up there in your hollow like

an old mountaineer. You've said it yourself, the sooner you can leave Marlett, the better."

"Kay, nobody's found the whiskey. I'm going to sell it and make the money, and then we're going to leave here and buy good farmland or a business somewhere, I don't know which or where we're going. All I know right now is they don't have any idea where that whiskey is located. They've looked, but in eight years nobody's found it."

Kay pushed herself up on one elbow. "Son, this isn't a game anymore you play with your neighbors. Frank Long is a federal officer."

"You're sure built. Look at them things."

"Honey, if you don't tell them where it is they can make it hard for you and send you to prison."

"They can do that quicker if I do tell them."

"But you didn't make it, your father did."

"That doesn't mean anything. He made it, but I got it. Thing is, they have to prove I got it." Son smiled a little. "They have to find it—Frank Long does. That's one man, and I don't know as he's any better at it than Bud Blackwell or your cousin Virgil or some of the other boys."

"I don't know why you don't see it." She was concerned, worried, and now a hint of anger crept into her voice. "You're dealing with the federal government, not just one man. He'll bring all the officers he needs and if they don't find it they can sit up in the hills forever and watch you, and you won't ever be able to sell the whiskey yourself. Don't you see that?"

"I see a man named Frank Long," Son said. "He's the only one I see and as yet I don't know what he has in mind. I mean I don't know if he's out looking for the government or just for Frank Long, and that makes a difference."

Kay said, "What if we went away for a while—a month or maybe even longer, go somewhere and then come back and see—" She stopped. Son had pressed a finger to his lips. He was looking at her but listening to something else, she could tell. Kay heard the sound then, through the living room and outside: someone on the front porch.

Son rolled away from her, off the bed. He felt funny walking out of the room without a stitch of clothes on. He sucked in his stomach and moved carefully, feeling Kay watching him. Son waited in the front room, listening, before he walked over to the front window. He didn't see anyone on the porch or in the yard but, as he waited, listening, he heard a car engine start, beyond the stand of cedars. A moment later the sound faded to nothing down the road. Son walked back to the bedroom.

Kay was sitting up in bed, holding the sheet in front of her. "Was it him?"

"I didn't see anybody."

"What if he was looking in the window?"

Son stepped into his pants. "He might have learned a new trick or two."

# 4

Before Son was all the way through Marlett, heading out the highway in his pickup truck, he knew Frank Long was following him—a black Ford coupe hanging back there, keeping its distance. If it wasn't Frank Long he didn't know who it was, so he'd take for granted it was Frank and maybe play with him a little bit—get him tensed up maybe and wondering what the hell was going on, get him off alone and see how he handled himself.

Son left the highway at the county road pointing to Broke-Leg Creek, held back to see the Ford coupe make the turn after him, then was sure he was going to be followed wherever he went. That was fine with Son. He drove past the road that led up through the hollow to his place, went about two miles past it and turned off on a road that skirted the edge of an old worn-out pasture and led back into the woods, narrowing in the dimness and

259

looking more like a trail than a road. His dad had used this road sometimes to haul in his corn and sugar, but it had not been used much in the past few years. Weeds grew tall down the spine of the road and brush closed in on both sides to scrape against the body of the pickup truck. Maybe Frank would be irritated, getting his car all scratched up. That, too, was fine with Son. He hoped to get Frank Long irritated.

Finally the road climbed up through dogwood and yellow pine and came out into the sunlight on the ridge that looked down over the Martin property: the pasture and the barn and sheds and the gray-weathered house, little squares way, way down below. Son's pickup bumped along in low gear, passing the place where Mr. Baylor had waited with his deputies the evening before, following the ridge trail through trees and clearings, until Son decided this was about far enough back and away from everything. He got out of the pickup and stood squinting in the sunlight, waiting only a couple of minutes before the Ford coupe came bumping along and pulled up next to him.

Frank Long's elbow stuck out the window. He said, "Well, here we are."

Son nodded. "Here we are." He watched Frank open the door and come stiffly out of the car and then press his hands against the small of his back and arch his body as he looked out over the land.

"It's a nice view," Long said. "But it don't compare to that cozy little setup you got back of town. That I'd say was about it for a Sunday afternoon—truck hid in a shed, jar of moonshine in the kitchen. Where was you, Son? I peered in, I didn't see nobody stirring anywhere. You all must have been down in the cellar putting up preserves." Frank Long grinned. "You helping that nice lady with her canning?"

Son grinned with him. "You aren't any little sneak, are you? You're a big tall skinny sneak. Grown man peeks in windows— what else you like to watch, Frank?"

"Being a little sneaky is part of my job, so I know what boys like you are up to."

"I'll tell you, Frank, anything you want to know."

"Anything?"

"Maybe just about anything."

"How's she, any good?" Long waited when Son didn't answer. "Well, is she? How many times you put it to her?"

Son kept watching him. Thinking, two steps, two and a half, fake with the right and come in with the left wide, hard against that bony nose and mouth, right where the hat-brim shadow cuts him. But Son knew he would have to keep going and finish it because if he didn't, the .45 would come out of the shoulder sling and he didn't know for sure what Frank had in mind, so Son held on. He didn't smile, he didn't go stone-faced either. He just looked at Frank, telling him he had better ask real questions if he wanted answers.

"All I wondered," Long said, "was if she's the local whore or Son Martin's special stuff. All right, now I know, we can get to other things."

"Like whiskey," Son said.

Long nodded. "Like whiskey."

"Come on." Son walked out of the clearing into the trees and scrub, Frank Long catching up to stay close behind him.

Frank wasn't worried; he had lived in the mountains most of his life. He knew the dank smell of the forest and the feeling of silence in the tree dimness—silence, though there were sounds all around them, high up in the trees and in the dense laurel thicket. The sound of their own steps in the leaves, the sharp brittle sound of twigs snapping. He could follow Son anywhere and he could keep up and keep his sense of direction in the thicket and if Son figured to lose him in here, Son had something to learn. Hell, he'd traveled these paths. They were just barely trails leading into where they hid the stills. A man could tramp these woods till he dropped of old age, but if he didn't know what to look for he'd have to be dumb lucky to find anything. Water, that was what to look for: cool stream water a stiller had to have in order to run whiskey. In this hollow it would be Broke-Leg Creek and if Son was going to show him anything he'd have to take him to the creek.

Son showed him a rock house up in the limestone cliffs where his dad had once operated a still: more of an open ledge than a cave, with water seeping in and staining the rock a copper color. He showed Frank Long the aqueduct system his dad had made: split logs hollowed into troughs and laid end to end a quarter of a mile from the spring to the outdoor still. That was another one his dad had used. The third one was in the house Son had built the year he got married, and that still was operating today.

"Where's the house?" Long was following Son through the laurel, speaking to the back of the man's tan shirt.

As they came out of the thicket, Son pointed and said, "Down there in the trees. You see the roof and the smoke. I guess Aaron's got the fire going."

"Where you and your bride lived, huh?"

"For a year, before I went in the Army."

"Was she from around here? Somebody you knew awhile?"

"From Corbin. I knew her a few years. Then we seemed to get married all of a sudden."

"I know how that is," Frank grinned.

"Elizabeth never had any children, which I guess is a good thing."

He could picture her; he could see the dark-haired girl with freckles, a strong and healthy-looking girl, who had never been sick in her life until the influenza came to Marlett and spread up into the hollows. Son did not see her in the casket. He got home from Camp Taylor the morning of the funeral and went directly to the funeral home where everyone was standing around waiting for him, and the undertaker was wishing they would hurry up and get done with expressing their sorrow, because he needed this parlor for somebody else. So they buried Elizabeth Hartley Martin, 1898-1919, in the churchyard. Son got on the train to Camp Taylor and was back in Marlett seven days later for his mother's funeral and burial in the cemetery, next to his wife.

Son could picture her, the twenty-year-old girl he had married, but he seldom thought of her as his wife; he could see her smile and her nice even white teeth with the freckles across her nose, a pretty girl he had taken to dances and out riding in a buggy. He didn't think of her as his wife and it gave him a start sometimes when he remembered he had once been married. He would probably marry again. It seemed natural, though it wasn't a simple thing to do now—with Frank Long standing with his hands in his pockets squinting down the slope at the little house where Son Martin worked his still. Son watched him. He said, "You want to look at the still?"

Frank Long turned, looking past Son, up the slope and to the dark ridges beyond. "Well, as you know, I'm more interested in old whiskey than new stuff. I'm interested to know where an old man would hide a hundred and fifty barrels." His gaze roamed over the slope studying the thickets and trees and the outcroppings of sandstone.

"Where'd the old man dig his coal at?"

"All over here," Son answered.

"I see where there might be some shafts. He worked all alone?"

"Usually. Sometimes Aaron helped him when he wasn't working the farm."

Long nodded. "The old man dug coal, Aaron farmed, and the both of them made whiskey. What I want to know, was the old man digging for coal or digging hiding places?"

Son was working a cigarette out of the packet in his shirt pocket. "There's only one way to find that out, isn't there? Go look in all the holes you come across, peer in and poke around and see what you find."

"That would take me some time, wouldn't it?"

"I don't know. Twenty years."

"Less I had some help."

"You think they can spare the men? I understand you Prohibition people are awful busy."

"I was thinking," Long said, "of getting people around here to help me, like the Blackwells and the Worthmans. I mentioned to Mr. Baylor this morning it might be the way to do it."

Son drew on his cigarette. "What'd Mr. Baylor say to that?"

"He said he'd like to be there when I ask them."

"I would too."

"Then I told Mr. Baylor I wasn't going to ask them, I was going to tell them."

"I see. Just order them."

"That's right. I say to them, 'You go out and find me Son Martin's hundred and fifty barrels. Find it or get him to tell where it's at, I don't care which. Because if you don't I'm going to start busting your stills one at a time, and I'm going to put all you boys out of business.'"

"Now you're telling me."

"Yes, now I'm telling you. Mr. Baylor said they need their stills to make a living and without the stills their families would go hungry and said something about the kids getting rickets and scurvy. You believe that?"

Son nodded. "They rely on their stills, that's the truth, with the good farmland washed into the creeks and river. I don't know anything about what would happen to the kids."

"But without money to buy food it would seem those folks would go hungry," Long said.

"It would seem so," Son agreed.

"So what are you going to do about it?"

Son looked at him, drawing on his cigarette. "I don't see as it's my problem."

"You don't care what happens to them?"

"I think the Blackwell boys and the others are big enough to take care of themselves."

"After I put them out of business?"

"If you can do it. You haven't showed anybody how big you are yet."

"How about when they see their stills in little pieces?" Long was working in gradually, keeping his gaze on Son now. "They see their equipment shot full of holes and all busted to hell and they see the smoke still curling up from your cooker. What do they think then? The Prohibition man hits them where they live, but he don't lay a goddamn finger on his friend Son Martin. How do you think that will set with them?"

"I think you got to bust a still first," Son answered. "And I think you got to have more than that army automatic hid under your coat."

"But let's say I can do it."

"Frank, we'll be here. Show us something."

"I just want you to realize what's going to happen."

"If I don't tell you where the whiskey is."

"That's right. It's in your hands," Long said. "I promise you, if you don't do the right thing your neighbors are going to come down on you like a herd of bulls."

"Frank, you should have stayed in the Army where you got somebody to think for you. You start using your own head it's likely to get blown off."

"You keep thinking I'm alone."

"All I see is you."

"And all I got to do is call Frankfort and you'll see more Prohibition agents than you can count. I'm offering the easy way, Son, because we soldiered together and were buddies. But if you want me to be mean about it then boy you got trouble."

"Because we were buddies," Son said. "I appreciate that. Listen, because we were buddies I'll do you a favor, Frank, I'll give you an ax and let you go down there and chop up my still and pour out any whiskey you find. You write a report and say you found only one still in Broke-Leg County and you busted hell out of it and your boss says, Frank, you did a dandy job, now we'll send you someplace else. Then you go there, wherever they send you, forget all about any hundred and fifty barrels a drunk soldier told you about. Figure it was drunk talk and go about your business and maybe you'll live to enjoy old age."

Frank Long grinned, shaking his head. "It is surely good to be talking to an old buddy again. Yes, I'm certainly glad I came here. Son, I'm not going to bust your still. I told you why. But I wouldn't mind taking a look at it—see where the best moonshine in the county comes from."

"Down there in the house." Son nodded toward the roof showing in the trees below.

"How do I get to it?"

"Path over there, through the bushes."

"Show me."

Son had dropped his cigarette stub. He paused now to fish another out of his pocket and light it. "Go ahead, I'm right behind you."

Long moved through the brush and stopped at the edge of a dry wash that came down from the slope above and dropped down steeply a good hundred feet to Son Martin's, where the bank of the wash had been lined and built up with stones, diverting the course of the gully away from the house. Frank Long looked down the open trough. It looked dry or crusted over; you couldn't tell about it this time of the year. He looked over his shoulder at Son coming up behind him.

"Is this all right?"

"That's the quick way, Frank. You can take it or go on over aways and find a switchback trail the ladies use to go down."

"I asked you if it's all right."

"Well, it looks all right to me."

Long would have to agree to that, but he didn't know when it had rained last and he didn't know if the wash was dry or only covered with a thin dry crust. He stepped down off the bank, took another step and one more before his foot went through the crust.

Long hopped as his foot sank into the mud, but with the next step his shoe disappeared and as he struggled to pull his foot out and keep his balance he went down, breaking through the thin dusty crust. He tried to get up and slipped again and rolled over to get his arms out and his hands in front of him, but he was going down the gully head first now, plowing open the thin crust, clawing at the mud, and taking chunks of it with him. Long had no chance against the month of spring rain that had seeped into the red dirt and turned the gully into a mud chute. He gave up, letting himself slide and roll until he came to a stop a hundred feet below, where the bank turned and was reinforced with stones.

He sat there a minute before pulling himself up, his clothes and one side of his face painted with the red muck. Long was still wearing his hat. He took it off, looked at it, put it on again, and stared up the wash, way up to where Son Martin stood waiting.

"A man has to be careful around here, Frank. Watch his step and know what's he doing. He'll find he can't rely on anybody's word." Son didn't raise his voice; his words carried clearly to Long, who unbuttoned his coat and drew the big .45 automatic, looking at it and then at Son as he held the gun in front of him.

"You want to get rough," Long said, "I can end this game right now."

"Maybe," Son said, "but not without getting the back of your head messed up. Put it away, Frank."

Long hesitated. Son wasn't going to trick him from a hundred feet away. He looked over his shoulder, hesitated, then slid the automatic back into its holster. Aaron covered him from the porch of the house, holding a 12-gauge aimed right at his head.

By Monday noon the story around Marlett was that Son had thrown Frank Long down the mud wash after Long pulled a gun on him. Aaron told it correctly at the Sweet Jesus Savior prayer meeting Sunday night; but it was natural for the story to take on weight in Son's favor. Son causing him to fall wasn't enough; Long deserved to be pushed. Lowell Holbrook told how Frank Long had given him the muddy suit of clothes and instructed him to throw it away—there was so much wet mud stuck to it, the suit would have to dry out for a week and then be beaten with a stick for another week. Lowell Holbrook said the suit was in a trash barrel back of the hotel if anybody wanted to see it. A few of Lowell's friends went to take a look.

By the time Frank Long appeared on the street that Monday, he was being referred to as the Hog Man, a nasty creature that liked to wallow around in wet clay mud. No one was sure who had made up the name, though later Bud Blackwell claimed he said it first. Maybe he did. It was Bud Blackwell who said it to Frank Long's face.

Bud and his brother Raymond, and Virgil Worthman were standing at the corner down from the hotel entrance, probably waiting for Long, when he came out and walked right up to them.

Long took them by surprise. He spoke first, asking if Mr. Baylor had talked to them.

"About what?" Virgil Worthman said.

"If you have to ask then he didn't," Long said, "so I'll tell you myself."

"I don't know," Bud Blackwell said, "if we should be seen talking to you. They say you tell a person by the people he hangs out with."

"You won't have to talk," Long said. "Just get the wax out of your ears and listen."

Bud Blackwell glanced at his brother. He said, "Hey, you know who this is? Somebody must have hosed him off, because this here is the Hog Man."

Frank Long hit him in the mouth. Bud might not have gone down, but the curb tripped him and he fell hard in the street. He got up, wiping his hands on his thighs; his right hand slid around to his back pocket and came out with a bone-handle clasp knife that he put to his mouth to pull the blade out with his teeth.

"Open it," Long said, "and I'll shoot you dead for assaulting a federal officer. You can come at me, boy, but if you use the blade or these others horn in, then out comes Sweetheart." Long patted the hard bulk of the automatic beneath his coat.

One thing about Bud Blackwell, whether it was to be knives or guns or a fist fight, he didn't stand around talking about it. He threw the knife underhand to his brother Raymond and went for Frank Long, who was waiting with his big bony fists and his reach advantage. He jabbed Bud hard in the mouth with his left and slammed the right into Bud's cheekbone; he took a couple of Bud's wild swings on his shoulder and forearm and waded in

267

again with the jabs and hammered Bud's bloody mouth with the right and held up from throwing it again as Bud went down on the sidewalk and this time didn't get up.

Frank Long waited for Bud's brother Raymond and Virgil Worthman to look at Bud—both of them stooping over him—then gave them time to look up at him and make up their minds whether they were going to take a turn or pick up Bud and go home. Evidently they weren't having any, Long decided, because they didn't say a word or make a move.

"When that boy wakes up," Long said, "take him over to see Mr. Baylor and you all listen to what he says. I've done enough talking for a while."

Long had come out to take a walk and look over the main drag and maybe stop in a cafe for his noon dinner. But he changed his mind now and went back to the hotel, up to 205. There was no sense in fooling around, he had decided in the past few minutes. If these hardcase boys were going to gang him, it was going to take more than conversation to make them think in the light of reason. He was going to have to bust a few heads as well as stills. In his room Frank Long took off his hat and suit coat and laid the .45 automatic on the night stand as he sat on the bed. He lighted a thin cigar and picked up the telephone. Those smart-aleck boys wanted a fight, Jesus, he'd order up more fighting than they could stomach. When the operator came in, Long gave her the number of the federal Prohibition director in Frankfort. The operator took his name and room number and said she'd call him back and he hung up the receiver. Long waited.

They'd be surprised to hear from him, since he was supposed to be on a leave of absence. He'd told them he was needed at home because of sickness in the family.

When the operator called back she said the circuits were busy but that she would keep trying.

He said all right and hung up again. When the operator did get through to Frankfort probably the line would be busy. Then, it wouldn't be busy, but the phone would ring for about an hour before anybody in the office decided to answer it. Then the fat woman clerk would get on and he'd tell her who he wanted and she'd say he was out and didn't know when he'd be back. He'd give another name and the fat woman clerk would sound put out as she said, all right, just a minute, and another hour would go by while the fat woman clerk stood over the water cooler talking to another woman clerk and the phone receiver lay on the desk, off the hook. He sure didn't enjoy waiting or taking crap like that from women clerks who thought they were the cat's ass. There hadn't been any women clerks in the Army, but Jesus there had been enough waiting. The Army was famous for it: hurrying a man up and then making him wait. Though it hadn't been a bad life, even with the low pay and usually lousy food and having to wear leggings and thick-soled shoes. In his life Frank Long had farmed, worked for a mine company, gone through the ninth grade of school, and had served twelve years in the U. S. Army, Infantry and then Engineers. He had made sergeant and had a pretty nice room of his own in the barracks, but they never let him go to Officer Candidate School and get a chance at the soft life. Hell, he'd probably be in today if they'd made him an officer. He didn't have anything against the service, but when someone told him they were looking for federal Prohibition agents it sounded good. You wore a regular suit and the pay wasn't bad; you were given a badge and a gun. Long wasn't sure what the gun would be, so he swiped a BAR he liked and took it along with him when he was discharged.

The old man, Mr. Baylor, had asked him, "What do you get out of this? A five-dollar-a-month raise?" Probably he wouldn't even get that. He'd put in his expense sheet and get a hard time from the fat woman clerk who would act like it was her money she was giving out.

The other way, keeping the whiskey himself—the minimum he stood to make—would be forty-five hundred gallons times five dollars a gallon. Or, at the bootlegger's price of five dollars a fifth, he could make over a hundred thousand bucks.

Hell yes, he had thought about it. He'd thought about it most of the time the last couple of days: find the whiskey, get some-body who knew what he was doing to ship the stuff out by truck to Louisville, and split the profit with him: some bootlegger who knew the market and ways to get to it. Long had a file on some pretty good boys. Some wanted, some in jail, some just released. One in particular Long couldn't get out of his mind, the perfect guy for a deal like this one, somebody who had the knowledge and experience to sell the whiskey and, at the same time, some-body who could be trusted. Hell, the man had been a dentist before becoming a bootlegger. You had to be pretty upstanding as well as smart to be a dentist.

Dr. Emmett Taulbee was his name.

Long got a two-ring binder out of his suitcase and sat down on the bed again as he opened it, flipping through pages of reports and "wanted" sheets until he recognized Dr. Taulbee's photographs, in profile and head-on.

There he was: Emmett C. Taulbee, D.D.S. Age fifty-one, a slight smile curling his lip and showing some of his upper front teeth. He must have thought they were something to show, though they protruded a little and were big horse teeth. Taulbee considered himself a ladies' man, and maybe there was some indication of that in the way he combed his wavy hair and let it dip down across one side of his forehead. He was also said to be a dude—wore expensive striped suits and detachable white collars on a blue shirt. His last known place of residence, Louisville, Kentucky. There was an address and a phone number, the typewritten phone number crossed out and another number written above it in pencil.

The photographs had been taken seven years ago, at the time of Dr. Taulbee's arrest for sexually assaulting a woman patient in his dentist chair.

At the trial the woman testified that she had been a patient of Dr. Taulbee's for several years. No, he had not made advances or displayed an interest in her physically, not until she was in his chair for the extraction of her molar. She said Dr. Taulbee placed the mask over her nose and mouth and told her to inhale the gas slowly. She remembered the sound of breathing in the mask and the awful suffocating feeling for a moment. Then she was asleep. After that she remembered stirring and feeling a weight and something white over her, close to her face. She did not realize at first that it was Dr. Taulbee partly on top of her on the chair. She thought perhaps she was dreaming, until she felt something and moved her body and knew that her lower body was bare and that her legs were apart. When she screamed Dr. Taulbee twisted off her. He stood with his back to her for a moment, then hurriedly left the room. The woman testified that she found her undergarment on the footrest of the chair. Her skirt had been pushed up around her hips, but her stockings and shoes had not been removed.

She was an attractive woman in her early thirties, the mother of three children. In questioning her, Dr. Taulbee's defense counsel played with the implication that the woman had made up the story as a means of smearing Dr. Taulbee's name. Though they gave no reason why she would want to, nor did they accuse her of it directly. The woman answered all questions calmly, candidly, looking at Dr. Taulbee from time to time to see how he was taking it.

Taulbee sat quietly most of the time. Occasionally he would smile or shake his head at the woman's testimony. His counsel did not put him on the witness stand, so the court did not hear from Dr. Taulbee. Though they did hear two additional women patients testify: one, that he had acted strangely and had touched her—held her arm or shoulder and had asked her if she was by any chance menstruating, because if she was the anesthetic might have an adverse effect on her. The other testified that upon leaving Taulbee's office, after having had gas for an extraction, she felt her clothes disarranged, as if she had been sleeping in them or as if someone else had dressed her. Dr. Taulbee's license to practice was revoked and he was sentenced to one to three years in the State Penitentiary at Eddyville. While he was there his wife of twenty years divorced him.

Prison, Frank Long decided, was what changed the man's life. He met bootleggers and whiskey runners and evidently something about their business appealed to him. Dr. Taulbee was released after a year and was a good boy during the two years of his probation. Since then—during the past six years—Taulbee had been arrested four times for the possession of illegal alcohol, but had not been convicted even once. He was making money and sure had better lawyers than the one he had at the assault trial. Taulbee was a businessman with a working force and a good profitable operation that reached from Kentucky up into Ohio and over into Indiana and he would be just the one for a deal like this one. Hell, Taulbee was the only one Long knew of who could handle a hundred thousand dollars' worth of grade-one whiskey.

He had met Taulbee twice, both times after raids on Taulbee's warehouses. The last time they had sat around the police station questioning Taulbee and waiting for his lawyer to come and Frank Long had got along pretty well with him. Taulbee didn't seem to be worried; he told some pretty good jokes and grinned when everybody laughed. Long liked a man who didn't let anything bother him. Sitting around there Taulbee gave everybody a cigar and said, well, now if somebody else could supply the whiskey and the girls, he'd as soon come to this jail as most of the speaks he did business with. He was honest, right out in the open, and they said he sure liked girls.

Long did not make a judgment about Dr. Taulbee's assault on the women. If he liked to do it to them while they were sleeping, that was his business, but Jesus, it was sure better when they were squirming around. It didn't seem enough to send a man to prison for. Those women had probably been asking for it anyway.

The more Long thought about it, the better it looked to him. Long and Taulbee, partners. One job, that was all. He wasn't about to turn criminal for life. One job and he'd take his cut and go to California or somewhere. Just one job and not do anything wrong ever again.

Before the phone rang, Long picked up the receiver and waited and then said to the operator, "Listen, never mind that call to Frankfort. I got a number in Louisville I want you to get me."

# 5

Dual Meaders told the filling station man ten gallons of ethyl and sat to wait, his elbow pointing out the window and his pale-looking eyes gazing straight ahead, half closed in the afternoon glare.

Behind him, in the back seat, Dr. Taulbee said, "Ask him where's a good place to eat."

The girl sitting with Dr. Taulbee, Miley Mitchell, a good-looking eighteen-year-old girl with brown hair and nice dimples, said, "God, around here?"

"Ask him," Dr. Taulbee said.

Dual Meaders got out of the La Salle; he walked back to where the filling station man was holding the nozzle in the gas tank opening and asked him where was a good place to eat.

"Right in front of your nose," the filling station man said, nodding across the highway to the white frame house with the FOUR STAR CAFE sign on a pole in front.

Dual Meaders didn't like the man's answer. If the man had been close enough to see Dual's light-colored eyes, he would have smiled or laughed or said something else to show he was just being friendly and not smart aleck at all. But he didn't see Dual's eyes and Dual didn't have time, at the moment, to show them to the man. He opened the rear door and said, "Across the street."

Dr. Taulbee squinted at the FOUR STAR, frowning, showing his front teeth. "Ask him how far to Marlett."

"I know how far," Dual said. "Corbin's another fifteen miles, Marlett's sixty, seventy more."

"We could wait till we get to Corbin," the girl, Miley Mitchell, said.

"Not the way my stomach's growling," Dr. Taulbee said.

Miley was studying the cafe. There were no cars parked in front. "I don't know. It's after three, maybe they're not serving now."

"Honey," Dr. Taulbee said, "get out of the car, will you?"

Holding the door open, Dual was looking at the filling station man who was watching the gauge on the gas pump. It still burned him the way the man had answered. Dumb hick saying right in front of your nose. Dumb hick pumping gas in his filthy dirty overalls.

At the edge of the road Dr. Taulbee looked around and said, "What're you waiting for?" Dual closed the car door and followed after them.

As he was crossing the road, the filling station man called out, "Hey, what about your car?"

Dual kept going. Over his shoulder he said, "Leave it where it's at."

The man called out something else, but Dual didn't pay any attention. Jesus, it was hot in the country already, a spring day, but like the middle of August. He headed for the shade of the cafe, opening the door that Dr. Taulbee, a few steps ahead of him, had let close.

The place was empty: counter, tables, and booths all empty. A radio was playing in the kitchen and there was the sound of voices, but no one appeared until they were seated at a booth.

The woman who came out of the kitchen looked them over as

she stood at the counter and filled three glasses of ice water from a pitcher, then smiled as Dr. Taulbee gave her a pleasant nod. From the city, the woman decided, judging by their suits and striped ties, the older one with a rounded stiff collar and a tiepin, but they seemed friendly. Probably father and son, or uncle and nephew—they looked enough alike to be related though the older one's hair was nice and wavy and the younger one's was slicked straight back and shiny. The woman didn't know about the girl. She could be the daughter of one or the wife of the other. Though the woman had a feeling the girl wasn't related to either of them. The girl was certainly pretty, a thin little thing but with a pair of grown woman's ninnies; if they were her own and not a pair of socks balled up inside her undies. They were travelers on the road, maybe going to visit kin or to attend a wedding or a funeral. It was too early in the year for them to be on a vacation.

They drank their ice water and asked for Coca-Colas and when the woman came back with the Cokes they ordered from the top of the menu, talking among themselves as they told her what they wanted: the older man ordering salmon croquettes and the salad and asking the younger one about Marlett and how far out from town was a certain place—"the Caswell place"—which sounded like somebody's farm. They made the woman wait talking about Marlett, but she didn't mind because then she would learn something about them. The woman looked at the girl for her order, but it was the one with the slick shiny straight hair who spoke up and told her he'd have the barbecue beef and two orders of fried potatoes; though he was so thin and pale, with sunken cheeks, he didn't look like he'd ever eaten a full dinner. He had a toothpick in the corner of his mouth he must have picked up at the cashier's counter coming in. He rolled the toothpick to the other side of his mouth and said, don't worry, Caswell would have enough room for anybody they brought. The young girl said she guessed she'd have the salmon croquettes also; but the Four Star Cafe woman was listening to the older one say they would learn soon enough if they needed the extra room or not and when they got there they'd stay at the hotel if the burg had a hotel. The younger man said if he remembered correctly it was called the Cumberland Hotel, and the young girl said again she would have the salmon croquettes, if the woman wouldn't mind, and another Coca-Cola. The woman had never been to Marlett, though she knew where it was and was pretty sure there were no tourist attractions over there like natural caves or mineral springs. With them mentioning this Caswell place, or whatever the name was, the woman was pretty sure they were going to visit friends or kin.

It was a little while after she had served them their dinner and was back with more bread and butter for the skinny slick-haired one that the young couple came in. They sat at a table after standing at the cashier's counter and looking around the empty restaurant for a while.

As she put the bread down the skinny one said, "Dog, I like that tan suit that boy's got on."

The woman went to the counter to pour two ice waters and studied the new couple as she took the waters to their table: nice looking, both of them in their mid- or late-twenties with city written all over them. They were trying to appear at ease, but the woman could tell they were self-conscious and knew the three people in the booth were looking at them. Yes, they sure were: the skinny one was looking this way and then laughed out and the young girl with the pretty dimples giggled and the wavy-haired man was grinning, showing his teeth. The young couple ordered ham sandwiches on whole wheat and iced tea. When the woman told them they didn't have any whole wheat the young man said white would be fine.

The Four Star woman took their orders to the kitchen. She was at the counter fixing their iced tea when the skinny slick-haired one from the booth walked over to the young couple. She heard him say something about the man's suit. The man looked surprised and said, "Well, thank you."

"Where'd you get it?" Dual asked him.

"I believe it was in Cincinnati," the young man said, fumbling with the button of his suit coat to open it.

As he did, pressing his chin to his chest to look at the label, his wife said, "Where else?" She opened her eyes wide and laughed brightly to show she was at ease. "You just bought it about a month ago."

"I like that kind of material," Dual said. "It's not as woolly or hot as some suits."

"Thank you," the young man said.

"It's gabardine," his wife said.

Dual frowned, cocking his head as he studied the light tan

double-breasted suit. "How much you pay for a suit like that?"

"This suit?" The young man trying to act natural, looked at the label again, as if the price tag might be there. "I think it was about fifty bucks."

"Forty-four," his wife said, "I remember because you wondered if you should spend that much."

"Forty-four dollars," Dual said, nodding, still appraising the suit. "Okay, I'll buy it off you."

The young man grinned, going along with the joke. "Gee, if I had another one I would, I mean I'd sell it to you."

"I don't want another one," Dual said. "I want that one you got on."

As his wife laughed, letting Dual know she had a good sense of humor, the young man laughed and kept smiling as he said, "What am I supposed to do, take it off right here and give it to you?"

Dual wasn't laughing; he wasn't smiling either. He said, "That's right." He pulled his wallet out of his back pocket, looked inside closely as he fingered the bills, and dropped two twenties and a five on the table. "You owe me a dollar," he said.

The young man let his smile fade, then smiled again with an effort, shaking his head and looking beyond Dual Meaders now toward Dr. Taulbee and Miley Mitchell. Raising his voice to a pleasant tone he said, "Is your friend serious?"

Dr. Taulbee took a bite of salmon croquette and rested his fork momentarily on the edge of his plate. "He's serious. If there's one thing you can say about him, he's serious."

"But you can't just come in and tell a person you want to buy his clothes—" The young man was appealing to Dr. Taulbee. "You just don't do it."

"You wouldn't think so," Dr. Taulbee said, buttering a slice of bread and folding it in half to take a bite.

Miley glanced over at the table and went back to her salmon croquettes. They were pretty good; a lot better than she thought they would be.

"I can't take off my suit. Right here."

"Why can't you?" Dual asked him.

"I mean why should I? You can't just come in here and take anything you want."

"I'm paying for the suit, ain't I?"

"But I don't want to sell it!"

"Mister, do you believe I care what you want? Take off the suit yourself so I won't have to do it and maybe tear it," Dual said.

The young man's wife wasn't laughing now. She seemed afraid to move and her face was white. She said in a low voice, but loud enough for Dual to hear, "Urban, call the police. Ask the lady to call."

The Four Star woman was watching from behind the counter, holding the two iced teas. The young man looked at her now, a glimmer of hope in his expression. He said, "Are you going to stand for this going on in your place? You allow anybody to come in here and threaten your customers?"

"I work here," the woman said. "I don't own it or anything. The owner is Mr. James C. Baxter, but he ain't here right now."

The young man's wife said, "Well, will you please call the police?"

"I don't know—" The woman stood rigid holding the iced teas. "I don't know what's going on here. I don't know if it's a joke or what."

"He's threatening my husband!"

"Well, I don't know what he's doing. I was to call, I wouldn't know what to tell them."

"Ruth," the young man said, "never mind. Let's forget it. Let's just leave. Are you ready?" He was keeping his voice low and controlled, doing a fair job of acting natural.

Dual Meaders let the young man push his chair back and stand up before he reached inside his coat and came out with a .38 revolver. The gun looked heavy in Dual's slender hand; his wrist bent with the weight of it so that the barrel pointed low on the young man.

"I'll put a hole in your suit," Dual said, "if you don't start taking it off."

The young man opened his mouth, but not to speak. The gun barrel and Dual's expression held him wordless. He couldn't believe this was happening; except that the skinny, pale-looking fellow was pointing a gun at him and it was the realest thing he had ever seen in his life. He didn't want to look at his wife. He was afraid she might say the wrong thing and make the fellow mad. The fellow seemed calm, even patient, but that was it, he was too

278

calm: his face was like a dead man's face with the eyes open, a skeleton man who was too small to wear the suit in the first place. It wouldn't even fit him. If he asked the fellow to try it on he'd see for himself. But if the fellow took it wrong, thought he was calling him a squirt, God, there was no telling what he might do. That's why the young man from Cincinnati looked straight ahead and took off his coat without saying a word.

When he hesitated, Dual said, "Now the pants. Hey, what size shoe you wear?"

"Nine B."

"Too big. Keep your shoes and them garters. Jesus Christ, I don't want no garters. The tie's all right. I'll take that and you don't have to pay me the dollar change." Then, studying the young man as he undressed, Dual said, "Take everything off, right down to your skin."

"What?"

"Come on, take off the drawers and the undershirt."

The young man pleaded, "There's no need. You don't want my *underwear*," and forced himself to smile.

"Please—" his wife said.

Dual's eyes moved to the woman. "Don't you like to look at him with no clothes on?"

"Please," she said again. "Take the suit and let us go."

Now Dual's eyes shifted to the young man. "You better step out of those drawers, mister."

Dr. Taulbee used a doubled piece of bread to push the last of his salmon croquettes onto the fork. He glanced over at the young man, then at Miley, and put the salmon in his mouth. "You're not looking," he said.

Miley's head turned to study the young man, briefly. "What's there to look at?" She was eating her salad, wiping the side of the bowl with a piece of bread. "They don't have enough mayonnaise in the dressing," she said.

"Do you like that outfit she's wearing?"

"Who?"

"The guy's wife."

Miley looked over at the couple again. "It's all right. I don't wear much brown."

"It might look good on you."

Miley shrugged. "Maybe. I think it's too small though."

Dr. Taulbee straightened in the booth, raising his head. "Dual," he said, "we'll take that dress too."

The young man's wife stared and hesitated as long as she could and said, oh please, and finally began to cry. Her husband put his hand on her shoulder and pulled down the zipper in back and helped her off with the dress.

"Pink teddies," Dr. Taulbee said. "I like teddies on a shapely woman."

"She's not much," Miley said.

"Well, we don't know for sure."

Dr. Taulbee straightened again. "Dual, we might as well see the whole show."

The woman pleaded until Dual turned the revolver on her and her husband again patted her shoulder and stood close to her. The woman pulled the straps from her shoulders, peeling the silk undergarment down and stepped out.

Miley was finishing her salad. "I told you," she said.

"No, they're not too bad."

"Are we going to have dessert?"

Dr. Taulbee continued to stare at the woman. "Ten, twelve pounds she'd be all right."

"I wouldn't mind ice cream or pudding," Miley said.

Dr. Taulbee touched his mouth with his napkin. "I think we'd better get along." He looked over at the Four Star woman holding the glasses of iced tea. "Miss, if you'll bring us a check please." Dr. Taulbee got up; starting for the door he paused to look at the couple standing naked by their table, the woman huddled close to her husband and sobbing. "Honey," Dr. Taulbee said, "there's nothing to be ashamed of. I've seen women get by just fine with a whole lot less than you got."

Dual paid the check. By the time he was outside with the suit over his arm, squinting in the sun glare and waiting for a truck to pass before he could cross the highway, Dr. Taulbee and Miley had reached the La Salle and were getting in. The car had been moved from the canopy of the filling station and stood off to the side in the hot sun. Another car was next to the line of three pumps and the filling station man was standing with one foot on the car's rear fender, holding the gasoline hose—the same one that had said to Dual Meaders, "right in front of your nose."

Dual approached the first pump, at the front fender of the car. He didn't pay any attention to the filling station man, though he noticed the guy in the driver's seat of the car watching him—an old guy, a farmer. Dual took out his pocketknife and slashed it through the pump hose as the guy watched. Then he gave the guy a look and walked off toward the La Salle. Dr. Taulbee would get sore if he had to wait too long.

Dual Meaders gave himself the gabardine suit as a birthday present. He turned twenty-five the day he drove Dr. Taulbee and Miley from Louisville across the state to Marlett. Dual had never been over in this hill country before. He was originally from Memphis, Tennessee; had left home when he was fourteen and had been back only once since—and then by accident, because some hobos had robbed him and thrown him off the freight as it was passing through Memphis. That's what he had intended to do, pass through, but they pushed him out of the boxcar near Chickasaw Gardens and he picked cinders out of his face and hands for a week. (There were still spots on the heels of his hands where the gravel had been ground into the skin.)

Not long after that, when he was eighteen years old, Dual was charged and convicted in Kentucky of assault with the intent to commit bodily harm, after he had poured gasoline on a sleeping hobo drunk and set him afire.

Dual had thought this was pretty funny and had even cracked a smile in the courtroom when the prosecuting attorney described to the jury the old man running down the street screaming. The old man lived, though he spent two months in the hospital. Good—Dual didn't have any use for hobos since the time he was robbed and thrown off the freight train and he admitted he was out to get them. What he got was three years in Eddyville and Dr. Taulbee as a cellmate during the last year of his sentence. They got along all right. Dual liked Dr. Taulbee because even though the man was educated and a dentist, he did not act biggety or think he was better than anybody else. He didn't act tough and he wasn't a fighter, but if a con got mean with him, Dr. Taulbee could usually quiet the man by talking to him. Only once did a con cause him real trouble. The con told him he wanted a sack of tobacco and cigarette paper every day or else he'd break Dr. Taulbee's arms, both of them. Dr. Taulbee gave the man what he wanted until Dual got the tin knife made in the metal shop and, on a rainy afternoon in the yard when a bunch of them were huddled in a doorway, slipped the tin knife into the con's side. Dr. Taulbee didn't have any trouble from then on. After he was released from Eddyville he wrote to Dual and told him to look him up. Five months later Dual was out, working for the doctor and having one hell of a good time.

Boy, things happened fast; and it seemed everything had a reason. If he hadn't been sent to Eddyville, he'd never have met Dr. Taulbee. If he hadn't been thrown off the freight train and got them cinders in his hands, he wouldn't have poured gasoline on the bum and lit him up. Hell, and if he hadn't been riding the rails, he wouldn't have been thrown off. Take it back all the way. If he hadn't killed that boy with the rock, he wouldn't have run away from home. (The fat son of a bitch was way bigger than he was and had been picking on him and beating him up all during the school year. So one day coming home Dual had got up on the garage roof with the rock that must have weighed twenty-five pounds and, when the fat boy came along the alley, Dual dropped it on his head.) So if he hadn't dropped the rock, he wouldn't be working for Dr. Taulbee.

He sure liked working for him. It was a good easy job with plenty of excitement and all the booze and babes he wanted. What he liked especially was the .38 Smith & Wesson. God it felt good holstered there under his arm: blue steel and a hard hickory grip and with it he could do just about anything he wanted. It was sure better than a heavy rock or a wavy tin knife.

Dual said to the rearview mirror, "This Frank Long is supposed to be at the hotel?"

As Dr. Taulbee looked up Miley stirred, her head resting against his shoulder, her eyes closed. "That's what he said."

"Marlett ain't very far now." Now Dual's eyes were on the uneven blacktop beyond the dark dusty oval hood of the La Salle. "The Caswell place is supposed to be up back of town. He said turn at the cemetery and keep going, you can't miss it, a two-story house, was painted white one time."

"You told me," Dr. Taulbee said, sitting patiently and looking out at the rolling green countryside.

"You remember Caswell at Eddyville?"

"The name more than the face."

"Boyd Caswell. It was something, I remembered him being from Marlett. You said we're going to Marlett, I thought of Boyd Caswell right away. You know what he said when I called him?"

"I think you told me that also," Dr. Taulbee said.

"He said, 'Jesus H. Christ, come on. There ain't nobody here but me and my old daddy and he's half deaf and full blind.'"

"We'll see how blind he is," Dr. Taulbee said.

Dual looked up at the rearview mirror. "Caz says it, it's a fact."

"You said he was in for armed robbery?"

"Sure, but me and him was friends. I mean if you can't trust Caz, you can't trust anybody."

"Now you're talking," Dr. Taulbee said. "Say that every night before you go to bed."

"What I was wondering—if we shouldn't stay there awhile, get the lay of the land before we see this Frank Long."

Dual held his gaze on the road and the voice behind him said, "No, we'll talk to Long first. We want to see whether he's real or wasting our time."

"Or setting a trap."

"Or that," Dr. Taulbee agreed.

"How do you tell?"

"You don't. You get something on him."

"What if he's playing square?"

"You still get something on him."

"I don't know." Dual shook his head. "I don't believe I remember this one."

"I remember him," Dr. Taulbee said. "I remember two different times meeting that boy and both times thinking to myself, If you went looking to buy yourself a Prohibition agent you'd find this boy sitting on the counter."

"He never came to you before this?"

"No, not till his telephone call the other day."

"It could still be a trap he's setting for us to walk into."

"Don't forget it either," Dr. Taulbee said. "Let's think about it in silence so this little girl can get her rest."

Dual straightened up to look at Dr. Taulbee in the mirror. "She sleeping?" Miley was cuddled against him with his arm around her now.

"Like a baby," Dr. Taulbee said. "Bless her heart."

A few minutes later Dual Meaders said, "You are now entering Marlett, Kentucky. Population two thousand one hundred and thirty-two."

Lowell Holbrook came down the stairs to the lobby and went right to the desk, where Mrs. Lyons was closing the register and putting it on the shelf under the counter.

He said, "I was sure the girl was with the younger guy; I mean I thought she was his wife. But she had me put her bag in the same room with the older guy." Lowell was frowning, looking at Mrs. Lyons for an explanation. "Is that her father?"

"Her husband," Kay Lyons said. "Dr. and Mrs. Emmett Taulbee, from Louisville."

She began going through a stack of mail that must have come in, Lowell decided, while he was upstairs. He said, "Well, the other one can't be her son."

"Mr. Dual Meaders, also from Louisville."

"They staying long?"

"They didn't say."

"Well the younger guy's in 208 and the married ones are in 210. Is that right?"

"That's fine, Lowell."

"Mrs. Lyons? The older one, upstairs, he asked me what room Frank Long was in."

Kay looked up from the letters, holding one in hand. After a moment she said, "Then he must be a friend of theirs."

"Don't you think it's funny?"

"No, I don't think so," Kay Lyons said. "Why?"

"Well, coming in and asking for a Prohibition agent."

"He could still be a friend."

"I suppose," Lowell said. Though all afternoon he kept thinking about them: seeing the man with the big toothy smile and the girl looking out the window and the younger one with a tan suit over his arm, like he was going to send it out to have it cleaned, though he never did. He would think about them and wonder if he should tell Mr. Baylor.

And Mr. Baylor would say, "These birds checked in and asked for Frank Long. Well, now what do you want me to do, put them in jail?"

That was it, what had they done outside of asking for somebody? Frank Long was a Prohibition agent, but he was also a person, with kin anyway, even though he might not have any friends.

So Lowell didn't tell Mr. Baylor about them. He told himself if Mrs. Lyons wasn't going to worry, he wasn't either. Hell, tomorrow they'd probably be gone and he'd never see them again.

Lowell found out that was wrong the next morning—when he saw the three of them walking through the lobby and out the front door with Frank Long. He watched them get into a big car that looked like a La Salle and drive away.

# 6

Son could hear the dogs down in the hollow, far below through the stillness of the trees, the clear, sharp racket of the foxhounds on to something. Son stood on the porch, at the edge of the morning shade, looking out across the yard to where the road came up out of the hollow. Aaron came around from the side of the house and both of them stood listening for a minute.

When he was sure he had located the sound of the dogs in his mind and could picture them bounding out of the thicket and coming this way, Son looked over at Aaron.

"There isn't any rabbit would run up the road, is there?"

"No rabbit I know of," Aaron said. "They chasing up a car."

"Whose car they say it is?"

The Negro cocked his head. "They don't say whose, only it's a car."

"I guess one. They're both right together."

Aaron nodded, looking at Son now. "Jes' one, but maybe full of dudes. You want me to go down aways?"

"No, go on up to the still. Hey, Aaron? With a shotgun."

Aaron came up on the porch, as tall as Son and heavier through the chest and shoulders. "Maybe it jes' a friend come for breakfas'," he said.

"I didn't invite anybody." Son waited while Aaron went inside and came out with the Remington 12-gauge. "Aaron," he said, "somebody comes in and wants to knock the still all to hell, let them do it."

"I'll be nice."

"But if somebody shoots at you or you think they're about to, don't hold back."

"No, sir, I let them make the intentions known."

"They can have the still if they want it."

"Tha's right."

"But they can't have us."

Aaron grinned. "Tha's right."

Son sat down on the top step to wait. He got up and went into the house and came out wearing a dark hat with a funneled brim that he pulled down close to his eyes—the way Frank Long wore his hat—and looked off at Aaron crossing a hump of the meadow, heading for the slope and the house up in the trees. Son sat down on the step again.

This is where he was when the La Salle came up out of the hollow with the foxhounds yipping, leading the way. Son didn't recognize the car, so he didn't get up. He didn't move. He sat with his arms on his raised knees and his hands hanging limp. He watched Frank Long open the front door on this side and get out.

He watched the driver in the tan suit come around the front of the car. Son had to look at that suit again, wondering why the man didn't wear a smaller size, so he wouldn't have to roll up the cuffs of his pants like that.

He watched the dude and the good-looking young girl get out of the other side and come around the back of the car: the dude wearing a straw hat cocked to the side and a brown striped suit that was snug around his heavy chest and stomach, the dude looking like he should be carrying a sample case of jewelry or ladies underwear. Next to him Frank Long looked like a skinny old-time Baptist preacher.

Son watched the four of them gather to stand looking up at him, Frank Long two paces in front, the spokesman. Well, he could talk if he wanted, though Son knew already who was in charge of the party. He had a fairly good idea about the boy in the tan suit also and wasn't fooled by the suit being too big for him. The only one he couldn't figure out was the girl, who stared right up at him and didn't look away when he shifted his gaze toward her. There was a bold little thing. Maybe not so little either. Son didn't nod or speak because it wasn't up to him, it was up to Frank Long.

Frank said, "I might as well introduce my associates here and get to it, seeing how you're so busy. This here is Dr. Taulbee, he's a scientific whiskey expert who's come to sample your supply for the government and give it a grade and tell whether it's any good or not. This little lady is Miss Miley Mitchell, who is Dr. Taulbee's expert assistant and secretary, you might say. And here you have Mr. Dual Meaders, come here as a special investigator to help us capture your daddy's whiskey, if you force us to do it that way. And folks," Frank said then, looking up the stairs, "this is Son Martin, my old army buddy."

Son still didn't move. From the top step he could see them all and didn't have to turn his head to study any one of them.

"Son," Frank went on, standing relaxed with his suit coat open and his thumbs hooked in his vest pockets, "Dr. Taulbee here has a proposition I think you're going to like. See, I got to thinking, why start a lot of shooting and trouble when maybe there's a simple legal way to settle this. Your daddy went to a lot of work to run a hundred and fifty barrels and maybe you, as his heir, are entitled to something for it, even though you're breaking the law by having it. As you know, possessing is as much against the law as making." Frank waited.

But Son didn't give him any encouragement.

"How's that sound to you? A proposition."

Dr. Taulbee shifted his weight and shook his head and moved up next to Frank Long to put his hand on Long's shoulder and give him a friendly shove. Grinning in the morning sunlight Dr. Taulbee said, "Frank, you old horse, you're doing as much good as a one-legged man in as ass-kicking contest. You ask him how it sounds, you haven't *told* him anything."

"I'm getting to it," Long said, standing straight now, serious.

"Well, you sure take a while." Dr. Taulbee looked up at Son Martin, giving him his honest-to-God, good-old-boy smile. "Don't he though? We could be out here till suppertime before he'd have it told, I swear." The down-home drawl rolled out naturally and Dr. Taulbee moved in closer to plant a polished shoe on the bottom step.

The girl had her hands on her hips and was moving about idly, a step this way and that, looking down at stones and kicking at them lazily with the pointed toe of her pumps, then looking up and squinting in the sunlight and brushing her dark hair from her forehead. She wasn't dressed for being out here; she wore a skirt and jacket and pearls and little earrings. She was really pretty. Son decided she was pretty enough to be an actress or a singer. While the one in the tan suit kept looking up at the porch, nowhere else. He wasn't dressed for being here either, but he didn't look like any actor or singer. Or like a federal man or a special investigator. He didn't change his expression or seem to be aware of the heat or the sun glare or the dust that would blow across the yard when the wind came up. He kept his eyes raised to the porch.

"My," Dr. Taulbee said, "but it's getting warm. I wonder if you would have a cold drink of water in the house."

"Water's over there." Son nodded toward the pump standing in the yard, a few feet from the corner of the house.

"Well, friend, if you'll let me have a cup then."

"Cup's on the pump handle."

"Yeah, I see it now," Dr. Taulbee said, maintaining, with an effort, his friendly down-home tone. "Miley, be a nice girl and fetch the old doctor a cup of spring water, if you will please."

Miley stared at him a moment before walking over to the pump.

Dr. Taulbee kept his friendly gaze on Son. "What I was thinking, if we could go inside, out of the heat, I'd like to tell you about this proposition Frank mentioned. I guarantee you'll be interested."

"I don't think so," Son said.

"Well, you'll want to hear it before you say yes or no for sure, won't you?"

Son shook his head.

Dr. Taulbee held on. "My friend, that doesn't make any sense.

289

A man comes to you with a deal, you want to at least have the courtesy to listen to it, especially if it's going to save you a lot of trouble and maybe even your life. You understand what I mean?"

"There's no deal," Son answered. "No chance."

Dr. Taulbee's easy expression vanished. "Mister, you get tough with me, I'll tear your goddamn scrub farm apart and if I don't find what I want, I'll hang you from that porch beam—you hear me?"

A smile touched the corners of Son's mouth as he stared at the man. They looked at each other and got to know each other without a word being spoken. It wasn't a long moment in the silence between them, but it was there and it was enough. The squeaking, air-sucking noise of the pump handle broke the silence.

Miley called over, "I can't get this thing to work."

"Forget it," Dr. Taulbee said.

"I haven't pumped water since I was a little girl."

"I told you forget it!"

Frank Long shifted his position, impatient now. He said, "Son, listen to us, all right? I guarantee you'll want to think on what we tell you."

"Is it your idea," Son asked him, "or this scientific whiskey expert's?"

"Both of us together thought of it."

"Frank, you showed us a badge when you marched in here." Son looked over at Dr. Taulbee. "I want to see the paper says he's a scientific whiskey expert."

"There ain't no paper says he is."

"Then get him off my place."

"Son, I'm telling you that's what he is, hired by the U. S. government."

"Or hired by you?"

"Son, you're getting into things that don't matter when all we want to do is lay this deal on you."

Dr. Taulbee said, "Dual, if you're tired of standing with your finger in your nose, look for where a man would hide a hundred and fifty barrels of shine."

"I been thinking about it," Dual said.

"Now wait a minute," Frank Long said. "He's going to listen to us. Aren't you, Son?"

"If you say it and leave," Son answered.

"Dual," Dr. Taulbee said, "do you take that kind of talk?"

"Not since I can remember. No, sir, I didn't ever take it from any east Kentuck farm hick."

"If he talks like that again, what're you going to do?"

"I could shoot his ears off."

"Show him your gun, Dual."

"Right here." Dual pulled the .38 out of his suit coat and pointed it at Son's face. "You see it, mister?"

Son didn't say anything.

"I asked if you see it."

"You better answer," Dr. Taulbee said.

Son nodded. "All right. I see it."

"There," Dr. Taulbee said. "He's going to be a good boy now and he wants us to go into the house and have some coffee and a nice talk. He's saying, 'Yes, sir, Dr. Taulbee, I certainly want to listen to your deal 'cause, god*damn*, I get my ears shot off I won't be able to listen to anything.' Isn't that what you're saying, boy?" Dr. Taulbee was grinning, his old self again.

"Come on," Frank Long said.

Dr. Taulbee looked at Miley who was sitting on the board cover of the pump well. "Honey, you'll make us some coffee, won't you?"

Dual shifted his position for the first time. He said, "I don't want any. I'm going to start looking around."

Dr. Taulbee reached over to slap him on the shoulder. "If that's what you want to do, you go ahead."

"It's what I come for," Dual said. "Seein's I'm the special investigator."

The way Dual Meaders had it figured, the one hundred and fifty barrels were hidden somewhere close to Son Martin's house. The stuff had been out of sight for eight years, though during that time people had been roaming all over the Martins' land playing find the whiskey. Most of them would have stayed up in the hills looking for two reasons. Because they'd be afraid Son would catch them if they got too close to his house. And because the old man had dug coal up in the hills and a mine shaft was the logical place to hide that much stuff—if it was all in one place. Dual wasn't sure about that. It could be spread all over.

Where he'd like to start looking was right in the house. While they were talking he'd kept studying the house, the way it was built against the side of the hill with its high front porch. Under the house itself was a cellar—and a stone wall of that cellar could be covering a mine entrance that burrowed straight into the hill, which wouldn't be a bad place to hide it; where you could live on top of it and know the second anybody came looking and got warm.

When they had all gone up the steps and into the house, Dual squatted down to look under the porch. There was no need to duck under; he could see there was no opening in the stone foundation—hunks of limestone chunked together with mortar. So Dual walked around, past the pump, to the side of the house.

There it was, the wooden door to the cellar angled against the base of the house. The door creaked on rusty hinges as he lifted it, then pushed it over to let it bang hard against the ground as sunlight filled the stairwell and formed a square of light on the floor of the cellar. Going down inside Dual had a kitchen match in his hand ready to strike, but there was enough natural light to show him everything there was to see: shelves of quart and half-gallon fruit jars, shelves of jars from floor to ceiling, cases of jars, and jars lined on the shelves and filmed with dust. All of them empty, waiting to be filled with moonshine. He didn't find any corn meal or sugar—they must have kept that at the still. He felt along the stone wall that would be against the hillside and didn't find any loose stones to indicate an opening: which shot his idea of the stuff being buried under the house.

But he did find something that surprised him: a new-looking Delco Farm Electrification System, the motor-generator and the row of glass batteries taking up half of one wall. Looking it over, Dual was thinking it was an expensive outfit to light up an old farmhouse that one man lived in. He felt along the wall and traced the wire going up through the ceiling to the room directly above him. Well, maybe this Son Martin was ascared of the dark and liked plenty of light. Dual grinned at the idea. He wished he could grin like Dr. Taulbee, showing teeth like big square pearls, but his own teeth were crooked and tobacco stained and he didn't much like seeing them himself. He had brushed them every day the first couple of months he worked for Dr. Taulbee, but the brushing didn't make them any whiter, so he had quit.

There wasn't anything else down here.

There wasn't much out in the barn either. Walking inside Dual could tell this wasn't the place: a back-country barn that wasn't much bigger than a two-story house, weathered and starting to fall apart; like the owner didn't plan to be here long. The floor was hard-packed dirt; no boards that might be covering a big hole underneath. A stack of baled hay filled a corner of the buildings. Something could be behind or under it, but Dual wasn't going to go pitching hay bales around with his new gabardine suit on. Some other time. There was nothing here in the dirty smelly place but the hay and some grain sacks, empty stalls and stiff harnesses and hackamores hanging from pegs. Up the ladder was half a loft. Stepping back to one side of the barn Dual could see there was nothing up there. Out the window were two mules in the yard, nuzzling the ground, penned in there by a split-rail fence that looked like they could knock over if they wanted to. Christ, get this job done and get back to Louisville where things were going on, that was the ticket. Dual never did care much for farms; there wasn't anything to do.

He had spotted the roof showing way up on the slope in the trees. As they drove into the yard Frank Long had said that's where the still was, in a house Son Martin used to live in.

So Dual Meaders trudged up there from the barn—a long walk in the open sunlight, the dusty pasture steeper than it looked— feeling the muscle-pull in his thighs and sweating under his new suit like a goddamn field hand before he reached the trees.

Dual noticed the grave over a couple hundred feet from where he stood: the grave and the post and the little fence, close to a steep rocky section of the slope. He studied on it a minute before saying to himself, "It's a funny place for a grave with a light post, but you ain't going to get a hunnert and fifty thirty-gallon barrels in a six-foot hole." This Son Martin was a spooky gink with his goddamn lights everywhere.

By the time Dual had made his way up through the pines and brush and had clawed through the tangled laurel, losing the path about every time he turned around, he had his new suit coat open and was wiping dusty sweat from his forehead and out of his eyes. Woods might look cool and fresh and from a distance, but he didn't like any part of them. In the trees and thickets, with hardly any breeze seeping through, it was close and steamy and, Christ, there was an awful sour rotten smell hanging over the place. Dual located the source of the smell: over to one side of the little house, where they had cleaned out their mash barrels and left the fermented grain to rot. Christ, there would have to be some awful drunk snakes and lizards around here.

The house looked like it was about to fall off its stone foundations that leveled the porch at the two front corners. There wasn't much of a slope here in this clearing; it was like a bench on the slope, with pines and stone outcrops towering way above. Dual looked at the two windows and the wide open door and the smoke wisping out of the chimney pipe: not much smoke, probably burning dogwood or beech. Two barrels of mash stood by the door. Dual glanced at them as he stepped up on the porch and went inside, expecting somebody to be here because of the smoke, but the still was working all by itself.

It was about as clean and orderly a still as he'd ever seen, a first-class copper outfit you could take a picture of and say under it here's how to do it, boys: fifty-gallon capacity cooker with a low fire burning in the grate and a gleaming copper gooseneck coming out of the cap to carry the steam over into the flake stand: an open barrel filled with limestone spring water, water so clear Dual could see the worm of copper that was fitted to the gooseneck and coiled down through the fifty-gallon barrel. Inside the coil the steam was right now being cooled by the water and condensed into the clear moonshine whiskey that dropped from the spigot into a half-gallon jar.

About six gallons a day they'd draw, Dual decided. He preferred aged amber-colored whiskey every time, but this stuff didn't look bad, probably because the place was so clean.

He stopped outside on the porch and looked over the small clearing, then noticed again the two barrels of mash by the door and bent over the nearest one. A crust that looked like dried mud covered the fermentation taking place inside the barrel.

"When the cap falls that mash is ready to run."

Dual came around with his revolver out of his coat and put it square on Aaron standing with the shotgun across the crook of his arm, standing a few yards away in the clearing that had been empty a moment before.

"You put your ear close on the barrel," Aaron said, "it sound like meat afryin'. Few mo' days we pour off the beer and cook it."

Dual said, "Boy, lay that shotgun down."

Aaron grinned; lazy, slow-moving, head-shaking nigger, he seemed barely to shift his stance, but in the movement he came around enough so that the double barrels on the Remington, angled across his arm, were pointing directly at the man on the porch.

"You want something in my house?" Aaron asked him.

"You're pointing that at me, boy."

"No, suh, it pointing out of my arm."

"I'm telling you you're pointing it at me." Dual held the revolver in front of him and hadn't moved. "No nigger points a gun at me, boy."

"Mister, I ain't pointing the gun, it pointing itself."

"Put it down."

"I like to, but my finger is caught in the trigger. I'm afraid to move it."

"I'll plug you right between the eyes, nigger. You see that?"

"Yes, suh."

"You want me to do it?"

"No, suh, cuz if you do, I'm afraid this old shotgun will fire off and blow them mash barrels all to hell and anything standing close to them."

Dual Meaders had never felt such a terrible sharp urge in him. He felt if he didn't fire, if he didn't squeeze his wet hand on the grip and keep squeezing it, he'd rush the nigger and tear him apart with his fingernails. But the twin barrels of the shotgun, the round black 12-gauge holes, were as real as the terrible urge and they held him, like a wild animal caught in a headlight beam, and saved his life.

It was not worth dying to kill a nigger. Not when there could be another time to do it. Any time he wanted. Let the nigger think about that for a while.

"No," Dual said, "I don't want anything in your house. But I'm going to come back again sometime. I expect you know that."

Aaron nodded. "I expect I do."

Dual holstered the .38 and rebuttoned his coat, lingering there, waiting for the nigger to make a mistake. Finally he stepped off the porch and walked past him into the thicket. He felt all right now, calm and himself again, but Christ, that nigger was going to pay for getting him worked up like that. He couldn't believe it, the nigger standing there holding the gun on him. Christ, what was the world coming to?

Son punched two holes in a Pet Milk can and set it on the table. He and Frank Long took some, but Dr. Taulbee and the girl drank their coffee black. Son took a sip of his as the girl watched him. It was weak and about all he could say for it, it was hot, but he nodded to the girl and gave her a little smile. She'd worked on the coffee like she was preparing a full dinner.

Son didn't push or ask questions; it was still their party. But nobody seemed ready to get to the point until the coffee was on the table. Then Dr. Taulbee sipped his and said, "Ahh—" and blew on it close to his mouth and sipped at it again.

Frank Long bit off the end of a cigar and said, "Goddamn-it," and picked shreds of tobacco from his tongue. "The proposition is this."

As he paused then to light the cigar, Dr. Taulbee said, "The proposition is we buy the whiskey from you."

"Who's we?" Son asked.

"We. *Us*. The United States government."

"I didn't know the government was in the business."

"Not in the business. But there is such a thing as government spirits. Didn't you know that? For various reasons, like medicinal use, and so on." Dr. Taulbee leaned in close to the table, his eyebrows raising. "Now, somebody has to be making what the government approves and buys, would you agree to that?"

"Whiskey don't make itself," Son answered. "I'll agree that much."

"Fine." Dr. Taulbee grinned. "We're starting to get along, aren't we?"

"Who pays me for the whiskey?"

"The government does."

"How much?"

"A fair price. You tell us what you want and you submit it like a bid contract through Frank here's office. Of course there's one thing." Dr. Taulbee waited for Son to jump up and say what, but Son just looked at him and Dr. Taulbee had to continue. "You have to pay a government tax on what you've produced, otherwise it's illegal whiskey." Dr. Taulbee sipped his coffee and eyed

Son over the rim. "First though, of course, I'd have to taste the whiskey before issuing a stamp."

"Buy it," Son said, "you can taste all you want."

Dr. Taulbee sat back and laughed. "My goodness, do you think the government is dumb? They aren't going to buy anything unless I tell them it tastes good."

"Then they don't buy it," Son said.

Frank Long bit down on his cigar, hunching in, and said, "Jesus Christ, who do you think you are holding up, the goddamn United States government?"

Son shifted his gaze to Long. "Frank, if you want to buy it, give me the money and I'll tell you where it is and get out of your way. Otherwise you're just blowing smoke out your ears."

"All right," Dr. Taulbee said, "now let's discuss this like gentlemen. I believe we're getting somewhere and there's no need to get excited, is there? Son here has a product for sale and we're the customers. Right? Now like on any deal it's a matter of the two parties getting together. Maybe there's a little give and take, but finally it's worked out to everybody's mutual satisfaction. Miley, honey, you want to pour a little more? That coffee just hits the old spot, doesn't it, boys?"

Son glanced over at Miley. He wasn't sure if she was still looking at him, or looking at him again.

She said, "Who cooks for you?"

"I do," Son answered. "Or Aaron. Whoever wants to."

"You aren't married?"

"Miley"—Dr. Taulbee's tone was pleasant but loud—"I said we'd like some more coffee—"

She got up to go to the stove. "It isn't very good, is it?"

Son watched her move, too slowly for a young girl; she stood with her back to them.

And Dr. Taulbee was saying, "Supply and demand is the golden rule of commerce, boys. When somebody has something other people want, then by golly he gets paid for it. Son, how much do you want?"

"Twenty-seven thousand dollars."

Frank Long started laughing, forcing it and shaking his head. He said, "Now who do you think's going to pay you twenty-seven thousand dollars for a hundred and fifty barrels of moonshine?"

"If you're not, Frank, we can talk about foxhounds or the price of corn or you can get the hell out of here and I won't mention it again."

"Now, wait a minute," Dr. Taulbee said. "The man says that's his price. All right, you got to start somewhere in working out this supply and demand business." He waited while Miley poured the coffee, then stirred his thoughtfully, though there was no sugar or cream in the cup.

"I was just thinking," he said. "If the government can't pay your price—I mean if they believe it's too high and just won't budge on it—what would you say if I was to offer to buy it as a private citizen?"

Son placed his spoon in his saucer. "I'd say you were a boot-legger."

Dr. Taulbee laughed now, curling his mouth and showing his big teeth. "Whoeee, my goodness, if the folks in Frankfort heard you say something like that. What I mean, if I bought it as a spec-ulator, paid you for it, but kept it right where it's at, gambling on repeal coming about during the next year or so. If the country stays dry, I lose my shirt. But if the Eighteenth is repealed—and I'll admit I got a hunch it's going to be someday—I buy me some tax stamps and market the booze before the big distillers get going again. Even with repeal it's chancy; somebody could un-dersell me and I'd end up drinking it all myself." Dr. Taulbee grinned his finest grin. "But if it's all as good as you say it is, then having to drink it might not be so bad either. Son, what do you say?"

He said, "What does this Prohibition agent think about it?"

"Frank's a reasonable man. Aren't you, Frank? If you believe like I do that repeal's coming, then it would be wasteful to pour off a hundred and fifty barrels of good stuff, wouldn't it?"

Son watched Frank Long pretend to consider this and nod thoughtfully.

"I guess it would be a waste at that," Long said.

Now it was Son's turn to nod. "Well, then," he said solemnly, "if you feel that way, Frank, I guess I'll just keep the whiskey myself and wait on this repeal you all are talking about."

Neither Frank Long nor Dr. Taulbee was smiling. They sat quietly for a minute staring at Son Martin. For what it was worth

Long said, "You can't afford to speculate, Son, but he can. That's the difference. That's why I could permit him to keep the whiskey, but not you. I mean I wouldn't let you take the chance."

Son didn't bother to reply and Long, in the silence that followed, added nothing to the statement. Dr. Taulbee was the thoughtful one now and he was not pretending or stalling or getting ready to present a new proposal. He was accepting reality, resigning himself to the fact that Son Martin was not going to be talked out of his whiskey. It was going to take work; no doubt a pretty dirty kind of work.

Dr. Taulbee was glad to see Dual Meaders coming up the steps. There he was, the sweet boy, coming right when he was needed, marching in on cue, looking hot and tired and meaner than usual, which was all right with Dr. Taulbee. Yes, *sir*, when in doubt turn Dual loose, and the meaner he felt, the better. Dr. Taulbee got up from the table.

"Boy," he said mildly to Son, "I see you're going to make us work, which Frank claimed right along would happen. I'm not opposed to work, but I am a little disappointed in you, at your hard-headed stupidity, because we're going to get your whiskey and I think you must know that, whether we have to break your legs to get you to tell or put you under and find it ourselves."

Son shook his head. "If I don't tell, you won't find it."

"Just a minute, boy. I'm not finished my speech. We're going to let you have a few days to think about it and watch the trouble start to come down on you, then we're going to come back and ask you again in a nice way, 'Son, where's the whiskey at?' I'll bet you ten dollars right now you tell us. If you don't tell, you win the bet and I'll put the ten-spot in your pocket when we bury you."

Son waited a moment. "Is that the end of the speech?"

"All I'm going to say," Dr. Taulbee answered.

"Then I'll see you in a few days."

Son waited on the porch as they walked toward the car. He had better not say anything else. He had better hold on and, when they were gone, get up to the still and see if Aaron was all right. He was looking that way, toward the hillside and the faint trail of smoke above the roof, when Dr. Taulbee called to him.

"One more thing, Sonny."

Son looked over.

"Dual here showed you his gun, but he never showed you what he can do with it."

Son waited. Let him talk; don't say anything.

"See that barn yonder? See the two mules in the pen? Watch."

Dual drew his revolver, standing in front of the car with one foot on the bumper, a good thirty yards from the split-rail fence at the side of the barn. He didn't hesitate. He raised the .38 and fired and fired again and one of the mules jerked its head up and side-stepped and, as its knees buckled, fell heavily to the ground.

Dual looked over at Son on the porch, the revolver still in his hand. Dr. Taulbee looked over and waved good-bye.

Frank Long rested his arm on the top of the seat cushion and shifted around to look at Dr. Taulbee in the back seat.

"He'll tell once we get done with his neighbors."

Dr. Taulbee's head moved with the motion of the automobile and he seemed to be nodding. "It might work."

"I'll guarantee it. If you can get the men."

"All we'll need."

"I think about eight anyway. You can get eight?"

"Dual," Dr. Taulbee said, "call when we get back to the hotel."

Dual looked up at the mirror. "Then I'll go out to Caswell's and see they have a place to stay."

"You're way ahead of me, aren't you, boy?"

Dual smiled with his mouth closed, his eyes on the road. He didn't know what to say to that.

Miley sat close to the side window, staring at the fence posts and telephone poles and thickets and empty fields.

She said, "Why doesn't he just run?"

Dr. Taulbee's head drifted up and down. "Who?"

"If he knows he might get killed, why doesn't he just give you the whiskey? Or run away and forget it?"

"You sweet little thing," Dr. Taulbee said. "Because he's dumb."

"I can't understand that. He seems smart to me." Miley was silent, picturing him, seeing him smile as he raised his coffee cup. "How come he's not married?"

"His wife's dead."

"When did she die?"

"I don't know. A long time ago."

"He never got married again?"

Dr. Taulbee was looking out the window.

"I'd think some Marlett girl would have got him before this." Miley was silent again. He was nice looking and owned land. Why wouldn't he just get married and forget about the whiskey? She said, "What does he expect to get out of it?"

"Pain," Dr. Taulbee said, "if he thinks a minute. And anguish."

"I can't understand him—"

"Sweetie, don't worry your pretty head."

"Why he'd risk getting killed for nothing."

"Some people are funny," Dr. Taulbee said.

Miley was turned to him with a serious expression. "Why don't you buy it from him?"

"Because we don't have to."

"You offered to buy it at first."

"Sweet thing, if he didn't believe it, why do you?"

"I thought you meant it."

"We were trying to get him to tell," Dr. Taulbee said, "without trying too hard."

"Maybe he would sell it to you though."

"Except now we're not buying." Dr. Taulbee showed his teeth. "Sugartit, why don't you just sit back and enjoy the ride."

Miley sat back. It seemed like they were always driving somewhere, always in the car looking at the same wire fences and telephone poles and plowed fields, always the same run-down farmhouses and the same filling stations at the crossroads, the same MAIL POUCH and NEHI signs and the same skinny old men in overalls looking up as the car passed.

It was hot in the car. Miley rolled the window down as far as it would go. She didn't care if the wind blew her hair. She was going back to the Hotel Cumberland, Room 210, and if the doctor was in the mood he'd have her hair all messed up anyway in five minutes, his too, with his waves down on his forehead or sticking out on the sides. She'd smell his hair tonic and the breath sweetener he used, sweet little things like bird shot he was always popping in his mouth. He had clean habits, but, God, his stomach was a size and after he was through doing it—all the while whispering dirty little sweet things in her ear—he would rest on top of her for a couple of minutes, sprawled out like a giant seal lying on a rock. She had to wait till he stirred and finally rolled off before she could go into the bathroom. When she came out, he'd be lying on his back with his eyes closed and his mouth open, the round white mound of his belly rising and falling in peaceful sleep. Miley would put on a kimono and maybe read a magazine, waiting to see if he wanted to do it again when he woke up.

Sometimes she wished she was still working in the house. If there were no customers or, like in the afternoon when usually only one or two would come by, the girls would sit around talking and laughing or she and another girl would go shopping and have lunch out. It wasn't ever boring. It was usually fun, and interesting to meet new customers, to see a group sitting in the parlor and wonder which one was going to pick her first. It was nice to get a good-looking young one, though some of the old boys, like Dr. Taulbee, fooled you and had little tricks the young studs hadn't learned yet. She hadn't met any man who was so ugly that he repulsed her, and only once in a while did she get one who was smelly or whose breath was so bad it was hard to smile at him. The clientele was mostly a higher class, who could afford clean habits and ten dollars a trick.

Dr. Taulbee had got in touch with her after the house in Louisville was closed by the police. Dr. Taulbee had been a customer of hers for almost a year; she liked him and she appreciated him taking care of her now. He was generous and it was a pretty interesting and exciting life. Even the automobile trips to different places weren't too boring. The only thing that bothered her about the arrangement was the feeling, lately, that she was being wasted. God, Dr. Taulbee was the only man she had gone to bed with in the past five months. It seemed a shame with all the nice-looking fellows around. Dual Meaders didn't interest her—ugh, he'd be quick and serious and never say a word or crack a smile; get up, get dressed, and go. But she had been wondering, since meeting Frank Long and knowing he was in 205, what he would be like. And now she found herself picturing Son Martin taking his shirt off and looking at her and smiling. He probably wouldn't say much but—Miley made a little bet with herself—he would be something to experience.

Dual let them out in front of the hotel. Going up the steps, Dr. Taulbee gave her a little pat on the fanny and said, as if he had just thought of it, "Hey, honey, I know what let's do before dinner."

Miley smiled and Dr. Taulbee winked at her, running his arm around her waist.

"He didn't have to shoot the mule," Aaron said. "What would he want to shoot a mule for?"

"He likes to shoot his pistol," Son answered. He was harnessing the other mule. They'd drag the dead one out of the yard and bury it somewhere down in the hollow.

"I got a gun I like to shoot," Aaron said. "Next time I do it too."

Son shook his head. "No next time."

"He shoot a mule, the mule don't even know what the man want. I had him in front of me," Aaron said. "I could have shoot him for going in my house. I didn't know he was going to shoot no mule."

"Forget about him."

"He say he coming back, I don't forget about him."

Buckling the harness, Son paused. "He'll kill you if you're here. It's his business."

"I let him try."

"No, you go away for a while. You got family in Tennessee, haven't you? A sister? Visit her till this is over."

"I got two sisters and a old uncle. But I live here thirteen years."

"I know you have."

"Since the time you go in the Army and your daddy hire me to help him."

Son shook his head. "This has got nothing to do with you."

"They want the whiskey I help make."

"And if they think you know where it is, they'll ask you and break one of your legs and ask you again."

Aaron stared at him, his broad shoulders sloping and his arms hanging at his side. "You afraid I'd tell them?"

"I know you wouldn't," Son answered. "So they'd have to kill you."

"If they want to try," Aaron said. He brought over a coil of rope to tie around the dead mule. "That's all the talking about it I'm going to do."

# 7

Five days following Dr. Taulbee's visit, E. J. Royce drove up the hollow to tell Son about the raid on the Worthman place:

How the dirty son of a bitches in their suits come in the dead of night without any warning and took all the moonshine they could carry off and tore up the still with axes and shot Uncle Jim Bob Worthman through the neck when he came outside with a shotgun that wasn't even loaded.

Mr. Baylor had sent E.J. with word that Son was to get over there, since it was Son's good old army buddy, Frank Long, who led the raid and Virgil Worthman would swear to it in court. Son said to E. J. Royce, what court? And E.J. said, he just wants you over there probably because nobody knows what to do. Their still was gone, smashed to pieces, and Uncle Jim Bob, with a hole going in his neck and a big hole coming out, would probably never talk again, if he lived.

304

The Worthman place was less than two miles away in a straight line over the hills, but more than five miles through the hollows and around by road. On the way E. J. Royce told Son everything he knew about the raid, which wasn't much. Mr. Baylor had sent him over just a few minutes after they got there. Other people were arriving, E.J. said, hearing about it and coming out. By the time they got to the Worthman farm the yard looked like a family reunion was taking place. There were a dozen cars and trucks in the yard and along the dirt road, a bunch of children climbing on one of the trucks. The grownups, mostly men, were standing around and staring at E. J. Royce's official car as it drove up. The men nodded or seemed to as Son got out and nodded to them, but nobody said anything. They stood with their grim serious expression and those that were in the yard, by the porch, stepped back so Son could walk up to the house and go inside.

He saw Kay Lyons first, who had probably not been out here since she was a little girl. She was helping her aunt, Mrs. Worthman, put cups and spoons and more sugar on the table where Mr. Worthman and Virgil and Mr. Stamper and Mr. Blackwell sat with Mr. Baylor. These men looked up, but it was Bud Blackwell, over against the wall in a rocking chair, his high-top shoes stretched out in front of him, who said hello to Son.

He said, "Well, Son, your old buddy was here last night." Bud was relaxed and seemed pleased with himself.

Son wasn't going to bother with Bud Blackwell right now. He kept his eyes on Mr. Worthman, in his overalls and old suit coat and top button of his shirt buttoned, who had lived here half a century and had made whiskey a quarter of a century and never in his life had realized trouble because of it. Mr. Worthman, staring at his cup as he stirred it, looked as if someone in his family had just passed away. Virgil Worthman had a cold mean look on his face, clenching and unclenching his jaw, that may have been the way he felt or may have been for the benefit of his friend Bud Blackwell, Son wasn't sure which.

"I seen him in the light," Virgil said. "There was no doubt as to who it was. They were carrying these high-powered flashlights. One of them said something to Frank Long; said, 'Frank—' and put a light on him and that's when I seen his face, right there in the yard after Uncle Jim Bob had been shot. They didn't bother coming over to look at him. Well, I'll tell you, I'm going to look at Mr. Frank Long after I shoot him 'cause I'm going to make sure the son of a bitch is dead."

"Virgil," Mr. Baylor said, "kindly shut up and let your dad tell it. I want Son to hear this, and then I'll tell you what you're going to do and what you're not going to do."

Kay Lyons handed Son a cup of coffee. She came back with milk and poured it in herself, looking at Son's face as she lifted the pitcher away, but not saying a word or telling him anything with the look.

"We never did see their cars," Mr. Worthman said. "They left them down the road. We heard the cars when they drove away, after, but not when they come. Some of them walked up to the house and the others went over across the crik to the still, knowing where to find it. It was a little washtub outfit we had setting deep in the trees but these people went right to it."

"So somebody knowing where the still was led them to it," Mr. Baylor stated, and there was silence in the room.

"They'd never found it in the dark," Mr. Worthman said, "without knowing where it was at."

Mr. Baylor was hunched over the table, his gleaming steel frame glasses holding on Mr. Worthman. "You heard them over there, did you?"

"We heard them. We heard some shots and we run outside. We don't know these other people are in the yard till Uncle Jim Bob come out with the shotgun. As he appeared somebody fired from the darkness, and Uncle Jim Bob made a sound like he was gargling and fell to the porch. After they was gone, we went over to the still and seen how they'd put bullet holes in the cooker, then taken axes and chopped up everything, the mash barrels, everything."

Mr. Baylor said, "They took some stuff you'd run?"

"Most of it. They broke some jars too. Didn't pour it out so we could use the jars again, broke them."

"Before they left, what was it the one said to you?"

"We were on the porch tending to Uncle Jim Bob, this one calls out, 'Worthman, you listening?' I said, 'I hear you.'"

"Was it Frank Long's voice?"

"I don't know. I don't remember his voice any."

"What'd this voice say?"

"It said if I was to rebuild my still, they'd bust it again. They said they'd bust every still in this county if Son Martin didn't hand over his hunnert and fifty barrels."

Mr. Baylor waited, giving the silence time to settle. His steel frames gleamed as he looked from Mr. Worthman to Son and back again. "What'd you say to that?"

"I don't remember I said anything."

Stretched out in the rocking chair, Bud Blackwell said, "I'd a told the son of a bitch something."

Mr. Baylor turned on him, a skinny bird with its neck feathers ruffled. "Like you told Frank Long the other day on the street corner? I know all about how you told him," Mr. Baylor said. "If you're through telling then I'll tell you a few things."

Bud's dad, at the table across from Mr. Baylor, said, "Now wait a minute before you say too much." Mr. Blackwell had once been as smart-mouthed and sure of himself as Bud; he was an older, smaller version, now balding and wearing a Teddy Roosevelt mustache to make up for his bare expanse of forehead. "Long had a gun on Bud when he hit him."

"Is that right?" Mr. Baylor said. "Well, if you were there, then you saw your little sonny boy pull a bone-handle knife before he got his ears beat off."

"Who told you that?"

"Your other boy, Raymond. Now, if you're through, I'm going to tell you how things are."

"They aren't going to sneak up on us," Bud Blackwell said. "You wait and see when they try it on us."

Every once in a while Mr. Baylor remembered his blood pressure and his seventy-three-year-old heart and would make himself breathe slowly with his mouth closed. To fall dead while beating Bud Blackwell with a pick handle wouldn't be too bad; but to go out screaming at him and slobbering and popping all the veins in his face would leave the memory of a mess they had to clean up before they put him in a box.

Mr. Baylor said to Bud, "What happens if you shoot a federal Prohibition officer?"

"They bury the son of a bitch," Bud grinned. "If'n they find him."

Mr. Baylor had breathed slowly in and out enough that he was still in control, a kindly and wise old man. He said, "Bud, honey, that's true. But you know what else happens? Whether they find him or not, you got the whole United States government after you, because they know where that boy was going and who he was to see."

"A man comes at you with a gun," Mr. Blackwell said, "you by God better meet him with a gun."

"Is that a fact?" Mr. Baylor asked pleasantly. "Man to man. He shoots at you, you shoot at him."

"If the man wants to keep his still," Mr. Blackwell said, "and isn't ascared to defend it."

"Fighting for hearth and home." Mr. Baylor nodded thoughtfully. "That's a noble idea, but let me remind you of one thing. Stilling is against the law of this land, and if you're caught at it and resist, they got every right to shoot you full of holes. We have never had any federal people here before but, boys, we got them now. Aggravate them and they will stay till this county is wiped clean of stills."

"If I can't sell moonshine," Mr. Worthman said, "how'm I supposed to provide for my family and feed them babies playing in the yard?"

"How're you going to provide if you're dead?" Mr. Baylor asked him. "Or if they send you to Atlanta for five years? Listen, do you realize, as a county law officer I'm obliged to help these people?"

"Jesus," Bud Blackwell said, "with all the whiskey you drink?"

"I'm telling you what I'm supposed to do. I'm saying you got to quit stilling till they get tired of hunting and go home."

"They wasn't hunting when they come here," Mr. Worthman said. "They walked right to the still like they'd been to it before."

"That's another point," Mr. Baylor said. "If there's some person among us who's telling where the stills are, then it's all over, boys. You don't have a chance."

With his solemn expression Mr. Worthman said, "I can't believe a person would do that. Somebody around here who's bought whiskey from me. It would have to be somebody around here."

"That's the first thing we do," Virgil Worthman said, "find the one's helping them."

Mr. Baylor turned on him. "Do that, Virgil. Find him out of the hundred people you know by name who come here and the hundred you don't know. You never had any trouble before so you'd sell to anybody's got four dollars. Well, there's trouble now, boys, and you got no choice but to leave off stilling till they go home."

"Or move your stills."

Everybody in the room including the women by the stove, looked at Son Martin.

Arley Stamper, who had not spoken a wod through this meeting, sitting next to Mr. Baylor, said, "Move them where?"

"Hide them," Son answered. "Your still's been sitting in the same place for ten years, with ruts and beaten paths leading to it. Now it's time to move the whole outfit and keep moving it every week if you feel the need."

Arley Stamper nodded, but Mr. Blackwell wasn't taking on any heavy work today. He said, "Move it where? How far you talking about?"

"Move it anywhere you want and cover your tracks," Son answered, "and don't tell anybody where it is. I mean don't even tell anybody here. Arrange some other place for delivery that isn't anywhere near the still."

"That sounds like pure nigger work, don't it?" Bud Blackwell said. "All that lifting and carrying and moving. Is that what you're going to do, Son?"

"If I decide to keep running."

Bud Blackwell shook his head like he was tired already. He said, "Hey, Son, 'stead of us doing all this moving and hiding, why don't you give them the hunnert and fifty barrels? That's all they want, ain't it?"

Right now if he had that pick handle, Mr. Baylor decided—in this quiet room with everybody staring at Son Martin—he would swing it at Bud Blackwell until he died of a stroke and went straight to heaven and would never hear what Son answered or stay around to see the end of this dirty business. But he didn't have that pick handle.

And he heard Son Martin say, "Bud, you tend to your whiskey business and I'll tend to mine."

Mrs. Lyons had hardly said a word since she got back from the Worthman place about one o'clock in the afternoon. She stayed in the office going through some figures—what looked like the same page of the ledger for quite a while—and it was like pulling teeth for Lowell Holbrook to get any information out of her.

"Well, what do you think's going to happen?"

"I don't know, Lowell."

"You think they'll hide their stills?"

"I haven't any idea."

"I mean didn't they say if they were going to or not?"

Then she would be concentrating on the figures and he would have to ask her again. He had to ask her three times was Son Martin there and what did he think of the situation? Finally she said yes he was there, but she didn't mention anything he said. Mrs. Lyons was acting funny. It was natural she would be worried; the Worthmans were kin and Uncle Jim Bob was her great-uncle or some such relation. But besides being worried she seemed to be acting funny, like something else was on her mind that had nothing to do with the Worthmans, or at least had not been mentioned.

A little before two o'clock Frank Long and Dr. Taulbee and his wife came down the stairs and went into the dining room. Lowell noticed the time. A pretty late dinner today.

He hadn't noticed Frank Long leaving the hotel the night before. Which didn't mean anything: he could have been on a room-service call or Frank Long could have been out all day. One thing Lowell was certain of, Dr. Taulbee and his wife hadn't gone anywhere. He'd taken some Coca-Colas and ice up to 210 just before going off duty and they had looked pretty settled: the doctor sitting up in bed smoking a cigar, reading the newspaper and his young wife standing by the window with a green silk-looking robe on brushing her hair.

The thing Lowell wondered about now: if Frank Long had been on that raid like they said, had he taken that BAR rifle with him? Was it up there in 205 now? If it was, could a person look at it and tell if it had been fired?

Lowell watched the three of them come out of the dining room at twenty-five past two. It gave him a funny feeling, thinking about the BAR rifle and seeing Frank Long. He expected them to go back upstairs, but they stood there a minute talking. Then Dr. Taulbee's wife turned to walk away, and Dr. Taulbee gave her a little pat on the butt. Lowell and Dr. Taulbee and Frank Long all watched her walk up the stairs with her fanny moving from side to side. Then the two men turned and walked out the front door.

If you think about it, Lowell said to himself, you won't do it.

He wasn't sure why he wanted to, except it was a scary thing to do and it would, somehow, put him in the middle of the excitement that was going on. Lowell tried not to think any more about it than that. He got the passkey on the brass ring from behind the desk and went up to 205, right to the door, and opened it and, Jesus, there was the big suitcase laying on the bed.

You're here now and another minute won't make any difference, Lowell said to himself. Will it?

He didn't answer that yes or no; he went over to the suitcase and unbuckled it and opened it and there it was, the big heavy beauty of a gun, broken down and strapped in snug. Lowell lifted a two-ring binder out of the suitcase so he could get a better look at the weapon, then leaned in close and sniffed it, getting a strong smell of oil in his nostrils. The gun certainly didn't look like it had been taken out and fired. Lowell wished it was put together so he could lift it in his bare hands and feel the weight of it. He looked at the binder in his hand—nothing written on the blue cover—and dropped it in the suitcase; then picked it up again and opened it. There were a few typewritten pages he didn't bother to read but, when he got to the pictures, his interest picked up and he started reading the men's names and descriptions and records of arrests and convictions. He was starting to skip through, just glancing at the pictures now, when he saw Dr. Taulbee's face looking up at him, grinning at him with those big white teeth.

Lord in heaven, Lowell said to himself, and started to read about Dr. Taulbee.

Frank Long turned at the Baptist Church and shifted into second gear as they started up the grade. Ahead, on the left side, he could see the stand of cedars and part of the small farmhouse showing. Frank waited until the car was almost to the front yard.

"That's where the woman from the hotel lives. Mrs. Lyons."

Next to Long, Dr. Taulbee turned enough to get a brief look at the house through the rear side window. "*Mrs.* Lyons, uh?"

"She's not married anymore."

"Well, now, maybe I should be nicer to her."

Long glanced over at him. "What would you do with two women?"

"The same thing I do with one."

"I mean you got Miley along. Isn't she enough for you?"

"If you mean by enough, all you want," Dr. Taulbee said, "little Miley can dish it up. But she is one woman and Mrs. Lyons is another and, mister, they are all different. Each one has her own little pleasures and secret tender places. Each one is potentially the best one you ever had."

"There's the Caswell place up on the right."

Dr. Taulbee was looking at Frank Long. "You wouldn't mind a little bit of Miley, would you?"

"She's a good-looking girl."

"Well, Frank, maybe when I'm through with her. How'd that be?"

Long had a tight grip on the curved top of the steering wheel. Past the ridge of his knuckles he was looking at the farmhouse: at the vines climbing its walls, at the yard grown over with weeds and brush, and the sagging barn that was missing boards and part of its roof.

"I was saying—there's Caswell's."

Dr. Taulbee studied the place. "They ain't much for farming, are they?"

"Not a blind man and anybody drinks as much as Boyd does."

"You tell me," Dr. Taulbee said, "because little Dual could be wrong about Boyd Caswell. Dual thinks anybody was at Eddyville is a first-class citizen."

"Boyd took us to Worthman's still last night," Long said. "I guess he's been there enough times he can find it drunk or sober."

Dr. Taulbee propped one hand against the dashboard as they turned into the yard. "Well, he's in it now, isn't he?"

"The cars are in the barn if you're wondering." Long drove past the side of the house and pulled up in back as Dual Meaders came out the screen door in his shirtsleeves and shoulder holster, his hands deep in his pants pockets.

"Bless his heart." Dr. Taulbee grinned and yelled out, "Hey, boy!"

Dual came over to the car and pulled a hand out of his pocket to open Dr. Taulbee's door, giving him his slight, closemouthed smile. "We're all in there waitin' on you," he said.

The old man at the kitchen table looked up with sightless eyes, with milk and wet crumbs in the thin stubble of his beard. He held a piece of corn bread soaking in a bowl of Pet Milk, the tips of his fingers in the milk covering the bread, as if hiding it from whoever was coming in the screen door.

Across the table Boyd Caswell's head raised with closed eyes that opened halfway, bleary, before his chin dropped to his chest again, as if he were staring down the front of his overalls. A quart jar of moonshine, almost empty, was on the table in front of him.

Dual's eyes shifted to Dr. Taulbee. "You recognize Boyd now you see him?"

"I sure do," Dr. Taulbee answered. "Though I'd forgot what a beauty he is."

"Boyd's resting after a hard night," Dual said. "This here is his daddy." Dual stared at the old man for a moment. "Daddy, you're losing all your pone in your milk. You ought to have Boyd fetch you a spoon."

The twelve men Dual had sent for were in the front room, sitting and standing around, some of them smoking cigarettes, patient and solemn, waiting expectantly, until Dr. Taulbee stepped in flashing his friendly smile, raising a hand in greeting and saying, "Well, looky at all the good old boys are here. Boys, I heard you done it last night like genuine federal Prohibition revenue agents, yes, *sir.*" Dr. Taulbee knew most of them and went around shaking hands and slapping shoulders and saying god-*damn*, you all are going to enjoy your trip, I guarantee, with fun and prizes for everybody. Dr. Taulbee loosened them up and told them to make themselves at home, while Frank Long unrolled his map of Broke-Leg County and thumb-tacked it to the wall.

Long stood by the map waiting for everybody to settle down and look his way. He recognized half the men in the room; he had pictures of them in his binder. They were stick-up and strong-arm men and ex-convicts, now in the bootleg whiskey business. Every man here was armed; two of them had brought Thompson machine guns. Frank Long was not afraid of any of them individually. But the dozen of them and Dual Meaders and Dr. Taulbee, all staring at him now, made him aware of himself standing in front of them, not part of them but with them, and he wanted to get this over with and get out as quick as he could.

He pointed out Marlett and traced the highway line east into the hills, to the spur roads that led to the areas he had circled and marked with a capital letter to indicate Worthman, Stamper, Blackwell, and Martin. He drew a line through the W and then pointed to the S for Stamper. That was the next place they'd hit, tomorrow night, unless Son Martin contacted him before then. Next, if Son didn't move, they'd hit the Blackwell place. That should do it, Long told them. By then there'd be enough pressure on Son he'd have to give up his whiskey.

They stared at the map for a while, until one of them said, "It seems to me a long way round the mountain. Introduce me to this Son Martin, I'll make him tell anything you want to know."

Dual Meaders said, "Jesus, yes. You shoot him in the knee, he'll tell."

Another man said, "What you do, you take his pants down and hold a razor over his business. I mean to tell you, you can learn anything you want."

Everybody thought that was pretty good. Dr. Taulbee made a face, an expression of awful pain, and seemed to be saying, "Whooooo."

"They's some good ways," the first man said. "I like to slip on this leather glove and punch 'em around a little first, have some fun."

Frank Long waited while they laughed and talked among themselves, offering sure-fire ways of getting a man to talk. Finally, when there was a lull, he said, "We're going to hit his neighbors. We get to the man through his neighbors. That's the way I want it and that's the way it's going to be. You're playing you're federal agents and for a while these hillbillies are going to believe it; but once you start torturing people or killing without any reason, that old man sheriff or the newspaper or *some*body is going to get on the phone to Frankfort and that'll be all for the fun and prizes."

Dr. Taulbee was grinning as he rolled a cigar in the corner of his mouth, wetting it before he bit off the tip. "Frank," he said across the room, "don't worry about it, all right? They just having a little sport with you, boy, that's all."

"I want it understood what we're doing."

"We're with you, boy, don't worry."

"They're supposed to act like federal U.S. officers."

"They will."

"If Frankfort hears and wants to know who they are, I say they're deputies hired by the sheriff."

"That's good thinking, Frank."

"But they make this a shoot-up with them goddamn Thompsons, we're done."

"I believe it, Frank," Dr. Taulbee said. "That's why we're doing it your way."

"No shooting unless the stiller shoots at us first."

"Right."

"No shooting at the stiller's house, where you're liable to hit one of his family."

"No, sir, we don't want any of that." Dr. Taulbee waited, then lighted his cigar and went up to Frank Long and took him by the arm, saying, "Come on, Frank, I'll walk you out to your car."

In the kitchen Boyd Caswell was still sleeping, snoring now, but the old man was gone. Outside they saw him walking toward the privy, his withered face raised to the sun.

"It's a terrible thing to be old and poor," Dr. Taulbee said thoughtfully, blowing out a thin stream of cigar smoke. "But Frank"—turning to Long now—"we ain't ever going to become a pathetic creature like that, are we?"

"I don't aim to."

"No, sir, not if we can get that load and sell it at five dollars a fifth. What'd we say that was? A hundred and twenty-two thousand five hundred dollars. A third for you and a third for me and a third for labor and bottles. Forty thousand dollars each. Which is no bad start on keeping out of the poorhouse, is it?"

"If we can pull it."

"If we can pull it?" Dr. Taulbee seemed amazed. "What's this pulling we got to do? Frank, all we need is to trust each other and lead a clean life and we shall get our reward." Dr. Taulbee let his grin form and gave Long a shove. "Now go on, get out of here, and see if Son's been looking for you."

Dual Meaders came out to stand next to Dr. Taulbee as Long turned around and drove out of the yard.

His gaze following the car, Dr. Taulbee said, "We're going to have trouble with that boy."

"How come?" asked Dual.

"He's starting to eat his own insides."

"He is?"

"He's getting nervous. He's starting to make rules. We don't need any of that."

"I don't see we need any of *him*," Dual said.

Dr. Taulbee seemed pleasantly surprised as he looked at Dual. "God*darn*," he said. "Isn't that something, both of us thinking the very same thing."

# 8

Arley Stamper's place was raided the evening of June 18, 1931. Arley said later it was right at dusk. He saw the cars coming up his road and the first thing he did, he got his children and his old woman down on the floor and cocked his Winchester. The cars didn't show any headlights, they came sneaking in black against the trees. But how could they have sneaked past his oldest boy who'd been down by the gravel road to watch and was to give the signal? The signal being three shots. Three shots and you'd know there was hell in the air. But there were the cars driving into the yard. The men got out and they had his oldest boy with them, walking him to the house on his tiptoes with his arm bent behind his back. They had seen him and drew down on him before he could give the signal. There was nothing to do then but drop the Winchester and put your hands in the air, Arley Stamper said.

Yes, he had recognized Frank Long. The others he had never

seen around here before and swore he had never sold any of them moonshine. He'd of recognized their clothes. One of them was dressed in overalls, but his hat was pulled down over his eyes and he wore a neckerchief over his nose and mouth like a bank robber. This one led them off to where the still used to be, off where the yard path went into the thicket.

Where it used to be, Arley said, because he'd moved the still. When they came back they acted sore and Frank Long asked him where the still was now. Arley Stamper said, what still? Then one of them, a big man, the one holding his boy and wearing one leather glove on his right hand, turned his boy around and hit him as hard as he could in the face. Frank Long said, don't you know what still I'm talking about? The one you moved. Arley Stamper said, oh, that still; and took them to it. They stood back and one boy used a tommy gun to shoot the outfit apart so it could never be repaired. It was something to hear that gun go off, but it was an awful sight what it did to the still and the mash barrels.

No, they didn't arrest Arley—like they hadn't arrested any of the Worthmans, which was a strange thing. No, Arley said, they went on up the holler and he figured they were going to his brother Lee Roy's place.

Mr. Baylor found Lee Roy Stamper at the doctor's house in Marlett, Lee Roy clenching his teeth while the doctor closed the gash in his right arm with seventeen catgut stitches. Lee Roy said he'd put his arm through a window trying to get the son of a bitch open. But outside the doctor's house, Lee Roy admitted that wasn't the way it happened at all.

He had heard the gunfire down at Arley's and knew they would be up to his place next; so he and his wife Mary Lou's brother, R. D. Bowers, grabbed a shotgun and a high-powered rifle and got over to the still, which he'd located in a gully section they had dug out and covered over with brush and vines. These federal boys had to come across a pasture field to reach them, Lee Roy said, so he and R. D. Bowers figured they would let go with warning shots to let these fellows know if they fooled around with Lee Roy Stamper they'd get their moldboards cleaned. Well, they let go, firing three shots over their heads and, God Almighty, it was like opening the door on a furnace, the fire that came back at them—bullets sniping through the brush leaves and clanging into the copper still, blowing up the mash barrels and the flake stand. When they dove for cover, Lee Roy said, he landed in a mess of broken glass and was laying there bleeding when the federal boys appeared on the edge of the gully pointing their guns at them. One of them said, well, according to the rules we can shoot these two, they fired on us. But another one, who sounded like he was in charge, told him to get a car over here and start loading moonshine. No, Lee Roy wasn't sure if it was Frank Long. No, he hadn't seen anybody with a neckerchief over his face that looked like a bank robber. Hell, the whole bunch of them looked like bank robbers. His brother-in-law, R. D. Bowers, got scratched up some and found a big wood sliver in his hip that was so deep it was like it had been shot into him. R.D. didn't say a word; he went home and nobody had talked to him since.

That Friday, June 19, Lowell Holbrook spent the morning looking for Mr. Baylor. He wasn't at his office in the courthouse; nobody was except the girl on the switchboard. He wasn't at his house. He wasn't anywhere having coffee. When Lowell went back to the courthouse just before noon, E. J. Royce was on the telephone. Lowell waited, trying to decide whether or not he should tell Mr. Royce what he'd learned about the friend of Frank Long's staying at the hotel, this Dr. Taulbee. E. J. Royce hung up and reached for his hat. Lowell asked him if Mr. Baylor was around. No, he was out on official business. Lowell asked him if he had a minute to listen to something that might be important, or at least seemed awful strange, this man who was supposed to be a doctor but had been to the state penitentiary. E. J. Royce said he would have to tell him some other time. There had been a bad accident out on the highway.

God no, it was no accident, Bob Cronin said. It's no accident when they shoot off your back tires and you go in the ditch and almost kill yourself.

When E. J. Royce got to the scene, there were cars parked along the shoulder of the road and people looking at the platform Feed & Seed truck that was tilted over and wedged against the inside bank of the drainage ditch.

Bob Cronin, age seventeen, employed by Marlett Feed & Seed,

had gone out about eleven with a load of deliveries to make east of town. He was carrying rolls of bob wire, he said, and hundred-pound bags of clover seed—what was left of them. God, look at the mess to clean up.

Driving along he had seen this car up ahead parked to the left side pointing toward town. Passing the car he had slowed up to see if it was anybody he knew, but it was three men he had never seen before, in suits. One of them was out behind the car like he was taking a leak. As Bob Cronin drove by, this one shouted something at him. Bob said he thought the man was yelling hi or making some funny remark; so Bob had waved his arm out the window and kept going. Well, actually he had given the fellow a sign out the window with his middle finger, but not meaning anything really insulting by it. The next thing he knew the car was coming up fast behind him and a fellow was leaning out the window firing a pistol at him. Bob had thought, oh my God, they must be highway patrolmen, and right away put on the brakes and started to shift down his gears. They came right up behind him, still firing and the next thing he knew he was in the ditch. When he got out, he was so scared he didn't say a word. The three of them were out of the car and one was holding a Thompson machine gun. Not him, but a littler one with a tan suit said, where are you taking that corn meal? To whose still? Bob Cronin told them it wasn't corn, it was clover seed. The one in the tan suit didn't say anything for a minute. Bob Cronin said he just looked at him, not blinking or moving a muscle in his face. A horsefly buzzed past his face and circled him and buzzed around his hair, but he still didn't move. Then he took the machine gun from the other one and fired it from ten feet away into the hundred-pound sacks, ripping them to shreds and blowing seed all over the truck and the highway. Then he picked up a handful of it and said, yeah, it's clover seed all right. That was all he said, yeah, it's clover seed. They got in the car and U-turned and headed for Marlett. Bob Cronin said he heard the highway patrol had tough boys, but God, he didn't know they were that tough. One thing though, they hadn't given him a ticket.

Saturday, June 20, was the longest day of Mr. Baylor's seventy-three-year-old life. It was Cow Day and it seemed like half the people in the county were in town to buy a raffle ticket, then walk around figuring how to stretch four bits or a dollar bill along five blocks of store windows.

He hoped no boys were caught swiping candy or combs over at Kress's. He hoped Boyd Caswell stayed home and didn't weave down the street looking to pick a fight. He almost wished he might start coughing and spitting and have to go home for his wife to rub his chest with Mentholatum and stay in bed a few days. Mr. Baylor had on his desk the unofficial eyewitness accounts as told by Mr. Henry Worthman, Arley Stamper, Lee Roy Stamper, his brother-in-law R. D. Bowers, and young Bob Cronin, and he'd be a son of a bitch if he knew what he was going to do about them. Only Bob Cronin seemed within the law. (Marlett Feed & Seed wanted to know who these officers were, so they could claim damages, taking it to Frankfort if they had to.) The rest of them were moonshiners and, by law, deserved to be raided and prosecuted. He had warned them, told them to cease operating. If they didn't, then it was their funeral. That was the trouble, it was going to be somebody's funeral before it was through.

There wasn't any mention of the raids in the *Marlett Tribune*. Because it was a weekly and they'd gone to press yesterday. But next week the accounts would be on the front page and Mr. Baylor's phone would ring all day Saturday and they'd be lined up out in the hall: newspaper people from other towns; friends wanting to know was anybody hurt; friends wanting to know where they were supposed to buy it now; temperance ladies saying it was about time somebody did something.

You've got a week before the dam breaks, Mr. Baylor told himself. Rest your mind.

Two o'clock that afternoon the editor-publisher of the *Marlett Tribune* came over for the facts. Mr. Baylor let him read the as-told-by eyewitness accounts.

At two-thirty a man from the Corbin newspaper called the office.

At ten to three the manager of the Kress store called; he had this boy in his office caught stealing a black leather wrist band and a dollar-ninety-five key case, a good one.

At three-twenty a man named McClendon, who had bought a

farm east of town just a year ago, came in dirty and worn-out, his face bruised and swollen, to tell how Prohibition agents had burned his barn to the ground.

It had happened early in the morning before sunup. He hadn't heard the cars drive up, hadn't seen them till these men broke his door down and dragged him outside and started asking him where his still was.

Mr. Baylor knew McClendon had never operated a still, though he had been on a couple of Saturday night moonshine parties, including the one two weeks ago at Son Martin's place. So he asked McClendon if he had recognized Frank Long. No; and he hadn't noticed a man with a neckerchief over his face either. They kept asking him where the still was; then one of them, with a glove on, started hitting him. They asked him if he had any moonshine. He told them part of a half-gallon jar out in the barn, but that was all. They laughed when he said that, and one of them said, that's where Caz said he's supposed to keep it, in the barn.

They looked all through the barn and when they didn't find more than the half jar, this little fellow lit a cigarette and threw the match in the hay. When they were sure it was caught good, they took McClendon outside to watch his barn burn down, his wife and children watching from the house. While they were standing there, the little fellow said, next time we come, Mr. Blackwell, we want to see your still. The man said to them, Blackwell? My name isn't Blackwell, it's McClendon. The Blackwells live three miles from here. The little fellow shook his head and said, no wonder he didn't have any shine in his barn.

Mr. Baylor was pretty tired by now. He told the man to keep quiet about what happened; because if they wanted to, they could send him to Atlanta on the strength of his having that half jar. It's a shame, Mr. Baylor told him, but, Jesus, don't go writing to your congressman about it, get busy on a new barn.

When McClendon had gone Mr. Baylor took his glasses off and rubbed his eyes, seeing little white spots floating around in the dark. He'd pull the shade and try to take a nap for ten or fifteen minutes.

At quarter to five the phone woke him up. Lowell Holbrook, calling from the hotel, said Bud Blackwell had shot and killed a man out in the street not five minutes ago.

\* \* \*

322

Bud Blackwell and Virgil Worthman came to town that Saturday afternoon with loaded .38s and twenty-four jars of moonshine. They parked the pickup truck back of Marlett Feed & Seed where the farmers would drive in to load their supplies. By four o'clock Bud and Virgil had sold out their stock and drunk a quart of the stuff between them.

Virgil had gone to get something to eat, but Bud was still back of the store when Mr. McClendon came out and started loading building supplies into his truck. Bud asked him if he was going into the contracting business. Mr. McClendon told him no, but he would be willing to build the Blackwells a new barn for a good price. Bud said they didn't need a new barn and Mr. McClendon said not to be too sure if he had not been home all day. After Mr. McClendon told him about the men coming and thinking it was the Blackwell place, Bud began to curse and swear that if he saw any of them he would teach them to fool around with a Blackwell. Well, Mr. McClendon said, he thought he saw one of them over in front of the hotel as he came by. Mr. McClendon followed Bud through the feed store out to the street. They walked down to a cafe where Bud went in and got Virgil Worthman; then they walked on toward the hotel where, from across the street, Mr. McClendon pointed out the car parked in front and the man sitting behind the wheel. The man was one of them who'd burned down his barn, Mr. McClendon said.

Lowell Holbrook told Mr. Baylor about the shooting, as he had seen the whole thing from the front door of the hotel.

About a half hour before, two men had come into the lobby: the one who was about to be shot and another one, whom Lowell had seen before, a short guy in a suit that was too big for him. The short guy went up the stairs to the second floor, probably to see Frank Long. The other one waited in the lobby for about fifteen minutes, then went outside and got in the car. He was sitting there when Bud Blackwell and Virgil Worthman came across the street and walked up to the car.

Lowell didn't hear what was said. Bud Blackwell was close to the car door, between this car and the one angle-parked next to it. Virgil stood back aways, almost in the street, with his hands in his pockets. Bud Blackwell seemed to be doing the talking. When he turned from the door Virgil Worthman walked on across the street. Bud was following him, but when he got into the middle of the street—there was no traffic at that moment—he turned to the car again and yelled something. The car door came open and the man started to get out, reaching into his coat with his right hand. That was when Bud Blackwell shot him, as the man was half out of the car. Bud fired three or four times and then ran across the street. Lowell didn't see where he went. The next moment there were cars in the street and people out on the sidewalk wanting to know what had happened and some of them pointing toward the car. The short guy came out of the hotel right past Lowell Holbrook. He stuck his head in the car, leaning over the man who'd been shot, then pushed him over and got in behind the wheel and drove away.

Mr. Baylor went into the hotel to call the doctor. The doctor said no one had been brought in with a gunshot wound, but he would let Mr. Baylor know if they did. Mr. Baylor told Lowell Holbrook not to talk about the incident until he made an official statement. Then Mr. Baylor went home; he sat down in his easy chair with the crocheted doilies on the arms and drank four ounces of Son Martin whiskey while his wife fixed him a nice supper.

He didn't want to have to go out to the Blackwells.

He didn't want to have to talk to Frank Long.

He wanted to go to bed.

His wife told him he looked like he was coming down with something. If he didn't rest it would knock him flat and he wouldn't be any good to anybody. So Mr. Baylor didn't go out to Blackwell's or look for Frank Long. It was too late this evening and tomorrow was a Day of Rest. He'd do it Monday.

Sunday afternoon, June 21, a delegation of neighbors and moonshiners came out to talk to Son Martin.

They all arrived at the same time, two old cars and two pickup trucks nosing cautiously up out of the hollow and rolling into the yard, careful of the foxhounds dodging in front of the wheels. The men got out of the cars—wearing their Sunday overalls and coats and shirts buttoned at the neck—and assembled in a straggling group, looking toward the house but holding back. None of them seemed in a hurry to walk up to the porch or get a step ahead of the others.

Son counted fourteen men; no women or children present, men and grown boys: Worthmans and Stampers and their kin, Mr. McClendon and some other people Son didn't know very well. Virgil Worthman was next to his dad. No Blackwells though— thank God for small favors. Son moved to the kitchen table and replaced his pistol in the drawer. Aaron had leaned the 12-gauge against the wall by the stove. He said, "You have more company in a week your daddy had in ten years."

When Son walked out on the porch they nodded to him and Mr. Worthman explained they had stopped by on their way home from church service.

"Now just the men go?" Son asked him.

No, they'd had a meeting after the service and these here fellows had agreed to come out and speak with him.

Son waited.

"We understand you're still making whiskey," Mr. Worthman said.

"Some."

"Then they haven't closed you down."

"Not yet."

"Well, they've closed the rest of us down; all but the Blackwells and we understand they're next."

"I'm sorry to hear it."

Virgil Worthman said, "You don't look sorry to me. You look like a man that don't care what happens to his neighbors."

Son didn't pay any attention to Virgil. He said to Mr. Worthman, "If there's something I can do, to get you started again, I'll be glad to help."

"There's only one thing you can do for us," Mr. Worthman said, "You know what that is."

"Give them my whiskey."

"The hundred and fifty barrels. It's the only way they'll leave us alone."

"It's that easy, uh?"

"I'm not saying it's easy. I'm saying how it is. If we build new stills they'll bust them again."

"Then hide the stills."

"Now you're making it sound easy," Mr. Worthman said. "Like if they don't find anything they'll go away. These federal people mean business. They aren't going till they get what they want."

"You think they're federal people?"

"They say they are."

"I say I was, would that make me one?"

Virgil Worthman was squinting up at him. "Who do you say they are, they're not federal?"

"Bootleggers," Son answered. "Gangsters hired to do a job on us."

"Your friend too?"

"I don't know about Frank Long, if he's real or not."

"Say it's true," Mr. Worthman said. "What do you do about it, call the law for help?"

"All right, if you were standing over here," Son asked, "what would you do? If you banked your future on that whiskey—knowing you could sell it for enough to buy good land or a business somewhere—what would you do?"

Mr. McClendon spoke up. "I'd look to see what it was doing to my neighbors," he said, "to people aren't even making moonshine but are suffering because of it."

"Everybody is certainly ready with advice," Son said. "Come on, Mr. Worthman, what would you do?"

"I'd give them the whiskey, Son."

"Mr. Stamper, what would you do?"

"I've seen them," Arley Stamper said. "I tend to agree with you thinking they're bootleggers."

"You'd give it to them."

"Yes, I would."

"Well, I'm not going to," Son told them. "They can try and take it, but I'm not *giving* it. You can come to me like it's all my fault, I'm still not going to give it to them. You want my advice—if I was standing where you are—I'd decide if I wanted to run a whiskey still or not run it and then I'd do one or the other. But, Jesus, I wouldn't go crying to anybody about it."

They stared up at him solemnly. Arley Stamper turned and walked through the group and the others began to follow him, walking over to the cars and pickup trucks.

"Son," Mr. Worthman said, "you don't have a family. That's the difference."

Son went into the house. He stood at the screen door until the cars were out of the yard and he could hear the hounds chasing them down the road.

"You didn't have to talk to them that way," Aaron said.

The yard was still, dust hanging in the sunlight. "What would you do?" Son asked him.

"I don't know," Aaron answered. "But I wouldn't have talked to them that way. They your friends."

Son turned away from the door. "We'll see," was all he said.

The doctor called Mr. Baylor early Sunday morning: a man with a gunshot wound had been brought to him late last night. The bullet had entered his side beneath his left arm, smashed a rib and tore a hole in his back coming out. If the man went to bed and didn't move, he would probably be all right. But the one who'd brought him in said, wrap him up good, Doc, because he's going to Louisville tonight. The doctor said the man couldn't be moved, but this little fellow insisted his friend wanted to go to Louisville to see his own doctor. Mr. Baylor asked him if he had the man's name and address. The doctor said yes, but he believed it wasn't his right name. No, neither of them said they were federal agents.

The editor-publisher of the *Marlett Tribune* called up later to find out what was this about a shooting in front of the hotel? Who had been shot? Was it true Bud Blackwell had done it? Mr. Baylor said he had not finished questioning people and for the editor-publisher to hold his horses and call him tomorrow or the next day.

You can't hide or run away, Mr. Baylor told his wife, and started to put his pants on. But his wife pushed him back in the bed and said she would have his son and grandsons come over and tie him to the bed if she had to. Mr. Baylor said well, he wouldn't mind seeing his grandsons—weren't those boys the captains though?

Monday morning Mr. Baylor slept in till seven-thirty, then got dressed and ate a good breakfast. He'd had all day yesterday and last night to decide what he was going to do. The first thing would be to see Frank Long and ask him some questions about these federal agents he had working for him. What district were they from? Where were they staying? How come they didn't arrest anybody? What happened to the man who'd been shot? If

Frank Long's answers sounded fishy, then by God he'd call Frankfort and find out what the hell was going on.

Before Mr. Baylor left the house E. J. Royce called him. They'd just got word the Blackwell place had been raided during the night. Mr. Baylor swore and told E.J. to pick him up. They'd better get out there.

# 9

Monday morning Dr. Taulbee and Dual Meaders were out in the Caswell barn looking over the whiskey that had been taken in the raids: mostly quart and half-gallon fruit jars and a few gallon jugs of moonshine with Coca-Cola labels.

"Not too bad for the work put in," Dr. Taulbee said. "What'd you get last night?"

"Just the few cases there," Dual answered. "They came shooting, we had to get out of there."

Dr. Taulbee frowned. "They drove you off?"

"Like they was waiting for us. We got to the still and commenced to smash it, and they let go from the bushes."

"Wasn't anybody hit?"

"Well, one boy was. I don't think too bad."

"What about the one Saturday?"

"Somebody's driving him to Louisville and is coming back with more men, like we talked about."

"Is he going to make it, the one was shot?"

"I don't know. But we'll have these others anyway."

"Maybe you should go back to this Blackwell place tonight. Finish the job."

"I was thinking that," Dual said. "Or start on Son Martin and quit wasting our time."

"You think you can bust him?"

"We go over there again I'll take care of him. Both of them."

"Both of who?"

"Him and his nigger."

"Do you think the nigger knows where the stuff's at?"

"That's what I'm going to find out next trip over there."

"It does seem like we're wasting some time," Dr. Taulbee said. He turned as the door opened and sunlight came into the dim enclosure. Frank Long stood in the doorway.

Dr. Taulbee said, "Hey, Frank, how you doing, boy?"

"We got something to talk about," Long said.

"Well, fine." Dr. Taulbee moved toward him. "Speak up, don't be bashful."

"I want to talk to you alone."

"We're alone. It's only Dual here with us."

"He's what I want to talk about mainly."

"Then he should hear it, shouldn't he?"

"I'll say it to his face if you want," Long said. "He's messing up this deal, him and his gunmen."

"Frank, you said you wanted guns."

"I said it had to be done my way or the whole thing will come down on us. All right, they shot up a feed truck. They burned down a man's barn wasn't even a stiller. They have a gunfight on the main street on Saturday afternoon—"

"You don't care for this business," Dual said, "what're you in it for?"

"Frank, when boys are carrying guns there's the chance they're going to go off," Dr. Taulbee said, like explaining it to a small child. "We know there's the chance somebody might get hurt, right?"

"And that somebody might get caught," Long said, "and start talking."

"Frank, we got that boy out of here was shot Saturday. He's home in bed."

"And the one last night," Long said. "Is he home in bed?"

"There's something I haven't heard about? Which one is that?"

"Boyd Caswell," Long said. "Have you seen him around here this morning?"

"Dual"—Dr. Taulbee turned to him—"what's he talking about?"

"You asked me was anybody hit, I said yes."

"What's he talking about!"

"Boyd Caswell got shot last night."

"Where is he now?"

"I'm not sure exactly—"

"You left him there? Jesus, of all the people you leave Caswell?"

"I didn't know at the time." Dual was frowning; he'd never heard Dr. Taulbee speak loud to him before. "We got out of there once we seen they had position on us. I guess it wasn't till we was back we noticed Boyd wasn't along."

"You left him!"

"We didn't *leave* him. It was just he didn't come back with us."

Dr. Taulbee stared at Dual. Then he put his hands in his pants pockets and walked deeper into the dimness of the barn. He turned around and came back and said, with only a slight tight edge in his tone now, "Dual, you're going to have to go out and get that boy."

"He might be dead, all we know."

"Yes, he might be," Dr. Taulbee said. "Or, he might be sitting up in bed telling them we're not federal agents at all, but just some old boys from Louisville."

"Well, what could they do about that?"

"They could tell the sheriff. They could do that, couldn't they?"

"I guess."

"Then the sheriff, he could pick up the telephone and call the state capitol. Couldn't he do that?"

Dual nodded slowly, thinking about it. "I guess he could. Listen, I better get a couple of cars and go back out there."

Dr. Taulbee was his old self again, swatting Dual on the shoulder as he started past him. "Hey, Dual, now you're talking. Go get him, boy."

The old man, Mr. Caswell, was standing in the yard facing the barn. As they came out, his head raised to them, following their sound.

"Boyd?"

Dr. Taulbee and Dual walked past Mr. Caswell; they didn't seem to notice him.

"Boyd, is that you?"

Frank Long hung back. He hesitated, then took the old man by the arm and walked him toward the house.

"I haven't seen Boyd all morning," the old man said. "The lazy som-bitch is supposed to give me my breakfast."

"Come on, we'll get you something. Nice dish of pone and milk."

"Lazy som-bitch, he's dead drunk, ain't he?"

"He's all right," Long said. "They're gone to fetch him."

"See, we knew they were coming," Mr. Blackwell explained, "because of what they done over at McClendon's Friday night."

Mr. Baylor and E. J. Royce followed Mr. Blackwell out to the still, located in a limestone cave, and back to the yard while he described how they had beat off the revenuers. You bet they were ready for them. Right after supper the women and small children had been sent over to Raymond's place to be out of the way. They cleared the house, set Bud out by the road as a lookout, while the rest of them—Mr. Blackwell's three younger sons, his three brothers, and an uncle who'd come over to help out—hid in the rocks by the cave. Along came Bud soon after dark to say the revenuers were turning up the road. Well, they waited and fired everything they had and chased them through the pines and back to their cars, then fired at the cars until they were out of sight down the road. Probably some of them had been shot; though there was only one they had been sure of hitting, because they had him and he was bleeding all over the ground back of the house.

Boyd Caswell was lying in the shade of a beech tree, a neckerchief loose around his neck and the front of his shirt and overalls stained with blood. He was the one who'd been leading them to the stills, Boyd Caswell, who'd probably drunk more of their whiskey than any man in the country. Well, he wasn't going to be drinking anymore.

Mr. Baylor said to E. J. Royce, "Bring the car up here." When Mr. Blackwell asked him what he planned to do, Mr. Baylor said, "Take the man to the doctor, what in hell you think I'm going to do?"

Bud Blackwell said, "Hey, now wait a second. We pumped five rounds in the son of a bitch to kill him, now let him die."

"And you pumped a round into another man Saturday," Mr. Baylor said, glaring at Bud Blackwell, "which you are coming to my office to tell me about. But right now just get the hell out of my way."

They got Boyd Caswell into the car, across the back seat, though he didn't open his eyes and Mr. Baylor didn't hold much hope for him. He glared at Bud again and told Mr. Blackwell to see that his son came in or he would swear out a warrant for his arrest on a charge of murder. With E. J. Royce at the wheel they drove away, taking it slow out of the yard so as not to jounce Boyd Caswell and start him bleeding all over the car.

As soon as Dual Meaders saw the car approaching them, still way down the road, he knew it was coming from the Blackwell place. This lonely stretch, a pair of ruts winding through the backwoods, didn't lead anywhere else; so the car had to be coming from there. If they were Blackwells they'd even up the score for last night. If it wasn't Blackwells they'd look and see who it was.

This was a good spot to take them, with trees and scrub falling away to one side and a steep bank on the other. Two cars could pass here, but barely. Though no cars were going to be passing right now. Dual braked, easing over to the right shoulder, then swung the wheel sharp to the left and came to a stop, angle-parked across the road as the oncoming car started blowing its horn, the driver leaning on it and not letting up. Dual had three men with him. They didn't ask what was going on. They kept their eyes on the car ahead of them and got out. One of them went back to the car behind, which was carrying four men, and now they all came up on both sides of the road, a couple of them moving around behind the blocked car.

When the horn stopped blowing there wasn't a sound until, further down the road, crickets started up in the dusty weeds along the ditch.

"Take a look," Dual said. He stood in front of the car, two faces staring at him through the windshield.

The man who approached on the driver's side paused with his hand on the door and motioned to Dual. "In the back," he said.

Dual walked over and looked in at Boyd Caswell. He studied him a moment, making sure he was still breathing, then shook his head and began to smile. Walking back to the front of the car he was still smiling; he couldn't help it and didn't care who saw his teeth.

But now the old man with the glasses was getting out the passenger side, holding the door open in front of him and pointing to the gold-lettered inscription, tapping his finger hard on the door sill.

"You see these words?" Mr. Baylor said. "If you can't read, it says Sheriff's Department, Broke-Leg County."

"I can read," Dual said. "You better get back inside, papa."

"You better show me your identification, then get your cars the hell out of our way. We got a prisoner needs a doctor's attention."

"He ain't going to make it," Dual said.

"You going to get out of my way?"

"I'll tell you what. You can give him to us and we'll take care of him."

"And you can throw your tail up in the air and hump at it," Mr. Baylor said, "because if I don't take this man in nobody does."

"You're right that time, papa," Dual said. He drew his revolver and shot Mr. Baylor three times through the chest, then emptied his gun at the windshield, at the face staring at him with eyes stretched wide open and the mouth trying to say something. "Somebody else will have to finish off Boyd," Dual said. "I'm empty."

They pushed the sheriff's car off the road and watched it roll down the slope, plowing through the brush clumps and snapping off the young trees.

# 10

Tuesday, June 23, Son drove into town to buy meal and stores.

He went to the grocery first, where he always bought his sugar, and asked for three hundred and fifty pounds. The clerk went out into the back room and returned and said they didn't have any sugar. Through the doorway Son could see the fifty-pound bags stacked up. He said, I can see the sugar, right there. The clerk said yes, it was sugar, but it had been special-ordered by somebody and couldn't be sold to anybody else. Son asked to speak to Mr. Hanks, the owner of the store. The clerk, trying to act natural, looking Son straight in the eye, said Mr. Hanks wasn't in today.

At Marlett Feed & Seed Son ordered eight bushels of yellow corn meal, a hundred pounds of wheat bran and a fifty-pound can of lard. The manager asked if he wanted to pick it up in back. Son looked at him and said didn't he always pick it up in back? The

335

manager said he'd tally it up then. Son told him to put the amount on his account. The manager was polite but he didn't seem to have an expression of any kind on his face. He told Son he already owed a hundred and eighty-seven dollars and he would have to pay it before he charged any more items.

"How long have I been coming in here?" Son asked him.

"I don't know. A few years I guess."

"My family's been coming in fifteen years. All of a sudden our credit isn't any good."

"It's a new policy," the manager said.

"Since when?"

"We got to pay our bills too, you know."

"Since when is this new policy?

"Just recently; the past week or so."

"Since the day before yesterday," Son said. "All right, I expect you know what you're doing, because you're never going to see me in this store again."

"It's a new policy," the manager insisted.

Son went to the bank and had to wait twenty minutes for the manager to get back from his dinner, then had to wait some more while the manager sat at his desk behind the fence and looked through papers. The open room was quiet; Son was the only customer in the place. He listened to the overhead fans for a while and every few minutes heard the bank manager clear his throat.

Finally Son got up and stepped over the fence. He said, "I want to borrow three hundred dollars. You going to give it to me or not?"

The bank manager looked up at him. He didn't say hello or, well, Son Martin, how're you doing? He said, "What have you got for security?"

"A producing still," Son answered.

"You know we can't accept that."

"How about forty-five hundred gallons of whiskey?"

"There's no such thing as whiskey these days," the bank manager said.

"How about my place?"

"I don't know what it's worth."

"Do you want to have somebody look at it?"

"Well, we're pretty busy right now."

Son could hear a fly close to him in the silence and the whirring of the overhead fans. He stepped over the fence and walked out.

At the Hotel Cumberland he again had to wait. The girl came out of the office to tell him Mrs. Lyons was tied up at the moment, but would be with him as soon as she could. He picked a chair away from the sunlight coming in the window and lit a cigarette. Then watched Lowell Holbrook coming down the stairs. Lowell didn't look over right away. He stood by the desk. Then when he did look over, Son was staring at him and saw his reaction; the sudden look of surprise and Lowell's eyes shifting away, but coming back now because he knew he had been caught and would have to acknowledge Son's nod. But he didn't come over until Son motioned to him.

"How're you doing, Lowell?"

"Pretty good, I guess."

"I'm waiting on Mrs. Lyons."

"Yes, sir, I figured you were."

"She's busy doing something, I don't know what."

"Yes, sir. Well, I better get back to work."

"Lowell, I wondered if I could have a glass of cold water."

"You can get one in the dining room," Lowell said. He crossed the lobby to the desk. Behind it, he leaned over the counter with a pencil in his hand, like he was checking a list of something. His head would come up and he would look out toward the front door, concentrating, deep in thought.

When Kay Lyons came out of the office, Lowell nodded toward Son and pointed the end of his pencil in that direction. Son watched her crossing the lobby, raising her eyebrows and putting on a little expression of surprise.

"What brings you to town?" She stood in front of him.

Son looked up at her. "Everybody's busy today. Did you know that?"

"It was something I had to finish."

"No, I mean everybody. Everybody's very busy. And serious. Boy they're busy, serious, hard-working people in this town. I never realized before how busy everybody was."

"Is that what you wanted to tell me?"

"No, I wanted to ask you something."

"What?"

"If you'd loan me three hundred dollars." He kept his eyes on her. He watched her eyes move away and come back and saw the little raised-eyebrow look of surprise again.

"Why would you want three hundred dollars?"

"I need it."

"That's a lot."

"You told me you've got over four thousand dollars in the bank."

"Well, yes, but that's my husband's insurance money. I mean he left it to me and it's all I have."

"When we get married, is it still his insurance money?"

"That's different—listen, tell me why you need it."

"To buy stores."

"Well, don't you buy on credit?"

"Not anymore. I found out today my credit's run out."

Her eyebrows closed together in a frown, then raised again. "They won't give you credit? I don't understand."

"Yes you do."

He waited, watching her, but she said nothing.

"I have to be a good boy," he said then, "and do what people want or else they start talking it over and saying, 'What kind of a neighbor is this man? He isn't any neighbor, he's only for himself and doesn't care about others.' Then they say, 'Well, a man like that sure doesn't deserve to run a credit. He won't be nice to the people he lives among, we won't be nice to him.'"

"Well?" Kay said.

"Why don't you sit down."

"I have to get back to the desk."

"Will you loan me three hundred dollars?"

"I told you—it's insurance money. I have to be very careful."

"Kay, yes or no?"

"All right. No."

"Don't you think I'd pay you back?"

Kay had stopped dodging, trying to evade him. "How would you pay me back?" she said. "Lying in a grave next to your father, how would you pay me? Would you leave it to me in your will? Three hundred dollars' worth of bootleg whiskey, is that how you'd pay?"

"It's nice to have things out in the open," Son said, "isn't it?"

Kay sat down now, on the edge of the sofa facing his chair; her hands were locked together on her lap, but her face was relaxed now and her eyes did not wander from his.

"You know what I want," Kay said. "I want to leave here. I'll leave tomorrow if you want to go and I'll give you every cent I have in the bank. But I'm not going to give you money to help you stay here and kill yourself. Wouldn't I be foolish to do that, pay for something I don't want?"

"Kay, you're not burying me. We leave here together it's got to be when I can take what I want with us. What *I* want. Doesn't that mean anything to you?"

"What you want isn't possible."

"I've got to find that our for sure. I'm not giving it away to any-body, not to federal people and least of all not to anybody pre-tending to be federals."

"What do you mean by that?"

"I don't think the ones making the raids are agents, I think they're bootleggers."

"Are you sure?"

"No, it's what I think."

"If it's true, it could be worse, couldn't it?—what they might do."

"I don't know. It's up to them."

"But either way, no matter who they are, you can't win. Be-cause what you want isn't possible."

"That's the way your uncle and the rest of my neighbors see it," Son said, "so I guess I can't explain it to you either. But I'm staying. They'll put me under or get tired and go away, I'm stay-ing. You want to wait around and see what happens, it's up to you."

Miley Mitchell didn't like going out to that farmhouse. She didn't like looking at the old blind man. He was depressing; the whole place was depressing and filthy dirty. The men would sit around looking at her, not being able to do anything about it. Once one of them said to her, "You ought to be upstairs and we could take our turns." And she had said, "Gee, that would be a lot of fun," and walked away from him. She could picture the old stained mattress crawling with bedbugs. No thank you. Dr. Taulbee said, then stay at the hotel if you don't like the place. They had been here nine days now and nine days were about eight too many in a town this size. Once you had walked five blocks up the street and five back and had dinner in the hotel dining room, you had been to Marlett. Sitting in the lobby had been kind of fun the first time; aware of the salesmen looking her over; though not one had worked up enough nerve to walk over and start a conversation. Even a dry-goods salesman could help pass the time. The fun would be in getting away with it without Dr. Taulbee knowing; the salesman letting her know he was a pretty slick article and not realizing he could get shot if they were caught. She had gone to the beauty parlor Friday for a wash and wave set. Saturday, Sunday, Monday, Tuesday—four days ago. She might as well go again today; get out of the hotel room before she started counting the designs on the wallpaper.

It was either while she was going down the stairs or walking across the lobby that Miley decided against the wave set. She just didn't think about it again once she saw Son Martin and the hotel woman talking. He was saying something and she was listening, at least not interrupting, not smiling either. Neither of them looked this way. The hotel woman never did smile or touch him; she got up and walked away.

Miley didn't wait for Son to notice her, she went out to the sidewalk and stood at the curb with her back to the hotel entrance. When he came out she followed him to his pickup truck; she opened the door and got in as he sat with his hands on the wheel staring at her, but she didn't look at him until she had closed the door and sat back with her hands in her lap.

Now she gave him a nice little smile that showed in her eyes and waited for him to say whatever he was going to say.

But he didn't. He didn't say a word. He looked at her for a moment, then backed into the street and drove west out of Marlett, past the stores and the church and the filling stations, past the section of old homes and trees lining the street, and out into the open sunlight of corn fields and telephone poles and shadowed hills in the distance.

Miley wasn't sure what she wanted to happen. She did feel it was working out better than she would have predicted. She had pictured Son getting mad and telling her to get out or asking her if Dr. Taulbee was sending a girl now to do his work—being grim and solemn about it—or saying something dumb, sarcastic, like this isn't a taxi, lady, or where is it I'm supposed to take you?

Nope, none of that. He drove along at forty miles an hour, looking straight ahead, not saying one word and Miley felt a little excitement and settled down to see what would happen, deciding
once they were out on the highway, she wasn't going to say a
word either and they'd see who could hold out the longest.

What happened, after about ten minutes Son turned off the
highway and came to a stop in a dense glade of trees. He helped
Miley out of the pickup, helped her take off her clothes, spread
his shirt on the ground for her to lie on and eased down next to
her. At one point Miley said, "Oh God—" and a little while later,
when he was stepping into his pants and she was looking up at
him, not ready to move quite yet, she said, "I guess you win."

Son was yanking the end of his belt through the buckle. "You
bet," he said.

"What're you mad about?"

"I'm not mad."

"You can tell by your big smile."

"I'm going to Corbin. You want to come?"

"When are you coming back?"

"I don't know, tonight if I can get what I want in Corbin."

"God, I don't know why you couldn't."

"You want to come or not?"

"I'd have to think of a good story to tell him."

"Like he doesn't know you're with me."

Miley made a face, a hint of disappointment. "Don't say anything dumb, okay? Up to now you've been perfect. I'll tell you
truthfully he doesn't know where I am and he didn't put me up to
this."

"Then what'd you come for?"

"I don't know. I guess just to see what you're like. Say, do you
go with that woman at the hotel?"

Son hesitated. "You could say that. Why?"

"She's not your type." Miley waited, but he didn't say anything. "She's too nice for you."

"What does that mean?"

"Did you ever bring her here? She'd die. She has to have
everything nice. You can tell by looking at her."

"I better take you back."

"If you want me to go to Corbin with you, I will."

"What will you tell him?"

"I don't know. I'll say I went for a walk and got lost in the woods."

"Are you—married to him?"

Miley smiled. "You're sweet."

"You like him?"

"He's not my type but he could be worse."

"Well, what're you living with him for then?"

"I guess I haven't had any better offers." Miley got up slowly and handed Son his shirt. "Would you care to make one?"

"Like I don't have enough trouble."

"Maybe I could help you. I don't know."

"Put your clothes on."

"Nervous?"

"Somebody's liable to come along."

"You didn't worry about that before. Come on, are you the strong silent type or aren't you?"

"How could you help me?"

"Well"—Miley stepped into her skirt—"let's see. I know enough about that big teddy bear to send him to jail for life. How's that?"

"He's a bootlegger, isn't he?"

"You haven't made an offer yet," Miley said.

"He's no more with the government than I am. Neither is that little mule shooter."

"Dual. Isn't he a cutie?"

"The one I'm not sure about is Frank Long."

"Well," Miley said, "make an offer and if it's any good I'll tell you about the doctor and Dual and Frank and the whole bunch." She turned her back to Son. "Zip me."

"You've told me," he said, "just admitting there's something to tell."

She came around, standing close, her face raised to his. "Then why don't you call the police? You can't, but I could, couldn't I?"

Son touched her face, holding it in his hand. She was a good-looking girl with soft skin and nice mouth and warm green eyes. And if you let her talk any more, Son told himself, you'll begin to believe her.

He dropped her off in front of the Baptist Church, turned around, and headed for Corbin as fast as the pickup would go.

# 11

Tuesday evening, a little before seven, Frank Long was in his hotel room waiting for Dr. Taulbee to call or come by or do something. He had been waiting all day for Taulbee to "think over the situation." Because the window was open a few inches to get some air in the room, Long heard the people below in the street. He didn't hear actual words, only the urgent sounds of words and the sound of hurried steps on the sidewalk. Long went to the window, pressed his forehead against the glass, trying to look straight down, then raised the window and looked out, leaning over the sill.

People were bunched around a pickup truck parked at the curb. In the box, lying side by side, were three bodies. Long recognized Boyd Caswell and the sheriff, Mr. Baylor, who seemed to be looking straight up at the window. A hat covered the face of the third one.

Long closed the window. He walked down the hall to 210 and knocked on the door. Miley opened it after he waited and knocked again.

"Is he here?"

Miley stood with her hand on the door. "I haven't seen him all afternoon."

"Where would he be, at the farm?"

"I guess so. I was out." Miley turned away from the door, pushing it open. "Unzip me, will you?"

Long hesitated a moment before following her into the room. Then he was close behind her, pulling down the zipper of her blouse, looking at her bare white skin. Miley said over her shoulder, "You can wait for him if you want. I'm going to take a bath."

"I might do that," Long said. "You think he'll be coming soon."

"He could come any minute." She turned, looking up at him. "Or he might not be here for an hour. I never know what he's going to do."

"Well, it's pretty important I see him."

"There's a bottle of liquor on the shelf in the closet."

"You want some?"

"I don't drink," Miley answered. Going into the bathroom and closing the door partway, she began to undress behind it. Long could hear the water running. He kept looking at the door, catching brief glimpses of her body, knowing she was expecting him to come in. He went over to the window: the people were still gathered around the pickup truck. What the hell were they waiting for? Why would they have the bodies on display in front of the hotel? Like they were waiting for him to come out and show him and say, "See what you done?"

Somebody would have to investigate it. Maybe the town police or the county prosecutor or whatever law enforcement they had here. They would sit him down and start asking questions.

Miley was singing something he had never heard before—a soft, little-girl voice—making sounds for the words she didn't know. She's going to ask you to hand her something, Long told himself. He'd go in and there she would be looking up at him, her big white boobies floating in the water. All wet and soapy, waiting for him to reach in and grab her.

Like hell, he said to himself, and went back to his room.

Inside of ten minutes his suitcase was packed and he was at the desk in the lobby to check out.

Mrs. Lyons looked a little surprised and he almost told her he'd received a call from his office and had to leave right away; but he caught himself in time, knowing she could check on his calls, and didn't tell her anything. She was saying she was sorry, but he would have to pay for tonight also, even though he wouldn't be here—when Lowell Holbrook came over.

"They took them away," Lowell said.

Frank Long turned to him, easing against the counter. "I could see something from my window—what was going on?"

"They found the sheriff and E. J. Royce and Boyd Caswell all shot dead."

"You don't tell me."

"Yes, sir. They said it looked like Mr. Baylor and E.J. were bringing Boyd in and he got one of their guns and they shot it out, all killing each other. They came here looking for the undertaker. He was having his supper."

"That's why they were out in front?"

"Yes, sir, looking for the undertaker," Lowell said. His gaze dropped to the suitcase. "Excuse me, but are you leaving?"

"Yeah, have to leave."

"They say it might have been moonshiners done it, besides Boyd Caswell."

"I'll have your total in a minute," Mrs. Lyons said. She walked off toward the office. Long watched her: she didn't seem too concerned and it surprised him. Three men were dead she must have known, but she went about her business and didn't even seem interested.

"Do you believe it could have been moonshiners?"

Frank Long's eyes came back to Lowell. "I guess it could."

"I don't know any of them would have shot Mr. Baylor."

"Well, maybe it was Boyd Caswell, like you said."

"Maybe."

"You got police here to look into it?"

"Just a constable," Lowell answered. "Mr. Baylor was the law. With him dead I don't know who it would be. I wondered maybe if you were going to do something about it."

"No, that wouldn't be my department. You know what I am, huh?"

"Everybody knows it."

"I expect people are talking about us raiding the stills."

"Yes, sir," Lowell said. "Since you're going, I guess you must be through raiding."

"I'm through," Long said.

Lowell watched him pay his bill, then touch his hat to Mrs. Lyons and walk out. Lowell didn't offer to help him with the suitcase. He watched him go through the door before he turned to Mrs. Lyons.

"Did he say where he was going? Back to Frankfort?"

"I didn't ask."

"It seems funny. Three men killed and he leaves the same day. Don't you think that's kind of funny?"

"I don't think about it at all," Mrs. Lyons said.

"I mean you can't help but wonder."

"Yes you *can* help it," she said then, with a note of irritation that took Lowell by surprise. "You can keep your nose out of it and let them all kill each other. That's what you can do." Mrs. Lyons turned from the desk and went back to her office.

"Long's coming," Dual said.

Dr. Taulbee got up from a chair and followed Dual through the kitchen. Out on the porch they watched Frank Long walking over from his car. Dr. Taulbee got his grin ready.

"Hey, Frank, I was fixing to come see you."

Long reached the porch. "Has he told you about killing the sheriff?"

"Dual? Sure he did."

"It doesn't seem to bother you any."

"Well, what was he going to do? That old man had Boyd Caswell in the back seat. He ever held a bottle in front of Boyd and started asking him questions, it would be all over before breakfast."

"It's all over now," Long said.

"What're you talking about? Listen, Frank, Dual didn't have any choice. He seen what he had to do and did it."

"That old man pulled his gun on me," Dual said. "I shot him too dead to skin."

"And then you finished Boyd."

"I didn't want to, he was a buddy of mine. But he was going to die and there wasn't anything we could do to help him."

"That's what I mean," Dr. Taulbee said. "He didn't want to shoot Boyd or that old man but, Frank, if he hadn't, you'd be heading for Atlanta next month. Heck, Dual saved your hide and you haven't even thanked him for it."

"I don't dare look at him," Long said, "I'm liable to grab him and wring his neck. We had a good plan that could have worked, but he starts shooting people and now we might as well piss on the fire and call the dogs."

Dr. Taulbee nodded. "I guess your part in it's done. I don't see any reason for you to stay around."

"I mean it's over for all of us."

"No, sir, Frank, it's over for you, but we got to find us that whiskey yet."

"If he pulls his gun," Long said, "I'll shoot you first."

"Nobody's talking about shooting anybody." Dr. Taulbee sounded hurt. "I'm saying it's time for you to go home is all."

"I guess it was going to come sometime," Long said. "I should've known the day you got here."

"Well," Dr. Taulbee said, "you can't know everything. You took a chance and you didn't make it. Dual here doesn't trust you. He's for putting you under; but I told him, old Frank's not going to sic the law on us. He knows if we get put in jail he's going to be right there with us, hoping and praying some accident don't be-fall him. Isn't that right? I said to Dual, hell, Frank was nice enough to tell us about that boy's whiskey, what do we want to hurt him for?"

"I guess that's it then," Long said. "Since there's not much I can do about it."

"There isn't anything you can do," Dr. Taulbee said, "outside of wish me luck. This next raid I'm leading myself."

Dusk was settling as Long drove away from the farmhouse. Reaching the gravel road he flicked on his headlights.

He told himself that he must be awful dumb. Taulbee must think he was about the dumbest boy he'd ever met. He had called Taulbee in and now he couldn't do a thing about it. What he couldn't figure out was why he had trusted Taulbee in the first place. Probably because he figured he had a hold on Taulbee and, if the man pulled anything, he'd put on his federal agent hat and arrest the son of a bitch. He hadn't thought about Taulbee having a hold on him at the same time. Maybe he should have stayed in the Army. Son Martin had said something about that, about staying in the Army where there was somebody to think for him. That hadn't made him mad at the time, but it did now, thinking about it, because he could picture Taulbee laughing at him and saying the same thing. Boy, he would sure like to think of a way of nailing Taulbee and that loony-head Dual and the rest of them. He had stayed calm and walked away, because he looked stupid enough without crying and kicking his feet and, because if he'd stayed any longer, he would have taken a swing at Dual and gotten shot full of holes before he cleared the yard.

Passing Kay Lyons's house he thought about her for a moment, picturing her, the dead expression on her face as he checked out—probably a cold fish underneath her woman's body; no life in there at all. The house, he noticed, was completely dark.

But there was a light farther down the road, off to the right side. He couldn't figure where the light was coming from: the church was down there and the cemetery.

It was a lantern hanging from the stubby limb of a tree. As he drew near the cemetery he could see the dull light beyond the fence and a man digging a grave. It was strange, like he had seen a lantern in a cemetery before somewhere, a little while ago, though he knew it had not been around here. Then he remembered what it was: the grave of Son Martin's father with the light post over it, a lonely grave up on the hill, all by itself.

Long stopped, skidding in the gravel, then backed up until he was even with the lantern light and saw the gravedigger looking over toward him. The man leaned on his shovel as Long got out and came through the fence.

"See you're working late."

"They's going to be some burials tomorrow."

"That's what I hear. I knew one of them."

"Boyd Caswell? I see you're coming from that direction."

"That's right. You knew him?"

"I knew them all that's buried here. Them or their children or grandchildren."

"I used to know that girl was married to Son Martin," Long said.

"She's over yan side of that big gravestone there. Her and Son Martin's old mother lying side by side. Next to them's his daddy's folks and I believe two little brothers passed on as babies."

"The whole family," Long said. "Except his dad."

"It's the family plot," the gravedigger said.

Long got in his car and drove on, asking himself, If they are all buried there, then why is that old man all by himself up on the hill? Answer me that.

Lowell got a pot of coffee and some cookies from the dining room and took them in to Mrs. Lyons, who was in the office making entries in a ledger book. She was not in a talkative mood and hadn't been for a few days, so Lowell didn't waste time trying to make conversation.

He went out to the lobby just as Frank Long was coming in the door with his heavy suitcase.

"Did you forget something?"

"No, I'm checking in."

"You just left here a half hour ago."

"Well, I got to thinking, since I've paid the room for the night I ought to get my money's worth, oughtn't I?"

"You'll have to check in again."

"I don't mind."

"How long you 'spect to be?"

"Oh, I don't know," Frank Long answered. "Probably just a short visit this time."

# 12

Son didn't get home from Corbin until almost noon Wednesday. He had spent the evening with his father-in-law, Mr. Hartley, and finally stayed at his house that night. In the morning he asked Mr. Hartley if he would loan him three hundred dollars. The man wrote out a check without comment or question. Son thanked him and left. He bought his sugar and grain in Corbin and, on the way home, stopped off at Marlett Feed & Seed to pay his past-due bill, counting off one hundred and eighty-seven dollars in front of the store manager, not saying one word, and walked out.

It was a dry, sunny day that June 24. The open yard and the outbuildings lay still in the noon heat. Son came to a stop by the porch. He turned off the ignition and sat there a moment in the stillness. In broad daylight it was quieter than night. There was no breeze and nothing seemed to move. What Son wanted to know right away: where were the hounds? How come they hadn't chased him up the road? Maybe it was always this still at noon on a hot day and he hadn't noticed it before. But he still wanted to know where those hounds were. Aaron was probably up at the still. The hounds could be with him; though Son couldn't remember Aaron ever taking them up there.

He went into the house. There was a pail of water on the sink-board and a pot of coffee, which smelled fresh, on the stove. He was upstairs, taking off his suit coat and about to change into work clothes, when he heard the hounds faintly, way off. By the time he got downstairs and out in the yard, Aaron was coming across the pasture. The hounds were close in front of him and Aaron's arm was extended, like he was pointing at them. It looked strange until Son realized Aaron had them on a rope leash. It was something else he couldn't remember Aaron ever doing. Or going hunting at noon; though Aaron was sure as hell carrying the 12-gauge.

"You get anything?" Son asked him. He reached for the hounds as they panted and sniffed and jumped up on his legs.

"We got us plenty," Aaron said.

Son looked at him, straightening, "Who'd you see?"

"They up in the woods."

"Who is?"

"The ones your friend brought. I saw one of their cars. I heard other ones making noise in the woods, 'Hey, where you at? Man, I'm *lost!*' They don't know what they doing up there, but I know what they come for."

"Why didn't they drive in the road?"

"I don't know that. I think they know you was away and they want you to come home and think everything fine before they come get you. But I took these two boys and sniffed like I was squirrel hunting and it ain't any surprise now."

"Maybe we still have time to get out of here."

"Is that what you want to do?"

"They've probably closed the back door by now."

"Sealed off the road. Nobody in or out," Aaron said. "Then they sneak up."

"Or they watch for a while. Think maybe we want to take some whiskey and make a run."

"Where'd we run to?"

"I don't know of anywhere," Son answered. "So I guess we stay."

Aaron nodded, at ease. "We here when they come."

They got ready for Dr. Taulbee, knowing he was watching them: two small figures through field glasses three to four hundred yards away, two boys doing the chores, taking their time in the afternoon heat.

They unloaded the pickup truck, carrying what looked like grain sacks into the house. And inside they stacked the heavy sacks beneath the two windows facing the open yard.

They hauled a load of old lumber from the barn to the porch. Son Martin looked like he was repairing the porch steps, replacing some of the boards. Yes he was, though from three to four hundred yards you would never see he was wedging in the two middle steps and not nailing them. And you would never see. Aaron, who was pulling lumber inside from off the porch and covering the two offside windows that faced the near slope behind the house.

Throughout the afternoon, every hour or so, they would carry a pail of water into the house until they had half-filled a thirty-gallon barrel.

On the kitchen table, pushed over closer to the windows, they laid out their weapons: the 12-gauge Remington and two rifles, a lever-action Winchester and an 0-3 Springfield, and all the ammunition they had in the house. Son put his Smith & Wesson .38 in his back pocket.

They parked the pickup truck on the offside of the pump in the yard, to give them some protection if they had to go out there again.

They pulled back the linoleum in the kitchen and pried up a couple of floor boards so Aaron could drop down into the cellar and bolt the door that opened from the outside. Then he pickaxed the hard-packed floor and shoveled the dirt into grain sacks and handed them up to Son.

At suppertime they ate biscuits and gravy and green beans and wondered if there was anything else they should do. If they had some bob wire, Aaron said, that'd be good, string it around the place when it got dark. They'd bring the dogs in the house. They'd stay by the windows and keep watch on the yard, because maybe those boys out there were tired from waiting and would feel like doing something. They'd be a moon tonight, Aaron said; that was good.

They went out to the porch after supper, to sit down and smoke and watch the hill slopes fading in the dusk, spreading their shadows over the pasture. The ridges were silent and almost black against the night sky. Son finished another cigarette and flicked the stub out into the darkness.

"What do you think?" he said.

"I think they decide to go home or come visit us," Aaron said. "They no reason to stay out in the dark."

A little while later, inside the house, in the kitchen, Aaron rose from where he was seated by a window. "All the getting ready we done, I forget the mule."

"The mule's all right," Son told him.

"It don't have any water I know of. If it be a while before we bring any out there, that old mule be thirsty."

Son looked out the window, at the moonlight that lay in the yard between the house and the deeply shadowed outline of the barn.

"Take the water out of the barrel," he said, "you won't make any noise at the pump." Within a few moments he was watching Aaron crossing the yard, his shadow following him until he was close to the barn and enveloped in silent darkness. Son heard the door creak and saw a faint movement. Aaron was inside.

Son waited. He knew how long it would take to walk through the barn to the stock pen and pour a bucket of water into the trough. As the minutes passed he told himself Aaron had decided to stay there awhile and keep watch from the barn. They could sneak up from that direction, using the barn for cover. Or they could have already done it and were inside the barn when Aaron walked in. After about ten minutes more, Son had to know for sure. He opened the door about a foot, letting the foxhounds run through the opening and down the steps. He watched them sniff around the yard. As they worked closer to the barn, they would sniff, then raise their heads and stand still. The hounds were about ten feet from the deep shadows when they started growling, then barking and howling, raising a racket to frighten off whatever the unknown thing was inside.

Son didn't see the half door in the barn open or make out the figure there until the repeating shotgun went off four times, louder than the howls that came from the dogs as they were cut down by the charges. By the time Son got his Winchester on the door it was closed and the deep shadow lay in silence.

Dual held out the shotgun. "Here, take it."

"I can't see where you're at."

"Then light the goddamn lantern. He knows we're here now, it don't matter."

"I guess you got them, I don't hear anything."

"Course I got them—what'd you think I was going to do?"

Aaron said, "They wasn't hurting you any."

"Jesus," Dual said, "who asked you anything?"

A gloved hand held a lighted match inside the lantern until the wick caught and the yellow glow showed Dual holding the shotgun and the heavy-set man with the glove and Aaron standing with a rope that was noosed tightly around his neck, reached up over a horse-stall beam and hung slack behind him falling to a tanagled coil on the floor.

The man who took the shotgun from Dual reloaded the magazine, then trained the barrel on Aaron.

The heavy-set man, with the glove on his right hand, went into the stall behind Aaron. He took a good grip on the slack end of the rope, coiling it around his hands. "Ask him again," he said.

Dual moved in close to Aaron. "You going to tell us?"

"I can't tell you if I don't know, can I?" Aaron gasped and reached up as the rope tightened, pulling him off the floor. The heavy-set man strained, leaning away from the rope, turning to get it over his shoulder and raise Aaron's feet another few inches from the floor.

"You should tie his hands behind him," the man with the shotgun said. "He's trying to pull himself up."

"Trying," Dual said. "You try raising yourself. In a minute your arms start waving crazy. Okay, Carl."

The heavy-set man turned, letting go of the rope and Aaron dropped to his knees.

"Hey, nig," Dual said, "you going to tell us or not?"

"I work for him; I don't know about no whiskey."

"We hear you helped make it."

"No, sir."

"Pull him up again."

"What if he doesn't know?" the one with the shotgun said.

"He knows."

"But what if he doesn't? Then he can't tell us. But the one inside the house can."

"Jesus Christ," Dual said.

"Listen, I mean we tell the one inside. He gives us the stuff or we string up his boy."

"Yeah?" Dual said, "then what?"

"Then he gives us the stuff."

"He gives us the stuff?" Dual was frowning, because maybe he didn't understand it right. "Why would he give us the stuff? All he's got to do is get himself another nigger."

The linoleum came up easier this time when Son rolled it back; the floor boards were already loose; all he had to do was lift them out. He took the Winchester and the 12-gauge Remington with him, dropped them to the floor of the cellar and lowered himself down through the hole. With the weapons he went up the steps to the slanting outside door, opened it as quietly as he could, and stepped outside. To his left was the corner of the house. Beyond it, several yards, was the pump, and beyond the pump the dark shape of his pickup truck, sitting in the open about thirty yards from the barn. Son stayed close to the house, listening. When he was ready he cradled the weapons in his arms and crawled on his elbows and knees out to the pickup.

"Take him up to the loft," Dual said. "There's a beam sticks out over the door; loop the rope around it and hold him there and we'll be right up."

The heavy-set one went up the ladder first. He said, "Come on," and Aaron followed, the rope trailing from his neck.

Dual said to the one with the shotgun, "We'll ask him again. If he don't tell us, we run him out the door."

"Hang him," the one with the shotgun said.

Dual shook his head. "That ain't any fun. See we don't tie the end of the rope. But he don't know it. We run him out and get a wing shot at him while he's in the air. Buddy, like shooting crow."

"What if you miss him?"

"Miss him? Listen, you stay down here. When I give you the

word, I'll say *now*. You pour it into the house and keep Son off us."

"Then if you miss the nig I can bust him, huh?"

"Miss him?" Dual said again. "Buddy, you got something to see."

Dual climbed the ladder, up into the darkness above the lantern. A crack of moonlight showed the edge of the loft door, not closed tightly. Dual positioned Aaron about ten feet from the door, facing it. He moved back to where the heavy-set one had tied the end of the rope to a support post, whispered to the man to untie it and hold it loose in his hands, ready to let go when he gave the word.

"Your last chance," Dual said to Aaron. "Or you go through the door with rope around your neck. You'll fall aways and then *snap*, the rope jerks tight and breaks your neck. You want that, it's yours."

"No, sir," Aaron said, "but I can't tell something I don't know."

"Well, it's up to you." Dual glanced back at the man holding the rope. "You don't want to tell us, then get ready to run, nig."

Dual drew his .38. He got a step behind Aaron, waited a moment, and yelled, "Now!" pushing Aaron, running him toward the closed loft door. The timing was dead on, the automatic shotgun opened up on the house as Dual stopped short and Aaron banged through the door, his arms reaching for moonlight. Dual fired twice and instinctively ducked back as the solid reports of a rifle filled the yard below.

Aaron had his hands in front of him as he hit the door and was through it falling and grabbing frantically for the rope above him as the gunfire erupted like it was all around him, like he was falling into it, and he hit the ground so hard the jolt went through his body, buckling his legs and throwing him forward. He got up to run and fell and started crawling and heard somebody say, "Aaron!" as the shotgun skidded across the ground and the stock bounced and hit him in the face. He knew the voice and knew the shotgun and knew what to do with it, grabbing it and finding the triggers as he rolled to his back and saw the figure in the loft door and let go one 12-gauge charge and the second on top of it and saw the figure pitch forward and hit the ground like a sack of

meal. Aaron could make out the pickup; he was crawling toward
it, hearing the rifle going off close to him, then Son had him by
the arm, raising him and running him around behind the pickup
to the cellar entrance. He fell down the steps and lay breathing in
the darkness with an awful pain shooting up his legs through his
knees, but he still had hold of the shotgun. Son almost had to pry
it out of his hands.

During the night Dr. Taulbee left Son Martin's still and moved
in closer, to a position in the rocks and brush above old man Martin's grave.

All the goddamn shooting and then silence. Nobody had come
back from the barn, so he didn't know what happened outside of a
lot of guns going off. Maybe Dual had him pinned down and was
moving in for the kill, the little fellow squirming up close to the
house and inside before they knew he was there. Maybe. Dr.
Taulbee wanted to know what the hell was going on; so he sent
five men down with two Thompson machine guns and moved to
a closer position to see what he could see. He watched them go
down the hill, circling to get behind the barn. In a couple of minutes they were down among the dark shapes and shadows and Dr.
Taulbee had to wait again. Though not long this time.

The gunfire came as suddenly as it had before, the Thompsons
going off now, tearing apart the stillness, sweet music that was
good to hear and set a grin on Dr. Taulbee's face as he stared expectantly into the darkness. There were rifle shots and again a
Thompson rattling the night. Then silence.

The first of the five to return had trouble locating Dr. Taulbee
in the rocks. Dr. Taulbee had to call to him. The man came
stumbling up the gravel slope out of breath.

Taulbee couldn't wait any longer. "You get them?"

No, the man didn't think so. There wasn't any way of telling.

"Then what the hell was all the shooting about?"

Well, the big guy, Carl, was in the barn and the boy with him
was shot dead. They didn't see Dual right away. They said to
Carl come on, show us where them two are. Carl pointed out the
pickup truck and both the boys with Thompsons let go at it until
their magazines were empty. That should do it, one of them said.
The five spread out in a line and went over to the pickup truck
that was shot through like a sieve. When they looked in and didn't

see anybody, my God, it was a terrible feeling being out in the open and knowing the two were in the house. It was either go back to the barn or rush the house—there wasn't room for all of them behind the pickup truck. Since nobody had fired at them so far, they decided to rush the house. The two boys with the tommy guns commenced to shoot at the windows, one of them going ahead, running right toward the porch and up the steps. But he never got up. It was like the steps collapsed under him and as he fell these two rifles opened up from both windows and everybody dove for the pickup truck. The boy by the porch was so close under them he was able to crawl out; all they had done was shot his hat off and grazed his skull. Nobody else was hit; they laid down cover fire with a Thompson and got back to the barn.

There, the others were coming now: the big guy, Carl, and the other four carrying two people and having a struggle getting up the slope. Dr. Taulbee called out, "You find Dual?"

Nobody answered until they were up in the rocks. Then one of them said, "We got him here," laying him down in front of Dr. Taulbee, "but I don't think he's moved."

Or ever would. Dr. Taulbee could tell by Dual's eyes he was dead: the fixed, wide-open stare, like somebody had given him the surprise of his life. It made Dr. Taulbee tired to look at him. He gazed down at the dark shape of the house for a while and then at the men waiting for him to say something. Then made them wait a little longer.

"Well," he said finally, "what I want to know, are you all going to bring that boy out of there or do I have to get somebody else to do it?"

The big guy, Carl, said, "Tomorrow, we're going to bring the nigger out dead and the other one with his hands in the air."

"I want to see that," Dr. Taulbee said. "Because to now it doesn't look to me like you've scared him one bit."

# 13

Upstairs, in the bedroom directly over the kitchen, Son used a big hand auger to drill through the floor plank and the board and batten ceiling below it. With his eye close to the hole, he could look down into the kitchen and see one of Aaron's swollen ankles extended out from where he lay against the grain sacks.

It was Thursday morning, June 25. As soon as Taulbee's men opened up on the house with rifles, snapping the shots in from the dense tree cover of the slope, Son went upstairs with a pair of field glasses. Crouched low, his glasses on the window sill, he studied the ridges and rock strains, making out movement here and there, but not seeing anything worth aiming three hundred yards to try and hit. They had better keep their bullets for the close-in business that would come as soon as Taulbee realized the snap shooting wasn't doing him any good, not telling him anything.

The bedroom, his own, was a good place to watch from. Son drilled the hole so he could call to Aaron in a hurry if they came across the pasture. Aaron had stayed awake most of the night and was trying to sleep now, with his knees turning blue and his feet and ankles swollen up like he had eight pairs of socks on.

Son kept his gaze on the slope because he wanted to see the first sign of a move from them.

Taulbee was probably in the stillhouse, giving orders. And Frank Long, where would he be? He hadn't been in the barn last night, though he might have been with the bunch that came later. They'd got one of them; Son had heard the man yell as he went through the steps. The sight to see again was Aaron blowing Dual out of the loft with the 12-gauge. That was one of them would never have to be shot again. Son was sure of it, though at first light they saw he wasn't lying in the yard.

A bullet went through the window, shattering the glass above him. Son continued to study the slope through the field glasses. It was hard to tell where the shots came from. The snap shooters were spread out in the trees. He would hear the far-away reports and the bullets hitting fragments of window glass and thudding into the timbered walls. They were telling him he wasn't getting out of here unless he gave up. Well, as far as Son was concerned, the first part could be true. He might not get out. But there was no chance of him giving up. He was sure of that.

Until he saw the cars appear on the ridge.

Inching his glasses across the hills and gulleys, he stopped on an open, grassy part of the slope. A car was parked there in the sun. It was a good hundred yards to the left of where Taulbee's men were hidden in the trees. Still, Son decided, it was probably one of their cars. Maybe a few more shooters had been called in.

Two more cars appeared. Son watched the men get out and he almost jumped up and yelled to Aaron because they weren't Taulbee people at all, they were boys in overalls and farm hats and goddamn if they weren't looking this way and figuring it out and deciding what to do. Son swung his glasses back to the trees and said to Taulbee, "Look over there, mister, and see what you're going to have on your hands."

As another car and pickup truck drove across the open slope, Son got down by the hole in the floor and called, "Hey, Aaron, look out over to that open piece, see who's coming!"

Son put his glasses on the ridge again. God Almighty, there were a dozen men up there now.

And a couple of women.

He couldn't understand why the women would be here. Less they wanted to see Taulbee run so bad they couldn't be kept home.

Now there was a wagon coming off the ridge trail, holding a car behind it, and a stake truck from Marlett Feed & Seed that looked like it was loaded with men.

Son kept his glasses on the stake truck. He watched men jump off the back end and saw young boys climbing the sides to get down. He counted several more women and young girls in the group. He inched his glasses over the slope and noticed a few other women he had missed. He saw the men standing in groups talking. He saw a couple of others spreading a blanket on the ground. He saw a man handing some folding chairs down from the stake truck. He saw friends, neighbors, acquaintances, and people he didn't know sitting and standing around on the open ridge in the June sun and he didn't see a rifle or a shotgun among the bunch of them.

They had come out to watch.

They had lost their stills because he had not given up his whiskey. Now they had come to see it taken from him.

Son turned from the window. He sat on the floor with his back to the wall, in this room where he was born and where he had slept almost every night for the past four years. He felt tired and his head ached. He hadn't slept more than an hour. He hadn't eaten since yesterday supper, though he wasn't hungry. He sat in the bedroom with his back against the wall and began wondering what in hell he was doing here, getting shot at, putting on a show for his neighbors.

That's the fact of it, Son thought. Whether they are up there watching or not anywhere in sight, what you're doing is putting on a show. Showing off. It's your whiskey and nobody can take it. So they tell how you never gave up and somebody says well, where is he now? And they say, he's buried, where do you think? Buried? You mean they killed him? Of course they killed him. Then he was awful dumb not to give up, wasn't he?

Well, he was brave.

Well, some call it brave, some call it stupid.

The only thing Son was sure of, he was tired. Sitting in the upstairs room looking at the bed—he'd like to get in it and pull the covers up over his head and stay there. But he had to decide something, what was brave and what was stupid. How he wanted people to talk about him. Or whether he cared or not.

Bud Blackwell and his dad and Virgil Worthman and a few other men were in one group. They squatted and sat in the grass at the slope of the ridge, where the hill fell away in a sweep of weeds and brush toward the pasture. They squinted in the noon glare and gazed around at the other groups, and occasionally one of them would get fidgety and rise up to stretch and spit tobacco. It seemed like it would be something to watch but, Jesus, there wasn't much happening.

The other groups felt about the same. One boy said if they didn't start something soon he was going home and pick bugs off his tobacco. Some others were getting hungry. They should have packed lunches, they said. A couple of the men had moonshine jars they were passing around, but nobody, it looked like, had thought to bring water. Somebody said, well, there's Son's pump right down there, and the ones near him got a kick out of the remark. Bob Cronin, from Marlett Feed & Seed, said he had a tarp in the truck; maybe they could rig up a tent as a couple of old ladies—fanning themselves with pieces of cardboard—looked like they were about to pass out. Finally they sent a boy over to the Worthman place to bring some water back.

A man would look out over the pasture toward the Martin place and give his opinion of the situation. Son was treed and there wasn't anything he could do about it.

Virgil Worthman said, he couldn't get out by the road down the holler; they'd laid trees across it to box him in.

Bud Blackwell said, down the holler? Shit fire, look at his truck. He couldn't drive it over to the privy.

What the federals ought to do was get up on the slope back of the house, light a hay bale, and drop it on the roof. Burn him out.

Drop it on corrugated tin, yes, sir, that was a swell idea cause everybody knew how tin burned.

It didn't look like any tin roof.

If it didn't then somebody needed glasses. No, the only way was to rush him or starve him out.

How long did anybody figure that would take? Son didn't look like he ate much anyway.

They'd have to rush him and that would be the show to see.

Somebody asked who had seen the Bengal Lancers picture and they got to discussing tortures, like sticking bamboo slivers under a boy's fingernails to get him to tell where something was. Maybe they'd do it to Son if they'd seen the picture.

The closemouthed son of a bitch, you could hardly get him to tell whether he thought it was going to rain or snow.

Somebody said, hey, look, and they all looked toward the house. No, over there coming out of the trees—tiny little ant figures running across the pasture, circling wide to get on a line behind the barn, four of them running in a single file, hurrying hunch-shouldered, the first one gradually gaining distance on the others. Everybody was watching the four men now. They heard the thin report of a rifle from the direction of the Martin house. They heard a muffled echoing report up in the sandstone rocks and they saw the first man go down and lay there, my God, dropped in his tracks from a good three hundred yards. They watched the other three men stop, looking toward the house, then run back as fast as they could to the cover of the trees. They were hidden from sight before anybody on the ridge moved or looked around. One man whistled softly and shook his head. He had a funny, startled look on his face. Others stared out at the tiny dark shape lying in the pasture but nobody spoke for a while.

They would look over at the trees, but they didn't expect to see anybody come out of there again in the daylight.

Lowell Holbrook had got a ride out in Bob Cronin's stake truck. Lowell was the first one to notice Frank Long. He hadn't seen him come; it must have been while they were watching the four men; but there he was. His car was parked just in from where the road came out of the trees into the open and he was standing by the door looking out over the hood, studying the Martin place and letting his gaze drift over to the wooded slope, getting the lay of the land. Lowell wasn't sure what to do, whether he should go over and say anything to him or not. Finally he didn't have to do anything.

Bud Blackwell saw Long. As soon as he did, he walked over with Virgil Worthman and a group came trailing behind.

Long threw them off balance. He nodded and said, "I've been

looking all over for you. I was out to your place and Worthman's before I learned everybody was out here watching." Long looked out at the pasture, then let his gaze move over the cars and groups of people in the clearing.

"Yes, I see a crowd of people watching, but I don't see nobody helping."

Bud shifted his weight, staring narrow-eyed at Frank Long. He wasn't sure what to say now, though he had part of it in mind and said, "It would look to me like you're in the wrong part of the woods. How come you're not leading your men?"

"I'll give you a simple answer. Because they're not my men anymore. They quit me to do it themselves and told me to go home or get put under." Long paused. He had them, they were staring hard at him and he felt only a little tenseness inside. "You wonder what I'm talking about, all right, I'll tell you. Those people over in the trees aren't federal agents at all. See, I wanted to do this job by myself; so I hired some boys, like deputies you might say."

Bud Blackwell and the others were listening, not moving their eyes from him.

"You can understand I got a job to do, to find the whiskey stills. Now then, I figured if I didn't call in any more federal people I'd get all the credit myself. That was bad thinking. But the worst part, I picked the wrong deputies and they want to shoot everybody they see. Well, I got to do a job, as I said. But not if it means shooting at honest men trying to make a living. You follow me?"

If they followed, no one was admitting it. They were letting Frank Long talk.

"I'm here to tell you," Long said, "I made a mistake of judgment. Those people after Son are cutthroat killers, every one of them, and you're standing here watching while they try to murder one of your own boys."

He wanted a short silence, to give his last words time to sink in. But Mr. Worthman spoke up. He said, "You're telling us this. A week ago you tell us you'll bust every still in the county if Son doesn't hand over his whiskey." ·

"Because," Frank Long said simply, "I thought it would be the way to avoid bloodshed."

"Our old uncle shed blood that very night," Mr. Worthman said.

Long nodded solemnly. "I know, and that's when I began to learn these people are killers and I'd made a mistake. A man can make a mistake."

"He surely can," Bud Blackwell said, "and you made your big one coming here thinking we'd help Son Martin. You want us to run the bad boys off so you can get down to bustin' stills again."

"No, sir—"

"So you can go after Son's whiskey yourself."

"No, I'm telling you the truth. If you don't help Son right now, they'll kill him."

"And you won't ever find his whiskey."

"I'm thinking of *him.*"

"Well, bein' you're so thoughtful," Bud Blackwell said, "ought'n you be down there with him?"

It took a couple of seconds for Virgil Worthman to catch on; then he couldn't help smiling. "Sure, he's a friend of Son's—how come he ain't helping him?"

"That's what I mean," Bud said. "He comes up here, says he sees a crowd of people watching, nobody helping. Well, I know one son of a bitch is going to help."

Lowell Holbrook watched them take hold of Long, a bunch of them crowding around so that Long was hidden for a minute. Then they had both of Long's arms twisted behind him and were running him toward the slope of the ridge. He was holding back, but not fighting; he was trying to say something. "Let me take my car down!" he said. God, thinking of his car.

They pushed him down the slope and he ran stumbling and then rolled aways, losing his hat and getting his suit covered with dust and briars.

He stood on the slope looking up, brushing at one sleeve. "Let me get my suitcase," he called out. "All right?"

Virgil Worthman had gotten his shotgun from the car and was aiming it at Long. "You'll get something else," he said, " 'less you start a-running." Long turned after a moment and started down the hill, brushing at his clothes.

Lowell watched him, thinking about the suitcase and the BAR rifle inside.

# 14

Aaron's shoulder was against the grain sacks, his Winchester pointing out the kitchen window. He looked over as Son came down the steps carrying the Springfield.

"You see who's coming?"

"Frank Long."

"How come you didn't shoot him? I 'spected to see him go down about at the stock pen."

"He's coming to join our side."

"Tha's nice," Aaron said.

Son opened the door as Long reached the porch. Through the field glasses he had picked out Long on the ridge and had watched them gang him and throw him down the hill. He said, "Watch the steps."

Long strolled in, looking around the room, at the shattered windows and bullet scars in the walls and cupboards. He was in no hurry. Finally, when he looked at Son, he grinned and said, "How you doing, buddy?"

Son almost smiled. "Not working out like you thought, is it?"

"Buddy, I couldn't stand to look at that man anymore. I come to help you run him off your land."

"Those people up there"—Son nodded toward the ridge— "they wouldn't help you, uh?"

"They got funny ideas, those people."

"Dr. Taulbee, he threw you out, too, I guess."

"We parted company when I learned he was nothing more than a bootlegger."

"You mean when he told you he'd have you shot if you didn't start running."

"Something like that," Long admitted. "But as you can see I didn't run, did I? No, sir, I've stayed to help you beat him."

Son watched him. "You've stayed for more than that."

"Well, you might say I've stayed to protect my interest."

"Your interest in what?"

"That's right, I haven't told you we're going to be partners." Long kept looking at Son with his easy, almost smiling expression. "We might as well be. Since I know where the whiskey's hid."

"Where?"

As Aaron said, "*Now* look-it what's coming—" Son turned to the door and as he saw it—the car bouncing and swerving coming fast down the slope from the ridge—he heard Frank Long say something and then almost shout it, "That's my *car!*"

It looked like the same one, coming dead on toward the house, cutting through the pasture weeds with a wispy trail of dust rising behind. They could hear the rattle of it and the sound of the engine, then the high whine of rifle reports as the car reached the yard, swerved toward the barn, and came around in a wide circle to pull in with the driver's side next to the porch. Lowell Holbrook looked up through the side window, his hands gripping the wheel like he was afraid to let go. Son got him out of there and Frank Long got the suitcase from the back seat. Once they were in the house the rifle fire stopped.

Lowell still looked scared, even as Frank Long patted him on the shoulder and said, "Boy, I think you got a tip coming."

"I don't know," Lowell said. "I don't believe it, but I guess I'm here."

Long had the suitcase on the floor now, like a boy pulling open a birthday present. "You sure are here," he said. "You and Big Sweetheart."

Son took a seat, resting his arm on the table, watching Lowell and Frank as he lit a cigarette. The boy had a good reason for coming or else he wouldn't be here. So there was no sense in asking dumb questions when it appeared the answer was in the suitcase. When he finally saw what it was—as Frank took out the parts of the BAR and began fitting together—Son waited.

He waited until the weapon was assembled and Frank was holding it up before he said, "I've got a few things to say about this party we're having, which I don't remember inviting anybody to. I've got some other things to say about this partnership you mentioned, Frank. But first, I think you better move your car out of the way, else Big Sweetheart isn't going to do you much good."

"That's sound advice," Frank Long said.

It was. Not twenty minutes later Dr. Taulbee came down on them.

"Jesus Christ," Virgil Worthman said, "look at the cars!" He jumped up as the first car came out of the trees wobbling from side to side, easing along in the ruts. The men squatting with him got up and people in other groups, seeing two cars coming toward them, moved out of the way and stood watching. There was an old lady a boy had to help; somebody else snatched her blanket from the ground before the first car reached it.

There was no doubt who they were, the cars coming out of the trees from that direction, from the trail that led around to Son Martin's still. But when Bud Blackwell saw there were just the two cars, with what looked like three men in each, he took his time moving aside and the driver honked his horn at him.

"You had enough?" Bud said. "You all going home now?" The man in the back seat of the car nosed a tommy gun out the window and Bud shut up.

As the cars crept by Virgil Worthman said, "They're going for something. Jesus, I thought for a minute they were coming at us, but they're heading out."

"Like hell," a man near Virgil said. And somebody else said, "They're going right the same way Lowell Holbrook did!"

They were, too, following his tire tracks in the weeds, straight down the slope.

Frank Long said, "Well, here we go, boys," and turned the BAR in the direction of the cars.

He had taken over Aaron's window—once he'd pushed his car away from the porch—and swiveled the BAR around in the windowsill, letting the sights roam over the yard and the barn. Holding the gun on an angle out the window, he could train it on the rocks above old man Martin's grave and sweep left into the trees. Dr. Taulbee was in for a surprise.

Lowell Holbrook was on the floor. Son and Aaron were at the second window, facing off the porch with a clear view of the two cars coming at them on a line from out of the pasture. The cars didn't belong to anybody in Marlett, Son was sure of that now, and Frank Long confirmed it. "Taulbee's fastest cars," he said. "But you can bet the doctor ain't in either of them."

Son could make out the barrel of an automatic shotgun sticking out the front window of the first car. He suspected the machine gun would be in back, but didn't see it until the first car was swerving at the corner of the house to cross in front of them and he was firing the Springfield at the sunspot on the windshield and Aaron's Winchester was going off in his ear as the BAR opened up, filling the room with its hard-pounding racket. Son was aware of a Thompson firing from the first car, but now he was swinging his front sight to the second car, firing twice to empty the clip, then brought up the Smith & Wesson to let go at the car's side windows. Now Aaron had emptied the Winchester; he grabbed the Remington and fired both barrels fast, without putting the gun to his shoulder, and the BAR kept pounding away. Son watched the first car veer off out of control and go through the front of the barn. The second car was running for open country with Long's BAR chasing it until the pan was empty and, in the silence, they watched the car bump and scrape its way to the far side of the pasture. Two men got out and ran for the trees. There were no sounds from the barn. Past the shattered frame of the opening, the rear end of the car was barely visible in the dimness.

They reloaded and sat watching the barn. Son looked over at

Frank Long a few feet away, then let his gaze move outside again. He said, "Where do you think the whiskey's hid?"

Long answered without looking over. "Under your old daddy's grave."

Son could feel Aaron and Lowell Holbrook watching him. "A hundred and fifty barrels," he said. "That would be some hole."

"If you dug it straight down," Long said, looking at him now. "But if the grave is sitting on a mine entrance or an air shaft, then it's something else."

"That's what you think, uh?"

"I think it's funny the old man is buried up there by himself when the rest of your kin are down in the graveyard."

"That's where he asked to be buried."

"You say it and people believe it. Like the light over the grave, you say he wanted it because he died in the dark of a mine shaft." Long turned from the window. "I say you rigged the light so you can keep an eye on your whiskey when it's dark."

Son watched him get up from the window and look around the room, the BAR under his arm now.

"What're you looking for?"

"The switch."

"Right behind you, on the wall."

Long turned. The light switch was near the window. He stooped then. "The tommy guns tore up your wall, didn't they? You can see the wires where they come in from outside."

As Son rose he glanced at Aaron, whose eyes shifted briefly and returned to Long. Past Long's shoulder they could see where the window frame and wall planks had been splintered by gun-fire. Long pulled away fragments of wood, then worked a board lose and twisted it out of the wall.

"It might have shot up your wiring," he said. His back was to them as he looked closely into the opening. "You've got a number of wires in there for one light post, haven't you? I see two wires coming in. One goes up to the switch. What's this other one for?"

"I guess it used to be part of the house wiring," Son answered. "Goes down to the Delco outfit in the cellar."

Long straightened, leaning the BAR against the wall. "It doesn't look like it to me. I learned wiring in the Engineers same as you did."

Son kept watching him. "Probably for something my dad had hooked up."

"You're telling me a story now," Long said. "That wire comes in from outside." His eyes moved over the wall. "Runs along there—I'd say over to that cupboard." He walked past the stove to the other side of the room; stooping, he opened the lower doors of the cabinet.

"Can goods," Son told him.

"That's all I see."

Long remained stooped, feeling inside. He jiggled the bottom board, then pushed the cans aside and lifted the board, wedging it against the shelf above it.

Aaron turned from the window, letting the barrel of the Winchester rest on Long. Son didn't move or take his eyes from the man.

"Well, now," Long said, "look-it here." He glanced over his shoulder, then noticed Lowell Holbrook watching him and motioned with his head. "Boy, you ever see one of these?"

Lowell came over. He didn't know if something was going to jump out of that dark space or what. "Get closer," Long said, and Lowell hunkered down next to him.

"Know what it is?"

"It looks like some kind of a box."

"What's it look like with this handle in the top?"

Son straightened slightly. "Be careful now."

"He means it," Long said. "For if I was to push this down—"

Lowell knew what it was now. "It's a dynamite thingumajig—an exploder!"

Long looked over at Son, grinning. "That's what it is all right—hey, Son?—a dynamite thingumajig, like we used to have in the Engineers. Boy," he said then, "why do you suppose he'd wire this up to his old daddy's grave?"

"I don't know," Lowell said. "To blow it up?"

"You believe he'd blow up his daddy's remains?"

"No, I don't think so."

"No, sir, his daddy ain't in that grave. Is he, Son?"

Son hesitated. "You're telling it."

"All right, I'd say his daddy's buried someplace else. That grave, what looks like a grave, covers up an old mine shaft that tunnels into the hill, and that's where the whiskey's at, set with charges, so that anybody was to dig there and find the whiskey, Son pushes the plunger and *boom*, nobody gets it. How many sticks you got in the hole, Son?"

"About a hundred and fifty."

Long stood up, looking at Son, smiling. "A stick a barrel. That's more'n you'd need to do the job. Let's see now, you got the two wires running out there under the ground. Insulated good, are they?"

"In some lead pipe," Son answered. He felt Aaron looking at him again, like he was crazy to admit anything. But Long was right and he was here. They couldn't get rid of him or shoot him for knowing.

"So every evening," Long said now, "you turn on your light. If it works you know your wiring's good and hasn't got corroded or chewed up by little animal creatures. Son, that's pretty good thinking. Though if you was to blow it, that would be a terrible way to treat good whiskey."

"I guess you can see the point of it though," Son said.

"Yes, sir, if you don't take the whiskey out yourself, nobody does. But things are different now, Son. You got a partner."

"How does that make it different?"

"You won't need to think about blowing up your whiskey. I mean *our* whiskey." Long stooped at the cupboard again. He took a spring knife from his pocket, reached in and cut the wire connected to the plunger. "So you won't blow up our business when I'm not looking," Long said. He lifted out the box, dropped it, and proceeded to smash it into pieces with the stock of his BAR. "Now then," he said, "let's figure out how we're going to run old Dr. Taulbee."

The only thing they decided for sure was that after dark Lowell Holbrook would slip out through the hollow and run home. If, Frank Long said, he wasn't afraid of being out in the dark. Lowell said he wasn't afraid of the dark, that wasn't the reason he wanted to stay. But Son told him no, he had done a brave thing, but he wasn't going to stay here to get shot at; it wasn't his affair. Frank Long told Lowell he was the best bellboy he had ever seen and gave him ten dollars for bringing his suitcase.

Son, with the 12-gauge, saw Lowell across the yard. Coming

back, Son approached the barn from the blind side, slipped through the fence rails and got up close to the building and pressed his ear against a seam in the boards. He listened for about ten minutes before going in and feeling his way to the car. He waited again, briefly, before striking a match. There were blood stains on both the front and rear seats, but no sign of the three men. Son went out the back, the way they would have left, and looked out over the open pasture in the moonlight, at the brush shadows and the dark mass of trees beyond. Then he circled back, around the barn to the house.

Later in the night, listening, watching the slope, Son touched Long's shoulder and pointed out into the darkness. "Straight up there," he said. "You know where the grave would be?" Long said he thought he did. "Then put your gun on it," Son told him. "Right above it."

Son put his hand on the light switch. "You ready?" As Long answered, Son turned it on.

A hundred yards away on the hillside, the grave and the light post and a moving figure were illuminated and the BAR hammered through the darkness until the figure disappeared and the light went off as Son flicked the switch.

"Buddy," Long said, "that's a good idea. It's too bad we can't pull it more than once."

"Maybe we can." Son was staring out at the darkness. One idea was leading to another, an idea that could end this; but he said no more to Frank Long.

# 15

Friday morning, June 26, Dr. Taulbee made a decision: this would be the last day he could afford to sit out here in the piney woods playing war.

It would be simple to outwait the man and starve him out. It had seemed simple before. But now, he realized, that could take a month for all anybody knew. Dr. Taulbee wasn't financing an extended campaign, or performing for the audience over on the ridge, or taking a chance that word of the siege wouldn't get in the county newspapers. That happened and before he knew it, the federal people would be driving up. No, thank you.

He had been out here two days and two nights. To show for it he had four dead, another who probably wouldn't last the day, two more shot up, two cars out of commission, and eight men left who gave him sullen stares, waiting for him to think of something. He asked them, don't you want to get that boy's whiskey?

Don't you want to get Frank Long? All right, a hundred-dollar bonus to the man that shoots him.

But he still had to convince them he knew what he was doing. He had to maintain their confidence. And, Jesus, if he didn't do another thing he had to keep them busy, away from the boy dying with the bullet in his chest. So this morning he kept six of them peppering away at the house with rifles while the other two men drove to town to get Miley. He might as well keep Miley busy too. He had an idea for getting his boys in the mood for an all-out fight and needed Miley to help him.

The image Dr. Taulbee presented to the world that Friday morning was one of relaxed confidence. He sat in a wicker-back rocking chair on the porch of Son Martin's still, smoking a cigar, rocking gently, letting his tough boys from Louisville know he had the situation under control.

When Miley walked into the yard, looking around, frowning in the sunlight, she said. "What am I suppose to do out here? I can't shoot a gun and I never was a campfire girl."

Dr. Taulbee smiled at her and said, "As soon as you finish being a little sour-mouth smart-ass, I'll tell you."

Miley shrugged and waited, and Dr. Taulbee said, what she was going to do, she was going to march down the hill and tell Son Martin he had one last chance to give up and save his life. And, if he acted at once on this offer, he would be paid a dollar a gallon for his whiskey.

Miley thought about it, picturing Son Martin. "And what do I do when he says no?"

"You come on back here."

"If you know what he's going to say, then what's the good of asking him?"

"Because of what you say when you get back."

"What is it I say?"

"In front of the men, you tell them all three of them down there are shot up and in pain, just barely dragging theirselves around with blood all over everything. They look to you like they won't last till night."

"Yeah," Miley said, "then what?"

"Then our brave boys, smelling easy victory, storm the house and finish them off."

Miley shook her head. "You sure are  a thinker."

375

"You cute thing," Dr. Taulbee said, "give us a kiss before you go."

"They all out there again," Aaron said. "More than yesterday."

Son looked out across the pasture to the cars parked on the open ridge. "Come to see the show."

"I don't understand them people."

Son made no comment.

"Something else I don't understand," Aaron said. "Why you told him about the grave."

"He figured it out."

"He was guessing."

"But he was right. Whether I said anything or not, he was right. If he gets out of this he'll dig for the whiskey and find it. But we can't shoot him because he knows where it is, can we?"

"I don't know," Aaron said. "Maybe *you* can't."

Son looked over at him, then at the ceiling. "There's something we can do if he stays up there long enough." He edged closer to Aaron at the window. "The light switch—"

"Hey, what're you two whispering about?" Frank Long's voice came from the hole drilled in the ceiling.

Son's eyes raised. "We were just talking about you, Frank. Arguing which one of us is going to shoot you."

They heard him laugh. "Son, you wouldn't shoot an old buddy."

"You ain't an old buddy of Aaron's."

"What're you talking about?" Long said. "Hey, Aaron, I meant to tell you. I'm giving you a cut of the whiskey take, boy, so don't be having any dark thoughts. You hear?"

Looking up at the ceiling, Aaron didn't answer. He said to Son, "You want him with you?"

"No."

Son had made up his mind. He could say yes, thinking about the whiskey, the work and the years that had gone into it. He could say, all right, Frank Long is a partner. Finish this with his help. Maybe. Get the whiskey out and sell it with half the county knowing and watching and split the profit with a crooked federal agent he used to know in the Army. Do all that before another gang like Dr. Taulbee's heard about the whiskey and came down with the guns to start another war. Or before the Prohibition agents heard and started busting stills all over again. Forty-five hundred gallons of eight-year-old whiskey was a good idea at one time. Now it was a dream a man would have with his head under the covers, while he wished all the trouble it caused would go away.

He knew he wasn't going to drink forty-five hundred gallons himself and it didn't look like he was going to sell the whiskey. So if he didn't want anybody else to have it, there was only one thing left to do.

Blow it up. Splice the dynamite wire to the electrical system and turn on the switch.

If he could think of a way to keep Frank Long busy while he made the splice.

Walk up to him and knock him cold; that was one way. Hit him with a gun stock or a hunk of kindling if he had to. Then wire the charge and blow it and hope Dr. Taulbee would look at the smoke and go home.

That was the trouble. Son couldn't be sure what Dr. Taulbee would do. He was a scary son of a bitch, with his big smile. He might look at the smoke and go right out of his head.

Frank Long came downstairs with the BAR under his arm. "What I want to know," he said, "is who you expect will be coming next? Look-it out there."

Miley looked up from the porch steps to the house. "You got a ladder or is somebody going to pull me up?" She could see Son in the window. She didn't know Long was here until he opened the door and stepped out. When he leaned down to give her a hand, Miley continued to stare at him. Finally she let herself be pulled up. On the porch she brushed at the front of her skirt before looking at him again.

"It doesn't appear you're being held for ransom."

"I switched over, honey, seeing the error of my ways. That's a terrible person you're playing house with."

"He must have thrown you out," Miley said.

Long grinned at her. "How about yourself?"

"I've come with a message."

"Well, come in, honey; we want to hear it."

Miley looked around the room before her gaze settled on Son Martin. "You look all right to me," she said.

"We're getting along." Son realized he was glad to see her. He couldn't help smiling and she smiled back at him.

"Emmett says if you all want to quit now he'll pay you a dollar a gallon for the whiskey."

"We're asking five," Long said.

"*We* are." Miley raised her eyebrows. "We fit ourselves right in, don't we?"

"You want to be on our side?"

"It's a thought, isn't it?" Miley looked at Son. "I doubt if he can pay your price."

"Even if he could," Son said, "and was willing, the whiskey's not for sale. Tell him that. Not for a dollar, not for ten dollars."

"So you're still the one to talk to," Miley said.

"Tell him if he wants it he'll have to come get it."

"I expect he will. Though he's running out of people."

"How many we get?" Long asked her.

"Four, I think. Maybe five by now."

"Hey, Son, that ain't bad, is it?" Long looked at Miley again. "You sure you don't want to be on our side?"

"I'd have to think about it," Miley said. "It looks to me like the odds are still way against you."

"But changing all the time."

"That's true." Miley nodded. "But I still think he's going to win."

"I'll tell you what," Long said. "You stay here awhile with us and see how you like it."

"If I don't get back he'll send them looking for me."

"He might at that. What if we tell him we'll shoot you if he doesn't clear out?"

Miley laughed. "Are you kidding?"

"That's what I thought," Long said. "So we'll just keep you here and won't say anything and see what happens."

Son almost overruled him. He almost took Miley by the arm to push her outside; but he saw something—the way Long was openly looking at her body, peeling her clothes off with his gaze. Son went over to the stove. "You're going to stay," he said, "you might as well fix us something to eat."

Miley followed him over. "If that's what you want." Long's eyes were on the nice little can moving in the tight skirt. Son noticed that too.

\*    \*    \*

"I'd like to see them run in there with the cars again," Bud Blackwell said. "Jesus, the one car went right through the barn."

"You hear that gun they got?" Virgil Worthman said.

"Like a machine gun." Bud pulled the weed stem from his mouth and made a noise like a machine gun firing.

Lowell Holbrook looked over at him. "It was a BAR rifle," he said, "belongs to Frank Long. Doesn't anybody know a BAR rifle when they hear one?" Gazing off at the house he walked away from them, like he wanted to study the house from a different angle. He knew the people were watching him.

Let them wonder what he was thinking. He had been in that house all yesterday afternoon until dark and he knew things nobody else knew. Last night and earlier this morning nobody would leave him alone, all the questions they asked. Why had he gone down there? Wasn't he scared? How were they doing? Had any of them been shot? Lowell told them the man was a guest of the hotel; the man had wanted his car and his suitcase, so he delivered them. That's all there was to it.

Now, every once in a while, somebody would ask him what he thought was going to happen. Lowell would study the house with his cool gaze and say, "Don't worry about Son Martin." A couple of times he wanted to add, "If you're so worried, why don't you go help him?" But he never did. If anybody wanted to help Son, but didn't do anything about it, it was their own personal business. A person knew what he should do and what he shouldn't do.

Lowell had a feeling for a while that Mrs. Lyons was going to do something. It had surprised him to see her drive up this morning. He would watch her when he remembered her being here. She stood by herself most of the time. Once she had asked him if he thought Son was all right and he gave her the answer, "Don't worry about Son Martin." She had looked awful worried; maybe it was true they were going to bed together. She had talked to other people, maybe trying to get them to help. But Lowell didn't see anybody getting any guns out of their cars. After a while Mrs. Lyons sat down on the corner of a blanket that a couple of ladies had spread. Lowell watched her holding a cup as one of the ladies poured coffee in it from a thermos.

Everybody was sure prepared today. They had picnic baskets

379

and coffee and Coca-Colas, blankets and folding chairs and canvas awnings built out from some of the cars. There was even a cook-fire for anyone who wanted to fix a hot meal.

"Somebody ought to sell tickets," Lowell said to Mrs. Lyons, and got a strange, sorrowful look from her, like she might be going to cry. Though she didn't.

The heavy-set guy, Carl, came over through the brush to tell Dr. Taulbee there was no sign of her yet, she was still in the house.

"They think they're pulling a stunt," Dr. Taulbee said. He blew a thin stream of cigar smoke toward the edge of the roof over the porch. "We start down there shooting and they tie her to the front door."

"If that was to happen, what do we do?" the man asked.

"You'd keep shooting."

"We been shooting, mister, for two days."

"Now when was it," Dr. Taulbee said, "somebody told me he was going to bring the nigger out dead and the other with his hands in the air? It seems to me it was the night before last. Well, buddy, I have been waiting for that to happen. I been watching you hotshots with your tommy guns and high-powered rifles, but I haven't seen any results. I don't know with all the shooting you been doing one of them is even nicked. Can you tell me that? If all this shooting for two days has hit anybody? No, you can't, buddy, because you haven't been close enough to that house to find out. Now tell me again how you're going to bring them out."

Carl's thick shoulders were hunched. He stood sullenly, looking up at Dr. Taulbee, who was rocking in the chair slowly back and forth. "We'll get them out," the man said.

"Yes, I know you will," Dr. Taulbee said. "Sometime. Tell me something, is there any hay in that barn?"

"Plenty of hay."

"And there's a car in the barn?"

"That's right."

"If you were to get down to that barn just as it's getting dark—start the car up and get it loaded with nice dry hay."

"Yeah?" The man's sullen expression came alive then. "Set the hay afar and run the car into the house!"

"That'd bring them out, wouldn't it?"

"God*damn* if it wouldn't."

"Buddy," Dr. Taulbee said, "I think you got an idea."

"Miley," Frank Long said, stretching as he got up from the table, "you ain't much at the stove; but then a girl can't be an expert at everything, can she?"

Her eyes moved to Son at the window. "Some people like my coffee."

"Some hill boys will drink anything." Long grinned. "Hey, Son, I'm just kidding you. You got fine taste and good grub. I'll sit at your table any time."

Son looked over. "I'd appreciate you more at a window. You going back upstairs?"

"I guess I better."

"We'll see you later then."

Long reached for his BAR leaning against the table, then hesitated. "Hey, Miley, why don't you come up and keep me company?"

"I was going to do the dishes," she said, looking over at Son again.

"You can do them later. Son, you don't care if she does them later, do you?"

Crouching at the window, waiting for Long to get upstairs, Son shook his head. "I don't care."

"Honey, you can stretch out on the bed if you want, take a little rest."

"I'll bet," Miley said.

"What do you mean by that?" Long's tone was meant to sound offended.

"Oh, come on," Miley said then, "get your gun and let's go up."

Watching the pasture and the hillside—and the light post far up on the slope marking the grave—Son listened to them mount the bare wooden stairs. He heard them in the room, the floor boards creaking. He heard Miley laugh. Long's voice came to them through the drilled hole in the floor. "Keep a close watch now, you hear?"

Son didn't raise his eyes. He said, "We hear," and waited in the silence of the room. He waited several minutes before glancing at Aaron, who crawled over and put a hand on the Springfield, holding it on the windowsill, as Son moved to the bullet-shattered opening in the wall and worked quickly with his knife, cutting the line to the light post and splicing the end of the dynamite line to the wire that led from the switch down to the battery-powered electrical system. He covered the opening with the board Long had pulled loose, then removed it again. Long might notice the board and wonder why it had been put back. Son reached for a kitchen chair. He set it against the opening, then put his .38 on the chair with a box of cartridges, as if he placed the chair close to have the gun within reach.

Son leaned back against the grain sacks under the window. Looking up at the ceiling he lit a cigarette, wondering if Frank was having a good time, wondering how long he'd be up there.

When Miley came down, she put the coffee pot on the fire and asked Son if he'd like a cup. He nodded and watched her turn to the stove.

"You want to go back to Taulbee?"

He saw her shoulders move. "I guess so. I mean, where else is there to go?"

"What if something happens to him?"

"I don't know."

"Do you think about it?"

"Sometimes."

"What do you think you'd do?"

Miley turned toward him now. "I guess I'd look around, wait for an offer. Are you making one?"

"I was just asking."

"Do you want to go upstairs?"

Watching her, Son shook his head.

"Why, what's the difference between right now and the other day?"

"Do you see a difference?"

"I guess so. Or I wouldn't have said it like that."

"You want to shock me," Son said.

She nodded, slowly. "Do you know why?"

"I'm not sure."

"Because if you ever made an offer, no matter what it was, I'd probably take it. But you're never going to make an offer. There," Miley said, pausing, then turning to the stove again. "You can take that and do whatever you want with it."

Son got up from the window. "Pour me a cup," he said. "I'll be back directly."

Up in the bedroom, Long was sitting on the bed facing the window where the BAR leaned against the sill. He looked over as Son came in. "You want me to clear out?"

Son went to the window. He stood next to it looking up at the slope. "You remember last night," he said, "you got a shot at the guy by the grave?"

"I mentioned it was a good idea," Long said, "but would only work once."

Son looked at him. "What if I got Taulbee and the whole bunch to line up right there."

"How?"

"Tell them where the whiskey is."

"He wouldn't believe it."

"I'd go up there and start digging. They see the shaft entrance and the first barrels, they know it's true."

Long nodded. "While they're standing there I open up with Big Sweetheart."

"How's it sound?"

"You're standing there too, buddy."

"I wait till they're looking in the hole, then I make a run for it."

"Maybe."

"As I take off, you open up."

"I'd have to hit them the first time, wouldn't I? If they get to cover, you're dead."

"You hit that boy last night."

"I think I did."

"But you'd have to be sure I was out of the way."

"Come on, buddy, you think I'd fire while you was standing there?"

"I just mention it, Frank."

Long nodded, squinting as he looked at the late-afternoon light filling the window. "It would be shooting the works, wouldn't it? If I don't hit them, they got the whiskey."

Son shrugged. "I don't see any other way."

"My, it's a chancy deal though, isn't it?"

"You want to try it?"

"How do we get the word to him?"

"Send Miley."

"I was just getting to know the girl."

"You don't have to shoot her."

"I was hoping not."

"She'd go out just a little way and call to them I'm coming."

"Well," Long said, "if you got the nerve, I got the gun."

Son frowned, making a face. "I hope I got the nerve. Maybe I'd better think about it a little more."

"What'd you tell me about it for if you don't want to do it?"

"I want to be sure, is all."

"Well, it's not something anybody can be *sure* of. Listen, we don't do it soon there won't be enough light. I want to be sure too."

"Let me study on it awhile."

"If you don't want to go up there," Long said, "I won't hold it against you, don't worry about that. But if you do want to go, we got to act quick. I mean it's your idea, buddy; it's up to you. I'll tell you what though. I think you can pull it off."

Son stared out the window, thoughtful. After a moment he said, "Why don't you go down and get some coffee. Let me think about it."

He remained at the window until the sun was behind the ridge and a shadow lay across the slope and darkened the sandstone wall above the grave. He waited until Long climbed the stairs again and stood in the doorway looking at him.

Son turned from the window. "I'm ready if you are."

"You want to do it?"

"I just made up my mind as you came up the stairs."

"Just a little too late," Long said.

"Why? It's still light out."

"Not over on the slope."

Son looked out the window. "You can see the post, the grave."

"But not clear; there ain't enough light."

Right now, Son told himself and looked over at Long again. "You know what you just said? Not enough light?"

Long was nodding, beginning to smile. "I was thinking the same thing. There's a light up there. All I got to do, as you start to run, is turn it on."

"That's all."

"You see any problems?"

"Not after that," Son answered.

\*     \*     \*

He waited on the porch, leaning on a shovel, while Miley went out to the edge of the hardpack, where the path started across the pasture, and called out to Dr. Taulbee.

She would point to the house and yell out as loud as she could, "He's coming out! He wants to talk to you!" There was no response from the hillside, no sign of movement, but Taulbee must have heard. Miley's voice carried across the pasture, each word hanging sharply clear in the evening stillness.

Son looked over at the window, at the barrel of the BAR sticking out, at Frank Long and Aaron watching him. "I'll see you," he said, and jumped down from the porch and started off, the shovel pointing up over his shoulder. Miley came toward him as she returned to the house.

"Take care of yourself, all right?"

"I'll be back," he said, not pausing, walking out to the pasture, his eyes on the trees and brush and the rock outcropping that towered above the grave, holding the slope in its shadow. He watched for signs of them, but saw no one until he was almost to the grave. Then a figure stood up among the rocks, a man pointing a rifle at him. Son kept walking until he reached the low fence around the grave and stepped over it. He saw several more men in the rocks now, but paid no attention to them. He began digging in front of the headstone. After a few minutes he could hear them coming toward him. Pushing the shovel into the earth with his foot, he looked up. Taulbee was coming out of the trees.

Son straightened now to wait, the handle of the shovel upright in front of him.

"I hope you're not pulling something," Dr. Taulbee said. "If you are, you're dead."

Son watched him come up almost to the fence. "I'm showing you where it is," he said, leaning in then and throwing out another shovel of dirt. "I'm going to take your offer, a dollar a gallon, and clear out. Then it's up to you what you do with it."

Dr. Taulbee was in no hurry. He stared at Son, as if trying to see something else behind his words. "You're telling me the whiskey's buried here, in a grave?"

"It's no grave, it's a mine tunnel. You'll see." He began digging again, aware of Taulbee's men moving in closer. Taulbee placed one foot on the fence and leaned on his thigh as he watched.

"All of a sudden you just give up, uh?"

"I don't see any point in dying for whiskey."

"What does Frank say about it?"

"He doesn't have any say. It's my whiskey."

"You just suddenly change your mind."

"Do you want to listen to me talk or see me dig it up?"

"Go ahead," Dr. Taulbee said. "We're all anxiously awaiting."

After a few minutes the blade of the shovel struck something hard. Son cleared the dirt away and lifted out a board. "Look down in there," he said.

Dr. Taulbee leaned over the fence. "I don't see nothing."

"Get closer. Down in there you see part of the first barrel."

Taulbee stepped over the fence now to peer into the dark opening. "It might be a barrel. Take some more boards out."

"I'm giving you the whiskey," Son said. "I'm not going to dig it out for you. What you see is the end of a ditch that leads over there to the shaft entrance, where the slope gets steeper."

"I got to see more of it," Dr. Taulbee said, " 'fore I know for sure what you're selling me."

Son looked right at him. "You got a flashlight?"

"Over at the house."

Now Son's eyes raised to the post. "Well, there's a light right here we can use."

Taulbee looked up, squinting. "Turn it on." As Son stepped over the fence he said quickly, "Where you think you're going?"

Son half-turned. "To get the light put on."

"You can't work it here?"

"No, the switch's in the house. I got to holler for somebody to turn it on." Son started down the slope, feeling Taulbee and the men with the guns watching him.

"Hey," Taulbee called out. "That's far enough!"

Son stopped. "They won't hear me less I get a little closer." He started walking again, taking his time, moving steadily down the slope. When Taulbee called again, he kept walking, holding himself to the same pace.

"You hear me!" Taulbee yelled.

Son kept going.

"Another step, boy, we shoot!"

Son came to a halt facing the house across the pasture, a deserted-looking house, the two front windows dark squares in the shadow of the porch. He wanted to look around, to see how far he was from the grave. He could feel Taulbee and his men standing by the mound, all of them facing this way. Son didn't look back.

He called out, "Hey, Frank!"

He was aware of the cars and the people on the ridge, way off to the right.

His eyes remained on the house. He was thinking, if you started running right now—there's a chance.

But then he said to himself, get your head out of the covers, boy. And he yelled, "Hey, Frank—turn on the light!"

There was a moment he would remember that stood alone, motionless, in dead silence. The moment ended and the hillside behind him exploded.

Frank Long's hand was still on the light switch as the sound rocked across the pasture and filled the hollows. As he looked out, the explosion shook the house and he saw the hill blown apart in a jarring string of eruptions that lifted smoke and earth into the air and billowed out to envelop the lone figure on the slope. As he watched, as the smoke thinned and rose against the sky, the first thing Long noticed was the outcropping of rock that crowned the heights of the ridge. Through the haze of dust he saw that the face of the wall was altered. Rock and brush had come sliding down in the explosion and now covered the upper part of the slope. There was no sign of the grave or Dr. Taulbee or his men.

The figure on the lower part of the slope was looking toward the rocks.

Long was outside before he noticed the people coming down from the ridge. A few remained by the cars, but most of them had started for the pasture, coming in straggling groups, coming almost hesitantly, but coming.

They stood looking past Son at the rubble covering the slope, at the place that had been a grassy hillside and the site of a man's grave. When he turned and walked down the grade toward them, they continued to gaze off beyond him and above him, staring solemnly in the dust haze.

Bud Blackwell seemed about to speak, looking at Son for a moment, but said nothing.

Frank Long was the only one who spoke. He said, "After all that work, uh?"

Son didn't answer. He was aware of Long and the others as he walked past them toward the house. Without looking at anyone directly, he was aware of familiar faces: the Blackwells, the Worthmans, and Stampers; Lowell Holbrook standing awkwardly; Miley Mitchell, alone, watching him; Aaron on the porch, holding on to a post, waiting for him. He wondered if Kay was here, though he didn't look for her among the solemn faces.

Son walked on until he was almost to the yard. It was here that he stopped and looked back and said, "I got a half barrel and some fruit jars if anybody feels the need."

# GOLD COAST

# 1

One day Karen DiCilia put a few observations together and realized her husband, Frank, was sleeping with a real estate woman in Boca.

Karen knew where they were doing it, too. In one of the condominiums Frank owned, part of Oceana Estates.

Every Friday afternoon and sometimes on Monday, Frank would put his spare clubs in the trunk of his Seville—supposedly to play at La Gorce, Miami Beach—and drive north out of Fort Lauderdale instead of south.

There were probably others, random affairs. Frank did go to Miami at least twice a week to "study the market" and play a little gin at the Palm Bay Club. He could have a cocktail waitress at Hialeah or Calder. He visited the dogtracks regularly, the jai-alai fronton once in a while. Cruised for gamefish out in the stream with some of his buddies; went bonefishing in the Keys, near

Islamorada, several times a year. Frank could have something going anywhere from Key West to West Palm, over to Bimini and back and probably did. The only one Karen was sure of, though, was the frosted-blond thirty-six-year-old real estate woman in Boca.

Frank's actions, his routine, were predictable; but not his reactions. If she confronted him, or hinted around first, with questions like, "Do I know her?" or, "Are you going to tell me who she is?"

Frank would say, "Who're we talking about?"

And Karen would say, "I know you've got a girl friend. Why don't you admit it?"

And Frank would say—

He might say, "Nobody told you I have a girl friend and you haven't seen me with anybody that could be a girl friend, so what're we talking about?"

And Karen would say, "The real estate woman in Boca," and offer circumstantial evidence that wouldn't convict him but would certainly put him in a corner.

He might deny it outright. Or he might say, "Yeah, sometimes I go to Boca. Not that it's any of your fucking business."

Then what? She'd have to get mad or pout or act hurt.

So Karen didn't say a word about the real estate woman. Instead, she drove her matching white Caddy Seville up to Boca one Friday afternoon, to the big pink condominium that looked like a Venetian palace.

She located Frank's white Seville in the dim parking area beneath the building, on the ocean side, backed it out of the numbered space with the spare set of keys she'd brought, left Frank's car sitting in the aisle, got into her own car again and drove her white Seville into the side of his white Seville three times, smashing in both doors and the front fender of Frank's car, destroying her own car's grille and headlamps, and drove back to Lauderdale. When Frank came home he looked from one matching Seville to the other. Karen waited, but he didn't say a word about the cars. The next day he had them towed away and new matching gray ones delivered.

Weeks later, in the living room, she said, "I'm getting tired of tennis." And said to the dog, sniffing around her feet, "Gretchen, leave, will you? Get out of here."

"Play golf," Frank said. He patted his leg and the gray and white schnauzer jumped up on his lap.

"I don't care for golf."

"Join some ladies' group." Gently stroking the schnauzer.

"I've done ladies' groups."

"Take up fishing, I'll get you a boat."

"Do you know what I do?" Karen said. "I exist. I sit in the sun. I try to think up work for Marta and for when the gardener comes—" She paused a moment. "When we got married—I mean at our wedding reception, you know what my mother said to me?"

"What?"

"She said, 'I hope you realize he's Italian.' She didn't know anything else, just your name."

"Half Italian," Frank said, "half Sicilian. There's a difference. Like Gretchen here"—stroking the dog on his lap, the dog dozing—"she's part schnauzer, part a little something else, so that makes her different."

"You don't get it, do you?" Karen said.

"Get what? She's from Grosse Pointe. I lived in Grosse Pointe one time. What's that? You buy a house."

"She wasn't being a snob. At least not when she said it."

"All right, what did she mean I'm Italian? What was she? Hill, maybe it was shortened from Hilkowski. Are you a Polack maybe? What're we talking about?"

"What she meant," Karen said, "the way you lived, what you were used to. You'd probably be set in your ways. You'd have your man things to do, and I'd have to find woman things to do. And she was right, not even knowing anything about what you really did, or might still be doing, I don't know, since you don't tell me anything."

"I'm retired," Frank said, "and you're tired of playing tennis and sitting around. All right, what do you want to do?"

"Maybe I'll just do it and not tell you," Karen said.

"Do what?" Frank asked.

"Not tell you where I go or who I see. Or make up something. Tell you I'm going to play tennis but I don't. I go someplace else."

"Stick to tennis," Frank said. He stopped stroking Gretchen. "You have a very hard time coming right out and saying something. You want to threaten me, is that it? Because you're bored? Are you telling me you're gonna start fooling around? If that's what you're saying, say it. A man comes to me and gives me some shit out the side of his mouth. I tell him that's it, get the fuck out or talk straight. Now I'm much more patient with you, Karen, you're my wife and I respect you. You're an intelligent, good-looking women. I tell you something, I know you understand what I'm saying. I'm not dumb either, even though I didn't go to the University of Michigan when I was younger or one of those. Especially I'm not gonna *look* dumb, like have people point to me and say, 'Yeah, that's the guy, his wife's ballin' the tennis pro, the dumb fuck's paying the bill,' anything like that. No—you get bored and a little irritable, okay, use your head, work it out some way. But don't ever lie to me, all right? Or threaten me, like you're gonna pay me back for something. I know all about paying back. I could write a book about paying back, then look at it and realize I left a few things out."

"My mother was right," Karen said. "You can do anything you want, but I can't."

"Your mother— You're a big girl," Frank said, "you were a big girl—what?—forty years old when we got married. You should know a few things by forty years old, uh, what it's gonna be like married to a half-Italian with varied and different business interests. You know what it's like? In the Bible. You got this house, eight hundred grand—sightseers come by the Intercoastal in the boats, look at it, 'Jesus Christ, imagine living in a place like that.' You got the apartment in Boca on the ocean. You got clothes, anything you want to buy. Servants, cars, clubs—"

"Go on," Karen said. "I have a dog—"

"Place in the Keys. Friends—"

"Your friends."

"I'm saying it's like in the Bible, you got anything you want to make you happy. Except there's one thing you're not allowed to do, and it's not even unreasonable, it's the natural law."

"What is?"

"A wife's faithful to her husband, subject to him. It's in the Bible."

"If I don't tell you what I'm doing, I'm being unfaithful?"

"What do you want to argue for? Haven't I been good to you?

Jesus Christ, look around here, this place. The paintings, the furniture—"

"Your first wife's antiques."

"I don't get it. Five years, you don't say a word—"

"Five and a half," Karen said.

"Okay, there's some very rare, valuable pieces here. I happen to like this kind of stuff," Frank said. "But anything you don't like, sell it. Redecorate the whole place if you want."

"Keep me busy."

"What's the *matter* with you?"

Saying she was bored and irritable—while he went off to visit his girl friend in Boca, a real estate women. Five and a half years of playing the good wife and now having the Bible thrown at her.

Karen made a mistake then, but was too angry to realize it at the time.

She gave Frank an ultimatum. She said, "No more double standard. If it's all right for you to fool around, it's all right for me to fool around. I may not want to, but I'll do it, buddy, as a matter of principle and you can see how you like it."

Frank seemed tired. He shook his head and said, "Karen, Karen, Karen—" and began stroking the dog again.

She did have misgivings later, twinges in her stomach whenever she thought about it and realized she had actually threatened him to his face. If that wasn't being a big girl, what was? She was relieved he never brought it up and would reassure herself with thoughts like, Of course not. Frank knew she'd never have an affair. Frank knew she had simply overstated, that was all, to make a point.

She would replay the scene in her mind and revise it as she went along, keeping her voice in control, maintaining poise. Relying more on innuendo than outright threat. Hinting that she might fool around rather than throwing it in his face. She would recall later that the scene, the argument, had taken place May 10. A date to remember.

On December 2, the same year, Frank was admitted to Holy Cross Hospital with an oxygen mask pressed to his face, a rescue-unit fireman pounding on his chest. He died that afternoon in the Intensive Care Unit at age sixty-one.

Karen couldn't believe it. Forty-four years old and widowed for the second time, having outlived two Franks, one an automotive engineer, the other with "varied and different business interests." Aware of herself and feeling—how? analyzing it—feeling relief after the funeral and the mile-long procession with police escort to Memorial Gardens. Feeling—afraid to admit it at first—great. Free. More than that, excited. No more wondering after five years if she'd made a terrible mistake. Off the hook and looking forward to a new life.

Then discovering within the next few months that Frank DiCilia had as tight a hold on her dead as he did when he was alive.

She would look back. How did I get here? Trying to see a pattern, a motive.

Restless?

Karen Hill. A nice girl. Polite, obedient, a practicing Catholic. B-student through Dominican High and the University of Michigan, arts major. Accepted popular ideas about happiness along with a list of shoulds and shouldn'ts.

But, looking back, did she?

Yes, pretty much. Meet a nice guy with a future and get married, raise a family. The nice guy was Frank Stohler, Michigan '52. Neck a lot but don't go to bed with him until married: June, 1954, at St. Paul's On-the-Lake. Reception, Grosse Pointe Yacht Club. Finally to bed with big, considerate Frank Stohler who never made a sound or said a word making love. Rhythm method, no Pill yet. A daughter, Julie, born September, 1956.

The period with the first Frank was a lump of time. What did they do? Lived in two houses. Joined Lochmoor, the Detroit Athletic Club. Spent an annual business weekend at the Greenbriar. Went to Chrysler Corporation new-model show, SAE conventions. Restless. Was this her role? Played tennis, racquetball, paddleball, a little bridge, argued with Julie. Worried about her. Went to the theater or a dinner party every weekend. Refused to let Julie go to Los Angeles to study drama. She went anyway and was now appearing almost daily in *As the World Turns* and was good in a young bitchy part. What else?

Death. Her father and the first Frank within ten months of each other; both cardiac patients a short time and then gone. A little over two hundred thousand dollars in life insurance and Chrysler Corporation stock. Restless. A chance to do something else, be someone else. Sold the house in Grosse Pointe and moved to Lauderdale. Why? Why not? Got a job in real estate. Boring. Quit. And was introduced to Frank DiCilia at the Palm Bay Club.

The real and authentic Frank DiCilia out of Detroit newspaper stories about grand jury indictments and Organized Crime Strike-force Investigations, linked to perjury trials, the Teamsters, Hoffa's disappearance.

The widow and the widower, both eligible, both eyeing each other, but for different reasons.

She said to herself, This isn't you at all. Is it? Fascinated by the man and all the things he must know but never talked about. She liked his hands, even the diamond on the little finger. She liked his hair, still dark and thick, parted on the right side. She liked the dreamy expression in his eyes and the way he looked at her—Frank DiCilia looking at *her*—and she liked to look back at him calmly to show she wasn't afraid. Not feeling restless anymore. She could not imagine the first wispy-haired Frank with the second dark Frank. Engineers said they were engineers and drew cross-section pictures on paper napkins of how things worked. Frank and his associates never said what they were or wrote anything down. She asked Frank DiCilia directly, "What do you do?"

He said, "I'm retired."

She said, "From what?"

He said, "Industrial laundry business."

She said, "Are you in the Mafia?"

He said, "That's in the movies."

She visited his home in the Harbor Beach section of Lauderdale—her present address, 1 Isla Bahía—and said, "The laundry business must've been pretty good."

He said, "I'm in a little real estate, too."

She said, looking at the decor, the Sotheby estate-sale furnishings and Italian marble, "You could charge admission."

He said, "If you're not comfortable I'll sell it." But did not mention it again until May, five and a half years later.

She remembered another girl by the name of Hill, Virginia

## ELMORE LEONARD

Hill, on television during the Kefauver investigations, the girl in
the wide-brimmed hat and sunglasses who was the girl friend of a
gangster. Karen had watched her, fascinated, wondering what it
would be like.

That was part of it. Finding out. To walk with Frank DiCilia,
aware of it; to enter La Gorce, Palm Bay, Joe Sonken's place in
Hollywood and feel eyes on her. Playing a role and enjoying it. It
was real.

Julie was married to a film stuntman. She was working and
couldn't come to the wedding, but wrote a long letter of love and
congratulations that ended with, "I knew you had it in you somewhere, you devil. Wow! *My* Mom!"

Karen's mother, only nine years older than Frank, came to the
wedding, drank champagne and said, very seriously, "But he's
Italian, isn't he?" Her mother went home, and Karen went home
three years later for her mother's funeral.

What was going on? Everybody dying. The first Frank and her
father, then her mother and the second Frank. Feeling close to
so many people for years and then feeling alone, the survivor.
Losing touch with old friends in Detroit. Living a different life.
Having no one to talk to with any degree of intimacy. Anxious to meet people, have at least one close friend. Preferably
a man.

She became more aware of the retired older people in Florida.
More women than men in the high-rises that lined the beaches
north and south of Lauderdale. Women driving alone in four-
door sedans. Women having dinner with other women. Karen
was forty-four. She said, I don't look like those women.

Do I?

No, even after all the hours in the sun, tennis in the sun, lying
in the sun, she was five-four, weighed exactly one hundred and
five and looked ten years younger than her age. Or maybe thirty-
eight or -nine; right in there somewhere. With sort of classic good
looks: dark hair, blue eyes, nice nose; facial lines that gave her a
somewhat drawn look but, Karen told herself, showed character
or wisdom or experience. She wore simple but expensive clothes,
dressed more often, in the past year, without a bra and looked
outstanding, tan and lean, in any of several faded bikinis. God, no,

398

she didn't look like those widows with their gaudy prints and queen-size asses.

Okay, but then what was she doing sitting home alone? Why did the few interesting, eligible men she had met since Frank's death show up once or twice and then seem to vanish?

# 2

In May, five months a widow—exactly a year from the time of the double-standard disagreement, the argument with Frank, the ultimatum—Karen was seated in Ed Grossi's private office on the thirty-ninth floor of the Biscayne Tower.

The sign on the double-door entrance to the suite said DORADO MANAGEMENT CORPORATION.

Karen could ask Ed Grossi what Dorado Management managed and he would tell her, oh, apartment buildings, condominiums; that much would probably be true. She could ask him who all the men were, waiting in the lobby, and Grossi would say, oh, suppliers, job applicants, you know. His tone patient. Ask anything. What do you want to know?

But if she were to probe, keep asking questions, she knew from experience the explanation that began simply would become complicated, involved, the words never describing a clear picture.

They sat with glossy-black ceramic coffee mugs on his clean desk, and Karen listened as Grossi said, "Well, it looks like you're worth approximately four million."

Karen said, "Really?" Noncommittal. She had thought it might be much more.

"There was a tax lien that had to be straightened out, some business interests of Frank's sold—I won't go into all that unless you want me to."

Four million.

She still had nearly two hundred thousand of her own in stocks and savings, plus the thirty-five thousand cash—in one hundred dollar bills—she had found in Frank's file cabinet.

"Do I get it in a lump sum?"

Ed Grossi seemed alone and far away on the other side of the clean desk, the Miami Beach skyline behind him, through a wall of glass. Mild Ed Grossi sitting on top of it all. He wore black, heavy-framed glasses and was holding them in a way to see through the bifocal area clearly, looking down at a single sheet of paper on his desk.

"According to the way Frank set it up, the money's held in trust."

"Oh," Karen said, and waited for the complicated explanation.

"In Miami General Revenue bonds, four million at six percent, two hundred and forty thousand a year. How's that sound?"

"Do I pay tax on it?"

"No, they're municipal bonds, the earnings are tax-free. Two-forty or, the way it's set up, twenty thousand a month as long as you live."

Karen waited. There was a catch, she felt sure, certain stipulations. "What if I want to take the entire two hundred and forty thousand, all at once?"

"And do what?"

"I don't know. I'm saying what if. Are the bonds in my name?"

"No, Dorado Management. You remember the lawyer explaining it? Frank appointed Dorado administrator of his estate."

"I thought he appointed you," Karen said.

"No, the corporation. Answer your question, yes, you can take the entire two hundred forty thousand for a given year in one payment but, for your own protection, it would have to be approved by Dorado Management."

"By you," she said again, insisting.

"Karen, I could cross Flagler Avenue and get hit by a car. The corporation is still the administrator of Frank's estate. You follow me? Like as a service to you."

"Then I can't just cash in the bonds if I want and take the four million."

"Why would you want to?" Quietly, with an almost weary sound. "Put it in what? Some hotshot comes along with a scheme—that's why Frank set it up like this. Dorado administrates the capital, does your paperwork, and you don't have to worry about it."

"What about when I die?"

"It stops. Your heirs are yours, not Frank's. But, in the meantime you get this money working for you, you'll have quite a sizable estate."

"What if I marry again?"

Ed Grossi hesitated. She saw him, for part of a moment, unprepared.

"I think it stops."

"You're not sure?"

"I don't recall. Maybe Dorado Management has to approve. I don't mean it like that, like you have to get permission. I mean in that case we'd have to assign the bonds to you, if there's no stipulation against it."

"Why would there be?"

"I'm not saying there is. I just don't recall all the details, how it's set up. Why?"

"Why what?"

"I mean are you interested in somebody?"

"No. Not at the moment. I've barely seen anyone," Karen said, with a little edge now in her tone. "I just want to know what my rights are, what I'm allowed to do and what I'm not."

"It was Frank's money, Karen."

"And I earned a share"—still with the edge—"wife subject to the husband, faithfully living up to my end—if you want to make it sound like a legal contract."

"Hey, Karen—come on."

She didn't say anything, but continued to look at him.

"He's dead, Karen. You want him to come back and apologize?"

The man left you a house, couple of other places, quarter a million a year tax-free— What do you want?"

"I don't know. I feel . . . tied down. Maybe I should get away for a few months."

Ed Grossi hesitated again, forming the right words or a relaxed tone. He said, "You don't have to run off, do you? Get involved in something here, some kind of club activity. Spend your money, enjoy it."

"You sound like Frank."

"That's very possible," Grossi said. "Frank and I were together a long time. He says something, this is his wish, then it's my wish, too. You understand what I mean?"

Karen was watching him, not sure, hoping he would say more and reveal something of himself.

"I don't have to agree with Frank entirely about something," Grossi said. "But he let me know this is the way he wants it, okay, it's the way it's gonna be. What I feel—well, it's got nothing to do with it, it was his business."

Karen waited.

"What're you trying to say?"

"Nothing. I'm repeating myself." Serious, then making an effort to smile as he pressed a button on his intercom. "What else can I do for you, Karen?"

Almost telling her something, how he felt. Then aware of it and backing off.

There had been no interruptions, no phone calls, until Grossi's secretary came in and asked if they'd like more coffee. Karen said thanks, no, and picked up her handbag from the floor. The secretary said, "Roland is here."

"Tell him to wait," Grossi said. He took Karen by surprise then. He said, "Vivian, you know Mrs. DiCilia? Karen, this is Vivian Arzola."

The secretary extended her hand to Karen and smiled. "I'm very pleased to meet you, Mrs. DiCilia. I've heard so much about you."

Like what? Karen wondered, still surprised; and yet she knew the girl meant it.

A very attractive Cuban girl, about thirty, neatly tailored, hair pulled back in a bun, large round glasses, a beige pants suit Karen decided was a Calvin Klein or a Dalby. Vivian seemed to linger. She said, "You are much more beautiful than your picture."

*Beautiful?* Karen raised her brows to show a little surprise. She said, "Well, thank you. I think I'll come back more often."

Vivian left them, and Grossi said, "What do you need? Anything at all."

Karen settled back. "Why don't you want me to go away? Do I have to have permission?"

"No, of course not. I didn't mean it that way. I'm suggesting why don't you take it easy. Anywhere you go now it's hot. Stay here by the ocean. But keep in touch. Let me know what you're doing and if I can help in any way."

"I'll tell you right now what I'm doing," Karen said. "Nothing. I see someone two or three times—like Howard Shaw, do you know him? He's an investment consultant, belongs to Palm Bay, recently divorced—"

Grossi was shaking his head. "Karen, you've only been a widow, what, a few months. What's the rush?"

"Almost six months," Karen said, "half a year. I've gone out to dinner a few times—Ed, I'm not jumping in bed with anybody. I've been out with three different men that I like, I mean as friends. We have a good time, we seem to get along. They say they'll call tomorrow or in a couple of days, then nothing, not a word."

"I don't know," Grossi said. "Give it time."

"Give what time?"

"Relax, don't worry about it."

Karen waited, staring at him. "Ed, what's going on?"

"You mean, what's going on? They're businessmen, they're busy. Maybe they're out of town."

"They're not out of town. I've seen them."

"Well, their wives found out. I don't know."

"They're not married." Karen waited again. "Is it because I was married to Frank DiCilia?"

"Some people," Grossi said and shrugged. "Who knows."

"I've thought about that," Karen said. "But they knew it, every one of them. I mean I didn't tell them and then they stopped calling. They *knew* I was Mrs. Frank DiCilia. It's my name. It didn't seem to bother them."

"Well, you don't know," Grossi said. "A guy's a lightweight, sooner or later it shows. He gets nervous, starts to look around; he thinks, Jesus Christ, maybe I'm over my head. You understand? Just the idea, going out with Mrs. Frank DiCilia."

Karen didn't say anything.

"If I were you I wouldn't worry about it," Grossi said. "You got everything. What do you need some lightweight for? Right?"

Roland Crowe stepped over from the reception desk to hold the door open for Karen. She said, "Thank you," and Roland said, "Hey, don't mention it." He stood hip-cocked in his tight pants and two-hundred-dollar cowboy boots watching her ass and slim brown legs move down the hall. When he turned, letting the door close, all the guys in the Dorado lobby were looking at him. Roland winked at nobody in particular. Bunch of dinks, waiting around for the grass to grow.

He went back to the desk to pick up fooling around with the little receptionist, but she told him he could go in now. Roland gave her a wink, too. She wasn't bad looking for a Cuban. That DiCilia woman wasn't bad looking either. He remembered her face.

In Grossi's office, Roland Crowe said, "Wasn't that Frank's woman just went out?"

Grossi was putting a sheet of paper in his middle desk drawer. He took out another single sheet that bore a name and a street address written in ink and locked the drawer.

"Was that who?"

"Frank's old lady."

"Her name's Mrs. DiCilia," Grossi said.

Shit. Little guinea trying to sound like a hardtimer, bit off words barely moving his mouth, more like he had a turd or something in there. Roland felt sociable—back in Miami after six months at Lake Butler State Prison, busting his ass chopping weeds, eating that slop chow—he felt too good to act mean, though he visualized picking the little guinea up by his blue suit and throwing him through the window—grinning then—hearing his guinea scream going down thirty-nine floors to Biscayne Boulevard.

"I met her one time about, I don't know, a year ago," Roland Crowe said, "I took something out to their house. Frank introduced us, but she don't remember me."

"Here," Grossi said, handing the sheet to Roland, who frowned looking at the name.

"Arnold . . . Rapp? What kinda name's that?"

Grossi's expression remained patient, solemn. "Address's up in Hallandale."

"Hiding out, Jesus Christ, in Hallandale," Roland said. "This dink know what he's doing or's he one of them college boys?"

"Arnold tells us the Coast Guard impounded the boat, turned nine tons of grass over to Customs. We see in the paper, yes, there was a boat, Cuban crew, pulled into Boca Chica two days ago."

"But was it Arnold's?" Roland said. "What'd you bank him for?"

"Five hundred forty grand, two and a half to one."

"Well," Roland said, "if he's telling a story he must've smoked a ton of it to get the nerve, huh?"

"Ask him," Grossi said. "The other matter, Mrs. DiCilia, Vivian'll tell you." He reached over to punch a key on the intercom box. "Vivian, Roland's coming out."

Like that, their business over with. There was no, "How was Lake Butler?" or "Thank you, Roland," for keeping his mouth shut, standing up to that asshole judge and drawing a year and day reduced to six months for contempt of court, having to live up there with all them niggers and Cubans.

Roland said to Ed Grossi, "Oh, how'd I make it up at Butler? Well, just fine, Ed. I kept my hands on my private parts, broke a boy's arm tried to cop my joint and came out a two-hundred-and-five-pound virgin. I lost some weight on the special diet of grits and hog shit they got."

Ed Grossi said, "Vivian's waiting for you."

"He's going to take so much and then fire you, you know it?" Vivian said.

Roland Crowe gave her a nice grin going over to the glass-top table where she was sitting, a place to talk away from her desk. Roland liked the setup, the glass, looking down through it at Vivian's crossed legs, the thin beige material tight over her thigh. He said, "You know what I kept dreaming about and seeing in my mind all the time I was at Butler? Cuban pussy. Man, all that black hair—"

Vivian said, "I know one Cuban *cocha* you never going to see. Sit down, Roland. Be nice."

He put his hand on his fly as if to unzip his pants. "Come on, you show me yours and I'll show you something you never seen down on Sou'west Eighta Street."

"Sou-wa-SAY-da," Vivian said. "Dumb shit, you never get it right. Come out of the swamp, what, twenty years ago, you still don't know nothing."

"I know I can make you happy," Roland said, having fun, sitting down now and laying his solid forearms on the glass. The cuffs of his flowered shirt were turned back once to show his two-thousand-dollar wristwatch and gold ID bracelet. "See, I got to find a new place. I thought I'd move in with you while I was looking."

"That's what I need in my life, a convict," Vivian said. She was straight with Roland but very careful and alert, as though he might slam a fist down on the glass table, and she would have to get out of there fast. She said, "You ready to listen, quit the bullshit?"

What he'd like to do was reach over and take off Vivian's big round glasses and pull her hair loose, but he said, "Sure. Tell me about it." Roland felt really good and could be obliging for a while.

"Mrs. Frank DiCilia, 1 Isla Bahía, Harbor Beach, Lauderdale."

"I been to the house."

"There's a tap on the phone line that goes into Marta's room from outside—"

"Wait a minute. Who's Marta?"

"Marta Diaz, the maid. Sister of Jesus." Vivian pronounced the name Hay-soos.

Roland said, "Sweet Jesus working on this?" and pronounced it Jesus. "I never knew he had a sister. I never knew *what* he had. He don't talk hardly at all."

Vivian said, "Listen, all right? The recorder is in Marta's room. Every night she takes the cassette out and gives it to Jesus."

"Then what?"

"Then—he was bringing it here, but now he gives it to you and you listen to it. You write down the names of men she talks to. If it looks like she's got something going with one of them, you find out about him, go see him, tell him Mrs. DiCilia would like to be left alone. You understand? You don't hit anyone unless you ask us first."

"For how long?"

Vivian shrugged. "Long as she lives, I don't know. She's not to see anyone in a serious way that she might go to bed with."

Roland squinted, like he was looking into sunglare. "Grossi want her for himself?"

"It's not his idea, it's the husband's."

"The man's dead." Still squinting.

"Is that right? But people still do what he wants," Vivian said. "He wants his wife to remain pure, true to him even after death, and we see to it."

"That's a good-looking woman," Roland said.

"Yes, very stylish."

"And she's not getting anything? Jesus, she must be dying."

"Everyone isn't a sex maniac," Vivian said.

"You don't have to be wild with the notion to want some poon." Roland saw the poor woman alone in her house at night, looking out the window. "Maybe she has some boy sneak in, give her a jump."

Vivian shook her head. "Marta says no one stays, they don't go in the bedroom."

Roland was thinking, You don't have to do it in the bedroom. Shit, he'd done it in a car trunk, in sand, weeds, an air boat in the middle of Big Cyprus Swamp, one time right on the Seventy-ninth Street Causeway like she was sitting on the railing . . . on floors—all kinds of floors, carpet, linoleum—on a table— He'd never done it on a glass table though.

Roland wanted to get it straight in his mind. "This is Frank's idea not Ed's."

"Like he left it in his will to Ed," Vivian said. "Watch her so she doesn't fool around with anyone, ever."

"Jesus—" It was a hard proposition to understand, cutting the poor woman off like that. But then these guineas did all kinds of things that didn't make sense. Serious little buggers with their old-timey ideas about honor, the *omerta*—no talking, man, keep your mouth shut—all that brotherhood bullshit.

Roland said, "It seems to me, an easier way—why don't Ed tell her, no fooling around. Here's what Frank wants, dead or not, and that's the way it's gonna be."

"Why do you ask questions?" Vivian said. "Ed doesn't like the idea but he's doing it, uh? For his friend."

"But he doesn't want her to know."

"He doesn't want to be involved," Vivian said. "The woman's also a friend. He wants her to be happy, but he has to do this to her. So he gives it to you because he gave his word to Frank. But he doesn't want to be in*volv*ed in it personally. You understand now? God."

"Who knows about the setup?"

"The three of us. See, he doesn't even want to hear himself tell you about it. I have to tell you."

"What about Jesus? He knows."

"No, he thinks the woman is being protected."

Roland liked that idea. He thought about it some more and said, "What'd Frank leave her?"

"None of your business."

"I bet a big shit-pile of money," Roland said. "And I bet that's part of the deal. She starts putting out, she gets cut off, huh?"

"Pick up the tapes and listen to them," Vivian said. "That's all you got to do." She rose from the table to walk over to her desk. It was not clean like Ed Grossi's, it was a working desk with papers and file folders on it. Vivian picked up an envelope that was thick and sealed closed, no writing on it.

"Protect her," Roland was saying, nodding, accepting the idea. "Keep all these dinks away from her who want to get in her little panties. All right, I guess I can do that."

Vivian came back with the envelope and handed it to him, saying, "Roland"—reading his mind, which wasn't difficult—"while you're protecting her little panties, don't try to get in them yourself. I told you, she's a very good friend of Ed's."

"We're all friends," Roland said, ripping open the envelope, "that's why we get along so good." He looked at the money, counting through it quickly, then at Vivian. "I don't get any extra? Shit, I just did six months at Butler, hard time, lady, and I pick up my paycheck as usual, huh?"

"Join a union," Vivian said. "What're you complaining to me

for? You got eighteen thousand dollars there, back pay for your six months."

"The way I see it, chopping weeds at Butler is worth more than that," Roland said. "Way more."

# 3

During the time Maguire was being held in the Wayne County Jail, downtown Detroit, he'd say to himself, If I get out of this—sometimes even beginning, Please, God, if I get out of this—I'll change, I'll get a regular job, I'll stay away from people like the Patterson brothers and never fuck up again as long as I live. At least not this bad.

Sitting there in his cell facing something like 15 to 25, Jesus, the scaredest he'd ever been in his life.

While over at the prosecutor's office they could push computer buttons and Maguire would appear in lights on the desk-set screen.

CALVIN A. MAGUIRE, Male Caucasian, a date of birth that made him thirty-six, tattoo on his upper left bicep, *Cal*, in blue and red, a list of arrests going back eleven years, one in Florida, but no convictions.

An assistant Wayne County prosecutor looked at the screen, frowning. No convictions? The guy had stolen automobiles, broken into homes, business establishments, once attempted to shoot a man, apprehended with a concealed weapon, one willful destruction . . . and no con*vic*tions? Well, they had the guy this time. Two eyeball witnesses who'd picked him out of a lineup, two positive IDs, man. Calvin Maguire was going away.

The prosecutor's office also had an impressive computerized light show on the Patterson brothers: Andre Patterson and Grover "Cochise" Patterson, both male Negroes, both with previous convictions going back to age thirteen and fourteen, and both picked out of line-ups by the same two tight-jawed no-bullshit witnesses. Bye-bye Maguire and the Patterson brothers. The assistant prosecutor was going to trial happy. He didn't see how he could lose.

Andre Patterson had come to Maguire with the deal. This man was going to pay them fifteen hundred each to go and take a hit at the Deep Run Country Club out north of Detroit. Mess the place up, but mostly mess up their minds, the people out there. Maguire didn't get it. A man was paying them to hit a place?

Paying them and furnishing clean weapons. The man had some reason he didn't like the place, or he wanted to pay them back for something, not anybody in particular, the whole place. Maguire said, At a club they *sign* for everything; there's no money at a club. Andre Patterson said, But the rich people who go there have money; put it in their locker, go out and play golf. See, they could keep whatever they took. The man didn't want a cut; it wasn't that kind of deal.

Maguire was uncertain. What's the matter with your buddies Ordell and Louis? Why me? And Andre answering that those two were away for a while. No, you my man, only man I know can do it cool, without a noseful. Maguire told Andre he was doing fine without the thrills; he had a job he thought he'd stick with at least until the end of the year, then take off.

Andre Patterson saying, Yeah, making the *cock*tails for the salesmen flashing around the hotel, listening to all the big deals, the *cock*tail music coming out the wall, standing at attention in your little red jacket, man, hair combed nice, yes, sir, what would you like? And for the young lady?

Maguire thinking of a snowbanked Durant Mall in Aspen, deep powder on the high slopes, the rich ladies in their snow-bunny outfits. Then thinking of the Pier House in Key West, sitting out on the deck with a white rum and lemon, six in the evening. Places out of the past. Thinking of fifteen hundred bucks and what they could scrounge out of the lockers, maybe two, three hundred more each. Thinking of islands and palm trees . . . get out of the cold, the slush, try the Mediterranean for a change, Spain, the south of France. Fifteen hundred guaranteed. Maguire liked to be outdoors. He liked to work outdoors, if he had to work. What was he doing in Detroit? Like a guilt trip, always coming back to Detroit, visit his mom and tell her yeah, everything was great. Listen to her describe her poor circulation and Detroit Edison rates and finally saying, Hey, thanks very much for everything, accepting the hundred dollar bill she always offered and getting out of there.

Andre Patterson saying, No security people. Walk in, pick up the wallets, watches. All right, everybody take off your clothes, get in the shower. Carry their clothes outside and throw 'em in the bushes—they all running around the club nekked.

Maybe wear ski masks, something like that?

Andre saying, Wear a tuxedo you want to. We going to the *club*, man.

That would be funny, tuxedos. It was good to keep it light, have a couple of drinks, smoke a joint before going in . . . lock the outside door after you . . . little details to think about. Watch the door that went from the locker room to the grill—

Maguire said, "I haven't done this in a couple years. I mean I haven't *ever* actually done it, Christ, gone into a country club."

Andre said, "Who has?"

They went in on a Wednesday, August 16, four o'clock in the afternoon, when all the doctors and sales reps would be out there playing golf, rolling Indian dice for drinks, talking their locker room talk with all the obscene words they couldn't say at the office.

They parked the van Cochise had picked up and went in a side door that led directly into the men's locker room—without the ski masks, too hot—Andre Patterson wearing a knit cap and faking some kind of Jamaican-Caribbean British-nigger accent, Cochise wearing a red and white polka-dot headband that bunched up his Afro like black broccoli. Maguire had quit his job at the hotel cocktail lounge, had a photograph taken for his passport application, then let his dark, black-Irish beard grow for three days. Once in the locker room he picked up a green Deep Run golf cap and set it on low over his sunglasses. He and Andre carried 9mm Berettas, brand new; wild-ass Cochise went in with a sawed-off double-barreled Marlin to scare the shit out of the members, get their attention quick and make them behave.

Maguire was nervous going in, Christ yes, but he wasn't too worried about the Patterson brothers overreacting, becoming vicious. There was a moment right in the beginning when they either grabbed control of the situation and it went smoothly, or they didn't grab control and it could turn into a fuck-up with a lot of yelling and jabbing. That moment of surprise—

The golf club members talking loud, their voices coming from the shower and the rows of lockers, middle-aged men in their underwear and towels, shuffling around in paper slippers . . . looking up and seeing, Christ, a wildman, a Mau-Mau, twin blunt holes of a Marlin pointing at them. Oh, my God! Sharp little startled sounds, seeing *two* mean-looking black guys with guns—

Then silence.

God Almighty, was it a revolution or a holdup? Hoping all they wanted was money. Andre Patterson telling the members in Jamaican to be cool, mon, and go in the shower room. Herding those wide-eyed, slow-moving white bodies in there, guns touching naked flesh—go on, mon, move your chickenfat ass—like a scene in a high-class concentration camp, moving them into the gas chamber. Getting the shit-scared locker room attendant to start opening up the lockers. Cochise going through the shoeshine room and the service bar into the ladies locker room—yeah, let's get everybody in here—the three of them actually grinning. Sure, because they knew they had it in their hands now. Unbelievable, Maguire thought, relaxing a little, already seeing himself and the Patterson brothers talking about it after, laughing, giggling at the scene, retelling parts of it one or the other might have missed.

Maguire dumping the clubs out of the golf bag, hanging it over his shoulder and throwing in all the wallets and watches, silver money clips with the club crest, a few pinkie rings, electric razors, hair-blower for Cochise—all the stuff he got out of the lockers. Unbelievable, the doctors and sales reps contributing something over twenty-five hundred in cash, like eight-fifty apiece.

Still talking about it the next day at Andre's, eating Chinese food, reading about it in the paper, ARMED TRIO ROBS COUNTRY CLUB. Bet to it, cleaned it out. All those chickenfat doctors out on the links, a man lining up a putt not knowing at that moment he was getting robbed.

They had fun talking about it. Maguire borrowed Andre's car, picked up his photos and a passport application at the post office, brought back some more scotch, shaved, cleaned up, and they went over the scenes again, waiting now for the man to send them the fifteen hundred each.

Talking about Cochise bringing the five women in through the service bar from the ladies locker room on the other side. Four ladies going to fat, holding their towels up around their titties. One not too bad, nice blonde, quiet, fairly calm, Maguire might've set up for a drink at some other time. Cochise pulling the towel off the last one, hearing her squeal as he poked her in the ass with the cut-down Marlin.

That was the highlight, making them all drop their towels, or take off their extra-size undies once they were in the shower with the men. The men standing there trying to hold in their stomachs, looking at the bare-naked ladies, at their big titties and bushes. So that's what so-and-so looks like without any clothes on, Jesus. Looking, making little mental notes. Couple of the women sneaking glances at the guy's shriveled-up joints. The shower room full of bellies and dimpled asses that looked like they'd been kept in a dark cave for years.

Andre Patterson saying, "I advise you all to go join Vic Tanney quick as you can, else you gonna die soon." Then saying to a little guy with muscles in his arms and shoulders, who kept staring at Andre, not interested in the naked ladies, "Don't do what you're thinking man, or you gonna die right now."

See, relaxed but very alert.

Cochise bringing in the two waitresses and the bartender, making them take their uniforms off and get in with the naked club members. Andre saying, Hey, I can't tell the rich folks from the help. Funny guys, half-stoned but they knew what they were doing.

Maguire saying, "Something like that, you could sell tickets to, you know it? I mean there some people would *pay* to see a show like that, fucking X-rated stick-up."

Maguire picking out a set of woods for himself, Andre taking a whole big bag of clubs that must've been worth eight hundred dollars, he said for playing at Palmer Park. Hey, shit, can you see it?

Sometime during the evening of the day after, Cochise went out to pick up some grass, trade in some of the country club items maybe.

He came back with about eighteen members of the Detroit Police Department, Christ, through the door with guns and kneeling on them before they knew what was happening.

So there was the robbery armed, something like 15 to 25 or possibly life, and a felony-firearm charge that carried a mandatory two years. More than enough to start Maguire praying and making promises in the Wayne County jail. In there from the middle of August to the end of November, with no way in the world of making the bond set at fifty thousand dollars or two sureties. Maguire saw Andre and Cochise once at 1300 Beaubien, police headquarters across the street, while they were waiting to appear in a line-up, and asked him, For Christ sake, the man got us into this, he's gonna put up the bond, right? No, the man couldn't get involved just yet. The man was under suspicion, using the bonding company to front him on some kind of deal in Las Vegas, so the man couldn't be seen to be paying the bonding company at this time. But hang on.

Hang onto what, for Christ sake? Hang on in the bus going to Jackson.

Maguire didn't think much of his court-appointed lawyer because the lawyer didn't think much of him. Maguire could feel it, the guy was going through the motions. The court was paying the lawyer, and he didn't give a rat's ass who won.

Maguire said, "What've they got on me? Some circumstantial evidence, that's all."

"Your photograph in Andre Patterson's car," the lawyer said. "The golf clubs in the trunk."

"I happened to leave my picture in the car"—shit—"that was the next day. Other people were in that car the next day. Andre's wife, she went out to get some Chinese food. Was she arrested?"

"You were ID-ed positively in a line-up by one of the victims," the lawyer said. "Possibly identified by four more. They saw you there. Now I'm representing you, not the jigs. You want to agree to testify against the jigs, maybe I can get you a deal."

"You can get fucked, too," Maguire told his court-appointed lawyer. What a rotten guy.

Something happened, several things, Maguire didn't understand.

The morning of the trial a different lawyer appeared in court to defend all three of them, a sharp young guy by the name of Marshall Fine, with styled hair and a pinched-in three-piece suit.

What's this?

Nice moves, very stylish; made the prosecutor look like a high-school football coach. Sent from the man? Andre nodding, pleased. Fine of fine and dandy, man. From the company does the man's legal business. Yeah, but the guy seemed so young. Was he practicing on them, or what? Maguire wasn't sure he liked it—putting his life in the hands of a young Jewish lawyer who looked about eighteen years old. He hoped to Christ the guy was an authentic hotshot young Jewish lawyer and not just somebody's nephew.

Marshall Fine didn't say much that morning, accepting the jurors one right after the other, very calm, courteous, but maybe wanting to get it over with. In the afternoon, first thing, the prosecutor put a witness on the stand. Oh shit, the little guy from the shower room with the muscles in his arms and shoulders—the guy describing what happened and saying yes, he saw the three in the courtroom, the white guy there and the two colored guys.

Marshall Fine got up and asked the club member where he was standing, in front or behind the others, what exactly took place during the incident and, in all that confusion, he couldn't be absolutely certain of his identification, could he?

Yes, the club member said, he could definitely be certain. He not only saw them in the locker room, he saw the white guy's picture a few days later when the police officer showed it to him.

Marshall Fine asked the club member what picture. Maguire noticed the prosecutor paying very close attention, frowning.

The club member said he was told the picture was found in their car.

Pictures of all three defendants?

No, just the white guy, the club member said. The officer showed it to him when he came down to 1300 Beaubien to look at the suspects.

Marshall Fine said, to no one in particular, "While Mr. Maguire was being held in custody." Then to the judge, "Your Honor, I'd like to request, if I may, the jury be excused. We seem to have a legal point to discuss."

Twenty minutes later Maguire was free. He couldn't believe it.

Marshall explained it to him in the hall, with all the people standing around outside the courtrooms, and Maguire had trouble concentrating. *Free,* just like that.

"What it amounts to, the cops fucked up. Once you're in jail they can't show anybody your picture unless your lawyer's present."

"They can't?"

"See, it used to be the cops would tell the victim, or a witness, they got the guy and then show the guy's picture. Then, when the witness sees the guy in the line-up, naturally he's gonna pick him out, the same guy, of course."

Maguire nodding—

"The prosecutor raised the point, this impermissible taint, what it's called in law, was irrelevant because there was an independent basis for the identification. I said what independent basis? Like knowing you from someplace else. I pointed out there was absolutely no independent corroboration that would provide a sufficiently acceptable alternative identification that comports with due process. And the judge agreed. It was that simple."

"Oh," Maguire said.

"So, good luck. Get your ass out of here." Young Marshall Fine turned to go back into the courtroom, then stopped. "I almost forgot. You need a job? What're you gonna do now?"

There it was. "I got some money coming in," Maguire said.

"I don't know anything about that," the lawyer said. "I guess

I'm only into rehabilitation, small favors, maybe something we might be able to do for you. Were you working?"

"I was a bartender, but I quit."

"I could get you something like that. How about Miami Beach?"

"Well"—seeing the black people standing around, all the victims, witnesses, relatives of defendants—"I used to live in Florida about ten years ago." Thinking in that moment, the Mediterranean, Florida, what's the difference? Seeing himself going to the cops to get his passport pictures back? No way. "Yeah, Florida sounds like a good idea."

"Get you into one of the hotels, bartender—what do you want to do?"

Thinking of the ocean, the sun, being outside, getting a tan—

"When I was there before I worked with dolphins. Maybe something like that'd be good." He felt funny talking to a guy younger than he was about a job.

"Dolphins," Marshall said.

"Porpoise. You know, they call them porpoise but they're really dolphins. Not the fish, they're mammals."

"Yeah, dolphins," Marshall said. He was nodding, thinking of something. "I believe we've got a client—yeah, I'm sure we have—they've got an interest in one of those places. You mean like Sea World, they put on the porpoise show, a guy rides a killer whale, Shamu?"

"Yeah, only the place I worked," Maguire said, "it was more a training school. Down in the Keys, with these pens right out in the ocean. They put on a show, but not with all the bullshit, the porpoise playing baseball and, you know, coming out of the water to ring a bell and the American flag goes up—not any of that kind of shit."

"But you've had experience."

"I worked there almost a year, down on Marathon. The pay wasn't anything, but I liked being outside." He thought about the fifteen hundred again. "What about this money somebody owes me?"

"I'm sorry, I don't know anything about it." The young hotshot lawyer did seem to want to help though. "You must've made some kind of an arrangement."

"Well, I guess so. But then some snitch sees Cochise walking in a place with a golf bag full of electric razors and that's it. We were picked up, you know, before anything was paid."

"I don't know anything about it, so don't ask, okay? But I'll see where we stand with the porpoise. You say porpoise or porpoises, plural?"

"Either way," Maguire said.

"Nice clean animals," Marshall said. "Give me a call in a couple of days." He turned to go back into the courtroom.

"What about the Pattersons? You think you can get 'em off?"

"I don't lose if I can win," Marshall said. He paused, hand on the door. "It's too bad they didn't pull the kind of dumb stunt you did, leave some snapshots in the car. I'll see you."

Andre and Grover Patterson drew 20 to life.

A few days before they were sentenced, Maguire gave Andre's wife a list of things to tell Andre and two questions, in particular, to ask him, when she went in to see him on visitor's day.

She came out of the Wayne County jail, Maguire waiting, and they walked the three blocks south to Monroe, Greektown, for a cup of coffee.

Andre's wife said, "Yeah, he understand. You out and he's in, that's all. That dumb, stupid man"—shaking her head, sounding tired—"he's always in. Must miss his friends at Jackson so much, got to get back to them."

"You tell him I got a job waiting for me, but I want to do something first?"

"Yeah, I told him."

"I'm gonna write to him all about it. And give you his money? You tell him that?"

"I told him."

"Good." Maguire sipped his coffee. "And you asked him the man's name? He told me once, but I wasn't sure. I might've got it mixed up with somebody else."

"Yeah, the man's name is Frank DiCilia," Andre's wife said.

"That's it." Maguire nodded. Right, Frank DiCilia. He knew it was something like Cecilia or Cadelia. Years ago the name had been in the papers a lot.

"And how about where he lives? Or where I get in touch with him?"

"His home's in Florida—"

"Is that right?" Maguire perking up. "That's where I'm going, Florida." Maybe it was a sign, things beginning to come together without a lot of sweat and strain. "Where, Miami Beach?"

"Fort something. For Laura—"

"Fort Lauderdale."

"Yeah, Fort Lauradale."

Jesus, it *was* a sign. That's where he was going for the job. The man was right there. No special trip required. It would give him time to think about it, how to approach a man like Frank DiCilia. Show him the clipping from the paper, ARMED TRIO ROBS COUNTRY CLUB, identify himself as one of the defendants—

"But ain't no way you gonna see him," Andre's wife said.

"What do you mean? Why not?"

"The man died about a week ago," Andre's wife said. "Andre say he heard about it. You didn't?"

# 4

Some of Roland Crowe's buddies were still sloshing around back there in the swamp, driving air boats, guiding hunting and fishing parties, poaching alligators, making shine; some others were doing time at Raford and Lake Butler. Bunch of dinks.

Roland had been that entire route and had poured cement for five years before going broke and learning the simple secret of success in business. Deal only in personal services. Not *things*. No lifting, no heavy work, no overhead, no machinery to speak of. Look good, listen carefully, take a minimum of shit, live close to the Beach and always make yourself available to people who called and said, Roland, there's this man owes us money. Or, Roland, we believe this man is going independent on us. Or, we believe he's telling us a story . . .

Like the guy laying up at Hallandale, Arnold Rapp. Financed

him like a half million dollars, and he says the Coast Guard con-
fiscated the shipment, nine tons of Colombian.

Say, Come on, Arnold, for true? Holding him out the window
by his ankles.

Get that done, then stop by Lauderdale on the way back and
say hi to the DiCilia lady. Look the situation over, lay in some
footings.

First thing though, Roland spent his back pay. He bought
himself four new summer suits the man told him were designed
in Paris, France, and specially cut for them by this tailor in Taiwan, Republic of China. He bought himself new three-hundred-
fifty-dollar hand-tooled, high-heeled boots. He bought an Ox
Bow wheat-colored straw hat with a high crown and a big scoop
brim that, with the cowboy boots, put him up around six-six. He
bought a cream-colored Cadillac Coupe De Ville, cash. And put
two months' rent down on an eight hundred dollar apartment in
Miami Shores.

Look good and you feel good. He picked up Jesus Diaz and
drove up to Hallandale.

"I bet what it is," Roland said to Jesus, "I bet anything Arnold
is a boy went to about five colleges, traveled all over, got busted a
couple of times, has his rich folks bail him out and he thinks he's a
fucking outlaw. You think I'm wrong?"

"No, you right," Jesus Diaz said. He was comfortable in the
air-conditioned Cadillac, he didn't want to argue with Roland.

"See, they get together, these snotty boys like Arnold? They
think shit, they been to college, dumb guineas financing the deal
don't know nothing. Tell 'em the load went down the toilet and
keep the money."

"Maybe so," Jesus Diaz said.

"No maybe. These little shitheads're pulling something." Jesus
Diaz did not reply and Roland said, "You don't believe it?"

"I believe it if you want me to," Jesus Diaz said. He knew he
should keep still, but he didn't like Roland's bright-blue pimp
suit or the big Lone Ranger hat touching the roof of the car. He
said, "Why they in business then? They make more selling it,
don't they?"

"They *do* sell it, you dink," Roland said. "But they tell Grossi
they lost it, and he's out his dough."

"They believe they can get away with that?" Jesus Diaz said.

"Jesus," Roland said, not meaning the little Cuban but the other Jesus. "You should never've gone in the ring, you know it? I think you got your brains scrambled."

Jesus Diaz agreed with that in part. To look like Kid Gavilan and fake a bolo punch wasn't enough. After thirty-seven professional fights, several times getting the shit beat out of him and almost losing an eye, he could still see clearly and think clearly and knew this man next to him was a prehistoric creature from the swamp—man, from some black lagoon—who wore cowboy hats and *chulo* suits and squinted at life to see only what he wanted. Maybe he could punch with Roland and hurt him a little, but before it was over Roland would kill him. Roland's fists were too big and his nose and jaw were up there too far away.

Jesus Diaz, looking up at the green freeway sign as they passed beneath it, almost there now, said, "Hallandale."

"Yeah?" Roland said. "Hallandale. You can read English, huh?"

What Jesus Diaz would like to do, take the man's cowboy hat from his head, reach over and grab it and sail it out the window.

This one, they should keep him locked up someplace with his mouth taped.

Then let him out to do the work, yes, because no one walked into a room and faced people the way Roland did.

Into 410 of the Ocean Monarch high-rise condominium on the beach, Jesus Diaz behind him, into the big living room of the apartment with the expensive furniture, where the four young guys were sitting with their beer cans and music and the smell of grass—a heavy smell even with the sliding door open to the balcony.

Arnold Rapp, the one they came to see, let them in, looked them over, turned and walked back to the couch. Jesus Diaz closed the door behind them. He liked the loud funk-rock music. He didn't like the way the four young guys were at ease and didn't seem to be scared. Yes, stoned, but it was more than that. They lounged, sitting very low in the couch and the chairs, no shoes on, each with long hair. They looked like bums, Jesus Diaz thought, and maybe Roland was right. Rich kids, yes, who didn't give a shit about anything. Man, a place like this, view of the

ocean, swimming pool downstairs in the court—these guys laying around drinking beer like they just came off a shift, not offering anything, waiting, like Roland was here to explain something
or ask for a job. That was the feeling.

Roland said, "Your mommy home?"

They grinned at him. Arnold said, "No, no mommy, just us
kids."

Roland said, "Well now—who're your little friends, Arnie?"

Arnold said, "Well now"—imitating Roland's cracker accent,
getting some of the soft twang—"this here is Barry. That there're
Scott and Kenny."

The young guys—they were about in their mid-twenties—
snickered and giggled.

The one called Barry, trying the accent, said, "And who be you
be?"

It broke them up, "Who be you be." The guys laughing and
repeating it, Jesus, who-be-you-be. They thought it was pretty
funny.

Roland walked over to the hi-fi. He brushed the stylus off the
record and the funk-rock stopped with a painful scratching
sound.

Arnold straightened up. "Jesus Christ, what're you *do*ing?"

"Getting your attention," Roland said.

Barry was still grinning. He said, "Who-be-you-be, man?"
And one of the others said, "He's the who-be-you-be man. Comes
in, who-be-you-bes your fucking records all up."

"No, I'm the man's man," Roland said. "Sent me to ask you
what happened to his five hundred and forty thousand dollars, I
believe is the figure."

"It's in the municipal incinerator," Arnold said.

The one named Barry said, "We already told it, man. Ask
him."

Roland tilted up his Ox Bow straw. He walked out to the open
balcony with its view of the Atlantic Ocean and leaned on the rail
a moment.

Jesus Diaz stood where he was in the middle of the room,
watching Roland, hearing the young guys say something and gig-
gle. Something like, "Hey, partner" and something about riding
here on a fucking horse, and another one saying, "A fucking
bucking bronco, man," and all of them giggling again.

Roland came back in. He said to Arnold, "How about you tell me what you told him."

"Coast Guard picked up the boat in international waters and brought it to Boca Chica," Arnold said. "He knows all that. The pot went to Customs and they burned it up."

"Pot went to pot," Barry said.

"The crew, the three guys, were turned over to Drug Enforcement," Arnold said. "Your man is out the five hundred forty grand and there's nothing I can do about it."

"It's a high fucking risk business," Barry said, "any time you get two hundred percent on your investment, it's got to be."

"Two and a half," Arnold said.

"Right, two and a half," Barry said. "You know it's high risk going in, man, if you're not stupid."

Roland walked over to where Barry was lounged in his chair. He said, "Is that right, little fella? You know all about high risk, do you? Stand up here, let me have a look at you."

"Jesus Christ," Barry said, sounding bored. "Why don't you take a fucking walk?"

Roland pulled Barry up by his hair, drew him out of the chair and an agonized sound from Barry's throat, telling him to hush up, turned him around and got a tight grip on the waist of Barry's pants that brought him to his toes, Levi's digging into the crack of his ass.

Jesus Diaz reached behind him, beneath his jacket—to the same place Roland was gripping the young guy's pants—and brought out a Browning automatic, big .45, and put it on the other three guys, sitting up, maybe about to jump Roland.

Roland said, "See it?" without even looking, knowing Jesus had the piece on them. "Now tell me about high risk," Roland said to Barry, walking him toward the open balcony, the other three guys rigid, afraid to move. "You want *me* to tell you?" Roland said, bringing the young guy to the opening in the sliding glass doors. "Fact I'll show you, boy, the highest risk you ever saw." And ran him out on the balcony, gripping him, raising him by his hair and pants and grunting hard as he threw the young guy screaming over the rail of the fourth-floor balcony.

Someone in the room cried out, "Jesus—no!"

There was silence.

Jesus Diaz held the gun on them, not looking at the balcony.

Roland stood at the rail, leaning over it, resting on his arms.

When he came back in adjusting his hat he said, "That boy was lucky, you know it? He hit in the swimming pool. He's moving slow, but he's moving. People gonna say my, what do those boys do up there? Must get all likkered up, huh?" Roland paused, looking at Arnold and Scott and Kenny sitting there like stones. He said, "Now, who-be-you-be, who be's gonna answer my question without getting smart-aleck and giggling like little kids? You see what I do to smart little kids, huh? Next one, he might hit the concrete, mightn' he?"

"The name of the boat in the paper was *Salsa,*" Arnold said quietly. "The same one I hired, I know, because I saw it in Key West two weeks ago."

"And the Coast Guard cutter hauled it in was the *Diligence,*" Roland said. "Same thing I'm gonna use till you pay us back the five hundred and forty thousand. You can take you time, Arnie, we're reasonable folks. Long as you understand the vig's fifty-four grand a week, standard ten percent interest."

Arnold began to nod, very serious. "We'll pay you, don't worry."

Roland said, "Do I look worried?"

He said to Jesus, in the car, driving away from the beach, "I told you, didn't I, them dinks'd pull something."

"But they weren't lying to you," Jesus Diaz said. "It was the same boat was picked up."

"Oh my oh my, you don't understand shit, do you?" Roland drove in silence to the federal highway, US 1, went through the light and pulled over to the curb. "Out you go, partner."

Jesus looked around. "What am I supposed to do here?"

"Hitch a ride or take a cab, I don't give a shit. I'm going up to Lauderdale."

Roland was looking at himself in the rearview mirror, squaring his new Ox Bow wheat-colored straw.

# 5

"He say he's a friend of Mr. Grossi," Marta said. "Mr. Grow. You supposed to have met him one time before."

"Crow?" Karen said. She felt Gretchen's tongue on her shoulder. The dog had come out with Marta.

"Yes, Grow," Marta said.

Lying on her stomach, Karen looked at the watch close to her face. Quarter to five already. It amazed her that time did go quickly. Time now to—what? Go in and dress. She didn't remember a Mr. Grow from anywhere. Turning, getting up from the lounge, Karen held the bra of her bathing suit to her breasts, fastened it, then reached for the phone on the umbrella table and dialed a number, Ed Grossi's private line.

"Ed? Karen." She paused, listening a moment. "Everything's fine ... No, no problems. Listen, do you know someone, a man by the name of Grow? ... Yeah, that's what I thought. That must be it ... No, I don't know what he wants. Is he a friend of yours?" Then listened to Ed saying well, yes, in a way. Roland Crowe was an employee. He'd probably stopped by to see if there was anything she needed, maybe take a look around—"For what?" Like a security check, Ed said, that's all. But listen, if the guy was imposing, taking up her time, tell him to get lost. That bluntly. Not someone whose feelings Ed Grossi cared about. "Thanks," Karen said. And Ed said sure, anytime.

Quiet Ed Grossi, trying to sound himself, but a little disturbed. By what? Her call, perhaps interrupting him? Or the fact Roland was here. Whoever Roland Crowe was. A man who worked for Ed Grossi but wasn't Italian or Cuban.

"Ask him to come out," Karen said. She reached for a white cotton robe as Marta went back to the house.

Roland walked along the seawall to the point of land where a boat canal joined the Intercoastal. He stood for some time looking across the broad channel to the homes on the far side, then turned and seemed to study the DiCilia house: the million dollar layout that resembled a California mission, tan brick and clay tile roof; red pyracantha bushes forming borders, screening the swimming pool and brick patio.

As Roland came this way across the lawn, Karen watching him, Gretchen ran out from the house, barking, coming to a sudden stop. Roland went down to one knee to take the dog in his hands, playfully roughing her up, saying something, repeating it, as the little gray dog licked and sniffed him.

Gretchen ran off toward the house and Roland squinted after her. Coming to the patio he said, "That's a nice little doggie you got. What's her name?"

"Gretchen," Karen said.

"Yeah, she's a nice little girl." Squinting up at the house again, then looking directly at Karen in the canvas chair. "I thought that was some view out there, but this one beats it." Giving her a friendly grin. "I've sure heard a lot about you."

Karen touched her knee to pull the robe over her leg, but let her hand rest there.

Roland caught it, the brown hand with three little gold rings lying there idle on the brown knee. Yes, sir, begin small and work up. No hurry. This woman might not even realize how bad she needed it. Like a starving person forgetting about food as the stomach began to shrink up.

Marta was hanging around back there in the shade of one of the archways, door open behind her, leading inside. Roland didn't know if Marta was keeping an eye on him or what. Maybe told by the lady to stay close.

The lady, he figured was near his age, somewhere around forty. The maid, twenty years younger, and with a little more meat on her but not as good-looking. Both of them in white. A short-skirt skimpy uniform; and the robe the lady wore, Roland bet, didn't cover no more than a little swim suit. She might even be bare-assed under there. Two women in white all alone in this place like a Florida castle. It sounded to Roland like something in a story-book. The fair princess with some kind of a spell on her that she'd have till her prince come along and fucked her.

All that going on in his head inside the summer cowboy hat. Hey, prince—Roland grinned.

"What's funny?" Karen said.

"Nothing. I was thinking of something." Then serious. "See, the problem, this place is pretty exposed, out here on a point."

"I don't see a problem," Karen said.

"What I mean, the place is tempting. Be easy for somebody to get in here, maybe clean out your jewel box." Roland kept staring at her with a grin fixed on his mouth.

"We have security service, it's around here all night," Karen said.

"Yeah, well those rent-a-cops aren't worth—they're mostly older retired fellas."

"What I don't understand—you walked all around—what exactly you're looking for."

"Any evidence somebody's been setting the place up," Roland said. Was she too thin? Naw, her hips looked a nice size, nice round white curve there. "See, I was originally from over in the Everglades. Used to track, hunt a lot, so I got a fairly keen eye for reading sign."

Karen studied him. She said then, "Would you like something cold?"

"Sure, that'd be fine."

She looked over her shoulder. "Marta? Bring out a couple of vodka and tonic, okay?" And continued to look that way until

Marta was in the house. Turning to Roland again, Karen said, "Mr. Grossi didn't ask you to come here."

Roland sank into a canvas director's chair and stretched out his boots, crossing his ankles—fairly close now with kind of a side view of her.

"He didn't?"

"Is this your idea, or did someone send you?"

"My idea, in a way."

"What do you mean, in a way?"

"Coming here is my idea, but I wouldn't be here, would I, if it wasn't for the situation."

"What situation?"

"Your being a widow, the way things've been going and all." Roland teased her with his grin, like he knew more and was holding back. They were getting to the good part quick, and he was enjoying it. This woman sure wasn't dumb.

"What situation exactly are we talking about?" Karen said.

"I'm not allowed to tell."

"But you're going to, aren't you?" Karen said. "Or you wouldn't be here."

She was aware of a curious feeling, wanting to urge him to explain, but knowing she didn't have to. She could sit back, and it would come out. She could show indifference, and he would still tell her.

Roland was squinting with a slight grin. "You figured that out, huh? I'm not just inspecting the premises."

"Well, otherwise you wouldn't have mentioned it," Karen said. "You're certainly not a little kid."

"No, I'm not little," Roland said.

"Sometimes little kids say, 'I've got a secret, and I'm not gonna tell you what it is.' What you said was, you're not *supposed* to tell." Patient, speaking to a child.

Roland shook his head. "Uh-unh, I said I'm not al*low*ed to tell."

Karen smiled, hanging on. "I guess there is a difference, isn't there?"

"But I'm gonna tell you anyway," Roland said. "I don't think it's fair you living like this, not knowing."

Marta was coming, Gretchen tagging along.

Karen was aware of another strange feeling, enjoying the suspense, waiting to learn something, wanting to make the feeling last, afraid the revelation would be something she already knew, or suspected. But right now an interesting, close-to-unbelievable situation, entertaining this backcountry gangster, who sat with his cowboy hat tilted low and his long legs stretched out comfortably as the maid served cocktail-hour vodka and tonic.

You can handle it, Karen thought. And you can handle Roland. Mr. Crowe. Out of a minstrel show.

She had handled—up to a point—someone much more potentially dangerous than this guy who worked for Ed Grossi but seemed to be venturing out on his own. Roland wanted something, that was obvious. Playing a nice-guy role that was about as subtle as his electric-blue suit.

Marta left them.

Roland was leaning forward playing with Gretchen on the ground, saying, "Yeah, you're a nice little Gretchie. You're a nice little Gretchie, ain'tcha, huh? Ain'tcha?"

"What is it you're going to tell me?" Karen said.

"Hey, Gretchie, come on, Gretchie, don't bite me, you little dickens. That ain't nice to bite people."

Karen decided to wait.

Roland looked up at her, his hands still fondling the dog. "You're not allowed to see anybody, what it is. I mean any man that might have serious or sexu'l intentions."

"I beg your pardon," Karen said.

"I'm supposed to keep 'em away from you. Any man believed to be serious—you know, not the grocery boy or something—I tell him to keep moving."

"Protecting the widow," Karen said. "That's what I was afraid of. I guess I'll have to have a talk with Mr. Grossi."

"Well, there's a little more to it."

"This is Ed Grossi's idea, isn't it?"

"No, it's your husband's idea."

"My husband's?"

"He left word, no man gets near you in a serious way or as a one-nighter just fooling around or anything like it as long as you live. In other words your husband's cut off your action."

Karen was frowning. "Are you serious?"

"It's what they tell me," Roland said. "I'm the one supposed to keep 'em away from you."

432

"Wait a minute," Karen said, "Frank?—" Staring at Roland, but going back in her mind—hearing it again, threatening Frank, angry, yes, but the threat less than half serious—and Frank saying in a weary voice, "Karen, Karen, Karen—" The man who could write a book on paying people back. Thinking she knew him, but, good God, not taking the time to understand exactly how literal the man was. He had allowed her to think she was an equal, wife to husband. He had allowed her to ask blunt questions and finally threaten him with her independence. And he had quietly locked her up for good.

"Keep the woman in the house where she belongs."

"What?" Roland said.

"You're not kidding, are you?" Like coming out of shock, beginning to see things clearly again.

Roland seemed surprised. "No, I'm not kidding."

"Something you dreamed up."

"It's been going on, ain't it?"

"Yes, but—what do you say to them? How do you let them know?"

"You mean the guys? We tell them you don't want to see them no more."

"And what do they say?"

"Nothing."

"I mean don't they want to know why?"

"I 'magine they get the point pretty quick."

"Do you threaten them?"

"Well, there's different ways. You put the boy against the wall and tell him something, he sees you mean it." Roland grinned. "I made a point with a boy today, didn't believe at first I was serious."

"What did you do?"

"Threw him in a swimming pool."

"You don't . . . beat them up or anything like that?"

"Whatever it takes," Roland said. "That's how Ed says handle it. See, he respects your husband's wish here. But he don't want to do it himself. Fact, all he wants to know it's in somebody's hands and being taken care of."

"I'll see Ed tomorrow," Karen said.

"You sure you want to do that?"

"We're going to quit playing games, I'm sure of that."

"Well, as I see it, the one you'd have to talk to'd be Frank," Roland said. "He's the only one can call it off. Ed, he's respecting the wish of his dead buddy. You know how them people are. He can't change nothing, it's the code, or some bullshit like that." Roland was feeling more relaxed, into it now. He liked the way the woman was hanging on his words. "But you go to Ed, tell what you know, then he's liable to take me off the job and put somebody else on ain't as sympathetic. You follow me?"

"I'm not sure. Why are you . . . sympathetic?"

"I'm not one of *them*, as you can see. I work for them, but I don't think the way they do. It's like you're a white woman got mixed up with these people, I come along—I didn't take none of their oaths and shit—so I can sympathize with your situation and maybe help you out."

"How?" Karen said. "Not tell if I go out with someone?"

"No, see, I'd still have to do my job. There's people watching me, too," Roland said. "But maybe I could ease up your situation some. Come around, talk to you. Maybe, put our minds to it, we could work something out."

"I'm not sure I follow you," Karen said, following every word, watching his eyes beneath the cool-cowboy curve of the brim and knowing exactly what he was talking about.

"I mean ease up your situation," Roland said. "I 'magine you might be getting a little tense and edgy sitting around here, your husband dead, no men you're close to. These dinks you went out with evidently didn't turn you on any."

She was tense, all right, watching him gradually moving in. She said, cautiously, "How do you know that?"

"It's my business to know. See, me and you are much closer than you realize. We got a lot in common."

"We do?" Karen said.

"See, I been thinking," Roland said. "Why would a deceased husband want to cut off his wife's . . . activity, let's say, less he was good and sore on account of she was messing around while he was alive." Roland gave Karen a friendly wink. "Just wanting to have a little fun. What's wrong with that? It's the way we're made, we got to keep active or we dry up, can't even spit."

"That's quite an assumption," Karen said. "I mean that I was cheating on my husband."

"Nobody's asking you to admit nothing you don't want to,"

Roland said. "It's between me and you and the bed. I mean the bedpost."

"Actually, Frank had no reason—" Karen began, and stopped. Why was she trying to explain?

"It's none of my business either way," Roland said. "You don't have to confess nothing to me, lady, to be born again. That's the way I look at this setup, like a new beginning. Here you are stuck here, starting to dry up. Here I am full of notions going to waste, shit, working for them guineas. It's like, I won't tell if you won't. You scratch mine and I'll scratch yours and we'll get something cooking here—see, once you give it some thought, realize how your dead husband and his buddy've got your knees tied together and there's nothing you can do about it less I help you. You follow me? I'm giving you your big chance, lady, and it's the only one you got."

"I said to her, 'Are you all right?' She didn't answer me," Marta said. "She went to the telephone and began to speak to Mr. Grossi."

"You could hear it?" Jesus Diaz, her brother, asked.

It was dark now. They were in the street in front of the house on Isla Bahía, standing by Jesus' car, Jesus holding the cassette tape she had given him.

"I could hear it because she was making her words very clear, not in a loud voice but with force, saying, 'I don't want to see him here again. Keep that animal away from here.' Then saying, 'Why didn't you tell me yourself? I have to learn it from someone like him.' Then listening to Mr. Grossi for a long time. Then saying again, 'Keep him away from here.' But she didn't tell him everything." Marta said.

"What didn't she tell him?"

"Your friend Roland said he wanted to help her in the situation, do something for her to relieve her being tense. But she didn't mention this to Mr. Grossi—I don't know why—only that she didn't want to see Roland again. Very disturbed, but cold in the way she said it, not screaming and shouting. I thought of the time she came home with her car smashed in front and Mister came home with his same car smashed in the side."

Jesus said, "All of that with Mr. Grossi is on this tape?"

"Yes, of course. Every phone conversation today."

"I give it to Roland, he'll hear it," Jesus said. "He'll know she told Mr. Grossi."

"Then don't give it to him," Marta said.

"You crazy?" Jesus said.

Roland heard about it the same evening, in Vivian Arzola's office. Vivian telling him he was lucky Ed Grossi had already gone home. Roland looking out the thirty-ninth-floor window at all that night glitter over the Beach.

"Why?" Roland said.

"Because maybe this time he would have killed you he was so angry."

Roland said, "Lady, I'm the boy didn't testify in court against somebody, and went to Butler. You remember? I just got *back* yesterday. He puts me on a job, I do it the way I see fit to. Does he want another boy? That's up to him. But don't start talking about him doing me harm. There's an old Cuban saying, you fuck with the bull, you get a horn in the ass."

"Where'd you get that suit?" Vivian said.

Roland grinned. "You like it?"

"It's the worst-looking suit I ever saw."

"That's my sweet girl," Roland said, coming away from the window to put a leg up on the edge of Vivian's desk, "your old self again. What else he say?"

"He's going to tell you himself. Keep away from Mrs. DiCilia."

"But not taking me off it."

"Do what you're told. Nothing more."

"You listen in and hear her talking to him?"

"It's recorded here," Vivian said. "I can listen if I want. You try to lie to him, he'll play it for you."

"I got nothing to hide. I told her her old man set up the deal, that's all. So everybody understands each other. I asked her if there was anything I could do for her."

"I can hear you," Vivian said, "the way you'd say it. Did she scream for help?"

"She was nice about the whole thing. What I'm surprised at, she went and called Ed."

"Well, stay away from her, that's all."

"Sure, that's how he wants it. What I better have, though, are all the back tapes. You think I come to see you, it's the tapes I need most."

"Why?" Vivian said.

"You want me to do the job or not?"

Vivian, sitting at her desk, studied him, trying to catch a glimpse of how his mind was working.

"See, now the woman knows she's being watched, she's gonna be more careful," Roland said.

"Thanks to you."

"No, it's better this way, let her know where she stands. But I got to listen to the back tapes. See, get to recognize voices if any of 'em call again and don't use names. You understand?"

"I understand that," Vivian said, "but I think I better talk to Ed first. He'll be back in a few days."

"He went out of town?"

"He'll be back."

"Meanwhile," Roland said, "we're sitting here humping the dog, huh? What I could do is return 'em before he gets back. Otherwise, something happens, Ed sees the work wasn't done properly, he looks around for who's to blame and, like that, you're back in your overalls picking oranges."

Roland walked out with a cardboard box full of cassette tapes. Fucking Cubans, he hadn't met one yet you couldn't hold their job over 'em like a club and get whatever you wanted.

6

If porpoise were really so smart, Maguire would think, how come they put up with all this shit?

The porpoise could ask Maguire the same question. Or Lolly the sea lion.

In the cement-block room off the show pool, Maguire and Lolly would look at each other. Maguire holding the mike to announce Brad Allen and the World-Famous Seascape Porpoise and Sea Lion Show. Lolly waiting to go on, the opening act. Maguire wondering if Lolly ever played with her beachball when no one was around. Lolly wondering—what? Looking at him with her sad eyes.

Maguire would announce the show, hearing his voice outside on the P.A. system as he looked through the crack in the door at the people in the grandstand.

"And now . . . here's Brad!"

After the show Brad Allen would say to Maguire, "Look, how many times? You don't say, 'Here's Brad,' for Christ sake. You ever watch Johnny Carson, the way they do it? You say, 'And now . . . heeeeeeeeeeere's Brad!' "

"I don't know why, but I have trouble with that," Maguire would say.

Brad Allen was show director, star, working manager of:

### SEASCAPE
### PORPOISE SHOW

### SHARKS * SEA LIONS
#### S.E. Seventeenth Street Causeway
#### At Port Everglades

### TURN HERE!

He would say to Maguire, "Are you stupid or something? I don't think it's that hard, do you?"

"No, it isn't," Maguire would say.

"I believe you're supposed to be experienced—"

"The thing is, down at Marathon we didn't have the same kind of show," Maguire would try to explain. "I mean it wasn't quite as, you know, showy."

"Down there, did you know the names of the dolphin?" Brad always got onto that. "Could you identify each one by name?"

"Yeah, I knew their names."

"Then how come you don't know them here?"

"I know them. There's Pepper, Dixie, Penny, Bonzai—"

"Robyn says yesterday you were trying to get Penny to do a tailwalk. Penny doesn't do the tailwalk, Pebbles does the tailwalk."

"I get those two mixed up."

"The other day you thought Bonnie was Yvonne. Bonnie's got the scar from the shark—"

"Right."

"—and Yvonne's at least two hundred pounds heavier, ten feet long, you can't tell them apart. Work on it, okay? Take Robyn over the tank with you and see if you can name them for her. Then come back to the show pool and do the same thing. Is that too much to ask?"

Or, Brad Allen would say:

"The Flying Dolphin Show, you keep leaving out the Mopey Dick part."

"I forget."

"He lays up on the ledge on his side, doesn't move a muscle. Wait for the laughs. Then you say, 'And that's' pause 'why we call him *Mopey* Dick.' "

"I'll try to remember," Maguire would say.

Five months of it, January through May.

Brad Allen waiting for him when he first walked in, pale, a Wayne County Jail pallor, carrying his lined raincoat and suitcase, right off the Delta flight. Brad Allen glancing at a letter the Seascape Management Company had sent him, holding the sheet of paper like it was stained or smelled bad.

"It says you've had experience."

"A year at Marathon," Maguire had said, adding on five months.

"What've you been doing since?"

"Well, traveling and working mostly," Maguire had said. "Colorado, I worked for the Aspen Ski Corporation, also at the Paragon Ballroom. I worked at an airport, a zoo, a TV station. I was the weatherman. I tended bar different places. Let's see, I was an antique dealer. Yeah, and I worked a job at a country club."

"Well, this is no country club," Brad Allen had said. The serious tone, making it sound hard because he had to hire the guy. "How old are you?"

"Thirty," Maguire had said, subtracting six years—after walking in and seeing how young the help was. Like summer-camp counselors in their sneakers and white shorts, red T-shirts with a flying-porpoise decal and SEASCAPE lettered in white. (Brad Allen wore white shorts and a red-trimmed white T-shirt with the porpoise and SEASCAPE in red. He also wore a white jacket and red warmups and sometimes a red, white, and blue outfit.)

"How long you been thirty?"

What was Brad Allen? Maybe thirty-two, thirty-three. The guy staring at Maguire, suspicious, wanting to catch him in a lie. For what?

"What difference does it make?" Maguire had said. "I'm an outgoing person, I like to be with people, I don't mind working hard and"—laying on a little extra—"I'm always willing to learn if there's something I don't know."

It took him a few days to get used to the white shorts and the red T-shirt—thinking about what Andre Patterson would say if he saw the outfit; like, man, you real cute. Within two months Maguire was as brown as the rest of them, and his sneakers were beginning to show some character. He did believe he could pass for thirty. Why not? He felt younger than that. He was out in the sunshine. The work was clean, not too hard. He was eating a lot of fruit. Smoking a little grass now and then with Lesley. Not drinking too much. The pay was terrible, two-sixty a week, but he was getting by. Living in a one-room efficiency at an Old Florida-looking stucco place called the Casa Loma, fifty bucks a week, next door to Lesley, who lived in the manager's apartment with her Aunt Leona. What else? Air-conditioned, two blocks from the ocean—

The people he worked with—R. D. Hooker, Chuck, Robyn and Lesley—reminded him of high school.

Hooker, a strong, curly-haired Florida boy, twenty-three years old. A clean liver, dedicated. Hooker would go down into the eighteen-foot tank, Neptune's Realm, with a face mask and air hose and play with the porpoise even when he didn't have to, *between* shows. One time Hooker said to Chuck, the custodian-trainee, "I don't know what's wrong with Bonnie today. First she won't let me touch her, then she butts me. Then she comes up and starts yanking on my goddarn air hose like to pull it out of my mouth. Knowing what she was doing."

Chuck listened to every word and said, "Yeah? How come she was doing that?"

Maguire said, "It sounds like she's getting her period."

Hooker said, "What's it got to do with her acting nasty?"

Maguire would listen to them talk, amazed, nobody putting anybody on or down. Maguire said, "R.D., you ever talk to them? I mean understand them?"

"Sometimes," Hooker said. "Like I'm getting so I can understand Penny when I ask her a question?"

"No shit," Maguire said. "What do you ask her?"

"Oh, feeding her I might say, 'You like that, huh? Isn't that good?'"

"And what does she say?"

"She goes like—" Hooker did something with the inside of his mouth and made a clickity-click, kitty-cat, Donald Duck sound.

"Oh," Maguire said.

Hooker came on his day off and worked with the two young dolphins in the training tank, hunkered down on the boards for hours, talking to them gently and showing them his hands. Dedicated.

Chuck was on his way to becoming dedicated. He personally wrote two hundred postcards to Star-Kist Tuna, Bumble Bee, VanCamp, Ralston Purina, and H. J. Heinz, telling them to quit murdering dolphins or he would never eat their products again.

Robyn was dedicated, though didn't appear to be. She was a serious girl and didn't smile much or seem to be listening when you said something to her. Unless it was Brad Allen who said it. Brad Allen could tell Robyn to dive down to the bottom of the show pool with Dixie, shoot up over the twelve-foot bar and do a tailwalk across the pool, and Robyn would try it. When Brad Allen told her she was doing a good job, Robyn became squirmy and maybe wet her white shorts a little. Nice tight shorts—

Though not as tight or short as Lesley's. Lesley's showed a little cheek. She never pulled at them though, the way Robyn did when she got squirmy. What Lesley got was pouty. She'd put on her hurt look and say, "It's not my turn to feed the sharks, it's hers. If you think I'm going in there every day you're out of your fucking mind." Lesley was dedicated, but not to nurse sharks. She didn't think it was funny when she was standing hip deep in the pool trying to feed a hunk of bluerunner to a shark, and Maguire, on the platform above, would say to the crowd, "Let's give Lesley a nice hand"—pause—"she may need one someday."

Lesley had a pile of wavy brown hair she combed several times an hour. One night, during Maguire's fourth month, Lesley said to him, "I think I'm falling in love with you." She looked so good lying there in the dim light with her hair and her white breasts exposed, Maguire almost said he loved her, too. But he didn't.

Brad Allen was *very* dedicated. Brad Allen was also serious and tiresome. He made Maguire tired. Maguire wondered why Brad Allen didn't get tired of being Brad Allen. Once, Maguire took a couple of puffs on a joint before announcing the show and said, over the P.A. system, "Heeeeeeeeeeeeeeeeeeeeeeeeeeeeeeeeeeeeeeere's

Brad," holding the "here's" almost as long as he could. And after the show Brad Allen said to him, "Now that's a little better."

Seascape, the layout, reminded Maguire of a small tropical World's Fair: round white buildings, striped awnings, and blue and yellow pennants among shrubs and royal palms.

There was Neptune's Realm you could walk into and look through windows to watch the porpoise and sea creatures glide past, underwater. Topside they put on the Flying Dolphin Show.

There was Shark Lagoon, a pool full of brown nurse sharks and a few giant sea turtles.

There was the Porpoise Petting Pool, where you could touch Misty and Gippy's hard-boiled-egg skin and feed them minnows, three for a quarter.

At the Grandstand Arena Brad Allen put on the main event, the World-Famous Seascape Porpoise and Sea Lion Show: "where these super-smart mammals perform that aquatic acrobatics."

Back in the Alligator Pit a Seminole Indian used to wrestle twelve-foot gators, but the Seminole quit and went to Disney World, and R. D. Hooker only tried it a couple of times; so the alligators and a crocodile were there if you wanted to look at them.

Yellow- and white-striped awnings covered the refreshment stand and gift shop. A fifty-cent Sky Ride in two-seater gondolas gave you a low aerial view of the grounds, the tanks and pools of blue water, the white cement walks and buildings among the imported palm trees: a clean, manicured world just off the S.E. 17th Street Causeway.

"If you don't like it, why don't you quit?" Lesley said, getting a little pouty.

"I didn't say I didn't like it, I said it wasn't *real*," Maguire said, Maguire driving Lesley's yellow Honda, heading home to the Casa Loma. "It's like a refuge. Nothing can happen to you there, you're safe. But it's got nothing to do with reality. It's like you're given security, but in exchange for it you have to give up your*self*. You have to become somebody else."

Lesley said, "Jesus, what's safe about getting down in the water, feeding those fucking sharks? I've done it every day this week, you know it? Robyn's off probably giving Brad some head."

Maguire said, "Come on, the sharks feed all night. You jiggle a piece of fish, it's for the tourists. I'm not talking about that kind of being safe. I mean *here*, you live in a little world that's got nothing to do with the real world. You're sheltered—"

"*I'm* sheltered?"

"*We* are, working there. What's a really big problem? Misty eats some popcorn, gets constipated. Pebbles is grouchy, won't imitate the Beatles. Everybody's going, 'Christ, what's the matter with Pebbles?' Spend *months*, maybe a year training a dolphin to jump through a hoop, come up seventeen feet in the air and ring the school bell."

Lesley said, "Yeah?" She still didn't get it.

"They're doing something that dolphins don't normally do, right?"

Lesley thought a moment. "Yeah—but they jump. Out in the wild they jump all the time."

"They shoot baskets? They bowl out there?"

"It's to show how intelligent they are," Lesley said, "how they can be trained."

"Here's the point," Maguire said, wishing the Honda was air-conditioned, wishing the lady in front of him would turn, for Christ sake, if she was going to turn, *turn.* "They don't normally, the dolphin, they don't pretend they're playing baseball out in the ocean or jump up and take a piece of fish out of somebody's mouth, right?"

"If you don't like it," Lesley said, "what do you do it for?"

Jesus, Maguire thought. He said, "Just follow the point I want to make, okay? I'm not saying I don't like it. I'm only saying it's like playing make-believe. The dolphin wouldn't be here, they wouldn't be doing the tricks if we didn't teach them. You see what I mean? They'd be out there doing something else, we'd be doing something else. But no, we made this up. The dolphins and us, we're playing with ourselves. We're going through the motions of something that doesn't have anything to do with reality."

"So?"

Oh, Christ. "So—if they're not real dolphins doing all that kind of shit, what're we? Reciting the canned humor, throwing them pieces of codfish—what're we?"

"I was a waitress, a place on Las Olas," Lesley said. "That was real, real shit. You like to ask me what I'd rather do?"

"I'd like to borrow your car this evening," Maguire said. "What're the chances?"

He poured himself a white rum with a splash of lemon concentrate, left the venetian blinds half closed and sat for a while, the room looking old and worn-out in the dimness. Fifty bucks a week including black and white TV, it was still a bargain. He could hear the hi-fi going next door, Lesley boogying around the apartment to the Bee Gees, ignoring her aunt, who was a little deaf. A nice woman, Maguire would sit and talk to her sometimes, listen to episodes from her past life in Cincinnati, Ohio, until he'd tell her he had to go to bed, wake up early. Lesley never sat and listened even for a minute. Lesley would roll her eyes when she saw an episode coming and get out of there. Lesley had no feelings for others; but she sure had a nice firm healthy little body.

Maguire showered and had another rum and lemon while he put on his good clothes. Pale beige slacks, dark-blue sport shirt, and a skimpy Dacron sport coat, faded light-blue, he'd got at Burdine's for forty-five bucks. He loved the sport coat because, for some reason, it made him think of Old Florida and made him feel like a native. (A Maguire dictum: wherever you are, fit in, look like you belong. In Colorado wear a sheepskin coat and lace-up boots.) He got the *Detroit Free Press* clipping out of the top drawer, from under his sweat socks, and slipped it into the inside coat pocket. He then went next door and asked Lesley's aunt if he could use the phone; he'd be sure to get the charges and pay for it.

He said to Lesley, "You want to turn that down a little?"

Lesley said, "Who're you calling, your hot date?"

"I don't have a hot date."

"I thought you were going out."

"Turn the music down, okay?"

Maguire gave the operator the Detroit number and waited. He felt nervous. He wished Lesley would quit watching him.

"Aren't you gonna clean up?"

"You want me to leave, say so."

"I get back, I'll take you out to dinner."

In the phone, Andre Patterson's wife said, "Hello?"

445

"Okay?" Maguire said to Lesley. "Go on, get cleaned up." Then into the phone:

"Hi, this is Cal Maguire. How you doing?" He had to listen while Andre's wife told him she was piss-poor, if he really wanted to know about it, having trouble getting her ADC checks, had her phone disconnected for a while. Maguire said yeah, he'd been trying to get hold of her, calling information. He said, "Listen, you know the deal at the club? . . . The country club, Andre and I and Grover. I asked you the man's name? Remember? . . . No, I've got it. What I was wondering, you know, Andre said the man was paying them back for something? At the club, something happened there to the man. I wondered if Andre ever spoke to you about it . . . If he mentioned to you what it was happened out there. Like maybe the man's wife was involved, you know, maybe she was insulted or something and that's what got the man upset." Christ, upset—willing to pay them forty-five hundred to go out there and hit the place. "Uh-huh, yeah, that's right . . . But he never said anything about the man's wife, huh? . . . No, I was just wondering. Hey, well listen, tell Andre I'm gonna write to him, okay? . . . Fine, I'll be talking to you." Shit.

"Very mysterious," Lesley said, holding a beach towel wrapped around her. "Who's Andre?"

"Friend of mine."

"What'd somebody get upset about?"

Maguire said, "I know it's your aunt's phone and you're letting me use your car and all, but how about if you keep your nose out of my personal business, okay?"

"Yeah," Lesley said, "well, how about if you keep your ass out of my car, you want to get snotty about it."

"You're a beauty," Maguire said. "You got the maturity of about a five-year-old."

"Keep thinking it," Lesley said, "walking to work every day." She turned, letting the towel come open, giving him a flash as she went into the bedroom.

There you are, Maguire thought, walking up the street toward A1A. The kind of question you'd climb all the way up the mountain to ask the old man sitting there in his loincloth.

In the light of eternity, is it better to sell out and ride or stand up and walk?

And the old man would look at him with his calm, level gaze and say—

He'd say—

Maguire was still trying to think of an answer, standing on the oceanfront corner, when the girl visiting from Mitchell, Indiana, picked him up, said, "Heck, it's nothing," and went out of her way to drop him off at Harbor Beach Parkway.

# 7

An appraiser friend of Maguire's, a guy who bought and sold pretty much out of his back door, once said to him, "You walk out with a color TV, you realize the mirror hanging on the wall there, gilded walnut, might be a George II? Early eighteenth century, man, worth at least three grand." Maguire went to the library, looked through art books, made notes and lifted a copy of *Kovel's Complete Antiques Price List* from the reference shelf. In his work—during the short periods he was into B and E, usually to pick up some traveling money—he'd come across a few antiques and art objects of value.

But nothing like the display in Mrs. DiCilia's sitting room. He was looking at a Queen Anne desk—four drawers, stubby little pedestal legs, worth at least four grand—when the maid came in again, a dog following her, and told him to please be seated.

Missus would come to him very soon. A sharp-looking Cuban, nice accent. Maguire said thank you and then, as the maid was leaving, "How you doing?"

Marta stopped. She said, "Yes?"

"How's it going? You like it here?" Always friendly to the help. "I think it'd be a nice place to work."

Marta, still surprised: "Yes, it is."

"But I wouldn't want to have to dust all this," Maguire said.

The maid left, but the little gray and white dog remained, watching Maguire apprehensively, ready to bark or run.

"Relax," Maguire said to the dog and continued looking around the sitting room.

Bird cage table, not bad. Worth about seven and a half.

Pair of slipseat Chippendale chairs in walnut. Now we're getting there. Seventy-five hundred, maybe eight grand.

Hummel figurines, if you liked Hummel. Fifty bucks each. A couple that might go as high as a hundred and a quarter.

Plates—very impressive. Stevenson, Enoch Wood's shell-border pattern. Six, seven thousand bucks' worth of plates on one shelf.

And *yes*, Peachblow vases, the real thing. Creamy red-rose and yellow. Jesus, with the gargoyle stand. Name your price.

A picture of Pope Pius XII. The Last Supper. And some real paintings, old forests and misty green mountains, a signed Durand, an Alvan Fisher, nineteenth-century Hudson River school. A few others he didn't recognize—sitting down now as he studied the painting—

And jumping up quickly to look at the chair—Jesus, feeling the turnings of the arms. Louis XVI bergère, in walnut. Pretty sure it was a real one.

He sat in the chair again, carefully, and began thinking about the woman who lived here and owned this collection. Before, he had pictured a dumpy sixty-year-old Italian woman in the kitchen, rolling dough, making tomato paste, a woman with an accent. He'd lay it out to her: Your husband owes us money. She'd pay or she wouldn't, and he could forget about it.

But if she knew antiques—maybe he could fake it a little, establish some kind of rapport, trust . . . confidence?

The dog came over and began sniffing.

"That's fish," Maguire said. He didn't stoop to pet the dog or say anything else.

Karen, in the doorway, saw this much. And the color of his pants and shirt beneath the jacket, making her hesitate a moment.

"Mr. Maguire?"

He looked up to see a slim, good-looking woman in beige slacks, a dark-blue shirt with white buttons, hand extended.

Maguire rose, giving her a pleasant smile, shaking his head a little. They shook hands politely and he said, seriously then, "You know something?"

Karen expected him to say, I've heard a lot about you, Mrs. DiCilia. Something along that line.

But he didn't. He said. "We've got matching outfits on. Tan and blue."

Karen said, "You suppose it means something?" Playing it as straight as he was.

"I don't know about you," Maguire said, "but I got all dressed up. This particular outfit is from Burdine's, up on Federal Highway."

"I've heard of Burdine's," Karen said, "but I'm not sure I've heard of you. You were a friend of my husband's?"

"Well, we weren't exactly close. I worked for him once."

Karen, said, "And you want to know if I'm all right? If I need anything? What else? Are you with Roland or on your own?"

"I don't know anybody named Roland," Maguire said.

"So you're an independent. All right," Karen said, "let's go out on the patio. That's where we hold the squeeze sessions."

"The what?"

"Come on, I'm anxious to hear your pitch." She walked past him to the French doors.

It had felt like a good start. But now, she wasn't being cool, she was ice-cold, assuming way too much. Maguire hesitated. He said, "You've got some very nice pieces here. The bergère, is it authentic Louis Seize?"

Now Karen paused at the doors to look back and seemed to study him a moment.

"The what?"

Maguire grinned. Was she kidding? She waited, looking at him, and he wasn't sure.

"The chair. If it's real, it belongs in a museum."

"It *is* in a museum," Karen said. She turned and walked through the doors.

Putting him on, Maguire decided. Not wanting to sound agreeable or give him anything. He followed her out to the patio, where a torch was burning and swimming pool lights reflected in the clear water, Maguire looking around, thinking, So this is what it's like. Sit out here at night, watch the running lights, the powerboats going by on the Intercoastal.

Ring for the maid, get her with some mysterious signal, because there she was. Maguire said rum would be fine, surprised, wondering why Mrs. DiCilia was being sociable, hearing her ask for a martini with ice. Put that down: not "on the rocks" but "with ice." Yes, very nice; sit out here on the patio of your Spanish-Moorish million-dollar home that was full of antiques and art objects and—what?

He was going to say he was sorry for coming so late, or early— one or the other—and hoped he wasn't inconveniencing her. But why? Why suck around?

He said, "Besides all this, what's it like to be rich?"

Karen didn't say anything.

"Never mind," Maguire said. "It doesn't matter."

"I was thinking," Karen said. "If you really want to know, it's boring. I guess it doesn't have to be, but it is."

"I don't follow you."

"You asked me, I told you, it's boring," Karen said. "Next question. Let's get to the point, all right?"

The dog was sniffing around his foot again. Maguire crossed his leg.

Mrs. DiCilia was on the muscle, a little edgy, yes; because she was waiting for him to pull some kind of scam. Out here for the squeeze session: probably one of a long line of guys who'd come to make a pitch, take advantage of the poor widow. The slim, good-looking great-looking widow. Maguire resented her assumption, being put in that category, somebody out to con her. The lady sitting there waiting for the pitch.

The goddamn dog pawing his knee, scratching the material. Maguire reached down with one hand and moved the dog aside.

Karen watched him.

Sitting back he took the newspaper clipping out of his pocket, unfolded it carefully and handed it to her.

Karen said, "What is it?" In the soft glow of torchlight she could only read the headline. ARMED TRIO ROBS COUN-TRY CLUB.

"That was myself and two associates," Maguire said. "Your husband offered to pay us fifteen hundred each to go in and hit the place. Make them look dumb or give it some bad publicity, I don't know. We did the job, but we never got paid."

Karen said, "Deep Run Country Club, Bloomfield Hills."

"That's the one."

"It happened when, last August?"

"Right. The sixteenth."

"We visited Detroit in August—no, it was July," Karen said. "Frank played golf there a few times as a guest. He liked the club, so he applied for a membership."

"And they turned him down," Maguire said. Karen nodded. "I thought maybe you'd been insulted out there. You know, some-thing personal."

"What do you think Frank DiCilia being turned down is, if it isn't an insult?"

"Yeah, I guess so. But how come if you were living here at the time?—"

"Why can't he have a membership in Detroit? That's what it's like to be rich," Karen said. "So what is it you want, fifteen hun-dred dollars?"

"Each, for the three of us. The other two guys were convicted. They're in Jackson, but I'll see they get theirs."

"You got off?" She seemed interested.

"It's a long story, and if you're already bored—" Maguire said.

Karen said, "That's all you want?"

"That's all we got coming."

"You could've said . . . ten thousand."

"And you could've known about the deal," Maguire said, "de-pending on what you and your hubby talked about. It was a straight fifteen hundred apiece, no sick pay or retirement bene-fits."

Now, yes or no? Waiting for her to make up her mind. She didn't seem as edgy. She said let's have another drink and that surprised him. The maid appeared and left, and when she ap-peared again Karen was asking him if he lived in Florida or was he visiting.

He told her he worked at Seascape. "You know, the porpoise show? Practically around the corner from here."

"I've passed it," Karen said. "You really work there?" Sounding interested and a little surprised. "Get the porpoise to jump through hoops, that kind of thing?"

"We get 'em to do everything but mate in midair," Maguire said.

"They won't do that for you?"

"I think they go to a motel. Five months, I've never seen one of 'em even, well, get aroused."

Now she was studying him and didn't say anything for a moment.

"Amazing."

"Well, I wouldn't like it either," Maguire said. "People watching."

"No, I mean that you work there," Karen said. "And you seem to know antiques— What else do you do?"

"Rob country clubs," Maguire said, "and have a hard time collecting. I'm enjoying the drink and the chat, but just for my peace of mind, are you gonna honor your husband's obligation or what?"

Karen said, "*Honor* his obligation—" and seemed amused now. "Is that what it is, honoring his obligation?"

"You can call it whatever you want," Maguire said, "as long as we're both talking about the same deal."

"Do you do this sort of thing often?"

"What sort of thing?"

"Rob country clubs?"

"This was the first time."

"But you've robbed other places."

He didn't say anything.

"Do you carry a gun?"

"Why?"

"I'm curious, that's all."

"Do you fool around?" Maguire said.

"What?"

"Do you pick up guys, take 'em to bed? Or you just ask a lot of questions about their personal life?"

"I believe you came to me," Karen said. "You're the one that wants something."

"And if I'm not polite and answer your questions I can go fuck myself, huh?"

Karen didn't say anything. She got up, walked from the patio to the house and in through the French doors.

Maguire waited. Shit. Thinking again of the old man sitting on top of the mountain in his loincloth.

In the light of eternity, is it better to take a bunch of shit with the hope of getting paid, or—

Karen came back to the patio carrying something in each hand, something wrapped in white tissue paper and, in the hand she extended to him, a packet of bills. He couldn't believe it. New one hundred dollar bills. They were sticking together, only about an inch of them, they were so new.

"Forty-five hundred dollars," Karen said.

Maguire thinking, the first thing in his mind: There's more. Right in the house.

"Can I ask you one more question?"

"Go ahead," Maguire said, putting the money in his inside coat pocket. He could feel it against his ribs.

She pulled her chair closer to his and sat down before extending the tissue-wrapped package.

"What is it?"

She watched him, but didn't say anything.

Taking it then, feeling the weight, he knew what it was. Maguire unwrapped enough of the tissue paper to see the gun, wrapped it together again and handed it back to her.

She said, "Do you know what it is, the make?"

"It's a Beretta nine-millimeter Parabellum, holds eight rounds in the clip. How much you pay for it?"

"I didn't buy it. It was my husband's."

"You could get something like four hundred for it on the street."

"I don't want to sell it," Karen said, "I want to know how to use it."

"For what?"

"Protection."

"It isn't a good idea," Maguire said. "People who don't own guns don't get shot as much as people who do."

"Will you show me how it works?"

"If I don't, what? You want the money back?"

"The money's yours. You've already earned that." She waited.

"It's got a little crossbolt safety above the trigger. You push it to off, slide the top back and forward again and you're ready to go," Maguire said. "Which is what I'm gonna do if it's okay. Take my money and run."

"You're very direct," Karen said, and seemed to be studying him again. "You admit some things and then you stop."

"It's not that I have anything to hide," Maguire said, "it's the feeling I'm on the carpet, being questioned."

She said, "I'm sorry, I really am." There was a silence, but she continued to look at him.

Maguire said, "That's okay. I guess—as you say, I walk in here, give you a story, why should you believe me?"

"I do though," Karen said. She seemed to smile then. "Will you tell me something else?"

"Probably," Maguire said.

"What's the difference between a porpoise and a dolphin?"


Maguire found a note on his pillow that said, in a forward-slanting Magic Marker scrawl, "Knock if you are not mad!!!"

He reached across the bed to the wall—to a fading garden at Versailles, green-on-yellow wallpaper—and rapped on it three times.

Lesley came in wearing a short see-through nighty and several rollers in her hair, head somewhat lowered to gaze up at Maguire with a practiced, hurt little-girl expression.

"I thought you were gonna take me out to dinner."

"I must've got mixed up, who was mad at who," Maguire said. "I had something over on the beach."

"I *was* mad," Lesley said, "but I'm not anymore."

"How come?"

"You didn't have to talk to me like that."

"Did you go out?"

"No"—pouting—"I sat there with Aunt Leona watching TV all night."

Poor little thing—he was supposed to comfort her, tell her he was sorry. He wasn't annoyed or upset. In fact, he didn't feel much of anything toward Lesley, one way or the other. He was catching glimpses of Karen DiCilia in the glow of the torch, part of her face in shadow, the light reflecting on her dark hair. Dark but not Italian-dark, the woman not anything like he'd imagined the wife of Frank DiCilia.

Lesley said, "Are you going to bed or you gonna read?"

It was strange, in that moment he did feel a little sorry for her, standing there in her see-through nighty and her curlers. He said, "It's late. Might as well go to bed."

"You want me to get in with you?"

"You bet," Maguire said, getting undressed as she turned off the light and pulled back the green and yellow spread.

"There," Lesley said. "God, isn't it good?"

"It sure is."

"Shit, I forgot my curlers."

She sat up, took out the ones in back and got down there again. "Ouuuu, that hurts. But it's okay. Now it's okay. Ouuuuu, is it ever." After a while she said, "Cal?"

"What?"

"If my aunt knew we did this, she'd shit. You know it?"

"I guess," Maguire said.

"We're watching TV? She goes on and on about in Cincinnati she's at a picnic with this guy named Herman or Henry or something and how he grabbed her and kissed her. God, it was like it freaked her out, and she was *my* age. In the guy's car. I want to say to her, 'Aunt Leona, you ever go down on him?' She'd actually shit, you know it?"

"I bet," Maguire said.

"No, she was twenty-*three*. It was just before she got married. But not to Herman. My uncle's name was Thomas. That's what they called him all the time, Thomas. I can't imagine them doing it. Can you imagine Aunt Leona doing it?"

"No," Maguire said.

"She's in there snoring away, all this beauty cream on. You should see her."

He didn't say anything.

"Well, I better get my ass beddy-bye. I'll see you in the morning."

"Night," Maguire said.

"Don't play with it too much," Lesley said.

"I won't."

The door closed.

He could see Karen DiCilia in shadow and firelight, the clean-shining dark hair, features composed. Karen DiCilia, Karen something else, Karen Hill originally. He'd found out a few things. If she could ask questions he could, too. And then she had asked a few more. Calvin, is it? Yeah. Calvin doesn't go with Maguire. It should be Al instead of Cal, Aloysius Maguire, a good mick name. Well, Karen doesn't go too well with DiCilia, does it? And the good-looking woman saying, No, it should never have gone with DiCilia.

Sometimes we're bored, willing to try something new and different. Change for the sake of change.

Maguire saying, Right.

Sometimes, then, we're too impulsive, we make up our minds too quickly.

True.

Sometimes we talk too much, say things we don't mean.

Very true. (Talking, but what was she *saying*?)

And we get into a bind, a situation that offers few if any options and then we're stuck and we don't know what to do.

Maguire saying, Uh-huh.

Maguire almost saying, If you want to tell me what you're stuck in, what the problem is, why don't you, instead of beating around?

Almost, but not saying it. Because what if she told him? And expected him to help her out in some way; man, with the kind of people who'd been associated with her husband and were probably still hanging around—Then what, chickenfat, sit there and grin at her or get involved in something that's none of your business?

This was a very good-looking woman. The kind, ordinarily, it would be a pleasure to help out and have her feel grateful. This one, he was pretty sure, could be warm and giving.

But right now she was in some kind of no-option bind and had a keen interest in firearms . . . while Maguire had a vivid memory of the six by eight cells in the Wayne County Jail and what it was like to go to trial facing 20 to life.

So he had said, when it was his turn again, "Well listen, Karen, it's been very nice talking to you," and thanked her again and got out of there.

Lying in bed he began to think, But maybe she just needs somebody to talk to. Somebody she feels would understand her situation. Or keep the local con artists away. It didn't necessarily have to be anything heavy. What was the risk in talking to her, finding out a little more?

She was a good-looking woman.

He wondered how old she was.

He wondered how many more new one hundred dollar bills there were in her house.

# 8

Arnold came from the bedroom carrying a yellow canvas bag that had a zippered flap on the side for a tennis racket. Roland was on the balcony looking over the rail, holding onto his cowboy hat due to the wind off the ocean. Arnold stared at Roland's back, at the bright-blue material pulled tight across the shoulders.

Roland turned. As he saw Arnold watching him, he said, "How's Barry?"

Arnold walked over to the coffee table and dropped the bag. "Fifty-four thousand," Arnold said.

Roland came in from the balcony. "I asked you how's Barry."

"He's in traction. He'll be in traction six months. Also his kidney and his spleen's fucked up."

"Tell him if he's gonna dive, he should do it in the deep end," Roland said. He moved past Arnold to the canvas bag and picked it up. "Wouldn't think paper'd be this heavy, would you?"

"You gonna look at it?"

"I know what it looks like," Roland said. "You're doing good, Arnie. Keep it up."

"You know I'm gonna pay you, right?"

"Sure, I do."

"Well, how about—you know, since this isn't strictly speaking a shylock deal—we make a different kind of arrangement."

"Like what, Arnie?"

"See, the way it is, I keep paying the vig, how'm I ever gonna get to the principle?"

"Beats the shit out of me," Roland said.

"You know what I mean? I didn't borrow the money. I'm only paying the man back his investment."

"Yeah? What's the difference?"

"It's *diff*erent. You got guys borrow money from you, they know going in what the vig is. But this was a business deal."

"They're all business deals," Roland said, "but vig's vig and the amount owed's something else. Didn't they teach you that at school, Arnie?"

"I tried to explain it to Ed—"

"I know you did. And he told you to talk to me," Roland said. "It's the same way, a man, a guy owns one of the biggest hotels on the strip, he borrows money, he pays the vig. Every week. He's got a problem, he comes to me with it. Man with a restaurant right here in Hallandale, shit, half a dozen appliance stores over on federal highway, picture show, bunch of motels—they all pay the vig, Arnie. They understand it's the way you do business."

"Right, shylock business, I understand that." Arnold moving around, bit his lip. "But this is *diff*erent."

"And I ask you how-so?"

"I didn't *borrow* the money, Ed *invested* it."

"But you lost it, so you have to pay it back."

"I didn't lose it—"

Roland had his palm up, facing Arnold. "We ought to agree on something here."

"Okay, I lost it."

"Now then," Roland said, "when you come to paying back, what's the difference? Paying back is paying back, whether it's money you lost or money you borrowed. See, your losing it—we give you money, we don't ask you what you're gonna do with it, like the bank. You can flush it down the toilet if you want. Long as you pay it back."

"Okay," Arnold said, "I owe you five hundred and forty grand. I can pay you back in time, you know that. But I can't if I keep paying the fucking vig. Look, ten weeks from now, fifty-four *thousand* a week, man, where the fuck am I? I will've paid out five hundred forty grand, right? And I'm still not into the fucking principle. I'm never into it. You know what I got to do? I mean to get what I'm paying you."

"I don't know," Roland said, "ask your mommy for it?"

"I got to deal in hard shit, man, and that's a totally different business. Get into that Mexican brown, nobody even likes it, I got to keep a line coming through here and beg, im*plore*, dealers to take the shit. That's what I'm into now, myself, that's all."

"Your little friends," Roland said, "where'd they go?"

"Who knows. Fuck 'em. I said to Ed, okay, then back me again on the Colombian thing. Three times, three loads, you take my cut as well as your own, I'm paid off."

"And he said?"

"Shit, you know what he said."

Roland buttoned his suit coat and switched the canvas bag from his right hand to his left, ready to go.

He said, "It's hard out here in the world of commerce, ain't it, Arnie?"

But rewarding to those who put their nose to the grindstone and their ear to a boxful of cassette tapes, the way Roland did for twenty-four hours and fourteen minutes spread over three days, listening to something like one hundred forty-six different cassettes.

And ninety-nine percent nothing. Somebody called the weather every day. The lady called her hairdresser once a week, this queer who scolded her and acted impatient. (What'd she take that kind of shit for?) She talked to some people in Detroit a few times; nothing. She talked to her daughter, Julie, in Los Angeles; listened to her daughter bitch about work and her husband fooling around, the daughter talking away, never asking how her mother was doing. ("Hang up," Roland would say to himself. "Whyn't you hang up?") There were calls to Marta, short conversations in Spanish. Then a woman calling from the *Miami*

461

*Herald* a couple of times, wanting to interview her, take some pictures of Mrs. DiCilia at home, Mrs. DiCilia saying not now, some other time.

Then the dinks started calling about the middle of February. Dinks asking her to go out. Dinks calling again and saying what a fun time they had. "Hey, that was a ball, wasn't it? Delightful." Laughing like girls. One dink giving her his golf scores for the week. This other dink boring the shit out of her (and Roland) with all these stock market reports. Another one, the only thing he talked about was his Donzi cigarette boat and off-shore racing, Miami-Bimini, Miami–Key West, how big the waves were, implying what a fucking hero he was out there at the helm. (Roland said to the voice on the tape, "You dink, I'd blow your ass off with a Seminole air boat. Put you smack on the trailer.") From the sound of them, it couldn't have been too hard to scare them off. The lady didn't know how lucky she was, saved from listening to them dinks.

Then the woman from the *Miami Herald* again wanting to interview her; DiCilia saying all right. Then a call from some Palm Beach magazine, the *Gold Coaster*, something like that, and Mrs. DiCilia agreeing to talk to them.

Then more conversations with Ed Grossi in May. (Roland would sit up and pay attention to these.) Then Ed inviting her to his office.

There, that was up to where Roland took over the tape concession and started getting them directly from Marta or Jesus Diaz. Nothing interesting yet, not the kind of information he was listening for.

Then the one, her call to Ed chewing him out. "I never want to see that man here again." Not loud, but a good bite in her tone. "Keep that animal away from here." (*An*imal? Hey now.) Then saying, "Why didn't you tell me yourself? Why did I have to hear it from him? Keep him away from this house. You understand?" (Roland saying, "Hey, take it easy, Karen.")

He listened to the end. Then played it back and listened again. No, sir, nothing about his proposition. Not a word. Blowing off steam, but not telling the whole story, was she? Keeping a possibility open. Roland grinned.

The next few tapes, nothing of interest. One he thought at first was going to be good.

The woman talking to the operator, asking for the number of Goodman and Stern in Detroit, telling the operator it was a law office. (Uh-oh.) Then talking to a guy named Nate. Nate telling her it had been too long and how sorry he was he couldn't make Frank's funeral and was there anything he could do for her. Then Karen asking him if the name Maguire and Deep Run meant anything to him. Long pause. The guy, Nate, saying yes, he believed they handled it. Why? Karen saying it wasn't important but she'd like some information about Maguire if they had it on file. She had met him, she said, and something about Maguire wanting a job recommendation. This guy Nate saying, after another pause, well, he'd have somebody named Marshall something put a report together and send it to her. But he'd advise her to use discretion and touch base with someone at Dorado, someone close by. And how was everything else down in the land of sunshine?

"Hot in the day, cool in the evening," Roland murmured to himself. Dink lawyers, you never knew what they were talking about.

Another tape. Another conversation with Ed Grossi. Ed back from his trip. That would have been yesterday. Roland paid attention, listening as Karen asked Ed about a trust fund, wanting to know what bank it was in. Ed told her.

KAREN: You said in bonds, I know, but I've forgotten the name.

ED: Miami General Revenue, at six percent.

KAREN: Don't I get records, something on paper? How do I prove they're mine?

ED: Well, as I told you, the bonds are in the name of the administrator of the estate, Dorado. The yield, the interest—what'd I say, two and a half?

("Here we go," Roland said.)

KAREN: Two hundred and forty thousand.

ED: Yeah, goes into the trust and the bank deposits it, or they credit it to your account, twenty thousand a month. Yeah, that's it.

(ROLAND: "That's it all right. Man, that is *it*.")

KAREN: But I don't have anything that describes me as the beneficiary, or whatever I am.

ED: You're getting the money, aren't you?

KAREN: Yes, but I'd like something on paper.

ED: I'll have Vivian get you a copy. We'll get you something, don't worry about it. How's everything else? Clara says she wants to get together with you sometime.

KAREN: That'd be fine. (Long pause) Ed . . . look, we're going to have to talk about this other thing. When can I come to your office?

(Roland, writing figures on a pad of paper, looked up.)

ED: What other thing?

KAREN: Ed, for God's sake. Maybe this happens in India or Saudi Arabia, but not Fort Lauderdale, Florida. You can't simply ignore it.

ED: Karen—

KAREN: You've got to *stop* it, that's all. If you won't, I'll take you to court. I'll do *some*thing—leave here if I have to.

ED: Karen—

KAREN: If you think I'm going to live like this you're out of your mind.

ED: All right, we'll have a talk. How about tomorrow, my office? Come on up, we'll go to lunch.

(ROLAND: "That's today.")

KAREN: I'll meet you at Palm Bay.

(ROLAND: "Shit.")

He looked at his figures again, scratched them out and started over, multiplying, dividing, trying different ways, *finally* then, coming up with the answer, what twenty thousand a month was six percent of. Jesus Christ, four million dollars the woman had!

# 9

Lunch at Palm Bay. Ed Grossi used a Rye Krisp and a spoon on his bowl of cottage cheese. Karen listened, sipping her Bloody Mary, picking at her shrimp salad, every once in a while shaking her head. Unbelievable. Having to threaten, almost hit him with something to get him to talk about it.

"You serve me with some kind of cease and desist order. From doing what? Karen, this is a very personal matter. You want to get something like this in the papers?"

"If I have to. Ed, this is my life we're talking about."

Almost to himself: "People wouldn't understand it."

"Of course they wouldn't. It's something out of the Middle Ages." Karen leaned closer, staring at the quiet little man across the table. "He told you this in the hospital? Was he lucid? How do you know he was even in his right mind?"

"It was before that," Grossi said, "in my office. Before a witness."

"Who, Roland?"

"No, not Roland. I said to Frank, you're kidding. He said no, very serious. I know his voice, his tone. Nobody goes near her. I asked him why. He said I didn't have to know that. Then Vivian came in, took some dictation. She witnessed my saying yes to him, it would be done."

"Vivian, your secretary?"

"She's more my assistant."

"And Roland?"

"Somebody to carry it out, do the work."

"You trust Roland?"

"He does what he's told and keeps his mouth shut," Grossi said.

You don't know him, Karen thought, but held back from saying it. "Who else knows about it?"

"Well, Jimmy Capotorto. I told him a little, but not everything."

Karen frowned. "Who?"

"Capotorto. Frank knew him. He's been with Dorado for years; one of the associates."

"Who else?" Karen said.

"That's all." Grossi paused. "But there are some stipulations I didn't mention the other day that I didn't want to get into all at once."

"Like what?" Karen said.

"Well, if you move, the payments stop. You have to live in Frank's house."

"Frank's house," Karen said. "And if I marry again—I asked you that the other day, you said you weren't sure."

"For some reason it's not a stipulation. I guess Frank assumed we'd see nobody got close to you."

"But there's nothing in the agreement that says I can't take the entire amount."

"Not in writing, no, but in the spirit of it, you might say."

"Sign the bonds over to me and let's forget the whole thing," Karen said.

Grossi said nothing, looking at Karen, then at his cottage cheese, touching it tentatively with his spoon.

"Do you know why he did it?" Karen said. "Because he was having an affair and I found out about it. With a real estate woman." A hint of amazement in her tone. "I told him—I wasn't even serious, I was mad—I told him if he was going to fool around, I would too."

"Well, he took it at face value and here we are." Grossi seemed hesitant, working something out in his mind as they sat at his regular table in the corner of the grill room. He said, "Karen, I'll tell you, something like this, I agree, it sounds like we're back in the old country."

"But we're not," Karen said; firm, knowing how far she was willing to go. "Ed, you're aware of the people in here, how they keep looking at us?"

"You get used to it."

"I go to the john I get looks, I hear my name, Mrs. Frank DiCilia, yes, that's her, people talking about me, not going to much trouble to hide it."

"Sure, you're like a movie star."

"All right, what if I stood up right now and made a speech," Karen said. "Tapped my glass with a spoon—'May I have your attention, please? I want to tell you something you're not going to believe, but it's the honest-to-God truth, every word.'"

"Karen, come on."

"Come on where? Goddamn it, I'm not going to play your game. I'm not in the fucking Mafia or whatever you don't call it. What do you expect me to do?"

"Keep it down a little, all right? I understand how you feel."

"Like hell you do."

"Yes, I do." Grossi nodding patiently. "Listen to me a minute. I acknowledge his wish, I'm thinking, Jesus Christ, nobody ever wanted something like this before. I try to remember. Maybe a long time ago, I don't know."

"But it doesn't matter, because you do whatever he says." Karen holding on, refusing to let go. "He tells you to kill somebody—what's the difference?"

"Karen"—the tired voice—"what is that? You think it's a big thing? Maybe sometimes it is, but there's a reason for everything. The man has a reason, I don't have to ask him why."

She leaned close to the table. "I told you why. Because he has this thing in his head about paying back."

"Listen to me and let me finish," Grossi said. "Even when I don't want anything to do with it, I have to satisfy my conscience I've done something, I've acknowledged, I've gone through the motions. You understand? Then I say to myself, okay, that's all you can do. You can't watch her the rest of your life. I say to myself, did he mean that long? Forever? I answer no, of course not. I get a heart attack, cancer, I'm gone. Who continues the agreement? Jimmy Capotorto? Well, if I tell him to, but what does he care? He's got enough to think about. So how can it be forever? I say, Frank wanted to teach her a lesson. All right, there's the lesson. Did she learn it? I don't know. Like a teacher—did the student learn it? What can the teacher do? So, I say, it's up to her, she knows what's going on. She knows his wish, stay away from men even after his death. Does she want to honor his wish? I say to myself, not to you, not to anybody else, only to myself. Maybe it should be up to her now. Something between her and her husband."

There was a silence.

"You have more to do than keep watch on me," Karen said.

Grossi nodded.

"Assign the bonds over and let's stop all this."

"I have to think about it a little more."

"But you will keep Roland away from me."

"Don't worry about Roland."

She sat quietly, aware of sounds, voices around her. She waited, wanted to be sure. Ed Grossi touched the cottage cheese again with his spoon, then put the spoon down and picked up his napkin.

"I won't have to go to court then," Karen said.

"No, you won't have to go to court, if you give me time, let me be sure in my mind it's all right."

"Thank you," Karen said.

Maguire's body, arms raised, a piece of fish in each hand, formed a Y. He stood on the footrung of an aluminum pole that dug into his groin, the pole extending from a platform on a slight angle, so that Maguire's fish-offerings were held some fifteen feet above the surface of the Flying Dolphin Show tank.

He said to the mothers and fathers and children lining the cement rail, "Okay . . . now this double hand-feeding can be a little tricky, considering the height"—looking up—"*and* the wind conditions today. The dolphins could collide in midair, with a combined weight of"—serious, almost grim—"nine hundred pounds. And you know who's gonna be under them if they do. Yours truly, standing up here trying to look cool. Okay . . . here they come. Bonnie on my right, Pebbles on my left—"

Or was it the other way around?

The pair of dolphins rose glistening wet-gray in the sunlight, took the fish from his hands and peeled off, arching back into the water.

"And they got it! How about that, fifteen feet in the air. Wasn't that great? Let's hear it for Bonnie *and* . . . Peb-bles."

Applause, as Maguire stepped down off the pole to the platform. He got three hunks of cod from his fishbucket, quickly threw two of them out to Bonnie and Pebbles, and waited for Mopey Dick.

Come on—

Mopey's head rose from the water, below the platform. A wet raspberries sound came from Mopey's blowhole.

"What? You didn't like the double jump, Mopey?"

Rattles and clicks and whines from the blowhole. The kids watching, looking over the rail, loved it.

"You say you can jump higher?"

More rattles and clicks.

"Well, let's just see about that." Maguire sidearmed Mopey the piece of fish he was holding, stooped to the bucket and selected a long tailpiece. "You think you're so good, let's see you come up *six*teen feet and take the fish out of my mouth. Okay, Mopey? Everybody want to see him try it?"

Of course. The kids yelling, "Yeaaaaaaa—" as Maguire, with a piece of dead fish hanging from his mouth, adjusted the pole, raising it a foot, thinking, Jesus Christ—

Karen came out of the round white building, Neptune's Realm, down from the Flying Dolphin Show. She waited on the walk, looking around, as the moms and dads with their cameras and kids moved on to the Shark Lagoon.

There he was. Across the lawn, walking with a girl brushing her hair. Both wearing the white shorts and red T-shirts. He must have come out another exit. Karen watched them go through the fence enclosing the shark pool. Maguire mounted the structure that was like a diving platform, playing out a mike cord behind him. The girl remained below: cute little thing with a lot of Farrah Fawcett hair. Karen wondered how old the girl was. Not much more than twenty. She noticed Maguire was quite tan, healthy looking; different than the man she remembered sitting in the dark. She approached the crowd that rimmed part of the cement lagoon. There was an island in the middle, a palm tree and several sleepy pelicans. Sharks moved through the murky water like brown shadows.

He looked younger in his white shorts. Good legs. His voice was different, coming out of the P.A. system. It sounded like a recording.

"Nurse sharks do not have a reputation as maneaters, but like all sharks they're very unpredictable. They might not eat for three months, then go into a feeding frenzy at any time. What Lesley is doing is jiggling that ladyfish on the end of the line to simulate a dying fish, which gives out low-frequency sound waves that can be detected by a shark as far as . . . nine . . . hundred . . . yards away. There's a shark coming in from the left . . . Look at that."

Karen watched Maguire, then let her gaze move over the crowd, pausing on some of the men. Which one would you pick as an armed robber? Maguire would be about the last one.

"Well, this time for bait we're going to use . . . Lesley. Yes, Lesley is going down *into* the lagoon in an attempt to hand-feed a shark with her bare hand . . . using no glove or shark repellent of any kind or . . . feed a bare hand *to* a shark if she isn't careful."

The girl's face raised, giving Maguire a deadpan look. Karen saw it. For some reason she thought of Ed Grossi, Ed eating his cottage cheese with a spoon—an hour ago at Palm Bay.

Then coming over the S.E. 17th Street Causeway and seeing the sign, SEASCAPE. Why not? She felt like doing something. She felt thoroughly herself, almost relaxed, for the first time in a week. And probably the only woman here in a dress. Beige linen, gold chain and bracelet. She should have gone home first and changed—remembered him saying, "Practically around the corner," and telling him she had never been here.

He was saying to his audience, "We're not having a whole lot of luck getting the sharks into the feeding area. As I mentioned

they can go as long as three months without feeding. There's one
. . . no, changed his mind. Well . . . let's give Lesley a big hand for
getting down in the shark lagoon"—pause—"she may need one
someday."

"You sound a lot different," Karen said.

"I know," Maguire said. "I hear my voice on the P.A., I think
it's somebody else. You want a Coke or something?"

"Don't you have to work?"

"The main event's on next. Go over there—see the yellow and
white awning? I'll meet you there in a couple of minutes." He
seemed glad to see her, but hesitant, almost shy.

Karen got two Cokes and sat down at a picnic table away from
the cement walk and the refreshment counter behind the grandstand. She heard, over the P.A. system, "Good afternoon, ladies
and gentlemen, boys and girls. Welcome to Brad Allen's World-
Famous Seascape Porpoise and Sea-Lion Show." Pause. "And
now, heeeeeeeeere's Brad!"

Karen said, "Was that you?" as Maguire sat down across from
her.

"I'm afraid so."

"You always do it the same way?"

"Well—no, not always."

"The other night, I couldn't imagine you working here."

"No—"

"I wasn't inferring anything by that."

"No, I understand. I'm a little out of place, but nobody's
caught on yet."

"Maybe I know you better than most people," Karen said. "Do
you like doing this?"

"It's all right. It beats tending bar."

"Why don't you quit?"

"I'm thinking about it."

"Did you—" Karen paused. "Well, it's none of my business. I
wondered if you sent your friends their share."

"Yeah, their wives. I sent 'em money orders. They can use it."

On the P.A. system in the background, Brad Allen was intro-
ducing Pepper, Dixie, and Bonzai to the audience.

"I still don't know the difference between a porpoise and a dolphin," Karen said. "You never told me, did you?"

"No, I guess we got into other things." Looking away from her and then back, hesitantly.

He'd been doing that since she approached him. Natural, but just a little shy. She liked it and smiled when he said, "You didn't have to get all dressed up to come here."

"I was having lunch with a friend. Then coming over the causeway I saw the sign and thought, Does he really work there or not?"

"See? I wouldn't lie to you."

"I love your routine. Do you ever vary it?"

"Only when I forget lines. Or leave something out."

Brad Allen was telling his audience that Lolly the sea lion was now going to balance the ball and *walk* on her front flippers. "Heeeeey, look at that!"

"I don't think you're going to last here," Karen said. "I mean I wouldn't think you'd be able to take it as a steady diet."

"No—" He smiled, shaking his head. "You're right."

"What will you do then?"

"I don't know. Go down to Key West, see if it's changed any."

"Not back to Detroit?"

"I doubt it."

"We haven't discussed Detroit yet," Karen said. "Have we?"

"What's to discuss? Have you ever been to Belle Isle? Greenfield Village?"

"How about where you went to school." No—she shouldn't have said that. Then, what year, getting into ages. He was younger than she was. A few years, anyway.

"I went to De LaSalle," Maguire said. "By the City Airport."

She had meant college; he was referring to a high school. "I know where it is," Karen said. "I lived on the east side."

"Where'd you go?"

"Dominican."

"You're a Catholic?" He seemed surprised.

"Sort of. Not the kind I used to be."

"Yeah, I've fallen off myself. It's funny, isn't it?"

"What is?"

"I mean I'd never of thought of you as a Catholic. Even with your name."

"Or with yours." Karen said. "The thing that messes up yours is the Calvin."

He was looking directly at her now.

"How old are you?"

Without a pause Karen said, "Thirty-eight. How old are you?"

"Thirty-six."

"You don't look it."

"You don't either," Maguire said.

She should have told him thirty-six.

He said, "I told them I was thirty when I came to work here; everybody looked so young. I almost—just now I almost said I was thirty-two. Why would I do that?"

"Well, no one wants to get old."

"But thirty-six, thirty-eight, that's not old. I figure it's about the best age there is."

"It's all right," Karen said, thinking, Thirty-eight; what year was I born? "I don't give it much thought one way or the other. You're as old as you feel."

"Right," Maguire said. "Usually I feel about eighteen."

"I like twenty-five," Karen said. "I wouldn't mind being twenty-five again. Do it right this time."

"What would you do different?"

"Lots of things. I'd travel first, before I settled down anywhere."

"Why don't you do it now?"

"I may."

"I've traveled," Maguire said, "but mostly between here and Colorado. I've been to Mexico. Next—in fact, I was gonna get a passport." He paused. "Then something came up."

"Where were you going?"

"Spain. The South of France, around in there. Get a car and drive, like Madrid to Rome. That sounds pretty good."

"I've always wanted to go to Madrid," Karen said. "Málaga—"

"You've never been over there?"

"We used to go to the Greenbriar. Or SAE conventions."

"Frank DiCilia did?"

"The other Frank, the first one. The second one, I couldn't get him out of Florida.

"Except go to Detroit now and then," Maguire said, "if I recall you saying."

"Eastern nine-five-two, Miami to Detroit, the dinner flight. Nine-five-three back again."

"Well, what do you sit around in that big house for, if you've got the urge and you can go anywhere you want?"

"Right," Karen said. "It's dumb, isn't it?"

"You want to have dinner with me tonight?" Maguire said. "Anywhere you want. I just came into some money."

Three times Roland dropped the wrought-iron knocker against the front door. When Marta appeared, he pushed the door all the way open and walked in past her.

"Missus isn't here."

Roland walked through the sitting room to the French doors and looked out on the patio.

"Where she at?"

"Missus isn't here."

Roland came back to the front hall and crossed to look into the living room, narrowing his eyes at the size of it—the white plaster walls and beamed cathedral ceiling—as if to make the room smaller and spot her hiding someplace.

"Where is she?"

As he moved toward the stairway, Marta said, "Let me see, please, if she is upstairs."

Roland said, "You stay here, honey. You call anybody on the phone I'll know about it, won't I?" He reached down as Gretchen came running across the polished floor to him. "Hey, Gretchie, how you doin', huh? How you doin', girl? You gettin' much?"

Karen was thinking, Thirty-eight from seventy-nine . . . forty-one.

Lying on the king-size bed in her robe, on top of the spread, ankles crossed, resting before her bath.

She would have been a war baby instead of a Depression baby. Forty-one and seventeen . . . fifty-eight. Graduated from high school in '58. From Michigan in '62. It wasn't going to work. Unless she was married to Frank—thinking of the first Frank—say, eleven years. That would make Julie—married, living in L.A.—about fifteen.

So don't mention Julie. Except what if he says—

She had already told him.

The other night, listing the two Franks, yes, and a daughter—my daughter the actress. Shit. She had already mentioned Julie.

All right. She could have been married at Ann Arbor, still in school. Say, freshman year. If Julie was born in '60, she'd be nineteen now.

Better stay away from it. Change the subject if he brings up Julie.

Somebody was coming upstairs. Marta?

Avoid talking about age or tell him the truth. What difference did it make? She wasn't even sure why she was going out with him. She liked him; he was different; relaxed, low-key but very aware. She liked him—it was strange—quite a lot. Right from the beginning. But how did you make room for someone like Maguire? How did you explain him? Walking into the Palm Bay Club—

"Hey, look-it her waiting for me!"

Roland was in the room. She saw his hat, the color of his suit. She saw him coming, arms raised, *diving* at her! Karen screamed. She rolled, reaching for the edge of the bed, and Roland landed next to her with the sound of the frame cracking, ripping away from the oak headboard, collapsing, the king-size boxspring and mattress dropping abruptly within the frame, to the floor.

Roland, on his elbows, close to her, hat low over his eyes, grinned at her.

"How you doin'?"

Karen screamed, "Marta!"

She tried to roll off the edge, but he caught her and held her to the bed beneath one arm across her stomach.

"Take off my hat for me."

"Get *out* of here!" And screamed again, "Marta!"

"I told her we wouldn't need anything."

Roland took his hat by the brim and sailed it away from the bed. His arm came down again to grab her as she tried to twist away, free herself, and now he lowered his face to her, nuzzling it against her neck, working aside the collar of the robe. "I ain't gonna hurt you. This hurt?" His voice softly muffled. "Feels kinda good, don't it." His face moving lower as he pulled her toward him to lie on her back, his face nuzzling into the robe.

Karen held herself rigid, staring at the ceiling, feeling his mouth on her, his face moving side to side, opening her robe. She could hear Gretchen in the room, license and ID tags jingling on her collar.

"We don't have nothing on under there, do we? Mmmmmm, you sure smell nice." He looked up then, turning his cheek to her. "Here, smell mine. Called Manpower. Little girl in the store said, 'For the man who knows what he wants.' You like it?"

Karen turned her face away, the perfumed astringent scent almost making her gag. Thinking, Don't move. Don't fight. Breathe. His face moved lower, and she was staring at the ceiling again, feeling his mouth, feeling her heart beating beneath his mouth.

"Don't that feel goooood? Yeaaaah, feels good have somebody holding you again, don't it? Been a long, long time." His mouth moving over her, voice drowsy, soft.

Thinking, Six months. Seven months. Thinking, There's nothing you can do. Close your eyes. It could be—his mouth moving—it could be anyone. It could be someone else. But her eyes remained open.

*Any*one else, for God's sake. But it wasn't going to be this one!

Karen rolled into him, jabbed against him as hard as she could and abruptly rolled the other way, reached the edge of the bed with her knee and one hand before he caught her again and she could feel the bulk of him, his weight, against her back.

"Where you goin', sugar?"

"I'm getting up."

"What for? You got to make wee-wee?"

"I'm going to call Ed Grossi."

"Hey, shit, you don't want to bother Ed. This here's between you and me. You feel it?" He pushed against her. "That's what's between us, if you wondered I had something in my pocket. You want me to tell you what it is?"

Karen didn't answer.

"It's my Louisville Slugger."

"You know I'm going to tell Ed," Karen said, seeing Gretchen now, white whiskers and sad eyes looking up at her, only a few feet away. "You must be out of your mind."

"With love," Roland said. "Listen, come on. I wouldn't hurt you for the world."

"I saw Ed today."

"You had a nice lunch, did you?"

Karen hesitated. How would he know that? She almost asked

him; but it had nothing to do with right now, with Roland pressing against her.

She said, "I think you'd better talk to Ed as soon as you can. You're going to be in a lot of trouble."

"I don't mind trouble. Shit, I like a little trouble. Keeps you thinking."

She wanted to jab her elbow into him as hard as she could, but she held on, keeping an even tone as she said, "Talk to him. He's agreed, I'm not going to be watched anymore. The whole arrangement—it's over with."

Roland lay heavily against her, silent for a moment. "No shit, Ed's calling it off?"

"Talk to him, will you please?"

"You cry on his shoulder or kick him in the nuts? Either way, I believe, might work."

"Call him. The phone's right behind you."

There was a silence again.

"But did he check with Frank? What's Frank say about it?"

"Let me up, all right?"

Roland took his time. As he rolled away from her, Karen was off the bed, pulling her robe together, moving across the room.

"Hold it there, sweet potato. Don't go running off. I want to tell you something."

"And I want you to leave. Right now."

Roland got up slowly. "Messed up your bed, didn't I?"

"Don't worry about the bed. Just leave."

"I can probably fix it for you."

"Please, I'm asking you—"

Roland picked up his hat. He walked over to the wall of mirrors that enclosed Karen's closet. "See, what Ed says, like half the time don't mean diddly-shit. Ed's getting old, little guinea brain becoming shriveled up from all that red wine."

"Please. Talk to him yourself, all right?"

"See, but it ain't up to Ed. What Frank DiCilia wants, it's still like hanging out there in the air somewheres. Frank didn't say okay, never mind. Just Ed said it. But Ed, his thinking's all fucked up, ain't it? So that means I have to take over." Looking at himself in the floor-to-ceiling mirror, setting his Ox Bow straw just right, little lower in front. "And see nobody gets close to you." Looking at Karen in the mirror now, Karen by the foot of the bed. "You follow me? Nothing's changed. You start seeing somebody, the fella's likely to get one of his bones broke, and he won't even know what for."

Karen said, "You know I'm going to call Ed."

Roland shrugged. "And he'll shake his little guinea finger at me. But you know I'll still be comin' around, won't I? And long as I do, I'm your big chance."

Roland winked at her in the mirror.

# 10

Maguire looked up the number, then had to go over to the TV set to turn down the volume. "Okay? Just for a minute." Aunt Leona sat watching Barbara Walters talking to Anwar Sadat; she didn't say anything.

It was ten to seven.

"Hi. It looks like I'm gonna be a little late. This girl lives next door said I could use her car; but she went somewhere. She isn't back yet."

"That's all right," Karen said. "Listen, why don't we make it some other time then?"

"The car's not that important," Maguire said. "I wanted to pick you up, but if I can't—we can meet somewhere, can't we?"

There was a pause.

"I guess we could."

"What's the matter?"

"Nothing. I was trying to think of a place."

"You sound different," Maguire said.

"Where do you want to meet?"

What was it? She sounded tired.

"If I don't call you back by . . . seven-thirty, how about if we meet at the Yankee Clipper? Is that all right?"

"Fine."

"You don't sound very enthusiastic about it."

"Really, that's fine. I'll see you there."

"About eight, if I don't call—"

She had hung up.

Jesus Diaz wore a clean yellow sport shirt and his white poplin jacket to go to 1 Isla Bahía. At twenty after seven he rang the bell at the side door. Marta let her brother in without a word, left him to wait in the kitchen several minutes, returned and handed him the day's cassette tape.

"What's the matter?" Jesus said.

"Your friend Roland, what else."

"He's not my friend."

"The pimp, he came today and attempted to rape her."

"How do you know?"

"I heard it, how do I know. He broke the bed. Two hundred years old, he broke it jumping on her."

"Maybe she wanted him to," Jesus said.

"Go," Marta said. "Get out of here."

Roland was on the balcony of his eight-hundred-dollar-a-month Miami Shores apartment that had a view down the street to the ocean, drinking beer with his boots off, feet in blue silk socks propped on the railing. He let Jesus Diaz in, took Ralph Stanley and the Clinch Mountain Boys off the hi-fi and plugged in his tape player-recorder.

"Lemme have it."

They listened to a woman's voice say, "Dorado Management . . . No, I'm sorry, Mr. Grossi has left for the day."

Jesus saw Roland wink at him; he didn't know why.

Another woman's voice said, "Hello?" . . . "Clara, is Ed there? It's Karen."

No, Ed had gone to some kind of business meeting. Roland

thought they might talk awhile, but Karen asked her to have Ed call and that was it.

Then the next voice, a man's, said, "Hi. It looks like I'm gonna be a little late."

Roland listened and played it again. He said, "Son of a *bitch.*" Looked at his watch and then at Jesus Diaz. "Yankee Clipper. Go see who he is."

"It's only the first time. Maybe it's nothing." Jesus said.

"How you know it's the first time?"

"I don't know his name. Like the other ones on the phone."

"Follow him then. See where he lives, look it up in the city directory."

"Maybe he rents a place."

"Jesus Christ," Roland said, "then find out where he works. You understand what I mean? Follow the dink till you find out about him. Let me know tomorrow, and I'll tell you what to do."

Jesus Diaz wanted to ask something about Mrs. DiCilia, but he didn't know how to say it. So he left to go to the Yankee Clipper.

They sat next to each other at a banquette table facing the bar and the portholes back of it that presented an illuminated, underwater view of the hotel swimming pool.

Karen said, "I just realized why you come here."

"I've never been here before."

"The windows, like in the dolphin tank."

"You're changing the subject again."

"No—I just noticed it."

"I'm not dumb—" Maguire stopped, reconsidering. "I mean I'm not that dumb. This afternoon you're very relaxed, you talk, you're interested. I call you—since then you're like a different person. More like at your house the other night. No, different. You're quieter. But tense like you were then, something on your mind."

"Okay, I have something on my mind," Karen said. Sitting next to him, she could look at the bar, the portholes, the people in the room, without obviously avoiding his eyes. Or she could look down at her menu open against the table, resting on her lap. "That happens, doesn't it? A minor problem comes up, something you have to work out."

"I don't think it's minor," Maguire said.

"There's a man at the bar, the one in the white jacket. I think I know him," Karen said, "but I can't remember where."

Maguire raised his hand to the waitress, impatient, trying to appear calm, glancing at the guy sitting sideways to the bar—*him?*—then looking up as the waitress came over. "Two more please, same way."

"That was two Beefeater on the rocks?"

The waitress checked their glasses, leaving Karen's.

"Beefeater and a white rum martini."

The waitress turned away and he said to Karen, "Look, I don't care about the guy at the bar—"

"I know who he is," Karen said. "Marta's brother."

"Okay," Maguire said. "I don't care about Marta's brother. I don't want to look at the menu yet, I just want to know what's the matter. Even if it's none of my business. The other night you hint around like you want to tell me something. You show me a *gun*, you want to know how to use it. I'll admit something to you. I purposely didn't ask you the other night, because how do I know what I'm walking into? I'll tell you something else. I've been arrested nine times and not one conviction. I mean not even a suspended. All kinds of sheets on me, but no convictions. The last time, I promised—I even prayed, which I hadn't done in, what, twenty years. Get me out of this one and I'll never . . . get in trouble again. I'll dedicate myself to clean living and not even *talk* to anybody who's been in that other life. So the other night—you don't mind my saying, with your husband's associations and all, here's Frank DiCilia's wife wants to know how to use a gun. She must have all the protection she needs, her husband's friends still around—what does she want a gun for? See, that's where I was the other night. But now I'm asking you what the problem is. I don't know why, maybe this afternoon did something. You came to see me, you were very warm and open. That's another thing. I feel something with you. I feel close, and I want to help you if I can."

"You were different this afternoon," Karen said. "You seemed almost shy."

"I don't know, maybe I was a little self-conscious in my camp outfit, you seeing me there. But now I've got my outfit on I feel good in. See, I'm *me* in this outfit. Tan and blue, it doesn't matter that it's cheap or what anybody thinks of it, I feel good in it, I feel like the original *me* before I ever screwed up or wasted time. Does that make sense? I don't know—"

"I should've worn mine." Karen was looking at him now, smiling. "You were funny this afternoon, with your carnival voice."

"And now I'm frustrated," Maguire said. "I want to know what's going on."

The martini made her feel warm, protected. Still looking at him she said, "You have blue eyes," a little surprised.

"See?" Maguire said. "We're both from the east side of Detroit, we're both sort of Catholic and have blue eyes. What else do you need?"

"There's a man," Karen said, and paused. "I think he's going to ask me for money. Quite a lot of money. And if I don't give it to him, I think he's going to kill me." Still looking at him. "You tell me what else I need."

"Me," Maguire said.

Jesus Diaz ordered another Tom Collins, his fifth one, the bartender giving him the nothing-look again, not saying "Here you are," or "Thank you, sir," or anything, not saying a word. The bartender looked like a guy named Tommy Laglesia he had fought at the Convention Center ten years ago and lost in the fifth on a TKO. If the bartender did thank him or say something like that, the bartender had better be careful of his tone. Jesus would take the man by the hair, pull his face down hard against the bar and say, "You welcome."

Shit. He was tired of looking at the empty green water in the windows, waiting for a swimmer to appear, a girl. Tired of looking around, pretending to look at nothing. He didn't like to drink this much. But what was he supposed to do, sitting at a bar? What else would he be here for? While they sat over there drinking. Nine-thirty, they hadn't eaten dinner yet, Jesus Diaz thinking, I'm going to be drunk. We are all going to be drunk. The two drinking and talking close together, looking at each other, talking very seriously, the woman talking most of the time, the man in tan and blue smoking cigarettes, talking a little, touching the woman's hand, leaving his hand on hers. Like lovers. Man, he was fast if they were lovers. Jesus Diaz had never seen him before.

Maybe he was an old lover from before, a lover from when she was married to DiCilia, yes, someone younger than the old man. Young lover but old friend. That's what he must be.

Ten-fifteen, still not eating. Not touching their drinks either. Now only a small amount remaining in the sixth Tom Collins, the fucking bartender who looked like Tommy Laglesia pretending not to be looking at him. Come over and say something, Jesus was thinking; tired, ready to go to sleep on the bar.

Almost ten-thirty. They were leaving. They must have already paid the girl without him seeing it. They were getting up, leaving!

The fucking bartender was down at the other end. Of course, talking to someone who wouldn't stop talking. Jesus Diaz stood up on the rung of the barstool.

"Hey!"

The bartender came to him and this time he said, "Like another?"

"Shit no," Jesus Diaz said. "I want to get out of this fucking place."

"We've got to eat something," Karen said. "Three martinis— you know what that does to me?"

"Four," Maguire said. "It makes you feel good."

They stood on the patio making up their minds, sit down or go back in. There was a breeze off the channel, the feeling of the ocean close by.

"No worries," Karen said. "No, you still have them, but they don't seem as real. Maybe that's the answer. Stay in the bag and forget about it. Whenever he comes over, Marta can tell him Missus has passed out. So—do you feel like a drink?"

"Not right now."

"Something to eat then? Why didn't we eat?"

"Lost interest, I guess. I'm still not hungry."

Maguire was looking toward the house, at the dark archway and the French doors. A lamp was on in the sitting room. He could see the back of the Louis XVI bergère. The windows of the living room were dark; the upstairs windows dark, except for one. He could feel her next to him. She was wearing a dark buttoned-up sweater now, over the dress he thought of as a long shirt, open at the neck, letting him see the beginning soft-curve of her breast when they were sitting at the table. He took her arm, and they began to walk out on the lawn toward the seawall.

"That's one way," he said. "Get stoned. But the other way, going to the cops—I'm not prejudiced, I just don't see it'll do any good. Unless he's awful dumb."

"He acts dumb," Karen said, "but I'm not sure. He's so confident."

"I doubt the cops'd put him under surveillance. They'll tell you they'll serve him with a peace bond and that should do it. Like a warning, stay away from her. But it doesn't mean anything because how're they gonna enforce it? He comes here. You call the cops. They come and he's gone. They pick him up, he says, 'Who, me? I never threatened the lady.' They shake their finger at him, 'Stay away from her.' That's about all they can do. But the way it is, he hasn't asked for anything yet."

"No."

"So it's not extortion. How do you know he wants money?"

"What else is there?"

"I don't know," Maguire said, "but I think he's interested in you more than the money. Or you *and* the money."

"You're kidding."

"Why not? What does he do? He worked for your husband?"

"He works for Ed Grossi, but I doubt if he will much longer."

"Why not?"

"*Why?* After what he did?"

"He jumped on your bed," Maguire said. "You can say he had rape in his eyes, but in the light of what he does for Ed Grossi— we don't know but it might be very heavy work, a key job—then all he did was jump on your bed. Ed Grossi says, 'Don't worry, I'll talk to him.' And he says to Roland, 'Quit jumping on the lady's bed, asshole,' and that's it."

"Ed's a friend of mine," Karen said.

"That's nice," Maguire said, "but in his business you're a friend when he's got time or if it isn't too much trouble; unless you're in the business with him and you've taken the oath or whatever they do—even then, I don't know."

Karen thought about it, walking slowly in the darkness, holding her arms now, inside herself.

"What if I told Ed, I insist I be there when he speaks to Roland?"

"Fine," Maguire said. "Then they put on this show. Take *that*, and *that*. Ed chews him out and Roland stands there cracking his knuckles. Even if Ed's serious, he wants the guy to stay away from you, how important is the guy to Ed? Or how much control does he have over him? That's the question."

They stopped near the seawall, looking out at the lights of the homes across the channel.

"Are you cold?"

"Hold me," Karen said. "Will you?"

He put his arms around her, and she pressed in against him. She felt small. He thought she would fit the way Lesley did and feel much the same as Lesley, but she was smaller, more delicate; she felt good against him. He wanted to hold her very close without hurting her. He became aware of something else—though maybe it was only in his mind—that this was a woman and Lesley was a girl. Was there a difference? He raised her face with his hand and kissed her. She put her head against his cheek, then raised her face, their eyes holding for a moment, almost smiling, and they began to kiss again, their mouths fitting together and then moving, taking parts of each other's mouths, no Lesley comparison now, Lesley gone, the woman taking over alone, the woman eager, he could feel it, but holding back a little, patient. There was a difference.

He said, "Why don't you show me the bed."

She said, "All right—"

"Do you know what I thought about? The maid catching us. Why? It's my house, I can do anything I want."

"Afraid she'll go down to Southwest Eighth Street, tell everybody."

They lay close, legs touching, the sheet pulled up now.

"But only for a minute," Karen said.

"What?"

"That I worried about the maid. By the time we got to the stairs I couldn't wait."

"I couldn't wait to see you," Maguire said. His hand moved over her thigh to her patch of hair and rested there gently. "To look at your face and look at you here"—his hand moving, stroking her—"and see both of you. I tried to imagine, before, what it would look like."

"Really? You do that?"

"No, not all the time. Most girls, I look at them and I'm not interested in what it looks like. I *know*, for some reason and, well, it's just there. It's okay but it's not that important. But every once in a while I look at a particular girl, a woman, and I don't know what hers looks like, because it's a very special one, it's *hers*, it's part of her and—I can't explain it. But that particular person I know I can feel very close to."

"And I'm one of those?"

"There aren't that many. Just once in a while I see a girl, a woman—"

"You're having trouble putting me in an age group," Karen said. "It's okay, girl, woman. Which do you want me to be?"

"No, see, I like the word *girl*. Giiirl, it's a good word. Woman, I think of a cleaning woman."

"And you like girls."

"Yeah, but I'm not preoccupied, if that's what you mean."

"What about the shark girl? Let's give her a hand because she may need one someday?"

"Oh. Lesley." That was one thing about girls, women, he'd never understand. How they could read your mind. "Lesley's"— what was she?—"sort of spoiled. She pouts, puts on this act if she doesn't get her way. Or, she's arrogant, very dramatic, and you have to wait around for her to come back to earth."

"Do you go out with her?"

"Well, I have. She's the one who lives next door. In fact it's her aunt's place, the Casa Loma. She got me the apartment. It's an efficiency really."

"Oh," Karen said.

"That's all. I ride to work with her."

"She's a cute girl."

"I guess so. If you like that type."

"Do you picture her pubic hair?"

Jesus Christ—

"No. She's not the type I picture. She's more what they're turning out today. Not a lot of individuality, but a lot of hair and a cute ass. If that turns you on, fine."

"Does she turn you on?"

"Lesley? I ride to work with her, ride home. We talk once in a while."

"But does she turn you on?"

"The only reason you pick her, you happened to've seen me with her."

"Are there many others?"

"No, what I mean, it's like if I picked out Roland because we were talking about him and I ask you, when he jumped in bed with you, did it turn you on?"

"He jumped *on* the bed."

"Yeah, but did it?"

"We sound like we're married," Karen said.

"This is what it's like, huh? I always wondered if I was missing something."

She turned her head on the pillow to look at him. "I think you were miscast. You should've been something else."

"Yeah, like what?"

"I haven't decided yet. But—you would've ended up in prison. You're smart enough to know that."

"That's why I got out of it."

"No, I think you're out of it because you finally realized you never should've been in. That's what I mean you were miscast. Some wild idea influenced you."

"Money," Maguire said.

"See, you pretend you're cynical, but you're not. It wasn't just money. Maybe the risk, or the excitement."

"Maybe," Maguire said. "I remember telling Andre I could do without any more thrills. Yeah, maybe you're right," his tone thoughtful, going back in his mind and beginning to wonder how he'd got into the life—always one more, just to raise traveling money—and how those years had gone by so fast. He said, "That wasn't me I was telling you about. It must've been somebody else."

Looking at him lying next to her in her bed she could say to herself, My God, who is this guy? Or she could say, Somebody I've known for a long time. She said to him, "You feel it, don't you? You said you felt close." Putting her hand on his hand.

"Like the other night was years ago," Maguire said. "Even dinner, the one we didn't have, seems a long time ago now."

"That's what I'll tell Marta, we're old friends," Karen said, and smiled. "Why do I worry about Marta? Even with Frank, I was never afraid to stand up to him."

"I guess you did," Maguire said.

"But I was alway worried—not worried, concerned, with what the maid thought of me."

"Because you think of her as a person and not just a maid," Maguire said. "Talk about miscast, the lady of the house. I don't see you that way at all. A *lady*, yeah, I suppose, the way it's used. But I don't see you just sitting around pouring tea."

"How do you see me?"

"Well, like in a sweater and jeans, doing something outside." He paused. "You want me to tell you, really?"

"Yes, I'd love to know."

"I see *us*," Maguire said. "I see us driving through Spain. I see us at a sidewalk table, place with a red awning. I see us looking at somebody, like some tourist, and nudging each other and laughing."

She turned to him as he spoke, moving closer and laying her hand on his chest.

"I see us picking up our maps and a couple bottles of red wine to take with us."

"What kind of car do we have?"

"Alfa Romeo. Convertible, with the top down."

"Where're we going?"

"Madrid to the Costa del Sol. And if we don't like it, we'll go to some other costa."

"I think we'll like it," Karen said.

She thought, briefly, But who's paying for it?

Then put it out of her mind. She felt safe. For the time being, she could close her eyes without imagining something happening to her. She could picture herself doing whatever she wanted. She tried to imagine the sidewalk cafe and the Alfa Romeo. But she saw herself coming out of a shop on Worth Avenue, Palm Beach, putting on her sunglasses, and someone saying, "That's Karen DiCilia."

# 11

"Then they go back to her house," Jesus Diaz said to Roland. "Then, you know, after a while, he goes home."

Roland was down on the floor in his undershorts doing push-ups, red-faced, tight-jawed, counting, "Ninety-five . . . ninety-six . . . Where's he live?" straining to say it.

Like the time on the toilet, Jesus Diaz thought. The time Roland, sitting on the toilet, grunting, making noises, had made him stand in the doorway of the bathroom while Roland talked to him.

"He lives up by Northeast Twenty-ninth Street, in Fort Lauderdale."

"One hunnert," Roland said, getting up, breathing heavily with his hands on his hips. Jesus Diaz tried to read what was printed in red on the front of Roland's white bikini undershorts, without staring at his crotch.

490

"You tell me she met him at the place. So then they both drive to her house?"

"No, he went in the car with her, the Mercedes."

"Then how'd he get home?"

What was printed on Roland's shorts, was *Home of the Whopper*. Jesus Diaz said, "He drove her car home."

"She let him use her car?"

"I guess so. He drove it to where he work, that place, Seascape."

Roland squinted. "Seascape? The fuck is Seascape?"

"That kind of porpoise place. They have the shows there."

"Jesus Christ," Roland said. "Seascape, yeah. I believe Dorado owns it, or did. What's he do there?"

"The tricks, you know, with the porpoise. Make them jump up, take a piece of fish out of his mouth. All like that."

"Well, you go on back and see him," Roland said. "Take somebody with you to hold his arms."

"Today you mean?"

"I mean right now, partner. Get on it."

"Man, I'd like to get some sleep first."

"What you need sleep for? Didn't you go to bed?"

"I'm just tired," Jesus Diaz said, and left to go do his job, tired or not.

Do it right or Roland would chew his ass out, tell him to quit chasing that Cuban *cocha*. Stay in shape like him.

Sure, but if he'd said he was awake all night, except for dozing off—sitting in the mangrove bushes across the street so the security car wouldn't see him—then Roland would say, All *night*? You mean to say the dink spent the *night*? Then Roland might go over there and do something to the woman again.

Man, he was tired though.

Go home, get the Browning to put under his jacket, just in case. Pick up Lionel Oliva at the Tall Pines Trailer Park; pull him out of bed. Hey, Lionel, you want to beat up somebody for a hundred dollars? How big? Not big. Shit, yes, he'd jump in the car. It shouldn't be hard. The porpoise man didn't look very strong. Also he'd be tired out after his night in the two-hundred-year-old bed.

Marta had said, handing the early-morning cup of coffee to him out the side door, "If it wasn't broken before, it is now." Saying it, not as a truth, but because she was happy for the woman.

Jesus Diaz was happy for her also. It was too bad he had to do this to her old friend.

Maguire said to the crowd on the top deck of the Flying Dolphin tank, "There's the trick it took us eighteen months to teach him. He lays on his side, raises one flipper and . . . that's it. You can see why we call him *Mopey* . . . Dick. Let's give Mopey a hand. That must've worn him out."

He had already noticed the Cuban-looking guy in the crowd, lining the cement rail. Yellow shirt, white jacket. The same one Karen had pointed to who'd been sitting at the bar last night. Marta's brother.

Maguire, on the aluminum pole, gave them the double hand-feeding with Bonnie and Pebbles, wondering if Marta's brother was here to give him a message.

And the other Cuban-looking guy with him, why was he along, what, to watch?

Maguire asked the crowd, the little kids, if they wanted to see a mouth-to-mouth feeding. They said, "Yeeeeeeeeees!"

No, he had seen too many like the other Cuban-looking guy. They were bouncers in go-go joints. They hung around sports arenas. Marta's brother looked like he'd been a fighter; the neck, the trace of scar tissue around the eyes. The other Cuban-looking guy was bigger; he could be a lightheavy sparring partner for a good middleweight.

"And that's our Flying Dolphin Show for this afternoon," Maguire said, and told everyone next, to kindly proceed to the Shark Lagoon area. Hooker was doing the color over there today. Maguire's next job, in about twenty minutes, was to announce Brad Allen and then he'd be through. He picked up the bucket of fish sections, looked over at the two guys as he stepped off the platform to the cement deck.

They were waiting. The only ones still up here.

Maguire walked toward the stairway. He heard one of them say, "Just a minute."

And thought, Your ass.

He put the bucket down without breaking stride, moving with purpose but not running yet or looking around, down the stairway to the dim second level, the underwater windows of the tank showing dull-green.

Now run. And if they ran after him, it was absolutely for certain not to deliver a message he wanted to hear. He began running as he heard them on the stairway, his bare feet patting on the cement, their running steps coming after him now, hitting hard, echoing. He ran past the tank windows, seeing gray shapes in the water, Bonnie and Pebbles grazing the glass, pacing him as he ran all the way around the circular second level to the stairway again and up to the top deck.

The bucket of fish sections was where he'd left it. Maguire picked it up and stepped back from the open doorway, hearing their steps coming up toward him now, stiffened his arm holding the bucket, let the first one come through to the outside, Marta's brother, and swung the bucket into the face of the other Cuban-looking guy, turning him reeling, took the bucket in both hands, fish pieces falling out, jammed it down over the guy's head and, still holding onto it, ran the bucket, the guy coming with it to the waist-high rail, hitting the cement as Maguire grabbed the guy's legs and threw him into the tank.

Marta's brother stood watching.

Maguire moved to the wire gate in the rail that opened to a small platform on the other side, close to the water, where Hooker would go into the tank with his mask and air hose. Maguire waited, looking from the gate to Marta's brother, who was fifteen to twenty feet away.

"What do you want?"

Jesus Diaz said, "This is a warning." He didn't know what else to say. "Keep away from the woman."

Maguire said, "What?" Not sure he heard him right. He looked past the gate to see the other Cuban pulling himself up on the platform. Wet-gray bottlenose heads came out of the water to watch. Maguire waited until the Cuban's hand reached the top of the wire gate, his face appearing, coming up slowly, and slammed a right hook into the face, sending the man back into the tank as the dolphin heads disappeared.

"I'm talking about Missus DiCilia," Jesus said. "Keep away from her or we gonna throw you in that tank for good."

Maguire scowled. His hand hurt something awful. He said to Jesus, "You work for Roland or what?"

Jesus said, "Be smart, uh? Stay away from her."

Or what? Maguire thought. He took two steps toward Jesus, saw the man's hands go behind his back and reappear with a gun, a heavy automatic, Colt or a Browning. The other guy was coming up out of the water again.

Maguire said, "Well, I got to go."

Jesus said, "Don't work too hard."

Maguire went down the stairway holding his sore hand, shaking his head.

# 12

"The first thing you better do," Maguire said, "is fire your maid, and anybody else around here. How about the brother?"

"No, he doesn't work for me."

Karen was wearing big round sunglasses and a brown and white striped robe, open. Maguire couldn't see her face, her expression, as she looked at him and then out across the lawn; but he could see her brown legs and firm little belly and the strip of tan material almost covering her breasts. Maguire wore jeans and a shirt over his red Seascape T-shirt. He had come here from work and now, on the patio, he was trying to make Gretchen go away so he could concentrate on Karen.

She said, "I can't believe it. Marta's been here as long as I have. I think she was seventeen when we hired her."

"Give her a reference then," Maguire said. He'd push Gretchen away and she'd come back to him, thinking he was playing.

"I can't just fire her."

"Can you get rid of her for a while? Send her on an errand."

"She did the grocery shopping yesterday—"

"Tell her you need some Spaghetti-O's, something. We've got to get her out of here."

"For how long?"

"An hour anyway."

Karen got up and went into the house.

Maguire watched her. She didn't seem worried or upset. She didn't have nervous moves to do anything with her hands. Andre Patterson would try to sign her up.

Maguire had told her about Jesus Diaz and the other one coming to see him, not telling her all of it, but making a point of the warning. That was clear enough, wasn't it? Jesus worked for Roland. If they knew things about Karen that Marta could have observed, then Marta was telling them. And if they knew things Marta couldn't have known, then the house was bugged or there was a tap on the phone. Probably a tap. Karen had said, "Really?" quietly interested. Was she different again? She seemed different every time he saw here.

There was a newspaper on the umbrella table, part of the *Miami Herald*, the "Living Today" section. Maguire reached for it. It wasn't today's "Living Today" though. It was last Sunday's, and he didn't immediately recognize the woman in the photo. Karen DiCilia and a man, her former husband—yes, somewhat familiar to Maguire from newspaper photos years ago—Frank DiCilia. Both dressed up, both wearing dark glasses, coming out of someplace, a doorman standing behind them.

The headline said, WHAT IS KAREN DICILIA'S SECRET? A smaller line, above it, said, WIDOW OF MOBSTER WON'T TALK.

In the Miami paper, taking up the top half of the page. He didn't know how he could have missed it.

The story below, with before-and-after shots of a woman, said, TWENTY-YEAR WAR ON FAT TAPERS OFF IN VICTORY, and maybe Aunt Leona had cut it out of the paper. There were usually things cut out of the *Herald* by the time he got it Sunday evening.

"Widow of Mobster . . ." Jesus, he bet she loved that. The photo with Frank was dated four years ago. She looked the same.

"Why would an attractive forty-year-old widow, comfortably situated, chic, outgoing . . ."

*Forty* years old?

And that was four years ago.

". . . give up her independence to marry a former (?) Detroit mob boss relocated in Fort Lauderdale's fashionable Harbor Beach area?"

Maguire's eyes moved down the columns. Background stuff. Formerly Karen Hill. Married to an engineer. Daughter an actress.

"Since Frank DiCilia's death, Karen has become virtually a recluse, seldom venturing out to the fashionable clubs or attending the charitable benefits that used to be de rigueur for her.

"Turn to Page 2D Col. 1"

Maguire turned.

"Woman of Intrigue"

And a current shot of Karen in a pale bikini, hands on her hips, white sunhat and sunglasses, a grainy photo that had been blown up or shot from some distance.

Maguire looked out past the lawn to the seawall, where she might have been standing in the photo.

The hands on hips defiant rather than provocative. The soft hat brim straight across her eyes behind round sunglasses. Nice shot. The slim body somewhat slouched, but in control; yes, with a hint of defiance.

A phrase caught his eye. "The mystery lady of Isla Bahía," and he thought, It's a good thing she doesn't live on Northeast Twenty-ninth Street.

It didn't look as though the reporter, a woman, had learned much about her. There seemed to be more questions than facts. Maguire was still reading the piece when Karen came out.

She said, "Oh," for a moment off guard.

"I didn't know I was with a celebrity," Maguire said. He held the newspaper section aside, looking up at her.

"You didn't?" Karen said. She took the paper from him and folded it into a small square, hiding something thousands of people had already seen.

"That's a nice shot of you in the swimsuit." The same one he was looking at now, the robe hanging open, very thin waist, tight little tummy curving into the tan panties that crossed her loins in

497

a straight line. Maguire moved in the canvas chair, reseating himself.

"It was taken here, wasn't it?"

"From a boat. I didn't know it was a news photographer."

"They're starting to move in on you."

She looked at him, but didn't say anything. Her expression almost the same as the one in the photo.

"The woman that wrote it," Maguire said, "why didn't you tell her what's going on?"

"How could I do that?"

"Why not? Get it out in the open."

"Don't you think I'd look a little stupid? The dumb widow involved in some Sicilian oath."

"Well, you're not dumb and it *is* happening, isn't it? What I'm thinking, you expose Roland and maybe he'll go away."

"And expose Karen DiCilia," Karen said. "Would you like to read about yourself, involved in something like this, in a newspaper?"

"I don't know," Maguire said, "if I thought it would do the job."

"I have to handle Roland," Karen said, "if Ed Grossi doesn't." She folded the newspaper section again and shoved it into the pocket of her robe. "I gave Marta the evening off."

"Good," Maguire said.

"She didn't want to go." Karen was watching him now from behind her sunglasses. "I told her we wanted to be alone. It doesn't matter now what she thinks, does it?"

"It never did," Maguire said.

He located the telephone line coming in from the street, through the mangrove trees, to the house, and pointed to the piece of metal clamped to the line, an infinity transmitter. A second line ran from the terminal point at the house to a corner window and entered Marta's room between the brick and the window casing.

In the room itself the line led to a voltage-activated recorder beneath Marta's bed. Maguire explained it—part of an accumulation of knowledge picked up along the way to nowhere; though sometimes bits and pieces came in handy.

"The telephone rings, the voltage on the line automatically

turns on the cassette, and the phone conversation is recorded on a cartridge tape. Marta gives the tape to her brother or Roland and they know who you talk to, where you're going—I guess they learn all they need to know."

Karen didn't say anything. She stared at the recorder, her words in there, the sound of her voice contained within the flat cartridge, with its window and two round holes. Telling what?

"You want to give Roland a message?" Maguire flicked a switch on and off.

Still she didn't say anything.

"Get rid of Marta," Maguire said.

"Or keep her. Let them listen," Karen said. "Which is better, if Roland finds out we know about it or if he doesn't?"

"That went through my mind," Maguire said. "I let it go."

Karen looked up from the recorder. "It might be to our advantage."

"We talk," Maguire said. "I phoned—that's how they knew we were meeting the other night."

"But what do they learn, really? We could use some kind of code."

She was serious, taking off her sunglasses now, her eyes quietly alive.

"The question is, what did Roland hear before?" Maguire said. "Something he might've learned that turned him on, you might say, to go independent."

"What do you mean, turned him on?"

"Like money," Maguire said. He hesitated, then took a chance. "Maybe he heard you tell somebody you keep money in the house." She was staring at him now, and he looked down at the recorder again, fingering the different switches. "It's just a thought. Or he heard you talking to your accountant, your banker, somebody like that. It'd be a way of finding out what you're worth."

"Maybe he's not the only one who's interested," Karen said.

"No, your maid, her brother—"

"What do you think I'm worth?" Karen said.

"I don't know, three million, thirty million," Maguire said. "You get into those figures, I don't see much difference. But how does he get his hands on it unless it's sitting there. You're not gonna write him a check."

499

"He hasn't asked for anything."

"No, but he's leading up to something. We're pretty sure of that."

"You haven't asked for anything either," Karen said.

"What am I, the help? You hiring me?"

"That's not an answer," Karen said.

"Why don't I go home and get dressed," Maguire said. "We'll go out, have dinner, hold hands, look at each other. You can tell me what you want, and I'll tell you what I want. How's that sound?"

"I'll tell you right now what I want," Karen said.

Maguire picked up a pizza on the way home (Were they ever going to go out and have dinner together?), took off his shirt, put a cold beer on the table, and began eating, starving.

There were three rattling knocks on the front-door jalousie. Lesley came in still wearing her white shorts, no shoes, and a striped tanktop. She said, "I just got in, too; I was out all evening. Hey, can I have a piece?"

"Help yourself."

"What kind is it?"

"Pepperoni, onions, cheese, a few other things."

"Yuk, anchovies."

Like they were worms. Lesley being sensitive, delicate. He wondered when she'd ask about the car, the silver-gray Mercedes 450 SEL parked in front. She took dainty bites, holding an open palm beneath the wedge, bending over the table to give him a shot of her breasts hanging free in the tanktop.

"You still have Sunday's paper?"

"How should I know?"

"Aunt Leona keeps newspapers, doesn't she? Gives them to some charity drive?"

"She sells them. She's so goddamn money-hungry. Where you going?"

"I'll be right back."

Maguire went in through the manager's apartment, past Leona asleep in her Barcalounger, with a TV movie on, to the utility room off the kitchen. There were several weeks of newspapers stacked against the wall. He began looking through the first pile and there it was, last Sunday's edition of the *Herald*, finding it right away. Sometimes that happened. He pulled out the "Living Today" section, glancing at Karen and Frank DiCilia, then took the sports section, too, and slipped "Living Today" in behind the sports pages.

Lesley was sitting now, her chair turned away from the table, one foot on the seat, a tan expanse of inner thigh facing him. A lot of flesh there.

"Why're you so interested in the paper?"

"There's a story on the Tigers I missed."

"I think baseball's boring. Nothing ever happens."

Maguire was eating. He didn't care what Lesley thought. He wondered, though, how she'd get around to the car.

She said, "Brad's really pissed at you, you know it?"

"Why?"

"You were supposed to stay after and work with Bubbles."

It sounded like she was talking about school.

"I forgot," Maguire said. He'd left without looking back, not wanting to see the two Cubans again.

"Brad saw you take off in the car. He goes, 'Jesus Christ, where'd he get that, steal it?'"

That was how she did it, indirectly. Maguire worked his way through another pizza wedge, not giving her any help.

"Brad goes, 'He didn't have it yesterday. He must've got it last night.'"

Maguire drank some of the cold beer: really good with the salty anchovy taste.

" 'Somebody must've loaned it to him.' Then he goes, 'But who would he know that owns a fucking Mercedes?' "

"I bet you said that, not Brad," Maguire said.

"I might've. Somebody said it."

"It's a friend of mine's," Maguire said. "I'm using it while he's out of town."

"Well, let's go someplace in it."

"I'm not allowed to take passengers. He's afraid it'll get messed up."

"You big shit, you're just saying that."

"It's the truth."

"Who's is it?"

"Guy by the name of Andre Patterson."

"The one you were talking to on the phone?"

Talking *about* on the phone to Andre's wife, but it didn't matter. "Right. He went on a vacation." Christ, 20 to life. He should write to Andre, tell him how things were going. He wanted to read the newspaper story again and look at the picture of Karen on the seawall.

"How would he know the difference?" Lesley said. "I mean just me, not a lot of people."

"Maybe," Maguire said. "You want some more?"

"No . . . I feel like—" She gave him a sly look. "You know how I feel?"

"How?"

"Horny. Isn't that funny? I don't know why." She looked over at the bed. "You want to lie down, see what happens?"

"Your feet are dirty," Maguire said.

"My *feet?*"

"Actually I'm awful tired. You mind?"

"Jesus Christ," Lesley said, getting up. "You have a headache, too?"

"No, but I don't feel too good. I think maybe the pizza." He said, "Why don't you catch me some other time, okay?"

"Why don't you catch this," Lesley said, giving him the finger, and slammed the jalousie door, rattling the frosted-glass louvers.

There were times, yes, when he didn't mind dirty feet. Or, there had been times. But going from one to the other, from the woman to the girl, he couldn't imagine ever having to try and compare them. Hearing Lesley's voice, "Brad's really pissed at you." Serious. A crisis because he'd forgotten to stay after closing to work with the young dolphin. "Brad goes, 'What'd he do, steal it?'" Brad and Lesley, the whole setup, like a summer camp. Then hearing Karen's voice:

"What do you think I'm worth?"

Karen's voice:

"I'll tell you right now what I want."

Not putting it on, trying to act sultry, but straight. Looking at him without the sunglasses. "I'll tell you right now what I want."

She wanted it, too. She had said the first time, "I could hardly wait." This time was like the first time multiplied, more of it, more free and easy with each other, fooling with each other in that big broken-down bed, then getting into it, picking it up, beginning to race, feeling the rush. It was as different as day and night, the girl and the woman. The girl okay, very good in fact, but predictable: the same person all the way, making little put-on sounds—"Oh, oh, oh, don't stop now, God, don't ever stop"—she must've read somewhere and decided that was how you made the guy feel good. The woman, the forty-four-year-old woman didn't fake anything. She watched him with a soft, slightly smiling look that was natural. She moved her hands all over him, everywhere, which the girl never did—as though the girl was supposed to get it and not give unless she gave as a special favor; the girl very open and, quote, together, saying, "You want to fuck?" if she felt like it; except that it had no bearing on how she was in bed—the girl not aware of the two of them the way the forty-four-year-old woman was. The woman in the photograph. The lady in the million dollar home. The lady. That was the key maybe. The lady, with a poise and quiet tone, easing out of the role as they moved over and around each other on the bed, not being tricky about it but natural, touching, entering the special place of the slim, good-looking lady, moving in and owning the place for a while, right there tight in the place, and the lady trying to keep him, hold on to him there. Yes, there. Now that was different. That was being as close to someone as you could get without completely disappearing into the person, gone. Man. To look forward to that for another—how many years? Wondering if it was a consideration, a possibility. Maybe not. But at least feeling close enough to be able to say, "They got your age wrong in the paper." Smiling.

"They got a number of things wrong," Karen said, "including the way it was written."

"All the questions. It was like a quiz." Kissing her shoulder, her neck, feeling it moist. "I don't care how old you are . . . we are. What difference does it make?"

"None that I can think of," Karen said.

Her tone was all right, but what did it mean? *None*, because the way they felt, it didn't matter? Or *none*, because nothing was going to come of this anyway?

"I'm almost forty," Maguire said. "It's just another number. Forty, that's all."

"Then why are you talking about it?" Karen said.

They went downstairs and sat in the living room, with drinks Karen made at the built-in marble bar. Maguire checked the room for hidden mikes planted behind figurines and paintings or in the white sofa and easy chairs. They talked about Roland, what he might ask for, wondering if they could get him to ask for it over the phone, make an extortion demand and hook him with his own device. Which wasn't likely. Sometime, Karen said, she'd like him to look at the antiques and art objects and tell her what they were worth. Maguire was ready to do it now, but they went outside instead, all the way out to the seawall. They stood looking at tinted points of light in the homes across the channel, at cold reflections in the water. He thought of the photo again that had been taken here, Karen standing with hands on hips, legs somewhat apart, sunhat and sunglasses—the slim, good-looking woman who was close to him, in a skirt now, barefoot.

He liked skirts. He liked the idea of lifting up a skirt, something from his boyhood, something you did with girls. She moved against him when he began to kiss her. She let herself be lowered to the grass where he began to bring her skirt up to her hips and put his hand under it.

Gretchen came out and hopped around them, sniffing their legs. Maguire told the dog to get the hell out of there.

Sitting on the patio, another drink; were they going to go out to eat or not? It was strange the way she brought up the question of the dog, surprising him, asking him why he wasn't nice to Gretchen.

He said, "What do you mean I'm not nice to her? What do you say to a dog that's not nice?"

She said, "You ignore her. Until tonight you only said one word to her, the first time you came here, you told her to relax."

"Well, that was nice," Maguire said. "What do I want to talk to a dog for? I talk to dolphins all day, and I don't ordinarily, you're right, talk to animals at all. I don't have that much to say to them."

She said, "You know who's nice to Gretchen?"

He said, "I'll talk to the dog when I have time. I'll be very happy to."

"Roland," Karen said. "He can't keep his hands off her."

Maguire said, "Well, I'd keep an eye on him if I were you."

He said that, and they were friends again. The strange part was feeling a little tension between them over the dog. Or else he imagined it.

No, the dog wasn't a problem. What mattered was, they always got back to Roland.

He said to her, "I guess I'm gonna have to meet him, aren't I?" A few moments later he said, "I don't see you having conversations with the dog."

# 13

The reason Roland served the six months at Lake Butler:

Dade County Criminal Division had charged Jimmy Capotorto with three counts second-degree and one count first-degree murder: the victims being the three employees who died in the Coral Gables Discount Mart fire and the star witness who died of gunshot wounds in the parking lot of the VA Hospital. Dade County *knew*, circumstantially, Coral Gables Discount had borrowed shylock money from Jimmy Cap. They had the written testimony of the star witness, the former Coral Gables Discount owner, that described how Jimmy Cap had taken over management of the company and had decided to liquidate. They lost their star witness in the VA Hospital parking lot, on Eighteenth Street Road. But they now had a second star witness, who described Jimmy Cap and revealed the license number of his two-tone red and white Sedan De Ville pulling out of the lot moments following the sound of several gunshots; this within two blocks of the Dade County Public Safety Department offices. Jimmy Cap's lawyer pointed out that the first star witness was a drug addict and had gone to the VA Hospital parking lot to purchase stolen morphine to relieve his tensions. The second star witness, however, was a one-legged ex-Marine who had come out of the hospital after visiting one of his buddies. He said on the witness stand, pointing to Jimmy Capotorto, "Yes, sir, that's him."

Jimmy Cap's lawyer put Roland Crowe on the stand, and Roland said Jimmy Cap had spent the evening with him visiting a Cuban lady out on Beaver Road off the Tamiami Trail. The Cuban lady was waiting to go on next if they needed her.

The state's prosecutor hammered away at Roland's credibility, bringing out the fact Roland himself had served eight years in Raford for second degree murder—objected to and sustained, but there it was—then asked Roland if he had spoken to their witness, the ex-Marine, out in the hall. Roland said, "No, sir." The prosecutor said hadn't he, Roland, said to the ex-Marine, "You only got one leg now. How'd you like to keep talking and go for none?" Roland said if the Marine had said that, then the Marine was a fucking liar. The judge warned Roland his language would not be tolerated. The prosecutor kept at Roland, trying to hook him. But Roland remained cool. He said to the state's prosecutor, "What you say, sir, is your opinion. The only thing is, opinions're like assholes, everybody's got one."

Roland was sentenced to a year and a day for contempt, reduced to six months following an appeal. But he had stared long enough at that one-legged Marine, who finally said maybe he'd been mistaken about his testimony.

Jimmy Cap talked about it all the time, describing Roland on the witness stand, even describing Roland to Roland himself, the way the gator had fucked their minds around with his you-all bullshit and had actually distracted them from the reason they were in court. Jimmy Cap, at one point, had said to Roland, "Hey, I owe you six months."

When Roland came to see Jimmy Cap, at his office in the Dorado Management suite, Jimmy Cap said, "Buddy"—meaning it—"what can I do for you?"

"I was supposed to see Ed," Roland said, "but I guess he's out of town."

"So talk to Vivian."

"Vivian's out too."

"Is it important?"

"He'll chew my ass cuz I can't find him."

"When they're both away," Jimmy Cap said, "they're shacked up at Vivian's for a couple of days. Ed tells Clara he's gone to Pittsburgh or some fucking place, they're up in Keystone."

"Yeah?" Roland grinned, tilted up his Ox Bow and sat down. "That reminds me. The company manages a condo up in Boca, don't it?"

"Oceana," Jimmy Cap said.

"And Frank DiCilia had a place there he used, if I ain't mistaken?"

"That's right."

"But I don't imagine anybody's using it much no more. I know the lady ain't cuz I'm the one watching her. You know about that?"

"Jesus," Jimmy Cap said, "that's a weird setup. Ed told me something about it, I said, Jesus Christ, we back in the fucking Sicilian Mountains or Miami, Florida? We got better things to do. She's not a bad-looking broad either, you know it?"

"Look but don't touch," Roland said. "I got one firmer and younger up in Boca just dying for it. But this problem, see, she's a waitress at a place up there? And she's married. She can get out of the house only maybe a couple hours in the evening; but I don't have no place to take her up there. You follow me? I mean a nice place, to impress her a litle bit."

Jimmy Cap said, "So you're thinking of Frank's apartment."

"If it's sitting there going to waste," Roland said. "I remember I took a piss in there once, it had this great big bathtub you walked up some steps to get in."

"Clean the little waitress up first," Jimmy Cap said. "Sure, I'll get you a key anytime you want."

"Now'd be fine," Roland said. He waited a moment. "Oh, hey, you got Vivian's private number up there in Keystone?"

"Is it important?"

"Life or death situation," Roland said. He grinned, but he meant it.

*    *    *

Maguire said, "I'm gonna make a phone call, that's all. I'll be right there."

Brad Allen said, "You come to my office right now or you're out of a job."

The camp director. The school principal. Tell him what to do with the job.

Maguire watched him walking away. Pretty soon, he thought. He followed Brad to the office beneath the grandstand, ten by twelve, with a wooden desk, one chair, four cement walls covered with photos of Brad Allen and dolphins—Brad & Pepper, Brad & Dixie, Brad & Bonnie—Brad feeding, patting, kissing, presenting, admonishing, cajoling dozens of different one-name dolphins that, to Maguire, all looked like the same one.

Brad, seated, looking up at Maguire standing at parade rest, said, "All right, here's the new routine. You ready?"

"I'm ready," Maguire said.

"Beginning of the Flying Dolphin Show, most of the people've just come in. Right?"

"Right."

"You say, 'Anybody notice that lion out there by the main entrance?' " Brad's tone become an effortless drawl.

Jesus Christ, Maguire thought.

" 'We got Leo—that's the lion's name—to keep out undesirables, anybody that might come in and cause trouble. But the trouble is, the lion's asleep all the time. Never moves. That's why you might not've noticed him.' Then you say, 'Leo did cause a problem, though, one time, back when, for some reason, our porpoises were all getting sick and dying on us. Well, this fella came along and said, "What you got to do is feed your porpoises seagull meat, and I guarantee they'll live forever." He said he'd supply it, too. Well, we'd try anything, so we told him okay, bring some gull meat. Well, the next day he's walking in with it, stepping over Leo, when all of a sudden about a dozen cops jumped out and arrested him. And you know what for?' You wait then, make sure you've got everybody's attention. Then you say, 'He was arrested for transporting gulls over the staid lion for immortal porpoises.' " Brad Allen grinned. "Huh? What do you think?"

"Can I use your phone?" Maguire said.

*    *    *

"Karen, how are you?"

"Who is this?"

"You know who it is."

"Let me see. Is it Howard?"

"Come on—"

"Don't you know when I'm kidding?"

"Well, I though I had a sense of humor, but I think it was just ruined for good. Like pouring sugar in a gas tank."

"Where are you?"

"I'm at work. Listen, let's meet tonight."

There was a silence. Karen wondering what to say.

"At the Yankee Clipper. No, I'll try to pick you up about eight, then we'll go there. Okay?"

Tentatively, "Okay." A pause. "Are you sure?"

"Yeah, there's somebody I want to see. So wait for me to pick you up."

"I understand," Karen said.

Jesus Diaz had taken Lionel Oliva to Abbey Hospital to get thirteen stitches in his head and four inside his lower lip. They were in the Centro Vasco the next day, in the afternoon, Jesus having something to eat, Lionel Oliva drinking beer, holding it against the swollen cut in his mouth, when Roland came in. Roland said, "What's the matter with him?"

"He hit his head," Jesus said.

"I want you to pick up the tape after supper and drop it off," Roland said.

Jesus looked up at Roland and said, "I'm going to Cuba."

"What d'ya mean you're going to Cuba? Shit, nobody goes down there. It's against the law."

Jesus had, only this moment, thought of Cuba. If he wasn't going there he'd go someplace else. "You can go there now," he said. "I got to see my mother. She's dying."

"Well, shit," Roland said, "I got things going on, I got to go up to Hallandale—" Roland was frowning; he didn't like this. "When you coming back?"

"I don't know," Jesus said. "I have to wait to see if she dies."

"Well, listen, you pick up the tape and drop it off 'fore you go to Cuba. Don't forget, either." Roland turned and went toward the front of the quiet, nearly empty restaurant.

"Where did he get that suit?" Lionel Oliva said, not moving his mouth. "It makes you close your eyes."

Jesus Diaz was still watching Roland, the hat, the high round shoulders, the light behind him as he moved toward the front entrance.

"I'd like to be able to hit him," Jesus said. "I would, you know it? If I could reach him."

"When you going to Cuba?" Lionel Oliva said.

"Fuck Cuba," Jesus said. "Man, I'd like to hit him, one time. I think I'd like a Tom Collins, too."

Roland liked Arnold Rapp's balcony view a whole lot more than his own. You could look straight down on the swimming pool and some palm trees or turn your head a notch and there was the Atlantic Ocean. It didn't make sense. Here was Arnold, about to have a nervous breakdown, with the good view. Whereas Roland, who had the world by the giggy at the present time, had a piss-poor view of the ocean down a street and between some apartments.

He said to Arnold, "You don't get outside enough. Look at you."

"*Look* at me?" Arnold said. "How'm I gonna get outside, I'm on the fucking telephone all day. Now, you know what I gotta do now? Borrow money, for Christ sake, a hundred grand, guy I know in New York—if he was here I'd kiss him, shit, I'd blow him, he says he's gonna come through. That's what I have to do, get deeper in hock so I can buy time to put together some deals, I ought to go outside."

"You got this week's?" Roland said.

"What're you talking about this week's? I don't owe you till Friday."

"Couple of days, what's the difference?"

"You kidding? Almost eight grand a day, man; it makes all the fucking difference in the world."

"Ed don't think you're gonna pay it."

"He doesn't, huh."

"He thinks you're gonna get on a aeroplane one of these days," Roland said. "He thinks we ought to settle up. So he said go on see Arnie, get it done."

"Get what done? Jesus Christ, now wait a minute—"

Roland reached inside his suit coat and brought out a .45-caliber Smith & Wesson revolver with a six-and-one-half inch barrel, one of the guns he kept stored for this kind of work.

"Now come on—Jesus, put it away."

Extended, pointed at Arnold sitting on the couch, the big Smith covered Arnold's face and half his body. Roland reached down to the easy chair next to him and picked up a satin pillow. He held it in front of the muzzle, showing Arnold how he was going to do it as he moved toward him, the poor little guy pressing himself against the couch, nowhere to go, looking like he was about to cry.

"I'm gonna pay you. Man, I'm *paying* you, haven't I been paying? I got some money now you can have."

"Shut your eyes, Arnie." Roland took the pillow away so Arnie could look into the .45 muzzle that was like a tunnel coming toward his face. "Close your little eyes, go sleepy-bye."

Those eyes wild, frantic, the gun right there in his face.

"Ready?" Roland said. "Close 'em tight."

Arnold grabbed the barrel, wrenching it, twisting, rolling across the satin couch. Roland yelled out something, his finger caught in the trigger guard, then grabbing the finger as it came free, holding it tight, the finger hurting something awful, and there was Arnold aiming the gun at him now, pointing it directly at his chest, Arnold closing his eyes, the dumb son of a bitch, as he held the Smith in both hands and pulled the trigger.

*Click.*

Pulled it again.

*Click.*

And again and again.

*Click, click.*

Roland grinned.

Arnold hunched over and started to cry.

Roland took the gun from him, lifting it between thumb and two fingers by the checkered walnut grip and slipped it back into the inside pocket of his suit jacket. He patted Arnold on the shoulder.

"It ain't your day, is it, Arnie? Come on out on the balcony."

Arnold pulled away from him, his mouth ugly the way he was crying without making much of a sound.

"You dink, I ain't gonna throw you off. We're gonna sit out in the air while I tell you how you can get born again."

"I don't see why I can't meet him someplace here," Arnold said. He was sighing, but starting to breathe normally again.

Poor little fella, his nose wet and snotty. Roland handed him a red bandana handkerchief.

"You got Drug Enforcement on your ass, you dink. Ed ain't gonna chance being seen with you around here."

"I don't see why Detroit."

"Arnie, I don't give a shit if you see it or not. That's where Ed says he'll meet you."

"When?"

"Tomorrow, maybe the day after. You go to the hotel there at the Detroit airport and wait for a call. Ed'll get in touch with you."

"Yeah, but when?"

"When he feels like it, you dink." Shit, maybe he ought to forget the whole thing and throw the dink off the balcony.

"Then what?"

"Then you meet someplace, you tell him your deal."

"What deal?"

"Jesus Christ, you told me to get Ed to bank a couple of more trips, and he could take it all. Didn't you tell me that?"

"Yeah, right. I wasn't sure."

"Listen, Ace, I'm standing here in the middle with my pecker hanging out. You better be sure you got a deal to make him."

"Don't worry about it."

Roland liked that tone of confidence coming back into Arnold's voice, the dumb shithead. He brought a folded Delta Airlines envelope out of his side pocket and handed it to Arnold.

"This here's your flight. Tomorrow noon. You'll be driving out to the airport in your Jaguar, huh? License ARN-268?"

"I'll probably take a cab."

"Drive," Roland said, "case somebody want to follow you, see that you go to the airport and not take off for the big swamp."

"Something's funny," Arnold said.

"Okay," Roland said, "let's forget the whole thing, asshole. I'll see you in two days for the vig. I'll see you next week and the week after—"

"It's just a little funny," Arnold said. "I mean it isn't *that* funny. Not nearly as funny as that shit you pulled with the gun. You got a very weird sense of humor, if you don't mind my saying."

"No, I don't mind," Roland said. "We were just having us some fun, weren't we?"

# 14

Marta's brother, Jesus, came for the cassette tape a little after seven o'clock, while Mrs. DiCilia was upstairs. He said this was the last time. No more.

Marta asked him if he had been drinking. He said yes, with Lionel Oliva. He said, Why are we doing this? It wasn't a question. Why should we make life difficult for the woman? What has she done to us? Why should we want to deceive her? Still not asking questions. Marta listened. No more, Jesus said. You're drunk, Marta said. Jesus said, How does that change it? No more. Doing this for Roland. How can a man work for Roland and live with himself? Still not a question. Marta said, All I do is hand you this. Nothing more. Jesus said, *No* more! You feel the same way I feel. (Which was true.) So no more. I'm leaving. Marta said, But if I leave—Jesus said, I leave to be away from Roland.

You don't have to leave. Talk to the woman. Help her for a change. Marta said, Where are you going? Cuba, Jesus said. Then why give him this one? Marta said. Because when I go to see him and give it to him, Jesus said, I may have the nerve to shoot him. Or I may not. But I think I'm going to Cuba.

Then the one named Maguire came in Mrs. DiCilia's car at five minutes to eight.

Marta thought Mrs. DiCilia was going out with him, but they spoke outside for a few minutes and then the one named Maguire drove away. Mrs. DiCilia returned to the house and went up to the room that had been Mr. DiCilia's office, next to the master bedroom. Mrs. DiCilia had gone to the public library today—she had told Marta—for several hours, then had returned to spend most of the day in the room.

Marta remained in her own room for nearly an hour, telling herself it wasn't wrong to record Mrs. DiCilia's telephone calls; it was for the woman's protection—which is what they had told her—to keep bad men away from her. But if the men who were supposed to be protecting her were worse than the ones they were keeping away— If she *knew* this— Yes, then she could say to Mrs. DiCilia she had just found it out or realized it. Not confessing, but revealing a discovery. There was a great difference. For then Mrs. DiCilia would trust her and have no reason to fire her. Marta wanted to help Mrs. DiCilia. But she first wanted to keep her job.

She went upstairs to the office-room, where Mrs. DiCilia sat at the desk holding the telephone and a pair of scissors.

There was something different about the room. The white walls were bare. The framed photographs of Mr. DiCilia and other men—Mr. DiCilia shaking hands with them or standing smiling with them—were gone. They had been taken down.

Marta waited.

Mrs. DiCilia was speaking to someone named Clara, saying all right, she'd phone him the day after tomorrow, then.

There were newspapers and pieces cut from newspapers covering the surface of the desk, pictures out of the paper, pictures out of magazines, that seemed to be of Mrs. DiCilia.

Mrs. DiCilia was asking if Clara had the phone number of Vivian Arzola.

Marta, looking at the pictures on the desk and thinking, It's being recorded. The telephone. Roland will come for the tape and—what would she tell him?

There were small snapshots in black and white on the desk, and newspaper pictures of another woman, not Mrs. DiCilia, that had been machine-copied and looked marked and faded.

Mrs. DiCilia was saying all right, she'd try to call Vivian at the office again, and thanked the one named Clara.

Mrs. DiCilia hung up the telephone, looking at Marta. "Yes?"

"I have something I want to tell you please," Marta said.

"Where's a cowboy get a hat like that?"

Roland turned his head to look at Maguire on the bar stool next to him. He said, "Right in downtown Miami. There's a store there sells range clothes."

"Like western attire," Maguire said. "I believe if I'm not mistaken it's the Ox Bow model." As advertised in the window of Bill Bullock's in Aspen.

"You're right," Roland said, touching the curved brim and looking at Maguire again, a man who knew hats.

"But you didn't get that suit there," Maguire said.

"No, the suit was made for me over in the Republic of China," Roland said.

Maguire shook his head. "No shit."

"Yeah, over in Taiwan. It cost you some money, but if you're willing to pay—"

"I know what you mean."

"—then you got yourself a suit of clothes." Roland's chin rested on his shoulder, looking at Maguire. "I bet I know where you're from. Out west."

"How'd you know?" Maguire said, giving it just a little down-home accent.

"I can tell. Where you think I'm from?"

"Well, I was gonna say out west, too," Maguire said. "I don't know. Let me see—Vegas?"

Roland straightened around, looking down the bar at the display of bottles and the portholes full of illuminated water. "Bartender, give us a couple more here, if you will please." Then to Maguire, "What're you drinking?"

"Rum," Maguire said.

"One Caribbean piss," Roland said to the bartender, "one Wild Turkey. Las Vegas, huh? Shit no, I'm from right here in Florida."

"Lemme see," Maguire said, "you a cattle rancher? Those brahmans with the humps?"

"Naw, I was in cement, land development. Before that I was a hunting-fishing guide over in Big Cypress. Take these dinks out don't know shit, one end of a air boat from the other."

"Over by Miccosukee I bet," Maguire said.

"Near, but more west, by Turner River."

"I drove through there one time," Maguire said, "I stopped at this place on the Tamiami for a cup of coffee?"

"Yeah."

"Little restaurant out there all by itself. This woman about thirty-five, nice looking, serves me the coffee and then she sits down in a chair right in the middle of the floor. I'm sitting at the counter?"

"Yeah."

"She says, 'I love animals. It tears me up when one gets run over by a car.' She says, 'I love cowbirds the most. They have the prettiest eyes.' With this dreamy look on her face, sitting out in the middle of the floor. She says, 'Their little heads go back and forth like this'—she shows me how they go—'pecking away; they'll peck at a great big horsefly.'"

"That's right," Roland said, "they will."

"She's sitting there—I said to her, 'You all by yourself?' She says, 'Yes, I am.' I said, 'You live here?' She says, 'Yes, I do.' I said, 'You want to go back to the bedroom?' She says, 'I don't care.'"

Roland hit the edge of the bar with his big hand. "Yeah, shit, I know where that's at."

"We go back there," Maguire said, "she never says a word all the time we're doing it. We get dressed, come back out, she pours me another cup of coffee and sits down in that same chair again in the middle of the floor?"

"Yeah."

"Hasn't said a word in about twenty minutes now."

"I know."

"She says, 'We found a little parrot was hit by a car once. We nursed it, we got it well again and kept it in the bathroom so it'd be warm. But it drowned in the commode.' "

Roland, shaking his head, said, "Je-sus, I know her and about a hunnert just like her." He opened his eyes and put on a blank expression, turning his head to look around slowly and drawled in a high voice. " 'Yeah, I was down to Mon-roe Station, les see, 'bout five years ago for a catfish supper.' Fucking place's a mile and a half down the road. Man, I had to get out of there 'fore I got covered over with moss."

"It ain't the Gold Coast," Maguire said, "nor afford you the opportunities, does it?"

"Make thirty-five hundred a year in the swamp and you're big stuff. Over here you turn that up every week or so and sleep in on Saturday."

"I guess if you know what you're doing," Maguire said.

"And got hair on your balls," Roland said "Right now I'm lining up a deal—when it comes off I'm gonna be set for life as long as I live."

"What is it, land?"

"Land, you could say that," Roland said. "Land, a house, a trust fund." Roland looked over his shoulder, studying the diners at the tables.

Maguire had a close look at the man's creased rawhide face, and it made him feel tired to imagine trying to hit that face and hurt it. Like kicking an alligator. The way to do it, have a friend waiting outside in the car. Start bad-mouthing Roland till he says come on, step outside. Go out in the parking lot and square off, get Roland turned to the right way and then the friend guns the car and drives it over Roland, hard.

He said, "You meeting somebody?"

"Yeah, some people I'm suppose to see," Roland said. "There's this dink giving me a bad time. But if they don't come real quick, I'm going."

It was getting too close. "I'm going myself," Maguire said. " 'Less I can buy you a drink." He was becoming anxious to get out of here.

"Well, one more," Roland said, and squared around to the bar. Looking at the portholes, the illuminated green water, he started to grin. "You know what'd be good? Pop one of them windows.

See all that swimming pool water come pouring in here"—grinning, enjoying the idea—"People jumping up, trying to get out, shit, the water pouring all over their dinner."

"Yeah, that'd be good," Maguire said. "Get everybody's dinner all wet."

# 15

When the phone rang, Vivian looked at Ed Grossi. Ed had her private number. Jimmy Cap had her number. Her mother in Homestead had it. Ed's lawyer—

Grossi heard her say on the phone, after she had answered in a hesitant voice and spoke to whoever it was for a moment, "What? . . . What're you talking about? I never gave it to you . . . I did not."

Tough lady. Very soft and good to him but a tough lady to keep between him and other people. Twelve years she had worked for him: in the beginning somebody to go to bed with, good-looking young Cuban broad; but too intelligent to remain only a piece of ass. More intelligent, basically, than himself or anyone in the organization; but a little weak in self-confidence because she had been a migrant farmworker and was sometimes intimidated by people with loud voices. Something she had to learn: Loudness did not mean strength or power. Though she could be loud herself sometimes and it seemed to work.

He liked to come here and be alone with Vivian for a few days at a time. Do some thinking. Wear flowered shirts and Bermuda shorts. Try investment ideas on her. Tell her things about his past life he had never told anyone, certainly not his wife, Clara. Go to bed with Vivian. Eat fried bananas. Smoke dope with her, which he never did anywhere else but here. Twelve years only. And yet thinking of his life before Vivian seemed a long time ago, or like looking back at another person named Ed Grossi.

She brought the phone to him, where he sat, in his favorite deep chair, his thin bare legs extending to the matching ottoman. "It's Roland."

Seeing her clouded expression, then hearing Roland's sunny voice: "Ed, hey, I hope I ain't taking you away from anything, partner, but I got a little problem come up."

Presenting a problem, but making it sound like it was nothing. Then becoming more serious, with a sound almost of pain, goddarn, not knowing how to handle it and wanting Ed to help him out if he wasn't too busy and could get away for a while.

Vivian waited, not sitting down, trying to read Ed's expression, which told her nothing, and learn something from his brief words, questions. Something about Karen DiCilia. She took the phone from him when finally he said, "All right, I'll be there," and hung up.

"Be where?" Vivian said.

"Boca. DiCilia'a apartment."

"He told me I gave him this number," Vivian said. "I didn't. I know I didn't give it to him. What's he doing there?"

"He says Karen was drunk, talking loud to some reporter, starting to make a scene. So he took her to the apartment."

"Why? Wait a minute." Vivian put the phone on the floor as she sat down on the edge of the ottoman. "Where was this, in Boca?"

"He says in a restaurant. Roland followed her—it looked like she was meeting someone, this woman he finds out is a newspaper reporter or writer, something like that."

"Yes?"

"But he thinks Karen was already drunk before she got there."

"She drinks much?"

"I don't know, maybe."

"Call her at home," Vivian said.

"What do you mean, call her? She's at the apartment."

"How do you know for sure?"

"I heard her voice. Roland said, 'Just a minute. I heard her say something.' Then Roland said she was sick and went in the bathroom."

Vivian said, "What restaurant was it?"

"He didn't say."

"You're getting old."

Grossi looked at her without saying anything.

"I'm sorry," Vivian said. "Let's call him back and find out the restaurant."

"Why?"

"Call and see if her car's there. If he says he drove her to the apartment. Why there? Why not home?"

"He says the woman reporter would probably go there. He says Karen is going to tell her everything if I don't speak to her first, Vivian. Christ, the bullshit things we get into."

"Let's call him back," Vivian said.

"It's an unlisted number. I don't know what it is." Ed Grossi pulled himself out of the chair and went into the bedroom.

"I can go to the office and get it," Vivian called after him. "Forty minutes."

After a moment Grossi appeared in the bedroom door without his Bermudas now, in striped undershorts. "You can drive me."

"Call her home," Vivian said. "See if she went to Boca."

Grossi was patient with Vivian because he understood her. "I heard her voice on the phone. She's at the apartment, we're going to the apartment. Okay?"

"I didn't give him this number," Vivian said. "I know goddamn well I never gave it to him."

If Ed or Vivian called back, Roland would say, "Just a minute," and put his hand over the phone. Then he'd say, "Shit, now she's passed out."

Or he'd turn his tape recorder on again and give them one of the snatches of Karen's voice he'd pulled off of yesterday's cassette and rerecorded, Karen talking to the newspaper lady who'd called.

Roland punched the recorder to hear it again.

"Why do you keep asking me that if you know what I'm going to say? Think of something else."

Roland would say first, "Mrs. DiCilia, will you talk to Mr. Grossi, please?"

Then punch the recorder and hold the phone toward it.

"Why do you keep asking me that if you know what I'm going to say?"

Maybe cut it right there. Then say to them, "Now she won't talk to nobody. You better come see if you can handle her."

Roland liked this Oceana setup. All modern, bigger than Arnold's place, top-floor view and that deep, square-cut bathtub in there. He just might at that run into a nice cocktail waitress. Bring her up here when he wasn't busy with Karen. Or bring her when he was. That bathtub'd hold three easy.

Roland went over to the closet by the front door, where he'd hung his suit jacket. He lifted the big .45 Smith out of the inside pocket and laid it on the hat shelf of the closet, against the back wall. He left the suit coat hanging in there, but kept his Ox Bow straw on, resetting it loose, straight over his eyes trooper-fashion. People would ask him, "You ever take you hat off?" He'd say, "Let's see. Yeah, I take it off when I wash my head." Then wait as if thinking till they said, "Well, don't you take it off any other time?" And he'd say, "Oh yes, every Sunday I do when I go to church."

It was eleven years ago last March, Roland had his serious hat trouble, the time he was pouring cement for the subdivision going in along the Fakahatchee Strand over by the west coast and he went into the restaurant in Naples to have his dinner. At that time he was wearing a white Stetson that was seasoned and shaped the way rodeo contestants were wearing theirs, curved high on the sides but sort of snapped down in front. Some college boys in the place, drinking beer, would look over at him eating dinner with his hat on. He knew they were making remarks, snickering and laughing, bunch of dinks wearing athletic department sweat shirts and numbered jerseys. On their way out, number 79 stopped by Roland's table, stood there with his powerful shoulders and arms, hands on his hips, and said, "You always wear your hat when you eat?" The others, behind him, snickering some more. Roland said to 79, not looking up from his din-

ner, "Get the fuck away from me, boy, 'fore you ᵥ
salad." Number 79 reached for Roland's hat, got a foᵣ
his forearm and was letting out a howl when Roland beₙ
across the salad bar, smashing the sanitary see-through top
sending the boy to the hospital for stitches, nearly as many as tₕ
number on his breakaway football jersey. Roland pleaded guilty
to aggravated assault, was placed on a year's probation and paid
hospital costs out of his pocket, $387, when they told him his Blue
Cross wouldn't cover it.

He was in that same Lee County Circuit Courtroom a year
later and this time they got him good. They told him to take off
his hat and charged him with second degree murder: brought in
witnesses who testified Roland had threatened to harm a land de-
veloper by the name of Goldman, who Roland had said owed him
money; had been seen arguing with Goldman, provoking a fight,
which was stopped; seen driving out toward Fakahatchee with
Goldman, in his pickup truck, the day before he was found in a
drainage canal, shot to death. No probation this time. Roland got
10 to 25 in Raford and served seven long years. Time to learn
how to use his head and make valuable connections. Then he got
out and never went back to the swamp again, outside of one time
when a hotel owner fell behind on his vig and Roland drove out to
the site of the Everglades jetport that was never completed, shot
him and dumped him in a borrow pit a couple of alligators were
nesting in. When Roland was called in for that kind of work now,
he'd borrow Lionel Oliva's quick little eighteen-foot cruiser and
head out toward the Stream, throw the guy over the side and take
potshots at him till he disappeared.

Ed Grossi was a different situation.

Sometimes, when Vivian would continue to insist, making her
point over and over, Ed Grossi would think, Yes, yes, yes. Talk,
talk, talk. She was intelligent, but she was still a woman. She had
insisted on driving him to Boca Raton; so he allowed her to, giving her that much, but not saying anything to her most of the way
up Interstate 95.

Vivian said, "Why are you mad?"

He said, "I'm not mad."

She said, "I know when you're mad, whether you admit it or
not."

He said, "If you know I'm mad, even when I'm not, then you should know what I'm not mad at." And thought, Jesus Christ, two grown people.

Grossi was mad—no, more irritated—because Vivian had said he was getting old. ("What restaurant was it?" "He didn't say." And because he hadn't asked Roland the name of the restaurant she had said, "You're getting old." Then had said she was sorry, but still wanted to know the name of the restaurant.)

He said now, "Let's forget it." Which meant they were finished talking about whether he was mad or not; though he could continue to feel irritated.

Give a woman a little, she'd try to become the boss. You had to keep her in line. As they turned into the Oceana, going down to the parking area beneath the condominium, Grossi said, "Let me off by the elevator and wait for me."

"I want to go with you," Vivian said.

"I said let me off by the elevator and wait."

Sit. Fetch. Sometimes you had to treat them like that.

"Maybe she needs a woman to be with her," Vivian said.

Grossi got out of the Cadillac and slammed the door. He had to wait for the goddamn elevator, feeling Vivian watching him. Then he was inside, the door closed, there, and he was in control again. He'd have a talk with Vivian, tell her a few simple rules. Like when a certain point is reached, keep your mouth shut, the discussion's over. Clara gave him no trouble, but he had to listen to her talk about her garden. Karen talked about her freedom. Karen—he'd give her anything she wanted and get that settled, not have to worry about her anymore. Ridiculous, having to stop and deal with woman.

Grossi knocked and Roland opened the door almost immediately, Roland holding a decorative pillow.

"I was sleeping," Roland said.

Grossi came into the living room. "Where is she?"

"She's in the bathroom. Sounds like she's a little sick."

"She sleep at all?"

"Little bit. She won't talk to me no more."

Grossi moved down the hall to the bathroom. The door was closed. He knocked and said, "Karen?" There was no response, no sound from inside. Roland was coming along the hall now, still holding the small pillow. "You sure she's in here?"

"She might've passed out again," Roland said. "Better look in there and see."

Grossi turned the knob, expecting it to be locked. He opened the door carefully, not wanting to startle Karen or surprise her sitting on the toilet.

"Karen?"

He saw himself in the bathroom mirror. He looked toward the empty walkup tub. He looked back at the mirror and saw himself and Roland behind him. He saw Roland looking at him in the mirror, not quite grinning, but with an alert, knowing expression.

In his mind, in that moment, Grossi heard Vivian saying, "You're getting old," and his own voice saying "Oh my God," and heard the heavy muffled gunshot hard against him, jabbing him, and saw in the mirror blood coming out of his shirtfront and on the mirror itself, his blood sprayed there as from a nozzle, seeing it in the same moment the sunburst pattern of lines exploded on the glass, his image there, his image gone.

Roland picked Grossi up, surprised how light he was, and dropped him in the deep bathtub.

He hadn't thought about the mirror breaking. He'd clean up the glass and the blood. Replace the mirror some other time, tomorrow maybe.

Right now he'd move Ed's car for the time being. Put it in a lot away from here, lock it up and walk back.

Wait till real late. Then the tricky part. Drop Ed out the window to land him in the sand. Better than taking him down the elevator in a box.

Drive him down to Miami International and put him in the trunk of Arnold's Jag, Florida ARN-268, parked in the Delta area.

Don't forget. Put the Smith in there too, grip and trigger wiped clean of prints, but with Arnie's partials all over the barrel.

Then drive Grossi's car to Hallandale, park it near Arnie's apartment.

Lot of work.

In the morning call the Miami Police. Change his voice to talk like a queer, one of Arnie's ex-buddies: Hi there. You don't know who this is, but I'll tell you where you boys can find a dead body. (Probably have to argue.) Just listen, asshole, or I'm gonna hang up and not tell you who done it or where you can locate him up in De-troit.

Work on that before morning.

What else?

Roland thought of something and he said, out loud, "Oh, my. Oh, my aching ass."

Something he had not thought of before and didn't know why he hadn't; but there it was, Jesus, the possibility.

What if Vivian had come here with Ed?

Vivian said, The son of a bitch. She backed the Cadillac up the parking aisle all the way past the street ramp, ready to turn and drive out.

But waited there and let herself calm down. What would it prove? Like stamping her foot or breaking dishes. Nothing. You won't change him, she thought. He's sixty-three years old, and he's the way he is. She put the Cadillac in "Drive" and, without accelerating, the car rolled down the aisle to the elevator door in the cement-block wall.

He would come down with Mrs. DiCilia and they would be busy attending to the woman, getting her home or someplace. And he won't even know you're angry at him, Vivian thought. The son of a bitch. He can ride up here all the way from North Miami without saying a word. But now when it was her turn to be mad, the son of a bitch wouldn't even know it.

Vivian again backed up the car to the street ramp.

Go get something. Let him be waiting when she got back, Oh, have you been waiting long? I had to get some gas, since you don't keep any in your car.

The gauge indicated half full. But he wouldn't know that. Or go get a cup of coffee instead of waiting here like a chauffeur. Say to him, When do I get my hat and uniform?

Looking down the aisle, perhaps sixty or seventy feet, she saw the cowboy hat come out of the elevator.

She said, Oh, God—

She hesitated. Ed could have sent Roland down to get her.

Roland was looking around, looking this way now. Staring, not sure if it was the right car. Then waving—Come on!—taking several steps into the aisle.

Vivian started up, with the Cadillac in reverse, and had to mash her foot on the brake to stop it—Roland coming toward her now—and had to look down at the automatic shift lever to get it into "Drive"—Roland running now, not waving Come on, what're you doing, but pumping his arms—as she pressed the accelerator, the car instantly leaping forward, and she had to turn hard to aim the front end up the ramp, scraping the concrete wall and hearing the tires shrieking and Roland's voice yelling something.

If she was wrong she would tell Ed later, I was wrong.

But she knew she wasn't wrong. She didn't know how she knew it but she did—going back in her mind, knowing she hadn't given Roland her telephone number. But at this moment having no idea where she could go to be safe.

# 16

Karen read about it and saw film stories on television.

Ed Grossi's murder featured as a gangland/drug-related killing. His body found in the trunk of a suspected drug dealer's car
at Miami International. The suspected drug dealer, Arnold Rapp,
had fled; but soon after was apprehended in Detroit by fast-mov-
ing FBI agents and handed over to the Miami Police. Arnold
Rapp had been charged with first degree murder—bond set at
five hundred thousand dollars—and was being held awaiting trial
in Dade Circuit Court, Criminal Division.

Karen ran, instinctively.

She went to Los Angeles to stay with her daughter, Julie. She
told Julie about Ed Grossi, about the arrangement, about Roland.
Julie seemed to listen. But they would talk and then Julie would
run to the studio, where she was doing voice loops for an Italian-
made film or she would take milk shakes to Cedars-Sinai, to her

530

husband, Brian, who'd broken his jaw doing a stunt in a car-chase sequence.

At night Karen would sit in the living room of the house off Mulholland Drive and look down at the lights of Los Angeles.

Julie said, "I don't know, I guess I don't see the problem."

Karen said, "Then I must've left something out. If Ed Grossi is dead, then he can't change the arrangement, the trust fund. It goes on and on the same way, and I have to stay there the rest of my life."

"Well, get somebody else to change it."

"I'm afraid," Karen said, "I have a feeling, it's going to be in Roland's hands."

"Yeah? Well, then get Roland to change it. God, it sounds like something out here, dealing with these fucking producers, trying to find out who's in charge."

"He won't want to change it," Karen said. "If he does, he knows I'll leave in a minute."

"Well, if you like it there—" Julie said. "It's a good address, isn't it?"

"You mean—what? Is it fashionable?"

"Like here," Julie said. "We're in L.A., right? But you don't just say you're in L.A. Christ, L.*A.?* You say you live in the Hills. Or you get it across you're in 90046."

"I thought this was Hollywood," Karen said.

"God, no. There isn't any Hollywood, really. Or maybe 90069, down around where all the agents are, it's called Hollywood, but it's really Los Angeles County. See, if you're in Bel Air or Beverly Hills, like 90212, you don't even have to know your zip. But L.A.—Brian wanted to moved to North Hollywood? I said, 'Brian, 91604 is *okay,* but it's not 90046 by any stretch of the imagination. It's living in the Valley, Brian.' They say where do you live, you tell them Studio City, Sherman Oaks, some fucking place like that, they think you're in wardrobe or an assistant film editor."

Try again. Karen said, "I like my house, yes. But do I want someone forcing me to stay there?"

"Are you asking?"

Was she? Karen said, "I told you a little about Roland. I haven't told you everything, or what I'm afraid he's going to do."

"Well, at least you can talk to him," Julie said. "The director on this great epic spaghetti picture not only barely speaks English, he hasn't the slightest fucking idea what he's doing. He's got this translation for the dubbed version, it's written by an Italian, he's got me saying things like, 'I hated him. I think it is swell that he was slain.' Honest to God. I mean if you can talk to him, what's your problem, really?"

For five days Karen phoned Vivian Arzola at the Dorado Management office. Each day she was told Vivian was not in and each time the girl on the phone refused, politely, to give her Vivian's home phone number. On the fifth day Karen watched a brief television coverage of Ed Grossi's funeral on national news. She saw Roland, in his blue suit, serving as one of the pallbearers, but didn't recognize him immediately without his hat. There was no sign of Vivian in the film clip of activity outside St. Mary's Cathedral.

Later in the evening of the fifth day Maguire called. He said he had stopped by her house every day and finally Marta had given him the number in Los Angeles.

"In the Hills," Karen said. "Nine-oh-oh-four-six."

"What?"

"Do me a favor, will you? Tell Marta to save the Miami papers. But don't call her."

"You think I'd do that? Listen, how come you haven't called me?"

"I didn't have your number. But that reminds me," Karen said, "do you know how to find phone numbers?"

"You look in the book."

"Unlisted ones. I need Vivian Arzola's number. Or maybe you could find out where she lives." Karen spelled the name for him. "She works for Dorado Management but hasn't been there all week. It's very important. Okay?"

"Vivian Arzola," Maguire said.

She asked then, "Have you seen Roland?"

"Only on TV."

"Yes, I saw it too."

"When're you coming home?"

"Tomorrow," Karen said. There was a pause. "Do you miss me?"

She sat by herself in first class, no one in the seat next to her; wore sunglasses much of the time; sipped three martinis and California red with her roast fillet; was polite to the flight attendants though she sidestepped conversation; read a book, *The Kefauver Story*, by Jack Anderson and Fred Blumenthal, which she had found in Frank's office, and reread a Xeroxed copy of an article from the June, 1951 issue of *American Mercury*, entitled "Virginia Hill's Success Secrets," she had got from the Fort Lauderdale Public Library. She thought of Cal Maguire. Don't tell him obvious things: like not to call the house or how to do his job. Be nicer. She thought of Roland Crowe and thought of Julie's line in the Italian film, changing the tense and applying it to Roland so that it came out, "I hate him. I think it would be swell if he were slain."

# 17

The question in Maguire's mind, coming up more frequently now: What was he getting out of this?

He would recall and hear again the sound of Karen's voice on the phone. Almost impersonal. Nothing about being glad he'd called. Then asking if he missed her. Not saying she missed *him*. He had said, "You bet I miss you, a lot." He should have said, "Well, I think I do, but I'm not sure."

Friday, the day she was coming home—his day off—he drove to the DiCilia house again, left the Mercedes over by the garage doors, next to Marta's car, and rang the bell at the kitchen entrance.

Marta seemed surprised. "She isn't home yet."

"I came to see you," Maguire said. "You got any coffee on?"

In the kitchen that was like a restaurant kitchen, pans hanging from a rack above the table, he had to ask Marta to sit down. He could see she was aware of being alone with him in the house. "You know I'm her friend," he said. "You know I want to help her."

"Yes," Marta said.

"And you want to help her, too."

"Yes, but she said not to give anyone the number where she was."

"No, that was fine. I talked to her, and she's glad you did. She just forgot to mention it was okay to tell me." Forgot to mention—Christ. "She's got a lot on her mind"—looking for a way to get to the point—"but you know she's very grateful you told her about the tape recorder and all."

"I had to," Marta said. "It bothered me so much."

"Has Roland been back since she's gone?"

"Two days ago he came. He asked me where did she go. I told him I didn't know."

"Yeah? What'd he say to that?"

"He walked all over the house like he owned it, looking around in places he shouldn't."

"He take anything?"

"No, I don't think so."

"But you're not sure," Maguire said.

"He might have, yes. But I don't know."

"You told him you didn't know where Mrs. DiCilia was. Then what'd he say?"

"He threatened to do something to me." Marta hesitated. "So I told him, California."

"That was okay," Maguire said. "He's been listening to phone calls, he could've figured it out that's where she'd go. That's okay." He sipped his coffee and sat back, showing Marta he was at ease, not worried about it. "What I'd like to do, if I could, is talk to your brother."

"My brother?"

"From what I understand— See, she told me everything you told her. How he's quit, doesn't work for them anymore, all that. But I was wondering, maybe he could tell me a few things about Roland, the people he works for. Like Vivian Arzola. You know Vivian?"

Marta shook her head. "No, only the name."

"Or maybe your brother could tell me something about Roland that might help us. You never know."

"I could talk to him," Marta said.

"Could you call him? See if he'll meet me somewhere?"

"I think he may have gone to Cuba. Or he's going, I don't know."

"So maybe we don't have much time. You want to call him now? No, you can't do that, call from here." Maguire waited, letting Marta come up with the idea.

"I could go somewhere and call him. The drugstore by the causeway."

"Hey, would you do that?"

"Only the man's coming to fix the bed. He was supposed to come yesterday."

"Nuts." Maguire waited, thoughtful. When he'd given it enough thought, he said, "Why don't I stay in case the guy comes?" He paused, beginning to grin. "I know where the bed is."

Karen had walked from the patio into the house that night, was gone only a few minutes, and returned with a gun wrapped in tissue paper and forty-five new one hundred dollar bills.

He assumed she had put the gun back, somewhere in the bedroom—(He had thought of it lying with her in the broken-down bed. In one of the nightstands? In the dresser? Or behind the wall or mirrors in the closet?)

And assuming there were more new one hundred dollar bills hidden somewhere—(Lying in the bed he had thought of the money, too; first beginning to wonder what he was getting out of this.)

Maguire stood in the bedroom, alone in the house, Marta gone to phone her brother.

He had not told himself he was going to take the money; because at this point he could say, What money? You don't even know it's here. No decision to steal had been made. What he was doing—he told himself—was taking advantage of an opportunity. Seeing where he stood. Surveying the situation. So that if, in the end, he did have to grab something and run as an act of survival, for traveling expenses, it would be something portable and not the Louis XVI bergère or the Peachblow vases he'd have to wrap in newspapers and pack in a crate.

Where would she keep a lot of money?

In a safe.

But there was no safe in the bedroom or in the closet. In the top dresser drawer he found a box of jewelry, unlocked, with some fine-looking pieces he assumed were real; though he'd never made a study of jewelry.

Next to the jewel box was the Beretta, still wrapped in tissue paper, loaded, a cartridge in the chamber. He rewrapped the gun, put it back in the drawer and told himself, okay, he knew where it was if he needed it, if he ever had to come running upstairs looking for a weapon.

But he was thinking mostly of 45 one hundred dollar bills, Series 1975, with consecutive serial numbers. Clean money, he assumed: thirty of the bills accepted at the post office without question when he'd bought the money orders. New but almost five years old, dating back to . . . Frank DiCilia. And thought of stories of how the wise guys always kept a lot of cash hidden away but handy, a stake, in case they ever had to run, their idea of traveling money. Sure, there had been a guy in Detroit, the feds had gone in with a search warrant, looking for something else, and found a couple hundred grand in the basement, hidden under the guy's workbench. Andre Patterson had said, "Hey, 'magine hitting a man's house finding something like that? Pick out one of those old Eyetalian guys supposed to be retired." Andre couldn't even talk Cochise into it.

But the man dead, and happening to come across his stake, that was something else.

Except it could be anywhere in the house. Assuming it was here.

Maguire tried the door leading into the next room. Locked. He went into the hall and tried the outside door to the room. Locked. And thought, What's going on? Jewelry in an unlocked bedroom; the next room, the mystery room, locked. He remembered something, went back into the bedroom to the dresser, poked around in the top drawer again and found a half dozen keys, most of them to suitcases, one for a door lock.

He tried it, felt it slide in and turn, and stepped into what had been Frank DiCilia's office at home. He saw the desk, the typewriter, the file cabinet—

He saw the photographs on the wall.

Photos of Karen. Enlarged photos or photostats, blowups of snapshots taped to the wall, blowups of newspaper photos in bold black and white.

He wasn't sure if they were all of Karen and then saw, that yes, there were shots of Karen alone, when she was much younger and not as good-looking as she was now, but with the same serious, secretive look. Karen in hats, Karen in dark glasses. Karen in summer dresses, bathing suits, wide-brimmed hats and dark glasses. Like a much younger Karen playing dress-up. There was one of a heavier Karen, which he realized, after a moment, wasn't Karen. It was someone else. A woman in a black wide-brimmed hat and dark glasses, black dress, and a fur stole. Dark glasses, though the picture had been taken inside, he was sure. There were several other shots of the woman he had not noticed before, mixed in with Karen's photos, blown-up grainy photos like the one of Karen in the sunhat and bikini taken on the seawall. Karen's photos and those of the other woman were mixed together on the wall so that when he looked at the entire display he could believe they were all of the same person. Karen.

What was going on?

Maguire turned to the file cabinet. The key was lying on top. Then he looked at the wall of photos again.

If you did something like that, he thought, put up about a dozen pictures of yourself and a few of somebody who didn't look like you but did in a way, the expression, the dark glasses—trying for a certain look maybe? Going back to earlier pictures and finding the look there? An attitude? Why would you do it?

He opened the filed cabinet—it was unlocked—began fingering through folders, papers. He came to a manila envelope, a big one, tightly packed, opened the fasteners, looked in and said, out loud, "My oh my." He took the envelope to the desk that was covered with newspaper pages, clippings, negative photostats— Karen in reverse; but didn't stop to look at them. Six packets of new one-hundred-dollar bills slid from the envelope. Five thousand dollars in each of five packets, five hundred in the sixth one. Twenty-five thousand five hundred dollars, 1975 Series bills, the same as the ones Karen had given him—right out of the sixth packet.

He thought of something. That the room had been locked because of the photos, not the money. He was sure of it.

He thought of something else. It was decision time. There is was, twenty-five grand, the most money he had ever seen at one time. Take it and run.

Or leave it.

Or lock it in the trunk of the Mercedes, which wouldn't be taking it because it was her car. The rationale: protecting it from Roland. But having it ready to grab.

Shit, if he was going to take it, take it.

He heard a sound, somewhere downstairs, a door slamming.

Marta came out from the kitchen to see Maguire in the front hall, at the foot of the stairs.

"I found him. My brother says okay. He'll meet you at Centro Vasco on Southwest Eighth Street. You know where it is? Maybe about Twenty-second Avenue, in Miami."

"I'll find it."

"But he doesn't see how he can help you."

"I've been trying to remember where I saw you before."

"At the fish place."

"No, I mean before that. Ten years ago," Maguire said.

He thought about it, looking past Jesus Diaz to the tables of people talking, having lunch at Centro Vasco, almost all of them Cuban.

"I know. The Convention Center, over on the Beach."

"Sure, I was there plenty times. I used to work out at the Fifth Street gym."

"You fought a guy by the name of Tommy Laglesia. He was doing something, I forgot what; everybody could see it but the ref."

"Butting me, the son of a bitch kept butting me in the face, the fucking ref don't say a word." Jesus straightened, and leaned on his arms over the table. "You saw that, uh?"

"Yeah, it's funny—I used to go to fights, but not so much anymore."

"No, well, who's there to see?" Jesus said. "You saw that, uh?"

He drank some of his beer, settling back again. "You know the other day—I didn't want to do nothing to you."

"No, I know you didn't," Maguire said. "But the other guy—I had to try and hit first, you know, try and get an advantage."

"Man, you hit him all right. He had to get stitches."

"I wish it'd been what's his name, Roland."

"Yeah, I wish it, too."

"Had enough of him, uh?"

"Man, forever."

"Have you seen him?"

"Last week. Then I see him on TV, but that's all. I don't work for him no more."

"Who else does?"

"Nobody. He's by himself."

"I was wondering," Maguire said, "with Grossi dead, what do you think might happen?"

"What do you mean, what might happen? To who?"

"Mrs. DiCilia if Roland, you know, is gonna still bother her."

"I don't know. He don't work for Mr. Grossi no more. Why would he?"

"Well, he sees a rich lady, all alone—"

"She got friends of her husband there. Mr. Grossi wasn't the only one."

"Yeah, maybe Vivian Arzola. You know where she is?"

"No, I don't know. She got a place in town; another place, I hear about in Keystone, but I don't know where."

"You know her phone number?"

"No, I don't know it."

"Mrs. DiCilia's anxious to talk to her." Maguire paused. "She have family in Miami?"

"No. Wait, let me think," Jesus said. "Yeah, I took something to her mother once for Vivian. She lives in Homestead. Vivian gives her, you know, the support."

"What kind of car does she drive?"

"Vivian? A white one with like a flower or something on the antenna. Some foreign car."

"You want to help Mrs. DiCilia find her?"

"I think I'm going to Cuba."

"If you don't go, I mean. She'll pay you whatever you think it's worth."

"Maybe I could do it," Jesus said.

"Sure, Cuba'll be there. You know where Roland lives?"

"Miami Shores. A place on Ninety-first Street called the Bay-view."

"He live there alone?"

"Man, you think anybody would stay with him?"

"You want to go see him with me?"

"I don't think so. Not even stoned."

"How about with a gun?"

Jesus' hand was on his glass of beer. Looking at Maguire he seemed to forget about it.

"You ever do things like that?"

"If I have to."

"Yeah? Is that right?" Jesus continued to study Maguire. "Mrs. DiCilia, she want it?"

"She wants it, but she doesn't know she wants it, if you understand what I mean."

"She don't want to think about it."

"Something like that. But she'll pay you to be on her side, whatever you think it's worth," Maguire said. "Like five thousand, around in there? It's up to you."

"Around in there, uh? Let me think about it," Jesus Diaz said.

# 18

After Ed Grossi's funeral, relatives and close friends came to Grossi's house on Hurricane Drive, Key Biscayne, to give Clara their sympathy and help themselves to a buffet. The friends and relatives who had not been there before, and even many who had, took time to walk up the street to 500 Bay Lane to see where Ed Grossi's neighbor, Richard Nixon, had lived. They came back saying shit, Ed's place was bigger.

Roland didn't care anything about historical sites. He got a plate of fettucini with clam sauce, a big glass of red and some rolls, and went over to sit with Jimmy Capotorto in the Florida room that was full of plants hanging all over, like a greenhouse.

Roland said, "It's a bitch, huh, something like this? Man, you never know."

Jimmy Cap had finished eating. He was smoking a cigar, looking out at the Bay, five miles across to South Miami. He asked Roland if the cops had talked to him.

Which was what Roland wanted to get over with. He said, "You kidding? Man, I'm the first one on their list. That Coral Gables Discount deal—shit, they picked me up before they even thought of you." Reminding Jimmy Cap, just in case.

Jimmy Cap said, "They tell me, say it was a setup, you know that. I say how do I know that? They say, this Arnold Rapp, he shoots Grossi and puts him in his own fucking car, come on, and leaves it at the airport? I say I only know what I read in the *Herald*."

"They give me the same shit," Roland said, "I didn't say it to them but I'll tell you, which you probably know anyway from Ed. This Arnie was a pure-D queer. I mean you look at him cross he'd piss his pants. I'd go over there to collect, have to shake him a little sometimes? He'd bust out crying. I'd say, Jesus Christ, you dink, cut your crying and pay up, that's all you got to do. See, he was a nervous little fella 'sides being a queer. It doesn't surprise me at all he fucked up, left Ed in his car. By then all he was thinking to do was run."

"Who fingered him?"

"I don't know for sure, but I believe it was a dink name of Barry used to work for Arnie. He got hurt and maybe he was pissed off, believed Arnie should've been the one hurt. See, it's hard to figure how these queers think."

"Don't do business with college boys," Jimmy Cap said.

"Hey, I told Ed that, the exact same words. Little fuckers, life gets hard, they go to pieces."

"Well, I'm not gonna worry about it," Jimmy Cap said. "What else you got?"

Here we go, Roland thought.

"Nothing important. Well, that DiCilia arrangement, you want to count that."

"Jesus, I don't want to even hear about it," Jimmy Cap said. "You handle it. Pay her off, forget about it. I don't give a shit where she lives."

"Let me look into it," Roland said. He dug into his fettucini, waiting to see if Jimmy Cap had anything else to say. No, it didn't look like it. Roland then said, "Vivian's been acting funny lately. You notice?"

"I didn't see her at the funeral," Jimmy Cap said.

"You haven't seen her around?"

"I don't know. I don't think so."

"She's in mourning or hiding or something," Roland said. "Nobody's seen her in a few days. She hasn't called or anything?"

"What would she call me for?"

"I just wondered. I don't know what's wrong with her. She's been starting to act strange."

"Fuckin' Cubans," Jimmy Cap said, "who knows? They're all crazy."

"I was thinking," Roland said, "she's liable to start bitching about this DiCilia arrangement. I mean when she finds out I'm handling it."

"Fire her," Jimmy cap said. "I never could figure out what Ed saw in that broad anyway."

"Well, I'll see," Roland said. "I guess if I have to, I'll get rid of her."

Marta could not see Roland's face through the stained glass window in the door, but she could see his hat. She didn't want to open the door. But if she didn't, he could go around to the patio side, break something to get in. She didn't want to tell him Mrs. DiCilia had come home today and was in her room unpacking. But he would find out himself if he wanted. There was no way to stop him. It was too early to be picking up the tape: four o'clock in the afternoon. Marta opened the door, trying to be composed.

Roland was grinning at her.

He said, "You know, standing here I was thinking about another Cuban lady I liked to visit. She lives out on the Tamiami on Beaver Road? I used to say to her, 'Honey, I just see your street sign I get a boner.' How you doing, Marty?"

"Mrs. DiCilia is very busy."

"Oh, she home? Well, we won't bother her," Roland said, coming in. "I just as soon fool around with you anyway."

"I have to go to the kitchen."

"Why don't we go your room instead?"

Both were down the back hall. Marta started that way and turned and didn't know where to go, Roland on her then, taking her from behind and pulling her in, Roland pausing to look up the stairway.

Marta said, "Please," and Roland said, "Mmmmm, you feel good," heavy workman's hands moving over the front of her white uniform, over her breasts, Roland saying, "We got a bra-zeer on under there? No, hey, we don't have no bra-zeer on, do we? Like our little titties free." The hands like old tree roots rubbing the white material, working down to her belly and thighs. "Let's see if we got any panties on." Grinning then, seeing Gretchen the schnauzer skidding across the hall floor at him. "Hey, Gretchie, hey, Gretchie, how you girl? How's my girl, huh? You want some of this, Gretchie? No, you don't. This ain't for little doggies, this here is for—shit, where you going? Get her Gretchie!"

Roland reached down to take some playful swipes at the schnauzer, getting her to growl in fun, then went after Marta, hoping she was heading for the living room where he'd nail her on that big white sofa. But she ducked into the sitting room full of antiques and was almost to the French doors when he grabbed the hem of her white uniform from behind, yanked it up and heard it rip. Marta bounced off him and Roland fell hard against a wall of shelves, flung out an arm and destroyed several thousand dollars' worth of Toby jugs and English china. Blueplate specials to Roland. He swiped at a Ralph Stevenson soup tureen ("View of the Deaf and Dumb Asylum") and there went another three grand . . . and Marta, half out of the uniform now, going through the French doors.

Karen heard the sound, glass shattering. She thought of a window, the French doors. She thought of Roland. Then heard another shattering of glass. Or china. From the sitting room. Voices, the sound coming faintly from outside. She heard the scream and knew it was Marta. Karen turned from the wall of photographs and saw them outside, below the window. Marta running, Marta in white panties, nothing else, running across the patio and past the swimming pool. Roland following after her, waving something white. Roland calling out, the words not clear. Karen raised the window. "I'm gonna get you, yes, I am, sugar, gonna eat you up." Roland stopping as Marta stopped, out on the lawn, and came around warily, holding her hands in front of her, beginning to circle back toward the house, facing Roland now, screaming again as he dug in and lunged toward her.

Karen turned from the window as if to run, to hurry. Then seemed to pause, almost imperceptibly, as she moved past the wall of photographs. She walked from the office into the bedroom, picked up the phone on the nightstand, dialed and said, "Operator, this is Karen Hill. I'm sorry, Karen DiCilia, 1 Isla Bahía. Would you call the police, please, and tell them to come right away. It's an emergency . . . Yes, Fort Lauderdale."

As soon as Roland heard the hi-lo sound of the police siren he walked away from the swimming pool and sank into a canvas patio chair. Marta remained in the pool, slightly stooped, in about four feet of water. Both of them watched Karen come out of the house with the two police officers in dark brown uniforms and visored caps, both young looking and in condition, with serious-to-deadpan expressions. One of them took his sunglasses off and hooked them on his shirt pocket. No one spoke. Karen picked up a towel from the lounge chair, carried it to the broad steps at the shallow end of the pool and held it open for Marta. Roland and the police officers waited.

"Come on, it's all right," Karen said.

Roland and the police officers watched Marta step out of the pool and turn into the towel, pulling it around her.

"Tell them," Karen said.

The two police officers came onto the patio, looking at the two women, glancing at Roland.

Roland said, "How you doing?"

They didn't answer him. One of them said to Karen, "Is this the man?"

Karen nodded.

The police officer said to Roland, "Could I see your identification?"

Roland said, "Uh-unh. You got no reason to see it."

Both of the police officers turned to Roland with their deadpan expressions and stood without moving. The one who had spoken to him said, "Stand up and turn around."

Roland said, "Hey, cut the shit. You got a complaint? Let me hear what it is."

"Get up," the police officer said. "Right now."

The other one had his hand on his gun or his cuffs, Roland wasn't sure which. He looked over at Marta, shaking his head, then raised his hand. "Now come on. Since you didn't see nothing—before you start acting mean, who's your complaining witness?"

Karen said to Marta, "Tell them."

Marta looked from the police officers to Roland.

"Tell them," Karen said again.

"Somebody, I believe, got the wrong impression," Roland said. "It's all right, Marty, tell 'em. Heck, we were just playing around, weren't we?"

One of the police officers said to Marta, "Is this man a friend of yours?"

"I believe you could say we're a little thicker than that." Roland looked over at Karen and gave her a wink. "All of us here. We're old buddies. Me and Marty and Karen. Me and Marty's brother're very close. I see him all the time. Keep him out of trouble."

"He's threatening her," Karen said.

"Hey, Marty, am I threatening you?" Staring at her from beneath the low hat brim. "Go ahead, tell 'em."

"No, he's not," Marta said.

"Do you want to make a complaint against this man?" the police officer said.

"No," Marta said.

"Was he bothering you in any way?"

"No."

The police officer looked at Karen. Roland looked at her, too. She said, "Can I make a complaint?"

The police officer said to Marta, "How old are you?"

"Twenny-two."

"If this lady says there was an assault and it was against you, then you'd have to file the complaint," the police officer said to Marta. "Are you afraid of this man? That he might hurt you?"

"No," Marta said.

"Or he might hurt somebody in your family?"

Marta shook her head. "No."

"You and him were just playing around?"

"Yes."

The police officer stared at her a little longer before turning to Karen. "If you want to make a complaint— Or maybe you ought to tell us what's going on here."

Karen said, "Do you really want to know?"

Roland liked that. He grinned, adjusting his hat, fooling with it. He said to Karen, "There you are. They want to hear the dirt." Roland's gaze moved to the police officers. He said to them, "You know who this lady is, Mrs. DiCilia? Was married to Frank Di-Cilia, good friend of Ed Grossi, recently passed away."

(Sure, they knew it. They'd have been sitting on Roland with a sap under his chin if it was some other backyard.)

"See, we have our disagreements, get into arguments like anybody else," Roland went on, as though he belonged here, part of the family. "But if we was to start ex*plain*ing everything to you, you'd be writing reports all night and on your day off . . . wouldn't you?"

Roland knew he had hit the nail on the head. The police officers stood there not saying anything. What did they see? A guy chases the maid into the swimming pool and the lady of the house gets pissed off. The lady hadn't yelled or had a fit. The lady was mad, yeah, but she seemed in control of the situation. ("Do you really want to know?") Pretty cool about it. It took the policemen off the hook and it made Roland happier'n a pig in shit. The lady saw clearly the position she was in. Call the police and then what? Call them every day?

Roland, in the front doorway, watched the white Lauderdale police car with its red bubble, drive over the bridge to Harbor Beach Parkway. He'd pulled it off, made his point.

Roland said over his shoulder, "I knew you were up there watching. You enjoy the show?"

No answer from her.

The cops had eyed his Cadillac and right now were probably calling the Communications Center to punch the code on his license number. Those guys were going to shit when they got the report; but they wouldn't come back now without a heavy charge and backup.

Karen, standing behind him in the hall, said, "Are we going to talk?"

Roland turned, closing the door. He studied Karen, trying to make up his mind about something.

"You're different'n before. You know it? You're a lot calmer. I don't mean you're ever excitable, but there's something different about you. You got something bothering you you're holding in?"

"You talk a lot," Karen said, "but you never get to the point." She turned and went into the living room.

Roland followed her, looking up at the high-beamed ceiling, impressed with the size of the room every time he came in here.

"I believe I owe you a few bucks. I broke some plates."

Karen said, "Tell me what you want." She stood by the fireplace. She felt like moving but didn't want to pace in front of him.

Roland eased into a deep chair. His hat brim touched the cushion of the backrest and he hunched forward a little.

"What're you offering me?"

"How about twenty-five thousand?"

"Cash? In new hundred dollar bills?"

Karen stared at him.

Roland stared back. He said, "How come you got all those pictures upstairs?" He pulled his Ox Bow down closer to his eyes so he could rest his head against the chair.

"Did you take the money?"

"No, it's there. I figure it's for cigarettes and bird feed, uh?"

"I'm waiting for you to come out and say it," Karen said. "What you want."

"I'm not bragging or anything," Roland said, "but ladies have asked me that before. 'What do you want?' they say, 'anything.' "

"I haven't said 'anything.' "

"Not yet. See the fact you got four million bucks, sort of—the proceeds of it—don't make you any different from the other ladies asked me what I wanted. And I was in no position to be as nice to them as I am to you. See, Ed Grossi passed on before he changed anything, and guess who they put in charge?"

"I don't believe you," Karen said.

"Call Jimmy Cap. Ain't nobody higher'n Jimmy."

Karen started to move from the fireplace. She caught herself, moving to be moving, made herself stand motionless, relax, and put her hand on the rough beam that served as a mantel. Why was it so easy for him? Roland. The way he'd handled the police;

refused to stand up or answer them. The convenience, the timing of Ed Grossi's death. She wanted to probe, ask questions, insinuate—

And found she didn't have to. Roland said, "You don't know for sure Ed was gonna change anything, let you off, as you told me one time. No, I believe he meant to leave it as is. So you're lucky, aren't you, the way things turned out. Now you got somebody you can see eye to eye with."

"The way it happened to turn out," Karen said.

"Yeah, I don't mean we should go out and celebrate Ed's passing, but it does make it easier for all concerned."

"That he happened to die," Karen said, staying with it.

"Hey, they got the guy," Roland said. "Don't try and mix me up in that. No, all I'm saying, you work hard and sometimes you get lucky. And here we are, huh?"

"You had something to do with his death," Karen said.

"I know the boy did it, that's all. Ask the police, I already talked to them."

Karen wanted to say, And Vivian, who's also in this. Where's Vivian? But she held back, aware of herself standing at the mantel, alone with the man who wore his hat in the house, the backcountry gangster, the Miami Beach hotdog, the good-ol' boy with his boots on the coffee table—God—making herself remain calm while she felt the stir of excitement, and thought, as she had the first time he came here—you can handle it.

Play it his way. You can take him.

Karen said, "You still haven't said anything, have you? What you want."

"Yeah, I said ladies have offered me things, wanting to be nice."

"How much is nice?"

"No, it's got to be what you *want* to give. You don't understand, do you?"

"I'm having a little trouble," Karen said.

"Look, you got four million bucks, the proceeds of it. You got everything you should want or need. But if you leave here you're cut off, the funds end."

"I'm aware of that."

"I'm reviewing the situation. I can't see you leaving and giving up four million bucks."

"I can't either," Karen said.

"But your fooling-around love-life is also curtailed, huh?"

"It looks like it."

"Unless you and me get something going."

"You mean all I have to do is go to bed with you?"

Roland grinned. "You mention it, I get horny. But see, I'm not going to force you. As I told you the first time I was here, I'm your boy cuz I'm the only one you got."

"I go to bed with you," Karen said. "Then what?"

"You *ask* me to go to bed."

"All right, I ask you. Then what happens after that?"

"We live happily ever after."

"You move in here?"

"Tomorrow, you want me to."

"It's not just money then. Even a whole lot."

"Money?" Roland said. "Shit, I want the money and everything that goes with it. You, the whole setup."

"But you're not going to use force, intimidation."

"Other than keeping your dink boyfriends away so's you become sex-starved."

"If it's simply between you and me," Karen said and paused. "You don't have a chance."

There was Roland's grin, showing he was enjoying himself and liked the situation. He said. "We might've got off on the wrong foot and all. But, listen, you're gonna find I'm really a sweet person."

# 19

Maguire saw the Cadillac Coupe de Ville in the drive as he turned onto Isla Bahía. He continued past the house, seeing the dead-end ahead at the canal, and came to a stop.

Nowhere to hide. He knew it was Roland's car in the drive: the same one he had watched Roland get in when they came out of the Yankee Clipper, Maguire hanging back so Roland wouldn't see the Mercedes.

He'd see it now. Maybe looking at it out the window right this minute.

Well, he could turn around and get out of here, quick. Or he could go in the house— Didn't we meet someplace before? He didn't know how to play it. He didn't know how Roland would react. But Roland was there and what if right at this moment Karen needed help? Shit. Andre Patterson said he had nerve; but that was going into a place ready, knowing what you were going to do, having a good idea what the reaction would be. This was way different. Goddamn Roland—he didn't know anything about him except he was built like a six and a half foot tree stump and had the hands and the reach and a hide it would be hard to even dent, 'less you hit him with a tire iron. From behind.

He could feel them watching him. Roland and Karen. Shit. He backed up the car, all the way past the drive, and turned in.

Marta's hair was combed but looked wet, like she'd just washed it. Maguire said, "Anybody home?"

"He's here," Marta said.

"I know he is. Where are they?"

"I think you better not come in."

"It's all right," Maguire said. "I'm not gonna hurt him."

Both of them watched Maguire make his entrance, appear and wait to be invited into the living room. Karen by the fireplace, Roland seated in a deep chair with his hat on.

Gretchen came over, sniffed at Maguire's legs and went back to Roland who reached down, giving Gretchen his hand to play with, saying, "You smell the dead fish on him, Gretchie? Huh, do you? Pee-you but it stinks, don't it?"

Karen watched without moving, though she didn't seem tense; her eyes following Gretchen to Roland, then returning to Maguire with a mild expression, Maguire thinking, what if the dog was a test and he had flunked it? Maybe that's what dogs were for. Maybe this was the time, just now, to stoop down and play with Gretchen and try to think of doggie talk. He wondered how Karen was going to handle it, what she'd say—

But it was Roland who invited him in.

"Hey, come on'n sit down. You son of a gun, you knew it was me the other night in the bar, didn't you?" Roland grinned. "You tell her that story about the woman with the parrot?"

"I don't believe he has," Karen said, a little surprised.

Roland waved his arm. "Come on in here and sit down, part-ner."

Maguire walked around to the couch facing the fireplace and eased into it at the end away from Roland. He looked at Karen: her eyes on him but not telling him anything; guarded, or only mildly curious. Then looking at Roland as he spoke.

"This woman had a sick parrot she kep' in the bathroom," Roland said. "Christ, spent weeks nursing it back to health, got it all well again, and the parrot, you know what it did? Tried to get a drink of water in the toilet and drowned."

Karen said, "That's the story?"

"He didn't tell it right," Maguire said. "You don't say the parrot was trying to get a drink."

"What was it doing," Roland said, "taking a piss?"

"No, it's the way the woman told it," Maguire said. "The idea, like this is a moving experience, she's been waiting for somebody to come by so she can tell it. But then when she does, it's at the wrong time. You know what I mean?"

"Christ, I know them women better'n you do."

"I don't doubt that. I'm talking about this particular woman. All alone, nobody to talk to."

"Waiting for somebody to come give 'er a jump," Roland said. "I know exactly what you're talking about. But what do you believe that parrot was doing in the toilet?"

Karen looked from Roland to Maguire.

"I believe it wanted a drink of water," Maguire said, "but that isn't the point."

"If that's what the goddarn parrot wanted, then say it," Roland said. "Otherwise it don't make sense what the parrot was doing in the toilet."

"You tell it your way, I'll tell it mine," Maguire said.

Karen looked from Maguire to Roland.

"Shit yeah, I'll tell it my way," Roland said. "You leave out the best part. Or you could say—yeah, you could say the parrot *was* trying to take a piss and it drowned. That'd make it a better story."

"You miss the whole point," Maguire said.

"Miss the point—you dink, I *lived* out there with those people half my life."

"I believe it," Maguire said.

"What's that mean, that remark?"

"You say you lived out there, I believe it. That's all," Maguire said, looking at the redneck son of a bitch sitting there like it was his house, feet up, playing with the dog. Be cool, Maguire thought. Take it easy. But Karen was watching, and he had to say something else.

He said, "You always wear your hat in the house?"

"You want to say something about it?"

"I asked you a simple question, that's all."

"You want to take it off me?"

"No, I think it looks good on you. Tells what you are."

Black metal tongs and a poker hung at the end of the fireplace behind Karen.

"And what do you say I am?" Roland said.

"Let's see. You wear a range hat and cowboy boots," Maguire said, "and that suit"—aware of Karen listening—"I'd have to guess you're with a circus."

"You guessed it," Roland said, starting to pull himself out of the chair, ignoring Gretchen jumping at his leg. "And you know what I do at the circus?"

Karen could say something now. Right now would be a wonderful time for her to get into it. But Karen watched them without saying a word.

Maguire paused.

Three steps to the black iron poker—if he could get it off the hook in time.

He said, "Let's see. Are you one of the clowns?"

Roland said, "No, I'm not one of the clowns." Standing now, ten feet away. "I'm the Wildman of the Big Swamp, and what I do"—moving toward Maguire now—"I take smartass little dinks that smell of fish and I tear 'em asshole to windpipe and throw 'em away."

Karen said, "Why don't you sit down?" But much too late.

Maguire pushed off the sofa, going for the fireplace. Roland reached him easily, swiveled a hip, caught Maguire in a headlock against his side and held him there. Roland squeezed his hands together to apply pressure, and Maguire gagged, feeling his breath cut off.

"Leave him alone," Karen said, in a mild tone. Maguire hearing it and thinking, Christ *tell* him! Make him! He couldn't move; he tried to push against Roland, tried to reach around to get a grip on the man's hips; but Roland squeezed, and Maguire felt himself grow faint.

"So this here's the porpoise man," Roland said. "Hey, partner, what do you do, play with them porpoises all day? They get you excited, watching 'em? Little shithead comes in here, starts flapping his mouth." Roland held Maguire with one arm around his neck and began to rub the knuckles of his free hand into Maguire's scalp. "Hey, shithead, how's that feel? Give you a knuckle massage. I'll give you a knuckle sandwich I ever see you around here again. How's that feel, huh? Kinda burns, does it?"

Karen said, "That's enough. Stop it."

Roland took hold of Maguire's right arm as he released him and bent the arm up behind Maguire's back, lifting him up, raising his face that was flushed and stung, trying not to yell out but, Christ, his shoulder was about to twist out of place.

"That way," Roland said. "Go on, toward the hall there."

Karen watched, still at the fireplace, remembering something like this from a long, long time ago: Karen Hill watching two seventh grade boys on the school playground. The headlock; the Dutch rub, they called it then; the arm bent behind the back—

"Go on, get your ass out of here." Roland in the hall now, giving Maguire a shove as he released him.

Maguire kept going to the front door. He saw Marta in the doorway that led to the back hall, watching him, sympathetic. Or maybe not. Maybe thinking, So much for him.

Roland called out, "Leave the car!"

Maguire was opening the door when he called again.

"Wait a minute!"

Maguire waited, looking outside at the faint, early evening sunlight, not turning around. Roland came up to him.

"I want to ask you something," Roland said, his tone mild again. "You're over there with them porpoises all the time—you ever see 'em do it?"

"Do what?"

"You know, *do* it."

"Every night," Maguire said.

"No shit, every night, huh? Hey, you suppose I could come over sometime and watch?"

Jesus Diaz said to the woman in the doorway, her TV on loud behind her, "I know he be coming home soon. See, I know where he is. He told me to wait for him."

Aunt Leona said, "It's all right with me if you wait. Sit anywhere you want." Pointing to some old lawn chairs.

"I mean I'm supposed to wait inside his place." In case Roland followed Maguire for some reason, Jesus wasn't going to have Roland see him sitting here at the Casa Loma. He'd go to Cuba right now before he'd let it happen.

"Well, I don't know," Aunt Leona said.

"See, we old friends. I'm not going to steal nothing."

Man, all that to get in his apartment. If it was dark he would have walked in himself. As it turned out it became dark as he sat watching Maguire's black and white TV and drinking some of Maguire's rum. A good-looking girl in a red T-shirt came in. Jesus stood up and said he was waiting for his friend. The good-looking girl said, "Lots of luck," and went out. Finally, when Maguire walked in the door he looked surprised, though more drunk than surprised.

"I saw your two cars at the DiCilia house," Jesus Diaz said. "But you're all right, uh? You want to know who I saw before that?"

Maguire poured himself a rum over ice. "I don't know, do I?"

"I saw Vivian Arzola. I look around Keystone all day. Nothing. I drive to her mother's place in Homestead. There she is."

"That's nice," Maguire said. "Tell the lady. Hold your hand out like this, she'll give you a tip."

"Right away Vivian's scared to death when I see her. I say take it easy, I'm not going to hurt you. I jes want to tell you Mrs. Di-Cilia want to talk to you. She look at me like she don't trust me. Something is strange about her. You know? I leave, but I wait around in my car. Pretty soon she come out with a suitcase. I follow her little foreign car back to Miami to a house on Monegro. You know where I mean? In Coconut Grove, little pink house there. She goes in, a little while later I go up, ring the bell. No answer. Shit, I know she's in there. But what's the matter with her? You listening?" Jesus Diaz looked at Maguire stretched out on the bed now, holding his drink. "I ring the bell again. Nothing. So I open the door with these keys I have, you know? I look through the house. She's hiding in the bedroom, man, in the closet. She say, 'Oh, please don't kill me.' I say, 'What do I want to kill you for?' She say, 'I won't tell, I promise you.' I say, 'You won't tell what?' You listening? We talk some more, talk some more, I'm very nice to her, we talk about our mothers, I tell her I quit the business, I'm going to Cuba. She say, 'I want to go with you.' I say, 'Why?' We talk some more. You know what she's scared of? Of course, Roland. You know why she scared? Hey, you listening? Because she know Roland killed Ed Grossi."

"I'm listening," Maguire said.

# 20

Lesley was saying into the mike, "That little hole there on top of Misty and Gippy's head is called their blowhole. It's just like your nose. If they get water in there they could catch pneumonia, pleurisy, or even drown. So please don't splash them. 'Sides if you do, they're gonna splash everybody back." Pause. "And no one has *ever* won a water fight with a dolphin."

Lesley, Karen decided—walking away from the Porpoise Play Pool—was cute but a little tacky. Probably not too bright, either.

She looked in at the grandstand show pool again, walked around to the refreshment stand and there he was. At a picnic table having coffee.

"Why aren't you working today?"

Maguire looked up. "I'm trying to get fired."

"I think I asked you once before, why don't you quit?"

"Pretty soon."

Karen said, "I'm sorry about yesterday."

"Yeah, I could see, the way you were standing there watching."

"What did you expect me to do, hit him?" Karen sat down at the picnic table. Maguire, stirring his coffee with a plastic stick, didn't look up. Karen watched him. "I just found out something you wouldn't tell me. 'These are Atlantic bottle-nosed dolphins. The porpoise is a much smaller animal, nervous and high strung, practically untrainable,' " Karen said, giving it a little of Lesley's southern Ohio accent. " 'But we call 'em porpoise so you won't get 'em mixed up the the dolphin *fish* you see on menus in some of Florida's finest restaurants. Don't worry though'—you all— 'when you order it, you are not eating Flipper.' You think I could get a job here?"

"Talk to Brad. Tell him you need the money."

"Are we a little pouty today? I thought you handled it pretty well, considering everything. At least you stood up to him."

"I did, huh?"

Karen picked up his coffee and sipped it. "Too much sugar." She put it down again. "I brought the car for you—if you can drive me back."

"What else can I do for you?"

Karen studied him, waiting for him to look at her. "Why're you taking it out on me? There wasn't anything I could do."

"I got the feeling you didn't much care," Maguire said, "one way or the other."

"Would it've helped if I'd screamed, kicked him in the shins?"

"It might've."

"The police were already there once, and did nothing."

"For what? You called them?" Maguire looked up, interested.

"Roland was making a point. That he could hit close to home and the police wouldn't do anything about it. He pretended he was going to rape Marta, and I got excited and called the cops."

"You got excited?" Maguire said.

"I was afraid he was going to hurt her. I didn't know it was an act."

"Then when you realized it," Maguire said, "you were Cool Karen again?"

"What're you trying to say?" She put on a little frown, but it didn't indicate much concern.

"You've got this guy hanging on you," Maguire said, "but you don't seem too worried anymore. Like, so what? What's the big deal? I don't know if you've given up or you don't care."

"Guess what he wants?" Karen said. "He finally said it. Everything, including me."

"See? That's what I'm talking about. You think it's funny or what?"

"He said I'll reach the point where I'll *want* to give him everything, because he'll be my only chance."

"You believe that?"

"Well—he's got more confidence than anyone I've ever met."

"He's got more bullshit, and that's what he's giving you. He's gonna look for the opening, set you up and take whatever he can. And if you're laying there with your head broken, that's tough shit."

"He likes me."

"He may, but that's got nothing to do with it."

"But you see, his self-confidence, that's the flaw," Karen said, leaning closer over the table. "What does he base it on? Not much. There's considerably less to Mr. Roland Crowe than he realizes. Watching you two yesterday—you know what it was like? Two little boys showing off in front of a girl. Arguing about the parrot—I couldn't believe it."

"You didn't get it."

"No, I assumed you were putting him on, but he was serious. I'd look at Roland. *This* is the one who's giving me trouble? I thought of something Ed Grossi told me once, about being concerned with people who turn out to be lightweights."

"Ed Grossi," Maguire said. "He told you that, huh? You want some more advice?"

"What?"

"Forget Ed Grossi's advice. Talk to Vivian Arzola."

Roland said to Lionel Oliva, "How can you live in this dump? Goddamn place ain't any bigger'n a horse trailer."

"We manage."

"Get her out of here."

Lionel turned to the woman cooking something for him on the tiny stove. She edged past them without looking at Roland and stepped out of the trailer. Roland bent down to watch her through the window—big Cuban ass sliding from side to side as she walked out of Tall Pines toward S.W. Eighth Street.

"You want the boat?" Lionel Oliva said. "Take somebody out?"

"Not just yet." Roland straightened up, making a face as he looked at Lionel. "You drink too much, you know it?"

"I like to drink sometime, sure."

"You like to live in this stink?"

"I don't smell nothin'."

"Jesus, look at the place. You work for me, you're gonna have to clean yourself up."

"I work for you know?"

"I want you to see if you can find Vivian Arzola. Her and you both used to pick oranges, didn't you?"

"Man, a long time ago."

"Well, go look up some of your old buddies still around. See if anybody's seen her lately."

"How come I work for you now," Lionel Oliva said, "you don't get Jesus?"

"He went to Cuba, you dink. You were sitting there when he told me."

"No, he never went to Cuba. I see him talking to a guy in Centro Vasco yesterday."

"You see him again, tell him to call me," Roland said. "Tell him I don't hear from him and run into him on the street, I'll bust his little bow legs and wrap 'em around his dink head."

Roland got out of that smelly house trailer. He'd look around some for Vivian; stop in and see Karen, make her day a little brighter. First, though, he was going to go home and pick up a firearm to carry on him or keep in the car. There was too much going on now not to be ready for what you might least expect.

Vivian Arzola said to Jesus, when he returned in the morning, "I have to think about it."

"Think about what? She wants to help you."

"How? All I do is endanger myself telling somebody else."

"Trust her," Jesus said.

"All right, but only Mrs. DiCilia. If she brings police, I don't know anything."

"Her and one other, a friend that's helping her. This is his idea, but I can't tell you anything else."

"You can't tell me, I'm supposed to tell him everything. All right, the two of them. And you," Vivian said. "Any more, I have to rent chairs. You see what they do to this place? Sneak out before the first of the month, leave all this crap. Look at the condition, the dirt. Five years I've owned this place, I've never made any money."

"What time?" Jesus said.

"Late, after it's dark. I don't know, nine o'clock. You drop them off—what kind of car?"

"I don't know yet."

"Forget the whole thing," Vivian said.

"Wait, let me think. Gray Mercedes-Benz."

"You drop them off. I don't want the car in front."

"What else?"

"Tell them I'm not going to the police. If that's what they want, they're wasting their time. No police in this. I see a policeman, I don't know anything you're talking about."

"If you say it. Anything else?"

"A gun," Vivian said.

"What kind?"

"What kind, one that shoots. I don't care what kind. A big one."

"Take it easy," Jesus said. "You got nothing to worry about."

# 21

Jesus, driving the Mercedes, dropped them off in front of the pink stucco house on Monegro Avenue within a minute or so of nine o'clock, telling them he would drive around and come back at exactly 9:30.

Maguire wondered if all this was necessary: like synchronizing their watches, everyone very grim, Karen wearing dark glasses—why? So who wouldn't recognize her?—but he didn't say anything. Or comment, make a harmless smart remark about Vivian letting them in with the lights off, taking them back to the kitchen and closing the door to the hall before turning on the kitchen light. Maguire was glad he'd kept quiet. Even seeing Vivian for the first time—not anything like the stylish woman Karen had described in the car—Maguire realized how frightened she was. Vivian looked like she had been on a drunk for several days; combed her hair maybe, but had forgotten about makeup. For the

first few minutes they were in the kitchen, he had never seen anyone so tense. Maguire poured the coffee. He lighted three cigarettes for Vivian, while she told them about driving Ed Grossi to
Boca Raton and seeing Roland and barely getting away from him.

"Why won't you go to the police?" Karen asked her.

Vivian said, "Because he'll kill me. Why do you think?"

"But he'll be in jail."

"He'll be out on bond, he won't be in jail."

"Well—the police will protect you."

"Excuse me," Vivian said, "but I worked for Ed Grossi twelve
years. If they want a person dead, the person's dead. This is what
Roland does, it's his job."

Karen said, "To kill people?"

Maguire watched her. She seemed more fascinated by the idea
than startled or shocked.

Vivian said, "Yes, of course. He can go to prison and pay somebody else to do it. Or, if he wants to himself bad enough, he waits
till he gets out. Don't you know that? They convict him, I have a
nice time for ten years. Then what?"

"They've charged someone else with his murder," Karen said.

"Arnold Rapp, I know that," Vivian said. "It's too bad, but I'm
not giving my life for Arnold Rapp."

"It's almost nine-thirty," Maguire said.

Karen, seated close to Vivian, looked up from the kitchen table.
"Why don't you go with him? Come back at ten."

Why? What were they going to talk about? He couldn't see
Karen's eyes behind the glasses. She sat in the dirty kitchen of the
house on Monegro in the Cuban quarter working something out.
As though she did this all the time.

Maguire went out to the curb and got in the Mercedes as it
came to a stop.

"Where is she?"

"We come back in a half hour."

Jesus drove off. "I went up to Eighth Street. I saw a guy there
he say Roland's looking for me. Shit. Man, I got to go to Cuba or
do something."

Maguire didn't say anything, looking at the people sitting in
front of their houses and the ones on the sidewalk watching the
silver-gray Mercedes-Benz driving by.

"What do you think about Vivian?" Jesus said.

"I think she's scared."

"No, I mean do you think she'd pay us something? Why not, uh?"

They picked up Karen at 10. Maguire slid behind the wheel and Jesus got in back as far as S.W. Eighth, where they dropped him off. Maguire cut over to 95 and headed north to Lauderdale. Karen had taken off her glasses. She sat holding them, silent.

"Well?" Maguire said.

Karen didn't say anything.

"What else you find out?"

"Nothing, really."

"She still won't go to the police."

"The day Roland dies, she will. If the other man is still in prison. He kills people," Karen said.

"You mean Roland."

"Yeah. He kills people."

Maguire said, "Do you want me to stay with you tonight?"

Karen took a long time to answer. She said, "Not tonight, okay? I'd like to do some quiet thinking."

"That's the only kind," Maguire said, keeping it light, but feeling a little hook inside him. Something was going on.

They drove in silence; left the freeway and headed east toward the ocean through light evening traffic, across the 17th Street Causeway and past Seascape, Maguire's other world, dark. Maguire picturing the dolphins by themselves, surfacing in moonlight within their pools and tanks.

He said to Karen, "When I worked at the dolphin place down on Marathon, ten years ago—I didn't tell you, did I, I got arrested for willful destruction of property?"

Karen didn't say anything.

"You listening?"

"You were arrested for willful destruction of something."

"The fences," Maguire said. "They didn't have tanks down there, they had wire fences built out from the shore and the breakwater. Like pens they kept the dolphins in. Different pens that were attached to each other. One night I went out there with some tinsnips and cut the fences."

Karen said, "You freed the dolphins?"

"Yeah. They swam out to sea."

"That's remarkable." She kept looking at him now.

"Unh-unh, the remarkable thing," Maguire said, "as soon as they got hungry they all came back to the pens and never left again. . . They didn't want to be saved. They just wanted to play games."

# 22

Jesus Diaz was taking his suit and some pants to the dry cleaner, getting ready for his trip, whenever it was going to be. He was walking past the place on the corner of Eighth Street and Forty-second Avenue that gave spiritual readings and advice, when the car turned the corner, stopped hard, and the voice said, "Hey!"

Jesus almost dropped the clothes and took off. But it was Lionel Oliva motioning him to come over to the car.

"I thought you went to Cuba."

"Pretty soon."

"I got your job. Man, it's a lot of work."

"Keep it," Jesus said.

"What's he want with Vivian Arzola?" Lionel asked.

Jesus moved in closer, stuck his head in the window, resting his clothes against the dusty car.

"He's looking for her?"

"He came to the trailer yesterday, insulted me, then hired me to find her. What does the pimp give you for a job like this?"

"Different amounts. What he feels like," Jesus said. "You have any luck?"

"That's what it was," Lionel said. "You know she owns some houses to rent. I was talking to this guy used to know her, lives in the Grove. He said yeah, this house of Vivian's on Monegro was vacant for a month. But then he saw a light on, and he thinks he saw her go in there the other day. So I went over, I look in the window. There she is in the hall, going into the kitchen or someplace. I knock on the door, no answer."

"She probably don't want to see anybody," Jesus said.

"Stuck up, owning all those houses," Lionel said. "Fuck that, I'm not going to bother with her."

"I wouldn't," Jesus said.

"Let Roland see if he can talk to her."

"You tell him yet?"

"Yeah, I just called him a few minutes ago."

Ten-fifteen, another fifteen minutes before show time, Brad Allen was addressing his "gang"—Lesley, Robyn, Hooker, Chuck, and Maguire—sitting around on the lower grandstand benches, while Brad, in pure white, stood between them and the pool. The main-show dolphins would surface and watch them from the holding pens along the side. Brad half-turned to point across the pool to the deck that served as the stage.

"What we'll do, we'll light some paper in some kind of shallow metal container. Maguire, you'll still be backstage. Wait there after the intro. So you'll ring the firebell."

Seascape opened at ten. There were people on the grounds already looking around, coming past the roped-off grandstand area and looking in, wondering what all those kids in the red T-shirts were doing sitting there. No, they weren't all kids, were they?

Robyn said, "Brad, it's a dynamite idea, but do you light the paper, and you're the one that yells fire?"

"No, you're right," Brad said. "*You* light the paper. That's good thinking, Rob. And I'll be distracting the audience, my back turned to you."

Maguire saw Jesus Diaz approach the chain across the entrance and the sign hanging from it that said: THIS AREA CLOSED

UNTIL SHOW TIME, Jesus looking at the sign and then looking in anxiously at the group sitting in the grandstand. Maguire raised his arm. He stood up.

"Sit down," Brad said.

"I got to talk to that guy for a minute."

The others were turning to look up at Maguire and then over to the Cuban waiting by the chain.

"Sit down till we get this straightened out," Brad said. "I turn around, I see it and yell, 'Fire!' Cue for the firebell. No, wait'll I say, 'This is a job for Smokey the Dolphin.' Yeah. Then ring the bell. Then Hooker? You've got the hat on Dixie, right?"

"Right," Hooker said.

"Maguire, sit down."

"I just have to see the guy a minute."

"When we're through," Brad said. "Okay, Hooker—you give Dixie the signal."

"Right."

"She comes over, gives a couple of tail flaps—"

Maguire was staring at Jesus, trying to read his mind.

"—and puts out the fire."

"He knows where she is!" Jesus called out to him.

Maguire was moving.

"Where you going? . . . Maguire!"

Brad and the "gang" watched him hurdle the chain—brush the sign with his foot, causing it to jiggle—and take off with the Cuban.

"Any idea where he's going?" Brad asked.

"He probably don't know himself," Lesley said. "He's weird."

Virginia Hill was really Virginia Hauser, or Virginia Hill Hauser; but no one referred to her by that name. She was Virginia Hill, who told the Kefauver Crime Committee in 1951 that men kept giving her money because they were friends. Period. She didn't know exactly how much she had. Yes, she knew Bugsy Siegel, he was one of the friends. No, she didn't know what he did for a living.

Karen wore a white scarf over her hair (tied in back), sunglasses, and a beige and blue striped caftan that reached to the brick surface of the patio.

She said to the feature writer from the *Goldcoaster*, a pleasant, nice-looking but unyielding girl by the name of Tina Noor, "I was Karen Hill much longer than I was Karen Stohler or Karen DiCilia, that's all I'm trying to say. I think of myself as Karen Hill." And only thinking about the other Hill, not mentioning her. "How do you think of yourself?"

"As Tina Noor."

"You're married."

"Yeah."

"But you don't think of yourself, ever, as who you used to be?"

"Yeah, but that's exactly the point. I'm not really that person anymore."

"Well, we're different," Karen said. "You want to sell magazines, and I want to maintain my identity. Karen Hill. Don't you think it sounds better?"

"It's a nice name," Tina Noor said, "but no one knows who Karen Hill is."

"I do."

"I mean everyone's familiar with Karen DiCilia. You were in the papers again when Ed Grossi was killed. People are interested in what you think about . . . what it's liked to be associated with those people and live a normal life."

"A normal life," Karen said.

She moved to the umbrella table, reached into a straw beachbag and brought out a pack of cigarettes. Tina's eyes remained on the bag, lying on its side, open now. She looked at Karen lighting the cigarette, Karen sitting down in one of the deck chairs. Tina's eyes returned to the straw bag.

She said, "Is that a gun in there? In the bag?"

Karen nodded.

"Can I ask why you have it?"

"Why does anyone have a gun?" Karen said.

"I mean, of course for protection; but do you feel for some reason your life might be in danger?"

"I'm Karen Hill, I was born in Detroit, Grosse Pointe. I'm forty-four. I was married to Frank DiCilia five and a half years. I never asked him what he did. I never asked him why he had a gun. That particular gun, as a matter of fact." Karen paused. "But now I know."

"Would you tell me?"

Karen drew on the cigarette, the smoke dissolving in the afternoon glare. Karen seemed unaffected by the heat, though she was perspiring beneath the caftan, and when the writer left she'd go in the pool . . . come out, shower, it would be time for cocktails. Wait for someone to come.

She said, "Until Ed Grossi's death, I hadn't had a cigarette in sixteen years."

Tina waited. "You feel the need?"

"It's something to do."

"Are you . . . in good health?"

"Why do you ask?"

"I don't know, I just wondered. You seem a little tired."

"Or bored," Karen said. "In a way, bored. In another way—well, that's something else."

"What is?"

"Why don't you ask what my hobbies are?"

"What're your hobbies?"

"I don't have any."

"Well, what do you do all day?"

"Nothing."

"You have friends—"

"Are you asking?"

"Yeah, don't you have friends?"

Karen drew on the cigarette, looked at it and let it drop to the brick surface.

"Not really."

"Well, why don't you go out more, do things? Travel maybe."

"There are reasons," Karen said.

"What reasons?"

"I told you you weren't going to get much of a story. I don't know why you insisted."

"Because something's going on," Tina said, "and I think if you had just a little more confidence in me you might tell what it is."

"It has nothing to do with confidence."

"All right, trust. I promise I won't write anything you don't want revealed."

"*Revealed,*" Karen said. "That's exactly the kind of word I don't want to see. Karen DiCilia's Secret Revealed."

"I don't know why I used it," Tina said, sitting forward in her chair, feeling close to something and forgetting her casual-re-porter pose. "It's a written word, but it's really not the kind I use.

I'm interested in your point of view, how you feel about things, rather than your effect on me. If you know what I mean."

"What is what? How do you see me?"

"Well, I'm not sure. I mean I haven't made any judgments. Right away I think of those words again. Karen DiCilia's Secret *Not* Revealed. A very smashing-looking woman who keeps to herself, has a gun—".

"Don't mention that."

"Isn't exactly hiding but seems watchful, guarded, quietly aware of something going on she won't talk about. You must realize you've got everybody wondering about you."

Karen didn't say anything. She sat with her legs crossed, one slender hand touching the side of her sunglasses.

"All right, if I do a Karen Hill rather than a Karen DiCilia," Tina said, "do you have any early pictures of yourself?"

"I may have," Karen said. "I'd have to look."

A woman by the name of Epifania Cruz, forty-two, had given her daughter and son-in-law a wooden chair that was over two hundred years old and originally from Andalucia. The chair and baby Alicia, her daughter, were brought to Miami from Cuba the night of April 27, 1961, following the defeat at the Bay of Pigs.

It was a low straight chair, more like a three-legged stool with a back support. Epifania gave it to Alicia and her son-in-law with apprehension because he was one of those who dressed like a disco dancer and spent his time at the Centro Español even though he never had a job. Epifania was in Abbey Hospital because of a problem with her colon, when she learned Alicia and her son-in-law, the pimp, had moved away quickly, getting out before they were taken to court, and had left much of what they owned in their rented home on Monegro Avenue.

Nearly a month had passed; but maybe the chair was still in the house. Epifania was told no one else had moved into it. Maybe she'd be lucky.

She went there at night. If she found the chair and carried it away, she didn't want people to see her even though she considered the chair her own property. She brought with her a large kitchen knife to use to pry open the door, but found she didn't have to. The door was unlocked.

With the street light shining in the window, Epifania could see well enough. The chair wasn't in the living room. It wasn't in the kitchen. She opened the door to the bedroom and stood in the opening. It was too dark back there to see anything. She raised her hand holding the kitchen knife, reaching for the light switch. There was an explosion and Epifania was blown back into the hall, almost to the kitchen.

Roland came out of the bedroom with the 12-gauge pump-action shotgun under his arm, reached into the kitchen to turn on the light and looked down at the woman.

He said, "Shit. You ain't Vivian."

# 23

Maguire said to Lesley, "Just tell him I'm whacked out, probably coming down with something."

"I don't wonder," Lesley said. "The three of you get it on at one time, or you and the guy take turns? Hey, is he Andre?"

"Yeah, it's Andre," Maguire said, "and his wife. We haven't seen each other in a while, so I want to take the day off, spend some time with 'em."

"He just loaned you his car a week ago, didn't he?"

"Hey, Lesley," Maguire said, "you're gonna be late for work. Tell him, okay?"

"Brad's pissed at you anyway for not coming back yesterday. He's gonna want to know where you went."

Maguire reached the end right there. He said, "Tell him whatever you want. I don't give a shit."

"Ca-al!"

She never called him Cal. Did she? What difference did it make? He went into his apartment, leaving Lesley standing by her yellow Honda. (The Mercedes was parked two blocks away.)

Jesus, hunched in front of the television set, adjusting the picture, said, "Look, the house on Monegro." A covered human form on an ambulance stretcher was being carried down the front steps as the voice-over newscaster described the mysterious shooting, the murder of a woman named Epifania Cruz. The newscaster said the police were now looking for the woman's daughter and son-in-law, the last tenants of the house.

Vivian Arzola, holding a coffeepot, watched from the stove. She said, "You know what it's like?" Neither Maguire nor Jesus looked at her, watching the woman's body being lifted into the van now. "Like in a movie, the people run out of the house, they reach safety just in time and the house blows up."

They were looking at a commercial now. When Maguire realized it he turned off the television set. Next thing they'd be watching Dinah Shore and Merv Griffin. He said, "We got to do it tonight. Figure out how and set it up—"

"If we're sure we're gonna do it," Jesus said.

They had gotten Vivian out of the house on Monegro yesterday. They weren't going to sit around here or take her from place to place. Vivian had said she wanted to get far away from here. It wasn't worth it, looking over her shoulder all the time. She had to go someplace else.

"It's *how* we do it, not *if*," Maguire said. "It's got to be at the DiCilia house."

"Why?" Jesus said.

"Because the police were there already"—Maguire speaking quietly, wanting Jesus to relax and listen—"when Roland tried to grab your sister. Okay, he comes to try again, armed, huh? Only this time we're there. You're defending your sister, you shoot him."

"*Me?* I though you were gonna shoot him."

"One or the other," Maguire said. "You know how to fire a gun, don't you?"

"Sure, I know that. But I never shot at anybody."

"Let's talk about—first, how do we get him there?" Maguire said. "He comes because he thinks Vivian's in the house."

"You're crazy you think I'm going there," Vivian said.

"You don't have to go there. I'm saying he thinks you're there because we get him to believe it. Like, say I call you from there later. I say, 'Okay, Vivian, it's all set. We'll pick you up, you spend the night here and take you to the police first thing in the morning.' You say something, he hears your voice, he knows it's you."

"I don't understand," Vivian said, then began to nod. "Yeah, the tap on the phone. I can't even think straight."

"What if he don't?" Jesus said. "If he's busy looking for Vivian and he don't listen to it?"

"I don't know," Maguire said, wondering if he had to tell Karen about it and not wanting to. Though if they had to wait around a few days until Roland picked up the tape—it might turn out he'd have to tell her. But he didn't want to bring her into it. He wanted to get it done and present her with it. There, the guy's off your back. Making it look, not easy exactly, but not too hard either. There. You have any other problems?

He said to Jesus, "What's the guy's name working for him?"

"Lionel Oliva."

"Okay, you tell Lionel you know where Vivian is. You say you found out Vivian's gonna be there tonight. Your sister told you."

"What if he asks why I'm telling him?" Jesus said. "He knows I won't do any favor for Roland."

"Tell him—what if you tell him you're setting Roland up for somebody?"

"Then what's Lionel get out of it? He says bullshit. If he tells Roland and Roland gets taken out, who's gonna pay him?"

"You tell him you'll pay him," Maguire said. "What's it worth to him?"

"He's gonna be scared. You miss, the first one Roland go sees is Lionel, knowing he was set up."

"How about a grand?"

"You kidding? He'd do it himself for a grand."

"And get some more stitches in his head," Maguire said. "I've seen Lionel. *That* Lionel? No, we do it. But he sets it up. All he has to do, tell Roland he knows Vivian's gonna be there tonight. That's all he knows. He heard it from you and you told him not to tell anybody, acting very mysterious about it. You think he can do it?"

"Yeah, he can do that."

"And act dumb?"

"Easy," Jesus said.

"Then Roland gets the tape, hears Vivian's voice, he knows it's true. Even if he doesn't get the tape, he's got to go find out after Lionel tells him. But it's better if he does, because then he hears Vivian's voice, hears she's going to the police—it's much better that way. We don't want Lionel telling him all that and mess it up."

Jesus said, "Okay, but what gun do we use? I don't want to use mine, have to get rid of it after."

"No, we don't get rid of it," Maguire said. "That's what I've been talking about. We call the cops, we have to have a gun to show 'em, right?"

"You want to call the cops?"

Jesus, Maguire thought. He said, "Look. The guy comes in to rape your sister. You shoot him. *Some*body shoots him. You don't throw his body in the Intercoastal, you call the cops and give 'em the gun. That's what you *do*. Okay, then Vivian reads about it in the paper. Roland Crowe killed in rape attempt. Vivian goes to the police, tells 'em she knows Roland killed Ed Grossi. The police let the other guy go."

"I'm telling you, he better be dead," Vivian said, "or I don't say a word to them, not even my name."

"He'll be dead," Maguire said. He looked at Jesus. "You don't want to use your gun—okay, tell your sister there's a gun upstairs in Karen's bedroom, top dresser drawer. Tell her to sneak it out of there, bring it down to her room. We slip in the house after dark, she gives it to us. It was Frank DiCilia's gun. They want to bust somebody for possession they can dig up Frank. But bring your own anyway, just in case."

"Then what?" Jesus said. "He comes in—when do we do it?"

"That part, we'll have to wait and see," Maguire said.

Karen watched him coming out from the house. She stood at the shallow end of the pool drying herself lightly with a beach towel. He was putting on his sunglasses now, taking her all in.

"Do you really have that much nerve," Karen said, "or're you showing off?"

"What nerve?"

"Using the phone. You know he's going to hear it. You disguise your voice or what?"

"He's got to do more'n hear me, he's got to catch me."

"Who were you calling?"

"The guy I work for. Find out if I still have a job."

"Does it matter?"

"Well, I guess I'd rather quit than be fired. But I don't feel like working. He was busy, so I still don't know."

"I can't imagine you being worried about it," Karen said, "the job."

"I'm not worried, I want to know how he feels."

Karen said, "I saw the news this morning ... the house. Strange, the woman wasn't Vivian."

"No, we got her out of there. I forgot to tell you."

"Something's going on," Karen said. "In fact I think there's quite a lot you haven't told me."

Maguire watched her walk to the table to get something out of a straw bag. The slim brown body. Effortless moves. The quiet tone. He'd bet she drove a car fast and without effort; he saw the two of them, briefly, in the white Alfa Romeo heading for southern Spain.

He said, "I've been thinking the same thing. Like you know something you're not telling."

"What's Karen DiCilia's secret," Karen said. "Read the latest speculation in next month's *Goldcoaster*. Though this one's going to be on Karen Hill."

"Who's she?" Maguire said.

"Who knows," Karen said.

"You going out tonight?"

"Like where?"

He wanted to say to her, It won't be long; hang on. But said, "I'll see you later then, okay?"

"Fine. Anytime."

He left Karen in her backyard world putting on sunglasses, lighting a cigarette. Maguire walked up S.E. Seventeenth toward the beach, where he'd left the Mercedes. He wondered if she did know something she wasn't telling. He wondered about the photos of her in the locked room. When this was over he'd ask her about them.

Was she lighting a cigarette when he left?

He wondered when she had started smoking. Maybe he hadn't been paying attention lately, looking but overlooking, missing something.

Karen had a glass of distilled water from the refrigerator. She left Marta in the kitchen cleaning vegetables for dinner. Moving along the back hall, Karen paused, looked around, stepped into Marta's room and quietly closed the door. The cassette recorder was still beneath the bed, with a box of cassette cartridges. Karen brought them out, hunching down on her elbows and knees. She changed the setting from "Record" to "Rewind," stopped it, pushed the "Play" button and within a few moments heard Maguire's voice.

"Vivian? Hi, it's all set. We'll pick you up at eleven-thirty and bring you right here. Then first thing in the morning we go to Miami."

Vivian's voice said, "I'm so afraid he's going to find me. I can't eat, I can't sleep. God, I can't *think.*"

Maguire's voice said, "Tomorrow it'll be over. The Miami Police'll pick him up, you identify him, that's it."

Vivian's voice said, "I'll be so glad when it's over."

Maguire's voice said, "Eleven-thirty, Vivian. See you then."

Karen played the tape back and listened to it again, twice.

She was surprised, puzzled.

Then annoyed.

Karen ejected the tape cartridge. Holding it in her hand, she got a blank cartridge from the box, snapped the new one in positon and pushed the recorder and the box back under Marta's bed.

# 24

Karen bathed and dressed. She had a martini in the living room while she watched the news. At a quarter to seven she went into the kitchen carrying a handbag and the keys to Frank's Seville, in the garage.

Marta looked at her, surprised. "I was going to ask if you're ready for dinner."

"I'm sorry, I thought I told you," Karen said, "I'm having dinner out." She looked at the salad greens drying on the counter. "You haven't started anything yet, have you?"

"No—" She seemed to want to say more.

"What's the matter?"

"I don't want to be alone," Marta said, "if Roland comes."

"I thought your brother picks up the tape."

"Remember, I tole you he doesn't do it anymore."

"Well, it's up to you," Karen said. "But if you don't want to open the door when he comes, then don't."

"That wouldn't stop him."

"Maybe not. It seems funny, though, to be offering you advice," Karen said. "I tried to help you before. You had a chance to have him arrested and you didn't."

"Of course. For the same reason I don't want to be alone with him. I'm scared, I don't know what to do."

"And I don't know what to tell you," Karen said. "You're afraid to let him in and you're afraid not to."

"I wish things would be the same, the way it used to be," Marta said.

"Wouldn't it be nice," Karen said. "So, are you going to give him the tape?"

"I guess so."

Karen jiggled her keys, getting the one for the Seville ready. She said, "Well, I have to go," but remained by the kitchen table, looking at Marta. "I think what I would do, I'd leave the tape for him outside the door and get away from here for a while. Maybe a few days. You know? Instead of putting yourself in the middle of something that really doesn't concern you."

"Leave here?"

"Why not? What's anyone done for you lately?"

Just in time.

Roland wheeled his Coupe de Ville into the drive as Marta was backing out, saw her brakelights flash, and, before she knew it, was pressed against her rear bumper.

Out of the car Roland said, "Hey, don't leave on my account. Where we going?" He looked toward the open garage doors and at the house, up at the second-floor windows, as though he might catch someone watching him.

Roland picked up the envelope with his name on it—RO-LAND, in big blue letters—from the steps and moved aside to let Marta unlock the door.

"There's nobody home," she said.

"Don't look like it," Roland said. "I ain't gonna play house with you today, sugar, I want to use your telephone." He dialed the one in the kitchen, waited, said, "Son of a bitch," and hung up. "Where's Karen at?"

"She went out to dinner."

"Who with?"

"Nobody. Alone."

" 'Less she's meeting him, huh? Let's go in your bedroom and listen to this one," Roland said, holding up the envelope. "Many calls today?"

"Only a few," Marta said.

Minutes later, in Marta's room, after playing the tape and hearing nothing, Roland said, "I'd say that's less than a few. Or else this here's the wrong one."

"I took it out of the machine," Marta said.

"And I know you wouldn't lie to me," Roland said, straightening up from the recorder on the chair, standing close to Marta, the bed behind her. "Would you?"

"I have no reason to lie," she said.

"You got a nice body, you know it?"

Marta stood rigid, her head turned away from his chest.

"But I don't have time just now to make you happy. Your tough luck," Roland said, going into the kitchen. He picked up the wall phone and dialed again.

This time he said, "You dink, where you been?"

Lionel's voice said, "I was in the toilet a minute."

"Drinking beer—how many you have?"

"I'm sitting here, I have to do something," Lionel's voice said, the sound of a salsa beat behind him.

"Hang on a sec." Roland looked at Marta. "Go on out in the living room." He waited until she was in the hall before saying to Lionel, "Get in your boat and bring it up to Bahía Mar."

Lionel's voice said, "Man, it's gonna be dark soon."

"I hope so," Roland said. "I'll meet you there by the gas pumps in about a hour." He started to hang up, then said, "Hey, Jesus say his sister told him or what?"

"No, he didn't say anything about his sister," Lionel's voice said. "He say it was Vivian."

Roland held the phone away from him, away from the Caribbean jukebox music behind Lionel. Sure as hell—the sound of a car starting up outside, revving up, then banging something and a terrible sound of metal scraping metal.

"Shit," Roland said. "You be there." He banged the phone into its cradle and ran out of the kitchen to the side door.

Marta had her car turned around on the lawn; she cut across the drive and was screeching away, leaving the front left fender of Roland's Coupe De Ville all torn to hell.

The Palm Bay waiter said to Karen, "The gentleman at the bar would like to join you for a drink, if he may."

Karen looked from the booth she was in to a man with gray-styled hair and a paisley jacket. Half-turned from the bar he raised his drink to her.

"Does he know my name?" Karen said.

"Oh, yes. He said, 'Ask Mrs. DiCilia.' "

"Tell him he's mistaken," Karen said.

The waiter smiled. "You don't want a drink with him?"

"I said tell him he's mistaken."

"Very good," the waiter said.

When the man with the gray-styled hair came over, Karen said, "I don't know you. I don't intend to. Would you go away, please?"

"If you're alone, no harm in having a drink, a nice chat—"

"Beat it," Karen said. She stared up at him until he mumbled, "Sorry," and went back to the bar.

See? Nothing to it.

The look was important. Icy calm, unwavering; the tone quiet, somewhat bored. Maybe a little more work on the tone, keeping the voice low.

Maybe another one would come along. The rescuers—

The Maguires.

Maguire was going to stick his neck out all the way, showing off, and never be heard of again. The natural-born loser. She could try to prevent it, within reason; but if he insisted on playing the rescuer, then she'd have to let him. Karen Hill DiCilia was at the Palm Bay Club the night it happened. Or she was home, but it wasn't exactly clear what had happened, Karen Hill's part in it. Karen Hill seemed cooperative. Yes, she knew the deceased, was acquainted with him. But Karen Hill obviously knew more than she was telling.

The waiter came over and said, "If I may disturb you, please. The gentleman at the table by the window—"

Karen looked over. "Does he know my name?"

\* \* \*

584

Marta drove all the way to Jesus' apartment on Alhambra, Coral Gables, and got in after she proved to the manager she was Jesus' sister and not some girl who wanted to rip him off. God, all the things there were to go through and worry about—walking back and forth in Jesus' living room, walking to the kitchen, walking to the front window, looking out at the street and the cars going by, some with their lights on already, the time passing so fast, rushing her and not giving her a chance to think. She got the phone number form her purse, the Casa Loma, and dialed, then had to wait as the phone rang at least twenty times. When the woman answered, Marta asked if she could please speak to her brother, the man visiting Mr. Maguire. Marta could hear sounds of voices talking and an audience laughing, applauding on the phone, having a good time, as she waited again.

When Jesus was on the phone she said, "I left there. I'm not going back."

"Where are you?"

"I'm at your place, but I'm leaving here, too."

"Did Roland come?"

"Did he come—he was gonna take my clothes off again and I ran out. I'm not going back."

"Calm yourself," Jesus said. "I can't hear you very well, this TV playing;"

"I'm not going back there," Marta said.

"You have to be in the house," Jesus said. "You understand you have to be there."

"What is it to me," Marta said, "or you? It's none of our business. What do we get out of it?"

"Listen, stay there," Jesus said. "I'll come soon as I can, and we'll talk about it. All right?"

"I'm gonna have to go get her," Jesus said to Maguire.

"Did he pick up the tape?"

"Yeah, but he tried something, so she ran out and went to my place. She'll be all right."

"You sure?"

"If I take Vivian's car"—looking at Vivian on the bed with the newspaper on her lap, watching them—"I can go get Marta, talk to her first. See, then bring her to the house and meet you there. Take maybe an hour, a little more."

585

"Did she put the gun in her room?"

"I didn't ask her, but I know she did."

Maguire didn't like it. He said, "Call Marta back. Have her come here."

"She won't. I have to talk to her first. Then everything be all right."

"You can't drive up to the house in Vivian's car."

"No, we leave it at my place, take Marta's. Roland comes, sees Marta's car, he thinks oh, she's back. Good."

Maguire said to Vivian, "Is it okay with you?"

"What do I have to say about it? Nothing," Vivian said. "All I want to know is he's dead."

"All right," Maguire said to Jesus. "But you got to get back by nine-thirty, quarter to ten, the latest."

"Easy," Jesus said. "Don't worry."

# 25

Maguire's plan was coming apart.

An hour ago it had seemed close to foolproof. Drop in on Karen, sit around till about ten. Say he was tired or didn't feel good and leave. Park up by the beach and walk back. Marta lets him in the side door. He and Jesus wait in Marta's room for Roland to come. Let him enter the house. Say hi, how you doing? Marta screams (optional). Hit him.

But Marta was in Coral Gables, and Jesus had to talk to her and get her back.

And Karen wasn't home. The house was dark, the three-car garage empy.

He could say to himself, No, it's going to work. Don't worry. Keep your eyes open. You see it's not going to work or too chancy, bail out. You don't *have* to be here.

But reassurances didn't relieve the bad feeling, the doubt beginning to nag him.

Maguire drove the Mercedes into the garage, closed the door from the outside and walked around the house, past the empty patio to the French doors.

There was some definition to the shapes in the darkness: the hedges, the pool, the umbrella table, the yard misty in a pale wash of moonlight. There were specks of moving light on the Intercoastal, the deep darkness beyond the yard. There was the sound of crickets. And now Gretchen barking, inside the house. There was no reason to be as quiet as he might be. Maguire pulled the sleeve of his jacket down over his hand, held it in his fist, punched through the pane of glass next to the door latch and he was inside, Gretchen running up to him, barking.

Moving through the sitting room, his hand feeling the crown of the Louis XVI chair, he told Gretchen to be nice and wondered: If Karen knew she was coming home after dark, why didn't she leave a light on?

Because Marta must've still been home.

Then why didn't Marta tell them Karen had gone out? If she did, why didn't Jesus mention it?

Because they had no practice in this kind of thing, that's why, Maguire thought. And you better get your ass out of here.

But he moved from the front hall to the back hall to Marta's room, pulled down the shades and turned on a lamp. Okay, Jesus had said yes, he *knew* Marta had gotten the gun from upstairs. But where would she hide it.

Roland said to Lionel, "Look, I ain't gonna argue with you. Go on get drunk, sleep on the beach, I don't give a shit where, and pick up the boat in the morning. Now hand the suitcase here and push me off, goddamn it." Man, to get through to some people.

The eighteen-footer rumbled away from the dock behind the thin beam of its spotlight, passing the fantails of the motorcruisers and sailers tied up in their slips, heading out into the channel now, Roland keeping the revs low, bearing to starboard as he pictured the map of the Intercoastal, this little section of it. Finding his way through canals and watercourses, natural or manmade, wasn't anything new. Across the Harborage and where it opened up at the river—hearing a cruiser honking at the drawbridge down there—head for the second point of land and the house sitting there. He figured about a five-minute ride. There were support stanchions along the seawall; he'd tie up to one of them. In the meantime—wedging a hip against the wheel and zipping open the canvas suitcase—he'd get his twelve-gauge put together.

It took Maguire nearly ten minute of looking through every drawer, the closet, and the bed to convince himself the gun, the one Jesus *knew* was in the room, wasn't.

Andre Patterson would look at him and shake his head, Man, the people you associate with. Say to Andre, But look. What do they have to do? Practically nothing. Andre would say, That's exactly what they doing. Nothing. Where they at?

They'll be here.

In the meantime, run upstairs and get the gun. Before Karen comes home. Wherever Karen went.

Maguire turned off the lamp, felt his way out to the front hall and moved up the stairway. Gretchen had gone off somewhere.

When Roland saw the house dark it made him wonder for a moment. How come? Then accepted it as he crossed the yard toward the house. They went to get Vivian, that's why. Both of them.

But at the French doors, about to put the rubber-padded butt of the shotgun through the glass, seeing it busted already, he said, No, they didn't.

Somebody was home, and he bet he knew who it was, too. Somebody besides little Gretchen panting, trying to climb his leg. Roland sat down in the Louis XVI chair to pull off his cowboy boots, whispering, "You like to smell my feet, do you, huh? Come on up here you little thing. I don't like to do this, Gretchie, no I don't, but I got to." He put his hand over Gretchen's muzzle, clamping it over her nose and mouth, and held the squirming furry body until it shuddered and became limp.

Roland went through the hall to the living room, looked in, came back past the stairway and paused. Was that a sound up there? Like a drawer being shut? Roland went through the back hall to Marta's room—no Cubans hiding under the bed—came out and turned into the kitchen. There was a soft orange glow on the telephone to show where it hung on the wall. Roland got an idea. He'd memorized Frank DiCilia's private number once. Now, if he could remember it—

Maguire closed the top drawer. He opened, looked through and closed every drawer in the dresser. He looked in the drawers of the two nightstand tables. He looked under the pillows and the mattress. Shit. Andre Patterson would say, Get you ass out, boy.

No, be cool. Where would she put it?

He went back to the dresser and got the key to the next room out of the drawer. It was possible—she'd decided to put the gun back with Frank's stuff, his papers, his money. Maguire unlocked the door and went in. No light showed in the window; the draperies were closed. He turned on the desk lamp. Straightening then, his eyes went to the photographs on the wall, the shots of Karen.

The telephone rang.

Maguire jumped and Andre Patterson, watching, would say, See?

The telephone rang.

Maguire went over to it sitting on the desk and looked at the number in the center of the dial. Not Karen's number, a private line.

The telephone rang.

He'd wait for it to stop. And then thought, What if it's Karen? If she knew, somehow, he was in the house—

The telephone rang.

—Didn't want him to answer on her phone and have it recorded, so—no, both lines would be tapped. That wasn't it.

The telephone rang.

But it still could be Karen. Or Marta. It could be anybody. It could be Marta with Jesus, knowing he'd be looking for the gun. No—why this phone?

The telephone rang.

It would stop.

The telephone rang.

The telephone rang.

Shit, Maguire said, and picked it up.

"How you doing?" Roland's voice said. "You coming down or you want me to come up?"

\* \* \*

"So this parrot went to take a piss, see, and drowned in the toilet. How you doing?" Roland said, coming out of the dark bedroom into lamplight, the pump-action shotgun leading.

"In the commode was the word," Maguire said, sitting in the swivel chair behind the desk, trying to look calm. Where the hell else was there to go?

"I think it sounds better toilet. Where's Vivian at?"

"I don't know any Vivian. Vivian who?"

"Shit," Roland said. "we gonna have a question-answer period or we gonna get to it?"

"I got nothing to tell you," Maguire said.

"Then you might as well be dead, huh?" Roland put the shotgun on him.

"Unless you want to try a few questions and see where they lead," Maguire said.

"I got one," Roland said, "only one. Where's Vivian?"

"I can't do it like that, have it on my conscience."

"How can you do it?"

"I don't see a way yet."

"Then die looking, you dumb shit. It's up to you."

"You want to go for two counts, is that it?"

"*Two?*" Roland said. "If I notched my gunbutt you'd get splinters running your hand on it, you dink. I don't care about numbers. You're just another one."

"But it's money what it's all about. Right?"

"What do you make, two bucks an hour? Want to give me about a hunnert?"

"I don't have it, no. But I know where I could get some." Maguire looked up at the photos on the wall.

Roland glanced over and back to Maguire, then turned to look at the display of photos again.

"What's this all about, you know? Puts up pitchers of herself." Roland stepped closer. "And somebody else there, huh? I thought they was all her when I first seen 'em."

"I think she comes up here and plays pretend," Maguire said. "Get her mind off things."

"Pretend what?"

"The mystery lady, I think. Like that other one."

"Who's she?"

591

"I forgot her name." Maguire heard the car then.

Roland heard it, too. He came around with the shotgun. "She bringing Vivian?"

"Or cops. You gonna wait and see?"

"Stay put," Roland said. He stepped into the bedroom.

Maguire heard a door, downstairs, open and close. He couldn't see Roland now. But heard his voice from the upstairs hall. "Come on up, join the party."

He could go out the window—if it opened and there was no screen to fool with. He didn't owe Karen anything. It was the other way around, all the time he'd put in. She owed him more than she'd ever know.

But he remained in the swivel chair. Probably wouldn't make it out the window anyway—Roland moved for a big man. So what could he do? Nothing. The hell with Andre Patterson there watching, shaking his head.

Karen was coming in, seeing him at the desk. Christ, Karen shaking her head, too. Roland came in behind her saying, "I hope we can get this cleared up, what's going on."

Karen took a cigarette out of a pack in in her straw handbag and laid the bag on the desk.

"You have a light?"

"I used to chew, but I never smoked," Roland said. "It's bad for you."

Karen took a lighter from the bag and snapped it several times. "I went to Miami for dinner. Alone." She dropped the lighter on the desk and raised her hip to sit against the corner, picking up the handbag and resting it on her lap now as she felt inside.

"You got a match?" Roland said to Maguire.

"I don't smoke."

"That's smart," Roland said. He looked at Karen. "I believe you. It's this dink here causing all the commotion. See, he was gonna bring Vivian here—the way I figure it—and try and get a lot of money out of you to help her get away." He stopped. "You know why?"

Karen looked up from the handbag on her lap, pausing. "Yes, I know."

"Then they did talk to you."

"Not really. I found out on my own."

Maguire kept looking at her as Roland said, "Don't believe everything you hear, it ain't required. So he comes to the house wants to talk to you, see if he can bring Vivian, and you're not home. So what does he do, he busts in."

"Why?" Karen said.

"To wait for you."

"Unh-unh, to wait for *you,*" Karen said. "That was the whole idea."

"Wait for *me?* Why would he do that?"

Jesus Christ, Maguire thought.

"To kill you," Karen said.

"Shit, he don't even have a gun."

"I do," Karen said.

Her hand came out of the straw bag gripping the Beretta and fired it point blank at Roland's bright-blue suit jacket and fired it again and fired in again and fired it again, until Roland stumbled against the file cabinet and went down on top of his shotgun, tried then as if to do a pushup and fell heavily and didn't move again.

Karen stood up, watching Roland. After a moment she laid the gun on the desk. She said to Maguire, who was staring at her, "How did you get in?"

"I broke in. The glass door in the sitting room."

"No, that's how he broke in," Karen said. "You weren't here."

"Look, I'll tell what happened, or anything you want. I'm not worried about being involved."

"You weren't here," Karen said, again. "So you'd better leave, okay? I have to call the police."

"Wait a minute," Maguire said, getting up. "This was my idea, right? The whole thing."

"It wasn't a very good one," Karen said. "What did you expect to get out of it?"

Maguire was confused now, frowning. Was she kidding? She couldn't be. "What'd we talk about all the time? Getting him off your back, going away, traveling together."

Karen picked up the lighter, flicked it once, and lit her cigarette. Looking at him she said, "Did I promise you anything?"

"It's all we talked about."

"We did?"

"Jesus Christ, I paid Jesus five grand—"

"Of my money. Don't you think I checked it? With you two in the house."

"Jesus Christ," Maguire said. He couldn't believe it. "*Us* two—I paid Lionel a grand out of my own money."

"And I believe I saved your life," Karen said. "But I'll pay you whatever you spent out of pocket." She walked to the file cabinet, stepping over Roland, and opened it.

Maguire watched her. He said, "You didn't want to get out of this at all, did you? You get some kind of a kick out of it, playing a role. Like the dolphins—they're putting up with all that shit, you turn 'em loose. What do they do? They come back to the phony world to play games. You're just like the fucking dolphins, you know it?"

"Here's your thousand," Karen said.

"You'll get your picture in the paper again, act mysterious—you gonna have room to put it up?"

"I enjoyed meeting you," Karen said. "Now beat it. Okay?"

F       Leonard, Elmore,
LEO       1925-

       Double Dutch treat

| DATE | | | |
|---|---|---|---|
| | | | |
| | | | |
| | | | |
| | | | |
| | | | |
| | | | |
| | | | |
| | | | |
| | | | |
| | | | |
| | | | |
| | | | |
| | | | |